VILLAGE SQUARE
by Linda Eberhardt

*Phyllis
To a fellow
member of RWA &
a sweet friend.
Happy reading!
Linda*

Village Square

LINDA EBERHARDT

JOVE BOOKS, NEW YORK

VILLAGE SQUARE

A Jove Book / published by arrangement with
the author

PRINTING HISTORY
Jove edition / October 1995

All rights reserved.
Copyright © 1995 by Linda Eberhardt.
This book may not be reproduced in whole
or in part, by mimeograph or any other means,
without permission. For information address:
The Berkley Publishing Group, 200 Madison Avenue,
New York, New York 10016.

ISBN: 0-515-11740-4

A JOVE BOOK®
Jove Books are published by The Berkley Publishing Group,
200 Madison Avenue, New York, New York 10016.
JOVE and the "J" design are trademarks
belonging to Jove Publications, Inc.

PRINTED IN THE UNITED STATES OF AMERICA

10 9 8 7 6 5 4 3 2 1

Village Square

Chapter One

S HE WAS ALMOST home.

Amanda Hall leaned out the open window of the train compartment and eagerly searched the horizon. The early summer breeze caught the brim of her hat and would have swept it from her auburn head had she not quickly snatched the loose ribbons and pulled it back. She laughed in delight at the thought of the cumbersome steam engine grinding to a halt so one of its passengers could chase after a straw hat, and then, with a slight blush, she cast a quick glance over her shoulder at her fellow passengers, only to find that the lady seated next to her was snoring softly, her graying head sunk onto her ample bosom, and the gentleman in the opposite corner was buried in his newspaper.

Only her traveling companion sitting across from her seemed aware of her actions. At her laugh, he lowered his book and craned his neck to look out the window, curious to see what had caused her mirth. Upon finding nothing of particular jocularity, he asked, "Are we there?"

"Nearly." Amanda ducked back inside the window. "I can just make out the courthouse spire. I hope Bonnie didn't give up on us. Poor dear, she's been waiting over an hour. Damned slow train!" At that, the gentleman in the corner lowered his newspaper to give her a disapproving frown.

"If your sister is anything like you, Mandy," Harper

1

leaned forward to whisper, "she's bound to be in a stew about it."

Amanda smiled. "Not Bonnie. She has the patience of Job. Oh, I can't wait for you to meet my family, Harper!" She leaned out again, feeling the warmth of the early summer sun upon her face, wishing she were in the cab of the noisy engine. They'd be in Wheatener in no time if she were at the controls.

Wheatener. Amanda propped her elbows on the window ledge and rested her chin on her hands. She had dreamed of coming back to Wheatener for four long years. And now she was almost there. Almost home. She could barely contain her excitement.

"Do you know how Wheatener got its name, Harper?" she called over her shoulder. "From the railroad engineers. Wheatener was nothing but a railroad junction until Grandfather Hall settled here. He used to tell me that when the engineers would stop to pick up a load of grain, they'd look out over the fields and say, 'T'ain't nothin' here but wheat'n air!' So that's what they named it. Isn't that funny?"

At Harper's silence, Amanda ducked her head in once again, only to find that he had resumed reading his book on the founding of Harvard University. "How can you possibly read when we're so close?" she asked.

Harper smiled patiently. "If we intend to found a college, Mandy, it would help considerably to know how others have done it."

It was against Amanda's nature to concede gracefully. With mock annoyance, she grumbled, "You've read enough to teach an entire course on the history of higher education."

"An excellent suggestion, Mandy. Perhaps we should include it in our schedule."

Amanda threw him a vexed look as she settled back against the seat, but Harper only smiled to himself and continued to read.

Watching Harper absorb the information with his seemingly unquenchable thirst for knowledge, Amanda recalled the evening she had first met him. Whether by providence, fate, or simple coincidence, it had changed the course of her life forever.

They had met at a coffeehouse after a suffragette rally, where Amanda and her friends had heard, among other things, a speech on free education for all people. There, while in a heated discussion about the speaker's unconventional ideas, a young man at the next table had pulled his chair right up to theirs and joined in the debate as if he had known the girls all his life.

At first put off by his forwardness, the girls were soon listening with interest to the intense, earnest young man who fervently believed in the right of all men and women, regardless of race or religion, to receive an education. To her surprise, Amanda had found herself sharing with him her dream of establishing such a college in her hometown, and when the others rose later to go back to their dormitories, Amanda had paid them no heed, so entranced was she by this person with the odd name of Harper Winston Beauregard Brown III.

Harper had come from Philadelphia, the grandson of a wealthy cloth manufacturer. He had a high forehead, a slim, intelligent face, light blue eyes, and silky, light brown hair, parted on one side and forever falling over his eye. He dressed with no concern for fashion, mixing the oddest colors and patterns, and he seemed not the least impressed with Amanda's good looks, but instead with her ideas. Her proposal of starting a college appealed to him and he had questioned her at length about it.

That was the start of a steady, if ultimately platonic, relationship. Amanda admired his intelligence and optimism and he admired her ambition and determination; neither felt the slightest inclination to move their liaison beyond that point.

At the coffeehouse one evening, just before graduation, Harper had surprised Amanda by proposing that they start a college in Wheatener.

"Just the two of us?" she had asked in surprise.

"We'll start a campaign to raise money for it this summer. You didn't really want to teach grade school, did you, Mandy? What is your major? History? Well, it's not as good as a business degree, but still, I think you'd be a good administrator. My grandfather would give us enough money for the building, so we'd only have to raise funds to hire professors and, of course, to buy textbooks, furniture, and such. If we work diligently, we might be able to open for the spring semester of next year."

"Would your grandfather give you that much money, Harper?"

"Without a doubt. He has more money than he knows what to do with. And when I turn twenty-five, I'll receive my trust money, which is well over fifty thousand dollars."

Amanda hadn't known how to respond to his plan. Starting a college had sounded like such a grand and noble idea; yet faced with the seemingly insurmountable task of actually doing it, she had serious doubts about their capabilities.

However, if they succeeded, she would finally have the money to fulfill the vow she had made at the time of her parents' death—to bring together her younger brothers and sisters and buy back their family home. It was a vow, a dream, that had sustained her through her lonely years away from home.

"It sounds wonderful, Harper, but I'm afraid I wouldn't be of much help this summer. You see, I have to work to afford a place to live."

Harper had reached across the table and taken her hands in his. "You needn't worry on that account, Mandy. I'll rent us rooms. I'll even hire you to raise funds for the college so you won't be without money."

"Can you afford to do that?"

"I receive a monthly allotment. It will be more than sufficient. What do you say?"

Amanda had smiled in delight. "I say we do it."

Harper had assembled his papers in a neat pile and tucked them under his arm. "I'll write my grandfather tonight and tell him of our plan. Can you find rooms for us?"

"I'll have my sister locate some immediately."

She had written Bonnie about their plans that very night and had received a letter back almost as swiftly saying rooms had been reserved for them in a brand-new apartment building, the first of its kind in Wheatener.

Now Amanda leaned her head against the seat, closed her eyes, and smiled, imagining Bonnie's wistful face eagerly watching for her. She hoped the others were waiting there, too. She was anxious to see how much her six younger siblings had grown in her absence.

She was also anxious to see the changes in Wheatener that Bonnie had mentioned in her letters, and more than a little apprehensive of them, as well. She could not imagine it as anything other than the unspoiled, picturesque town she had left. Her father, Vernon Hall, had been one of Wheatener's foremost leaders and had been the driving force behind the construction of the white limestone courthouse that stood in the middle of town, as well as the attractive, gas-lit streets that surrounded it, forming a village square filled with a variety of shops where a lady or gentleman could buy most anything they desired.

Wheatener also had a hospital due to Vernon Hall's generous donation from his own inheritance. It had been his parents' home, one of the first mansions in Wheatener, a rambling Victorian with high ceilings, winding staircases, and a multitude of rooms. Amanda could not pass by Hall Hospital without being reminded of her family's dedication to the town. It was one of the first things she intended to show Harper.

Wheatener's bucolic period had come to an end two years ago. Bonnie had written that a sprawling iron mill had been put up on the outskirts of town, employing over one hundred men, two-thirds of them newcomers. The owner of this mill, a Matthew Blake from New York, had also built a lumberyard of a much larger size and with many more employees than Engstrom's lumberyard. Blake's business milled and sold lumber at low prices, forcing the old yard to shut down from lack of business.

Now there were blocks and blocks of new, inexpensive homes on the northern edge of town, close to the iron mill, all built, of course, with Blake lumber for the express purpose of housing Blake employees. There was also a brandnew four-story luxury hotel, which had been financed by none other than Matthew Blake, who lived in a deluxe suite on the second floor—when he wasn't staying with his mistress, Amanda thought with a sniff of disdain.

According to Bonnie, Matthew Blake had become quite popular with the ladies in town, especially with the doting mamas who invited him to every soiree and dinner in the hopes that one of their daughters would snare the wealthy bachelor. So far, their plans had come to naught, for Matthew seemed to prefer the company of Dixie Nightingale, a voluptuous widow in her mid-thirties, who lived in a neat, white-fenced house on the south side of town.

Amanda scowled, imagining this arrogant rake, this East Coast stranger who publicly flaunted his immoral lifestyle. He was antiunion, too, a stance that went against everything her college years had taught her.

At least he's done his damage on the outskirts of town, she thought with a scowl, although she still couldn't understand why the town board hadn't ridden him out on a rail. If her father were alive, that's exactly what he'd have done. He wouldn't have let a stranger decimate the town he loved.

And neither will I! Amanda thought with fierce determination. She would pick up the reins her father had dropped. She would make sure their town stayed as perfect as it was when he died. If the New Yorker didn't like it, he could pack up and head back where he belonged.

Before the cumbersome train could lumber to a halt, Amanda had snatched her hat box and satchel and hurried down the narrow aisle to be the first to disembark. But once off, she stood in the crowded depot and stared around in dismay as Harper clumsily propelled himself, his baggage, and an armload of books toward her.

"Dash it, Mandy! You don't give a fellow a chance to catch his—what's wrong?"

"I don't see a single familiar face, Harper. Who are all these people?"

Harper was fighting a losing battle with the books, which were slipping through his arms. "I couldn't say, Mandy. Think you could lend a hand here?"

Amanda turned to look at him just as the whole pile fell, scattering books and loose papers all over the wooden planks. They both dropped their bags and hurried to gather them, only to find themselves buffeted about by the passing crowd. Outraged by the pairs of dirty feet trampling on Harper's precious load, Amanda jumped up and began to wave her arms as if to scatter a flock of hens.

"Would you kindly move around us? Can't you see he's dropped his books? Go away!" she cried, stamping her foot in annoyance when no one paid the least bit of attention to her.

She swung around to see how Harper was faring, only to find herself facing a very broad, white-shirted chest. Abruptly, Amanda's head snapped up and she inhaled sharply at the sight of the tall, strikingly handsome, dark-haired man before her. As distraught as she was, she nevertheless couldn't help but give him an appraising glance.

He wore freshly shined brown leather boots and well-made brown tweed trousers. His tan frock coat was slung over one broad shoulder of his boiled white shirt. He had a strong, lean jaw, generous mouth, dark brown hair, and the most penetrating, sensuous, dark eyes she had ever seen.

"May I be of help?" the stranger offered, his bold gaze sweeping over her trim figure, sending a tingle of excitement down her spine. Amanda couldn't quit staring at him. She'd never in her life felt such an immediate and powerful attraction to a man. And by the warm flicker in his eyes, she guessed the feeling was mutual.

Remembering suddenly where she was, Amanda said with some embarrassment, "Thank you, yes, you may. You may keep these—these *people* away while we retrieve our books."

The stranger's mouth curved up at one corner as he turned and motioned to another man who had been standing nearby, and then the two of them effectively blocked anyone from coming within yards of Amanda and Harper.

When the books and papers were once again safely in Harper's arms, Amanda retrieved her own belongings and turned to thank the stranger with a smile. "It was so kind of you to offer your assistance. Kindness seems to be in short supply today, no doubt due to all the strangers in town."

The man lifted one dark eyebrow, as if baffled by her statement. Harper cleared his throat and said quietly, "Mandy, do you think we could find a hack before I lose my hold again?"

"Michael!" the stranger called suddenly in a deep, booming voice, startling Amanda, "hail a hack!" As the wiry little man scurried to do his bidding, the stranger picked up Harper's baggage in one hand and lifted Amanda's out of her grasp with the other. "I'd offer you the use of my carriage," he told Amanda as he swept the two out to the street in front, "but I came on horseback."

Amanda cast him a quick, sidelong glance, imagining him sitting astride a horse. He'd cut a fine figure, she was sure.

Michael waited at the curb beside a hackney, and at their approach, helped load their bags in the boot. The stranger held out his hand to help Amanda into the buggy, fastening upon her his penetrating, dark-eyed gaze.

Her pulse racing dizzily, Amanda put out her gloved hand. His fingers closed over hers, sending a tremor throughout her body and color into her cheeks. She quickly stepped inside and sat down, adjusting her skirts to hide her discomfiture.

"Thank you again, sir," Harper told the stranger as he took his seat and shut the door.

Matthew Blake smiled. "You're quite welcome. I hope we'll meet again sometime."

Amanda leaned forward to peer at him around Harper's shoulder, and finding the man smiling at her, she blushed and sat back. As the hack pulled away, she pulled out her fan to cool her overwarm face and turned to peer at him through the narrow window cut in the back of the hack, watching avidly as he strode back into the train station.

"I hope we'll meet again sometime, too," she murmured

to herself. But only minutes later, the meeting was forgotten as the carriage turned the corner onto the village square.

"Look, Harper! Here is our courthouse on the right," she exclaimed as the horse's hooves clopped loudly down the brick street. "Isn't it splendid? And I can't wait to show you the hospital. It was my grandfather's house—" Amanda glanced at Harper only to find him staring amazedly through the opposite window.

"I'd no idea you had anything so grand in your town, Mandy."

She leaned forward to see past him and her mouth fell open at the sight of the white, marble-fronted hotel, situated directly opposite the courthouse. Her eyes fell on the words inscribed in marble over the door.

"The Blake?"she cried in outrage. "Why that—that egocentric New York buffoon! How dare he build his hotel here in town, across from our courthouse!"

Her outrage increased as the buggy clattered past the gambling halls, saloons, and dance halls that now marred the once perfect village square. They were brought to Wheatener, no doubt, as everything else seemed to have been, by Matthew Blake.

But what awaited her around the next corner turned her outrage to anguish. "No!" she cried in horrified disbelief, her hands pressed to her face.

"What is it, Mandy?"

Amanda pointed through the window. "That's not Hall Hospital! Someone tore it down and built that—that *monstrosity* in its place." She choked back a sob, seething inwardly at the man she knew was responsible.

"Why do you suppose they tore it down?" Harper asked.

"Not *they,* Harper," she said through gritted teeth. "*He.* The New Yorker. None of the members of the town board would ever dream of tearing down Hall Hospital. Matthew Blake must have the entire town under his control." She pulled her handkerchief out of the sleeve of her traveling jacket and wiped her wet cheeks. "Well, it's a good thing I'm back. A very good thing. Someone's got to stop him."

Chapter Two

THE JEFFERSON ARMS apartment building was a somber, dark, red-brick edifice that sat three blocks east of the square. It was a long, rectangular, two-story structure with two entrances on the west and one on the south. As the hackney drew up to the south entrance, Amanda leaned out and hailed Bonnie, who had positioned herself and their youngest sister, Gabrielle, at the corner so as not to miss their arrival.

"There they are!" she cried to Harper, thinking at once that Bonnie looked too thin and her clothing somewhat shabby. But then, Alice Ripley, their guardian, was known to be of a frugal nature, and no doubt did not spare much for her sister's clothing.

Gabrielle, however, now eight years old, seemed the picture of health and fashion, and her plump face glowed with happiness as Amanda alighted from the carriage.

"Mandy!" Bonnie cried, her delicate features shining with joy as she threw herself into her oldest sister's arms.

"Oh, Bonnie, how I've missed you," Amanda whispered through her tears. She leaned back, her hands on her sister's shoulders. "Let me look at you. Why, you're a lady now! You've grown up."

"Haven't I grown up, too?" her youngest sister asked.

Amanda gathered Gabrielle into their circle. "Yes, Gabby. You've grown, too." Her smile faded as she remembered the horrors that had greeted her arrival. "Bonnie, why didn't you tell me about the hospital?"

Bonnie dropped her gaze. "I couldn't, Mandy. I knew how terrible you'd feel. I was afraid you'd leave school to try to stop it."

"Was Matthew Blake behind it?" she asked bitterly.

Bonnie nodded, her head bowed.

"That house was a landmark. A piece of Wheatener's earliest history. And now it's gone! Destroyed by that monster from New York, along with our village square. Father would be devastated by what that man has done to Wheatener."

"But, Mandy—" Bonnie began.

"Matthew Blake will regret ever coming here, Bonnie. I promise you that. I'll make life so miserable for him he'll pack up and be gone by Christmas."

"But, Mandy—" Bonnie tried again, only to give a start at the sound of Harper clearing his throat behind them.

"Oh, Harper, I'm so sorry," Amanda said, pulling him into their midst. "Let me introduce my sisters, Bonnie and Gabrielle Hall."

"How do you do, Miss Hall?" Harper said, enthusiastically pumping Bonnie's hand. Then turning to the youngest sister, he said, "And you, too, Miss Hall."

Gabrielle giggled behind her hand. "Please, Mr. Brown, you must call me Gabrielle, or Gabby, if you prefer, which is what everyone else calls me, except for Aunt Alice, of course, who is not really my aunt at all, but Mrs. Ripley, the mayor's wife, who considers Gabby a very vulgar and unladylike name."

Amanda put her arm around her little sister. "And now you see why the name Gabby fits her so well."

Bonnie glanced shyly at Harper as she said to Gabby, "Why don't we take Mandy and Mr. Brown in to see their rooms. We can talk more privately there."

Amanda's room on the first floor consisted of a tiny kitchen, a parlor with two windows facing south, a narrow bedroom with just enough space for one slim bed and a bureau, one closet, and a small bath. It was rather stark, but being new, it seemed very luxurious to Amanda.

Harper's room was on the floor above, and was identical to Amanda's. He did not seem to think the rent was outrageous when Bonnie quoted him the monthly rates, as Amanda feared he might; rather, he blithely suggested they spend the afternoon shopping for furniture.

"But I did want to see my brothers today," Amanda said with some dismay. "Bonnie, why don't you and Harper go into town to select some furnishings for us?"

Bonnie blushed pink and said in her soft voice, "Mandy, I think you should have asked Mr. Brown first."

"I'd be delighted if you'd accompany me, Miss Hall," Harper said, bestowing his wide smile on Bonnie.

"And Gabby shall come with me," Amanda announced. "I'll stop to tell Mrs. Ripley, then I'll bring Curt and the others back here so we can all have dinner together tonight."

There were seven children in the Hall family. At twenty-three, Amanda was the oldest, followed by Bonnie, a sensitive twenty-one-year-old; Curtis, a fearless eighteen; Daniel, a sixteen-year-old musical prodigy; Ethan, at eleven, a sturdy copy of his adored older brother Curt; Frederick, an exuberant ten-year-old; and eight-year-old Gabrielle, the delightful pet of the family. From oldest to youngest, their charming, doting mama had named them in alphabetical order, a fact that had either tickled the townsfolk's funny bones or set their teeth on edge.

It was said by many that the Hall children had been spoiled, for they seemed to have had every luxury imaginable. But if they had been spoiled, they had also been dearly loved by their parents, Vernon and Rachel Hall. The family had been very close, and though they argued and teased, it was never done maliciously but out of genuine affection for one another.

Vernon Hall had been a well-respected doctor in their small town and was known for his boundless energy and modern ideas. Rachel had been a parson's daughter, at her best among throngs of people. Her pretty face, lilting laugh, and sunny disposition had made her a favorite among men and women alike.

The Halls had been considered the epitome of the perfect family. They had symbolized all that was good about Wheatener, from their prosperity and handsome looks to their philanthropic goals and Christian values. Their friendships had been highly desired, and once won, had been nurtured like fine wine. They had been Wheatener's darlings.

Then came the night of the tragic sleigh accident that had claimed the lives of Vernon and Rachel Hall. In that one swift stroke of fate, the Hall children had suddenly discovered the hard truth about their good townspeople. They had very short memories.

Hall House, mortgaged to the hilt to pay for hospital equipment, had been abruptly put up for sale by the bank and its furnishings sold to pay the debts. Long-time friends of the family had looked the other way as Amanda struggled to care for her siblings, buy food, and pay for the meager rooms in which the seven of them were forced to live.

Abandoning her plans for college, Amanda had found jobs for herself, Curt, and Daniel, leaving Bonnie to care for the youngest. To children unused to such labor, daily living became a constant chore, yet all had agreed that it was preferable to being separated, and soon they had begun to take pride in their independence. But they were still an embarrassment, a reminder to family friends of failed duty, and so a committee was formed to decide what to do about them.

The committee was composed of Vernon's closest friends, Mayor Ripley and Judge Douglas; the Hall's attorney, Jeffrey Gable; and, although it was not widely known, the mayor's wife, Alice. They decided that the six younger children were to be placed in separate homes, with Gabrielle going to the Ripleys, and Amanda going away to school as her father had intended each of them to do, using the trust money set up for that purpose. All this was for the benefit of the children, of course.

But Amanda had not seen it that way. She had lost her

parents and her home and was on the verge of losing the rest of her family. She fought their decision with every resource she had available. She reasoned, accused, demanded, and finally pleaded broken-heartedly with the committee that her siblings not be separated. She even wrote to her Uncle David, an archaeologist working in Egypt, asking him to come home immediately to help her, but she had no idea how long it would take for the letter to reach him, or even if he would be able to get back in time to help.

In the end, the only concession made to Amanda's demands was to let Bonnie serve as nurserymaid to the bewildered, terrified, four-year-old Gabrielle at the Ripley's home, which Amanda suspected had been conveniently arranged to suit Alice Ripley's pleasure.

Alice was a lanky, horse-faced woman with a pinched mouth and dull brown hair that was streaked heavily with gray and worn in a tight bun on the very top of her head. As the wife of the mayor, Alice saw herself as an extension of his office, voicing her many opinions as proclamations. What she was, in truth, was a busybody, but because she was the mayor's wife, everyone pandered to her—everyone, that is, except for Amanda, who had never liked or trusted Mrs. Ripley.

The Ripleys had only one child, Clara, a girl of Amanda's age, who had been a bitter disappointment to her overly ambitious mother. But with sweet, malleable Gabrielle under her dominion, Alice had been given the perfect opportunity to start over again.

Now, Amanda couldn't wait to get Gabrielle away from that lady's influence. She knew she wouldn't be able to take her sister to live with her until she had the financial resources, but she could exert her own influence on the child and instill in her the values and standards their parents had held dear. It was her foremost objective, and she intended to start on it that very day.

"Sugar, Amanda?" Alice Ripley asked sweetly, holding out a small, crystal bowl.

"Thank you. I believe I will." Amanda spooned two lumps out of the bowl and stirred them into her cup, listening politely as Alice filled her in on four years' worth of gossip. Over the course of the hour, it became apparent to Amanda how fond Mrs. Ripley had become of Gabby. It seemed that Gabby had become the focus of her life, and Amanda feared the damage it had wrought on the child's personality. She wondered how badly Clara felt about it.

"How is Clara, by the way?" Amanda asked, as Alice pushed a ginger cookie on Gabby.

"She's getting along splendidly! She has a very good position at the courthouse, you know."

Yes, Amanda did know, for Bonnie had written that Clara had been turned down by every college at which her mother had applied for her. After two years, the woman had finally admitted that her daughter was not college material and had persuaded Mayor Ripley to find a spot for her in his office.

As for Clara's very good position, she was a glorified office girl, nothing more. But she seemed happy, and as long as Gabrielle was around to occupy Mrs. Ripley's attentions, Clara was left alone.

"Now, what are your immediate plans, Amanda?" Alice asked her with a fey smile.

"My immediate plans are to gather together my brothers and sisters and have dinner with them."

"I meant your future plans," Mrs. Ripley said with a forced smile.

Amanda shrugged evasively. "I'll have to see. Now, Gabby, are you ready to go? We still have to pick up the boys."

Alice was not satisfied with Amanda's vague answers, but could not very well insist she tell all, so she saw them to the door with a last reminder to have Gabrielle home by eight. As she closed the door, she heard Gabrielle say to Amanda, "Will we all come to live with you now that you're home, Mandy?"

Alice pressed her ear to the door.

"Yes, Gabby," she heard Amanda say, "as soon as I am

able to support you. But first, I need to make enough money to buy back Hall House."

"Will we really be able to live there again?"

"Oh, yes, Gabby. We will indeed."

"We'll see about *that,* Miss Amanda Hall!" Alice sneered as she yanked viciously on the bellpull. "Have my carriage brought around at once!" she commanded the girl who answered her page. She would see her husband immediately and have him put a stop to any foolish notions Amanda might have.

Alice had always considered Amanda a troublemaker and had hoped she would meet a nice boy out East, marry him, and settle far away from Wheatener. But it had not happened. And now she was back.

But she was *not* going to take away her little Gabrielle!

Chapter Three

POLLY'S INN WAS a cozy, wood-paneled eating establishment that sat on a corner diagonally across from the Blake Hotel. The hotel boasted a much finer restaurant, but Polly's was still the most popular gathering spot in town. It was there that Amanda and her siblings had their first chance to become reacquainted.

As they talked, Amanda's gaze fell lovingly on each face, memorizing the features that had changed over their four years apart and yet seemed as familiar to her as her own. Her heart swelled with happiness to be with them at last, if only for that one evening. It could only have been better if her parents had been there.

Amanda blinked back the sting of tears, thinking how unfair life had been to her brothers and sisters. It made her more determined than ever to reunite them permanently. This time, no one was going to stop her. All she needed was the money to buy back their family home.

"Were you able to find everything you needed for your apartment?" Amanda asked Harper during a momentary lull in the lively conversation.

"Yes! Your sister is amazingly efficient, Mandy." Harper bestowed a grateful smile on Bonnie, who blushed and smiled down at her lap. "We'll have to hire her to work for us; I could use someone with her organizational abilities to keep me in line."

Amanda laughed and explained to her siblings that Harper was well known for his absent-mindedness.

Curt gaped at him. "You don't mind being called that, sir?"

"I'd rather be called forgetful than sir," Harper replied with a kind smile.

"Harper, I'm afraid we can't hire Bonnie until she finishes school," Amanda informed him.

Harper turned to Bonnie. "Where do you attend?"

"Oh, I don't, yet."

"She's been waiting for me to finish," Amanda explained. She leaned toward Harper and said in an undertone, "She didn't want to leave Gabby alone with Mrs. Ripley until I returned."

"I see. Well, then, Bonnie must be our first enroller!"

Amanda was puzzled by the bewildered faces staring at them. "Bonnie, haven't you told them what Harper and I have decided to do?" And when Bonnie sheepishly shook her head, Amanda proceeded to describe their plans to build a college.

Daniel shyly spoke to Harper. "May I attend your college?"

"Daniel, you wanted to go to a music school," Amanda reminded him. "I'm afraid ours won't be set up for that."

Daniel looked crestfallen. "Oh, I see."

His mouth full of food, Curt asked, "Where do you intend to build your college, Mandy?"

"I've been thinking about that meadowland near Shale Lake, the old Hovarth farmstead. Remember it, Bonnie?"

Bonnie smiled ruefully. "That's where Mr. Blake built his ironworks, Mandy."

"That beautiful meadowland is gone?" Amanda cried. "Why didn't the town board stop him?"

"Because they realized Mr. Blake's mill would be good for Wheatener," Curt replied defensively.

Amanda nearly choked on her food. "Good for Wheatener!"

"There are more jobs available now," Curt explained,

"and at decent wages, too, and we've got new roads and a park and—"

"Saloons, dance halls, and gaming rooms!" Amanda cut in, throwing down her napkin. "Well, it's quite clear to me that Mr. Blake has the board members in his pocket. I can't bear to think of that dirty iron mill sprawled in the midst of that beautiful meadowland. Poor Father. He wouldn't recognize Wheatener if he were to see it now. And just thinking about Hall Hospital makes my blood boil."

Curt thrust his chin forward defiantly. "It's progress, Mandy. You know what Father thought about progress."

Amanda's amber eyes glittered angrily. "Of course I know. But do you remember what Father said was the key to progress? Pay attention now, Gabby. Controlled growth. He said as long as Wheatener's growth was monitored by sensible people, there would be no problem with a few new businesses coming into town. But where are those sensible people, Curt? And where is the control when a perfect stranger can come in and randomly destroy a wonderful old house, a beautiful meadow, and probably the lake, as well?"

Amanda took their stunned silence to mean she had won her point. "And as for Mr. Blake," she continued, "in my opinion, he should be run out of town for what he's done to Wheatener. And I, for one, shall be glad to take up that task myself."

At that, there were exclamations of protest. Finally, Bonnie hushed them to silence and turned to her older sister with a worried frown. "Mandy, you should meet Mr. Blake before you say such a thing. He's not the ogre you reckon him to be."

"Oh, I intend to do much more than meet him, Bonnie. And I promise it will be an event he won't soon forget." Amanda looked around at her shocked siblings. "Being the oldest, I suppose it falls to me to pick up where father left off. But I expect you to do your part, as well, and that means to stop defending the person who has ruined this town."

"I like Mr. Blake!" Freddie declared defiantly. "And I'm going to work for him when I get older."

"Hush, Freddie," Bonnie said quickly.

"He even said I could. Besides, Curt works for him."

The other five siblings held their breaths as Amanda turned to stare at the oldest of her brothers. "Curt!" she cried in a shocked voice.

"It's just a part-time job at the lumberyard," Curt mumbled, his eyes on his plate.

"Daniel likes Mr. Blake, too," Freddie pointed out. "He bought Dan a piano."

Amanda glanced at the second oldest of her brothers, but Daniel would not meet her eyes. It was no wonder her brothers and sisters defended the man. *Was that how he controlled the board?* she wondered. *Had he bribed them, too?*

"Well, there's nothing we can do about the piano, but Curt, you'll have to quit immediately. If I'm going to fight the man, you can't very well be working for him." She sighed wearily. "I should never have left Wheatener. It makes me heartsick to see what's happened to it."

Curt and Bonnie exchanged worried glances. It seemed that their beautiful, beloved older sister, by being sent off to school so quickly after the death of their parents, had been denied the opportunity they'd had to come to terms with the changes in their lives.

Curt sighed, feeling as if a deep gulf now separated them from Amanda. They had grown up and so had Wheatener, and Amanda couldn't accept it.

Bonnie glanced at her watch fob. "It's getting late. We should get back."

Amanda gathered her handbag and gloves. "You're right. Mrs. Ripley is sure to have a conniption fit if I'm tardy bringing Gabby home."

After the children were returned to their respective homes, Amanda and Harper rode back to the apartment building in contemplative silence. Harper saw her to her door, then walked away, lost in his own thoughts. He was halfway down the hall before he realized he had not said good night. He turned around and called, "Oh, good night, Mandy. I'll see you tomorrow."

Again, Harper walked away, only to pause, turn around, and add with a grin, "I like your sister. She's a fine person." Then he spun around and disappeared into the stairwell.

With a puzzled frown, Amanda stared at the spot where he'd stood, then shrugged her shoulders and unlocked her door. Inside her tiny apartment, she took off her gloves and looked around at the unfamiliar walls. She was a stranger here—a stranger in her own hometown—all because of Matthew Blake.

She gave a determined tug on her hat ribbons and removed the hat from her head. "Everything will be put to rights once that New Yorker clears out and we're all back together in Hall House."

The first order of business the next morning was to open a bank account in Harper's name. Amanda took Harper to the Wheatener Building and Loan on the square, where he deposited the first of his grandfather's generous endowments. Amanda thought it prudent as long as they were there to enlist the bank president's help for their endeavor, so she asked to see Fred Moore.

As they sat in the sparsely furnished waiting room on the second floor watching the minutes tick by on the case clock, Amanda began to fidget, thinking of all she had to do. She was so preoccupied with her plans that she didn't notice when the president's door opened, but at the sound of his voice, she jumped to her feet and sailed across the room, giving not a passing thought to the dark-haired stranger who had strode out ahead of him.

"Good morning, Mr. Moore."

Fred Moore turned and stared in some surprise, looking her over from head to toe. "Amanda? Amanda Hall?"

Amanda laughed. "I wondered if you'd recognize me. I've just returned."

Absorbed in his own plans, Matthew Blake had not noticed the pair sitting across the room as he strode toward the hallway, but at the mention of Amanda's name, he came to an abrupt halt. Intensely curious, he turned, catching her in profile. He was surprised to see the comely young lady from the train station.

So that was Amanda Hall!

She was slender and graceful and slightly taller than he'd expected, with large, golden brown eyes that fairly sparkled with vitality. Her auburn hair, except for the softly curling wisps around her face, had been pulled back and topped by a navy straw hat adorned with a wide, white ribbon that hung down her back. His gaze took in her prim navy blue serge dress, from the trim skirt and tiny waist up the delightful swell of her breasts to her slim throat enclosed in a high white collar, to fasten on the most desirable pair of lips he had come across in a long time. *Soft and generous,* he thought to himself, *and ripe for kissing—and completely at odds with her conservative attire.*

Fred Moore hooked his thumbs in his waistcoat pockets and rocked back on his heels, smiling broadly. "You're looking mighty pert, Amanda!"

"How very kind of you to say so. You're looking well, yourself. I came to see you this morning because I—that is, my business partner and I—have a proposition for you."

Amanda glanced around to signal Harper to join her, only to discover that he had found a magazine and was now totally absorbed in it. Moreover, she realized she had an audience. Amanda turned fully around, only to discover it was her benefactor from the train station.

Amanda started to give him a smile, but finding his dark eyes studying her figure as a predator might study his prey, a blush stained her cheeks and she promptly lifted her chin and turned away with a huff, leaving no doubt as to how she felt about his rude behavior. She leaned toward the president and lowered her voice. "Might we speak in private?"

Fred peered over her shoulder at Matthew, who raised one dark eyebrow in amusement. "Certainly, Amanda," the president said. "Come into my office."

"Harper?" Amanda called, purposely ignoring the nosy

stranger. She waited for Harper to join her, then allowed Fred to usher them into his office. Fred paused to close the door behind them, stopping long enough to exchange a meaningful look with Matthew Blake.

After a moment's deliberation, Matthew turned and strode out of the bank and down to his waiting carriage, where he sat rubbing his smoothly shaved chin reflectively. It was hard to reconcile the prudish beauty he had just encountered with the courageous, steadfast, grief-stricken young heroine he'd looked forward to meeting ever since he had heard the story of how she had tried valiantly to keep her family together. Somehow this aloof, prim female didn't fit his image. It also didn't fit with what he knew of her father and siblings.

Matthew had known Vernon Hall for only a very brief time before his death, yet he felt he owed the man a large debt of gratitude, for it had been Amanda's father who had not only encouraged Matthew to build his iron mill in Wheatener, but had also coerced the town board into allowing him to build.

They had met while on the train from New York to Chicago. Vernon had been returning from a medical conference; Matthew had been scouting locations for his iron mill. Vernon, always with an eye to the future, had been impressed by the young man's determination and had described Wheatener as the ideal place to build a mill. They had corresponded for a short time afterward concerning that very subject.

When Matthew finally moved to Wheatener to build his mill, he had attempted to look up his new friend, only to learn of the terrible accident that had befallen him and of the tragedy of his children's separation. Unbeknownst to anyone, Matthew had appointed himself guardian of the children to ensure they were being properly cared for, and in that way he felt he was repaying a kindness. He had also made it his goal to transform the town into the booming industrial area Vernon Hall had envisioned.

Matthew wondered what Amanda's business proposition was about. He had always imagined that she would return from school more determined than ever to reunite her family. Had she abandoned that goal for some new cause, or was this proposal merely a means of achieving her objective? He trusted Fred would fill him in on the details that afternoon.

Amanda thought the meeting with the bank president went very well. Fred seemed quite enthused about having a college built in town and promised he would see that they were put on the agenda for the next town board meeting.

"We'll need to consult the architect immediately to have our proposed plans drawn up," Amanda told Harper over lunch. "We'll also need to prepare a speech. I'll leave that to you, and I'll go see the architect first thing in the morning."

"Why not this afternoon?"

"I have to see a lawyer this afternoon."

"A lawyer?" Harper asked in surprise. "What for?"

Amanda calmly pulled on her gloves. "I've decided to sue Mr. Blake for tearing down Hall Hospital."

Chapter Four

SITTING IN A straight-backed chair facing Jeffrey Gable's massive oak desk, Amanda tilted her head to smile up at the tall, thin attorney as he came forward and took her hand. "It's very good to see you again, Miss Hall."

"It's good to see you, too, Mr. Gable."

Jeffrey straightened his cravat as he walked around behind his desk, wondering if she knew how utterly charming she looked peering up at him from beneath the brim of her navy straw hat. "How may I help you today?" he asked, easing his long-boned frame into the leather chair.

"I want to hire you to file a suit against Matthew Blake. On a contingency basis, of course."

Jeffrey Gable sat forward in his chair. "Sue Mr. Blake? On what grounds?"

"On the grounds that he destroyed the hospital my father donated to the county."

"Miss Hall," the lawyer said, tugging on his cravat, "Matthew Blake financed the new hospital. The town board was all for it, including the judge. You wouldn't have a chance of winning."

Amanda chewed her thumbnail for a long moment, her forehead wrinkling in concentration. "Well, then, couldn't we sue him on the grounds that the house had historical significance, being one of the first built in Wheatener?"

"The house was never declared a historical landmark."

Amanda pursed her lips. "Surely there's something we can do, Mr. Gable!"

"I know the hospital had sentimental value, Miss Hall, but legally, Mr. Blake is on solid ground. He's got the town board behind him, as well."

"Don't you mean in his pocket, Mr. Gable?"

The attorney ignored her barb. "Believe me, Miss Hall, it would be a waste of time and money." Seeing Amanda gather her gloves and handbag, Jeffrey rose to assist her. "I wish I had another suggestion for you, but I'm afraid what's done is done."

"And what if Mr. Blake decides he doesn't like the courthouse anymore?" she asked tartly. "Will you all sit by while he tears that down, as well?"

"Ah, now there you would have some recourse. The first would be to get a petition signed by as many concerned voters as possible. The board won't do anything that will keep them from being elected again."

Amanda pulled on her gloves in quick, angry motions. "I appreciate your seeing me on such short notice. What do I owe you?"

The attorney waved his hands in front of him. "Absolutely nothing, Miss Hall. And please feel free to come see me anytime you need my assistance."

Amanda left the building, inwardly fuming. Matthew Blake did have the town board in his pocket and Jeffrey Gable knew it. Perhaps she didn't have the grounds to sue Mr. Blake, but there was always more than one way to skin a rabbit, as her Grandfather Hall used to say. She would just have to watch for an opportunity.

"What is that sister of yours up to?" Alice Ripley questioned Bonnie over supper that evening. She ignored a warning glance from her husband, who was now sorry he had mentioned what he had learned from Fred Moore that afternoon. "I hear she wants to build a college. Is that true?"

"Yes, isn't it exciting?" Gabrielle squealed, earning her a warm smile from Alice.

"Whatever made her come up with that idea?" Alice mused.

"I believe she intends it to be a place where the less fortunate may attend," Bonnie answered in her soft voice.

Alice's thin lips curved down. "I see."

"Father, do you intend to let Amanda bring that kind of people into our town?" Clara demanded.

"By 'that kind of people,' I presume you're talking about those who have the brains to attend but not the funds?" her father pointedly replied.

Turning an unflattering shade of red, Clara fell silent. Her mother, however, took up the subject with relish. "You know what Clara means," she said, eyeing her husband disdainfully. "It's bad enough with the kind of men that ugly iron mill has brought in. Do we want more riffraff coming into town?"

"Riffraff?" the mayor asked incredulously. "I hardly think the sort of person you mean would be likely to aspire to a higher education, my dear. Personally, I think Amanda has a very good idea. There are many deserving youth who simply do not have the funds to attend." He patted his round chin with his napkin. "I wish there had been such a college when I was a lad. Now, if you will excuse me, dear ladies, I have some paperwork to finish."

Alice Ripley did not like to be reminded that her husband was not a college graduate. She seethed silently. Waiting until he had gone, and after excusing the girls, she called, "Bonnie, would you wait just a moment, please?"

"Yes, Mrs. Ripley?" Bonnie asked, waiting quietly in the doorway with her hands folded in front of her. She, unlike Gabby, had never felt comfortable calling Alice "Aunt."

"Come sit down again, dear. Thank you. Now, is it true that Amanda intends to bring all the children to live with her?"

Bonnie glanced away uneasily. "She hasn't said so."

Alice's eyes narrowed. Bonnie knew well enough what Amanda was planning. What a pity they didn't know what *she* was planning. Coyly, she asked, "Is it also true that Amanda is sharing a room with a man?"

Bonnie stared at her aghast. "No! No, it's not true at all!" she gasped, covering her flushed cheeks with her hands.

"Nevertheless, from what I heard today, Bonnie, your sister has moved into the Jefferson Arms with a young man she met at college."

"But not into the same apartment! Amanda is only friends with Mr. Brown. It's true they met at college, but she would *never*—" Bonnie stopped, unable to even think those horrid thoughts about her sister.

"Now, Bonnie, I didn't mean to upset you," Alice said in annoyance. "It's just that rumor has it that this man is, well, shall we say, paying for your sister's accommodations, and naturally one assumes when that is the case that they—oh, never mind. I can see that you don't wish to discuss it."

"My sister is a lady, Mrs. Ripley," Bonnie said firmly, drawing up her slender body in indignation. "I think that is all that needs to be said on the subject."

But once Alice had planted the seed of that idea, Bonnie could not put the matter out of her mind. She had never considered that Amanda and Harper might be—No! She would not think it! Amanda would never consider living with a man out of wedlock. Would she? But did she really know Amanda after being separated for four years? Could college have changed her thinking so much?

"Morning, Mr. Blake."

Standing at the counter at the tobacconist and bootery the next morning, Matthew turned to see Clark Randall, the young, red-headed architect whose office was on the floor above, smiling at him from the doorway. "Morning, Clark."

"I'm ducking out for a moment, Sam," Clark said to the shopkeeper.

Sam waved him on. "I'll keep my eye on the door for you." He turned back to Matthew with a smile. "What can I do for you, Mr. Blake?"

"I need a pair of tan shoelaces, fifty-seven inches."

Sam searched the shelf behind him but didn't see any in that size. "I'll look in the back. I'm sure I have some."

While waiting for the shopkeeper's return, Matthew

walked to the front window and stood looking out at the traffic passing by. A hackney drew up and Amanda Hall stepped down, smoothing out the skirt of her crisp, mint green and white striped dress before turning to pay the driver. Matthew stepped back out of sight as she walked past the window; when she opened the outer door to the shop, he straightened his cravat and adjusted his white shirt cuffs. Instead of turning into the bootery as he had thought she would, Amanda went up the stairs to the architect's office.

Matthew started to alert Sam, but then thought better of it. Fred Moore had briefly filled him in on Amanda's plan to build a college, but not enough to satisfy his curiosity; now he saw an opportunity not only to satisfy that curiosity, but also to become better acquainted with the oldest of his charges. So, after making sure the shopkeeper was still occupied, Matthew slipped out the door and quietly climbed the stairs to the second-floor office.

Amanda opened the door at the top of the stairs and peered into the cluttered office. "Mr. Randall?" When no on answered, she walked in. "Mr. Randall? Are you here?"

"I'm sorry. I had to step out for a moment."

Amanda swung around with a smile, but at the sight of the dashing stranger from the train station, her eyes widened and her mouth opened in surprise. "You're the architect?"

He held out his hand and, when she lifted hers, it was enveloped in a strong, warm clasp. "Well, it seems we meet again."

"Yes," Amanda murmured breathlessly, gazing up into his devastating eyes. Her insides quivered like jelly at his touch and, with a blush, she gently eased her gloved hand from his grasp.

He smiled down at her. "How may I help you?"

Amanda quickly collected her wits and launched into her purpose for coming, pulling off her gloves as she spoke. "My name is Amanda Hall. I'm going to build a college, and I need an architect."

He glanced around the room, then shoved a pile of catalogs off a hard-backed chair and pulled it up to a long table littered with drawings and blueprints. "Please, sit down, Miss Hall." Taking a seat opposite her, he grabbed a pencil lying nearby, turned a paper to its blank side, and said, "Now, tell me about this college."

Amanda sat forward in her chair and began to describe her vision for him in vivid detail. He made notes as she talked, giving her an excellent opportunity to study him at close range. She marveled at the lean line of his jaw and the charming way his dark brown hair waved around his ears. His eyes were the deepest brown she had ever seen, and his nose was long and straight, exactly the way a man's nose should be. He also had the merest shadow of a beard on his smooth face, giving him a dangerous quality that she found quite appealing.

Amanda admired the expensive cut of his beige linen frock coat, too, and remembered how powerful he had looked that day at the train station with his white shirt-sleeves rolled up to the elbows. It seemed odd that a man who spent most of his day sitting at a work table would have such a well-developed torso. For some reason, she thought he'd be much younger, perhaps in his early twenties. Was it something Fred Moore had mentioned?

When she finished talking, the architect stopped writing but continued to study his hastily scribbled notes, a frown of concentration on his face. Amanda's eyes flickered once again over his handsome features, thinking how pleasurable it would be to work with him. She wondered if he were married and wished Fred had told her more about him.

When he looked up, the seriousness of his expression puzzled her. "I'm afraid your idea is just not feasible, Miss Hall."

Amanda blinked in amazement. "Why not?"

"Because no one in town will finance a free school, I guarantee you."

"No one?"

"No one."

Amanda narrowed her eyes at him. "And just how would you know that, Mr. Randall?"

The architect seemed completely taken aback by her question. "I guess you'd have to call it a gut feeling, Miss Hall, if you'll pardon the expression."

Amanda gave him a coolly appraising look. Fred Moore had spoken highly of Clark Randall's abilities, yet there was something about this man that didn't sit right with her, handsome or not. "I think we should leave the financing of the school to those who understand such business matters, Mr. Randall, and the designing of the school to you. Perhaps it would be best if you gave me the names of the buildings you've designed so that I may judge your work for myself."

The architect looked flustered. "Well, ah, there's the Blake hotel, for one, and the Blake lumberyard, and, of course, the iron mill. And then we'll soon begin to dismantle the old grist mill."

Before he could continue, Amanda interrupted him. "Why would you want to dismantle Mr. Wagner's grist mill? He didn't pass on, did he?"

"No, not at all. What I want—that is, what *Mr. Blake* wants to do—is to build a new and larger blacksmith shop on the premises."

"Indeed. And do you think Mr. Blake cares what that new blacksmith shop will do to Bill Yates's smaller shop in town? Well, you needn't go any further, Mr. Randall. It's quite apparent that you work for Mr. Blake and therefore would not be suitable to build my school."

"What?" he sputtered, sitting upright. "Look, Miss Hall, Clark doesn't—that is, I, Clark Randall, do not *work* for Mr. Blake. I have worked *for* him, but not exclusively."

"Are you presently designing anything for Matthew Blake?" she asked, eyeing him skeptically.

The architect settled back against the chair and folded his arms across his chest. "Would it bother you if I were?"

Amanda leaned forward as if to share a confidence. "I don't know how you feel about Mr. Blake personally, Mr. Randall, but I despise him."

"I see." He rubbed his chin, watching her. "You know him, then?"

Her eyebrows lifted. "I know *of* him."

"And it seems you don't like what you know *of* him. May I be so bold as to inquire why?"

Amanda was beginning to wonder why Fred Moore had spoken so highly of this man. "He tore down Hall Hospital, for one thing."

"And built a better hospital in its place."

"Better for whom? The man supplying the lumber, who just happened to be Mr. Blake? Tearing down that house was a travesty, Mr. Randall. It had historical significance."

"It also had termites, Miss Hall. And it was virtually impossible to carry patients on stretchers up and down those winding staircases."

Amanda was momentarily taken aback. She had never considered that the house wasn't particularly suited for the injured. But she wasn't about to concede.

"Four years ago, Mr. Randall, Wheatener was a quiet, lovely place to live. Then Mr. Blake moved here and . . ." She shrugged eloquently.

The architect's eyes narrowed to icy slits. "And *what*, Miss Hall?"

Amanda rose gracefully and, with a silken rustle of petticoats, moved to the window overlooking the street below, filled now with horse-drawn vehicles crowding each other for parking space, hack drivers shouting at slower conveyances, and pedestrians trying to cross the dusty, rutted street without being run down. "Take a look for yourself, Mr. Randall."

He walked up behind her and gazed down. "I see a prosperous, progressive, growing town, Miss Hall."

"And I see a dirty, congested street filled with objectionable establishments and—and strangers!"

"Perhaps you need a good pair of spectacles."

Amanda swung around, an angry exclamation on her lips, and found the architect standing only inches away. His face was so close she could see the window reflected in his irises. His arms came up on each side of her to brace themselves against the window frame, trapping her there, his unsettling dark eyes watching her like a hawk.

Amanda's heart began to thump loudly against her ribs, and to her dismay, her knees suddenly grew weak. She backed away, only to find herself pressed against the window pane. She summoned her bravado and lifted her chin, trying not to betray her trembling limbs. "I'm afraid I can't do business with you, Mr. Randall. We obviously don't see eye to eye on things, especially where it concerns Mr. Blake."

The architect's penetrating gaze searched her face, as if he couldn't understand her aversion to a man she had never met. Suddenly, there was a knowing gleam in his dark eyes and his mouth curved into a slow grin. "It's not that you despise Matthew Blake for what he's done, is it, Miss Hall? For somewhere in that attractive head of yours, you know that progress is inevitable. You're just annoyed because Wheatener didn't stand still for you while you were away at college."

An alarm sounded in Amanda's brain. Her amber eyes grew round, and in a breathless whisper she asked, "How did you know I'd gone away to college?"

He smiled like a pirate closing in on his victim. "I know a lot about you, Amanda Hall." His gaze dropped to her mouth, and then he bent his head toward her.

Amanda did not believe the architect would actually kiss her, and when she felt the firm pressure of his lips on hers, she was too amazed to move. His strong hands gripped her shoulders, holding her steady as his kiss grew more heated. She tried to think, but found it impossible; indeed, she seemed to have lost all control over her reactions, for she was quite enjoying the feel of his mouth ravishing hers.

When his hands slipped down to her waist and his lips left hers to forge a trail of hot kisses down her throat, Amanda dropped her head back with a sigh. "Mr. Randall," she said in a breathless voice, "Someone may come in. This isn't seemly."

"Do you truly care, Miss Hall?" he asked huskily, and raised his head once again to cover her mouth with his own, kissing her hungrily, impatiently, until Amanda was quite dizzy with excitement. She'd never felt such an undeniable attraction to a man before, or such strange sensations blossoming inside her. There was a tingling in her nipples that carried all the way down to her belly and a delicious throbbing between her thighs that shocked her. She knew she should push him away, yet she hungered for more.

Suddenly footsteps sounded on the stairs and a moment later, a bright red head appeared at the door.

"Mr. Blake! I didn't remember we had an appointment this morning." Clark Randall gaped in amazement as Matthew abruptly turned, giving him a clear view of an attractive young lady who was standing almost flattened against the window.

Amanda looked from the red-haired young man at the door back to the dashing, dark-haired stranger who held her in his arms, and in a barely controlled voice she exclaimed, "*Matthew* Blake?"

Matthew grinned, stepped back, and bowed. "At your service, Miss Hall."

Amanda's eyes blazed with fury. Her sworn enemy had fooled her. And what's more, he had made a fool *of* her. To think the arrogant brute had actually kissed her and *made her enjoy it!* She pulled back her hand and swung at his grinning face with all her might, only to have her wrist caught and held in a steely grip.

"Let go of me, you loathsome toad!" she cried, struggling with him to free her arm, and suddenly finding her other wrist caught as well. "How dare you impersonate Mr. Randall! I should call the police and have you arrested!"

Matthew laughed and released his hold. "It would have been well worth the embarrassment, Miss Hall. Good day, Clark." He strode out of the room and was gone.

Both Amanda and Clark Randall stared at the empty doorway, and then, when Amanda sagged weakly against the wall, Clark rushed forward to assist her to a chair. "Please, sit down and allow me to get you some water. I'm so sorry this happened. I can't think of why Mr. Blake would play a trick on you. He normally doesn't do things like that. Will you be all right while I go for the water?"

Amanda put one shaking hand to her brow. "Thank you, Mr. Randall. I would appreciate a drink of water."

Clark dashed into the other room while Amanda sat in shocked silence. The *audacity* of that New Yorker! Impersonating Mr. Randall. Ruthlessly taking advantage of her. She accepted the glass of water from the flustered architect and took a long, shaky drink.

More than anything Matthew Blake had done, however, it was what he had said that now upset her the most, for she did indeed despise him, but not for changing Wheatener in *her* absence. No, it was that he had dared to turn it so abruptly from the path on which her father had set its course. To its own detriment, Wheatener had gone forward without Vernon Hall's loving guidance, and that thought suddenly overwhelmed her with the grief she had suppressed for over four years.

Amanda put her hands to her face and wept as she had not done since her parents' death. It was like facing the tragedy all over again.

After a time, she dried her eyes, reassured the nervous architect that she would be fine, and rescheduled their meeting. She left his office and began to walk, blindly at first, weaving through the throngs that crowded the wooden sidewalks, seeing her hometown as though through a stranger's eyes.

Soon Amanda began to focus on the familiar buildings, however, and a sense of peace began to seep through her misery as she saw her father's loving spirit all around her. "Yes, Mr. Blake, progress is inevitable," she whispered, "but not your kind of progress."

With new determination, she hailed a hackney and ordered the driver to take her to Wagner's Grist Mill. "Wait for me," she instructed, and with an obstinate swish of her skirts, she marched inside. Fifteen minutes later she emerged, smiling triumphantly. "Now, Mr. Blake, you shall see what it means to make a fool of me."

Instead of returning to the apartment, Amanda instructed the driver to take her to see her family home. She had been putting it off, fearing she would be unable to bear it if she found that Hall House, too, had changed. But she decided it was time now to face her past.

As soon as the driver turned the horse onto Willowbrook Lane, a lump formed in Amanda's throat. She sat on the edge of the seat and gripped the drawstrings of her handbag as the buggy proceeded down the wide tree-lined street, slowing before the stately brick home. Amanda could barely see it through her tears.

The driver stopped beneath one of the two giant maple trees that shaded the front lawn and sat quietly there, sensing Amanda's need to be undisturbed. She wiped her eyes with her handkerchief, then took in every detail of her family home, starved for the sight of it.

There were different draperies in the tall windows of the Georgian-style two-story home, but otherwise little on the outside had changed. She stared at the front door, imagining what lay inside. In her mind's eye, she saw the Christmas party her parents had given the night before their accident. It had been her first adult gathering, and the house had been alive with lights, music, and laughter. That night, Amanda had felt as though she were on the brink of an exciting new life, with endless possibilities before her. Two days later, her parents were dead and her life had become a nightmare.

Amanda bowed her head and gave way to her tears once again, remembering how she had fought to keep Hall House. She would never forget the day they had left it.

All seven of them had stood in the front hall in mute shock as piece after piece of their parents' furniture passed by on its way to the freight wagons parked in front of the house. Daniel had wimpered upon seeing their beautiful piano carted out, and Bonnie had pulled him against her so he wouldn't cry.

Everything but the family portraits, the precious jewelry, and a few mementos, which Amanda had hidden away, had been sold. When the house was finally empty, Amanda had walked through it one last time, stopping at the first room at the top of the stairs, her parents' large suite, to cross to the fireplace where once their wedding portrait had hung.

"I'll get Hall House back," she had vowed through gritted teeth, her hands gripping the edge of the walnut mantelpiece, tears trickling down both cheeks. "I swear I will. And we'll all come back to live in it."

Now Amanda lifted her head and gazed at the house through swollen, red-rimmed eyes. "I *will* get it back," she whispered, "and then everything can be the way it was."

Chapter Five

AMANDA COULD NOT help but notice the wan complexion and dark circles under Bonnie's eyes the next day when they met at the apartment to sew curtains for her windows. Bonnie had been unusually quiet as they worked, and even when Harper had come by at noon to share a luncheon with them, Bonnie's mood failed to improve. In fact, when Harper bestowed a brotherly kiss on Amanda's cheek upon entering the apartment, she seemed to grow even paler.

"Didn't Bonnie do a marvelous job on these curtains?" Amanda asked, holding up one panel for Harper's inspection, hoping a compliment would cheer her up.

"They're dandy. Think you could do some up for me when you're finished here?" he asked Bonnie, and for a moment, she brightened.

"Why, yes. I'd be happy to."

"What a lucky fellow I am to find someone with such a swell sister," Harper declared, but it seemed the wrong thing to say, for Bonnie averted her eyes and withdrew even further.

Harper cast a questioning glance at Amanda, who shrugged her shoulders.

"Don't forget about meeting with Mr. Randall at four o'clock this afternoon," Amanda reminded him, the memory of that other meeting bringing a stinging blush to her cheeks. She hadn't yet told anyone of her encounter with

Matthew Blake; the embarrassment was still too fresh in her mind. And she had yet to recover from the disturbing feelings he had aroused in her.

"I'll be ready, Mandy. Good day, Miss Hall."

Bonnie mumbled a reply, seeming to be absorbed in her sewing.

As soon as Harper had gone, Amanda put down her work and went to kneel in front of the chair where Bonnie stitched. "What is it, Bonnie?" she asked, and when Bonnie shrugged and continued to sew, Amanda gently drew the work from her hands and held the trembling fingers in her own. "Something is troubling you. You can tell me; you know I'll help in any way I can."

Bonnie caught her lower lip between her teeth and took a shaky breath. "Mandy, is it true that you're—that you and Mr. Brown . . ."

"What, dear?"

Bonnie could not meet her eye. "Is he keeping you?"

"Keeping me?" Amanda asked in puzzlement. Her face cleared and she said incredulously, "*Keeping* me! Do you mean to ask if I am his mistress? Why, Bonnie! How could you think such a thing?"

Tears trickled down Bonnie's white cheeks as she looked into Amanda's golden-brown eyes. "Oh, Mandy, I didn't want to believe it, but someone is spreading a rumor to that effect. And you've never said exactly what your relationship is."

"We're only friends and business partners—or we soon will be. Now, who told you such an evil thing?" And when Bonnie looked down in shame, Amanda knew immediately who it was. "Listen to me, dearest, you tell Mrs. Ripley that your sister will never be anyone's kept woman."

"But is he paying for this apartment?"

"Yes, but only until I can repay him—I insisted on that. Harper is a very generous person. It would be easy to take advantage of his kindness, but you know I would never do such a thing. Harper is highly intelligent, but not very practical. If I seem protective of him, it is only because I know how he is. And if he feels anything for me, it's only a brotherly affection." She smiled. "Now do you feel better?"

"Yes," Bonnie said with a sigh. "And I'm sorry I accused you."

"It's not your fault, dearest. I should have made our relationship clear when I first wrote you about getting rooms for us."

Amanda was relieved to see her sister's mood improve drastically after that, and secretly she vowed to give Mrs. Ripley a good piece of her mind the next time they met. But she didn't seriously believe the woman would spread such nonsense, and so she put the matter aside. Unfortunately, the harm had already been done, for within a week, the entire town was buzzing about Amanda Hall and Harper Brown.

When the rumor reached Matthew Blake's ears, he was at first disinclined to believe it, especially after seeing Harper and sizing him up as an earnest young man, but not necessarily a romantic one, and definitely not Amanda's type (although he wasn't sure how he knew it).

For a short time he even thought it rather amusing that people would think the girl would have the audacity to come home with a lover in tow, but that ended the following evening. Over a game of cards at Porter's Saloon, he heard the rumor again and found himself snapping at the tale-bearer and reminding him of what decent, upstanding people Amanda's parents had been, and daring him to quote one single episode in which any of the Hall children had been anything other than conscientious and well behaved. It was only Dixie Nightingale's calming influence that prevented Matthew from calling the offender out.

"Whatever got into you tonight, Matthew?" Dixie asked him as he drove her back to her little house on the edge of town. "You jumped all over poor Henry just because he mentioned that girl and her lover."

"I don't like malicious gossip," Matthew said irritably, drawing Dixie's buggy to a stop in front of the house. "And it has yet to be proved they're lovers. It happens that

Amanda's father was a friend of mine. He was a kind, honest man who helped me get my start in this town, and I hate to see the good name of Hall maligned." *And if Harper Brown is her lover,* Matthew thought with a furious scowl, *I'll throttle the silly chit myself for ruining her family's name!*

"Well, goodness, honey. I didn't mean to get you riled up about it. Why don't you come inside for a nice hot toddy to ease your tension?" Dixie suggested, stroking his arm with her practiced fingers.

Matthew sighed and rubbed his forehead, rubbing away a vision of sparkling amber eyes and a soft, voluptuous mouth, wishing it *were* the ruination of the Hall name that bothered him. He was even loath to admit the real reason. He was, after all, the Hall children's self-appointed guardian, although one could hardly call Amanda a child.

Before ever setting eyes on Amanda, Matthew had admired her. He had even felt protective of her. He hadn't expected or wanted to desire her. He had long ago placed his idealized version of Vernon's oldest child on an imaginary pedestal, to be held up as an example of womanhood at its most courageous, to be applauded, admired, and even pitied for the hardships she had suffered.

His desire for Amanda was even more surprising in light of her obvious dislike of him. Perhaps it was the challenge of overcoming that dislike that made her all the more desirable. He knew for a fact that Amanda felt the same potent attraction for him that he did for her. She had proven it quite effectively in the architect's office. But that was before she knew who he was.

A sudden heat filled his loins as he imagined turning that feisty, hot-headed temper of hers into a blazing, unbounded passion. But why was he even thinking that way? His conscience wouldn't allow him to take Vernon Hall's daughter as a lover, and he wasn't about to consider marrying her. The very mention of marriage made him break out in a cold sweat.

If there was going to be any relationship at all between them, Matthew decided, it would have to be straightforward and aboveboard. He was there to watch over Amanda's interests, just as he had her siblings'. Any other thoughts about her would have to be buried immediately.

"I think I'll need something stronger than a hot toddy," Matthew muttered hoarsely.

On Sunday morning, Amanda collected her brothers and took them to church with her, where they were to meet Bonnie and Gabrielle. But it was Bonnie alone who waited for them in the vestibule. She explained in a worried whisper that Alice had insisted that Gabby sit with her instead.

Amanda's amber eyes blazed with fury as she marched her siblings down to the front of the sanctuary to take the pew directly across from the Ripleys. *Alice might have succeeded in breaking my family apart,* she thought angrily, *but she will not keep us apart.*

As she waited for the boys to file into the pew, Amanda leaned over to whisper to Alice, "How kind of you to sit with my sister until we arrived. Come, now, Gabby. We've saved a seat for you."

Alice kept her eyes fixed straight ahead but Amanda could almost feel the anger radiating from her skinny frame. With a smug smile, she sat beside her little sister and covered the chubby hand with her own. *That* would teach Mrs. Ripley a lesson.

After the service, Amanda cornered her nemesis before the lady could escape in her carriage. "If you think to hurt me by spreading lies about me, Mrs. Ripley, you'd better think again, for you're hurting yourself, as well. When Gabby finds out what you're saying, she'll despise you; and I promise, if you spread any more lies, she *will* find out. She's *my* sister, Mrs. Ripley, *not* your daughter. Never forget it."

Alice glared at Amanda's back as she sailed off toward her waiting family.

"What did Amanda want, my dear?" the mayor inquired as his wife settled inside their carriage.

Alice pursed her thin lips and turned her head to fix her husband with her most intimidating glare. "Lucas, you must swear to me that you will never allow Gabrielle to return to live with Amanda."

"But I already told you—"

"You told me you would *try*. I want you to *swear*."

Lucas Ripley knew that look only too well. With a sigh, he said, "I swear."

The next afternoon, Matthew's office assistant tapped lightly on his office door at the iron mill, and at his boss's command, the young man stepped halfway in. "Curtis Hall is here to see you, Mr. Blake."

Matthew replaced the pen in its holder on his desk and leaned back in his chair. "Send him in."

Standing outside the office in the huge, noisy iron mill, Curt jumped when the assistant tapped him on the shoulder. "You can go in."

Curt adjusted his shirt and smoothed back his thick, auburn hair. He wanted to make a good impression on the man inside; Matthew was Curt's hero.

"Good afternoon, Mr. Blake," the eighteen-year-old said in a serious voice, offering his hand before he had even reached the large walnut desk.

Matthew rose and shook the boy's hand. "Hello, Curt. Thank you for coming down. Have a seat." He waited until Curt had settled in a chair facing his desk, then he asked amiably, "You're about done with school, aren't you?"

"Yes, sir. This coming year will be my last."

"How are your grades? The job isn't interfering, is it?"

"No, sir. I'm carrying straight A's."

"Your father would have been proud of you, Curt."

Curt smiled and relaxed his rigid posture. "Thank you, Mr. Blake."

"What do you want to do when you graduate?"

"I'm supposed to go to college, but . . ." He shrugged unhappily.

"But?"

Curt hung his head. "I'd rather go into commerce." He looked up, his eyes sparkling with excitement. "I've been reading everything I can about the lumber industry."

"You find that interesting?"

"Yes, sir."

Matthew studied him for a moment, his pen tapping the desktop. "If you want to learn about lumber, Curt, I can teach you. But you'll still need to go to college." He rubbed his jaw for a moment, then stood up. "Let me see what I can do."

"Thank you, Mr. Blake," Curt said happily.

Just as the youth reached the door, Matthew said on impulse, "Tell me something, Curt. What is your opinion of Mr. Brown?"

Curt scowled thoughtfully, pleased to have his opinion asked. "Harper's a good sort." He smiled Amanda's impish smile. "Somewhat absent-minded, though."

"Is he going to marry your sister?" Matthew asked with deliberate nonchalance.

Curt shrugged. "They haven't mentioned anything about it. All they ever talk about is their college."

Matthew smiled. "Thank you, Curt. That's all."

Amanda knocked on Harper's door late the next afternoon, almost bursting with excitement. When it was opened, she threw her arms around Harper's neck, heedless of any prying eyes, and told him the good news.

"We're on the agenda for tomorrow night's meeting!" she said excitedly. "Oh, Harper, we'll succeed yet in getting our school built."

"That's terrific, Mandy. Come listen to my speech and tell me what you think, then we'll round up any of your family who want to join us, and go out for dinner."

An hour later, Amanda, Harper, Bonnie, and Gabrielle were gathered around a small table at Polly's Inn. Harper opened the bottle of wine he had ordered and poured a glass for everyone but Gabby. "Here's to a successful presentation tomorrow," he proposed.

Bonnie gazed at Harper with her large, admiring eyes. "And here's luck to the speaker," she added softly.

"To success!" Amanda seconded as the three touched glasses. She laughed as her wine sloshed onto her hand.

"Good evening, Mr. Blake," Bonnie said suddenly, gazing with a smile above Amanda's head.

"Good evening, Miss Hall," a husky voice behind her said.

Amanda glanced around and her own smile instantly dissolved. Matthew Blake stood three feet away from her, his dark eyes regarding her with a look that made her blood suddenly run hot.

"Miss Hall," he said to her with a nod of his head.

It wasn't until his companion cleared her throat that Amanda noticed the well-dressed woman on his arm. Her eyes narrowed as they swept up the voluptuous figure clad in a sable brown and cream dress to the most beautiful, peaches-and-cream complexion Amanda had ever seen. Her blond hair had been meticulously coiffed and topped with a stylish white hat sporting two creamy ostrich feathers. She looked every inch the lady. But Amanda knew better.

"May I introduce Mrs. Nightingale?" Matthew said to them.

Harper jumped to his feet and extended his hand. "Harper Brown. It's a pleasure to meet you. And you, too, Mrs. Nightingale." He took Dixie's hand and pumped it up and down, causing her to stare at him in surprise.

"My, that's a strong handshake you have, Mr. Brown."

"Dixie, that charming lady opposite us is Miss Bonnie Hall," Matthew explained to his companion, "and that vision in pink is Miss Gabrielle Hall. And this," he concluded, meeting Amanda's furious glare with a flicker of a grin, "is Amanda Hall."

Dixie looked down at Amanda and gave her a smug smile. "How *interesting* to meet you at last, Miss Hall," she purred.

"How peculiar, Mrs. Nightingale," Amanda replied with a frosty glare, "I was about to say the same thing to you. Now, if you will excuse us, I believe we're ready to order our dinner."

Seething at the verbal slap, Dixie turned to Matthew to come to her aid, but he only put his hand under her elbow and guided her around their table. "Enjoy your meal," he said to Bonnie and Gabby, and then, with a nod to Harper, he escorted Dixie to the far side of the restaurant.

"Of all the impertinence!" Amanda muttered.

"Mandy, I've never seen you behave this way before," Bonnie said in a hushed voice.

"You know I can't abide that man. And as for his companion, the less said about her the better. *'How interesting to meet you at last.'* Whatever was that supposed to mean?"

"I thought she was pretty," Gabby blurted.

Amanda's mouth dropped open. "Gabby, that is enough. We want no more talk about either one of them."

Unfortunately for Amanda, however, they were placed directly in her line of sight, where she could not help but see Dixie and Matthew talking and laughing, their heads close together. A tremor shook her body as she remembered vividly the taste and feel of Matthew's arousing kiss, and for an instant she actually found herself envious of Dixie.

As if he sensed her thoughts, Matthew lifted his head and looked straight at her. For a breathless moment their gazes locked, making Amanda feel as though they were the only two in the room. Then his mouth curved into a grin and he raised his wineglass to her. Amanda blushed hotly and looked away, but not before witnessing Dixie's venomous look.

"You have nothing to fear from me," Amanda murmured under her breath. "*I* certainly don't want him."

Chapter Six

O N THE MORNING of their presentation to the town
board, Amanda stood indecisively before her small
wardrobe and pondered a suitable costume, finally choosing her most businesslike outfit, a light blue and dove gray
plaid suit with a bias skirt and leg-of-mutton sleeves, a
solid waist in gray, and a prim blue lace collar. She swept
the sides of her auburn hair to the top of her head, leaving
soft wisps to frame her oval face. To this she added her
mother's pearl earbobs, the only piece of jewelry she hadn't
given to her sisters or sold for rent money years before.

Harper had been ready for some time, and when Amanda
joined him in her parlor, she thought he looked quite dignified in his newly pressed gray frock coat and matching
waistcoat, white shirt, and black striped trousers. He carried
a brown leather case.

"What do you think?" Amanda asked, pivoting for his inspection.

"I think we'd better hurry. The meeting is due to start in
an hour and we still have to set up the plans."

With a resigned sigh, Amanda followed him outside,
where they set off for the courthouse at a rapid clip.

"Mandy, first thing tomorrow, I'm going out to buy us a
buggy," he panted as they stopped at the door to catch their
breath.

They were shown into the meeting hall and left to prepare. A long, well-used pine table dominated the front of

the white-walled room, and rows of wooden, folding chairs faced it. Four large oil paintings hung on each of the walls, one the portrait of Vernon Hall. Amanda stood before the painting for a long moment, then turned with a sigh to find Matthew Blake watching quietly from the back of the room.

He wore dark pinstriped trousers and a gray satin waistcoat with a white shirt beneath, and as before, his frock coat was slung over one shoulder. His dark hair was neatly combed to one side, and there was the usual faint shadow of a beard on his face. She took a breath to steady her racing pulse. "What are you doing here?" she demanded.

Harper glanced up at her in bafflement. "Pinning the blueprint to the easel."

Matthew laughed. "I think she means me." He walked forward, his dark eyes on Amanda, setting off a nervous fluttering in her stomach. "It's an open meeting, Miss Hall. Is there any reason why I shouldn't attend?" He stopped directly in front of her and folded his arms across his chest, looking down at her from his superior height.

It was there again, that flicker in his dark eyes that brought back in vivid detail the memory of his kiss and caused Amanda's breath to catch in her throat. Annoyed by such unwelcome feelings, she hid behind an armor of indifference. "Do whatever you like, Mr. Blake." She turned away with a toss of her head.

The cherry case clock on the front wall ticked solemnly as Amanda and Harper sat in the first row of chairs and waited. Matthew had taken a seat at the end of their row, where Amanda could feel his eyes on her.

Finally the door opened and the board members walked in, talking among themselves in jovial voices. Fred Moore took the first chair at the end of the table. Next to him sat Carolyn Tanner, a widow and a proprietress of a dressmaker's shop. She was followed by Judge Douglas and Mayor Ripley. Next was Dr. Wright; Joe Porter, owner of the general store and Porter's Saloon; Bob Egley; Leon Risk; and Jonathan Jenkins. A clerk had also come into the room and was now sitting near the table, ready to take notes.

Matthew lounged unconcernedly in his seat for most of the meeting, but when Harper began to speak, he sat forward, watching the board members for their reactions. By their expressions, it seemed Harper's proposal was being well received, but Matthew knew better than to trust appearances.

He wasn't disappointed. Upon Harper's conclusion, there was a sudden, loud burst of objections. Voices crossed one on top of the other, growing more strenuous, until some of them had worked themselves up into such an indignant frenzy that they were arguing with each other.

Matthew glanced at Amanda again and found her sitting rigidly in her chair, twisting her gloves in her hands, her eyes wide with concern. He'd tried to warn her this would happen, but she had been to stubborn to listen. This time, he wagered, he'd have her undivided attention. He rose and waited to be recognized.

The mayor pounded his gavel on the table to bring the noisy group to order. "Matthew, you may have the floor."

The other members fell silent as Matthew addressed them.

"Mrs. Tanner, gentlemen," he began, "I think you're all in agreement that an institution of higher learning is needed in this area; and I also think Mr. Brown and Miss Hall should be admired for their desire to provide free education for all."

There was a begrudging murmur of agreement around the table. With a satisfied gleam in his eye, Matthew continued. "However, my guess is that you would be more interested in seeing the school turn a profit."

At his remark, several board members shouted, "Hear, hear!"

Matthew turned to face Harper and Amanda. "Wouldn't you rather your school be self-governing, as well?" he asked. "For surely you understand that if the town were to fund your school, they would naturally insist on a voice in its operations."

"But that's not necessarily a bad idea, Matthew," Mayor Ripley interjected, rising from his seat. "No matter what type of institution it would turn out to be, we would, after all, need some kind of overt control."

Judge Douglas rose, his thumbs hooked in the pockets of his waistcoat as if he were about to deliver a speech. "I concur with Matthew's assessment. The school should be profitable *and* self-governing."

Two others stood to voice their opinions while Amanda and Harper sat helplessly by as the matter was taken out of their hands. Amanda risked a glance at Matthew and found him watching her with an arrogant smile. She frowned and looked down at her lap as Carolyn Tanner offered a proposal.

"What if the school were to be partially funded by the town? Then the board could choose a representative to monitor it, tuition could be reduced to a minimum amount, and perhaps scholarship money could be raised by charitable associations for those most in need."

There was a moment of thoughtful silence, then everyone began to speak at once. Amanda looked to Harper for help, but he was listening intently to the discussion. Finally, the mayor stood up and rapped the gavel.

"Well, it seems we're all in agreement on the need for a school, and now we have some idea as to how it should be funded. Mr. Brown, Miss Hall, are you agreeable to Mrs. Tanner's proposal?"

Before Amanda could voice her opinion, Harper stood and replied for both of them. "Yes, Your Honor, we're agreeable."

Amanda gaped at him as the mayor continued. "Well, then, since Mr. Brown and Miss Hall have the particulars as to how to set it up, I think the next thing to do is to appoint our representative to work with these young people and report back to us on a regular basis. Matthew, you seem to have a good grasp of the situation. Would you accept the responsibility?"

Amanda's face drained of color and she almost feared to breathe. *Please, anyone but him!* she prayed silently, keeping her eyes focused on her paper.

"It would be my pleasure."

Amanda's head snapped up, but before she could protest, several of the board members began to talk. She turned to Harper to see if he would intervene, but he was already moving toward the table.

Traitor! she thought, gathering up her supplies and thrusting them in Harper's open case. Not only did Matthew Blake have the entire town under his thumb, but now Harper as well. Was there no end to his intervention in her life?

"Well, Miss Hall," said a deep voice behind her. "It seems we'll be working together."

Amanda rounded on Matthew, bristling with disdain. "Not if I can help it."

With a puzzled frown, Matthew watched her march over to Judge Douglas. He hadn't expected her to throw her arms around his neck to thank him for intervening, but he had expected a *little* show of gratitude. Obviously, she was still miffed about that stolen kiss in Clark's office. He rubbed his jaw. That kiss had been a mistake. He never should have let his control slip. Now he had to convince the little spitfire he was truly trying to help her.

"Judge, surely you don't think Mr. Blake is the best person to work with us," Amanda began imploringly.

The judge peered at her through rheumy eyes. "I don't harbor any doubts about his capabilities, if that's what you're hinting at, Amanda."

"But just look at what he's done to Wheatener. Gaming parlors. Dance halls. Saloons! Is that the kind of man you want supervising a college? A man who would ruin Bill Yates's business by building a bigger blacksmith shop?"

The judge hooked his thumbs in his vest pockets. "Seems to me I remember hearing Bill say he wanted to retire, anyway."

Amanda stared at him, dumbfounded. "Doesn't anyone care about what Matthew Blake is doing to this town? Do you think my father would have been as complacent as you are, meekly allowing everything he worked so hard for be destroyed?"

"Amanda, you're overwrought. When you calm down, you'll begin to see things clearly."

"My vision is perfect, judge. I see that Matthew Blake controls this town like a master puppeteer." She turned on her heel and left as Harper spread the architect's rendering onto the table so that the group, who had at first almost unanimously rejected the plan, could better see it.

"The next thing they'll want is to name it Blake College," she said aloud, turning the key in her lock. She gave the door a good slam and sank into the nearest chair, where she moped for the better part of an hour.

At lunchtime, there was a timid knock on the door. Amanda rose and opened it to admit Harper.

"Why did you leave?" he asked, following her into the room.

"You didn't need me."

"But, Mandy, this is your idea. You should have stayed to listen to their suggestions."

"It *was* my idea. Now it's their idea. Oh, Harper, this isn't at all the way I'd pictured our school operating!" Amanda resumed her gloomy position in the chair.

"I know, Mandy," Harper said gently, coming to crouch in front of her. "But what Matthew Blake said made very good sense."

"Good business sense, perhaps. It's quite clear that all he ever thinks about is making money; you can be sure he's not in it for altruistic reasons."

"You wouldn't want to see the school collapse several years down the road for lack of money, would you? Not after putting in all the hard work it will take to see it completed."

Amanda sighed petulantly. "I suppose not."

"And we'll still be able to offer a reasonable education to those most in need of it."

"I suppose so."

"Cheer up, Mandy. We're going to build a college!"

Amanda turned her head and studied Harper's face. Seeing his happy glow, she reluctantly conceded. "All right,

Harper. Just promise me you won't let them name the school after Matthew Blake."

"I promise. Speaking of whom," Harper suddenly remembered, "Mr. Blake will be here tomorrow morning at nine o'clock to pick us up so we can inspect those properties Mr. Moore found for us."

"You'll have to go alone, Harper. I refuse to ride in the same carriage as that pirate."

Harper studied her intently. "Mandy, you wouldn't back out on me now, would you?"

"Harper, Matthew Blake has single-handedly spoiled the character of my hometown. Not only that, but he's greedy, rude, and arrogant and keeps company with shameless females. Why, he even had the nerve to—" Amanda put her hands to her cheeks to hide the blush, wishing she could forget that awful moment in the architect's office. "How can you expect me to work with him?" she spluttered.

"This fuss about having to work with Mr. Blake—you're not by any chance attracted to him and afraid to own up to it, are you?"

"Harper, that's preposterous! You know I can barely tolerate the sight of him."

Harper suddenly turned and looked around the room, a baffled expression on his face. "Where did I put my leather case? I didn't leave it at the courthouse, did I? Dash it all, I must have! I hope no one picked it up by mistake!" He strode rapidly to the door, yanked it open, and muttering to himself, left without a word of good-bye.

Amanda stared after him. Harper couldn't possibly think she was attracted to Matthew Blake, could he? Because she wasn't and never would be. He was a scoundrel. A pirate.

And, unfortunately, a damned good kisser.

When Amanda saw Matthew alight from his carriage the next morning, she ran from her window to check her appearance in the pier glass, then made a face at her reflection. "Balderdash!" she said to the frowning girl who faced her. "I don't care how I look!"

She picked up her handbag and white ruffled parasol, ad-

justed the short, cuffed sleeves of her pink and white afternoon dress, and tied the ribbons of her white straw hat, then
walked out into the hall where Harper was just coming to
collect her.

"Mr. Blake's waiting at the door," he told her.

"Yes, I know. Do you have the information Mr. Moore
gave us on the properties?"

Harper patted his coat pockets, looked puzzled, then
dashed off toward the stairway. "I must have left them on
the table. Tell Mr. Blake I'll be right down, will you?"

With a huff of annoyance, Amanda proceeded down the
hallway and around the corner to where Matthew Blake
waited just inside the entrance, leaning against the door-
jamb, looking just a trifle impatient and annoyingly dashing
in his fawn colored coat, white shirt, and brown pants.

"Miss Hall," he said with a polite nod.

"Mr. Blake," she returned, thinking how pleasurable it
would be to see his face when he learned she'd scotched his
blacksmith shop plans.

"Is Mr. Brown ready?"

"He'll be right down." She caught his surreptitious ap-
praisal of her outfit and wondered what he thought of her
appearance.

"You look particularly fetching today, Miss Hall."

Could the man read her very thoughts? She smiled politely and forced herself to reply as her mother had taught
her, "That's very kind of you to say so." Then she was instantly angry with herself for being so pleasant.

With a grin, Matthew checked his watch, then tucked it
in his waistcoat as Harper came flying around the corner,
his frock coat flapping behind him. "Good morning, Mr.
Blake," he called cheerily.

"Good morning." The two men shook hands, then
Matthew opened the door for Amanda and she sailed
through it. At the street, Matthew's driver handed her into
the elegant black and silver landau, whose twin roofs had
been put down to take advantage of the pleasant weather.
Amanda and Harper settled on one side of the carriage and

Matthew took the leather upholstered bench directly opposite her, behind the driver's high perch.

As the landau started away, Harper opened the folded papers he had retrieved from his room and began to give Matthew the particulars. Amanda kept her gaze fastened on the scenery, well aware of Matthew's dark eyes upon her.

At their first stop, Harper hopped down and strode off, leaving Matthew standing ready to assist Amanda. She lifted her skirt with one gloved hand and placed her other hand on his warm, strong one, dismayed to feel her pulse leap at the contact. As she stepped down, she raised her eyes to his face. For a brief second, his intense gaze locked with her own, bringing that sudden fluttering in the pit of her stomach. Appalled that he should have such a disturbing effect on her, Amanda removed her hand and hurried away, deciding then and there to remind Harper to assist her in the future.

The first site they explored was a cow pasture with rolling hills and a grove of pine trees on one side. The second required traveling down a narrow, curving, rutted road to reach it. It was a large parcel of flat, rocky land, owned, but unused. Being the largest site of the three, it seemed to Amanda to be the best.

Their last stop was at an apple orchard on the west side of Wheatener, halfway between the village square and the iron mill. As she had done on the previous properties, Amanda accompanied the two men as they paced off the grounds, but she found herself slipping on rotting apple blossoms and grass still wet with dew. So while the men finished their inspection, Amanda waited in the shade of one of the apple trees, until a loud buzzing near her ear made her jump.

She quickly moved away from the tree, but the bee, attracted by the pink silk roses and blue forget-me-nots adorning her white straw hat, followed. Amanda finally swatted the bee with her parasol only to have the angry insect sting her on the underside of her wrist just above her glove.

"What happened, Mandy?" Harper called as the two men

came striding toward the landau where she sat cradling her wrist.

"A bee stung me."

Matthew and Harper both inspected her wound. "Looks like the stinger is still in there," Matthew remarked. "Dr. Cook lives nearby. Let's stop and let him see it."

"It's not that bad," Amanda scoffed, although it was starting to swell and did, indeed, hurt. But Matthew insisted, and soon they were all seated in Dr. Cook's examining room, where the elderly, white-haired doctor seated himself on a stool to take a look.

"The little bugger got you a good one, didn't he? Looks like we're going to have to operate," the old doctor said to Amanda with a wink. He started to probe the underside of her swollen wrist with a pair of tweezers, but Amanda gasped and pulled her arm back.

"Now, now, Mandy, it'll only be a minor operation," the doctor admonished, taking a scalpel from his tray and holding it up to the light, "something you've probably seen a hundred times in your father's surgery. Mrs. Cook!" the doctor called to his wife who was working quietly in her kitchen. "I do believe we have a man here who is about to faint."

Amanda glanced up at Matthew, who was standing nearby, watching the proceedings with interest. He in turn glanced over at Harper, who had sagged against the ladder-back chair, his face a strange ashen color.

"Harper, are you all right?" Amanda called at the exact moment his eyes rolled up in his head. Matthew caught him before he slid to the floor.

"If you can see him into the kitchen, Mr. Blake, Mrs. Cook will make him a bracing cup of tea," the doctor directed. "Now, young lady, let's take care of you." He swabbed the site with carbolic. "I believe you may be allergic to bee venom. You'd best avoid them in the future unless you want to swell up like a ripe gooseberry. As for this, I'm going to have to make a tiny incision in the skin.

"Mr. Blake," he said, aware that Matthew had returned,

"will you lend Mandy your hand? That's a good fellow, just keep her hand rock steady on the table."

Matthew pulled up a chair as Amanda said stiffly, "I'm perfectly able—" She drew in her breath as the doctor touched the scalpel to her wrist, then she raised dubious eyes to Matthew's face.

"Mr. Blake?" the doctor said.

Matthew grinned and took a firm hold of her hand. Startled by the intimate feel of her bare hand in his rough, warm-fleshed one, Amanda blushed and looked away.

As the doctor made his incision, Matthew asked quickly, "Which of the three sites do you favor for the college, Miss Hall?"

Amanda clenched her jaw and scrunched her eyes closed as the doctor probed. "Any but the orchard," she answered faintly as the sharp stinger was withdrawn, drawing a laugh from Matthew.

"There you are," the doctor said proudly, holding up the object of torture. "Wouldn't think such a tiny thing could inflict so much pain, would you?" He dropped the stinger on the tray and reached for the antiseptic swab. "You can let go of her hand now, Mr. Blake," he said, the corner of his full, white moustache twitching with amusement.

Amanda hastily drew her hand away. "I hope Harper is all right," she muttered, keeping her eyes lowered.

Matthew rose and strode off to find out.

"You were very brave, Mandy," the doctor said as he finished bandaging her wrist.

"Thank you, but I could have kept my hand steady without Mr. Blake's assistance," she reminded him.

Dr. Cook leaned closer. "I know that, but I can't stand to have someone looking over my shoulder while I'm operating." He winked, then stood up to carry his tray to the counter as Amanda laughed behind him. "Shall we join the others for some tea?" he said, turning to offer her his arm.

Chapter Seven

B Y THE TIME they left Dr. Cook's house, Amanda's wrist was feeling much better, though she herself was misty eyed. The old doctor had been a friend of her father's, and as they drank their tea, Dr. Cook had recounted stories about him she had never heard before.

"A good man and a fine doctor, your father," Dr. Cook had said before they left. "It was a dark day when we lost him."

The ride back to town was a silent one. Harper had removed a pencil from his coat pocket and was making notes on the three properties, while Matthew sat across from Amanda and observed her as she sighed deeply and pressed her lips together in a valiant effort not to cry. Still, the tears slipped silently down her cheeks. "How is your wrist?" he asked her.

Amanda looked up and quickly dabbed her tears with the back of her hand. "Better."

"Good thing it's your left hand," Harper murmured.

"A good thing indeed!" Amanda huffed, throwing Harper an accusing glare. "You know I'm left-handed!"

"Left-handed?" Matthew repeated in amazement. "How did you slip through school using your left hand?"

"I was incorrigible," she said.

"I don't doubt that," Matthew replied, drawing forth the intended scowl.

"My father and mother were completely on my side,"

Amanda told him. "My father used to say, 'If the child can write easier with her left hand, why make her struggle with the right?' "

Matthew smiled at her. "Your father was a wise man."

Amanda turned her head to look out the window, simmering silently. How dare he compliment her father! If Matthew Blake thought so highly of him, then why was he systematically destroying the town her father had created?

Suddenly, she sat up and looked around, noticing for the first time that the carriage was not headed toward the Jefferson Arms. Immediately suspicious, she demanded, "Where are we going?"

Matthew crossed an expensively booted foot over his knee. "I thought we'd discuss the three sites over dinner. It might help keep your mind off your wound."

Amanda was in no mood for his charity. It was hard to keep her resentment sharp when he was kind. "I'm sorry, but I can't," she curtly informed him. "I promised my sisters we would meet at my apartment to work on Harper's curtains."

"Then we'll take them with us."

Amanda was about to protest, but as Matthew turned to give the driver new instructions, she noticed that Harper seemed to have brightened at the prospect of dining out, so she fell silent.

Bonnie was kneeling on the floor of Amanda's apartment, measuring out material, when Amanda swept inside. "Oh, good, you're here. Call Gabby and let's go."

Bonnie glanced up at her sister and her large brown eyes widened in alarm. "What happened to your wrist?"

"It's a bee sting. Hurry, Bonnie. We're going out to dinner with Harper and Mr. Blake." She quickly checked her appearance in the pier glass, tucking in wisps of hair that had escaped the golden pins.

"Mr. Blake!" exclaimed Bonnie, who had risen from the floor. "Why, only the other day you told me you couldn't abide the man."

"Oh, I still intend to make his life as miserable as possible, but the dinner is for business reasons, so please hurry.

The sooner we get this over, the better. Now where is Gabby?"

"She didn't come. Mrs. Ripley decided Gabby had to have new clothing today. Am I dressed all right?"

"You look very sweet." Amanda closed the apartment door behind them and dragged her sister down the hall to the waiting landau. "I'm terribly disappointed that Gabby didn't come with you. Didn't she tell Mrs. Ripley she wanted to come?"

"No, she didn't," Bonnie replied breathlessly.

At the carriage, Harper offered Bonnie his hand and helped her in. Amanda watched in dismay as Bonnie settled beside him, leaving only the seat next to Matthew free.

"May I lend a hand?" Matthew offered with a smile, leaning over to extend his hand to her.

"Thank you, but I'm quite able to climb up myself." Holding her skirts with one hand, Amanda grabbed the carriage frame and hoisted herself up, then sat down as far from Matthew as the space of the carriage would allow, frowning at her sister as the carriage pulled away.

Harper gazed at Bonnie with limpid, blue eyes. "How are you today, Miss Hall?"

Bonnie gave him a shy smile in return. "Fine, thank you, Mr. Brown."

Amanda sighed morosely and turned to gaze out at the scenery. Matthew, observing all three, smiled to himself and settled back to enjoy the view.

He took them to the Peacock Room of the Blake Hotel, which Amanda judged to be too gaudy for Wheatener, but she allowed that it could have been due to her perverse mood. She resisted the urge to gape at the sumptuous decorations only to show Matthew she didn't care for his fancy hotel.

As soon as they were seated at a table covered in blue linen, Amanda pursued the subject of her youngest sister. "Did Gabby seem upset when she couldn't come?" she asked Bonnie.

"Not at all. In fact, she seemed quite happy about being fitted for new clothing."

Amanda leaned toward her sister, her expression earnest. "Mrs. Ripley has done this purposely, Bonnie. She's trying to buy Gabby's affections!"

Harper looked stymied. "Is there a problem with Gabby?"

"I'm afraid the problem is Mrs. Ripley's," Bonnie replied with a sigh. "She seems to have developed a strong attachment to my little sister."

"Strong attachment or no, Gabby is not her child," Amanda declared.

Matthew put down his wineglass and leaned back, studying her with his dark gaze. "Can your sister's affections be purchased?"

"Absolutely not!" Amanda declared. "She's a Hall through and through."

"I wish I were as confident," Bonnie said quietly. She paused while a waiter refilled their wineglasses. "Gabby has developed a decided preference for fineries, and she enjoys all the attention she gets when she wears her fancy clothing."

Amanda's forehead creased as she pondered the problem. "We'll have to work on her, Bonnie."

"But you'll be busy with the school."

"School or no, my family comes first."

Harper lifted his wineglass. "As they say, 'blood is thicker than water.' Here's to family."

There was a clink of crystal as the four glasses met over the center of the table. Matthew drank down the contents of his glass, and not to be outdone, Amanda followed suit.

While the girls discussed their campaign to win back their sister, Matthew and Harper discussed the three sites. At the end of the first course, Harper informed Amanda that they had chosen the apple orchard as their preferred location.

"Not the orchard, Harper," Amanda implored. "We'd have to cut down all the apple trees."

"But the orchard is located more conveniently to town and to the neighbors from which you hope to draw your students," Matthew explained. "Also, that land is more valuable, which will make your investors happy."

Amanda ignored Matthew to direct her comment back to Harper. "It seems a crime to chop down good fruit trees, Harper, especially when we have all that unused land on the northeast side available."

"That rocky land would cost a fortune to build on," Matthew again cut in, "and we'd have to do something about the road, as well, which would entail acquiring even more funds."

Amanda's eyes blazed with anger. "You needn't say anything more in the apple orchard's favor, Mr. Blake. I'm well acquainted with your policy on the destruction of beautiful land."

As Bonnie dropped her gaze in embarrassment and Harper gaped at her in shock, Matthew lifted one dark eyebrow and said coolly, "I wasn't aware you'd developed such a fondness for bees, Miss Hall."

Before Amanda could volley another riposte, Harper intervened. "Mandy, you must see the sense in his argument."

"Why must I, Harper? Why does everything have to be done Matthew Blake's way?"

"It's not only my way, Miss Hall, it's also the most logical way. Do you have money for a deposit on the land?"

"It was transferred to the bank two weeks ago," Harper informed him.

"Good. Then we should make an effort to see the owner tomorrow and begin negotiations with him."

Goaded by his taunting remark and another full glass of wine, Amanda became argumentative. "What is there to negotiate? You know his price; you have the money. Just buy it outright!" She hiccuped and pressed her fingertips against her lips, hastily mumbling an apology.

His mouth twitching in amusement, Matthew swirled the wine in his glass and watched it tint the sides a translucent red. "A good businessman never settles for the first price, Miss Hall. People set their price expecting to haggle over it."

"Perhaps that's how it's done in New York, Mr. Blake,

but that's not how it's done in Wheatener. Unlike you, we value our—" Amanda paused as a sudden wave of dizziness swept over her, "—integrity."

Matthew leaned forward, studying her closely. "Are you feeling ill, Miss Hall?"

Amanda was indeed suffering the effects of the glasses of wine she had consumed in close order, but she wasn't about to admit it to him. "Perfectly fine," she said, trying to hold Matthew's face in focus. She braced her hands on the table to keep from sliding off the chair, for the room seemed to be leaning to one side.

"It's getting late," Matthew announced with one eye on Amanda. "I think it's time we left."

"And because you think so, everyone is expected to jump up and do as you say!" Amanda hiccuped again and quickly covered her mouth.

"Mandy, shall I help you up?" Bonnie asked, a worried frown on her face.

But before either Harper or Bonnie could rise from their seats, Matthew was there to assist her. "You're right, Miss Hall. I should have asked if you were ready to leave."

"You needn't patronize me, Mr. Blake. You may have the town board jumping through hoops, but you'll never win me over."

He smiled as she clutched his sleeve to keep from tilting. "We'll see."

Once Amanda was in the carriage, Matthew sat close beside her, keeping watch over her lest she begin to feel unwell and ruin his expensive moroccan leather seats. But he had no need, for before they were even a block away, Amanda had fallen asleep, her head against the side of the vehicle.

Matthew's gaze traveled over the delicate contours of her face, down her long, ivory neck to where the top button of her dress was fastened. In his mind's eye, he saw himself pressing kisses up that slender column to the sensitive flesh beneath her jaw, up to those petal-soft lips, brushing across them with his own lips until they parted for him.

Matthew let out his breath slowly and looked away. He could not allow himself the luxury of those thoughts. His role was guardian, nothing more. And, he thought wryly, nothing less, either, the way she disliked him. Everything he did to make peace with her seemed only to make the situation worse. He regretted deeply his little joke in the architect's office. He was sure if they'd met under different circumstances, he could have easily won her over. As it stood now, however, changing Amanda's opinion of him would be next to impossible.

The carriage stopped and Harper and Bonnie got out, walking to the Ripleys' door together. Jolted by the sudden halt, Amanda turned toward Matthew, settling comfortably against his shoulder. She sighed peacefully and curled one arm around his waist, bringing a rise of desire in him so strong he found himself gritting his teeth against it as Harper climbed back inside the carriage.

Once they reached the Jefferson Arms, Matthew lifted Amanda in his arms and carried her to her apartment, with Harper close behind. "We should have brought Bonnie with us," he told Harper as he laid the limp figure on the bed. "I don't think Amanda would appreciate either one of us removing her clothing."

Harper looked worried. "I think you're right. Perhaps we should just remove her shoes and stockings."

"Take off her hat and open a button at her neck so she'll be more comfortable," Matthew directed as he sat down at the foot of the bed. He unlaced her low-heeled boots, dropped them to the floor, then gingerly reached up beneath her skirt to expertly loosen the silk garters and roll the stockings down over the shapely calves and off each foot.

"Well, that's done!" Matthew said, relieved that Amanda had not stirred and caught him at his task, although he couldn't deny there had been a measure of enjoyment in removing such an intimate article of her clothing. Nevertheless, it wouldn't do to admit that to Harper.

Matthew stared down at Amanda's finely detailed features—her soft, ripe mouth curved into a serene smile, the long, dark eyelashes lying as softly as butterfly wings across her smooth ivory cheeks—down over her dress, imagining the silken flesh underneath, to her bare ankles and feet, and it took the utmost willpower to turn away.

He cast a quick glance at Harper, hoping he hadn't been able to read his thoughts. "Think she'll be all right alone here in this condition?"

"I'm right above, you know. She'll knock on the ceiling with a broom handle if she needs me."

"Listen, Harper, there's no need to tell her I was here," Matthew gallantly suggested as he pulled the bedroom door shut. "She wouldn't be at all pleased about it."

"No, I expect not." Harper stuck his hands in his pockets and rocked back and forth on his heels.

Matthew smiled ruefully. "She doesn't much care for me, it seems."

Harper shrugged and gave Matthew a sheepish grin.

Matthew stared at him, wishing he had denied it, then he turned and left the apartment. He instructed his driver to take him back to the hotel, but the image of those shapely calves and that soft, tempting mouth haunted him so much that he ordered the carriage be turned around, feeling a sudden urge to visit Dixie.

Even after fulfilling his needs in Dixie's welcoming arms, Matthew found himself thinking about Amanda. Would she have any recollection of him being in her bedroom? Would she see him and begin to tremble, remembering the feel of his fingers sliding down the velvety skin of her leg?

"My, you're amorous tonight!" Dixie exclaimed as Matthew suddenly rolled toward her and pulled her against his taut body. Fortunately for his own well-being, Matthew thought, Dixie didn't know the reason behind it.

On the morning that ground was to be broken, a crowd gathered in the newly cleared orchard, including a photographer from the newspaper, who was on hand to record the event for posterity. The temperature had been fairly cool for late June, but now, as Amanda stood beside her siblings in her navy serge dress, her white straw hat covering her head, she felt the sun's rays hot on her back and wished the mayor would arrive.

Mayor Ripley had been awarded the honor of shoveling out the first spadeful of earth, a matter that annoyed Amanda to no end, for she felt that by rights the honor should have gone to Harper and herself.

"You'd better smile, Miss Hall," she heard a deep voice say behind her, "or these good townspeople will get the impression you're unhappy with today's proceedings."

Amanda tensed as Bonnie, Gabby, and her brothers turned to greet Matthew with exuberant smiles. She had only seen him from a distance that morning, standing with Tom Bowers and two men she didn't know and couldn't describe if she had to. But she could have described how dashing Matthew looked, his dark hair ruffled by the warm breeze, his tweed frock coat slung over one broad, white-sleeved shoulder as he shielded his eyes from the sun.

Amanda also could have said exactly how high his shirt-sleeves were rolled on his bronzed forearms, and how dark his face looked in contrast with the whiteness of his collar. She even knew the moment he first became aware of her presence there, for when his eyes had found her, she had averted her gaze, pretending to study the crowd around him.

She knew it all, she realized unhappily, every detail of his appearance. But why? She hadn't seen Matthew since that evening at the Peacock Room, yet, for some, unexplainable reason, her feelings toward him had subtly altered. She no longer felt that intense loathing that she had before, and she had no clue as to why. Now, just the sound of his voice was enough to cause her pulse to race excitedly and her stomach to flutter—and she didn't like it one bit. He was, after all, still the man who had ruined Wheatener.

"I can't imagine why anyone should get the impression I'm unhappy," Amanda replied evenly, keeping her back to him in case he should notice the heat that had spread to her face. "Just because Mayor Ripley—who was not in favor of the school to begin with—was given the honor of breaking ground is no reason for me to be unhappy."

"Sarcasm doesn't become you, my sweet," Matthew leaned close to say, making her heart thump like a drum. "Mayor Ripley is, after all, *the mayor,* and as such, he is partially responsible for getting your school built. So smile pleasantly, Miss Hall, and pretend to enjoy it."

Amanda tried to think of a retort, but the unfortunate fact was that Matthew was right.

Suddenly, the mayor's carriage came into view, causing a cheer from the bored crowd. Harper joined Amanda and Matthew as the rotund little mayor helped his wife out of the carriage. Then, his chest puffed out with importance, Lucas Ripley walked briskly over to the builder, smiling and waving at the crowd, mopping his brow with a large, white handkerchief. Posing for the photographer, he accepted the silver spade Tom Bowers presented him, then summoned Amanda, Matthew, and Harper to his side for another picture.

From her position on the sidelines, Alice Ripley glared at Amanda as she joined the men. "Just look at her!" Alice hissed to her dearest friend, Marylou Egley, whose husband was on the town board. "Any time you have a group of men, Amanda Hall is sure to be squarely in their midst. It purely breaks my heart to think that my poor, sweet Gabrielle is being poisoned by her sinful ways."

"Is Amanda still living with her lover?" Marylou asked.

Alice's gaze shifted toward Gabrielle, remembering Amanda's warning. "I can't say. Amanda had threatened to turn Gabrielle against me if I say anything more about her."

"No!" Marylou gasped.

"Oh, yes," Alice sniffed tearfully. "I've just been beside myself with worry."

"You poor dear. Well, you needn't fear that I will say anything."

Alice patted her arm. "I knew I could count on you." She turned her attention back to the group in the center of the field. Moments later, she saw Marylou edge over to Constance Porter and begin to whisper. A smug smile spread across her narrow face. She could *always* count on Marylou.

Her gaze narrowed as it shifted back to Amanda. "I'll teach you to threaten me, Amanda Hall!" she sneered under her breath. And tomorrow she'd buy Gabrielle those fancy opal earbobs she'd been wanting for so long.

Once the photographer had finished, Amanda started back toward her family, only to find Matthew on her heels.

"I'm leaving in the morning on a business trip. I doubt there'll be any problems while I'm away, but just in case you need me I'll leave an address where I can be reached."

"*Need* you? It's a relief to know you won't be under-foot."

Amanda suddenly found herself facing his angry glare, his fingers locked around her arm. "Look, Miss Hall, since we're going to be working together on this school, you could at least be civil to me. It will make the days a little more pleasant."

Amanda gave an exasperated sigh and looked pointedly at his hold on her arm until Matthew finally released her. She was tempted to walk away from him, but she knew he was right. There really was no need to bicker with him all the time, as long as he understood why she was agreeing to his request. "You realize the only reason I'm working with you at all is so this college can be built."

"I realize that."

"Well, then," she said, adjusting her sleeve, "in that case, I'll be civil to you if *you'll* be civil to me."

Matthew's dark eyebrow lifted. "I was not aware I had ever been uncivil."

"You have a very short memory, Mr. Blake. Or should I call you Mr. Randall?"

He laughed. "Actually I'd prefer you to call me Matthew, and I apologize for impersonating Clark Randall. *Now* do we have a deal?"

Amanda eyed him skeptically. "I suppose so."

"Shall we shake on it?"

Reluctantly, Amanda extended her hand toward him. She watched his long fingers close around hers, suffusing warmth and something she could not define through her hand and deep into the very core of her.

"It's a deal then," Matthew said huskily.

Amanda lifted her eyes to his, and for several moments she could only stare at him. His dark eyes watched her hungrily, possessively, causing her knees to grow weak and her blood to pound in her veins. She dropped her gaze and removed her hand, swallowing hard in order to speak. "It's a deal."

It wasn't until she was on her way home that Amanda realized he had never apologized for the kiss.

Chapter Eight

O VER THE NEXT month, Amanda watched excitedly as the college took shape, each day's work bringing her that much closer to seeing her dream become a reality. In a few more months, she told herself, she would begin to draw a good salary, and then, according to Jeffrey Gable, she could petition the court to regain guardianship of her brothers and sisters.

The attorney also recommended she get signed affidavits from the present guardians consenting to the transfer. Amanda knew Alice Ripley would never agree to it, but as long as she had four of the guardians on her side, she was confident the woman would pose no threat. She hoped that within a year's time she would have enough money to put a down payment on Hall House.

The only thing to mar her happiness was that Bonnie was due to leave for college in September. Bonnie was her best friend, her sounding board, and her conscience. Without her, Amanda felt she had no one in which to confide, and it made the loss of her mother even more acute. But as that day drew nearer Bonnie began to equivocate, arguing that she had to stay at the Ripleys' for Gabby's sake because Amanda had too much to do for the school.

It was Harper who finally convinced her to go by suggesting that Amanda bring Gabrielle to stay with her a few days each week for the time Bonnie would be gone. Amanda had happily concurred, seeing it as an opportunity to free her little sister from Mrs. Ripley's domination. The only problem was in convincing Mrs. Ripley to allow it.

At her visit with Gabrielle the next morning, Amanda gave it her best try. She stopped at the Ripleys' under the pretext of delivering a promised book, and as she had expected, Mrs. Ripley made sure to be present while the two sisters met in her parlor. There, in a rare display of tact, Amanda carefully broached the subject of Gabby coming to stay with her.

"And even though I'm thrilled for Bonnie," Amanda concluded, "I shall miss her. She has been such a comfort to me these past several months. After growing up with so many brothers and sisters, being alone can be so dreadfully—lonely." She attempted to look properly miserable, then cast a quick, sidelong glance to see if her speech had produced the desired effect, but her little sister merely reached for a piece of glazed seed cake, and Mrs. Ripley was only too happy to give it to her.

Amanda sighed heavily. "I don't know what I shall do in those long, dark evening hours by myself."

"Harper lives right upstairs," Gabby blithely offered, licking the icing from her fingertips. "He can keep you company."

"But he is so busy writing, reading, et cetera, that he doesn't have the time or the inclination to keep me amused every evening. Besides, what would people say if he spent so much time with me?"

"No more than they're already saying," Alice Ripley quipped under her breath, quickly taking a sip of tea.

Amanda couldn't be sure of what the woman had muttered, and so she ignored the jibe and forced herself to smile dulcetly at her sister. "I thought perhaps *you* might come now and then to keep me company, Gabby."

Alice was immediately on the alert. "What do you mean by now and then?"

"Oh, perhaps several evenings a week."

"On school nights?" the lady demanded, the fleshy skin under her chin wobbling with indignation. "I won't hear of it."

Amanda smiled sweetly. "Oh, you needn't worry on that score. I'd see that she did her homework and was in bed at a decent time. And I'd take her to school in the mornings, too."

Alice Ripley's cup clattered to its saucer. "Do you mean to have her spend the night? In your apartment?"

Amanda's temper was rising with each passing second, but she swallowed her ire and attempted a calmness she didn't feel. "Yes, that's what I mean. What's wrong with that?"

Alice was not quite brave enough to cast aspersions on Amanda's character with no one there to support her, so instead she sat back in a huff and replied, "Well, it just won't do, that's all."

"I don't see why not—if she wants to."

"The mayor and I are her legal guardians. We shall decide what she can and cannot do."

"And I am her sister. Surely the mayor would not object to Gabby spending a few nights with her own sister."

"Well, we shall see about that!"

"Indeed we shall!"

Both ladies clenched their fists and glared at one another, while the subject of their argument obliviously stuffed herself with more cake.

Amanda rose regally and pulled on her gloves in short, furious motions. "I shall be back as soon as I get the mayor's consent."

Alice Ripley huffed indignantly. "I shan't hold my breath."

Like a miniature tornado, Amanda descended on the courthouse and stormed across the spacious lobby toward the center staircase, ignoring curious glances from the building's other occupants. In her fury, she did not even see Matthew step out of an office on the main floor near the staircase until he reached out and pulled her to a stop.

"Let go of me!" Amanda exclaimed, jerking her arm in an unsuccessful attempt to loosen his grip. "Can't you see I'm busy?"

Matthew laughed. "Busy! You look like you're about to declare war on some unlucky soul."

"And so I am. Now, will you please release me?"

"I can see that you're wondering what I'm doing here," he said dryly, "so I'll tell you. I'm paying taxes on your land. It seems that Harper is out of funds for the present, and since these have to be taken care of before the construction may proceed any further, I thought I should go ahead and pay them."

Amanda's struggling abruptly ceased. "I wasn't informed of any taxes due."

"Don't look at me as if I'm to blame. I suggest you ask Harper about it. He received the final notice ten days ago."

"Ten days ago! Land sakes! As if I didn't have enough to worry about. Well, I'm sure Harper will wire for more funds right away, so you needn't worry on that account. You will be paid back, Mr. Blake. Now, please let me pass. I have to see the mayor immediately."

Matthew released his hold and watched as she straightened her hat and hurried up the staircase. When the last of her skirt had disappeared at the landing, he casually followed her up the steps.

Standing just outside the mayoral office, Matthew was able to satisfy his curiosity about Amanda's purpose for being there. He took out a wooden toothpick and chewed on it, lounging lazily against the wall as she vociferously argued her case, thinking to himself that she was being much too demanding to do herself or Gabrielle any good. The mayor, on the other hand, spoke in such hushed tones that, had it not been for Amanda's indignant exclamation afterward, Matthew probably would not have guessed his reply.

He waited for Amanda to burst into tears; instead, she stormed out the door and ran straight into his broad chest. "Oh, I beg your pardon!" she cried, one hand steadying her hat, and then, upon seeing it was Matthew, she stepped back with a scowl. "Have you been eavesdropping?"

"If you will stop snapping at me, Miss Hall," Matthew

said quietly, leading her some distance from the office doorway, "I will attempt to help you solve your problem."

Amanda eyed him mistrustfully. "How?"

"Have you ever tried cajolery?"

She gave him a disdainful look. "Yes. Today. And it didn't work."

"And who did you try it on? Alice Ripley? Well, no wonder it didn't work; she's wise to that game. No, you have to choose your victims carefully. Now, why don't you try it on the mayor and see what happens?"

"It won't work. I'm no good at it."

Matthew regarded her petulant mouth and downcast face, thinking that it was far better that she wasn't good at it or she'd have the entire town eating from her hand. Indeed, it wouldn't take but a smile and a flutter of her eyelashes to make his own heart beat faster. "Just come with me, will you? And go along with whatever I say."

Amanda studied him skeptically, wondering why he should want to help, but seeing no other recourse open to her, she finally allowed him to escort her back to the mayor's office.

"Your Honor?" Matthew called, tapping on the open door.

"Yes? Ah, Matthew! Come in, come in. How are you?" the little man began merrily, but upon seeing Matthew's companion, his smile quickly disappeared.

"Mr. Mayor, I ran into Miss Hall just now and found her very much in distress. It seems she feels she behaved quite badly toward you and wishes to apologize, but fears you will reject her apology."

Standing beside Matthew, Amanda blushed and cast her eyes down, not out of shame, but out of anger at his presumptuousness. The mayor, obviously misreading her embarrassment, came over to her and took her hand.

"Of course I will accept your apology, Amanda. You should know me better than that."

"Thank you, Mayor Ripley," Amanda choked out, keeping her furious gaze lowered.

"The fact is," Matthew explained, giving her a gentle

nudge in the arm, "Miss Hall has been greatly upset over her sister's imminent departure for college; so much so, in fact, that she hasn't slept well in weeks, which has played havoc with her temper, as you have discovered. You know as well as anyone that she has suffered some painful separations in the past; now, to be left alone again is more than she feels she can bear. Naturally, she wishes for the comfort of Gabrielle's company—on occasion, of course— which I'm sure you can understand."

Lucas Ripley gazed at Amanda through sympathetic and slightly besotted eyes. "Of course I can. Poor girl, I hadn't thought how Bonnie's leaving would upset you or I surely would have agreed to Gabrielle's visits in the first place. Please forgive me, Amanda. I only want what's best for both of you; you know how fond I was of your father."

Matthew certainly knew what he was about, Amanda thought ruefully. Playing along with the game, she gave the mayor a sad smile. "You don't know how much this means to me."

Lucas folded her into his plump embrace. As soon as he released her, Amanda edged closer to Matthew, wanting to put distance between herself and the little man and suppressing the desire to shiver from that altogether too intimate hug.

"We trust you will explain the circumstances to your wife to spare Amanda another painful ordeal," Matthew suggested tactfully.

"You needn't worry on that account," the mayor vowed, running his finger under a collar that suddenly felt too tight. "Now when would you like to have your sister visit, Amanda, my dear?"

"Bonnie leaves at the end of August," Amanda told him. "Perhaps Gabby could come the first of September. It would make our parting much easier to bear if I had that to look forward to."

"Consider it done. Now, Matthew, did you come to see me about something, too?"

"Actually, I was in the building to pay a tax bill," he replied, glancing pointedly at Amanda, who ignored him.

"Thank you again, Mayor Ripley," she said as she sailed blithely toward the door. "Good day."

Matthew cut short his visit and also bid the mayor good-bye. "Miss Hall, may I see you to your buggy?" he asked before she could get away.

Over her shoulder she replied evenly, "No, Mr. Blake, you may not."

Matthew rarely lost his temper, but he could feel it simmering now just below the surface. He took Amanda firmly by the elbow and steered her toward the staircase. "You are the most ungrateful—" he caught himself before he said "child," and finished, "—*person* I've ever had the misfortune to meet."

"Let go of me!" she cried, trying to pull free from his grip.

"Be civil, Miss Hall," he warned through clenched teeth. "Remember our deal." He led her down the stairs, out of the courthouse, and around the corner of the building, stopping at last under the sheltering, low-swept arms of a towering evergreen. "Now then," he said, turning her to face him, "you may thank me for helping you."

Amanda glared at him through narrowed eyes. She hadn't asked for his help. He had eavesdropped. And then he had practically insisted on butting in. However, she'd never get away from him unless she tossed him something to satisfy his giant ego. "You were kind to help," she said begrudgingly, then couldn't resist adding, "even though you weren't asked."

Matthew blocked Amanda's way as she tried to pass. "Not good enough."

A biting retort on the tip of her tongue, Amanda was suddenly seized with an idea. A mischievous gleam leaped into her amber eyes. Cajolery! She would beat the blackguard at his own game.

She lowered her head as if in shame, and then very seriously, chewing her lip, she raised solemn, troubled eyes to his. "You're absolutely right, Mr. Blake, and I'm sorely aggrieved by my rude behavior." Coyly, she laid her palms on the lapels of his frock coat, smoothing them in slow, seductive movements, then leaned close to gaze into his suddenly wary gaze. "*Bless* you for interceding on my behalf, Mr. Blake. Bless you! And a wonderful day to you, *kind, gentle sir.*"

Unable to stifle her impish grin any longer, Amanda twirled and would have fled, but Matthew's hand clamped around her upper arm, yanking her back to him. Before she realized his intentions, he had pulled her into his arms and was kissing her.

The shock of his firm mouth on hers squelched Amanda's cry of protest and sent her heart thudding crazily as a pulsing heat spread through her veins out to the tips of each finger and toe. His lips claimed hers, hard, demanding, and so relentless she thought she would swoon. Never had she experienced such a kiss. Never had she felt more alive—or more confused. She could no more think rationally than fly to the moon, so overwhelmed was she by the taste and feel of him, by the shock of his body against hers, by his undisguised desire.

But when she found herself wrapping her arms around his neck and leaning fully against him, feeling the stimulation of his hard chest against her breasts, of his swollen sex through the layers of material, Amanda's thoughts came into sharp focus and she abruptly stepped back, staring at him in surprise. She had *wanted* him to kiss her! Land sakes, what was happening to her?

It was a full second before Amanda was able to speak, and then she cried breathlessly, "How dare you accost me!"

She was further stunned when Matthew laughed at her. "*You* were the one who wound your arms around *my* neck, sweetheart, not the other way around. If you don't want to be kissed, I suggest you act like it."

Amanda gaped at him. He was blaming *her* for the kiss! But dear heaven, she *had* encouraged him. Blushing furiously, she turned and fled to the buggy.

"Rakehell! Reprobate!" Amanda swore indignantly as the buggy clattered over the brick street. Yet, even as she voiced her outrage, she could not help running a finger over

her still burning lips, remembering all too vividly the delicious feel of Matthew's mouth possessing hers.

Amanda sighed forlornly. She wasn't doing a very good
job of making Matthew's life miserable. Indeed, from the
look of things, it seemed to be quite the opposite. Certainly
she *had* provoked him into a rage, but she hadn't expected
him to react in quite *that* way. And she would most certainly have to take care not to provoke him that way again.
Those kisses could become habit-forming.

Matthew climbed into his landau and called an order to
his driver, then settled back on the seat and picked up a
folded newspaper. Five minutes later, he discovered he
hadn't absorbed a single word he'd read.

He rubbed his eyes with his thumb and finger. What had
come over him? Where was his control? Why did Amanda
arouse him so? He had never met a female as hell-bent on
having her own way as she. In fact, he'd always had quite
the opposite experience. Ladies usually fell over themselves trying to please him. Not that he wanted Amanda to
be one of those simpering, clinging females. But if she
were sweet-natured like her sister, or soft-spoken and ever
mindful of a man's needs like Dixie, he might be able to
understand his lustful feelings.

He turned his attention back to the news. He had to get
his mind off his amber-eyed charge and her problems; she
was beginning to dominate his every thought. Negotiations
with Timothy Wagner for the grist mill had come to a
crashing halt, and yet he had done nothing about it. He'd
have to put Michael on it as soon as he got back to the mill.

His eyes scanned the front pages of the paper, stopping
briefly to read items of interest. A new wave of strikes had
hit the country, and worker dissatisfaction was at an all-
time high. Matthew turned the page with a muttered curse
and perused the business page, noting with satisfaction that
his railroad stock had gone up. He turned to the back page,
skimmed the real estate section quickly, and was about to
put it down, but something made him take a second look.

His sharp gaze moved over the columns again until he

found what he was looking for. He removed a pencil from his coat pocket, circled an advertisement, then carefully folded the paper and put it under his arm as the carriage came to a stop at the lumberyard.

"Where's Michael?" he asked one of the workers as he strode across the yard toward the low wooden building that housed his office.

"In the storage barn, sir," the man replied.

"If you're going that way, send him to me."

Michael O'Day was a blue-eyed, scrappy, sentimental Irishman who was the same age as Matthew and the only person he trusted without reserve. Their boyhoods had been complete opposites. Matthew had come from a well-to-do Upstate New York family. He had attended the best schools, and had his financial future secured by his father before he was twelve.

Michael was one of thirteen children brought up in a three-room shanty in Brooklyn, had six years of schooling behind him, and was lucky to have had that. Michael owed his livelihood to Matthew and had stuck by him through good times and bad. There wasn't anything he wouldn't do for the man who had saved him from a life of drudgery and poverty.

Matthew was seated at the long wooden table that served as his desk at the lumberyard when Michael sauntered in.

"You're a bit late today," Michael noted with a grin. "Female trouble?"

Matthew ignored his attempt at humor. "Mike, I want you to go see the land agent and inquire about a property for me."

Matthew strolled around to look over his shoulder, pointing to the newspaper ad that Matthew had circled. "This one?" he asked.,

"Yes, and *be discreet*. I want my name kept out of it as long as possible."

Michael leaned back to study him. "You've a sudden urge to settle down, have you?" he asked in his lilting brogue.

Matthew scowled. "It's an investment, that's all. And see

if you can find out why Tim Wagner is suddenly afraid to do business with me."

"I'll get on it immediately." Michael turned and sauntered out, a twinkle of amusement in his bright blue eyes.

Chapter Nine

S UPPER AT THE Ripley household that evening was a tense affair. The mayor gulped his soup nervously as Gabrielle chattered on about her friends. He kept his gaze averted, hoping he could finish his meal and slip away to the library for a steadying glass of bourbon before he had to tell his wife what he'd done.

"Don't you think so, Lucas?"

With a loud clatter, he dropped his soup spoon into the bowl. "Huh? What was that you said?"

Alice eyed him suspiciously. "I said that our Gabrielle is becoming quite a little lady."

"Oh, yes. Yes, indeed!" He gave Gabby a quick smile and glanced guiltily at Alice. He felt like a prisoner eating his last meal. He barely tasted his food, drank down his wine, and excused himself with a hasty murmur, sighing deeply when he reached the safe haven of his library.

He had no sooner seated himself in his chair, a glass of bourbon in his hand and his feet on the needlepoint footstool, when Alice walked in and closed the door behind her. "Out with it!" she demanded, standing against the door with her arms folded across her chest.

"Out with what, dearest?"

"You know what, Lucas Ripley! Whatever is making you behave like you gambled away your last nickel."

The mayor mopped his forehead with his handkerchief.

"Now, Alice, it's nothing as terrible as that. In fact, I believe you'll see that it's quite beneficial—for Gabrielle."

Alice's mouth fell open. "You didn't!"

"See here, Alice. Gabrielle is, after all, Amanda's sister."

"You fool!" she screeched. "Do you think I've protected and cared for Gabrielle all these years to have Amanda taint her with her wicked ways?"

Lucas slunk out of his seat and moved some distance away, feeling safer on his feet. "I merely promised Amanda that Gabrielle could spend a night—or two—each week in her apartment. And I don't think Amanda would do anything to taint her."

Alice bore down on him, shaking a skinny finger in his face. "You lied to me! You promised me this would never happen!"

"And it won't," he offered with a tentative smile, backing up against his desk. "You won't lose Gabrielle. We'll just consider this a temporary loan while Bonnie is away at school."

"We'll *consider* that you'd better be right, or you and Amanda Hall will both be sorry!" With a furious huff, Alice marched out, banging the door behind her.

The day Bonnie left for college was a wrenching one for Amanda. Harper, Gabrielle, Curtis, Daniel, Ethan, and Freddie all turned out in front of the apartment building to say good-bye to their sister, but Bonnie had requested that only Amanda accompany her to the train station.

"You will write to me often," Bonnie said in a voice thick with emotion as they stood on the platform amid the hissing locomotives and people hurrying to catch the train. "I want to hear every detail of the progress on the school."

"I promise," Amanda replied, straightening Bonnie's straw bonnet.

"And you must be patient with Gabby."

"Yes, dearest. Now you'd better get aboard. There's the last whistle."

"I'll miss you, Mandy," Bonnie whispered, throwing her arms around her sister's neck.

Amanda hugged her tightly, too distraught to reply. Through a haze of tears, she watched Bonnie climb the steps, and then she walked down the platform, peering up at the windows until she saw her sister's face appear at one of them.

Bonnie lifted the glass to call to her as the train began to pull away. "Good-bye, Mandy. Take care of yourself and Mr. Brown, too! And try to be kind to Mr. Blake."

"Has he been talking to you about me?" Amanda demanded, trying to keep pace with the chugging locomotive as she wiped tears off her cheeks.

"Good-bye!" Bonnie called, sticking her handkerchief out the window to wave at Amanda.

Amanda stood on the platform watching the train until it disappeared around the bend. "Good-bye, Bonnie," she whispered through a throat choked with tears. "I'll miss you, too, more than you know." She turned and walked back to the buggy, lost in her melancholy thoughts, oblivious to the stares and whispers of passersby.

She wished she had a female friend. Not one of the ladies in town had gone out of her way to be friendly. No one had called on her or invited her to a luncheon or had even taken the trouble to speak to her on the street. She attributed their lack of courtesy to the changing times, for in her mother's day, there had been no dearth of invitations. Now she could only look forward to Bonnie's return.

By the following morning, Amanda had regained some of her cheerfulness, for she was to collect Gabby for her first overnight visit immediately after school that day. She waited impatiently in the black buggy outside the schoolhouse until she saw Gabby walk out the door, giggling and talking with several other girls, and then she lifted her hand. "Gabby! Here I am!"

Amanda had intended to take her for ice cream, then to Carolyn Tanner's dressmaker's shop to see about having matching outfits made, and then straight out to the construction site. She was anxious to share with her sister the progress the carpenters had made on the classrooms, sure that Gabby would find it equally as interesting as she; but on that point, as well as many others, Amanda discovered she was quite wrong.

After first announcing that Amanda had embarrassed her by calling her a babyish name in front of her friends, Gabby then clambered up into the buggy, refused Amanda's offer of having matching frocks made, and sulked all the way to the college. Once there, she dragged her feet as they toured the ground-level rooms of the three-story central building, and asked repeatedly when they would be finished so she could have her ice cream, until Amanda's patience had worn to a fine frazzle.

It finally snapped when her youngest sister plopped down in the middle of a pile of sawdust and flatly refused to walk into another room.

"Oh, for heaven's sake, you spoiled thing!" Amanda cried, rounding on her. "Get up and let's go then!"

As Amanda pulled her through the halls, lecturing her about her rude and inconsiderate behavior, Gabby whined loudly about how cruel Amanda was, causing several of the carpenters to stop hammering and listen. As the sisters drew closer to the entrance, two men stepped out into the hallway in front of them: Tom Bowers, the builder, and Matthew Blake.

At the sight of Matthew, Amanda's heart began to beat faster and she was sure her face betrayed her embarrassment. She hadn't seen him since their heated kiss under the pine tree, but it hadn't kept him from her thoughts. She had to keep reminding herself that she was supposed to make life miserable for him. The truth was, however, that she was finding that task more difficult all the time.

And now, coming face to face with him after the shameful way she had behaved, Amanda wanted to turn and run. But she couldn't very well do that with Gabby in tow.

Upon spotting the men, Gabby wailed louder. "You're hurting me! You're mean and hateful, just like Aunt Alice said you'd be."

"She's not your aunt," Amanda whispered near her ear. She straightened and smiled at Tom Bowers, ignoring Matthew. "Good afternoon."

"Good afternoon," the two men answered together.

"Er, Miss Hall, as long as you're here, would you have a look at the stage?" Tom Bowers asked.

"Yes, of course, Mr. Bowers. Gabb-rielle, I'll be right back." Amanda gave her sister a warning glance before following the builder into the large room behind him.

When she emerged ten minutes later, her sister was nowhere to be seen. Neither was Matthew. Amanda walked to the door to find Gabby sitting under one of the remaining apple trees beside Matthew, watching curiously as he made her a bracelet out of long stems of wild grass.

His head was bent to his task, a lock of his dark hair falling down over his eye. His white shirt was open at the neck and his sleeves rolled back to the elbow. Amanda watched enviously as he picked up the bracelet and slid it gently over Gabby's wrist, his long fingered hands tan against her sister's white skin. He looked up at Gabby and spoke to her, smiling easily at something she said.

Amanda imagined herself in Gabby's place, feeling his fingers against her flesh, remembering how warm and strong his hand had been at the doctor's office. Annoyed by her thoughts, she steeled herself to face him, wishing there was some way she could avoid it.

"I'm ready to go now, Gabrielle," she called as she approached them, keeping her eyes fixed on her sister. She came to a stop as the two rose to meet her. Remembering Bonnie's request to be kind, she added without meeting his eye, "Thank you for keeping my sister entertained, Mr. Blake."

"It was no bother at all. I always enjoy entertaining beautiful ladies."

"So I've heard," she said under her breath.

Gabby danced around her excitedly. "Mandy, Mr. Blake has offered to take us for ice cream!"

"That's very kind of Mr. Blake, but it's much too close to dinner now. We'll have to make it another time." She took her sister by the arm and tried to lead her away, but Gabby planted her feet and refused to budge. Amanda gave her an exasperated huff. "What's the matter this time? And how is it that you can call me by my pet name, young lady, and not allow me to call you by yours?"

"Oh, please, Mandy," Gabby begged. "It's Mr. Blake's birthday. He shouldn't have to celebrate it by himself."

"I'm sure he won't," Amanda replied. "Come along, now."

Gabby folded her arms, stuck out her lower lip, and turned her back on Amanda. "I won't go unless you say we can go with Mr. Blake!"

Matthew folded his arms and leaned against the tree trunk, watching the sisters' battle of wills. He was quite sure the reason for Amanda's reluctance to dine with him as well as for the heightened color on her cheeks was due to their intimate encounter outside the courthouse, and it amused him to watch her try to get out of it.

"If you will allow me to take the two of you to dinner, Miss Hall, we can have ice cream afterward," he suggested.

Gabby swung around and grabbed Amanda's hand in both of hers. "Please, Mandy?"

Amanda didn't know what to do. Her mind and body were at odds; her brain told her to refuse while other parts seemed to hold a different opinion altogether. The happiness sparkling in her sister's eyes finally swayed her. "Fine," she said at last. "But I'll have to stop for Harper, or he'll forget to eat."

At Amanda's request, they ate at Polly's Inn, rather than the Peacock Room at the Blake Hotel, which Matthew had suggested. For some reason the mere mention of that place gave Amanda a queer feeling.

"How old are you today, Mr. Blake?" Gabby asked as she scooped up her first spoonful of peppermint ice cream.

"Gabby!" Amanda said in exasperation. "You should never ask a person his age. It's rude!"

Gabby stuck out her lower lip. "It's Gabrielle, not Gabby, and why is asking someone's age rude? I don't mind someone asking *my* age. Aunt Alice asks people theirs all the time."

"As for *Mrs. Ripley*," Amanda corrected, "she should

know better. When a person advances in age, Gabrielle, he doesn't like to be reminded of it."

Matthew hid his laugh in a cough. "Your sister is right, and a person *especially* doesn't like to be reminded of his age when *he* is a female. And to satisfy your curiosity, I'm thirty."

But it was Amanda who exclaimed in surprise, "Thirty!"

"Does that surprise you?" Matthew asked.

"Well, I only supposed you to be much older," Amanda admitted, regarding his attractive features in a different light and noticing, suddenly, that he did have a certain boyish look about him.

"And now you see why it's so rude to ask someone his age," Harper pointed out to Gabby. "It can be very insulting."

Amanda turned on her sister and said sternly, "You see what your rude question did? Let that be a lesson to you, young lady."

At that, Matthew burst out laughing.

Once they left the restaurant, the four strolled together along the sidewalk as they headed for their conveyances. Gabby stopped to admire several dolls in the general store's window, and Harper politely waited with her while Amanda and Matthew continued slowly ahead.

"I think you're going to have your hands full with your sister," Matthew remarked quietly.

Amanda sighed. "Mrs. Ripley has done a marvelous job of spoiling her. I can't wait until I can get Gabby completely away from that old goat. Unfortunately, it will be some time before I have enough money to buy Hall House."

Matthew turned his head to stare at her. So the valiant heroine *had* set her sights on Hall House. He saw her amber gaze shift to the horizon and soften to a dreamy stare and her petal-pink lips curve into a wistful smile. No doubt she was imagining her homestead once again filled with the sound of children's laughter. Before ever setting eyes on her, this was the Amanda Hall he had always envisioned—

warm, loving, and very vulnerable—and seeing this side of her caused a sudden stiffening in his lower regions.

A slight glance over his shoulder told him Gabby and Harper were still at the window. How easy it would be to pull Amanda against him, to taste those invitingly sweet lips again, to feel the softness of her breasts against his chest, to savor the curve of her thighs pressed intimately to his groin.

He let out his breath slowly. And how wrong. He was supposed to be her protector, not her seducer.

They stopped beside his carriage and he turned to face her. "This has been a most enjoyable evening, Miss Hall. Thank you for having dinner with me."

His voice was husky and intimate, and when Amanda looked up at him, she found his dark gaze on her, a hungry flicker in their depths that sent that same pulsing heat throughout her body. Her lashes fell, hiding her discomfort. "You're welcome. And—happy birthday."

He lifted her chin until she was forced to look at him. With his back to the street lamp, Matthew's face was almost hidden in shadow, but Amanda could tell he was smiling at her. He took a step closer, bringing their bodies into the slightest contact. "That was almost as good as a gift."

He was so close she could smell the scent of soap on his skin. Amanda glanced at his mouth, remembering the feel and taste of it, and of the strength of his arms as they held her. She cast a nervous glance over her shoulder, hoping Matthew would kiss her quickly before Gabby saw them.

Land sakes! What am I thinking? With a twirl of her skirt she was gone, calling for her sister to hurry.

As Harper helped both sisters into the buggy parked half a block farther up the street, Amanda saw Matthew's landau drive past at a fast clip. He was obviously in a rush to get home, she thought, until she noticed that he was not headed for the hotel but for the south side of town where, she remembered, Mrs. Nightingale lived.

Happy birthday, indeed!

Chapter Ten

"MATTHEW, DARLIN'," DIXIE whispered into his ear, snuggling against him, "in two more minutes your birthday will be over. Don't you want to celebrate it with me?"

In reply, Matthew mumbled something unintelligible and rolled onto his back in the middle of her soft canopied bed.

"What did you say, darlin'?" she cooed, propping herself up on one elbow to bend down and kiss his cheek.

Matthew's head turned and his mouth sought her lips. After a lingering kiss, with his eyes still closed, he flung his arm over his eyes and sighed one word. *"Amanda."*

The next thing he knew, he was lying on the hard wooden floor alongside the bed. With a curse, Matthew picked himself up and glowered at Dixie. "What the hell did you do that for?"

Dixie was standing on the other side of the bed, furiously pulling on her silk wrapper. "You two-timing bastard! How dare you come here to satisfy your lust for someone else!"

Matthew was in no mood for riddles. He had celebrated the remainder of his birthday with Dixie that evening with a bit too much liquor, and now, when he should be fast asleep—it had to be at least midnight—he was standing stark naked on a cold bedroom floor being called a two-timer! He was around the bed in three strides and grabbed her by both arms. "You'd better explain that accusation, Dixie."

She jerked free of him. "You have a lot of nerve, Matthew Blake, coming here and getting drunk—too drunk to make love to me, I might add—then calling me by someone else's name! Go on. Get out. I don't want you here."

"You're insane, do you know that?" Matthew yelled as he stepped into his trousers. "Even if I were seeing someone else, it wouldn't be any concern of yours. I've never insisted you be faithful to me, have I? I don't know what you thought you heard me say, but you're dead wrong about that accusation, lady."

Dixie flung his shirt at him as he fastened the buttons of his trousers. "Then would you care to explain why you called me *Amanda* when I kissed you?" she sneered.

Matthew yanked the shirt off the top of his dark head and stared at her, his face incredulous. "What did you say?"

"You heard me! Now, get out!"

He left in a rage, only to have the door slammed soundly behind him. He had no carriage at his disposal because he had instructed his driver to come for him in the morning. Now he would have to walk into town, which was a good four miles away.

"A fine birthday this turned out to be," he grumbled as he strode along. If this was what his thirties were going to be like, then he'd just as soon skip them. Thirty years old! A man expected to be treated with a little respect when he hit thirty, not dumped on the floor in the middle of the night and thrown out of a house *he* owned.

He had half a mind to go back and throw Dixie out. The gall of that woman to accuse him of calling Amanda's name. *She* must have had the dream, because why on earth would he—

Matthew came to a sudden halt. There *had* been a dream; bits of it were flitting across his subconscious even now, just beyond reach. All he remembered of it was Amanda wishing him a happy birthday—or had that really happened? He rubbed his jaw in bewilderment. But surely she hadn't called him "darling"! He must have dreamed that part.

"Happy birthday, darling," Matthew repeated to himself,

and suddenly he remembered his dream, or at least the end of it. Standing in the shadow from the glow of the street-lamp next to his carriage, Amanda had wished him a happy birthday and then she had slid her arms around his neck and kissed him—a long, hot, deep kiss that had made his loins ache with his need for her and had sent his arms around her back to crush her against him. She had been completely willing, too—until he had tumbled to the floor.

It must be a punishment of some sort, he decided.

Matthew shivered against the brisk autumn night and pulled his frock coat more closely about his neck. *Thirty years old,* he mused again. He wondered if his mother had remembered his birthday. Her mind had deteriorated greatly since her last stroke. Each time he visited, she seemed worse than she had been the time before.

He was due to go to New York and see her, but he'd been putting it off because of the pain it brought him. At least she was happy, for the damage to her brain had left her believing she was living in the past. She talked to her dead husband as if he were sitting across from her, and when she saw Matthew after a long absence, she would chide him as if he were a young boy. "Now Matthew," she would say, "you must leave your brother alone so he can attend to his studies."

Matthew shivered again, but not from the cold. Perhaps he should leave for New York right away and put some distance between himself and Dixie. Even as he thought it, he realized that he was bored with her, although she was certainly more than enough female for any man.

Her possessiveness was annoying, too, for he had made it perfectly clear to her right from the beginning that he would not be tied down. Lately, however, Dixie had been dropping subtle hints that she'd like to get married and have kids before she got too old.

Matthew had always planned to have kids, too, *someday,* but did he want them with Dixie? She made a fine companion, but he couldn't picture her as a mother. She was older than he was as well, and if he wanted a big family, they'd have to get started right away, which brought him right back to the fact that he didn't want to get married. If she was so intent on marriage, she'd better start looking for another man.

Strangely enough, that thought didn't bother Matthew a bit. In fact, by the time he'd reached the hotel, he was almost grateful for their little spat, for it had given him a chance to put their relationship into perspective, and it settled a few other things in his mind, as well.

When he finally reached his deluxe suite of rooms on the second floor of the hotel, he fell into his bed with his clothes still on and his eyes shut immediately. But he was denied the sleep he desperately needed when, an hour later, the old nightmare returned to haunt him.

He woke up drenched in sweat, the acrid smell of burning flesh and the bright glare of flames still vivid enough to make him rub his eyes in an attempt to wipe out the terrible vision in his head. He swung his feet to the floor and sat with his head in his hands, fighting the painful memories that the dream had brought to life.

"Dear God, Josh, why did you have to be so stubborn?" he muttered hoarsely.

Michael O'Day was working at Matthew's desk at the lumberyard the next afternoon when Matthew opened the door with an impatient thrust and stalked in.

"Just the man I needed to see," Michael said with a smile. "The wagons are geared up to leave tonight for the north country. All we need is your chicken scratch on this paper."

"I need a cup of coffee first," Matthew growled.

Michael cast him a dubious look, walked to a small coal stove and picked up a pot to pour the strong brew into a tin cup. He handed it to Matthew, twirled a chair around, straddled it, and studied his friend.

"You look like a herd of cattle ran roughshod over you. Didn't you sleep last night?"

Matthew took a sip of the brew and grimaced as the heat seared his tongue. "No."

"Well, now," Michael replied, his brogue becoming purposefully thicker, "I can take a hint as well as the next fellow. If you don't want to discuss it, we won't discuss it. No one can say James Patrick O'Day raised a boy who didn't know when to keep his trap shut. Like me sainted mother used to say, 'Tis a wise man who can keep his own counsel.' "

Under normal circumstances, Michael's banter would have restored Matthew's good humor, but he only rubbed his eyes with his thumb and finger and sighed wearily.

Michael dropped his teasing tone. "What is it, Matthew?"

Matthew scowled at the papers before him. "The dream."

"What brought it on?"

Matthew tipped his chair back on two legs and ran his fingers through his hair. "Tension, I suppose. I'm leaving tomorrow morning for New York to visit my mother. I'll be back in a week. See to everything here, will you, Mike?"

"It goes without saying, Matthew." He watched his friend sign his name on the paper in front of him, then hand it across the desk. "Why don't you go back home and get some sleep?"

"Too much to do, Mike. Maybe later."

Comfortably ensconced in a soft mint green slipper chair in the fitting room of Carolyn Tanner's shop, a cup of tea in hand, Amanda watched Carolyn pin a new peach-colored wool frock on her youngest sister.

"Gabrielle, you're going to have to start refusing those cakes and cookies Mrs. Ripley feeds you if you want to have a nice figure when you grow up," Amanda told her bluntly.

Gabby started to pout, but one look from Amanda's stern face stopped her. "Yes, Mandy," she said with downcast eyes.

"You're a lovely young lady, Gabrielle," Carolyn said smoothly, "and you have beautiful skin, but to keep it that way you must avoid an excess of sweets."

The proprietress turned to wink over her shoulder at Amanda, who gave her a grateful smile in return.

Carolyn was an attractive widow in her mid-forties, her

blond hair only just showing signs of graying. She was tall, elegant, and soft-spoken, yet she exuded confidence and authority. When Amanda had been at her lowest after Bonnie's departure, Carolyn had invited her to tea. Before long, the two were fast friends, filling a deep void in Amanda's life.

Amanda looked at Gabby and smiled. She was finally coming around. She minded her manners, at least in Amanda's presence, and was outgrowing some of her selfishness. If only she wouldn't eat so many sweets. But that would change once she was back under Amanda's control.

Dixie Nightingale picked up the navy leghorn hat that had been sitting on a display stand in Carolyn Tanner's front window and tried it on, turning her head from side to side to study her reflection in the window's glass. In that same reflection she saw Carolyn Tanner part the back curtains and come into the main room of the shop. She swung around with a smile and opened her mouth to speak, but the words died on her lips as Amanda came into the room behind her.

Dixie's eyes narrowed menacingly. Amanda looked young and lovely and supremely confident, and it was all Dixie could do not to claw her eyes out. Matthew had never laid name to it, but Dixie was absolutely certain that Amanda was the reason he had bid her adieu. And now Dixie was after blood.

"Why, good afternoon, Mrs. Tanner, and you, too, Miss Hall," she said sweetly.

"Good afternoon," Amanda murmured coolly, and directed her attention elsewhere.

"What may I help you with today, Mrs. Nightingale?" Carolyn asked.

"I was passing by and saw this hat in your window, and I wondered if you had one just like it in a dark green color."

"I'll check for you," Carolyn told her.

When the proprietress had disappeared through the curtain, Dixie turned to Amanda, who was doing her best to ignore her, and said, "And how is your college coming, Miss Hall?"

"Fine, thank you."

Dixie moseyed closer to Amanda and said in an undertone, "If I were you, I wouldn't look down my nose at someone unless I were sure my reputation could stand the comparison."

Without turning her head, Amanda replied, "I don't know what you're talking about."

Dixie smiled cagily. "I know what kind of woman you think I am, Miss Hall, but I wonder if you realize people in town have put you in the same category."

At that, Amanda turned her head, her amber eyes narrowing. "What do you mean?"

"Why, you're a loose woman, just like me! Birds of a feather, so to speak. Haven't you heard? They've been talking about you since the day you brought Mr. Brown home. So I don't see any reason at all for you to put on airs every time you meet me, do you?"

Dixie paused to assess the effect of her speech on Amanda. Seeing the stricken look on the younger woman's face, she said, "I'm so glad we had this little talk. It'll be a real pleasure having someone to discuss *private* matters with. The *ladies* in town find such subjects much too coarse to even think about, let alone discuss. Why, we can have tea one afternoon. I've been dyin' to know if other men are as *forceful* and as *passionate* as my Matthew is."

The curtain parted and Gabby came into the room, chattering gaily. Carolyn followed her, a tall hat box in her hands. Amanda swung around, her eyes huge, her features stiff from shock. Woodenly, she mumbled a hasty good-bye to Carolyn, grabbed her sister's hand, and whisked her out of the shop.

With a satisfied smile, Dixie turned to say to a bewildered Carolyn, "Oh, good, you found the hat! Suddenly, I'm in the mood to spend a whole pile of money."

Amanda rounded the corner into an alley and came to a stop, trembling so hard her teeth were chattering. A loose woman! Birds of a feather! She dropped Gabby's hand and covered her face, sick with humiliation. Was it true? Did people really believe she was a loose woman? She felt light-headed and took deep breaths to steady herself.

"What's wrong, Mandy?" Gabby cried, shaking Amanda's elbow. "You're frightening me!"

Amanda dropped her hands and saw her sister's terrified face. "Oh, Gabby, I'm sorry." She wrapped her arms around the girl's shoulders and held her tightly until her own trembling stopped. "I just felt ill all of a sudden, that's all."

"Do you want me to fetch a hackney?" Gabby asked.

"No, I'm fine now." Amanda straightened her shoulders, took Gabby's hand, and they continued on their way. But it suddenly seemed that people on the sidewalks were averting their eyes as she passed them by.

"Are we going to eat supper with Harper?" Gabby asked as they neared the Jefferson Arms.

"I don't know," Amanda replied distractedly.

"But who will feed him if we don't?" Gabby pressed.

"All right, Gabby, we'll invite him to supper."

But the thought of seeing Harper made her stomach heave as the woman's unpleasant words rang loudly in her mind. How naive she had been to think Alice Ripley would never spread such a vicious lie. Yet now that it was all over town, what could she do about it?

Chapter Eleven

Despite her threat to Mrs. Ripley, Amanda could not bring herself to tell Gabby about the rumor, not only because of her humiliation, but also because she refused to use her sister as a pawn in her fight with Alice. For the next few days she kept to her rooms under the pretense of headaches as old feelings of helplessness surfaced. She even avoided going to the college, not only because she dreaded hearing the workers snicker at her, but also because she feared that any connection she had with the school would damage it. She was afraid no one would attend a school run by a notorious woman.

Carolyn Tanner surprised Amanda with a visit one afternoon, and as Amanda poured tea for her in her small sitting room, she couldn't help but wonder if Carolyn had come because she had heard the rumors, too.

"What I have in mind, Amanda," Carolyn told her as she accepted a cup of tea, "is to throw a charity ball to raise scholarship money for the college. I'd be willing to plan it, and I thought perhaps we could hostess it together."

"I think your idea is splendid, Carolyn, but it would be best if you didn't include me."

"Is it because of that ridiculous rumor?"

Amanda nodded and dropped her gaze.

"Amanda," Carolyn said gently, "I know how much gossip can hurt. I came to Wheatener from a small town in Virginia just to escape a rumor such as that."

"You, Carolyn?"

Carolyn laughed. "Do you find it so amazing? The rumor concerned myself and my husband's brother, who had consoled me after my husband's death. It was nothing more than that, but people chose to believe otherwise until it nearly destroyed my brother-in-law's marriage. At that point, I decided it would be better for both our sakes for me to leave and start anew."

"How dreadful!"

Carolyn smiled. "At the time it seemed so, but I'm perfectly content now. However, I shouldn't think you'd have to take as drastic an action as I did to stop the rumor. Just go about your business and it will blow over."

Amanda lifted her chin. "I'll try, Carolyn. Where do you intend to hold this ball?"

Carolyn's eyes shifted to the window as she pondered the question. "It does present a problem. Being a winter ball, we couldn't very well hold it at the fairground pavilion, and the ballrooms at the larger houses in town wouldn't hold nearly enough people for what I have in mind." Her eyes suddenly brightened. "I know—the dance hall."

"Land sakes, we couldn't hold it there!" Amanda exclaimed. "Why, people would be offended if we dared invite them to such a place."

"Perhaps you're thinking of how Wheatener was before you left. Half of Wheatener's populace have only lived here two years or less. I guarantee that if you invite them to a charity ball at the dance hall, they'll come." At Amanda's look of dismay, she rose and smiled. "Leave everything to me. I'll be in touch soon."

By the end of the week, Amanda could stand her self-imposed exile no longer. On an overcast Saturday morning, when she knew the school would be deserted, she finally ventured out. She parked her buggy around in the back and walked quickly to the front. Once inside, she pushed her worries to the back of her mind and took note of the progress that had been made in a week's time.

It still amazed her that she and Harper could effectuate something as grand as a college. She felt as maternal about the building as if it were their child, but that thought sent her mind spiraling back to Dixie's spiteful words and her elation faded into despair.

From force of habit, Amanda walked through each room, a pencil and writing tablet in hand to jot down notes. She stopped at the auditorium, where she discovered that all fifty rows of seats had been installed and the heavy curtains on the stage had been hung. But as she mounted the three temporary steps at the front of the stage, she caught the heel of her shoe between two boards and nearly fell.

"Damnation!" she muttered, and gave a hard yank on the heel only to have it tear completely off. She tried to walk with one flat sole, but it proved to be so awkward that she took off both shoes and walked across the stage in her stocking feet instead, until a sliver of wood caught the fibers of one stocking and tore it, at which point, with another muttered curse, she removed them as well.

As Amanda gingerly retraced her steps across the rough stage toward the stairs, she was so intent on avoiding splinters in her bare feet that she failed to see a piece of lumber sticking out from the scaffolding and banged her forehead on it.

Suddenly she heard voices in the hall coming toward the auditorium. She stepped backward to hide, knocking the lumber again as she did. She rubbed her aching head and pressed her back against the wall of the stage's west wing, praying no one had heard her.

In a matter of minutes she heard the voices again as footsteps sounded on the auditorium floor. At a closer distance, she was able to identify some of the voices, Matthew Blake's among them, as well as Judge Douglas's and Mayor Ripley's. She guessed it was the town board come to take a tour of the premises.

Hugging the shadows against the wall, Amanda scrunched her eyes shut and held her breath as someone walked up on the stage, paused, turned around, and walked down. After a few minutes the footsteps and voices faded, but Amanda waited until she was certain they were well away from the auditorium before leaving her hiding place.

Cautiously, holding her shoes and stockings in her hands, she descended the steps and tiptoed across the floor, peering into the hallway before proceeding farther.

From a classroom window across the hall, Amanda watched two carriages pull away, and then she breathed a heavy sigh of relief. She turned around and gave a small cry of alarm at the sight of Matthew Blake lounging in the doorway, his arms folded across his white-shirted chest, a bemused look on his face.

"Playing games, Miss Hall?" he asked dryly, until the sight of her bleeding forehead brought his dark eyebrows together. "Now what have you done to yourself?"

"If it's any of your business, I broke the heel of my shoe." She held up her shoes for him to see as she moved toward the doorway, intending to slip past him before he could ask any more nosy questions.

Matthew stepped in her way. "That doesn't explain your head. Hold still so I can see." He parted the soft curls on her forehead and whistled at the sight of her injury.

"There's another bump in the back," Amanda admitted begrudgingly.

He grinned as his fingers slipped to the back of her skull. "Why isn't Harper with you?"

"Why should he be with me?" Amanda retorted, and at his raised eyebrows, grumbled, "He's writing letters today and—ouch!" She winced as he felt the lump. "Land sakes, they're just little bumps. Leave them alone!"

Matthew removed his handkerchief from his coat pocket and carefully wiped the blood from her forehead. "I'd better see you home. These little bumps, as you call them, look mighty ugly. I wouldn't be at all surprised if you started to feel dizzy."

"I've never been dizzy in my life and I'm perfectly able to see myself home. I wish you'd stop accosting me every time we're alone." Amanda pushed away his hand and slipped past him into the hallway, hoping her show of temper covered her agitation, for the truth was, the very sight of him had sent her pulse skidding out of control and started a trembling inside that she couldn't seem to stop.

"The fact of the matter is, Miss Hall," Matthew said, fast on her heels, "I need a lift to town. I passed up my ride to come back and check on you."

They came to the front entrance and Matthew grabbed her upper arm before she could start out the door. "Aren't you forgetting something?" He smiled and looked down at her bare feet. "In case you haven't noticed, it's been raining. Surely you're not going to walk through that mud in bare feet."

Amanda turned to gaze out in dismay at the muddy terrain, but before she had a chance to reply, Matthew scooped her up in his arms. "I'm not accosting you; I'm only doing this to be civil. Is your buggy in the back?"

"Yes." Amanda clutched her shoes and tried to ignore the heat that suffused her body from his nearness, yet her voice was slightly breathless when she spoke and she was sure her cheeks were pink. "How did you know I was here?"

"I heard a noise on the stage, went up to investigate, and there you were, bare feet and all."

"I'm surprised you didn't call everyone up to see me."

One corner of his mouth twitched in amusement. "Now who's not being civil? Besides, I've seen you in worse states."

"I'd hardly call a bee sting worse than a broken heel and two nasty bumps on the head!" Amanda declared.

"Ah! So now you admit they're nasty. And I wasn't thinking of your bee sting."

"What, then?" Amanda asked as he approached her buggy. "I can recollect no other time."

"That doesn't surprise me, given your condition at the time."

She was growing increasingly vexed with him. "Would you explain that remark, please?"

Matthew came to a stop beside the buggy and smiled down at her, his eyes warm and amused. "I don't think you'd appreciate it if I did."

"You're making this up to irritate me." Amanda kicked her bare feet impatiently. "Put me down."

"You'll muddy your feet," he warned.

"I don't care."

His eyes glittered devilishly. "As you wish, Miss Hall." In a sudden movement, he withdrew one arm from beneath her legs, startling her so that Amanda gasped and turned toward him, flinging her arms around his neck to keep from falling into the mud.

When her bare toes came to rest on the tops of Matthew's boots, Amanda glanced up at him in astonishment, belatedly realizing that he still held her securely around her waist and had never intended to let her fall. And then a slow blush suffused her cheeks as she became aware of her thighs pressed intimately to his groin, and the soft peaks of her breasts thrust boldly against his muscular chest. He must have become aware of it as well, for she felt the sudden hardening of his sex against her belly, stirring her blood as nothing had ever done before.

Slowly, Amanda lifted her eyes to meet his. At the raw, animal hunger reflected in those dark depths, her entire body began to throb with desire. She wanted him to kiss her, to touch her where no one had ever touched her, but she was at a loss to understand why. Matthew was supposed to be her enemy.

Confused, embarrassed, and chagrined by her own wantonness, Amanda removed her arms from around his neck and dropped her gaze. In a subdued voice she said, "I think we should go."

For a moment Matthew didn't move, making her fear he did intend to kiss her. But then he lifted her up, placed her on the seat of the buggy, and climbed in to sit beside her.

Away from the warmth of his arms Amanda shivered in the cool air and pulled her black stockinette jacket tightly about her. As Matthew guided the horse back to town she bent to pull on her shoes, acutely aware of his muscular thigh so near her own, miserable that he should have the ability to affect her so. When they arrived at the Blake Hotel, she kept her eyes fixed straight ahead as Matthew handed her the reins.

"The next time you decide to venture to the college when

no one is there," he lectured as he climbed down, "take Harper with you. It's not wise to go alone."

She sighed unhappily, remembering the reason she had gone there alone. "It wouldn't be wise to go with Harper, either."

Matthew's eyebrow lifted. "Why?"

Amanda hadn't intended to tell anyone, least of all him, but now she was almost glad for the chance to find out if he, too, had heard the horrible lies being spread about. "Because the whole town is talking about us."

"And what is the whole town saying?"

An embarrassed flush colored her cheeks and she dropped her gaze as she spoke. "That I'm a loose woman."

Matthew threw back his head and roared with laughter. "A loose woman! I can't imagine anyone farther from that description than you!"

"Sh-h-h!" Amanda glanced around to see if they were being overheard, and spotting people farther down the sidewalk, she leaned toward him and whispered, "Then you haven't heard the rumors about Harper and me?"

Matthew's smile instantly dissolved. If someone were spreading new lies about her, he'd hunt down the guilty parties and wring their necks. "I think this merits further discussion. Come into the hotel and have a cup of coffee with me."

"Why can't we talk here?"

"Do you want it spread all over town that you were seen whispering secrets to me in the dark?"

"In case you forgot, I broke my shoe. And don't say I should go barefoot, for I won't do it and cause further scandal. And whatever you do, do *not* try to carry me or you'll be sorry."

"Wear your broken shoe," he said as he opened the door for her. "If you tiptoe, no one will notice."

With a huff of annoyance, Amanda allowed him to help her down and escort her into the hotel. Conscious only of maintaining a graceful gait so as not to draw attention to herself, she didn't realize his intention of taking her to his suite until he stopped before two large white doors and slipped his key into one of them.

Amanda stepped back in alarm. "Where are we?"

"Home," he replied, guiding her into his sitting room.

Amanda's angry retort was immediately stilled as she gazed about in wonder. While Matthew walked around turning up the lamps, her eyes swept across deep blue walls and creamy silk draperies to the ivory marble fireplace at the end of the room, then to the twin ivory camelback sofas facing each other before the hearth, and finally to the thick blue, green, and ivory patterned carpet beneath her feet.

Matthew turned up a gas lamp next to one of the sofas and walked toward her. "Have a seat, Miss Hall. I'll get the coffee."

Amanda was too curious to sit. When Matthew left the suite, she took off her shoes and wandered around the sitting room, examining the pieces of sculpture that had been placed on the odd oriental-style tables. Then she turned her attention to the oil paintings in their gilded frames.

When Matthew returned, it was to find Amanda standing before a newly acquired painting, quietly contemplating the dark-haired girl in a white dress and white straw hat, sitting under an apple tree in the middle of a meadow with a basket of wildflowers in her lap and a faraway look in her eyes.

Matthew stood quietly behind her, a silver tray in his hands, studying her trim back and slim neck appreciatively for a few moments before asking quietly, "Do you like it?"

"Yes, it's lovely." She cocked her head to one side as she considered it. "It reminds me of something—or someone."

Matthew gazed at it with her, then abruptly turned away. "How do you take your coffee?"

"What? Oh, cream, please." Amanda followed him to a small table set with an ivory linen tablecloth and brass candlesticks. "I shouldn't have come here," she told him, accepting the delicate white china cup of coffee. "I can't think what it would do to my reputation if someone should spot me leaving."

"Tell me exactly what you've heard."

"That Harper and I are—" She blushed hotly and looked down. "—more than just business partners."

Matthew leaned back in his chair and sipped his coffee. "That rumor is old hat. I'm surprised you haven't heard it before."

"I haven't run into your *mistress* before!"

Matthew set his cup down with a bang. "*Dixie* told you?"

"Do you have other mistresses? Yes, Dixie told me, and she took great delight in doing it, too!" Remembering the woman's crude suggestion that they compare lovers, Amanda pushed aside her cup with a grimace of distaste and rose.

"Wait." Matthew stood before her, his eyes as hard as flint. "I want to know all she said."

"She said we were birds of a feather!" Amanda exclaimed indignantly. "And now I can barely stand the thought of anyone seeing Harper and me together, imagining what they're whispering about us." Her fingers twisted together. "Poor Harper, from the way I've avoided him lately, he surely believes I'm angry with him, but I don't have the heart to tell him the truth. To think I went about town all those weeks without knowing. And I can't bear to think what it will do to the school, or to my family."

She felt the first prickle of tears and blinked them back. "Mrs. Ripley is responsible for this," she said through gritted teeth. "She'll do anything to ruin me so she can keep Gabby."

Amanda was suddenly embarrassed that she had confided so much to him. "Is there a way out where I won't be seen?"

"There's an exit into the alley from the rear stairway," he told her, walking with her to the door. "And you shouldn't fear what others say about you if your conscience is clear. Just hold up your head and go about your business."

Amanda's hand was on the doorknob, but at his words she paused, and when she turned, her eyes were bright with unshed tears. "That's just what my father would have said," she whispered in amazement.

Matthew moved closer and lifted his thumb to her face to

wipe away a solitary tear. "I'll take that as a compliment, Amanda." His gaze dropped down to her mouth and his thumb slid across her cheek to trace the outline of her lips.

Amanda placed her hand on his to halt him, but the warmth of his fingers beneath hers was too enticing. Her hand stilled, and, for an expectant second, neither one moved; then Matthew raised her chin and bent his head for a kiss.

At the first touch of his mouth on hers, Amanda forgot the hateful rumors. The taste of his lips, the scent of his skin, the faint stubble of beard against her chin, the heat of his body, all combined to fill her with a longing she was at a loss to explain. *Resist him!* her conscience warned.

Matthew's lips moved hungrily over her own. His hands slid down her back to her derriere, pressing her against him. She felt his arousal and moved her body in answer to it. With a deep, throaty growl, Matthew swept her up and carried her into his bedroom, his mouth never leaving hers.

He pressed her down into the bedcovers, his thighs hard against hers, his erection at the juncture of her legs. Amanda moved restlessly under him, trying to seek relief from the tension inside her. His tongue seared the line of her lips until she opened to him, and when he plumbed the depths of her mouth, she felt a throbbing heaviness deep inside that caused her hips to thrust upward against him.

She threaded her fingers in Matthew's hair as he trailed hot kisses down her throat. His hand covered her breast and his thumb circled a swollen peak through the material of her bodice, causing it to tighten and pucker.

"Mr. Blake!" she said in a breathless gasp.

Matthew raised his head, his dark eyes smoldering with an intensity that both frightened and excited her. "Matthew! Say my name."

"Matthew," she whispered, and gasped when he lowered his mouth to gently nip the tender peak with his teeth. His hand sought the inner curve of her thigh, pressing into the folds of her skirt, delving into the tender flesh beneath, bringing on a longing so great that she groaned in frustration.

At that, Matthew tore himself away from her and began to strip himself of collar and cuffs, his eyes never leaving her face. He loosened the studs of his shirt in short, hurried movements and dropped the garment carelessly at his feet. But when he tugged off his undervest, leaving his muscular chest exposed to her gaze and began to undo the buttons of his trousers, Amanda sat up in alarm, appalled that he should think her willing, and even more horrified to realize she very nearly was. She sprang off the bed and fled the room, more shocked by her own behavior than by his.

But Matthew was quicker, and as she yanked on the doorknob to let herself out of his suite, he grabbed her arm. "Amanda, wait. Let me explain."

Amanda jerked free and opened the door, stopping outside long enough to throw him a hurt and accusing glare. "You *do* believe what the gossips are saying about me or you wouldn't have tried to take advantage of me!"

"No, Amanda, you're wrong," Matthew called, but she wouldn't even look back. He watched her disappear down the back stairs, then he shut the door with a bang and raked his fingers through his hair. His desire for Amanda had risen beyond his control. He could hardly look at her without wanting to feel her body beneath his—without wanting to possess her.

Matthew took a deep, shuddering breath. He had to rein in his emotions. He wasn't the type of man to force himself on a woman, but Amanda's passionate response had fogged his thinking. The wisest course, obviously, would be to steer clear of her to avoid further temptation. As her guardian, it was the least he could do.

If he could do it.

Chapter Twelve

"MANDY, HERE YOU are at last!" Harper called. He had been pacing impatiently in the hall in front of her apartment, and as she entered the building, limping in her broken shoe, he strode forward to meet her. "You'll never believe the news! Twelve professors have replied to my advertisement!"

Amanda was astonished that he could not see her distressed state. She opened her door, and after a quick glance down both sides of the hall, she said quickly, "Come in, Harper."

Harper shut the door and started toward the kitchenette. "I'll put the kettle to heat while you look over the replies."

Amanda pulled out a chair and sank into it, staring unseeingly at the stack of mail before her.

"What took you so long?" Harper called.

"I . . . I had a slight mishap." Amanda's heart raced with frightening speed at the memory of her passionate encounter, and her stomach knotted when she thought of how close she had come to letting Matthew make love to her.

She was removing her shoes as Harper carried in two cups and placed one on the table in front of her. "Did you see the application from Professor Hildebrandt?" he asked excitedly.

"No, I didn't. Harper, what could Matthew Blake have meant when he said he'd seen me in a worse state than my bee sting?"

"I'm afraid I don't know what you're talking about. Look, Mandy, an application from *the* Professor Hildebrandt!"

"Yes, I see. Listen, Harper, today at the school, I bumped my head and broke my heel, and, well, one thing led to another and I ended up in my bare feet. When Matthew Blake saw me, he said he'd seen me in a worse state, but that I hadn't been in any condition to remember; and he wouldn't explain what he meant. Do you have any idea? Harper! Are you listening?"

He looked up and his eyes widened in surprise. "Mandy! You've injured your head! Let me get you a cold cloth."

"Harper, you didn't answer my question!" Amanda exclaimed in exasperation. Suddenly she sat forward, staring at the letter in front of her, then she reached for the others and began to leaf through them. "All of these applications are to Wheatener College. Harper, we haven't named the school yet! Where did this name come from?"

Harper walked in with a cloth in hand, which he applied to her bruised forehead. "I couldn't very well ask someone to apply to a college with no name, so when Mr. Blake suggested Wheatener, I thought it made perfect sense and I used it."

Amanda yanked the cloth away from him, irritated beyond reason to find yet another example of Matthew's influence. "The least you could have done was to ask my opinion of it."

"Don't be put out with me, Mandy," Harper pleaded. "I had to make a decision before I sent them, and since you were on one of your inspections . . ."

"You went to Mr. Blake's office and asked his advice."

"It wasn't that way at all." Harper frowned at the ground like a petulant child.

Amanda sighed. "I had wanted to name it after you, Harper."

He looked up in surprise and then put his arms around her and gave her a gentle hug. "Thank you, Mandy," he said softly. He leaned back to smile at her, then bent his head and kissed her very swiftly on the mouth. And in the next second, he was lunging for the rest of the mail.

"I've found four top-notch men so far," he said, oblivious to the fact that Amanda was staring at him in bewilderment.

Was Harper in love with her? He'd never acted as though he were, but then he was not a conventional person, she reminded herself. He wouldn't show it as others would. Her forehead wrinkled as she considered what to make of the situation, and then, suddenly, her face cleared. Perhaps there was a solution to those horrid rumors after all. She and Harper could get married. Surely, if he loved her even a little bit, he wouldn't mind marrying her.

But more to the point, she thought suddenly, do I love him? Amanda studied his earnest face as he bent over the applications. Harper was kind, intelligent, attractive in a studious sort of way; and she was very fond of him. And then there was their shared commitment to the college to consider. But was that enough? She thought back to his kiss. It had been given, she knew, from the bottom of his heart, but it hadn't felt as she had always thought a kiss from a beau should feel. It lacked . . . emphasis; yes, that was it. It was a sweet kiss, but it lacked emphasis.

The memory of Matthew's highly arousing kisses jumped into her mind, and with a furious shake of her head, she pulled half of the stack of applications to her side of the table and began to read them. She would not think about Matthew Blake. He was a scoundrel and a rake. Thank goodness the school was nearly finished. Then she need not see him ever again.

One morning a week later, Amanda rose from her bed and went to the window to gaze disconsolately at the sights beyond. The sky was gray with the threat of rain, the trees were bare and ugly, and the street was a mire from yesterday's downpour. With a sigh, she leaned her forehead against the cold glass.

It was her twenty-fourth birthday, and on mornings such as those, she missed her parents so much her heart ached from loneliness. Her mother had always made a fuss over their birthdays, preparing a huge family dinner where everyone dressed in their Sunday best. There was a special buttermilk cake, too, decorated with colorful frostings and candles, and a present in gaily colored tissue paper to open.

Amanda's eyes filled with tears as she recalled the special gift she had received on her eighteenth birthday. It had been the pale green silk gown she had worn to her very first—and last—social evening at Hall House.

"No! Not the last!" she said aloud. She shoved herself away from the window, stirred the coals in the little stove, and began to dress. So what if it was her birthday? It was a day like any other. Her only concession to the day would be a supper at Polly's Inn with Gabby and her brothers.

After she had eaten a light breakfast, Amanda went to the post office at the back of the general store to pick up her mail. Standing outside the store, she shuffled through the envelopes, and when she found one in Bonnie's handwriting, she hurried to the privacy of her buggy to read it.

Bonnie was coming home in three weeks! Bonnie, unlike Amanda, was near enough to come home to Wheatener relatively easily. Amanda smiled as she skimmed her sister's precise handwriting. Her exams would be over on December fifth, and she had already booked a seat on the train leaving the next morning. Would someone meet her at the station?

Amanda stuffed the letter into its envelope and hurried back to Harper's apartment to share the news with him.

"We'll have to celebrate," she told him before he'd even finished reading it. "We'll throw a Christmas party for Bonnie. We can make taffy, and cookies, too. And we should buy everyone presents. Oh, Harper, it will be almost like old times again." She paused and added wistfully, "If only we had Hall House."

Harper put his arm around her shoulders. "We'll do it up right, Mandy. We'll make sure it's a special Christmas for everyone, even without your house."

Amanda tried to thank him, but her throat was too thick

with emotion. She threw her arms around his neck and hugged him instead.

Harper patted her back sympathetically. "It's all right, Mandy. I know how much you miss your parents. In fact, I've been missing mine lately, too. I was even considering taking a quick trip out to Philadelphia to visit them before things really get busy at the school. You wouldn't mind, would you?"

Amanda pulled away and smiled through a haze of tears. "Of course not. Why would you think I'd mind?"

Harper looked down sheepishly. "Well, you've been rather standoffish for the past month. I thought you were angry at me for not pulling my weight with school business."

It was Amanda's turn to look embarrassed. "Oh, Harper, you do more than your share for the college. And you know how fond I am of you. It's just that there has been a terrible rumor going around about me. I didn't know how to stop it, so I thought it would be better for the school's sake if I kept away from you as much as possible."

"Why didn't you tell me this before?"

"I didn't want to worry you."

"I suppose the rumor concerns our relationship."

When Amanda averted her gaze, Harper sat down heavily on the chair. "No wonder you've acted oddly around me. Poor Mandy. How it must have hurt you to be talked about in such a vicious manner by people in your own town."

"Matthew said there wasn't anything to do but ignore the rumor."

"Yes, I suppose he's right."

Amanda knelt by Harper's chair. "There is another way," she said, her eyes sparkling with excitement. "If you're agreeable, Harper, we could get married."

Harper stared, open-mouthed. "Married? But, Mandy—"

"We can say we've been engaged all this time. And if we marry just after the new year, before the college opens, no one can say anything evil about us working so closely together. What do you think?" She smiled at him.

"I . . . I think . . ." He rubbed his forehead, his brow wrinkling in consternation. "I think we need to think about this some more."

Amanda studied his concerned features, then pushed to her feet. He didn't want to marry her.

Harper grabbed her hand. "Mandy, please don't take offense. I'd be honored to marry you, but . . . there's so much going on right now that I wouldn't want to rush a wedding into the midst of it."

"But we could at least announce our intentions, couldn't we? Then we can turn our Christmas party into an engagement party." She hurried to the table for a writing tablet and pencil to begin making her lists, calling over her shoulder, "Won't Bonnie be surprised?"

"Yes, I'm sure we shall surprise her." With a heavy heart, Harper sank into a chair.

At Polly's Inn that evening, when Harper, Amanda, and her siblings had all finished their meal, Harper rose from his seat at the end of the table and cleared his throat. "Mandy, your sister and brothers have a surprise for you. Close your eyes and don't peek."

Amanda scrunched her eyes shut and heard excited whispers all around her. "You may open them now," Harper said.

She opened her eyes to see a small, round, blue and pink frosted cake before her, alight with small, flickering candles.

"Happy birthday, Mandy!" everyone shouted at once.

Amanda rose slowly from her seat, her eyes filling with tears. "Thank you, Curt and Daniel, Freddie, Gabby, Ethan, and," she smiled at Harper, "thank you, too, Harper."

Harper laughed and came around to put his arms around her. "I believe the custom is to make a wish and blow out your candles."

"Make a wish, Mandy!" Gabby cried, clapping her hands.

Amanda stared into the flickering flames for a long moment, then blew out the candles in one breath.

"Tell us what you wished," Ethan insisted.

"But then it won't come true," Freddie argued.

"I'll tell you what I wished just this once, because in our case, it will come true." Amanda smiled. "I wished we could all be together again at Hall House."

For a moment, everyone was silent; then Gabby spoke up. "But Aunt Alice says we can't live with you because it would be unseemly. She says you're keeping company with Harper when you're not married."

"Hush, Gabby!" Curt ordered, giving his sister a cold look.

Amanda's hands balled into fists at her sides. "That insufferable, old—"

"Mandy," Harper cut in smoothly, "perhaps we should cut your cake. It's getting late."

Amanda huffed at Harper's intentional interruption, but said nothing more. Gabby, however, was going to get a good lecture before going back to the Ripleys.

Before they left the restaurant, Curt surprised Amanda with a request to speak to her privately. Under the pretense of needing fresh air, they went outside, where Curt tucked Amanda's arm through his and strolled with her down the street. "Don't let Mrs. Ripley upset you, Mandy. No one listens to her gossip."

Amanda sighed. "It still hurts, Curt."

"You know what father would have said," he reminded her.

"Yes. Matthew told me the same thing."

Curt waited until they had turned back, and then he nervously cleared his throat. "Speaking of Mr. Blake . . ." He winced as Amanda eyed him warily. "He's offered to help me learn the lumber business. I'll be leaving shortly to go up to his camp in northern Michigan so I can watch the lumberjacks."

Amanda stopped and swung to face him, her expression incredulous. "Curt, you can't! Why, you could be killed! You know nothing about cutting down trees."

"I'll only be helping them load the lumber," he assured

her. "Mr. Blake says it will be good training if I want to go into the business myself."

"Mr. Blake is not your parent, Curt."

"Neither are you, Mandy. You're not my guardian, either, and Mr. Green says it's okay. And you may as well know now that after I graduate from high school, I'm going to take a year off from school to work in Mr. Blake's lumberyard."

Amanda felt as though he had slapped her. "But it was Father's wish for all of us to go to college."

"It's only for a year. I'm not giving up my education."

"Once you become used to drawing a steady wage, I hardly think you'll want to give it up to go off to school and become a student again."

"Then I'll go to *your* school part time."

"It will take you years and years to finish. And what if you meet a girl and decide to get married? Please, Curt. You must not even consider it."

"I've already made up my mind," Curt announced defiantly, and at the determined set of his jaw, Amanda fell silent. How could she battle as powerful an influence as Matthew Blake?

She pressed her lips together as an idea came to her.

When Matthew walked into his office at the iron mill the next morning, he found Amanda waiting for him, her black skirt sweeping the floor as she angrily paced to and fro in front of his desk. A muscle in his jaw twitched as he crossed the room. He was in no mood for one of her snits. He had learned only the day before that it had been Amanda who had killed his deal with Tim Wagner. If he hadn't vowed to protect her, he would have seriously considered throttling her.

But it was safer to let Amanda believe her plan had succeeded. It had taken him the better part of an evening and a bottle of bourbon to get old Tim to agree to start negotiations again, and he wasn't about to let her ruin it a second time.

"I was wondering what time you'd show up," he growled, his back to her.

Amanda was taken aback by his uncustomary ill humor. "How did you know I was coming?"

"The desk clerk at the hotel said a wicked-tempered female stormed in last night looking for me; I assumed it was you. Luckily, I was playing cards at Porter's Saloon."

Ignoring his jibe, Amanda said, "I came to see you about Curt."

"What about Curt?"

She moved closer. "I don't want him going to your lumber camp."

"Fortunately for Curt, he's old enough to make his own decision. Now, if you will excuse me," he said, keeping his back to her, "I have work to do."

"He's too young. He could be hurt!"

"He's eighteen," Matthew grumbled. "That's a man in my book."

There was a pause, and then Amanda said in a small voice, "Men can be hurt, too."

Matthew turned, ready to snap at her, but the anguish in her golden-brown eyes drained away his anger. Amanda the tigress, he thought ruefully, protecting her cubs.

"He'll be safe, Amanda," he reassured her. "The men will watch out for him."

"What about Curt's education? He's supposed to go to college next year."

"Taking a year off from school won't harm him. In fact, it will help him decide if he really wants to make a career of the lumber business."

"What if he never wants to go back?"

"I've talked to him about it. He sees the sense in having a college education."

Amanda pressed her lips together. Why had Curt told her nothing of his plans? Did he feel more confident discussing his future with a stranger than with his own sister? Her eyes narrowed. This was all Matthew's fault. "I've had to swallow what you've done to Wheatener," she ground out, "but I *won't* let you decide what's best for my family."

From the doorway to his office, Matthew watched Amanda make her way through the noise and general commotion of the iron mill to the front of the building, her head high and her back ramrod straight. He shook his head and went back to his desk. It would have been easier to give in to her demands, but he would not betray Curt's trust in him, no matter how badly he hurt Amanda.

Chapter Thirteen

STANDING ALONGSIDE THE still belching train, Amanda eagerly scanned the disembarking passengers. "There she is, Harper!" she called over the commotion. She ran to her sister and engulfed her in a hug, causing Bonnie to drop one of her satchels and grab her hat to keep it from flying away. "Hello, Mr. Brown. It's good to see you again," she said breathlessly over Amanda's shoulder.

"Miss Hall," he said with a broad smile, crushing his hat to his chest, "it's a pleasure to see you again, too."

Amanda picked up Bonnie's satchel and started toward the buggy. "Come on, you two. It's nearly dinnertime. Oh, I've got so much to tell you, Bonnie!"

As they drove Bonnie to the Ripleys' house, Amanda filled her sister in on everything that had happened since her last letter, including Curt's decision to go north.

"Perhaps Mr. Blake is right, Mandy," Bonnie said. "Once Curt sees what's involved in running a lumber business, he might change his mind."

Amanda didn't want Bonnie to agree with Matthew, even though she knew there was sound logic behind his reasoning. "I just hate the way Matthew interferes in our business."

"Are you sure Curt didn't ask for his help?"

At Amanda's huff, Bonnie placed her hand on her sister's arm. "We must consider what's best for Curt. Would you want him to aim for a career he would come to hate?"

"I suppose not," she conceded reluctantly.

"Then go see Curt and tell him you're behind his decision. You wouldn't want him to leave with bad feelings between you."

Amanda sighed. "You're right, Bonnie, although it pains me to admit Matthew's idea is sound. I'll try to go see Curt in the morning."

But for the next few days, Amanda had no time to think of anything other than the final preparations for their fundraising ball. As she dressed for the event on Saturday evening, Amanda had a sudden attack of nerves. What if she were shunned because of Mrs. Ripley's awful lies? What if no one danced with her? Or spoke to her?

"Hold still, Mandy," Bonnie pleaded as she attempted to put the combs in her sister's hair. Her fingers trembled from nervous excitement, and Amanda's agitation was not helping. "I wish I'd paid more attention when Mother fixed your hair."

"There's not that much to it." Amanda watched in the mirror as her sister fastened the last comb. She had decided it would be better to wear her long auburn hair in a simple style for the ball, curled and pulled back by mother-of-pearl combs, accented only by her pearl earbobs. She had already arranged Bonnie's fine brown hair in long banana curls, which were gathered on either side of her small, oval face. All that remained was to put on their dresses.

"Do I look all right?" Bonnie asked for the third time as Amanda leaned in front of her at the pier glass to pinch her cheeks for color.

Amanda turned to examine her sister. Bonnie stood nervously before her, twisting her gloved fingers as her sister scrutinized her pale peach satin gown with its deep apricot trim and matching slippers of apricot satin. "You look sweet, as always," she pronounced, and turned back to examine her complexion. Too pale, Amanda decided, turning her face to the side, yet she didn't dare wear any cheek rouge. The last thing she wanted was to attract attention.

"I wish I were as beautiful as you," Bonnie said with a sigh.

Amanda paused in her examination and glanced at her sister through the glass. At the love and admiration reflected in her sister's eyes, Amanda's throat tightened and she said guiltily, "Don't wish that, Bonnie. You're much kinder and prettier than I."

Bonnie scoffed. "My nose is too short, my chin is too pointed . . ." She paused to glance down the front of her gown, ". . . and I have no shape at all!"

Amanda laughed. "I've never heard you complain so much. Whatever has gotten into you?"

Bonnie blushed shyly and turned away from the glass. "I'm just nervous about the ball, I suppose."

Amanda tucked her arm through her sister's. "There's no reason for you to be nervous. I'm the one the whole town is talking about."

"Well, they'd best not say anything bad about you in front of me," Bonnie vowed.

Other than the servants setting out the food, Amanda, Harper, and Bonnie were the first to arrive. As Harper took their wraps to the cloak room, Amanda and her sister curiously inspected the infamous dance hall. "This must be a reception room," Amanda said to Bonnie as they gazed about the small room lined with oak settees. Opposite the door stood a rectangular table covered in a linen tablecloth, where information about the college would be displayed.

"Mandy, just look what Carolyn has done in here!" Bonnie called from the adjoining room.

Amanda walked through the wide doorway and gazed around in awe. What had formerly been a common, dusty-floored, dance hall had been transformed into a formal ballroom. The generous use of black and white decorations lent the large, dimly lit room a scholarly, dignified appearance. Black spiraling streamers hung from the gaudy chandelier in the center to all four corners, and every gas lamp along the two side walls sported ribbons of black and white.

Narrow tables draped in white linen sat end to end at the back of the enormous room to form one long banquet table. Tall red tapers burned brightly at each end of the table and a shiny, black vase of white carnations flanked by more candles graced the middle.

Nearby stood the refreshment table, and along each side of the dance floor, simple, wooden folding chairs sat side by side, linked together by intertwining black and white streamers draped in scallops across the backs, creating a lacy effect when viewed from the opposite side. At the front of the room sat the chairs for the musicians Carolyn had engaged.

Amanda returned to the reception room, where Harper and Bonnie were carefully arranging their display, working side by side, but saying very little. Carolyn arrived looking beautiful in a dark plum velvet gown, her blond hair drawn back in an elaborate chignon.

"Everything looks wonderful!" Amanda told her.

The lady smiled enigmatically. "Did you doubt it would? Has the food arrived?"

"Yes, they're setting up now."

At the sound of male voices, Amanda looked around to see Mayor Ripley enter with Jonathan Jenkins and Matthew Blake. She moved closer to the table and pretended to help Bonnie with the brochures, while from the corner of her eye she watched Matthew walk to the wide doorway and survey the room.

Matthew wore black trousers and a matching swallowtail frock coat, nipped in at the waist, emphasizing his trim middle and broad shoulders, with a maroon cravat tied around a stiff, white collar. His hair was dark and gleaming, and when he turned and caught her gaze with his dark eyes, her breath caught in her throat as she forgot her anger and remembered how passionately he had kissed her, how intimately he had touched her, and how she had very nearly made love to him in his bed.

She turned away, her heart pounding furiously, and nearly jumped out of her skin when someone tapped her on the arm.

"Good evening, Amanda."

"Oh, Mayor Ripley, it's you!" She looked over his shoulder to see that Matthew had stopped a few feet away to talk to Harper. "Where is your wife tonight?" she asked distractedly.

"Home with a terrible head cold," the little man said with a sad shake of his head, although Amanda could have sworn there was a glimmer of relief in his eyes. "You're looking pert this evening, my dear," he said, his brown eyes darting over her gown. "I hope you'll allow me to sign your dance card."

"Of course," she murmured nervously.

Several of the board members entered then, and the mayor went to greet them. Amanda heard Carolyn's soft voice behind her and turned, certain her red face betrayed her thoughts.

"We should take our place at the door, Amanda. Our guests are beginning to arrive."

Amanda cast a quick glance back at Matthew, but he had stopped to talk to someone else.

"Amanda?" Carolyn called.

"Coming."

For the next half hour, Amanda and Carolyn greeted guests. When the hall was full, they stood at the entrance to the dance hall and observed the crowd.

"Quite a turnout," Harper remarked as he joined them.

"I'd venture to say we'll make enough profit tonight to send a few students through the school," Carolyn said. "Well, shall we mingle?"

Amanda was so busy watching Matthew dance with an attractive young lady that she failed to hear Carolyn's suggestion. "Harper, let's dance," she said suddenly, taking his sleeve and leading him to the dance floor.

She gazed around the room as Harper led her into a turn. "You know, I've never seen the inside of a dance hall before."

"Hmmm?"

Amanda glanced at him to find his eyes fixed on a point over her shoulder. When they turned again, she scanned the side of the room to see what had caught his eye, but all she saw was Bonnie sitting quietly by herself.

"Harper, you must ask Bonnie to dance next. She looks lost over there."

His face lit up. "I'd be happy to."

When the dance ended, Harper took Amanda across the room to where Bonnie sat, then bowed gallantly before her sister.

"Miss Hall, may I have the next dance?"

Bonnie shyly lifted her eyes to his face, her color heightened by an attractive blush. With an exultant smile, she rose, took his arm, and allowed Harper to lead her to the dance floor while Amanda stood on the side and watched.

After a few moments, Amanda began to search the faces on the dance floor, hoping Matthew was not still dancing with that attractive lady. She couldn't understand why he hadn't asked to sign her dance card. After the way he had nearly ravished her, she thought he'd at least have come over to say hello.

The crowd shifted, allowing her a view of Matthew dancing with a different young lady and enjoying himself immensely, if the look on his face was any indication. Amanda opened her fan to cool her face. Why did she care who he danced with? He *was,* after all, her enemy. Yet an enemy would not kiss her as he had. An enemy would not make her tremble with desire.

If he wasn't her enemy, then what was he?

With a sigh, Amanda turned to find Carolyn beside her, the woman's shrewd gaze fixed on her blushing face. "Well," Amanda said with forced brightness, "you were right after all, Carolyn. No one seemed to mind coming to the dance hall."

"Of course I'm right. One of the few benefits of getting older is greater wisdom." With a serene smile, Carolyn left.

When the dance ended, Bonnie and Harper came across the floor toward Amanda, laughing and talking animatedly. "Shall we get something to eat?" Harper suggested.

"Oh, yes! I'm parched after all that dancing," Bonnie exclaimed, looking livelier than Amanda had ever seen her.

Trailing behind Harper and Bonnie as they made their way down the long buffet table, Amanda selected a few

morsels of food here and there to fill her plate. Her mood
was growing more dismal by the moment, though she didn't
know why. She only wanted the ball to be over as quickly
as possible so she could go home.

As she ate, her eyes searched out Matthew's tall form
and found him dancing once again with the same young
lady she had noticed him with at the start. They moved
smoothly to the music, his dark hair gleaming under the
chandelier's sparkling lights, one darkly clad arm around
her slender back, and when he smiled down at her, Amanda
realized the reason for her melancholia. *She* wanted to be
the one in his arms.

But that was illogical. She certainly didn't love him. In
fact, she didn't care one whit about him. There had to be
some other explanation. So while the dancers whirled past,
and Bonnie and Harper chatted gaily beside her, Amanda
sat and picked at her food, wishing she were anywhere but
in that dance hall.

She finally took her plate to an empty table to be rid of it,
but when she turned to go back to her seat, she saw Harper
lead Bonnie once again onto the floor. Rather than return to
sit alone, Amanda took a glass of wine from the refreshment table and stood there instead, watching enviously as
couples whirled around the floor.

Every lady, it seemed, except herself and the very eldest,
were dancing. Even Carolyn was dancing. Where was
Mayor Ripley? He had asked her for a dance. Why hadn't
he come to claim it? But then she spotted him dancing with
Joe Porter's wife, and having a merry time of it, too, and
she sighed forlornly.

Sipping steadily at her wine, Amanda stared at the dancing figures until they blurred. When her wine was gone,
and yet another dance had begun, she took a fresh glass,
only to find it lifted from her hand and placed on the table
behind her.

"I think you should dance instead."

At the sound of Matthew's voice, Amanda tensed. "I
don't want to dance," she said petulantly.

He smiled wryly. "Yes, you do. You've been watching

the dancers like a child with her nose pressed to the window of a sweet shop." He held out his arm for her.

"Well, then, I don't want to dance with *you.*"

"It would seem you have no other choice; men haven't exactly been standing in line to sign your dance card."

Amanda's cheeks flooded with heat. "It's probably because of that horrid rumor."

"Ah! The rumor again. But that can't be the reason, because a rumor such as that would make men *want* to dance with you, if only out of curiosity."

"Not in front of their wives, it wouldn't."

Matthew chuckled. "A man determined to discover your charms for himself would only have to tell his wife he was dancing with you because it was his Christian duty; and afterward, he'd swear he hadn't enjoyed a minute of it. No, my sweet, I believe you frighten you."

Amanda scoffed, "Do I frighten *you*?"

"Definitely not."

She gave him a sidelong glance. "You haven't said why *you* asked me to dance."

Matthew's gaze raked over her, and, in a husky voice, he replied enigmatically, "It wasn't the rumor, Amanda."

She scoffed at him. "You're only asking me out of pity, not because you really want to dance with me."

"Pity is one of the few emotions you don't arouse in me. Now, stop fishing for compliments and take my arm." One corner of his mouth twitched slyly as he waited. Finally, she put her hand on his arm and they walked onto the floor.

Matthew took her slender hand in his, and put the other hand on the small of her back, the lush, rippling velvet sensuous to the touch. He gazed down at her, noting how her gown, the color of summer bluebells, emphasized the creamy whiteness of her throat, and, although her V-cut neckline was modestly framed by white lace, he could well imagine the gentle swell of breasts beneath.

Her leg-of-mutton sleeves fastened from elbow to wrist with tiny, crystal buttons, and his heart beat quicker at the thought of unfastening them one by one, his lips forging a path up the virgin whiteness of her arm. Just below her trim waist, an overlay of deep blue silk emphasized the gentle curve of her hip and formed a luxurious waterfall bustle that trailed to the floor in the back.

Dainty blue satin slippers peeked out beneath the hem of her skirt, reminding him of the broken heel on her shoe, and then of her passionate embrace on his bed.

His emotions were turbulent. He had watched her covertly all evening, wanting her with a hunger and intensity that frightened him. But he had made a vow to avoid her and he was determined to stick by it. Yet, seeing her standing alone and miserable, he hadn't been able to stay away.

Now the problem was how to keep his desire in check when she felt so good in his arms, when all he could think of was how good she'd feel lying naked beneath him.

The answer came to him immediately. All he had to do was make her angry. It was hard to desire someone who was bristling with hostility.

"Have you been to see Curt recently?" he asked.

Amanda's gaze slid away. "No, but I've been meaning to. It's just that I've been busy—"

Matthew laughed. "Busy? Stubborn is more like it. You're still angry with Curt for going against your wishes. If you want to see him before he leaves, you'd better swallow your stubborn pride and get over there. The wagons will be heading north in three days."

By the murderous look in Amanda's golden eyes, Matthew knew an angry retort was forthcoming. But the dance ended just then and people began to leave the floor. Instead of arguing, Amanda turned abruptly and began to march away.

Matthew caught her arm and pulled her back toward him. "I'm not finished with you yet."

With a firm hold on her back, Matthew led Amanda into the next dance. His next words surprised her so much that, had he not had a secure hold on her arm, she would have stumbled.

"I hope you're not serious about marrying Harper."

Amanda stared at him incredulously. "Who told you that?"

"What difference would it make?"

"Why shouldn't I marry him?" she cried defiantly.

"Because he's in love with your sister."

Amanda gazed at him in disbelief, then quickly turned her head to where Harper danced with Bonnie not three yards away. The look of adoration on Bonnie's face was so obvious that Amanda was momentarily stunned.

"You're wrong about Harper. He and I have already discussed it; we'll announce our plans at Christmas."

"You'll break Bonnie's heart if you do."

Amanda blinked in surprise. "She'll understand our reasons."

"Yes, she'll understand, and she will even forgive you, whether you deserve it or not, because she loves you and Harper without reserve; nevertheless, you'll break her heart. Would you do that to your sister, *Miss Hall?*"

Amanda was shocked into silence. Matthew was categorizing her as a cruel, selfish woman for wanting to marry Harper when all she had was the good of the college and her family at heart. She felt the first prickle of tears and blinked to dispel them.

Matthew seemed to sense the direction of her thoughts. "If you're only marrying Harper to end those foolish rumors, then let him marry Bonnie. It will serve the same purpose."

"How do you know he wants to marry her?" she demanded.

"How do you know he wants to marry you?" Matthew countered, and when Amanda had no reply, he said, "It's just as I thought; you coerced him into this betrothal."

Amanda's throat began to ache from holding back tears. "I did no such thing!"

"Who suggested the marriage?"

"He agreed to it."

"Did you give him a choice? No, I don't imagine you did, poor fellow. And he's too kind-hearted to tell you the truth, so he'll walk down the aisle with you and suffer through a disastrous marriage with the wrong sister."

Amanda tossed her head, looking away from his cruel gaze, blinking furiously to hold back the tears that threatened to fall. Was Bonnie in love with Harper, and she hadn't even suspected? Did Harper feel the same about her sister? Had she really coerced him into a betrothal? How like Matthew to want to humiliate her in front of a room full of people.

"You're cruel," she said in a choked voice. "You'd say anything to hurt me."

"I'm only being honest." At the sight of a stray tear leaking from the corner of her eye, Matthew remarked sardonically, "Tears, Amanda? That's very unlike you, resorting to tears to win your point. Usually it's your sharp tongue you wield against your enemies."

Amanda glared at him through a blurry mist, and her voice quivered when she spoke. "Do you think I have no feelings?"

His smug smile cut her to the core. "You have only two that I know of: anger and arrogance. By the way, thank you for putting a crimp in my plans to buy the old grist mill. Now Tim Wagner stands to lose a comfortable nest egg for his retirement, which he was looking forward to. I'm sure he'll be eternally grateful to you for your advice."

Amanda pulled free of him and began to weave her way through the crowded dance floor, brushing the tears off her cheeks so no one would notice them. Bonnie in love with Harper. Curt leaving town. Tim Wagner losing retirement money because of her interference. She could barely see the door through the haze of tears.

From across the room, Marylou Egley stopped in the midst of her sentence to watch Amanda slip from the hall. "Would you excuse me, please?" she said to her companions. With Alice unable to attend the ball, Marylou felt a certain responsibility to her. Quietly, she made her way to the receiving room at the front. If she were lucky, she'd have some juicy gossip to take back to Alice in the morning.

Chapter Fourteen

WHEN AMANDA REACHED the sidewalk outside, she stopped, shivering from the cold, and looked about for someplace to go. Spotting Carolyn's beige and brown carriage not far down the street, she hurried to it and climbed inside, where she indulged in a good, heartfelt cry.

She hadn't meant to coerce Harper into marriage. Hadn't he kissed her first? And she certainly hadn't realized Mr. Wagner wanted to retire. She hiccuped. Anger and arrogance. How little Matthew understood her.

When she paused to wipe her eyes with her fingertips, a handkerchief was thrust into her hand. She looked up in surprise to find Matthew leaning in the door. "Go away!" she cried, and turned her back on him.

As usual, he did exactly the opposite. She felt the carriage shift as it took his weight. He settled on the leather seat next to her and shut the door.

"Come now, Amanda, stop weeping," he said gruffly. "It doesn't suit you."

"You don't know anything about me."

"Now, there you're quite wrong."

She turned to glare at him through red-rimmed eyes. "I despise your cryptic remarks, and I despise you!" She crossed her arms and turned her head away, still hiccuping.

Matthew gave an exasperated sigh. "Look at your face; you're in no shape to go back inside. Turn around."

When Amanda refused to move, Matthew pried the

handkerchief from her clenched fist and, taking her chin in his hand, turned her face toward him to dry her wet cheeks. "I apologize for what I said about your feelings," he said, a note of tenderness creeping into his voice. "I had no right to say that to you."

Amanda's lower lip quivered and she caught it between her teeth. "No, you didn't have the right. But the truth is I do have a bad temper, and no one likes me because of it." On the verge of crying again, she dabbed her eyes with his handkerchief.

"This little bout of self-pity won't get you any sympathy from me. Your family loves you in spite of your temper, which you very well know, and, that means, I suppose, that there's something beneath all those thorns, if one cares to look hard enough."

Amanda stopped sniffling to listen, and then said petulantly, "Can't you ever say anything nice to me?"

Matthew laughed. "You never cease to amaze me. You have attacked my morals, my business ethics, and my iron mill—Am I leaving anything out?—yet you take offense when I offer you the truth. Since you profess not to like me, Amanda, why should what I say bother you?"

Yes, why should it bother her? Amanda huffed and looked away. Since she had no answer for him, she offered a question of her own. "Why did you follow me out here? And don't you dare tell me it was your Christian duty and that you haven't enjoyed a minute of it."

Matthew stared at her in astonishment, and when Amanda began to giggle at her own joke, he laughed with her. Finally, Amanda heaved a shaky sigh and said, "We should go back inside. Bonnie and Harper will be looking for me, and I'd hate to give the gossips something more to talk about."

Matthew gazed at her, thinking how very alluring she was when she smiled, which was something he rarely saw. "I can think of worse things to happen," he said huskily, his gaze dropping to her mouth.

He could not stop himself. He cupped her chin and bent his head to meet her soft lips, and when Amanda did not protest, his kiss grew deeper, hungrier, until he was lost in the feel and taste of her. His tongue parted her lips and sought the sweet hollows of her mouth. He broke the kiss to taste her throat and feel the pulse that beat rapidly in its hollow.

And when he felt her arms entwine themselves about his neck, Matthew's ardor increased. His hands slide down to support her spine as he pressed her back against the seat, his mouth leaving fiery hot kisses on the tops of her breasts.

He slid one hand around to cup a firm globe, his thumb caressing the hardening nipple through the material, bringing a soft moan to Amanda's lips. He moved up to take possession of her mouth once again, pulling her against his body, letting her feel his desire for her. He was surprised when she moved sensuously against his erection, and so overwhelmed with need that he broke the kiss, breathing hard, and whispered into her ear, "Come back to the hotel with me, Amanda."

Amanda repeated his request as if in a daze, "Come back to the hotel with you?"

"I want to make love to you," he said in a voice thick with passion, his mouth seeking hers yet again.

He was roughly shoved to the floor of the carriage. "Are you also asking me to marry you?" Amanda cried.

It was the second time he had been pushed to the floor. "Marry you!" he bellowed as he brushed off his coat in furious swipes. "Do you think I'm insane?"

Amanda's chest heaved in indignation. "Did you think to make me your next mistress then?"

Matthew stared at her in surprise. His mistress? Amanda Hall? Good God, what could he have been thinking?

"Oh, how I hate you!" Amanda cried, thrusting open the carriage door and stepping over him. She started to walk away, but changed her mind and swung around to leave him with a parting shot. "You once told me you couldn't imagine anyone farther from a loose woman than I, yet you were willing to make me one, weren't you?"

Matthew opened his mouth to refute her accusation, but she had turned her back on him and was marching toward the dance hall. He swore profusely at himself as he adjusted his clothing. Amanda's accusation had been true. Had he convinced her to go back with him, he would have proved the gossips correct.

Matthew dropped his head to his hands with a groan. He never should have followed her out to the carriage. He couldn't trust himself alone with her. Now Amanda was so furious with him that she was likely to confront Harper about his feelings for Bonnie just to prove him wrong.

How could Amanda not see how much in love Harper and Bonnie were? He only hoped Harper had the good sense to tell Amanda how he felt and not make a mistake that would ruin his life, for, if he married Amanda, he would surely do that. Matthew hopped down from the carriage, slammed the door, and stalked back to the dance hall. Amanda was *not* going to force Harper to marry her. He would make damn sure of *that*.

Marylou Egley watched from inside the doorway, and quickly stepped back out of sight as Amanda stormed through the door. A few moments later, Matthew strode in, his features as dark as a storm cloud. Putting a pudgy hand to her mouth to stifle an excited giggle, Marylou hurried to join her friends in the hall. Oh, what she had to tell Alice! She couldn't wait for the morning. With one eye on Amanda and the other on Matthew, she joined right in the conversation as if she had never left.

Before she entered the dance hall, Amanda paused to smooth her gown and take a deep breath, determined not to let anyone see how upset she was. In truth, she was feeling more than a little guilty for her own impassioned response to Matthew's kiss. If he had treated her as a loose woman, then she had surely behaved like one, as well.

Pasting a wooden smile on her face, she walked through the crowd to Harper's side. And as for that situation, Amanda thought to herself, she'd have to speak with Harper first thing in the morning. It would do no good to let

Bonnie grow more deeply in love with him when nothing could come of it.

With a twinge of guilt, she remembered Matthew saying, *"You'll break her heart if you marry him,"* but she justified her decision by telling herself that Matthew had made up that balderdash just to hurt her. Bonnie and Harper were merely friends. She would know if Harper was in love with his sister. She glanced across the room, her eyes sweeping the crowd until she saw Matthew talking to Carolyn Tanner. He turned his head toward her just then and caught her watching. Amanda tossed her head and looked away. She'd show that liar.

As soon as he had finished talking to Carolyn, Matthew walked outside to where some of the guests were waiting for their carriages to take them home. He located his driver standing around a portable coal stove talking to other drivers, and sent him back to the hotel. Then he went back to the dance hall and waited until Carolyn had diverted Amanda's attention, before cornering Harper and Bonnie. "I've just been informed that my driver took ill and had to go home. Think you could give me a lift back to the hotel?"

"Of course," Harper replied. "We'd be happy to. We only have to wait until Mandy finishes helping Mrs. Tanner and then we can leave."

"That won't be necessary. Carolyn has offered Amanda a ride home," Matthew told him.

Bonnie turned to Harper and laid a slender hand on his coat sleeve. "Perhaps we should stay and help Carolyn, too."

"Oh, I'm sure it's something the two ladies can manage," Matthew quickly added, "otherwise Carolyn would have asked for more help."

Bonnie looked uneasy, but accepted his reasoning without further comment.

"Then we'll see you home now," Harper said, smiling. "We were thinking of leaving anyway. I'll get Miss Hall's wrap and then we'll be off."

"We'll meet you at the door." Matthew held out his arm and Bonnie accepted it with a smile.

Once Bonnie had been delivered safely back to the Ripleys', Harper headed the buggy toward the Blake Hotel to take Matthew home. When they arrived, Matthew said, "Come inside for a nightcap, Harper. There's something I'd like to discuss with you."

"About the college?"

"Something of a more personal nature."

Harper hitched the horse and followed Matthew to his suite. He tested one of the suite's overstuffed ivory sofas while Matthew poured them glasses of brandy. "You mentioned something about a personal problem?" Harper asked after settling himself comfortably on the cushions.

"Yes, I did." Matthew handed him a glass as he silently contemplated his best strategy. "Suppose a fellow were considering marriage," he began, sitting on the sofa opposite Harper with one booted foot across his knee. "What qualities do you feel to be the most important for his intended wife?"

Harper looked perplexed. "That's hard to know, having never been married myself." He chuckled at his own attempt at humor and took a sip of his brandy as he mulled over Matthew's question. "But I would have to say that she should be kind, loving, intelligent . . ." He paused as a face conjured itself in his mind, bringing a wistful smile to his lips. "And she should be pretty, with a sweet nature that would be like a soothing balm to a man's soul."

Matthew lifted his glass to his mouth to hide a grin.

"Who is your intended?" Harper asked suddenly. "Mrs. Nightingale?"

Matthew nearly choked on his brandy. "What? Mrs. Nightingale?"

Harper laughed. "You needn't try to hide it. I know the fellow is you, and I just wondered who your intended is to be. Mrs. Nightingale, is it?"

Matthew stared at him, dumbfounded.

"Ah ha! I thought so. Your answer is as plain as the nose on your face."

Matthew downed his drink in one swallow. "You're too clever for me, Harper. I hope you'll keep all this in the strictest confidence."

"Of course."

"Now, tell me, what do you think about the love aspect? Do you think love is necessary for a successful union?"

Harper's pale eyebrows drew together in a thoughtful frown. "I should think so, yes. I would surely want that to be true in my case."

Matthew watched him carefully. "Would you?"

Harper studied Matthew, and suddenly he saw not the man before him nor the sweet face in his daydream, but Amanda, dear Mandy, his best friend and partner, telling him they should get married. His face drained of color. "Yes, I would," he said faintly.

"I think you're right," Matthew told him. "I surely wouldn't want to marry someone without being in love with her. Marriages of convenience are becoming quite rare; I suppose people have awakened to the fact that a marriage without love is senseless, no matter what the circumstances."

"Yes," Harper answered distantly, nodding his head. Then his eyes came into sharp focus and he said exuberantly, "Yes, dash it all!" He rose with renewed vigor. "I hope I've been of some help. I really have to leave now; I have important business to attend to first thing in the morning." He strode to the door and picked up his hat. "Good luck with your marriage."

"What? Oh, yes. Thanks." Matthew stood at the door and watched Harper charge down the hallway to the stairs and disappear from view, and then he closed the door and walked across the sitting room to his bedroom, whistling jauntily as he pulled off his cravat.

As soon as Amanda had finished counting the scholarship donations with Carolyn, she set off to find Harper and Bonnie.

"Amanda," Carolyn called, "if you're looking for your

sister and Mr. Brown, they left to take Matthew home. It seems his driver took ill."

"But they wouldn't leave without me."

Carolyn waved away her concern. "I told him I'd see you home."

As soon as she arrived at the Jefferson Arms, Amanda marched straight up to Harper's apartment, determined to talk to him about their plans, but no one answered her knock. She lay in her bed for a long while after that, wondering where Harper had gone, listening for him to tap on her door to let her know he was home. But her eyes finally shut before she could discover the answer.

Chapter Fifteen

A MANDA SLEPT FITFULLY that night, and when she awoke in the early hours of the morning, she lay in bed for a long time, thinking about the dream from which she had just surfaced. In fact, it had been a series of short dreams, all about Bonnie and Harper, bits and pieces of events that had escaped her attention while they were happening, but when strung together one after the other, like clothes on a line, they had presented a clear image—one she had not wished to see. When she finally climbed from the bed, it was with a heavy heart, for she knew now that she couldn't force Harper into a marriage with her when it was Bonnie he loved.

She had just dressed and eaten a light breakfast when someone tapped on her door.

"Good morning, Mandy!" Harper called cheerily as Amanda opened the door. "May I come in?"

"I'm glad you came by, Harper. I wanted to talk to you, anyway."

Harper bounded straight into the kitchen, where Amanda had a pot of coffee warming on the hob. "Do you mind if I help myself?" he called over his shoulder as he took a cup and filled it with the steaming beverage. "My, but it's cold out this morning. Snow's in the air. I can feel it."

She stood in the doorway and watched him. "You've been out already?"

He nodded as he sipped his coffee.

Amanda was surprised. He'd stayed out so late that she had expected him to sleep late as well. "Where did you go last night, Harper? I waited for you to come home, but you never did."

Harper poured Amanda a cup of coffee and handed it to her. "I stopped at Mr. Blake's apartment for a nightcap. You must have been asleep when I came home." He took a sip of his coffee and sighed blissfully.

Amanda put down her cup and paced to the end of the room, then turned and looked straight at him. "Harper, how do you feel about my sister?"

"Well, it's funny you should ask, because that's what I wanted to talk to you about. You see, Mandy—"

"You're in love with her."

Harper gave her a sheepish smile. "Yes, I am."

Amanda sank into the nearest chair. "Why didn't you tell me earlier, Harper?"

"How could I? You were dead set on us marrying to save the college."

"I didn't mean to coerce you."

"You didn't, Mandy," he replied gently.

"Have you asked Bonnie to marry you yet?"

"Well, yes. Just now, in fact. That's why I wanted to see you. In light of the rumors going around about us, Bonnie and I have decided to marry the day after Christmas. But if you'd rather we waited, we'll go along with whatever you think is best."

"No," Amanda said in a flat voice, "That's for you two to decide. But you know we have no money for a wedding."

"That won't be a problem. We only want a simple ceremony, anyway. I'm going to wire my father and mother today to let them know."

Harper walked over and picked up her hands, kneeling down to face her. "You know I wouldn't hurt you for the world, Mandy. You've been hurt enough in your life. But I couldn't see any sense in our marrying when we're . . . such very good friends. After all, why should we ruin a perfectly sound friendship?"

Amanda was close to tears, but she was determined to put his mind at ease. She smiled bravely. "You're right, Harper, and I'm happy for both of you. Now, go wire your parents so we can begin to make plans."

When Harper had gone, Amanda walked to the window and stared out at the street, where the first snowflakes of the season drifted lazily to the ground. What Harper had said was true; they were very good friends. And it was also true that his marrying Bonnie would put an end to the rumors. Why, then, did she feel such emptiness inside?

Pressing her lips together in determination, Amanda took up her paper and pen and sat down at the table to make a list of things to do. It would take all of the small savings she had put aside, but she would have to have dresses made for Bonnie, Gabrielle, and herself, and new suits for the boys, as well. She chewed on the tip of the pen, then dipped it in the ink bottle and began to write. "I'll have to find Mama's cherry punch recipe," she murmured as her pen scratched the surface. "It wouldn't be a proper reception without it."

Amanda filled the paper with notes, then lifted her head and gazed through the window. There was so much to do. If only her mother were there to help her. And she had Christmas to plan for, as well, the first Christmas in five years when all seven of them would be together. She had wanted to make it a special one for all of them, and now it would be, for there would be a wedding to celebrate.

With a horrified gasp, Amanda jumped to her feet. Curt! Curt didn't know about Bonnie and Harper, and Matthew had said he would be leaving to go north in a day or two. She ran to the coatrack and grabbed her mantle. She had to stop him. He couldn't be gone for Bonnie's wedding!

When Amanda arrived at the Greens' house, Mrs. Green courteously admitted her, yet there was a glimmer of disapproval in her eyes. "Curtis is gone, Amanda," she said.

"Gone?" Amanda cried faintly.

"He left this morning for the north country."

"But he wasn't supposed to leave for another two days!"

At the woman's shrug, Amanda turned and walked

blindly to her carriage. Curt hadn't even come to say goodbye.

And Matthew had lied to her.

Alice Ripley smiled at her friend as she poured them both a cup of tea in her front parlor. She had been feeling under the weather for a week, but that morning, Marylou had brought her news that had cheered her immensely.

"It doesn't surprise me one bit that Amanda is after Matthew Blake," Alice sneered, liberally stocking her tea with sugar cubes. "She knows she has a better chance to get custody of Gabrielle if she's married." She leaned closer to quip, "I still can't believe that insipid sister of hers stole Mr. Brown right out from under her nose. Who would have dreamed the little mouse had it in her?" She sat back with a satisfied smile and sipped her tea. "So Amanda enticed Matthew into a carriage for a tryst, did she? What a pity she hasn't heard what a devout bachelor he is."

"And to think what good people her parents were," Marylou commented, shaking her head.

"I can't wait until the judge hears about this." Alice paused to sip her tea. "It's a very good thing you kept your eyes open, dear. I shudder to think what would happen to my sweet Gabrielle if she were returned to that trollop. Why, Amanda could be with child even now."

"Oh, do you suppose?" Marylou cried, aghast.

Alice smiled smugly. "It wouldn't surprise me one whit. And it would be just what she deserves.

Matthew was walking among stacks of timber, checking inventories with Michael, when he heard Amanda call his name. He turned in surprise to find her hurrying toward him. Her face was partially hidden by a fur-trimmed hood, but he could see the anger glittering in her amber eyes.

"I'd like to speak with you," she said curtly.

Matthew turned to the man standing to his left. "We'll have to finish this later, Mike. Amanda, this is Michael O'Day, my right-hand man. If ever you should need something of me and I'm not here, Mike will see to it for you."

Amanda's gaze flickered over the wiry, freckled man with the dimpled smile and the brilliant blue eyes. "How do you do, Mr. O'Day?" she said in a clipped tone.

" 'Tis a grand pleasure to meet you, Miss Hall," Michael replied, sweeping off his brown work cap and giving her a deep bow. When he straightened, his blue eyes twinkled at her. "But if it's all the same to you, ma'am, it's Michael, plain and simple, like me."

Matthew cast him a dour look, and taking Amanda's arm, led her to a small shanty, out of the wind.

"Well, what is it I've done this time?" Matthew asked, leaning against a table, his arms folded across his chest.

"You lied to me! Curt is gone, and you said he wouldn't be leaving for another two days!"

"I didn't lie to you. Until last night, that was the plan. But a rider came in with a message from the logging camp that heavy snow is headed their way. I sent all my wagons out early this morning to bring back the men and the timber before they're trapped up there."

"When will they be back?"

"In about ten days."

"Ten days!" she cried. "You've got to bring him back now!"

Matthew's eyes narrowed. "Why?"

Amanda pressed her lips together and glared at him. She wasn't about to tell him Harper and Bonnie were getting married. He would only gloat.

"Why, Amanda?" Matthew repeated, stepping closer.

"Because Christmas is four days away, and it's to be our first Christmas together," she blurted.

"There'll be others." He walked to the door, ready to dismiss her. "You can celebrate when he gets back."

Amanda stamped her foot. "Curt *has* to be home by Christmas! Harper and Bonnie are getting married the next day."

Matthew lifted one dark eyebrow. "Well, what do you know. Did you give them your blessing, or are they marrying against your wishes?"

Amanda's hands curled into fists at her sides. "Will you bring Curt back or not?"

"Even if I wanted to bring Curt back, I'd be a fool to try it. Winter storms are too unpredictable up north. A light carriage could be stranded and all my heavy wagons are already on their way."

"You could if you really wanted to," she retorted. "You just don't want to help me."

"I *can't* help you, Amanda." Matthew paused and said more kindly, "Bonnie and Harper will understand."

Her blazing amber eyes locked momentarily with his, then she turned without another word and left. With a small stab of guilt, Matthew stood in the doorway of the wooden shanty and watched her as she pulled the fur-trimmed hood of her mantle closer about her face and hurried across the frozen ground.

Two days later, Matthew arrived at the lumberyard to find Harper and Bonnie deep in conversation with Michael. "I hear congratulations are in order," he said as he joined them.

Bonnie swung around and clutched his arm with her gloved hands. "Oh, Mr. Blake, thank heavens you've come! You have to help us. Mandy is gone!"

Chapter Sixteen

"A MESSENGER BROUGHT this to me only an hour ago," Bonnie told Matthew, handing him Amanda's hastily written note.

Matthew read it quickly and crumpled it into a tight ball, his features stiff. "When did she leave?"

"Early this morning," Michael volunteered. "She stopped here and asked me to draw her a map to the logging camp. I told her she hadn't ought to attempt it, bound as those roads are with snow, but she insisted she only wanted it for reference."

"Well, she won't make it far," Matthew growled. "The roads north of here are nearly impassable by buggy, and another storm is on its way."

"She'll be stranded!" Bonnie turned to Harper, her brown eyes shadowed with worry. "What can we do?"

Matthew checked his watch and, with a muttered curse, shoved it into his waistcoat pocket. He had stopped at the lumberyard only to take care of a last-minute errand. He had already been to the iron mill and had his bags in the carriage, which now waited to take him to the train station. He had received a telegram from his mother's cousin saying that his mother had suffered another stroke and was failing fast. Matthew was on his way home to spend what would probably be his last Christmas with his mother, though he doubted she would be aware of it.

There were thirty minutes until his train was due. If he

went after Amanda, he'd never be on it. But if he didn't go after her, if something happened to her, he'd never be able to live with himself.

"I'll find Amanda," he told them.

An hour and a half after he had left the lumberyard, Matthew was on his way, sitting easily on his huge, black gelding, galloping in a northeasterly direction past acres of snow-covered fields, passing orchards and a few scattered farms on the narrow road that would take him to his logging camp in Michigan. He glanced over his shoulder at the northwestern sky and frowned. There was a snowstorm coming, and it looked like a bad one. He only hoped it would hold off until evening when they would be safely back home.

But by three o'clock in the afternoon, the air was thick with snow, the wind was fierce and biting, and Matthew still hadn't seen any signs of Amanda's black buggy. At the speed he was traveling, he should have overtaken her. Could he have missed her? Had the buggy overturned in a ditch and been covered by snow?

He heard a far off jingle of harnesses and through the whiteness saw the faint glow of a lantern ahead. "Hello!" he shouted over the wind.

"Hello, yourself!" came a far-off reply.

He galloped toward the faint light and soon a wagon appeared through the curtain of snow. He reined in his horse as the wagon rumbled to a halt.

"Have you seen a lady in a black buggy pass this way?" Matthew called to the farmer sitting on the wagon bench.

"Haven't seen anything but trees and snow for miles," the man replied, holding up one arm to shield his face from the driving snow. "She couldn't have gone much farther north, though. Snow's drifted waist high back there by now."

Matthew turned to gaze at the road behind him. "Then somehow I missed her."

He retraced his trail, riding into the storm, until he reached a junction where the road split. The other fork veered off in an easterly direction, but in the storm,

Amanda could have become confused. He pulled his hat lower to shield his eyes and folded his sheepskin coat closer about his throat, then urged his horse up the other road.

For an hour, Matthew continued along the unfamiliar route, until the winter light began to wane and the wind blew up so strong he couldn't make out the path before him. He stopped under a bare-branched tree, coated now with a thick layer of snow, and pondered his next move. It would be dark soon. He would have to seek shelter, wait out the storm and try again in the morning. With a sigh, he turned the horse around and started back the way he had come. He had passed what looked like an abandoned barn several miles back, and it was there he headed.

With bitter wind and blowing snow stinging his face and coating his eyelashes, Matthew walked the horse slowly along the road, keeping an eye for any sign of Amanda's black buggy. As he passed a high, snowy mound of what he at first thought was a haystack sitting several yards off the road on lower ground he noticed a barely visible black top protruding from beneath it.

Urging his horse down the incline, Matthew approached the object and, seeing that it was indeed a black buggy nearly buried in a snowdrift, he jumped down and peered inside only to find it empty, with no sign of a horse nearby.

"Amanda!" he called, cupping his hands around his mouth, but his voice was carried away by the wind. He mounted his horse and began walking the animal through the deep snow, heading in the direction of the old barn which he knew had to be close.

When he finally spotted it, he urged the horse into a gallop and jumped down at the barn doors to pull them open against the wind. He led the horse inside and the doors slammed shut behind him.

It was a full minute before his eyes would focus in the dim light, and then Matthew saw a woman's form huddled in a corner, her mantle pulled close, her large, amber eyes staring at him in surprise.

"Amanda," he said with a sigh, his relief mixing with

anger. He pulled off his hat as he strode quickly across the barn and stood towering above her. "What the hell did you think you were doing coming out here alone?"

Her voice shook with cold and emotion, and tears welled in her golden-brown eyes, spilling down her white cheeks. "I wanted to bring Curt home for Bonnie's wedding."

When she put her hands to her face and began to sob, Matthew dropped down on his knees and pulled her into his arms, holding her against his damp coat. "Damn it, Amanda," he said gruffly, "you could have frozen to death in this storm. Then what would your family have done?"

"I'm s-so c-c-cold," she whispered against his shoulder, and, indeed, Matthew could feel her body shaking through the layers of clothing. He held her close until she stopped trembling, and then he said gently near her ear, "I'll build a fire. That'll warm you."

Matthew felt her nod and then he left her to see his horse. He led the animal into an old stall and removed the saddle and bridle. Amanda's mount was in the next stall. Thank God she'd had the good sense to bring him in with her, he thought.

After unstrapping his bedroll and removing his saddle-bags, Matthew took them over to where she sat and shook out a large woolen blanket to wrap around her. He spotted a low, slatted pen in one corner, pried off the thin slats of wood, and set them aside until he had hollowed out a spot on the earthen floor. He laid the wood in it, lit it with his matchsticks, and fanned it into a good blaze. Then he took out bread and beef jerky to share with her.

"It's hardly a feast, but it'll fill us for now," he told her. She accepted it silently, her eyes continuing to follow his movements. He brought in snow in an old, galvanized bucket someone had left behind, and melted it near the fire, then gave her his drinking cup and poured water into it. After she'd drunk her fill, he, too, drank to quench his thirst.

Soon it was warm enough that Amanda threw off the blanket and removed her bonnet. Some color had come back into her cheeks, he was relieved to see, yet she remained quiet, almost as if in shock.

"Do you want to sleep?" he asked, and when Amanda nodded, Matthew spread the blanket for her to lie on. She was asleep in minutes, and then he sat down next to her, stretched out his legs, and leaned his back against the wall, turning his head to study her. She wanted to bring Curt home for Bonnie's wedding. He shook his head. Was there anything she wouldn't do to get her family together?

Amanda was an exceptional woman, he decided. She was fiercely loyal, beautiful, intelligent . . . and also stubborn, quick-tempered, and self-righteous. Then, again, what female wasn't? But there was that other side of her, too, that warm, uninhibited, passionate side that filled his loins with searing heat and caused him to lose all reason.

But it was dangerous to dwell on those feelings. He had come to find her and take her back home, and nothing more. With any luck, she'd sleep soundly through the night and they'd be on their way at first light.

With a yawn, Matthew eased his body down onto the blanket beside her. She was lying on her side facing away from him, and he would have liked nothing better than to curl himself around her, but he resisted. A long lock of auburn hair lay near his face and he picked it up, feeling the silky texture of it against his fingers. He liked having Amanda beside him, not only because of the desire she aroused in him, but also because it made him feel—hell, he wasn't sure what he was feeling at all, other than tired.

In a few minutes, the crackle of the dry wood and the warmth of the fire worked their spell on Matthew and he, too, fell sound asleep.

Amanda let herself in the barn the next morning just as Matthew awoke. He sat up and ran a hand through his hair as she carried a bucket of snow to the fire.

"We were out of water," she told him, too embarrassed to admit she had also needed some privacy.

"How's the weather?" Matthew asked as he rose to his feet and set about building up the fire.

"Not much better than last night, though the wind has died down a bit. But the snow has drifted up around the barn so much that I almost couldn't get out the door. Luckily, I didn't have to go far."

Matthew smiled at that as he crouched over the bucket to wash his hands and face. His movements were so sure and capable, Amanda thought as she watched him. He never seemed to hesitate. She remembered awakening while it was still dark, wondering where she was. But then she had turned and found him lying beside her, and she had been able to go back to sleep almost at once.

It was a strange feeling knowing she had slept with Matthew. Amanda had always thought the first man to share her bed would be her husband. But then again, she and Matthew hadn't truly shared a bed. Her cheeks blazed red at the turn of her thoughts.

Matthew opened a paper-wrapped bundle and broke off another chunk from the half loaf of bread he had brought with him. Then he reached into the saddlebag and removed a smaller fold of paper, which, when opened, revealed a dollop of a deep berry red, glistening substance.

"Raspberry jam?" Amanda asked in surprise.

"My weakness," he confessed with a grin. He smeared a little on a piece of bread and handed it to her. "I bribed the hotel's baker into giving me some of his precious hoard."

Amanda bit into the bread and chewed slowly. "I wish you'd bribed the baker into giving you coffee, too," she said with her mouth full.

He watched her lick the last traces of jam from her fingertips. "I had no idea we'd be having a party," he said huskily. His eyes traveled over her long auburn hair lying loose and tangled on her shoulders, and her clothing, which was in disarray from sleeping. He couldn't remember her ever looking as beautiful as she did at that moment.

As if aware of his scrutiny, Amanda ran her fingers through her disheveled locks. Matthew leaned back on the blanket to watch her, imagining what she would look like sitting before her dressing table in a soft, filmy nightgown,

combing out those long tresses. He let out his breath between his teeth, rose quickly, and strode toward the horses.

"Where are you going?" Amanda called.

Matthew removed his rifle from the saddle, slipped on
his heavy coat, and replied over his shoulder. "I've got to
find something for the animals to eat, and for us, too. I
don't know how long it will be before we can get out, and
I'd hate to starve to death in the meantime."

"Be careful!" she called, as he slipped out the door and
disappeared into the whiteness.

Amanda had nothing to do to occupy her time but tend
the fire and pace, waiting for his return. How ironic, she
thought, that Matthew of all people had been the one to
come after her. She smiled to herself as she bent to poke
the wood with a twig, remembering how she'd vowed to
run him out of town by Christmas. Well, she'd gotten him
out of town, all right, but not the way she had planned.

Amanda walked to a small, four-pane window in the
back wall and peered through the dusty, frost-covered
glass, but all she could see was more snow. As she turned
to walk back, she noticed what appeared to be wooden
rungs built into the wall, leading to an opening the ceiling
above her.

Her curiosity got the better of her. She gathered the hem
of her skirt, tucked it into her waistband, and climbed the
rungs to peer into the loft overhead, but all she discovered
was a mound of hay. She hoisted herself up and gathered a
good sized bundle in her arms, then tossed it down and
climbed after it.

The horses nosed the old hay a bit, as if dissatisfied with
their meager fare, but finally began to chew it. Amanda
talked to them, stroking their warm necks, then left them to
their food and went to sit by the fire.

The sound of a shotgun blast brought her to her feet.
Minutes later, Matthew pushed through the heavy wooden
doors proudly bearing a snowshoe hare.

"Dinner," he announced.

Amanda smiled with relief. "I found hay up in the loft."

"Good girl." He shrugged off his heavy coat and sat

down to skin the hare. "That will save me digging through three feet of snow. Better stay away," he warned her when she moved toward him. "This might turn your stomach."

Amanda busied herself near the fire as Matthew cleaned the animal and readied part of it to cook, wrapping the rest and placing it under the snow outside the door for a future meal. Her stomach growled as he impaled the meat on twigs stripped from a bush and held it over the flames.

Amanda had never eaten rabbit meat; she had always considered it peasant fare, but now she found it to be delicious. They washed it down with more water, then sat on the blanket, leaning their backs against the wooden planks, and waited for the storm to abate.

Alice Ripley let the lace curtain fall back into place and hurried to stand next to the closed parlor door as the front door opened and Bonnie swept in. Alice pressed her ear against the wood and listened.

"Did you find Mandy?" she heard Gabrielle call from upstairs.

"No, dearest," Bonnie said in a hushed voice. "But we will soon. Harper and I went to see . . ." Her voice faded as she hurried up the staircase. Alice opened the door a crack to hear more, but Bonnie was already out of earshot.

"Horsefeathers!" she muttered. Where had that Amanda Hall gone? Chasing after Matthew Blake, no doubt. She'd heard he was leaving for New York to see his mother. She'd have to pump Gabrielle for more information in the morning.

Alice tugged the bellpull, then began to hum tunelessly as she waited for a servant to bring her tea. Whatever Amanda was up to certainly wasn't going to help her custody suit any. It was just like her mother used to say, give a person enough rope and she'll hang herself. All Alice had to do was sit back and watch.

Chapter Seventeen

SEVERAL TIMES DURING that long day, Matthew went outside to check on the weather conditions. Finally, toward the end of the afternoon, when the light had already begun to fade, he told Amanda he thought the clouds were thinning. "I think the storm is blowing over," he said with a sigh of relief.

Amanda noticed his mood seemed to lighten after that, as if he were relieved he would soon be able to escape her company, and his conversation, which had been stilted, became friendlier. As the darkness closed in on them, leaving only the comforting glow of the crackling fire, Amanda found herself telling Matthew more and more about her childhood, and finally, about the accident that had taken the lives of her parents.

"I could have managed the children," she said afterward. "We could have gotten by if Alice Ripley hadn't interfered." She frowned, remembering the day she had learned the judge's decision. "Stable homes! That's what the judge said they needed most, but I can't help thinking that if *I* had raised my sisters and brothers, Gabby wouldn't be the spoiled creature she is, Bonnie would be more than halfway through college, and Curt would be in his first year at Harvard."

"And you wouldn't have met Harper," Matthew reminded her, "or started a college, or even gone to one yourself."

"But we would have been together." She sighed heavily. "I so wanted all of us to be together this Christmas. Now Bonnie is to be married and Curt will miss that, too." She stopped talking, her throat closing with emotion.

"Amanda," Matthew said in a warning voice, "Don't you dare cry. I told you before that tears don't suit you."

"And I told *you* that you didn't know me very well!" she retorted, angrily brushing away her tears with the back of her hand.

Matthew pulled out his handkerchief and offered it to her. "And I said you were wrong about that," he challenged.

Amanda snatched the handkerchief from his hand. "I still don't understand what you meant."

"If I remember correctly, you were supposed to ask Harper."

"I did, but he wouldn't give me an answer. Tell me now," she demanded.

"I'm not so sure you'll thank me for it."

"I don't care about that. *Please,* Matthew!"

He sighed and stretched out his legs. "Remember the night we had dinner with Bonnie and Harper, when you were all put out over Gabby not coming along?"

"I remember."

"Ah! But do you remember how many glasses of wine you consumed at dinner? Can't remember, can you? Well, you drank enough to make yourself dizzy. And then you fell fast asleep in my carriage on the way home. Harper and I carried you to your apartment and put you to bed."

Amanda pressed her hands to her hot cheeks. "I don't remember any of that!" But after thinking over his embarrassing revelation, it did not explain how Matthew could say he knew her so well. Unless . . .

"Was that all that happened?" she asked quickly, unable to meet his gaze.

Matthew didn't reply immediately, and when he did, it was in a husky voice. "Not quite. Harper suggested we make you more comfortable before we left."

"Oh!" Amanda cried, bringing her hands once again to

her burning cheeks. "How could you!" She threw his handkerchief to the ground and would have jumped to her feet, but Matthew grabbed her arm and drew her down.

"You've drawn the wrong conclusion, as usual. All Harper did was to unbutton the top button of your bodice."

Amanda stared straight ahead, waiting for him to finish, but when he said no more, she turned to give him an accusing glare. "And you?"

There was a devilish glimmer in his dark eyes. "Your shoes and stockings."

"My stockings?" Her gaze dropped to her legs, hidden now by her black wool skirt. "But then you would have had to . . ." She was too mortified to say *"lift my skirt."*

Matthew smiled. "No, Amanda, I did not have to."

Amanda was silent as she considered this. He hadn't needed to peer beneath her skirt to unfasten her garters, and that should have been a relief—and was! Yes, it most certainly was! Furthermore, she had no call to be annoyed that he could remove a lady's stockings without looking; after all, it was no secret he was well versed in that area. "I see," she said finally.

Matthew smiled wryly. "Judging by the sound of your voice, that bit of information just damned me to eternal hell."

Amanda kept her gaze fixed on the dancing flames. "It's not for me to condemn or condone your behavior. Anyway, I don't see that it really matters one way or the other."

Matthew folded his arms and studied her. "So nothing has changed between us."

Amanda gave him a sidelong glance. "I don't know of any reason why it should have. Do you?"

"I take it that saving your life has no bearing on the subject?"

She scoffed at him. "You didn't save my life. I came here to wait out the storm, which is exactly what we're doing now."

A muscle in Matthew's jaw twitched angrily. "For your information, Amanda, I was supposed to go to New York yesterday afternoon. I was on my way to the train station and just happened to stop at the lumberyard while your sister was there. I *volunteered* to come out in this storm to find you, and this is the thanks I get!"

"Well, it was only right you should come looking for me since it's your fault I had to go after Curt in the first place," Amanda said, adjusting her sleeves. "Your conscience must have bothered you something fierce."

"Back up just a minute! It's *my* fault you came up here?"

"You gave Curt that job against my wishes," she reminded him, "and then refused to bring him home for Bonnie's wedding."

"I explained to you why I couldn't bring him home," Matthew snapped. When she huffed and turned away, he ran his hands through his hair in exasperation. "All right, if it makes you feel better, I'm to blame for everything that's happened and that's why I came to find you. Are you happy now?"

"I'll be happy when you stop butting into our affairs!"

"Butting into your affairs?"

Amanda got to her knees and glared at him. "Did you think I wouldn't figure out why you asked Harper to take you home from the dance hall?"

"Well I wasn't about to stand by and watch you hurt the very people you love just to spite me."

Amanda's mouth fell open. "You listen to me, Matthew Blake, no matter how angry I was, I would *never* intentionally hurt my sister. My family means everything to me. And for your information, I had already decided to call off the wedding plans when Harper came to tell me about their engagement."

Matthews anger faded as he remembered the cruel things he had said to her that night. He knew Amanda would never hurt Bonnie. He had only said those things to make her angry because he was afraid of his own desire for her.

He let out a heavy sigh. "I don't know what to say, other than to apologize. You have every right to hate me for the callous things I said."

Amanda's shoulders sagged. "I should have realized how Bonnie and Harper felt about each other, but I was too concerned about my own problems to notice, and poor Harper was too kind to mention it. I suppose I should thank you for opening my eyes before he—" she slanted him a glance, "—married the wrong sister."

Matthew grinned sheepishly. "I could have used a little tact."

Amanda gave a little "humphf," and looked away.

"I want you to understand something, Amanda. If I've interfered in your family's affairs, it's only because I wanted to help. I thought it would be a way to pay back the debt of gratitude I owe your father."

She turned her head and narrowed her eyes at him. "Gratitude for what?"

"For helping me get my business established. The town board was completely opposed to my iron mill until your father intervened on my behalf." At Amanda's stunned look, he said, "You didn't know that?"

She was instantly on her feet, her chest heaving in indignation, her hands balled into fists. "How dare you use my father's name to justify ruining beautiful land! He would have been appalled to see what you've done to that meadowland, not to mention the village square and his parents' home. And I resent you bribing my brothers and sisters to make them like you!"

"I *bribed* them?" he spluttered in outrage. "How the hell did I bribe them?"

"You gave Daniel a piano, for one thing. And you let Curt come up here against my wishes. And don't you ask me to believe my father would have wanted that big, fancy, eyesore of a hotel in our town, either!"

Matthew's voice grew louder to match hers as he rose to his feet and stood glaring down at her. "I bought Daniel a piano because he had none available to him, and Curt *begged* me to let him come up here! And for your information, sweetheart, your father encouraged me to build in Wheatener. I'd never even heard of the damned town until he told me about it. What's more, I can't believe he would object to a modern hospital replacing that crumbling, termite-infested, old mansion. And as for my fancy hotel, *your* shabby one-horse inn was lacking the conveniences of every other accommodation I've ever stayed in! Wheatener *needed* a hotel like The Blake, dammit! And it is *not* an eyesore!"

"The Blake," she scoffed. "How conceited to name it after yourself."

Matthew looked as if he were about to choke. His fists clenched at his sides and his voice dropped to a low, deadly snarl. "It was named after my brother!" He glared at her for a long moment, then jammed his hands in his pockets and stalked across the barn floor to the other side, where he paced back and forth muttering curses to control his fury.

In fact, Matthew's outrage was so great that, watching him, Amanda was assailed with doubts. Could it be true he had bought Daniel a piano solely out of kindness? What benefit could it possibly have brought him otherwise? And she was quite aware that when Curt set his mind to something, he could not be dissuaded. It seemed to be a family trait.

But could it also be true that her father had encouraged Matthew to build in Wheatener? She didn't want to believe it, yet how else but through a native would a New Yorker have heard of their nondescript Indiana town?

Amanda sighed. It wouldn't have been out of character for her father to encourage Matthew to build there in order to ensure Wheatener's growth. Her eyes followed him as he paced, and she suddenly regretted her unkind remark about the hotel, for she knew very well that the old inn had been a disgrace.

From the opposite end of the barn, she heard Matthew snarl, "Well, go on, Amanda. You haven't mentioned yet how I turned the lake into a quagmire. And what about my workers? Have you heard how I mistreat them?"

Amanda lowered her head as he strode toward her. What a muddle she'd made of everything. She had failed to bring Curt home; she had lost her way; and when Matthew had tried to make peace between them, she had only caused more animosity.

"Does your silence mean you're finished with your little

tirade?" he sneered, coming to a stop before her. "Or is there something else you don't like about me?"

She looked up slowly, ashamedly. His brown eyes were hard as flint. His mouth was set firmly and the muscles of his strong, lean jaw twitched under the stubble of a beard. In that instant Amanda realized there was much she *did* like about Matthew Blake, even when he was as angry as a hornet, even when she tried to convince herself he didn't deserve to be liked.

Amanda's gaze faltered; her thoughts were in turmoil. She had convinced herself that there was an ulterior motive for his every action, only to have him strip away those convictions one by one, until she was forced to recognize his acts of kindness for what they truly were. How could she have been so blind?

Bonnie had seen it all along, and so had Curt; and, as she looked back, she knew that she had been the only one among both friends and family to regard Matthew as an enemy. And now to discover that her father had helped him indicated that he, too, had seen something admirable in Matthew's character.

She had blamed Matthew for turning Wheatener off the path her father had set for it when it had been her father's idea to bring the mill to Wheatener in the first place. How foolish she must look in her family's eyes. How unjust she had been to Matthew when he had tried time and again to help her. She was so deeply ashamed that tears welled in her eyes and her chin began to quiver.

Matthew's dark eyebrows drew down in bewilderment. "What is it, Amanda? What's wrong?" He took a step toward her, but when he reached out to comfort her, Amanda backed away. She wanted time to think, to sort out her new feelings. She couldn't do that with his arms around her.

At her rebuff, Matthew spun around and left the barn, slamming the big door behind him.

Chapter Eighteen

AMANDA WAS AT the window when he returned some fifteen minutes later. She turned at the sound of the creaking door and watched as he stalked across the barn to warm himself by the fire. Squaring her shoulders, she walked over to where he crouched before the blaze, rubbing his cold hands together.

"Matthew."

He stood up slowly, his wary gaze searching her face. "What is it?"

"I have something to say to you."

She saw his jaw tense, as if he were bracing himself for another attack.

Amanda took a steadying breath and plunged into her speech. "You spoke earlier about laying blame, and that's exactly what I've done ever since I returned from school, when I should have been thanking you, instead, for your kindness to my brothers and sisters—and to me. And I do believe what you said about my father. He was a staunch advocate of progress. He never would have wanted Wheatener to stand still while every other town around us boomed. I just refused to see it because"—she paused to swallow the lump that had come to her throat,—"because it took him farther away from me."

Matthew tried to interrupt, but Amanda ignored him, wanting only to finish quickly and be done with it. "I'm sorry for interfering with your negotiations with Mr. Wagner, too." She dropped her gaze as tears gathered behind her eyelids. "And I didn't mean what I said about your hotel. It's actually very pretty."

Matthew could not help but laugh at her last admission.

Amanda's head jerked up, causing tears to spill down her cheeks. "Do you find my apology funny?"

Matthew reached out to wipe a tear from her cheek with his thumb. "No, Amanda, I don't find it funny at all. I just never thought to hear those words coming from your lips."

"Then you forgive me?"

"Yes." At his smile, Amanda's gaze softened. She knew for certain now that her feelings for Matthew had gone far beyond liking. She raised herself on tiptoe, resting her hands against his solid chest for balance, and lifted her head to press a kiss against his cheek. "Thank you, Matthew," she whispered, inches away from his mouth.

And, suddenly, his arms were around her back and he was kissing her with an intensity that would have thrown her off balance, had she not been leaning into him. He kissed her fiercely, hungrily, yet with a tenderness that made her heart sing. His tongue was hard and forceful, yet he stroked the hollows of her mouth with such sweetness that Amanda eagerly wrapped her arms around his waist and pressed her body even more tightly against him. She was in love and she didn't ever want those kisses to stop.

Matthew kissed her deeply for a long time, until they were both panting. He held her close as they paused to catch their breaths. Amanda leaned her head against his chest, listening to his heartbeat, feeling a contentment she'd never known before. She lifted her head to gaze at him and said softly, "Was it guilt that made you come looking for me?"

Matthew's eyes were dark with desire as he smiled down at her. "What do you think, Amanda?" He bent his head and kissed her again, taking her down with him to the blanket, where she lay pressed against his long, hard form, her lips joined with his, her tongue meeting his with equal enthusiasm. She thought no further than wanting to be held and kissed. Nothing existed for her beyond the glow of the firelight and Matthew's strong arms.

But as his kiss intensified, so did Amanda's desire. With shivers of excitement, she welcomed the feel of his hands sliding over the curve of her derriere and up the sides of her ribs. When Matthew broke the kiss to unfasten the buttons of her blouse and part the material to expose the creamy flesh above her camisole, she arched her head back so he could more easily trace the hollow at her throat with his tongue and cup her breasts with his hands.

Amanda closed her eyes in ecstasy as his mouth traveled lower. Her breasts seemed to expand and grow hot beneath his caresses, so hot she wondered if he felt it through the material. His touch was liquid fire, making her body throb to a primitive beat that left her aching with need.

Matthew's kisses took him down farther still, until her camisole impeded him, and then Amanda let out a small gasp as he tugged the material down over her swollen nipples. Her breath came quicker as the lace dragged across one peak, and when he bent his head to take it in his mouth and bathe it with his tongue, she bit her lip and turned her head to the side to stifle a moan.

His hand slid down her thigh and up the inside, into the juncture, bringing a quick gasp of surprise from her. He cupped his fingers into her, pressing into the sensitive folds of her womanhood, and when she moaned and arched against him, innocently seeking the relief she wanted so badly, Matthew lifted her skirt and petticoats and began to tug impatiently at the ties that held up her drawers.

Amanda heard him curse softly at his own ineptness, and then she felt the cool air on her bare thighs as he lowered her undergarments to her ankles. Slowly, he began to touch her with light, feathery strokes of his fingers on her calves, her knees, her thighs. She trembled with desire, even as he drew closer to that aching throb.

He raised himself up to kiss her as his fingers trailed over the soft mound of curls. With a moan, she arched against his hand as he stroked the hot epicenter of her arousal. She was near delirious with pleasure. She kissed him feverishly, wanting more, needing more, the tension within her so great, she thought she might scream.

Suddenly, the stroking stopped. Her eyes flew open to see Matthew stripping off his own clothing. She watched hungrily as he bared his chest to her gaze. But when he stepped out of his trousers, leaving only his clinging long johns, Amanda gulped and averted her eyes. She had never seen a male fully aroused and was suddenly afraid to do so now.

In a moment, Matthew was beside her, dark-haired, golden-skinned, and nude. Amanda's breath came in short gasps as he hurriedly unfastened the remaining buttons of her blouse and peeled it off her shoulders, then unfastened her skirt and petticoats and pushed them down to her ankles. Her stockings and corset followed, and finally her camisole.

"Amanda," he breathed against her bare shoulder, pressing kisses onto it. "My sweet Amanda." He ran his hands over her naked breasts, molding them with his fingers, rubbing his thumbs over the sensitive peaks, bringing one sigh after another to her lips. "God, how I want you," he groaned.

"Kiss me again, Matthew," Amanda whispered, suddenly frightened by the size and strength of him.

He pressed her back against the blanket, spreading her thighs with his muscular legs. His mouth devoured hers as he rubbed himself against the soft mound of auburn curls, until she whimpered and writhed beneath him, and then he teased her with the tip of his shaft until she was ready to accommodate him.

Stretched to the limits of his own endurance, Matthew groaned deep in his throat and shuddered, trying to hold back as long as he could. "I'll try not to hurt you, Amanda," he whispered hoarsely. He had to resist the urge to take her quickly, and instead, pushed slowly inside until he felt Amanda's maidenhead give under the pressure. Her body tensed suddenly beneath him, but only momentarily, as her need soon made her forget the quick pinch of pain.

Gradually, Matthew increased his rhythm until he felt

her grow rigid beneath him and dig her fingers into his back, then gasp in surprise as she found her release. He moved inside her still, hard and fast, until he came in a shuddering climax. When he opened his eyes, her own were closed in quiet rapture. He leaned down to kiss her, wishing it had not been over so soon.

Her golden-brown eyes opened slowly to gaze at him and a sultry smile lit her features. Amanda reached up to trace his mouth with a slender finger, then she lifted her head to nibble his lower lip. "I liked that, Matthew."

He was surprised to find himself hardening again. With a groan, Matthew lifted himself off Amanda and lay down beside her, afraid to hurt her by taking her so soon. But at that thought, he rolled onto his back, a wrinkle creasing his brow. He had made love to Vernon's daughter, to the very person he'd sworn to protect, and he was planning to make love to her again. He should feel guilty as hell. Why didn't he? What was wrong with him?

Amanda stretched her muscles and smiled. How marvelous it felt to be in love, to *make* love. She'd never felt so wild and uninhibited. She turned on her side and ran her hands up the springy, dark hair of Matthew's chest, admiring the breadth of his shoulders, the strength in his arms, the gentleness in his hands.

As he turned his head to look at her, she lifted one of his hands to her lips and pressed kisses in his palm, then raised herself up and leaned over him to nibble his neck. "I had no idea it would be like that," she whispered. Her nipples brushed against the rough hair on his chest, and she found she liked the sensation. She parted the hair with her fingertips and bent to tease one of his nipples with her tongue and teeth. She felt him shudder and marveled at her newfound power.

"Amanda," he said hoarsely, "don't start something unless you want to see it finished."

Growing more daring, Amanda kissed him lower, following the slender line of hair down to his flat belly. But when she looked down and saw his swollen member, she gasped.

"Loose woman, indeed!" Matthew teased.

Amanda was fascinated by the evidence of his desire. She ran her hand down it, pulling back when it jerked at her touch. Then bravely, she stroked it again. He was huge and hard, yet the tip was velvety soft. She heard Matthew's sharp intake of breath and slanted him a mischievous look. "Did you like that?"

In answer, Matthew pulled her up with a lusty groan and rolled her onto her back. He bent his head to her breast to take a sensitive bud in his mouth and wrap a long, muscular limb around her own, pulling her into the vee of his legs. "As much as *you* liked *that*."

Amanda ran her fingers through Matthew's dark hair and closed her eyes, smiling as a deeper, more stirring feeling took possession of her. His mouth sought her other breast while one hand traveled down the plains of her stomach to her velvety inner thighs, sliding his fingers between the folds, stroking that tender, aching nub of desire until she could stand it no longer.

"Matthew," she gasped, "now, please!"

He cupped her buttocks and entered her, plunging into the hot wetness faster and faster until she was in a frenzy of passion. She clamped her arms around his neck and strained against him, wanting more, wanting all of him, until at last she was granted a powerful, blissful release.

They lay together on the blanket for a long while, until Matthew suddenly lifted his head. "I don't hear the wind anymore." He rolled to his feet and pulled on his pants and a shirt. "I think I'll take a look outside."

Embarrassed by her nakedness, Amanda quickly donned her camisole and underdrawers, abandoning the stiff corset as too uncomfortable to sleep in, and finally buttoned her blouse and skirt as Matthew returned and came to warm himself by the fire.

"We should be able to get out tomorrow morning," he told her.

Tomorrow morning. Amanda gazed into the flickering flames, unexpectedly saddened. She should be relieved to be going home, but she suddenly wished they would be snowbound forever.

For a long time that night, Amanda lay awake listening to the sound of Matthew's even breathing next to her. His question came back to her: *"So nothing has changed between us?"*

Everything had changed between them. As Bonnie had once told her, Matthew was not the ogre she thought him to be. He was a human being, with all the faults and virtues of any man. He could be harsh, but now she knew the other side of him as well, the gentle, loving side.

She had been surprised to discover he had a brother. She had never thought of Matthew Blake as anything but a ruthless businessman; except for his relationship with Dixie, he had always seemed a loner. Now she wondered whether he had any sisters, and if his parents were still alive.

But thoughts of Matthew's family made her think of her own. She rolled away from Matthew and went across the floor to stand by the small, dirty window, staring up at the heavens. Usually, gazing at the stars made her feel closer to her parents, but now she could only think about how her plans to reunite her family for Christmas were ruined.

"Can't you sleep?"

Amanda gave a start. She hadn't heard Matthew come up behind her. He put his arms around her waist and rested his chin on the top of her head.

"I was just thinking," she said with a sigh, leaning back against his strong shoulder. "I had these grand dreams of coming home from school and stepping right into my father's shoes." Her throat tightened painfully. "But I've made such a muddle of things. Mrs. Ripley is fighting me for Gabby, Curt doesn't want to go to college, I nearly forced Harper to marry me, and I've ruined your deal with Mr. Wagner." Her throat was so tight, she had to whisper, "My parents would be so ashamed of me."

"You're expecting too much of yourself, Amanda," Matthew said gently. "No one could fill your father's shoes."

She swallowed her tears. "My sisters and brothers look up to me. I can't disappoint them. You have no idea how our parents' deaths hurt us."

There was a long moment of silence. Then Matthew answered quietly, "Yes, I do."

Amanda turned to look at him, but he was staring past her through the window. Amanda put her hand on his arm. "Did you lose your parents, Matthew?"

His dark eyes shifted back to her face, and then he turned away. "My father and my brother Joshua." He walked back to the fire and crouched before it, staring into the flames. Amanda followed and knelt beside him, waiting for him to tell her the story.

He spoke without looking at her. His voice was tight, controlled. "Go lie down, Amanda. You need to sleep so we can get an early start."

She stared at him for a long moment, then did as he told her, turning on her side to watch him, wishing he would share his sorrow with her. After a few minutes, Matthew came to the blanket and lay down beside her, staring at the roof overhead until his eyes closed.

Amanda wanted to put her arms around him and comfort him as he had her, for obviously he had been greatly distressed by his loss, but he had made it clear he didn't want to speak any more about it. *Had his brother been younger or older than Matthew,* she wondered. *Had it happened when they were boys or as men?*

She felt deeply guilty for accusing him of conceit. She understood now that The Blake Hotel had been built as a memorial, and that knowledge brought forth a fresh burst of love.

Matthew looked so young in sleep, Amanda thought as she gazed at him—this man whom she had once professed to hate. Had she truly ever hated him? Could she have responded to his kisses if she had loathed him? And what did she feel now? Was it love?

Yes, it was surely love, but of a different and more powerful kind than she had ever known before. This love made her heart swell to fill the cavity of her chest, made her omnipotent even as she quaked with fear. It made her feelings for him seem poetic, yet rendered her tongue-tied when she thought of giving voice to them. This was the deep, abiding love her parents had shared, a love that she and Matthew now shared and would continue to share throughout their life together.

Studying Matthew's handsome profile, she reached out to lovingly smooth back a lock of his thick, dark hair. But as she touched his forehead, Matthew caught her hand and drew it to his lips, pressing a light kiss in her palm.

"You're awake!" she said in surprise.

He rolled over, smiling at her. "So are you."

She was mesmerized by his gaze. "I can't seem to fall asleep," she said, laying her hand on the side of his face.

He put his arm around her and pulled her closer. "Neither can I, but I think it has something to do with you lying next to me."

Amanda's arms wrapped around his neck as he kissed her deeply, passionately, the warmth from his taut body rekindling the desire within her, making her love for him almost too beautiful to bear.

"Amanda, I want you," he breathed into her ear, nuzzling the tender lobe as he cupped her derriere and pulled her against his groin, letting her feel his need for her. "Now."

"Yes," she whispered against his shoulder, unable to tell him how much she wanted him, too. She undressed as quickly as he and fell on the blanket with him, delighted to hear him laugh at her eagerness.

Later, as they lay with their bodies entwined, their passion momentarily sated, Amanda said softly, "Will you tell me now about Joshua?"

There was a long moment of silence, and then Matthew said in a low voice, "He died in a fire."

"How old was he?"

"Twenty-five."

She stroked the hair on his chest. "And you?"

"Twenty-two."

Then Matthew had been the younger brother, she thought. He was lying very still, as if he hoped she would let the subject drop, but Amanda persisted. She had a fierce desire to know everything about him.

"How did the fire start?"

Matthew rolled away from her and sat up, running his fingers through his hair. "Amanda, this is something I cannot talk about. If I do, I can promise you that neither of us will sleep the rest of the night."

Amanda stared at his features, shadowy now with his back turned toward the firelight, but even so, she could see that he was shaking, his face tight with grief.

"I'm sorry," she whispered.

With a sigh, he lay down and pulled her into his arms. "Someday," he said in a weary voice, "someday I'll tell you about it."

Chapter Nineteen

WHEN AMANDA AWOKE in the morning, it was to the smell of meat cooking. She stretched languorously and opened her eyes to see Matthew crouched beside the fire, roasting the rest of his rabbit. She watched him with adoring eyes. She felt so alive she wanted to laugh with joy; she felt as though she had crossed an invisible barrier into womanhood and emerged a new being. She sat up, remembering belatedly that she wore nothing under the mantle that had covered her while she slept.

"Good morning," Matthew said, smiling at her as his eyes devoured her ivory flesh, which she now hastened to cover.

"Good morning."

"Hungry?"

"Yes." She glanced around for her undergarments, spotted them, and pulled them beneath the covering, where she struggled to put them on and still retain some modesty.

Matthew watched her futile efforts and laughed. "If you're trying to spare my eyes, please don't. If it's merely your pride, take my word, you've nothing to be ashamed of."

Amanda blushed and, after a few more minutes of struggling, emerged to quickly step into her skirt. Matthew stepped up behind her and wrapped one arm around her waist, murmuring close to her ear, "Will you always be this shy with me?"

She closed her eyes as his hand moved up to cup her breast and his lips caressed her neck, bringing delicious shivers up her spine. As her passion flared white-hot within her, Amanda turned and slipped her arms around his neck as her mouth met his, their tongues intertwining as their bodies pressed tightly together. Remembering the feel of him inside her, her hips moved sensuously against him, seeking out his hardness, bringing a groan of agony to his lips as he took her down to the blanket.

In his urgency, Matthew lifted her skirts, untied the drawstring, and pulled down her drawers as Amanda's fingers flew down the line of buttons on his trousers and tugged them low on his hips. Unable to hold back any longer, they joined together, racing for fulfillment, panting as their bodies met and separated time and again, until their passions were finally slaked and they lay together, breathing hard, savoring the intimacy.

Suddenly, Amanda sniffed the air. "Is something burning?"

Matthew jumped to his feet, buttoning his trousers as he called back, "Our breakfast."

Amanda finished dressing and joined him by the fire, where she had a twig handed to her, with brown, crispy meat hooked to its end.

He contemplated her as he took a bite of the well-cooked food. "I've never seen a female who looked as good as you do first thing in the morning."

His bald admission rankled her. "Really? And just how many females have you seen first thing in the morning?"

Matthew gave her a lazy grin. "Enough to know."

Amanda bit angrily into her meat, then realized how hungry she was and ate more carefully so as not to drop any of the succulent flesh on the ground. Matthew dipped his tin cup into the bucket, drank half the water, and handed her the rest, watching her as she drained the cup.

"We'd better pack up," he said afterward, as he tamped down the fire. "Sky's clear now, but I'd hate to wait too long. The weather is too unpredictable."

While Matthew got the horses ready, Amanda bundled

herself up as best she could, then followed him as he led
the animals outside. After digging out the nearly buried
buggy, Matthew hitched his larger horse to the front and
tied her horse to the rear.

"Did you know you'd turned off on the wrong road?" he
asked as they plodded along.

"I thought so, but it was snowing too hard to turn back."

"I'm going to take you to Carolyn Tanner's."

Amanda turned questioning eyes to his face. "Why?"

Matthew slipped one arm around her back and pulled her
close to nuzzle her ear. "My love, you look beautiful to me,
but to anyone else, you look like you've slept in a barn."

"Well, so do you!"

"My point, exactly. In fact, I've been thinking it would
probably be best to say I found you only this morning. That
way, we won't have to worry about your reputation being
further tarnished."

Amanda's heart slowed to a dull thud. Matthew had no
reason to be concerned about her reputation if he were
going to marry her. And he *was* going to marry her. He had
told her how much he wanted her. Their night together had
meant more to him than just physical pleasure. Her eyes
filled with tears. He loved her. He *had* to love her. They
had made love four times.

But Matthew had never told her he loved her. Only that
he wanted her. Just as he had in his bedroom, and in the
carriage after the ball. Amanda turned her head away from
him as bitter tears rolled down her cheeks. Matthew had
gotten what he wanted. That's why he was leaving her on
Carolyn's doorstep.

Her heart felt as though it were crumbling, and the joy of
her newfound womanhood was replaced by a bottomless
shame. She couldn't begin to imagine what her parents
would have said about her behavior.

An even more horrifying thought sprang to mind. What
would her brothers and sisters think of her if they were to
find out? What if, even now, she were carrying Matthew's
child? How would she bear the shame? She tried not to

think of it, but soon her throat ached from holding back her tears.

What a gullible fool she had been to mistake Matthew's lust for love. Her hands curled at her sides and her lips pressed together determinedly. She had learned her lesson. She would never be so foolish again.

After hours of traveling, it was a blessing to see the town come into view, and even more so when Matthew pulled the buggy up to Carolyn's house. Amanda accepted Matthew's hand without a word and walked quickly to the house.

Carolyn was shocked to see them and ushered them into her parlor. "My dear, what happened?" she asked Amanda.

Amanda's eyes met Matthew's briefly, then she looked away as he began to tell Carolyn the story he had invented about her rescue. He left soon afterward, promising to come back for Amanda in an hour.

"You look all done in," Carolyn remarked as Amanda sat glumly on her sofa.

"It's been a very trying experience," she replied despondently.

"Wasn't it fortunate you had Matthew to look after you?"

Amanda lifted her head in surprise. How did she know? Carolyn smiled kindly and said, "We'd better get you cleaned up and send you back. You must be anxious to see your family and put their minds at ease."

Amanda took a hip bath while Carolyn went to find her a fresh blouse and skirt to wear. When she came into the bedroom carrying the clean clothing, Amanda was combing her hair before the fire.

Carolyn set the clothing on the bed. "I think these should fit. Call me if you need anything else."

Amanda watched her friend cross to the door. "Thank you, Carolyn."

Carolyn paused, and after a moment's thought, turned back. "Amanda, I would not presume to guess what happened between you and Matthew, nor would I want you to tell me. However, I can see that it has affected you deeply—both of you. I think you recognize that; Matthew, I think not—not yet, so you must be patient. Men are stubborn creatures, not amenable to change. But sooner or later, they come around." With a smile, she quietly left the room.

Before leaving Carolyn's bedroom, Amanda stopped to gaze at herself in the cheval mirror. With her hair put up and clean clothes on, she looked like the Amanda of old; yet, as Carolyn had wisely observed, she had changed a great deal. She was a different person inside: older, wiser, and deeply scarred by the man to whom she had given her most precious gift.

Amanda's chin came up defiantly. She was not going to sulk over her loss. She would pick up her life as if the incident in the barn had never happened. She only prayed no one would ever find out about it.

When Matthew returned to Carolyn's house, it was as the serious businessman. Amanda stood still, feeling dead inside, as he looked her over. His eyes returned to study her face and a tiny furrow appeared between his brows, as if her solemn expression puzzled him. Amanda turned away, unable to bear his scrutiny any longer.

"Thank you for your help, Carolyn," she said tonelessly.

Carolyn smiled graciously. "Give your family my love."

Amanda took her hand and squeezed it, then followed Matthew to her buggy. They rode together as before, but with his horse tied behind, instead of hers. Neither one said a word. It seemed to Amanda that Matthew was preoccupied, his mind, no doubt, already turned back to his work, shutting her out of his life with no more thought than if he were snuffing out a candle.

Matthew walked her inside the Jefferson Arms and up the hallway to her door, where, just before she entered her apartment, he pulled her into his arms for a kiss. She stood stiffly in his embrace and said nothing when he released her, only turned her back on him and reached for the doorknob.

"Merry Christmas, Amanda," he said softly.

A sob welled up in her chest. "Merry Christmas," she whispered. The apartment door opened, spilling light and excited chatter into the hallway. Amanda found herself surrounded by her brothers and sisters who were all trying to talk at once, asking her questions and telling her what had happened while she was away.

And all she could think about was that Matthew did not love her.

Matthew was indeed preoccupied as he left Amanda and strode outside to where he had parked the buggy. After he had removed his traveling bag from the boot and strapped it onto his saddle, he mounted his horse and urged him into a gallop. He had only minutes to catch the last train, but it was urgent that he do so, for upon his return that afternoon he had found a telegram saying that his mother was near death.

As the train steamed eastward, Matthew's thoughts kept returning to Amanda, and he pictured her again as he had found her in the barn, huddled in the corner, frightened and cold. Then the image changed and he smiled, imagining her lying beside him on the blanket, seeing once more her delicately featured face with its masses of auburn hair fanned out beneath her, and the smooth ivory body that he now knew so well. He could almost feel the silken texture of her skin and taste the sweetness of her.

With a little smile, Matthew leaned his head against the back of the seat and closed his eyes, reliving those moments when she was in his arms. He had known it would be good with Amanda. He had known from their first kiss that she would be as passionate in love as she was in anger.

He no longer worried that he should feel guilty over what had happened. On the way back to Wheatener, he had developed a plan that would allow him to protect her as well as satisfy his desire for her. He had purchased Hall House months ago, with no particular purpose in mind, or so he had told himself at the time. Now he would have it restored and take Amanda there to live with him.

He chose not to examine the flaw in his thinking, so

caught up was he in his daydreams. He pushed aside the fact that Amanda had almost married Harper to protect herself from a rumor which, if he carried out his plan, would finally become true.

Upon reaching New York, Matthew sent a telegram to Michael O'Day, with explicit instructions on what to do in his absence. Then he turned his attention back to his reason for the trip, and hired a hack to take him to the big brick home where his mother lay dying.

Amanda tiptoed over sleeping bodies, quietly making her way to her bedroom. Their Christmas Eve celebration had lasted until the early hours of the morning, until Amanda finally bedded them down on blankets on the floor. Harper had gone back to his apartment and Bonnie was asleep on the sofa. But when Amanda closed her eyes and tried to sleep, she found herself thinking about Matthew.

Where was he now? Was he celebrating with Dixie? Amanda's heart twisted in misery as she conjured up the image of the voluptuous blond lying in his arms.

She tried to convince herself she could forget Matthew. But how could she ever forget what had happened between them? She had bared body and soul to him. She had given herself in total trust. And in return, he had invented a story to save her reputation and left her on her doorstep on Christmas Eve.

Chapter Twenty

SATURDAY MORNING, THE day of Bonnie's wedding, dawned clear and crisply cold. Amanda dressed and ate quickly and was ready to set off for the Ripleys' to help Bonnie prepare for the wedding when there was a hesitant knock on her door and a man called out, "Amanda Hall?"

His voice was very familiar. Amanda opened the door to see a tall, distinguished, sun-bronzed gentleman with thick white hair and a luxurious handlebar mustache smiling down at her, a mahogany cane dangling from one arm.

"Mandy, my dear child," he said in a gentle voice, holding out his arms.

For a moment, Amanda thought she was looking at her father. She clutched the door frame for support as her knees sagged weakly.

"Don't you know me? It's Uncle David!"

With tears in her eyes, Amanda began to laugh and threw herself into his arms. "Uncle David! Oh, how happy I am to see you! Please come inside."

She closed the door and leaned against it, watching him with an exultant smile as he walked into her sitting room and looked around for the most comfortable chair to sit in. Tears spilled down her cheeks. Uncle David, her father's brother who had been in Egypt when her parents had died, had finally come home.

"I'm afraid I only received your letter six months ago,

and it took forever to book passage to get back," he told her as she moved a footstool up to his chair.

She smiled at him. "Would you like coffee? Or tea?"

"Tea would be nice."

"Where have you been all these years?" she called from the kitchen.

"Oh, goodness! All over. After Egypt, I went to Persia, Mongolia, and then on to India. Luckily, a friend of mine in Egypt held your letter until I returned." He accepted a cup of tea, took a sip, and said, "I was terribly upset when I read about the tragedy. I wish I had been able to help you, Mandy. If only I had received your letter sooner . . ." He stopped to take another drink, glancing around the apartment. "I see the children are not living with you."

Amanda came in and sat down. "They were placed in homes here in town and I went away to college."

"You weren't able to keep the house, either?"

Amanda looked down and shook her head, but immediately brightened. "I've filed a petition for custody, and as soon as we have a hearing, I'll be able to bring them all to live with me. But I don't have the money yet to buy the house.

"Well then, I shall do whatever I can to help."

"Oh, Uncle David, your timing couldn't have been better! Bonnie is to be married today!"

"Today?" he exclaimed, sitting forward on the chair. "Well, there's no time to lose. I must air out my good suit and go find her a suitable gift. You'll have to tell me all about her young man on the way. But, for now, is there somewhere I can have a bath, do you suppose?"

Amanda prepared a bath in the tin tub and left him to his privacy while she went upstairs to inform Harper of this new turn of events. When she returned, it was to see a slim, dapper gentleman in his fifties dressed in a black, pin-striped swallow-tail frock coat and trousers, sitting calmly on her sofa reading the newspaper.

"It seems Wheatener has grown since I was last here," he remarked, turning the page.

Amanda laughed. "You won't recognize it."

On their short drive to the square to buy Bonnie a wedding present, she told her uncle as much as possible about their lives. From the square, they went to the Ripleys' for a joyful reunion with Bonnie and Gabby, the latter of whom didn't even know this exotic uncle of hers. Later, while Mayor Ripley entertained David in the study, Amanda and Bonnie disappeared upstairs to prepare for the ceremony.

"Well, you know what their uncle's return means," Clara Ripley whispered to her mother as they stood outside the closed doors, listening to the men talking within. "It means that Amanda can now bring her family back together."

Alice pulled back to stare at her in horror. Then she scoffed. "Horsefeathers! That man is a wanderer. He'll be off on another one of his expeditions in a month's time."

"Mama, you're forgetting how determined Amanda can be. What would you bet she doesn't already have a plan?"

"There will be no betting in this house, young lady!" With a huff, she left Clara with her ear pressed to the door and slipped quietly into the parlor, where she paced and fretted for over an hour. What if David Hall *did* stay in Wheatener?

"I won't let her take my little girl!" she said aloud, yet worry ate at her. Amanda was currently considered a heroine, having braved a blizzard trying to fetch her brother so the family could be together on Christmas. An editorial in the newspaper had praised her courage, as well as Matthew Blake's bravery in rescuing her. What judge would deny her custody now?

Alice stamped her foot. "There has to be a way to stop her!"

The wedding went off without a hitch. Harper was a properly solemn and dignified groom, although when Bonnie appeared on her uncle's arm, he could not prevent an enraptured smile from spreading across his face. Amanda had never seen her sister as beautiful as she was that day.

After the ceremony, everyone retired to the fellowship hall in the basement for wedding cake, coffee, and Rachel Hall's famous cherry punch recipe, which hadn't been used

in over five years. The mood was gay; children ran in and
out between the adults, who talked and laughed and wished
the newly wedded couple well as Harper and Bonnie
strolled among them, arm-in-arm. All the while, Amanda
kept a determined smile on her face and somehow made it
through the day. Her only salvation was that Matthew hadn't
come. She could not have managed if he had.

The next day, Amanda took her uncle around town,
showing him all the changes and additions since he had last
seen it, and then she gave him a tour of the college.

"I'm impressed, Mandy," he said, standing outside the
large main building with his head tilted back to see it all.
"It reminds me of a small college I once taught at in Virginia."

"What a marvelous idea!" Amanda exclaimed, linking
her arm in his as they walked back to the buggy. "You can
teach an archaeology course for us."

David stopped to stare at her. "Now, Mandy, you know
I'm retired."

"But what will you do with yourself all day? You're
much too young to sit in a rocking chair and stare out the
window. Why not teach a few courses? You can choose
your schedule; it would be perfect."

David looked thoughtful as they resumed their walk. "I
don't know. Let me think about it, will you?"

"Uncle David," she said as the buggy bumped over the
rough roads on their way back to the Jefferson that afternoon, "if you do stay, have you given any thought to where
you'd want to live?"

"Not really."

"Good. I have just the place." Brimming with excitement, Amanda turned the horse toward Hall House. Now,
at last, she had the resources to get it back.

She pulled the buggy up to the hitching post in front of
the house and climbed down, where she stood gazing at her
former home with eyes full of love. She did not see the
missing roof tiles or the chimney that needed tuck-pointing
or even the overgrown shrubbery across the front.

Rather, she saw the house as she remembered it, with her

father standing in the open doorway waiting for his evening paper and her mother calling for her from upstairs. And Curt racing out the door to meet his friends in the backyard. And Daniel's music floating from the open windows.

"Is it for sale?" David asked, staring at the huge, solidly built home with dismay.

"Yes, it's been empty for several months, when the last owners moved away. We'll have to see Fred Moore at the bank to find out who has title to it now."

But as they walked up to the house, the door opened and two men in painter's overalls came outside, heading for a wagon that Amanda had not noticed before, parked along one side of the street. There, the men picked up scaffolding from the back of the wagon and carried it inside.

Amanda followed them in and found other workmen bustling in and out of rooms, carrying ladders, buckets, tools, and sawhorses. The sound of their labor echoed throughout the house.

"What's going on here?" David asked loudly, trying to be heard above the noise. Several of the men stared at them as they crossed the wide hallway and stood at the drawing room doors.

"Pardon me," Amanda called to a painter inside, who halted his brush strokes to look at her. "Who ordered this work done?"

"The owner, who do you think?" he replied crossly, going back to his work.

"Do you know his name?"

The man shook his head.

"We'll have to ask Fred Moore," Amanda told her uncle. "But as long as we're here, let's look at the rest of the house. It's been so long since I've seen it, I've almost forgotten what the rooms look like."

When their tour was finished, they stood outside looking over the facade. David sighed, thinking longingly of the quiet little cottage to which he had always pictured coming home. "I think this house would be to big for us, Mandy."

Amanda stared at him in surprise. "Too big for seven of us?"

"Curt will be going to college in a year," David reminded her. "And it won't be long until Daniel goes, too. And sooner or later, you're bound to marry, and—"

"I don't think you'll have to worry about that," Amanda cut in, causing David to raise his eyebrows in surprise. She turned to him with a pleading expression. "Please, Uncle David, say you'll think about it. This house means the world to me!"

Looking at her hopeful face, David could not say no. "All right, Mandy. If it's that important to you."

"Oh, it is!" Amanda threw her arms around his neck, standing on tiptoe to kiss his cheek. "Thank you, Uncle David. Thank you so much! I can't wait to tell the others!" She turned and sailed toward the buggy, her mind already filled with plans for the house. "I'll go right now to find out who has title to it. Whoever it is, I know I can persuade him to sell it to us."

David sighed. If there was one thing he had learned from his years of traveling, it was that no one could stop a determined woman.

After depositing her uncle at the Jefferson Arms, Amanda went to the bank to see Fred Moore. She had to wait until he had finished a meeting, then she was shown into his office.

"Well, Amanda, this is a pleasant surprise." The bank president smiled as he offered her a chair across from his desk. "News about the college?"

"No, actually I came to inquire about Hall House."

He frowned. "Hall House?"

"Yes, my uncle would like to buy it for us, but when we rode past today, it looked as if someone were preparing to move in." She smiled impishly. "I hope you're not going to tell me I'm right."

Fred Moore pursed his lips, his eyebrows drawn together. "I'm afraid it was purchased some months ago."

Amanda's heart sank. "By whom?"

"Matthew Blake."

Amanda clutched the arms of the chair so tightly her

knuckles turned white. Matthew had bought Hall House and hadn't even bothered to tell her! But why would he keep it from her? Could it be that he intended to install Dixie there to live with him?

In her mind, she imagined the regal blond floating down the staircase as the new mistress of Hall House, and the bile rose in her throat. She thanked the bank president in a stilted voice and walked out as waves of nausea swept over her. She went straight to the lumberyard and demanded to see Matthew, only to learn he was not there. She was told to see Mr. O'Day in his stead.

"Michael?" she called as she swept across the dirt floor of the warehouse past rows of freshly milled timber.

The little Irishman stepped out from between the stacks of lumber, sweeping off his sawdust-covered work cap when he saw her, his merry blue eyes twinkling. "Good afternoon, Miss Hall. And how may I be of service to you today? Another map, perhaps?"

She ignored his teasing. "I must see Matthew at once."

"Would that I could help you, Miss Hall, but you see, he's gone back to New York."

Amanda felt suddenly lightheaded. "Gone back? For good?"

"Not that I'm aware of."

"Do you know when he'll be back?"

"That I can't say."

Obviously, Michael would give her no more information unless specifically directed to do so by Matthew. "Well, when you see him, tell him I was here," Amanda said firmly. "And you can tell him it's strictly a business matter!"

Michael watched Amanda's skirts switch angrily as she retraced her steps across the warehouse, thinking to himself that she was a match for Matthew if ever there was one.

Harper and Bonnie returned from their honeymoon on New Year's Day, a day after Curt's return. Amanda had planned to surprise them with a homecoming dinner that evening and had invited her brothers and sisters, but Bonnie turned up on her doorstep at one o'clock in the afternoon when she was in the middle of cooking and ruined her surprise.

"Bonnie! What are you doing back so early?"

Bonnie laughed and threw her arms around her sister, hugging her tightly, her face radiantly happy. "We took an early train. Where Uncle David?" she asked, looking around.

"He went to visit an old friend of his."

Bonnie walked into the sitting room and twirled around. "Oh, Mandy," she said with a sigh. "I can't tell you how happy I am. Harper is wonderful." She danced over to where Amanda now sat on the sofa and dropped to her knees in front of her. "He's kind and gentle and so patient with me." Bonnie blushed. "I was such a stupid girl, Mandy. But the awful things I'd heard about the wedding night, things Mrs. Ripley had hinted of, well, they're just not true, that's all. Remember that, Mandy, when you marry. There's nothing at all to be frightened of. Oh, Mandy, my dearest wish is that someday soon you'll have a husband who can make you as happy as I am."

Amanda averted her gaze so Bonnie wouldn't see the shame there. "I'm so happy for you, Bonnie. Now, I'm sure you have things to unpack. You run along and tell Harper he has to bring you down for supper at five o'clock."

Bonnie floated to the door. "All right, dearest. We'll be here."

Amanda stared at the empty doorway, her heart heavy with regret. If Bonnie knew the truth, she would not be so optimistic. What man would have her now? But if she could get Hall House back, it wouldn't matter if she never married. Having her family back together again was all that she needed.

Over dinner that evening, Amanda told her family of her visit to their former home and of her plans to buy it for them. "Uncle David said he'd help us financially," she told them, "but the problem is—"

The sudden rush of excited conversation drowned out the

rest of her sentence. Amanda held up both hands to silence them. "You didn't let me finish. Hall House has been sold."

Bonnie looked at the stunned faces around her and then turned to Amanda. "Do you know who bought it?"

Amanda's mouth tightened. "Matthew Blake."

"What does he need it for?" Freddie asked. "He doesn't have any children."

"Or a wife," Gabby added.

"I don't know why he bought it," Amanda told them in a bitter voice, "and I haven't been able to ask him because he went to New York."

Harper cleared his throat, a sheepish expression on his face. "I can explain his reason for buying the house and for his trip, as well. I believe he's decided to marry Mrs. Nightingale. He undoubtedly went back to inform his family."

Amanda felt the room tip beneath her. "Matthew's going to marry Dixie Nightingale?" she said in a faint voice.

"He told me the night of the ball," Harper said. "But you mustn't breathe a word of it. I promised him I wouldn't mention it to a soul."

Amanda was too stunned to speak. She tried to focus on the plate before her, but found herself staring through a watery blur. How could he have made love to her when he was going to marry another woman?

How could she have thought she loved him?

Chapter Twenty-one

MATTHEW RETURNED HOME a week later, arriving at the station late at night and wanting only to collapse in his own bed. He was now the only surviving member of his family. His mother had not even known he had come home, but she had lingered in an unconscious state for two long weeks after he had arrived and finally passed away in the night.

It had been difficult seeing his home again; it held such painful memories for him, memories he had hoped to bury. Now he shut out the past and looked forward, instead, to getting back to his businesses and to seeing Amanda.

He drove to the iron mill early the next morning and spent hours there going over weeks of work with his manager. After lunch, he went to the lumberyard, where he found Michael O'Day shouting encouragement to six sweating men carrying a huge log across the yard to be loaded onto a wagon.

"Ho! Michael!"

The little Irishman spun on his heel, his face lighting up with a broad smile. "Matthew! Good to have you back!"

"Everything coming along all right here?"

"You'll be happy to know we've had our share of problems. They're all waitin' for you on your desk." He paused and then asked, "Have you run into Miss Hall, by any chance?"

Matthew frowned. "Amanda? No. Why?"

Michael lifted his cap to scratch his head. "She came here one day to see you. And you may as well wipe that grin off your face, because she wasn't comin' to blow kisses at you. She was fit to be tied, and she said to tell you her call was strictly business."

"Another bee in her bonnet, no doubt," Matthew muttered good-naturedly as he strode off to his office. He decided to go see her as soon as he finished at the lumberyard.

But before he had finished there, Michael brought him news about Hall House. "John's outside, Matthew. It seems the back porch of your house is rotten. It'll have to be rebuilt. And he wants you to take a look at the bath. He's having problems putting in the plumbing."

"All right," Matthew said tiredly. "Tell John I'll be there in an hour."

Curt rapped on Amanda's door that evening, calling excitedly, "Mandy, open up!"

Amanda pulled open the door and he rushed in. "Mr. Blake is back," he panted. "I saw him at the lumberyard today. I thought you'd want to know so you could go see him about the house."

"Land sakes, Curt. You didn't need to run here. Sit down and rest a minute. I'll get you a glass of water."

"I have to go. I'm expected for supper." He gulped down the water and was off.

So Matthew was home, Amanda thought grimly. And if he'd received her message from Michael O'Day, he had ignored it. But he wouldn't be able to ignore *her*.

Amanda's work at the college kept her occupied most of the following morning. When she finally stormed in to see Matthew, he was having a quick lunch in his office at the lumberyard while he dictated orders to Michael.

When the door opened, both men looked up in surprise and then smiled, but seeing the angry set of her face, Michael stood up, picked up his sandwich, and slipped past her, saying quickly, "Good afternoon, Miss Hall. You're looking as lovely as ever."

Amanda ignored him.

When he had gone, quietly shutting the door behind him, Matthew came toward her. "Good lord, Amanda. By the look on your face, I'd say you intended to murder me."

She dodged his hands as he reached out to pull her into her arms, and said spitefully, "You bought my house!"

"So you found out about it, did you?" Matthew said with a grin.

"Yes, I found out. And about your other secret, too."

"My other secret?"

"Your engagement!" Tears sprang to her eyes and her voice shook with emotion. "How could you have taken advantage of me when you were engaged to marry Dixie Nightingale?"

"Is that what you think I did? Take advantage of you?" he asked with mounting anger. "And where in the hell did you hear I was marrying Dixie?"

She blinked furiously to dispel her tears. "From Harper!"

"Amanda, Harper didn't have the full story."

"You intended all along to marry Dixie and install her in *my* house. That's why you didn't tell me you bought it."

"Amanda, you'd better stop trying to tell me what I intended or I swear—"

"What will you do, Matthew?" she cried, glaring up at him. "You've destroyed my hometown, you've stolen my virginity, and now you've taken my family home. What more can you possibly do to me?"

"Stolen!" Matthew gripped her by the arms, drawing her close. "By God, you'd better listen carefully or I'll shake you till your teeth rattle."

"I'll listen," Amanda sneered, "but don't think I'll ever believe a word you say again."

"I bought the house for *us,* you foolish woman. For you and me. I wanted to surprise you."

Amanda blinked in bewilderment. But then her eyes grew hard. "As you have already pointed out, I *am* a fool, but not so foolish that I'd fall for *that* story."

Matthew ran his fingers through his hair, then he picked Amanda up by the waist and set her on his desk, looking her squarely in the face. "Dixie is gone. *Gone,* Amanda. I sent her packing months ago. If you don't believe me, ask Carolyn Tanner."

"But Harper said you were going to marry her!"

"That was Harper's idea, dammit. I was trying to encourage him to marry Bonnie, and he thought I was speaking of myself. Now do you see?"

"You bought the house for us?"

"Yes!"

Amanda stared at him in dazed disbelief as joy flooded her soul. He had sent Dixie away months ago. He *did* love her! "Oh, Matthew!" She flung her arms around his neck and hugged him. "I'm sorry I doubted you. Oh, I can't wait to tell Bonnie. Can we set a date right now?"

"A date for what?"

Amanda leaned back and searched his eyes, her elation turning to uneasiness. "For our wedding. That's what you meant, wasn't it?"

His perplexed look was replaced by one of embarrassment. Amanda suddenly couldn't breathe. She ran to the door and threw it open, stopping only long enough to add in a choked voice, "I thought you cared about my reputation, if nothing else. At least that's what you professed on our way home from Michigan." The door shut behind her with a resounding bang.

Two days later, Jeffrey Gable sat across from Matthew in his office at the iron mill, squirming in discomfort. Jeffrey respected and liked Matthew. He hoped Matthew would understand that what he had to say was purely business.

"Matthew, I am here today as legal counsel for Miss Amanda Hall, Mr. David Hall, Mr. Curt Hall, Mr. Daniel Hall—"

"Yes, yes," Matthew interrupted impatiently. "I'm familiar with all their names. Let's get on with this, Jeff. I've got a busy day ahead of me."

"All right, Matthew." Jeffrey cleared his throat, shifted

in his chair, and started anew. "It seems that Amanda's uncle, David Hall, would like to buy the property you own on Willowbrook Lane. He's willing to pay you whatever you paid for the house and land plus an additional five percent."

"It's not for sale."

Jeffrey sighed. He could tell within two minutes' time when a person was stalling for more money and when they were not; and now he saw no sense in continuing with the negotiations, yet he had promised Amanda he would do his best.

"In that case, I'm prepared to raise the price an additional five percent."

"It's not for sale, Jeff. Now, I suggest we end this conversation before we waste any more time."

Jeffrey rose, extending his hand across the desk. "Thank you, Matthew, for seeing me. No hard feelings?"

"No hard feelings." Matthew walked him to the door. "When you report back to Miss Hall, tell her for me that if she wants to live in *my* house, she knows my terms. And if she wants to negotiate, she can do it in person or not at all."

After Jeffrey had gone, Matthew walked back to his desk and tried to resume his work, but his thoughts were on the lawyer's visit. What had made him say such a preposterous thing? He knew Amanda would never live in that house under his conditions. He wasn't even sure now why he wanted to hold onto the cursed house.

But, dammit, he hadn't meant to insult Amanda. He just wanted her to live with him. She should have taken his offer as a compliment, and then wheedled and flirted and schemed to trap him into marriage like any normal, self-respecting female.

But when had Amanda ever behaved like other females? Not that it would have done her any good anyway. He simply wasn't ready for marriage. Marriage was for two people deeply in love, and love was a risk he was not willing to take.

Amanda was waiting anxiously for Jeffrey Gable's return, and when she saw his buggy pull up outside the college, she hurried out of her office and down the wide, tiled hallway to the double doors at the front entrance.

"Well, Mr. Gable, what did he say?" she asked, walking beside him as they proceeded toward her office.

"He said it wasn't for sale. I'm sorry."

She paused outside her office and stared at him. "That's all?"

Jeffrey waited for her to go in, then he followed, closing the door for privacy. "Mr. Blake said if you wanted to live in the house, you knew his terms, and any further negotiations would have to be handled in person."

Amanda simmered with rage. She would fight him. She had to get her home back somehow. "What can we do next, Mr. Gable?"

"Nothing, I'm afraid. The house is his. You can't force him to sell."

Amanda paced to the window and swung around. "Then I'll appeal to the mayor. Surely *he* can persuade Mr. Blake to sell."

Jeffrey took his leave, glad to be out of it, but he felt sorry for the mayor, who was about to be caught between two extremely stubborn people.

"Please, Mayor Ripley, talk to Matthew," Amanda pleaded the next morning, sitting in one of his leather chairs in his office. Matthew had shown her how to handle the sentimental little man, and now she used all her wiles to win him over. "You know how much the house means to me and to my brothers and sisters. You know how we struggled to keep it—and how we've always wanted to be together," she added, prodding his guilt. She saw him flinch and knew she had hit a nerve.

"Of course I shall speak to Matthew for you," he said, coming around to take her hand.

"Thank you, Your Honor," Amanda said in a husky, almost reverent whisper, rising to kiss his cheek, leaving a waft of rose scent in her wake as she swept toward the door.

Mayor Ripley ordered his carriage at once. No sense delaying the confrontation with Matthew, he decided. He would get to see Amanda again that much sooner.

He sighed dreamily, remembering how large and trusting her amber eyes had looked gazing out at him from her fur-trimmed hood. She was such a lovely young thing. Why, if he weren't already married to Alice, he would have considered courting her himself, even though she was his own daughter's age.

When the carriage stopped at the iron mill, the mayor shook himself out of his daydream. Imagine being infatuated at his age. Nevertheless, it did add a lift to his day.

"Thank you for seeing me, Matthew," Mayor Ripley said, his short, plump legs carrying him quickly across the room to shake hands. He removed his heavy top coat and drew out his handkerchief to wipe his perspiring face. No matter what the weather, any activity made him perspire.

"Now, Matthew, I've had it brought to my attention that you've purchased Hall House."

Matthew's friendly smile faded. Amanda certainly worked fast, he thought irritably. "It's Blake House, now, Your Honor," Matthew replied stiffly.

"Whatever," the mayor said, dismissing the matter. "But, does that particular house mean so much to you? Couldn't we help you find another good property to invest in?"

"I didn't buy it for investment purposes. I'm going to live there." Matthew hadn't actually decided that fact until that very second, but now that he thought about it, he liked the idea. Yes, he would live there—alone, too! The hell with Amanda. In fact, he would have the master suite done up to suit his tastes and move in as soon as possible.

"Now, Matthew, surely you know what that house means to Aman—to the Hall children."

"The Hall children will be leaving home within a few years. With all due respect, Your Honor, I refuse to believe the house means that much to them at this stage in their lives. And as for Amanda, I've already told her my conditions."

"Your conditions?"

Matthew made a temple of his fingers and studied the mayor from behind it. "Yes. It's a private matter between us. You can ask her about it if you wish."

But she'll never confess, he thought to himself. It would be too embarrassing.

Within the hour, the mayor was heaving his rotund body from the carriage and huffing up the steps of the courthouse, up another flight to his office on the second floor, wondering how he'd ever got himself involved in such a dilemma. He sent a message to the college asking Amanda to meet him at her earliest convenience, and then he went to the conference room where the town board awaited him.

But the messenger did not find Amanda at the college. She had finished her work there and had gone home to the four-bedroom house Uncle David had rented not far from the school.

At supper that evening, Amanda relayed her conversation with the attorney and with the mayor to her uncle, ending on a positive note. "I'm sure Mayor Ripley will be able to use his influence to persuade Matthew Blake to sell."

Uncle David shook his head. "It seems an awful fuss to be making about a house, Mandy."

"It's *Hall* house, Uncle. The house we were raised in."

"Nevertheless, it's only a building, and buildings don't matter as much as the people who live in them. You would have been happy anywhere your parents were, Amanda. I think you've attached too much importance to this particular building. Were you to get it back, you would find, I think, that it isn't the same because your parents aren't there."

Amanda sighed. It was so hard to explain her feelings for Hall House. She sometimes felt as if she were the only one who truly loved that house.

After supper, the mayor arrived, looking grim, and asked to speak to her privately. She showed him into the parlor.

"Come sit by me, my dear." He patted the settee. When she had seated herself beside him, he took her hand between his two plump ones. "I'm afraid I have bad news for you. Matthew refuses to give up the house, and insists that he intends on living in it."

Amanda dropped her gaze and he was sure she was about to cry. "Cold-hearted monster!" she said in a choked voice.

Lucas Ripley's heart beat faster at her distress. He wished he dared put his arms around those supple young shoulders. "Amanda, my dear," he said gently, patting her hand nervously, waiting until she raised her lovely golden gaze to his face, "there is a way. Matthew mentioned something about having given you a condition by which you might live there, although he wouldn't tell me what it was."

Her lashes fell for just a moment, and when she lifted them again, he was astonished at the hate that blazed in her eyes. She jerked to her feet, clenching her fists at her sides. "How dare he!"

The mayor was at her side immediately, taking her hand, drawing her back down. "What is it? Can you tell me? You needn't be afraid of shocking me."

Amanda knew she needed him on her side. Matthew could not afford to have both the mayor and the town board turn against him. "He wants me to live with him," she said, blushing hotly. "He says I may live in the house, but only as his mistress."

Chapter Twenty-two

LUCAS RIPLEY STARED at Amanda, his mouth open in shock. Matthew's proposal was an outrage, if only because Matthew had the freedom to pursue her, while he did not. "How could he even think to suggest such a thing to you!" he cried, jumping to his feet. "Why, he barely knows you, except for business concerning the college!"

He paced across the room, his mind busily turning over various theories. "Did you know he felt this way?" he asked at last, coming to a halt in front of her.

Amanda kept her gaze lowered. "We did become acquainted—somewhat—when I went to bring my brother home."

The mayor thought back. Yes, it had been Matthew who had found Amanda and brought her home. Found her stranded in a barn, if he remembered correctly. Alone, cold, defenseless—he could picture it well. Yes, Matthew would have known how to become better acquainted with her under those conditions. But it was reported he only found her that morning, and they were home by afternoon—if one could believe the press.

Lucas gazed down on her bent head, thinking angrily that she had surely been ill-used by Matthew. And now this! What would Vernon Hall have said about such an outrageous proposal? Well, by gum, in good conscience, he would not allow it!

He dropped to his knees in front of her and gazed up into

her lovely, stricken face. "I shall straighten everything out, my dear, dear girl. Rest assured of that."

He rose, and Amanda rose with him. "Thank you," she said gratefully. "You don't know how much I appreciate your kindness." She leaned forward to kiss his round cheek, but he turned at the last second so that her kiss fell on his lips. He gripped her hands fervently, wishing he dared pull her against him. And then he was shocked by his behavior, and with a red face, hurried out of the house, stopping only to pick up his hat and umbrella by the door.

Amanda, too, was shocked by his actions. She ran to her bedroom and stood in front of her dressing table mirror, studying her reflection. Would she always attract men who wanted to make love to her but not marry her?

For a moment, she closed her eyes and gave in to a fantasy that she had until then refused to acknowledge. She pictured herself as Matthew's mistress. Long evenings by the fire. Nights spent in his arms.

But reality intruded and Amanda imagined ladies turning their heads from her in the street, crossing to the other side so as not to sully their shoes by walking on the same sidewalk as she. She would be scorned every time she entered a shop or restaurant. Parents would withdraw their offspring from the school. Her brothers and sisters would be shunned for her sins. The Hall name would be ruined and there would be no hope of ever living together as a family.

Living in Hall House under Matthew's conditions would not be worth ruining everything she had worked for. She would have to trust the mayor to get the house back for her.

Alice Ripley carefully patted her mouth and chin with her dinner napkin, then dismissed her ward with a fond smile. She waited until she heard the dear child's footsteps going up the front staircase, then, with a gloating smile, looked down the table at her husband. "Gabrielle tells me Amanda has run into a problem buying Hall House."

The mayor's fork stopped in midair, then shook slightly as he raised the bite of peach pie to his mouth. He chewed quickly, swallowed hard, took a big gulp of coffee, and began to splutter. "Hot!" he rasped, his eyes watering.

Alice's foot tapped impatiently under the table. Finally, clearing his throat, the mayor's eyes met hers, then quickly darted away. "Yes, there's been a hitch—from what I understand."

Alice's eyes narrowed. She could always tell when he was hiding something. "And what else have you come to understand about the situation, Lucas?"

"N-nothing." He shook his head rapidly back and forth, his chins shaking, his round face turning beet red. "Just that there's been a hitch."

Foolish man, Alice thought with a contemptuous sniff. Didn't he know she could read him like a book? "You mean you didn't know that Matthew had bought the house?"

"Well, yes, I suppose I did hear that."

"And did you also hear that he intended to marry Mrs. Nightingale and take her there to live?"

He gaped at her, his heavy lips hanging open. "Marry Mrs. Nightingale, you say?"

Alice smiled. It seemed he didn't know much about the situation after all. "Don't you find that odd, Lucas? Mrs. Nightingale left Wheatener months ago."

"I—yes, I suppose that would be odd, then."

"I want you to be sure and keep your ears open, Lucas. I want to know everything you hear the minute you hear it. Do you understand? It's vital I know exactly what Amanda is up to so I can stop her in case she decides to pursue that custody petition."

"Yes, dear. I understand."

"Then stop staring at me, Lucas, and finish your pie before it grows mold."

When Matthew was informed that Mayor Ripley had come back to see him the next morning, he threw his pen to the desk, scraped his chair back, and stood up, banging his fist on the oak top as he did. He had no doubt as to the reason why the mayor had come. Damn that female, anyhow!

"Show him in," he barked to his clerk.

Lucas Ripley took one look at Matthew's face and beads of sweat broke out across his forehead. "Matthew, I've come with an ultimatum." He stood opposite Matthew on the other side of the desk and mopped his brow.

"An ultimatum!" Matthew had not expected this. His dark brows drew together and his eyes narrowed warily. "What is it?"

Mayor Ripley tucked his handkerchief in his pocket and leaned over the desk, bracing himself on his hands. "You must either sell Hall house back to Aman—Miss Hall, or marry her."

Matthew was incredulous. "What?" he roared.

"You heard me. And I want you to know I am shocked. Yes, *shocked* that you would make such an—an *outrageous* proposal to her!" he spluttered.

"You cannot think I would take your ultimatum seriously."

"Oh, you'd better take it seriously, my boy, unless you wish to feel the repercussions I can bring down on your head."

Matthew gaped at him, stunned by his declaration. He and Lucas were friends. How could the man treat him with such hostility?

Amanda must have talked the mayor into it. Yes, that had to be it. He had taught her how to use her feminine wiles to wind the foolish man around her finger, and now she had used it against him. It was plain to see the fool was smitten by her.

"Your Honor, I am not a marrying man, as you know. Surely you wouldn't force me to marry her against my wishes."

The mayor rested his hands on his ponderous belly and smiled confidently. "I believe I gave you a choice."

Matthew was incredulous. "You expect me to sell a house in which I've already invested hundreds of dollars? It's *my* house, damn it all! I've owned it for months. And no one has said a word about it until Miss Amanda Hall suddenly dances into the picture and decides she wants it back. Don't you see how unfair this is to me? Don't you see how she's using you?"

The mayor's face turned an angry red. "How she's using *me?* You dare say that after you—after you—" He paused to lower his voice, "after you shamelessly took advantage of her when she was stranded, when she was cold and frightened and vulnerable to your advances?"

Matthew could not believe his ears. "Amanda told you that?" he exclaimed hoarsely.

The mayor collapsed in a chair, mopping his perspiring face. "She didn't have to. I guessed it, and you just confirmed it for me."

Matthew, too, sank heavily into his chair, his arms lying limply on the armrests. What could he do? Give in and sell her the house—*his* house? Never! His pride would not allow that. Moreover, he had a hunch that if he were to take the alternative, she would refuse on principle.

"Well?" the mayor asked. "What's it to be?"

Matthew's eyes narrowed cunningly. "Tell Miss Hall that I will marry her."

Matthew swore under his breath as he rode to the lumberyard, urging the big gelding into a hard gallop as if to outrun his troubles. When he reached the yard, he left his horse and strode into the low, wooden building toward his office, stalking silently past the young man who clerked for him, his expression stormy.

As if he didn't already have enough problems without the mayor adding another! He slammed his door, jerked his chair out from under the table, and threw his weight on it. A group of union organizers had come to town only two weeks earlier and had succeeded in stirring up his workers in the hopes of forcing a union into his mill. He'd been able to counteract their propaganda and pacify most of his men. Still, there had been trouble with one man in particular, a burly, bald, giant of a man named Obediah Marley. Matthew had finally dismissed him, but Obediah had reacted so violently that he had to be forcibly removed by four men.

Now there was this nonsense about an ultimatum. It was enough to make a weaker man sell his business and leave town. But there was one thing Matthew would never do and that was to let out-of-town unionist bullies tell him how to run his business or a mayor tell him how to run his life.

A memory darted across his mind. He tried to push it away, but the pressures around him had been building, and the image always returned to haunt him when he was under stress. He shut his eyes to block out the sight, but it only became sharper in the blackness behind his eyelids.

He began to perspire, smelling once again the odor of burning wood and roasting flesh, hearing the groans of timber collapsing and the cries of men in agony, feeling the white-hot flames licking his arms and legs as he lay caught under a collapsed wall. His heart began to pound as he saw again his brother's sweating, blackened face braving the intense heat and the collapsing roof to drag him to safety. He heard his own voice calling out to him, pleading with him not to go back inside the incinerator that had been his father's iron mill.

"Mr. Blake?"

Matthew's eyes opened and he found himself standing at the window, his teeth clenched and his hands gripping the window frame with all his might. He had not even remembered rising from his chair. He turned toward the clerk at the door.

"Yes?"

"I thought I heard you call."

"No, Joseph. I didn't call."

"Then I'm sorry, sir." Blushing, the clerk shut the door.

Matthew pulled out his handkerchief and wiped his face. He was no longer in the mood to sit inside his office. He decided to go see how his house was progressing instead.

The mayor sat in his deep leather chair in the library, his feet on the needlepoint footstool, sipping steadily at his glass of bourbon, his eyes fixed unseeingly on the fireplace. How had it happened? He had thought himself so clever, yet Matthew had managed to outsmart him. How was he to

explain to Amanda that what he did had been for her benefit?

"Oh, dear," he moaned, then jumped when his wife suddenly moved toward him from the doorway. "See here,
Alice. Don't sneak up on me that way! Do you want me to
drop dead on this very spot?"

"What's the matter with you, Lucas? You're as twitchy
as a cat's tail. You've been moping around ever since you
came home." She pulled a chair next to his and sat facing
him, her arms folded across her sagging chest, a determined
look on her long, fleshless face. "Well? I'm waiting."

Lucas sighed wearily. There was no sense trying to keep
anything from Alice. She would nag him unceasingly, for
days and days if need be, making his life a hell on earth
until he told her the truth. Ah, if only she were Amanda . . .

Alice Ripley listened with growing pleasure as her husband confessed everything. She would have liked to rub her
hands together in glee. Instead, she pretended to sympa-
thize with her silly husband, while silently plotting her final
blow to Amanda's custody petition. First thing in the morning, she would pay a call on Jane Douglas, the judge's wife.
And after that, Marylou, of course. And then Constance
Porter. She almost cackled aloud with happiness. Gabrielle
was safe.

"You did what?" Amanda cried, her face draining of
color.

"Now, my dear, you won't faint, will you?" the mayor
asked nervously, patting one of her slender, cold hands.
"Should I send for smelling salts?"

Amanda pulled her hand from his grasp and rose, almost
knocking the poor man off his knees in her fury. She stood
in the middle of the parlor and glared down at him. "I *never*
faint, and I cannot believe you gave Matthew Blake an ultimatum! *That* ultimatum!" Her copper-colored skirt swished
angrily as she crossed the room.

The mayor was distraught. "Amanda, dear girl, I never
thought Matthew would choose marriage. He's a confirmed
bachelor; everyone knows that."

"You could have used anything other than marriage!" she cried.

"Amanda, please forgive me," he begged, crawling forward on his knees to grab her hands and press them to his lips. "I would never purposely hurt you. I—I am too fond of you."

"Mr. Mayor, please get up!" Amanda commanded, embarrassed by the fool he was making of himself.

The mayor heaved himself to his feet, pulled out his handkerchief, and mopped his face. "Amanda, you must go see Matthew yourself. It's the only way to settle your differences now."

"No! I never want to see him again!"

"Then how will you get your house?"

"I won't!" she cried, sinking into the sofa, covering her face with her hands. "I've lost Hall House!"

Amanda sobbed quietly into her hands as the mayor slunk out of the room. She knew Matthew was calling her bluff so she would concede. And what choice did she have now but to concede? She would never marry a man who would give her his name just so he could keep her house. A marriage like that would be a farce.

Angry tears replaced sorrowful ones. Matthew had won. Hall House was his. She hoped it collapsed on him.

Matthew received the news of Amanda's decision the next morning when a messenger delivered a letter from the mayor. He laid down his pen and opened it, confident of what it would say. He grinned as he read the mayor's hasty note, then tossed it aside. A moment later, he reached for it again, his smile gone. Regret flickered briefly in his eyes, then he crumpled the note into a ball and sent it flying across his office.

Chapter Twenty-three

WHEATENER COLLEGE FORMALLY opened its doors on January 31, 1885, with an enrollment of three hundred thirty-seven students. For the first two weeks, Amanda and Harper worked grueling sixteen-hour days to ensure that everything would run smoothly and efficiently for both students and professors. Bonnie worked with them, but only during the day, for Harper would not let her push herself as they did. Her constitution was not as strong as theirs, he insisted.

Amanda returned to her house late each night to fall into her bed in a deep slumber and wake groggy and out of sorts to an early alarm each morning. After more than ten days of the punishing routine, it took a determined effort to rise from her bed.

And there was still the dedication ceremony to get through, which Carolyn, in her usual, efficient manner, had organized. The ceremony was to take place at a ball given by the town board and was to be held in Jenkins Hall.

Amanda groaned and swung her legs over the side of the bed. She had made an appointment to see Jeffrey Gable at nine o'clock to confer about the upcoming hearing on her petition, and she had an appointment to see Carolyn during her lunch hour to have a gown made for the ball.

She hated the thought of attending the ball because it meant seeing Matthew again. Since her last conversation with the mayor, she had studiously avoided any and all situations where she might come into contact with Matthew, but at the ceremony, she knew it would be virtually impossible not to see him.

"I think we have a good chance of getting your petition granted, Miss Hall," the attorney told her later that morning. "Now that your uncle has returned and is providing a home, I can't see any reason why the judge should deny it. I've talked to all the guardians and, with the exception of one, none will oppose it."

"I warned you Mrs. Ripley would never agree to it," Amanda replied.

"Yes, you did. But it will be up to the judge to decide. I'm going to advise that you keep your distance from Mrs. Ripley, however. Don't do or say anything she might be able to use against you at the hearing. Agreed?"

Amanda smiled. "Agreed."

Two ladies were paying for their purchases when Amanda sailed happily into Carolyn's shop. She smiled at them as she passed by, but received only cold nods in return. As she stepped through the curtained doorway to the rear fitting rooms, she heard them begin to whisper about her.

"To think she came from such good parents."

"First that man from Philadelphia, now *him!* It's scandalous!"

"The strumpet! I've heard you don't dare leave your husband in the same room with her."

Amanda stood on the other side of the curtain trembling from shock. They couldn't mean Matthew! He had taken care to prevent any such rumors from spreading.

"Amanda, are you feeling ill?" Carolyn asked as she came from her back office.

Amanda looked up, her eyes large in her face. "The rumors are starting again."

Carolyn scowled. "Come with me."

She ushered Amanda into one of her private fitting rooms and pulled the curtains together. "Sit down, dear," she said, indicating the two slipper chairs in white silk that faced a tea table at one side of the pretty room. "I'll send for tea."

In minutes, a tea trolley was wheeled in and Carolyn swiftly poured the hot beverage into rose-patterned china cups. "Sugar?" she asked Amanda. Carolyn added a lump of sugar to one cup, stirred it, and handed it to Amanda. "Now, dear, I hope you consider me a good enough friend to tell me what you heard."

Amanda raised the cup to her lips and then set it back on the saucer without tasting it. "Your customers—the ladies outside—they insinuated that I have another lover. And they made a cruel remark about not trusting me alone with their husbands."

"And is any of that true?"

"No, but you know that Matthew and I—"

"If none of it is true at the present, then you should not pay attention to it. Let people say what they will, Amanda; your behavior will prove them wrong. Now, I do not want to hear any more about it. Hold your head up proudly. It is not every young woman who founds a college."

Carolyn rang for her assistant, who brought in layer upon layer of beautiful fabrics and spread them out for Amanda to see, but she could not seem to keep her mind on the task at hand. *"First that man from Philadelphia, now him. It's scandalous!"* The words seemed to burn themselves into her heart.

"I can't go to the dedication ceremony!" Amanda told her sister for the third time that evening. "What if Mrs. Ripley is there? What if she's heard the rumor and makes a stink about it? I can't risk losing the custody suit!"

"Please, Mandy, listen to reason," Bonnie begged, sitting down on Amanda's bed beside her. "You don't have to go near Mrs. Ripley. And anyone who knows you would only laugh at that silly rumor, anyway. Everybody knows how virtuous you are. In fact, I dare you to name one person who can prove you are not."

Amanda cringed inwardly at the trust in her sister's eyes.

*Oh, Bonnie, if you only knew the truth, you would not de-
fend me so.*

"Come back to the parlor, dearest, and tell them you've
changed your mind," Bonnie urged. "Why, Harper was so
distressed by your announcement at supper that he vowed
he would not attend, himself, if you were not there."

"Then he's a fool!" Amanda snapped, and immediately
regretted her hasty remark. "I'm sorry, Bonnie. I love
Harper, you know I do; but you have no idea how it feels to
be talked about in such a vile manner."

"I wish it were me they were talking about," Bonnie told
her, tears welling in her large brown eyes. "You've done so
much for us. I'll stay at your side the entire evening, and if
anyone dares say anything unkindly toward you, why I'll—
I'll do something terrible, I swear I will!"

Amanda was touched by her sister's concern. "Hush,
now," she said, turning to draw Bonnie's trembling body
against her shoulder. She held her for a minute, then kissed
the top of her head. "Come on. Let's go tell Harper he can
rest easy. We Halls are made of sterner stuff than that."

Nevertheless, on the evening of the ceremony, Amanda's
hands trembled so that she could not fasten her silver locket
around her neck and her stomach knotted in apprehension.
She finally enlisted Bonnie's aid to fasten the locket.

"How do I look?" Amanda asked her nervously when she
was finally dressed. She turned a full circle in her emerald
green velvet dress, peering over her shoulder to gage her sister's reaction. Both the back of the dress and the neckline had
been cut in a V-shape, exposing a hint of cleavage in the front
and smooth white skin in back. There were no sleeves, just
full puffs of green velvet material at her shoulders, exposing
long, slender arms clad in emerald green gloves. The skirt had
a modest, draping bustle of pale green silk and a waspish
waist with a slim skirt that showed off the top curve of a hip
and fell in graceful folds to her pale green satin slippers.

"Oh, Amanda," Bonnie whispered. "You look beautiful!"

The gravel lot was nearly half filled with conveyances by
the time they arrived at Jenkins Hall. Amanda had to hold

onto David's arm for courage as they paused just inside the door to get their bearings.

The large hall at the rear of the building had been gaily decorated with multicolored streamers and balloons. Silver paper covered the long tables, which formed a U-shape around the outside of the floor. A podium had been placed at the top of the U, and a refreshment table had been set up close to where Amanda and her family now stood. Behind the podium, the musicians were setting up. A quick look around at the faces told Amanda that Matthew had not yet arrived. She hoped he had decided not to come at all.

The hall filled up quickly. Most of the people congregated near the refreshment table, talking and laughing as they sipped their drinks. Smaller groups assembled in the open center of the room, their voices mingling with the clatter of plates as the dishes of food were set out. Still others sat talking at their seats, waiting for the meal to commence. The evening seemed to be off to a good start, and Amanda began to feel at ease in the midst of it.

All at once, the laughter and merry voices quieted and people moved closer in their circles to talk in whispers. Amanda noticed the sudden hush in the room and turned to follow the direction of their curious glances.

Matthew stood just inside the doorway, dressed in a formal, black swallowtail cutaway coat and pants, with a white shirt and vest and a white stock tied in a bow. There was a look of indifference on his handsome face and his dark hair gleamed. She watched as his eyes swept the room, coming to rest, at last, on her.

Amanda's heart gave a lurch and she quickly turned away, but not before noticing that those same people who had turned to stare at Matthew were now watching her. With a jolt, she realized that she and Matthew had been the cause of those whispered conversations. She prayed he would not come near her and give those watchful eyes and gossiping tongues anything more to feed on. She was relieved when a hasty glance told her he'd stopped to talk to Jonathan Jenkins.

Someone touched her arm and she jumped.

"Good evening, Amanda," the mayor said with a sheepish smile. "You're looking lovely tonight."

Amanda smiled back in relief. Here was another person who didn't care what others were saying about her. "Thank you, sir. That's very kind of you to say."

The mayor glanced nervously over his shoulder, then said hurriedly, "I was hoping you'd allow me to sign your dance card."

"Why, of course you may."

"Thank you, dear girl," he said as he scribbled his name. He wiped his brow with his handkerchief and slipped into the crowd.

Harper rejoined her some minutes later with Bonnie smiling at his side. When neither behaved as if anything unusual had happened, Amanda began to wonder if she had only imagined those surreptitious looks and whispered conversations.

Once the guests were preoccupied with their meals, Amanda ventured a look around the room. Seeing so many familiar faces, she began to feel foolish for believing her every movement was being noted, thinking that it was just her guilty conscience at work.

As waiters cleared tables, the musicians tuned up and began to play. People assembled once again into conversational groups or drifted onto the floor to dance. Amanda had promised the first dance to her uncle, and when they had finished, she danced with Jonathan Jenkins. But she was uncomfortable dancing with him, for he seemed to study her with a wily, knowing expression, as if slyly promising to keep a secret for her. She excused herself after that, and slipped away for a glass of punch.

As she walked up to the refreshment table, Amanda saw several women turn their heads from her and click their tongues in disgust, women she had known since her childhood: Jane Douglas and Constance Porter, Helen Warren and Marylou Egley. And then she knew her imagination had not played tricks on her.

Her cheeks flushed with color. She finished her punch

and looked around for her sister. She was intercepted by Mayor Ripley, who came to claim his dance.

"This one is ours, my dear girl," he said with a smile.

Amanda cast a hasty glance over her shoulder to see if she were still being watched. "I—I'm not feeling particularly well. I was thinking of going home."

"You wouldn't deny me one dance, would you?" he pleaded, taking her hand between his moist, plump ones.

The dance floor was crowded, and Amanda felt relatively hidden from the sight of those condemning faces as she danced with the mayor. He held her as if she would break and gazed into her eyes like a lovesick puppy. Amanda ignored his longing looks, thinking, instead, of the ladies at the refreshment table, praying that she had only imagined their hostility.

But there at the side of the floor stood Alice Ripley, her hands planted on her hips, watching Amanda and her husband as her thin lips flapped in rapid conversation. Jane Douglas, the judge's wife, stood beside her, a disapproving look on her broad face as she nodded in agreement.

When the dance ended, the mayor escorted Amanda back to her table, only to find that Alice had arrived there ahead of them. She glared at Amanda and then turned on her husband and said in a hiss loud enough for those standing nearby to hear, "How dare you dance with that hussy!"

"Now, Alice," the mayor said in a hushed voice, "please remember where you are. As representative of this town, it was my Christian duty to dance with her. After all, she *is* one of the college's founders. I couldn't very well let her stand alone all evening, could I? If it makes you feel any better, I didn't enjoy a minute of it." He cast a sheepish glance at Amanda, who was red with mortification, and hurried away.

"Well, *miss*, you've certainly done it this time!" Alice said, rounding on her.

Amanda's chin went up defiantly. "Just what is it you believe I've done, Mrs. Ripley?"

"Where would you like me to begin? In the barn?"

Amanda gaped at her, aghast. There was only one person

who would have told her about that: Mayor Ripley. She couldn't believe he had betrayed her that way. Her face burning in humiliation, she turned and started to walk away.

"Harlot!" the woman called loudly. "Do you think you can walk away from your sins as easily as you can from me?"

A hush fell over the people standing nearby, but Amanda was so angered by Alice's words that she failed to notice. Her quicksilver temper flared. She turned abruptly, her fists clenched at her sides, and said in a low sneer. *"You're* the one who is spreading such vicious tales about me. Only you would say I'm not to be trusted alone with a man. Shall I tell you how the mayor kissed me when we were alone in my parlor, Mrs. Ripley?"

Alice gasped and took a step backward, one hand clutching her scrawny throat. "Amanda Hall!"

Bonnie suddenly stepped between them. "Mrs. Ripley, go back to your husband," she said in a hushed voice. "This is no place to air your ridiculous accusations."

"Oh, you poor girl," Alice crooned for the benefit of those watching. "To have to bear the shame of your sister's sins. To think that your fine family name has been besmirched by this common *trollop.* To think that your baby sister, that sweet, innocent child, may have to grow up under *her* influence."

At the gasps and whispers from the growing crowd, Amanda suddenly recalled the attorney's warning and her heart leaped to her throat. "Bonnie," she said in a low voice, trying not to betray her panic, "let's go find Harper."

Bonnie ignored Amanda, her voice quivering with indignation. "No, Mandy, I will not let her malign you. Apologize at once, Mrs. Ripley. At once, do you hear?"

"Please, Bonnie!" Amanda implored.

"Apologize for speaking the truth?" Alice spluttered. "Never! If you doubt my word, ask Amanda to deny spending two nights in a barn with Matthew Blake!"

Chapter Twenty-four

A MANDA'S HEART SANK. She could feel Bonnie's shocked eyes on her, but she could not meet her gaze. Her worst fears had been realized. Now her whole family would know her shame. She felt a hand on her arm and suddenly Carolyn was beside her.

"Mrs. Ripley, you are making a spectacle of yourself," Carolyn said firmly. "Think of your husband's reputation. Go back to your table and sit down."

"My *husband's* reputation?" Alice sneered loudly. "It's not *his* reputation in question!" She looked at the people around her and received nods of encouragement.

A lively polka played in the background as Harper elbowed his way through at least twenty onlookers to reach his wife's side. "Oh, Harper," Bonnie whispered tearfully. "Do something!"

"Alice!" the mayor exclaimed, coming through from the opposite direction, posturing for the onlookers. "That will be quite enough. Bonnie, Amanda, I apologize for my wife. She's had too much wine."

"I speak the truth!" the woman screeched loudly as he took her firmly by the wrist. "You told me so yourself. Amanda Hall and Matthew Blake are *lovers!*"

At the sound of her shrill cries, the dancers halted and began to move toward the commotion, the musicians stopped playing, and guests in far corners craned their necks to see the cause of the mayor's wife distress.

"There's nothing to see here," Carolyn said, walking toward the people, smiling as if nothing of great importance had occurred. "Please go back to your dancing."

Mayor Ripley led his wife away as fast as his fat legs would carry him, his neck bright red, his face beaded with perspiration.

"You kissed that hussy!" Alice shrieked. "You stupid, deceitful pig. How dare you betray me! How dare you!"

As the guests reluctantly turned away, whispering among themselves, Carolyn said quietly to Harper, "Find David and ask him to bring his buggy around so Amanda can go home."

Matthew shouldered his way through the retreating crowd, his face set in a stony mask. From his position on the opposite side of the room, he hadn't noticed anything amiss until the music had stopped, and then he'd heard enough of Alice's loud lamentations to realize what was happening. He wasn't sure exactly what he was going to do once he reached Amanda's side; he only knew he had to get there.

He nearly collided with Constance Porter and Marylou Egley, who had their head together, deep in conversation.

"Alice was hoping for this opportunity," he heard Marylou say. "With David Hall's return, she'd begun to fear Amanda would win her custody battle."

Matthew came to a dead stop. *Alice was* hoping *for this opportunity?* He turned to catch the rest of their conversation and heard Marylou's childish giggle. "Now Amanda's certain to lose. Imagine. Having an affair under our very noses! Alice was right. She's not fit to care for those children."

Matthew's hands clenched as unreasonable anger gripped him. Amanda's dream was about to be destroyed by a conniving old biddy, and they were laughing!

"Wait, Harper. There's no need to send for the buggy."

Amanda's head jerked around as Matthew came out of the crowd and halted before her. His dark eyes met her terrified ones. "Amanda is going to dance with me."

She took a step back. "Are you mad? Haven't you heard what they're saying?"

"That is exactly why we're going to dance. We've got to put an end to this." He took her by the wrist and led her to the center of the deserted floor, where he nodded to the conductor to begin the music again.

For several agonizing minutes, they danced alone to a waltz. Amanda's legs felt as though they were made of stone. She was frightened, angry, and humiliated, and the memory of Bonnie's anguished look brought tears to her eyes. She stared straight at Matthew's dark lapels and wished the floor would open up and swallow her.

From the corner of her eye, she saw Harper and Bonnie join them on the floor, and then her uncle and Carolyn, and finally some of the board members and their partners, until, slowly, the dance floor filled up again.

"Save your tears for later," Matthew growled threateningly, glaring down at her. "You've made a big enough mess of this as it is."

"*I've* made a mess of it?" she whispered, staring up at him.

"Who went to the mayor for help? You should have figured it would only be a matter of time until his busybody wife found out. Now you're certain to lose your petition."

"No!" Her words came out as a strangled cry. Amanda bowed her head. "What have I done?"

"It's not what you *have* done that matters now. It's what you're *going* to do." He paused only briefly, then blurted, "You're going to marry me."

The instant the words were out, Matthew's thoughts began to spin at a dizzying speed. Sweet Jesus! He had just proposed marriage! Was he mad? A glance at Amanda's stunned expression presented the slim hope that she would refuse this offer as she had the last. But she hadn't been desperate the last time. He caught the last strains of the music and looked around. The dance was nearly over. There was no time to think it through.

"Come with me and try to smile," he told her. "How you

behave in the next hour will determine whether my plan works or not."

Matthew stopped to speak quietly to Harper, and then walked to the podium with Amanda at his side, holding her there by a steely grip on her wrist, although he doubted she would try to flee. She seemed to be in a state of shock. He waited while Harper rapped on the wood to get everyone's attention.

When the music and conversation came to a halt, Harper said curtly, "Mr. Blake has an announcement to make."

Matthew stepped forward. His gaze swept the crowd, silently daring anyone to challenge his announcement. "We've been saving this for our own celebration party, but since some of you have already heard the news, we may as well tell you all tonight. Miss Hall and I are to be married next month."

There were audible gasps of surprise from the ladies who had scorned Amanda, and an immediate buzz of conversation, while others moved forward to congratulate the couple. Amanda smiled woodenly and murmured replies she would not even remember later, and all the while, she was kept a prisoner at Matthew's side. Her brain felt numb. *Why is he doing this?* she kept asking herself. She had no answer.

When the dancing began again, and before Amanda could protest, Matthew swept her out on the floor for another dance.

"You can relax now," he told her. "No one will scorn a bride-to-be, knowing there will be a lavish wedding party to attend."

"You have a lot of nerve deciding my future for me!"

He smiled wryly. "It's my future, too."

"Why should you suddenly be so gallant? You said yourself you weren't a marrying man."

"But I do pay back my debts. And I've invested a good deal of time and money in the college, as well. I don't want to see it ruined by vicious gossip. So consider yourself fortunate, sweetheart. There aren't many people I'd do this for."

Amanda's face flushed angrily. He was only marrying her to keep from losing his money and to pay back her father for his help. She almost laughed at that. After what Matthew had done to her, her father was probably turning in his grave.

"So," he said, studying her grim features, "It seems we are to be married. I think I'll see you home, then go out and get pickled. I have a feeling I'm going to regret this when I wake up in the morning."

"No more than I," Amanda said bitterly.

When the dance ended, Matthew escorted her off the floor, but rather than head for the exit, he led her in the opposite direction.

"Where are you taking me?" she whispered in distress. "The door is the other way."

"You'll need to say good night to your family before we leave."

"Can't we just slip out?" she whimpered, tugging at her trapped arm. "I can't bear to face them now."

"You should have thought of that before you confessed your sins to the mayor."

Matthew stopped before Bonnie and Harper and smiled graciously while Amanda stood at his side, keeping her gaze averted.

"I'm taking Amanda home. She's a bit overcome from all the excitement, and we have a few things that need to be discussed privately. Enjoy the rest of the evening. Good night, Mrs. Brown," he said, bowing to Bonnie. He turned to Amanda. "Did you have something you wanted to say?"

She shook her head, unable to look at them, afraid of what she would see in their eyes.

Matthew ushered her out, stopping to say good-bye to at least twenty people as if nothing out of the ordinary had happened.

"How could you be so cruel," she cried once they were outside, yanking her hand free at last, "making me speak to all those people when I could have died from the humiliation?"

"Would you rather have slunk out and made yourself look as guilty as they believe you to be?"

Amanda was silent as they waited for his landau to be brought around. After he had handed her inside and she had settled as far away from him as possible, Matthew said, "I'll leave the wedding arrangements to you. You can buy everything you need and put it on my account."

"How do I know what you want?"

His teeth were a flash of white in the darkness. "It's your wedding, my love. You may make of it what you will."

"I trust you'll be there for the ceremony."

"Sheath those claws, Amanda. I'm not your enemy any longer."

"At least I'll get my house back."

"Yes, there is that," he said blithely.

When the carriage drew up to David's house, Matthew pulled her roughly into his arms.

"What are you doing? Let me go!" she cried, struggling to escape.

"You haven't given me a betrothal kiss, yet, my sweet bride-to-be."

And then his hard mouth crushed hers, his hands deftly unfastening her cape, slipping around to the bare skin of her back to push the shoulders of her gown down around her arms, freeing her breasts to his roving hands. Against her will, desire coursed through Amanda's veins, crumbling her resistance, leaving her as helpless as a babe to his potent charm.

As his fingers cupped the silken mounds, molding them beneath his warm palms, his lips left hers to forge a hot trail down the slim white column of her neck to nuzzle the hollow of her throat. Amanda sighed in ecstasy when his greedy mouth found the soft peak of her breast. She wound her fingers in his hair and closed her eyes, moaning at the throbbing ache that overwhelmed her with need.

Suddenly, cold air shriveled her exposed, damp flesh and her eyes flew open to find him staring into their amber depths. "A promise of things to come," he said. "If our marriage is a disaster, at least our nights together will be pleasurable."

He abruptly left her to climb out of the carriage, where he waited to hand her down. Amanda stared at him for a long moment, her surprise changing to humiliation, and then she pulled her cape together and lifted her chin as she stepped down, ignoring the proffered hand and marching past him to the door.

"Sleep well, sweetheart," he called mockingly.

Sleep well! Amanda thought bitterly as she struggled to undo her gown in the solitude of her bedroom. Sleep well, when Matthew had just decided her future? Yet what else could she have done but go along with him?

Her only consolation was that now she had a chance to make her dream come true. Hall House could be hers and her family could be reunited at last. Matthew wouldn't care as long as his nights were pleasurable. That was, after all, what he had wanted from her all along. But would it make up for the emptiness in her heart, knowing he had only married her to save his investment and pay back a debt?

Matthew had his driver take him to Porter's Saloon, where he found Michael O'Day playing cards. As he had promised, Matthew drank himself into oblivion and was carried back to his suite by his driver and his faithful friend.

"Well, Himself has finally come around," Matthew heard a scornful Irish voice say the next day. He attempted to open his eyes, but shut them again when they were stabbed by hundreds of sharp prickles of light. He groaned and reached up to cover his face with his hands.

"I've seen you corned a few times, Matthew Gideon Blake, but nothing like last night. And now we'll all suffer for it."

"Close the curtains," he croaked.

"Close the curtains, is it? Will there be anything else, yer majesty?"

"Yes, get out."

"And who'd see to curin' your hangover, I'd like to

know?" Michael came closer and sat on the edge of the bed. "So, 'tis marriage at last, is it? Well, I can't say I'm surprised, for I predicted some time ago if anyone could land you, it'd be Miss Hall."

Matthew finally opened bloodshot eyes to glare into the twinkling gaze of the man who smiled down at him. "Damn you, go away!" he whispered furiously.

"Well, now. You're finally awake. Will it be honeyed tea or dry toast you'll be wantin'?"

Matthew ran his thick, woolly tongue around the inside of his mouth. "Tea."

Michael walked to the table, poured a cup, stirred honey into it, and returned. "I thought so. Need a hand?" he asked when Matthew struggled to lift himself into a sitting position.

"No."

Michael waited until Matthew had finished every drop, and then, setting the cup aside, he asked, "And when's this momentous occasion to be?"

Matthew glared at him, but when the man continued to smile patiently, Matthew finally snapped, "In a month."

"A month! Not much time."

"Not enough time!" Matthew growled. "In thirty days, my freedom will be gone forever."

"Such a pity. To gain such a comely wife and lose your freedom at the same time." Michael shook his head, his eyes sparkling with mischief. "Now you won't be able to carouse with all those other females you've been seeing for the past two months."

"What other females?"

"And she'll saddle you with all those Hall brats, too, not to mention a few of your own."

"You'd better shut your mouth, Michael, or I swear—"

"Go ahead, knock me teeth in. I dare you to try it in your condition."

"I could sack you!" Matthew threatened.

"And lose the best lumberyard manager you've ever had or will have? Well, come on, my friend. Stand up and fight like a man."

Matthew glared at his friend, who now stood poised to defend himself, his wiry arms bent, his fists clenched in front of his face. Matthew began to laugh, and Michael with him, but that brought on such a severe pounding in Matthew's head that he pressed his fists to his temples and sank back into the pillow. "I can't marry Amanda," he groaned. "I'm not husband material. It wouldn't be fair to her."

Michael snorted. "What a bunch of malarkey!"

Matthew was silent for a moment, then said softly, "I don't love her, Mike."

"Don't? Or won't?"

Matthew's answer slipped out on a sigh. "Can't."

"Then why did you propose?"

Matthew dug his fingers into his eye sockets. "If I hadn't acted quickly, she would have lost her chance to reunite her family. I couldn't let everything she's worked for be destroyed. And that's just what Alice Ripley has been planning to do, the old biddy, to keep from losing Gabrielle."

"So you proposed out of pity, then."

"Don't make me out a saint, Mike. I had a few reasons of my own."

"You don't love her. You don't pity her. Is it nothing but pure lust, then?"

Matthew's hands dropped to his sides. "Now you're making me out to be a heel. I don't know what I feel for her. Lust? Definitely. I've wanted her from the moment I laid eyes on her. But I admire her, too. Amanda has more gumption in her little finger than most of the men in town."

His expression changed as he remembered the scene at the hall, and with some pride, he said, "You should have seen her face Alice and that unfriendly crowd, Mike. Her chin was so high and her back so straight I thought she'd snap in two. It was only in her eyes that I could see how terrified she was. She knew she stood to lose everything— her reputation, her family, the college—yet she refused to show fear. You have to admire a woman like that, Mike."

"Well, you've done a noble thing, Matthew."

"Noble." He gave a harsh laugh. "What's the price of nobility, Mike? Freedom?"

"I'd settle for a good meal at that fine restaurant on the first floor."

"What time is it, anyway?"

"Four o'clock in the afternoon."

Matthew stared at the ceiling, wondering briefly how Amanda was feeling about the whole situation.

Chapter Twenty-five

Amanda splashed cold water on her face and lifted her head to gaze at her reflection in the oval pier glass above the basin, groaning at the sight of the dark circles beneath her eyes. She needed sleep, but sleep had eluded her as she twisted and turned in her bed, frantically seeking another way out of her predicament. She had come up with nothing.

She wanted to talk to Bonnie, but could not bring herself to face her. She had finally decided to consult Jeffrey Gable in the hopes that he would be able to advise her.

The attorney looked grave as he ushered Amanda into his office. "I was just about to send a message to you," he told her as she perched on the edge of the chair opposite his desk. "I've asked the court to continue the hearing. I don't feel this is the best time to present your case to the judge."

"Have I ruined my chances, Mr. Gable?"

"Not if you truly intend to marry Matthew Blake."

Amanda took a deep breath and said quickly, "Then you think it would be best if I did marry him?"

"Judge Douglas likes Matthew. That's a plus for our side. And don't forget, we have signed affidavits from the other guardians. If you can prove to the judge the two of you can provide a good home for the children, he may be persuaded to grant your petition. I'm not promising anything—Alice Ripley is sure to fight us all the way—but I wouldn't call it a lost cause, either. We'll ask for the hearing to be set in two months. You'll need that time to prove to the judge that the two of you *are* compatible—if you're certain you want to go through with the marriage."

Amanda's gaze shifted forlornly to the window. "It doesn't seem that I have any other choice."

Amanda stood at her sister's bedroom door, her heart twisting at the sight of Bonnie lying so still and pale in her bed.

"She's had the headache since last night," Harper whispered. "I don't know what to do for her."

"It's my fault. I've made her ill."

"Amanda," Bonnie called, holding out her hand.

"Oh, Bonnie," she whispered through her tears. "How you must despise me." She fell to her knees at her sister's bedside and buried her face in her hands.

Bonnie reached out to stroke Amanda's head. "You haven't made me ill. I'm just a bit under the weather. Please don't cry. It's not as bad as all that."

Amanda raised her head, tears streaming down her face. "How can you say it's not bad?"

"Tell me what happened with Matthew, Mandy. Please."

Amanda stared at her for a long moment, and then, in a tremulous voice, told her of Matthew's rescue in the storm and of her fight with him over Hall House. When she was finished, she hung her head, waiting for Bonnie's rebuke. But Bonnie only said in an anguished voice, "I wish you had confided in me sooner."

"You've always looked up to me; I couldn't bear to let you think badly of me."

Bonnie threw her arms around Amanda's shoulders and pressed her cheek against her sister's. "You could never, never do anything to make me think badly of you!"

Amanda gritted her teeth. She deserved scorn, not sympathy. "I slept with Matthew Blake. I welcomed him with open arms. I'm a fool, Bonnie. A wretched fool. I believed he would marry me; I believed he loved me."

"Surely he does love you, Mandy, since he's offered to marry you. It's no secret he's always been marriage-shy."

Amanda scoffed at her. "He's marrying me to protect his investment in the collage and pay back Father for his help. He told me so. But it doesn't matter, because I'm marrying him for reasons of my own, and they have nothing to do with love."

"Mandy, no!" Bonnie exclaimed softly. "You *do* love him. Don't hide those feelings. If he doesn't love you now, he'll come to love you in time."

Amanda pressed her lips together in a hard line. "I've learned my lesson, Bonnie. I won't be so foolish ever again. I'm marrying Matthew because its the only way I can avoid scandal and get guardianship of the children. And I hope I can count on you to help me plan the wedding, because Matthew wants no part of it."

"Of course I shall help you! We'll make it a beautiful ceremony. One you'll both remember forever."

Standing in the hallway outside Alice's suite, Lucas Ripley pleaded with his wife for the seventh time that morning to open the door. "You must let me explain about the kiss, Alice," he said in a hushed voice. "You can't lock yourself in there forever."

"Go away!" She began to moan again, a sound that seemed to reverberate through Lucas's skull. He clamped his hands to his ears and fled to his study.

Moments later, there was another knock on Alice's door. "I said go away, you philanderer!" she cried. "It's too late for apologies."

"Mrs. Ripley, you have a visitor," the maid called. "Mrs. Egley."

With a groan, Alice swung her legs off the chaise longue and rose to her feet. She moved slowly toward the glass above the bureau, feeling as if she had aged twenty years overnight. To think that her own husband had been unfaithful to her! And with Amanda Hall, no less! It was more than a person should have to bear. She checked her appearance to see that she looked properly aggrieved, then shuffled back to take up her position once again. "Show her in."

As Marylou tiptoed across the threshold, Alice moaned, bringing her friend hurrying across the room. "Oh, you poor dear! How utterly dreadful you must feel."

"You have no idea," Alice whimpered, draping her skinny arm across her eyes as she continued to moan softly.

"First to find out about your husband and Amanda," Marylou went on, "and then to learn about Amanda's engagement!"

Alice's moans stopped abruptly. She lifted her arm and turned suspicious eyes on her friend. "*What* engagement?"

"Her engagement to Matthew Blake, of course. Why, Matthew made the announcement right after—oh!" With a sheepish giggle, Marylou pressed her gloved fingertips to her lips. "You'd probably gone by then. Well, we were all stunned, to say the least. I mean, who'd have reckoned it? Now it looks like she'll be able to bring her family back together at Hall House after—"

Marylou stopped talking and stared as Alice's mouth worked frantically, but the only sound to come out was a strangled cry. Marylou fled to the door to call for a servant, then turned and stood clutching the door frame with both hands, watching Alice's contorted face, fearing she had brought on a seizure. In a few moments, a maid bustled in and waved a bottle of smelling salts under Alice's nose. Alice inhaled, then began to cough, and finally sank back onto the chaise as the mayor came puffing across the room.

"What happened? Has she had a stroke?"

"She's just learned Matthew has offered for Amanda," Marylou whispered.

"Matthew Blake?" he spluttered in surprise. "For Amanda?"

Alice's eyes opened and fixed on his perspiring face. A bony finger lifted shakily and pointed at him. "If I die, at least I'll go to my grave knowing *you* can't have her!"

By the end of the week, Bonnie and Amanda had seen to it that the invitations had been ordered, the wedding dress and Gabby's and Bonnie's gowns had been started, and the food had been selected for the wedding dinner. Matthew's only request, delivered in the form of an impersonal note, was that they not have the traditional wedding cake and punch in the church basement, but have a formal dinner reception instead. There had been new suits ordered for Uncle David and her brothers, and a trousseau for herself.

Carolyn and Bonnie had taken over the planning of her trousseau; it held no special significance for Amanda. And when they had consulted her about it, she had been ambivalent about their selections, even when they had described the nightgown they thought she should wear on her wedding night.

"A transparent lavender sheath, soft and clinging, with the thinnest of satin ribbons to hold it up," Carolyn had insisted.

"I rather thought a white opaque lawn, gathered just below lacy shoulders to fall in long, graceful folds would be nice," Bonnie had maintained.

"Why bother?" Amanda had quipped sarcastically. "He'll only remove it."

They had clucked their tongues and gone ahead with their plans.

Amanda had sent a curt note to Matthew asking where they would go for their wedding trip, or if there was even to be one. Matthew's reply had been that it was up to her to decide. Amanda had decided there would not be one. There seemed no point in it.

A week before the wedding, Matthew; Michael O'Day; John, his construction manager; and two of Matthew's most trusted men met at Porter's Saloon to celebrate his last week of bachelorhood. It had capped off a week of tension at the iron mill, wherein Matthew had finally forced a showdown with the union sympathizers and had ordered all men who wanted to establish a union in the mill other than the organization he had set forth to hand in their resignation. Almost everyone had stayed and the few who left did so reluctantly.

There had been several minor incidents after that, bricks thrown through windows at the mill, a delivery wagon stolen from the mill yard, and water barrels spilled, but no serious repercussions had occurred as a result of the firings, nor had any evidence been left to point to the offenders. Matthew suspected, though, that Obediah Marley was behind it, for the man had been heard talking against him in every saloon in town.

Matthew took the precaution of having reinforced water barrels set up every thirty feet along the inner walls of the mill, along with hatchets and heavy blankets, for the thing he feared most was a fire. It would be the perfect way for a man to take his revenge; the large wooden structure would ignite like a pile of dried kindling and be reduced to ashes within minutes. Matthew had seen it happen once, and went to great lengths to ensure it would never happen again.

Because of the trouble at the mill, Matthew had been plagued by the old nightmare again, which left him drenched in sweat and wide awake every time it occurred. He hadn't been the most pleasant person to deal with, either; so now, as he sat at the poker table surrounded by men he trusted, he felt more than ready for a relaxing night out.

"Three kings," he said, slapping down his cards. A groan went around the table and Matthew laughed, sweeping the pile of coins toward him. "Another round of drinks," he bellowed toward the bar, and when the barmaid came with her tray, Matthew took it from her and pulled her onto his lap.

"For luck," he told his friends, flashing his handsome smile at the girl as he reached his arms around her waist to pick up the new hand. The girl put one of her smooth, bare arms around his neck and leaned against him so he could see her full, white breasts bulging from her garish red dress. The black feathers that held up the dress tickled his chin and he tried to scratch it, but found one hand occupied with the cards and the other around the barmaid's waist. He rubbed his chin on her shoulder instead. She giggled and whispered something in his ear.

"Ah! A room upstairs," Matthew repeated, ogling the

voluptuous mounds that jiggled when she laughed, the whiskey he had consumed pleasantly muddling his thoughts. "And what time do you get off, my sweet?"

When the girl again whispered in his ear, making Matthew laugh lustily, Michael frowned at the scene they were making and laid down his cards. He came around the table, pulled the girl off Matthew's lap, shoved a coin into her hand, and sent her away.

"What do you think you're doing?" Matthew bellowed.

Michael calmly took his seat and picked up his cards. "She's not the one for you, my friend. This is experience speakin'. She looks for the men who are too drunk to know if anything happened or not and then she takes them upstairs, strips them naked, and robs them blind with no one the wiser; and I'm not about to sit here and let that happen."

"So it's happened to you, has it, Michael?" one of the men asked, sending the others into loud guffaws.

"Not to me," Michael said good-naturedly over the noise. "No, not to me. This lad's too smart for the likes o' her."

"What you need, Michael, me lad," Matthew quipped, stabbing his finger at his friend, "is a wife!"

The others agreed vociferously while Matthew pounded on the table to be heard. "Not just any wife, mind, but one that's smart enough for the likes o' ye," he mocked. "Take my future wife, for example. Smart as a steel trap, boys. Started a college, by God!"

"She's too smart for you, Matthew," one of the men jested.

"That's what you think," Matthew said, tossing down a royal flush to their groans and grumbles. "That's what my future wife thought, too. But I outsmarted her. Both her *and* the Honorable Lucas P. Ripley. Neither one thought I'd ever marry her. And I wouldn't have, either, if she hadn't gotten herself into such a pickle."

Michael choked on his beer. "*She* got herself into a pickle! *She* did, you say? 'Tisn't the way *I* heard the story, my friend."

Matthew shot him a dark glance.

John winked at the other players. "If you're so smart, Matthew, how is it you let yourself get hornswoggled? You've always said no female would ever get a ring through your nose." He mooed and pretended to paw the ground, sending the others into gales of laughter. Matthew stared at his cards, his eyes narrowing.

"She caught you, Matthew," John ribbed him. "She caught *you* and you didn't even realize it."

"By Jesse, I'm not caught yet!" he roared, hitting his fist against the tabletop causing a clatter of coins and glasses. "How much time do I have left, Mike?"

"Eight days, Matthew. Today's Friday. You have until next Saturday."

"You'd better keep me corned till then, my friends, or I might come to my senses and call it off."

Michael laughed with the rest, but he had been watching Matthew too closely over the past months to take him seriously. He knew his boss was quite aware of what he was doing. It was just that he couldn't admit the true reason why.

On Monday afternoon, the two men shared their usual hurried lunch together at the lumberyard. Michael finished his sandwich while Matthew dictated orders, and then, when Matthew stopped to eat, Michael tipped his chair back on two legs to study him.

"Well, you seem to have recovered from Friday night," Michael commented.

Matthew threw him a black look. "Why did you let me drink so much? Took me till Sunday eve to get rid of my headache."

Michael laughed. "Ah, you're gettin' old, Matthew. Time was when you could drink me under the table and get up for church the next mornin'." He paused, watching his boss carefully. "Speakin' of churches, Matthew, thank you for the invitation."

"What invitation?"

Michael's chair clattered forward. "What do you mean, what invitation? You haven't forgotten you're gettin' married on Saturday, have you?"

"With you carrying on about it constantly, how can I forget?" Matthew snapped in reply. "And you thank my future wife for the invitation. She's handling everything."

"She has a name, Matthew; but, then, you've been havin' a hard time usin' it lately, haven't you?" Michael remarked, casting him a reproachful look. When Matthew ignored his comment, Michael shook his head. "Have you forgotten that you're the one who insisted on this marriage, and not the other way around? You should be decidin' these things, Matthew Blake, not her. I hope you've at least chosen the destination for your wedding trip."

Matthew scowled at the papers before him.

"May the saints preserve us!" Michael exclaimed. "How do you think the poor girl feels with you behavin' the way you are? You ought to be ashamed of yourself, Matthew Blake."

Matthew slammed his fist on the table. "You're beginning to sound like my mother! For God's sake, stop lecturing me!"

"Ah-ha! There's a guilty conscience talkin'."

Matthew came to his feet with a jerk, strode to the door, and opened it. "Our meeting is over."

When Michael had gone, Matthew sat down again and tried to work, but found his conscience would not let him concentrate. Damn that Michael O'Day! *She has a name, Matthew. You should be ashamed, Matthew.* Michael was *worse* than his mother!

Matthew ran his fingers through his dark hair, thinking about the forthcoming wedding. Jeff Gable had warned him that he and Amanda would have to prove their compatibility if Amanda was to win her custody fight. Compatible. Hah! With Amanda?

He wished he hadn't sent Dixie away; he could have used her now to soothe his taut nerves. He thought of the comely barmaid who had invited him up to her room, and then he frowned, recalling Michael's warning. Hell, he thought, I'm not drunk now. I'd know whether she tried to rob me or not.

But the image of Amanda lying asleep on the blanket beside him, with nothing but her mantle to cover her nakedness, flashed through his mind, making the barmaid seem lewd and dirty. He felt that familiar throb of desire that plagued him whenever he thought of Amanda in that way. Virginal and pure, until that night in the barn. He had been the first man to ever touch her, and by God, he'd be the *only* man if he had anything to say about it!

His sudden feelings of possessiveness caught him by surprise. He didn't want to marry her, yet he didn't want anyone else to have her, either. "What kind of hell am I getting myself into?" he groaned.

Chapter Twenty-six

THE FIRST SATURDAY of March was one of those rare, sunny, late winter days that gives promise to the warmth of spring to come. Outside Amanda's window, purple, yellow, and white crocuses opened their blooms for the first time and a robin sang to its mate. A happy bride would have taken it as a good omen.

Amanda was merely numb. While she stood mutely in front of her cheval mirror, Bonnie and Carolyn fluttered and fussed over her appearance as if they were entering her in a blue ribbon competition at the fair. When there was nothing more they could do, the two women stood back and had Amanda turn slowly for them.

The full-skirted wedding gown was made of the finest white satin Carolyn could find. It was hemmed with a deep ruffle at the bottom, and had an overskirt of Brussels lace that covered the back and sides of the skirt down to the ruffle, and opened at the front in ruffled scallops edged with white satin ribbon, trimmed at the inner point of each scallop with tiny bouquets of miniature silk roses in pastel colors.

The bodice of the gown was an off-the-shoulder style trimmed with a deep ruffle of Brussels lace that met at the cleavage of her breasts. The sleeves were created entirely from another even deeper ruffle of gathered lace.

Amanda's tulle veil, which hung to the floor in the back and hid her face in a double layer of netting in front, was fixed to her hair with mother-of-pearl combs festooned with white silk roses. She would carry a bouquet of white roses.

"Carolyn, you've designed such a lovely gown," Bonnie said. She turned to her youngest sister, sitting in a mass of pink ruffles on the edge of the bed. "Gabby, what do you think of our Mandy?"

"She looks like a princess," Gabrielle sighed.

Amanda gazed at her reflection for a moment and then said in a resigned voice, "Shall we get on with it?"

She had reconciled herself to a loveless marriage by thinking of all she had to gain by it. She would not admit to any other feelings; she was afraid to hope that Matthew might, after all, love her just a tiny bit, for fear of being severely disappointed a third time. It was better to be prepared for the worst.

Yet there were still those annoying butterflies in her stomach every time she thought of walking down that aisle and facing Matthew, and they were not helped by the lurching of Carolyn's carriage. Would Matthew think her beautiful? Would his gaze be cold or would he look at her with the warmth of which she knew him capable? And the thought of spending that very night with him sent shivers of anxiety down her spine.

The streets around the church were lined with carriages. Amanda leaned forward to look at them as Carolyn's driver pulled the team of white horses to a halt in front of the building, and then she stepped down, assisted by her uncle, and waited for the others to follow.

Bonnie carried the end of Amanda's long veil as the nervous bride walked up to the church and stepped inside, pausing at the sound of organ music coming from the sanctuary. Amanda took a deep, shaky breath. There was no turning back now. Her only prayer was that Matthew had not jilted her.

At the front of the sanctuary, Michael O'Day stood silently beside Matthew, watching the people slowly fill the pews. Harper and Curt stood to Michael's left. Freddie,

Ethan, and Daniel had been pressed into service as ushers. All wore gray, swallowtail suits and white boiled shirts with white stocks.

The guests were old friends of the Hall family and friends and associates of Matthew's, the latter list gathered with Michael's help. Amanda had refused to consult Matthew because of his seeming disinterest in the affair; and, other than Michael, she had known of no one else to ask.

But Michael had been more than happy to oblige. "No need to go mentionin' this to Matthew," he had told her, glancing cautiously over his shoulder one morning in the office at the lumberyard. "Matthew never was one for detail work; he's always left those things to others."

Amanda had seemed to appreciate his help and warmed to his charm. "Have you known Matthew a long time, Michael?"

Michael's blue eyes had twinkled at her question. "A very long time. Since we were wee pups. My father was a laborer at Blake's Iron Mill, you see, back in New York."

"Matthew's father owns a mill, too?"

"Owned. He . . . passed on some years back. Blake's Mill was a prosperous mill in its time. I worked there from the age of eleven until Matthew sent for me to come help him with the lumberyard here in Wheatener."

"Eleven!"

Michael had laughed at her surprise. "You'd think my folks would have spared a scrawny lad like me, wouldn't you? But we needed the money, you see. Thirteen in our family, so you can understand how one breadwinner wasn't enough. But eleven was a common enough age to start. Don't think I was alone in it." He had smiled then, his thoughts far away, seeing himself and Matthew as boys.

"I used to watch Matthew taggin' along after his father through the big mill, actin' all businesslike and important, and sometimes I'd throw a tiny scrap of iron in his direction, tryin' to provoke the boss's son, don't you know. One time I hit his shiny new boots and he came after me. Madder than a stuck pig he was, too; but the sight of my skinny arms flailing away made him laugh so hard he took pity on me. We've been friends ever since."

And then Amanda had looked over the list he had prepared. "You didn't include his mother on this list, Michael."

He had sighed regretfully. "Matthew's mother passed on this past Christmas, the poor lady. She was in a very bad way. Matthew barely made it back in time to see her."

"So that's why he went to New York," she had mused.

Michael was surprised she hadn't known. He had paused at that, wanting to tell her more, but honor bound him not to reveal any more than Matthew would have allowed. Finally he had said, "You should know, Miss Hall, Matthew has had some rough times, and they've hardened him, you might say. He keeps his feelings to himself now. But even a hard-boiled egg can be cracked. You might have to pick away at that shell for a while before you hit that soft, white meat underneath, but as long as you know it's there, you can find it."

Now Michael cast a covert glance at the groom standing solemnly beside him. Matthew seemed outwardly calm, but Michael knew him well enough to sense the tension within. After that angry meeting on Monday, Matthew hadn't mentioned the wedding all week, but Michael knew it had weighed heavily on his mind.

The organist began the wedding march. Amanda waited out of sight, outside the sanctuary, as Bonnie, Amanda's matron of honor, began her slow, measured walk down the aisle. A sudden panic made her heart pound and her palms grow clammy. *Am I doing the right thing?* she cried inwardly.

Carolyn was next, followed by Gabby, who walked to the front sprinkling flower petals from a basket onto the white runner. As Amanda waited for Gabby to finish her walk, her grip on her uncle's arm tightened. The music grew louder, signaling the bride to enter. Their guests rose expectantly. Amanda looked up at her Uncle David, who gave her a reassuring smile, a smile just like her father's, making her parents' absence all the more painful. She caught her lower lip between her teeth to still its quivering.

All at once, she felt a warmth surround her, a presence comforting her, giving her encouragement, and instantly she knew her parents were very close. *I must be doing the right thing. That's why they're here with me now.*

"Ready?" her uncle whispered.

Amanda nodded, grateful for the veil that hid her face. They moved forward as one, into full view of the congregation, and walked slowly up the aisle. There were gasps and sighs over her gown. She focused on Bonnie, whose large eyes were overflowing with tears. Gabby was smiling proudly, while her brothers looked slightly purple under the eyes. Amanda bit her lip harder.

And then she looked at Matthew.

He stood tall and serene before her, this dashingly handsome man who would be, in a matter of minutes, her husband. Amanda's heart seemed to stop for a brief second and then fill with the love she had tried to deny. His dark brown hair was neatly combed off his forehead. His dark eyes were upon her, serious, watchful. His formal, dove gray, cutaway suit with its long, deeply cut swallowtails fit him like a glove, the white collar and cravat making his face look even tanner than it normally was. He was the groom of every bride's dreams, Amanda thought. How sad that it was all for show.

In the next instant, it seemed, she and Matthew were married.

At the back of the church, Amanda stood stiffly beside him as guests poured out of the pews and stood in line, waiting to congratulate them. At Jenkins Hall, there were more guests to be greeted before the dinner could be served, and then toasts to be made, until Amanda's empty stomach began to burn from the champagne she had drunk and she felt an odd floating sensation whenever she turned her head.

At last, Michael stood up and announced that he would make the final toast of the evening. "May your days of happiness be as countless as the hairs on your head," he began, lifting his glass high in the air, "and your days of sorrow be none." He paused, his blue eyes twinkling as he turned toward the bride and groom. "May there be a host of wee Blakes to fill your hearts, and thank God that the toasts are done."

Laughter filled the room and many glasses clinked together. Amanda blushed uncomfortably. Matthew coughed. Michael noticed that neither looked at the other. He shook his head and sighed as he resumed his seat. They just couldn't see how right they were for each other.

After the meal, Daniel performed at the piano. He had written a song just for Amanda, he announced shyly. Amanda listened with tears in her eyes as his long, skillful fingers danced over the keys, sometimes playfully, sometimes somberly. When he finished, he came toward her, holding out his hands so that she had to rise and embrace him.

"I love you, Mandy," he said in a whisper near her ear. "I hope you'll be happy now."

"I will try," she said, gulping back a sob.

When the orchestra began to play for the bride and groom, Matthew pushed back his chair and escorted her to the floor. She held herself rigidly straight and kept her eyes fixed on his shoulder as he swept her around the room.

"Well, it's done," he said, letting out his breath as if he'd been holding it for hours. "No one can hurt you now. And in two months, you'll have your family back."

Amanda shifted her eyes to his face. "*If* we can prove we're compatible."

His mouth curved up at the corners, as if he doubted they could. Amanda looked away, her jaw set stubbornly. They *had* to prove they were compatible.

Somehow she made it through the seemingly endless rounds of dancing, smiling with forced gaiety until she thought her face would crack. She only stopped smiling when she climbed into Matthew's carriage, her new husband close behind her, and felt the vehicle begin to move away. With a shiver, she slipped on the velvet cloak that

had been left there for her. She turned to find Matthew
brushing rice from his sleeves.

"We'll probably find rice in our undergarments tonight,"
he remarked. "You've got it caught in your veil. Would you
like to remove it?"

"I hate to litter your carriage with rice. I'll wait . . ."
Amanda could not finish her thought. . . . *until I undress.*
She stared out her window for a long time, hating the silence, but not knowing what to say. *Thank you so much for
rescuing me once again. I hope I'll prove to be as worthy
an investment as the college.*

Suddenly, she realized they were not headed toward Hall
House. She turned with a jerk. "Where are we going?"

"To the hotel."

"The house isn't ready?"

"Ready enough, I suppose."

"Then, why—"

"Because, Amanda, this is our honeymoon, and I have no
desire to spend it with ghosts. I understood that you had decided against a wedding trip, so my rooms at the Blake will
have to do."

Amanda was silent. She had thought she would at least
have her dear house around her that night, comforting her,
soothing her, telling her that marriage to a man who didn't
love her had been worth it.

Chapter Twenty-seven

MATTHEW UNLOCKED THE doors to his suite, pushed them open, and stepped back to allow Amanda to enter. When she saw that he had no intention of carrying her over the threshold, she swallowed her hurt and swept into the room ahead of him.

Once inside his luxurious sitting room, Amanda had no idea what to do next. Should she begin to undress? She removed her gloves and placed them beside the cloak, which Matthew had thrown over a chair, then sat primly on the sofa with her hands folded in her lap as he walked around the room turning up the lamps. At a knock on the door, he strode over to it and admitted a boy carrying Amanda's traveling cases.

"Put those in the bedroom," he ordered.

Another boy entered behind the first, rolling in a tea trolley. Matthew again pointed toward the bedroom. When they had both gone, Amanda looked at Matthew from across the room and suddenly had the urge to run and lock herself in his bath.

"I ordered a light meal for us," he told her, his voice casual, as if sensing her panic. "I noticed you only nibbled at your plate this evening."

"I hope you didn't order more champagne," she replied, sounding sharper than she intended. "I don't tolerate it well. I feel as if there is a hole in my stomach now."

"Let's see what they sent." He walked to the doorway

and waited for her to come. She rose, smoothed out her skirts, and walked across the floor on trembling limbs. She entered his room slowly, as if a tiger waited to leap out at her, and then stared around curiously.

The room was painted and carpeted in the same pastel colors as the sitting room, with the exception of the enormous bed, which was draped, canopied, and covered in material of a dark blue satin, with gold tasseled tiebacks and gold fringe. The whole effect was that of an ornate ship floating above the foamy surface of the sea.

Matthew walked over to the linen-covered table in front of the window, where the contents of the tea trolley had been laid out for them. Lifting one of the domed silver lids, he observed, "Freshly baked muffins with butter, honey, and apple butter on the side." He lifted another lid. "Pastries filled with something creamy, whipped cream perhaps." He checked the contents of the silver teapot. "Tea," he assured her with a wry grin. He pulled out one of the ivory lacquered chairs with its upholstered seat of nubby, ivory silk and waited for her to be seated.

Amanda gathered her voluminous skirts and settled on the chair, where she accepted the cup of tea he poured for her. She stirred sugar into her cup and watched as he removed a muffin from one dish, split it, and spooned apple butter onto it. When he looked up at her across the table and lifted one dark eyebrow, she realized she had been staring.

"Would you like half?"

"No, thank you." She reached for her own muffin, and when she bit into it, she discovered she was famished.

"Daniel played beautifully this evening," Matthew commented as Amanda downed her second muffin. "He's incredibly talented."

"We knew it from an early age," she said, her mouth full of the crumbly bread. She stopped to drink her tea. "At the age of five, Daniel was able to play a song after hearing it only once. My mother always thought he'd be famous someday." She looked down, her throat tightening. "She had great plans for us all."

Amanda took a deep breath, willing herself not to cry.

Her parents seemed very far away from her at that moment. Indeed, she had never felt more alone.

"More tea?" Matthew asked.

Amanda shook her head, her eyes awash with tears.

He pushed back his chair and came around to raise her to her feet. *Does he understand?* she wondered. Could he see the loneliness, the doubt, in her eyes?

But he only reached up to unpin her veil and drop it onto the chair behind her. She stared at him numbly as he removed her golden hairpins, one by one, until the intricately woven knot on the back of her head loosened and the heavy auburn tresses fell around her bare shoulders. His eyes met hers then, and there was no mistaking his intent. *If our marriage is a farce, at least the nights will be pleasurable.*

He didn't understand at all. He was just making the most of the situation.

Amanda forced herself to show no emotion as Matthew turned her around and unhooked the long row of pearl buttons down her back. If she couldn't deny her feelings for him, at least she could keep from showing them and looking like a fool.

But when he ran his hands over the bare skin of her shoulders, then bent his head to kiss the nape of her neck, Amanda began to tremble as memories of their passionate night together came flooding back. *Dear God,* she cried inwardly, *how will I ever be able to hide my love or my desire from him?* He had only to walk into a room to start her heart racing. He had only to kiss her to ignite the embers of passion deep within her.

She closed her eyes as he pushed the lacy sleeves down over her arms and let the heavy gown puddle on the floor around her slippered feet. The layers of petticoats followed, then the corset, yet still Amanda forced herself to stand impassively before him.

When she was unclothed, Matthew turned her around and stared at her, his eyes moving up and down her body with deliberate slowness, as if assessing his new possession. Amanda curled her fingers into her palms and looked away. He had paid dearly for this right, she reminded herself. She would have to bear it for her family's sake.

He cupped her shoulders, then slid his palms down over her full breasts. Her nipples hardened at his touch, but she forced herself to show no reaction. One hand slid down her ribs, following the curve of her waist, over her hips to her inner thighs. His fingers brushed the triangle of curls, causing her knees to grow weak. He leaned over to press kisses down her neck as one finger slid between the folds and stroked her, preparing her for their joining. Had the clock on the wall not chimed at that very moment, Amanda knew he would have heard her strangled moan.

He left her to turn down the comforter on the bed, then to remove his own clothing. When Matthew called to her, Amanda swallowed, her throat unbearably dry, and tried to brace herself for what she had to do.

Yet, lying beneath Matthew's hard, virile body, she nearly lost her resolve and sighed aloud when he found the tender peaks of her breasts. His tongue bathed them in silken warmth. His lips covered one, then the other, drawing each fully inside his hot mouth. She reached out to run her fingers through his hair, but stopped herself, dropping her hands to her sides to grip the bed linen, instead.

She bit her lower lip when his fingers stroked her intimately and squirmed in delicious torment as his movements became faster and faster, until she arched her hips against his touch and whimpered.

It seemed to be what Matthew had been waiting for. Quickly, he claimed her mouth as he pushed her thighs apart with his long legs. His shaft found entry and thrust deep within, slowly at first, then with increasing speed, until she found herself matching his movements, thrust for thrust. Amanda clung to him helplessly until a tremendous explosion of pleasure made her oblivious to everything around her.

When she opened her eyes, Matthew had rolled to the side and was reaching for his undergarments, as if he'd accomplished what he set out to do and was glad to be finished. He hadn't even felt it necessary to speak to her.

Tears gathered in the corners of her eyes. Amanda told herself it shouldn't matter, but it did, and she despised herself
for caring. She pulled the covers to her chin and turned on
her side, praying he would fall asleep quickly before her
silent tears became sobs.

Matthew slid under the covers and lay on his back, his
arms folded beneath his head, staring at the ceiling. He was
married. The very idea of it was still a shock, but even
more shocking was that he didn't feel at all the way he'd
expected. He had expected to feel angry, resentful, trapped.
At the very least he should have felt exhausted from the
long day. Instead, he was restless, agitated. Aroused. He
thought of dressing and going into the sitting room for a
brandy, but he didn't want to disturb Amanda.

Matthew turned his head to regard her, lying now with
her back to him. He'd forgotten just how long and silken
her limbs were, how tight she was inside. Indeed, under the
strain of his impending marriage, he'd forgotten just how
much he'd enjoyed making love to her.

But he wanted *Amanda,* not this silent martyr beside
him. She hadn't refused him his marital rights, but neither
had she responded as she had when they were trapped in
the barn. She had made love—or rather had let him make
love to her—as if she were a wooden marionette and he the
puppeteer, as if she had locked up her passion and her spirit
and left him only the shell.

Yet he couldn't truly fault her for it. After the impersonal
way he had treated her since the night of the ball, he supposed he deserved her silent resentment. After all, hadn't
he made it perfectly clear how he felt about their marriage?

Tomorrow, Matthew vowed, he would make it up to her.
He didn't want a lifeless shell or a marionette. He wanted
the fiery, proud beauty he'd lusted after since the day they
first met. They might not love each other, but there was no
reason they couldn't enjoy each other.

In the morning, Amanda heard a timid knock from the
outside hall. She rubbed her eyes and turned to find the bed

beside her empty. A moment later, she heard Matthew say from the outer room, "Come in, Mrs. Stone. I want you to meet someone."

She scrambled to sit up and pull the blanket up to her neck just as Matthew strode in, followed by a shy, middle-aged woman who bobbed her stocky body and gave Amanda a quick smile.

"Mrs. Stone, this is Amanda, my wife. I'd like you to see that she has whatever she needs when she is here. Right now, I'd like you to run the bath."

"Yes, Mr. Blake," the woman said with a smile. "Pleased to meet you, Mrs. Blake," she said to Amanda. And with another bob, she turned and hurried to the bathroom.

Amanda gave Matthew a scowl as she sank back under the covers. "Would you please warn me before you bring guests into the bedroom?"

"She's not a guest, she's a maid."

Amanda opened her mouth to argue the point just as another knock sounded at the door. Matthew strode out of the room and returned with a waiter pushing a tea trolley. After two large, covered plates were set out on the round table and their coffee poured, the man asked, "Will there be anything else, sir?"

"No, that'll be all." When the man had gone, Matthew pulled out a chair for Amanda, but she wouldn't budge from under the blanket.

"I don't have my wrapper," she declared, not admitting to not having a nightgown either, which he knew very well. "It's in my case, if you'd care to fetch it."

Matthew opened one of her traveling cases, rummaged through the contents, and discovered the sheer lavender nightgown. He held it up to admire it, then gave Amanda a questioning glance.

"Not that. A wrapper!"

Matthew again rummaged through the contents, finally pulling out a delicate white wrapper made of lawn, the front held together with satin ribbons of varied pastel colors.

"Yes, that will do, thank you."

Matthew tossed it to her and she slipped it around her shoulders. She was tying the ribbon ties when Mrs. Stone came out of the bathroom.

"It's done, sir. Is there anything else I can do for you?"

"Yes, see that we're undisturbed for several hours."

"Thank you, sir." Mrs. Stone bobbed and hurried out, keeping her eyes averted, missing the hot blush that had sprung to Amanda's face.

Amanda took a seat at the table as Matthew uncovered their plates, revealing thin, crispy slices of bacon, eggs cooked to a turn, toasted bread with jam, three links of sausage, and a large, fluffy, buttermilk biscuit topped with thick, golden gravy.

The breakfast looked delicious, making Amanda's mouth water, but her stomach gave a nervous jump whenever she thought of his orders to the maid. No interruptions for several hours?

After they had finished their coffee, Matthew set the plates back on the trolley, rolled it to the hallway outside the suite, and came back to the bedroom, holding something behind his back. "I have a surprise for you," he said, pulling out a small, black velvet box.

Amanda opened it and found inside a perfectly matched pair of teardrop-shaped diamond studs for her ears. *Surely they had cost a fortune!* she thought. Why had he spent so much money on her? At a loss for words, she looked up at him.

Matthew looked pleased with himself. "Wear them for me."

Amanda hurried to the pier glass over his bureau and put them on, turning back to show him. "They're beautiful, Matthew."

He took her hand and led her into the large bathroom, where the immense, claw-footed tub had been filled with warm water.

"What are you doing?" she cried when he began to untie the ribbons of her robe. He pulled the garment off her body, swept her up in his arms, and lowered her into the tub.

"It's called a bath," he said, settling on his knees beside the tub.

"No, Matthew, I can't!" Amanda cried in a panic. She didn't want to be caught off guard. It was difficult enough to hide her feelings in the dark of the bedroom. How could she ever manage in broad daylight? In a tub!

"My hair!" she exclaimed. "It—will take too long to dry." She started to rise, but he jumped to his feet and strode toward the bedroom.

"I'll bring your pins," he called.

Matthew knelt behind her at the end of the tub as Amanda reluctantly fastened her hair in a twist on the back of her head. "Shouldn't I take off the diamonds?" she asked, but he stayed her hands before she could remove them.

"I want to see you wearing only your diamonds."

His words made her feel like a harlot. Amanda wondered if it was intentional.

Matthew picked up a bath sponge and began to draw the water up over her shoulders, letting it cascade over her breasts.

"Matthew, I'm perfectly able to bathe—" Amanda paused and closed her eyes as he leaned over to nibble her neck, "—myself," she finished with a shiver.

"I know," he breathed against her flesh, his mouth moving down her neck to her shoulder. "But it's so much more enjoyable to have someone else do it." He soaped his hands with the cake lying in a gold dish and began to lather her body, cupping her breasts in his hands, working the lather slowly into her skin in lazy, circular motions.

"I want to apologize for the way I behaved before the wedding," he said in a husky whisper. His hands slid down to her taut belly, his thumbs strumming the dewy peaks of her breasts. "I was a cad. I sprang the marriage on you and then acted as if someone had put a gun to my head. You have every right to resent me."

Amanda was finding it very hard to concentrate, especially when his hands slid into the juncture of her legs. "Don't resent me, now," Matthew whispered in her ear.

"Desire me. We don't need love to make this marriage succeed if we have desire."

All the warmth left Amanda's body. It wasn't true. She *did* need love. She didn't want to be only a mistress to him. She watched numbly as Matthew slipped off his robe and stepped into the tub with her.

He settled at the opposite end, stretching his muscular legs out to brace them on either side of her. Amanda looked away as he began to lather his chest, the sight of his body stirring feelings she did not want. He reached for her and turned her around until she settled her back against his chest.

"Matthew, please don't," she whispered, stiffening as his hands moved up to fondle her breasts.

"Why?" he said huskily. "Don't you like it?"

When she said nothing, Matthew rubbed the puckered nipples between his thumbs and fingers, remembering how willingly she had opened to him that night in the barn, and how tightly she had sheathed him. That was what he wanted from her now, not this rigid resistance, nor the remoteness of the night before. He had thought an apology would clear things up between them. He'd forgotten how stubborn she could be. "Answer me, Amanda."

"It doesn't affect me one way or the other."

Matthew frowned. His hands moved lower to stroke her more intimately, wanting to feel the heat and wetness of her, wanting to hear her soft moans of pleasure. "How do you feel about this, Amanda?" he said, pressing his lips against her slender neck. He heard her swallow hard and felt the slippery wetness on his fingers.

"It doesn't affect me," she whispered hoarsely, "one way or the other."

Amanda was fighting her passion. He could see the cords in her neck as she strained against him. Damn her control! She was ready for him, yet she refused to admit it. What game was she playing? Was she still trying to punish him?

Whatever the reason, Matthew could control his own desire no longer. He turned her around and guided her down on him until he was fully inside her. He closed his eyes, his breathing ragged. Sweet Jesse, he had never been so aroused. Amanda was so tight around him, so liquid, so hot, that he had to exert the utmost control not to spill his seed instantly. But when he opened his eyes and looked at her, the misery in Amanda's face nearly unmanned him.

He gripped her shoulders and said through clenched teeth, "Pretend for me, Amanda. Pretend you want me." He searched for something else to say, a reason for her to throw away her restraint. "Pretend you're my mistress, that your only desire is to please me. I'm giving you the chance to get your family back; can't you give me something, as well?"

Appalled, Amanda stared at him. She had never deceived herself about his reason for marrying her, but neither had she expected him to admit it in such a shocking fashion. Yet, she knew he was right. She did owe him more than stiff compliance. In truth, his request was a blessing, an answer to her dilemma. She wouldn't have to hide her passion. He would believe she was merely pretending.

She braced her arms on his shoulders and began to ride him. When he bent his head to capture a swollen peak with his mouth, she didn't try to stifle her moan of pleasure. Her hips undulated faster and faster, driving him into a frenzy of desire, until she felt spasms shake his body. And then she, too, came in a shuddering explosion of ecstasy—that she kept to herself.

Chapter Twenty-eight

WHEN MATTHEW ENTERED the bedroom again, freshly shaved, with his robe around him, Amanda was sitting on the foot of the bed, brushing out her hair. Her eyes were closed, her face serene. Her hair lay in shining waves over her shoulders. He felt himself stiffen as he watched her. It hadn't been but half an hour and he wanted her again, even if she had to pretend to want him. But she had wanted him once. Perhaps, in time, he could make her want him again.

He sat beside her and took the brush from her hand. "I've always had a mind to do this," he said as he began to run the brush through her heavy tresses.

He was too rough at first, and earned himself a slap on the knee twice, but then his motions gentled, the brush stroking from the crown of Amanda's head to the middle of her back. When her eyelids began to drift shut, he laid down the brush and slid his hands around to the ribbons that held her robe closed, noticing with a frown how she tensed as he untied them. He cupped her breasts, breathing in the sweet scent of her skin.

"I want you, Amanda," he said huskily, his breath hot against her neck.

To his surprise, Amanda slipped off her robe and turned to face him, untying the sash at his waist and tugging the satin material off his broad shoulders, pushing him back against the bedcovers.

She straddled his hips, stroked his shoulders, and kneaded the heavy muscles in his upper arms, traveling next to the dark, springy hair on his chest. And then she bent and kissed the hollow of his neck, feeling his pulse throb wildly, then her tongue was licking the tiny, hard nipples almost hidden in the hair.

Matthew felt as if he were drowning in pleasure. His plea had worked—brilliantly. It was a shame Amanda's family would never know how she had sacrificed herself for them, he thought wryly. Amanda slid lower still, touching him more intimately, stroking the silky firmness of his manhood, tasting the saltiness of him, until he groaned and drew her on top of him. They made love quickly, fiercely, and afterward, she fell asleep in his arms.

Gazing down at his sleeping wife, Matthew felt a strange, new feeling of protectiveness come over him that had nothing to do with the vow he'd made to Vernon's children. Amanda was his. The valiant, young heroine, the fiery-tempered hoyden, the sultry vixen, belonged to him.

A frown crossed Matthew's brow as he considered the responsibilities that entailed, responsibilities to care for and protect her above all others, something he'd never worried about with a mistress. He picked up an auburn curl lying near his face. He *would* care for Amanda. There was no risk involved in caring for someone. When that person no longer needed your care, you simply let her go.

Amanda woke late in the afternoon to an empty bedroom. Stretching languorously, she called, "Matthew?" But no one answered. She rose slowly, her muscles stiff, and in the bathroom, she found a washcloth and towel and cleaned herself, then dressed in one of her new gowns, a robin's egg blue heavy cotton strewn with sprigs of white, with a white shawl collar and cuffs of lace.

Her mood was surprisingly jubilant. Now that she had found a way to satisfy Matthew's needs and still keep her pride intact, she could see no obstacle in convincing Judge Douglas that she and Matthew could provide a good home for her brothers and sister. For the first time, she felt confident that she would at last achieve her dream.

For just a second, Amanda imagined how happy she would be if she also had the love of her husband; then she began to brush the tangles from her hair in short, angry motions. She had to stop such foolish daydreams.

She tied her hair with a white ribbon, sprinkled on the new toilet water Carolyn had given her as a wedding present, and began to wander about the bedroom, stopping to examine the articles on the bureau, picking up Matthew's comb and clothes brush, polishing his silver shoe horn with a handkerchief she found there. She was about to open a drawer to peek inside when she heard the outer door open.

Guiltily, she jumped away from the bureau and met Matthew at the bedroom door, almost colliding with him.

"Where did you go?" she asked, stepping back in surprise.

He shrugged off his heavy greatcoat. "To get a newspaper and order supper for us. Someone will be bringing up a tray soon; then I thought we'd read the newspaper over coffee."

It sounded so domestic, so cozy. So perfectly normal. Amanda could remember her parents doing the very same thing. Except that her parents had loved each other.

That night, Matthew made love to her again, slowly, sensuously, until Amanda was purring with pleasure. She had no reason now to hide her passion. His shocking request had given her permission to be as bold and as passionate as she wanted, and he would never know the truth. There was only one thing she could not do, and that was to let him see how much she loved him.

On Monday morning, Amanda was awakened by a kiss on the cheek. "Good morning, sleepyhead," Matthew whispered with a grin.

She smiled lazily and stretched, then opened her eyes fully to see that he was dressed for work. "Where are you going?"

"To the mill. I'll be back by suppertime."

Dismayed, she sat up as he strode to the door. "I would have breakfasted with you," she called.

"You were sleeping so soundly, I hated to disturb you. Go back to sleep."

Amanda watched him leave the hotel from her window high above the street. Matthew hadn't even arranged to take an extra day off work, she thought miserably. She turned to survey her temporary domain. What was there to do all day?

Within the hour she was on her way to the college.

Alice Ripley lifted the cool cloth from her eyes and peered at the woman tiptoeing across her sitting room. Marylou's steady stream of sympathy was beginning to grate on Alice's nerves.

"Feeling any better today, dear?" Marylou whispered.

"No."

"I brought you a jar of my pickled beets," she offered, opening up her basket. "They'll cheer you right up."

Alice rolled her eyes heavenward and replaced the cloth.

"It was quite a to-do Saturday," Marylou commented, settling on a slipper chair nearby. "It was a beautiful wedding. Why, Amanda's dress, alone, must have cost a fortune. And the wedding feast—"

Alice snatched the cloth away and sat up. "Not another word about that wedding, do you hear? Not another word! I've had my fill of it! Gabrielle's done nothing but jabber on about it for days."

"There's no reason to be sharp with me, Alice Ripley," Marylou said, looking hurt.

"And just tell me how you would feel if your dearest child was about to be lost to that strumpet."

Marylou made a sad face and shrugged. "I suppose you're right. But it's not definite yet, is it? Surely there's something you can do to prevent Amanda from taking Gabrielle."

Alice sniffed. "Short of proving she's a murderess, I haven't the faintest idea."

Marylou rose and went to set the jar of beets on a side

table. Suddenly, she turned, an exultant look on her plump face. "I have it! You'll go into a decline!"

"A decline?" Alice gave a snort of disgust.

"But don't you see? The judge will never take Gabrielle away and risk your death from a broken heart."

Alice stared at her for a moment, then a wide smile split her narrow face. Marylou was absolutely right. Judge Douglas was an old friend. He'd never jeopardize her health by taking away her only source of comfort. "You know, my dear, I do believe I feel a decline coming on."

When Amanda returned to the hotel at four o'clock, Matthew was standing by the window in the sitting room, staring at the street below. He heard the door open and swung around, relief filling his soul at the sight of her. "Where have you been?"

He saw the look of defiance spring into her eyes and immediately regretted his sharp tone. He hadn't meant to be angry with her; in fact, he had returned early to surprise her. But he'd panicked when he'd found the suite empty, fearing she might have been Obediah Marley's next target for revenge.

"At the school," Amanda retorted. "Is something wrong with that?"

Matthew knew he was being unreasonable, but his nerves were frayed, and, on top of it, she had ruined his surprise homecoming. His day had started badly, and now it seemed as if it would end that way, as well.

He had returned to the mill that morning to find a warning message scrawled on the outside wall threatening his life, and inside, more damage: smashed windows, holes shot in the water barrels, and the floor a muddy mess from the water that had gushed onto it. He had gone immediately to the sheriff, but, as usual, no evidence had been found to accuse anyone. Now two armed men would guard the mill at night—his men.

"I'm sorry, Amanda. I didn't mean to snap at you." He slipped his hands around her waist and pulled her against him. "Let's not argue. I came home early to surprise you. I thought we could have dinner downstairs at the restaurant and then return here for a nice, hot bath."

To Amanda's annoyance, her body responded instantly to his suggestive words. He truly didn't care what she did with her time, she thought, as long as she was there to satisfy his needs. "I'll have to change first," she told him.

"I'll come help you with your buttons. My hunger for food seems to have been replaced with something more urgent." And with that, he swung her up and carried her into the bedroom.

When Matthew came out of the bathroom the next morning, Amanda was waiting for him at the table, with his breakfast laid out and his coffee poured.

"You're up early," he commented. He sat down and opened the newspaper she had laid beside his plate, deliberately keeping his voice neutral as he asked, "Are you going to the college?"

There was a pause, as if she wasn't sure what to say, and then she answered warily, "Yes."

"Take the carriage. I'll ride my horse."

She seemed to relax. "Don't be silly. I'll call a hack."

Matthew folded the paper abruptly and put it down. "No hack, Amanda. You'll take the carriage from now on. I want my wife to ride in style." He sipped his coffee and observed her over the rim. His order clearly chafed her, especially for such a seemingly arrogant reason, but he couldn't protect her in a hired hackney and he couldn't tell her the truth without frightening her. He had no choice but to let her stew about it.

Matthew had given his driver orders to guard her, and had posted one of his men outside their hotel and another at the college, as well. He had also begun carrying a pistol with him. He was taking no chances, either with his own life or hers.

"When will we move into Hall House?" Amanda asked as he prepared to leave.

"On Saturday." Matthew didn't bother to correct her. He

would, however, when they moved in. She would have to adjust to the fact that it was now Blake House.

That night, for the first time since their wedding, Matthew had the nightmare. His thrashing woke Amanda, who at first thought he was feverish, but when she felt his forehead, it was clammy and beaded with sweat. Suddenly, he snatched her hand from his head and held it tightly, moaning, "No! You mustn't try it. Please don't go!"

"Matthew, wake up," Amanda said gently, lying on her side, propped on one elbow. She tried to pull her hand free, but he only held it tighter. "Matthew!" she called. "Wake up. You're hurting my hand."

Matthew struggled to hang onto his brother, afraid to release him for fear he would return to the burning mill. His eyes opened slowly and he was filled with a sense of relief at the sight of Amanda's concerned face hovering above his. There was no fire. He pulled her against his chest and tangled his fingers in her thick hair. She was real.

As the week passed, Matthew could see Amanda's excitement building as she waited for the day when she could go home. By Friday evening, she could talk of nothing else. He was sorely tired of it.

On Saturday morning, he heard Amanda humming in the bedroom and flinched as he nicked his chin with the straight razor. For some reason, her humming grated on his nerves. Matthew scowled at his reflection in the small pier glass above the basin. He knew his perverse mood was due to their imminent return to the house. At the hotel, he'd had her undivided attention. He had no idea how she would respond to him once she was home.

But why should that bother him? Once the judge granted her petition, it would be only a matter of time until Amanda asked for a divorce, anyway. After all, she'd have no further need of him. He'd even sell her the house, just so he could say with a clear conscience that he'd done all in his power to take care of her. And then he'd be a free man again.

Matthew nicked himself again when Amanda suddenly popped her head in the doorway. "Are you nearly ready?" she asked.

He had to stop himself from snarling at her. "Just about." He watched her in the glass. Her mouth was curved in a delightful smile and her eyes sparkled with a radiance he'd never seen before.

She turned and danced out, calling excitedly, "Oh, I can hardly wait, Matthew!"

He scowled at his reflection again. Amanda was happy at last. She was going home.

Chapter Twenty-nine

BEFORE THE CARRIAGE had come to a complete stop,
Amanda was out and running, the hem of her heavy
wool dress whipping her legs in the brisk, early spring
wind. She ran up the flagstone path to the steps of the wide
porch and across the porch to the door. If she could have
embraced the house, she would have. Instead, trembling
with excitement, she waited expectantly for Matthew to un-
lock the door.

When he did, she started inside, only to have him stop
her. "Not that way," he said, and she frowned at him in
puzzlement.

Matthew swept her up in his arms. "This way." He
stepped across the threshold into the large front hall and set
her down.

*So this is why he didn't carry me over the threshold the
night of our wedding!* she thought. *He was saving it for our
home.* Impulsively, Amanda pressed a kiss against his
cheek.

She turned to find a housekeeper, a butler, and three
maids standing in a line, smiling broadly, and her elation
died. He had done it all for show.

"Amanda, this is Mrs. Burns, our housekeeper. And this
is Prentiss, our butler."

Amanda smiled as the housekeeper and the maids—
Matthew hadn't mentioned their names—bobbed. Then the
butler bowed deeply before her.

"Welcome to Blake House, madam," he said, his long face beaming proudly.

Amanda's smile faded and she swung to face Matthew. "*Blake* House?"

Seeing the mutinous look in her eyes, Matthew took her arm and led her into the empty drawing room, closing the double doors behind him.

"What did you do that for?" she asked, jerking away from him with an angry motion.

"Because I didn't want you to start an argument in front of the servants. Yes, Amanda, it's Blake House now. It's yours and mine, at least for the time being, and we are both Blakes, whether you like it or not."

Amanda was stonily silent. It had always been and would always be Hall House to her, no matter what he said. She turned to look around her and felt a surge of disappointment. "It's empty."

"I'm leaving it to you to decorate. It's been painted and plastered and refinished, but I stopped short of furnishing it, except for the dining room and our bedroom."

She eyed him skeptically.

"Would you like to see it?"

Together, they proceeded out into the hall and up the stairs. Amanda glanced down once and saw the maids peeking at them. "What are their names?"

"I can't remember. Michael saw to the hiring. You can ask Mrs. Burns later."

Amanda would have passed by the first door at the top of the stairs, but Matthew halted there. *This could not be it,* she thought to herself. *This is Mama's and Papa's room.*

Matthew opened the door and stepped inside, then turned to observe his wife. With an expression of growing disbelief on her face, Amanda slowly walked in, taking in the rich Turkish carpets, the deep blue walls with ornate white trim, the white lacquered oriental-style furniture, the layers of gauzy blue bed curtains, the lush burgundy satin quilted bedcover on a bed strewn with pillows in oriental designs, and the gauzy white draperies at the windows. It was a beautiful, sensuous room, making her feel as if she were in a Far Eastern land.

In a harem.

But she was in Hall House. In her parents' room. She turned on him angrily. "What have you done to this room?"

One dark eyebrow rose warningly. "Amanda, it *is* my house."

"You had no right to take their room!"

"I have every right, as I just told you."

She turned and stared around her, seeing what he could not, unaware of the tears that spilled down her cheeks. "There used to be a carpet here on the floor in emerald and cream, and a lovely, dark oak bedstead over there against that wall, with a pink slipper chair beside it.

"And right here," she said with a sob, pointing to where a low, sleek, white dressing table now stood, "was an oak table where my mother brushed out her hair at night. I used to sit on the foot of the bed and watch her; she had such beautiful, long hair . . ." In a choked voice, she said, "It was such a lovely room—before they took everything away."

She turned to face him. "Dear God, Matthew, why did you choose this room?" She collapsed into his arms and wept brokenheartedly.

He picked her up and carried her to the bed, where he lay her gently on the cool bedcover and stroked her hair until she grew calm. Then he bent to kiss her salty cheeks and soft lips, his mouth moving down her throat as his hands began to unbutton her bodice, slipping inside to stroke her breasts. He would make love to her, to exorcise the ghosts. Then she would see that it was their room now and not her parents'.

But when Amanda realized his intentions, she shoved him away and sat up. "No! Not here! Anywhere but here!" And with that, she slid off the bed and ran from the room.

Their midday meal was a silent one. Amanda knew the cook had gone to much trouble to make a special meal for them, but she could only pick at it. Matthew sat at the opposite end of the new dining room table, a table of deep red cherry, covered by a white linen cloth edged with fine Irish lace, and glowered at her. Amanda would not meet his gaze.

The doorbell buzzed and Amanda rose, but Matthew stopped her. "Prentiss will get it."

She lowered herself to the chair, waiting impatiently for their guests to be announced. Finally, the butler came to the door. "Mr. and Mrs. Brown, sir."

"Show them in here."

Harper and Bonnie came in, both talking excitedly about the house, but Bonnie fell silent immediately upon seeing her sister's stricken face. She glanced questioningly at Matthew, but he said nothing about it.

"Sit down," he told them congenially. "Have some dessert with us. I'm afraid we'll have to sit in here until we buy furniture for the other rooms."

"We don't mind," Harper announced, pulling out a chair for Bonnie. "Well, Mandy, does it feel good to be back home?" he asked, looking down the table at her. He was taken aback when she met his innocent gaze with an icy glare.

"Did we come at a bad time?" he asked Matthew.

"Not at all. Your timing couldn't have been better, could it, Amanda?" Not bothering to wait for her reply, he added, "Harper, come outside and help me decide what to do about the old gazebo."

Harper and Bonnie exchanged curious glances, and then Harper rose to follow Matthew as he strode angrily from the room.

As soon as the men had gone, Bonnie sat down beside her sister and placed her hand on Amanda's arm. "What is it, Mandy?"

"He's ruined their room, Bonnie. He's taken our parents' room and *ruined* it!"

Bonnie stared at her in surprise. "Mandy, you mustn't say that—"

"Come see it, if you don't believe me." Amanda was up and moving before Bonnie had a chance to finish her sentence.

Bonnie stopped just inside the bedroom door and, as Amanda had done, stared slowly around her. "Why, it's lovely! It's not ruined at all. It's only that you remember it the way it used to be."

"It's lewd. Matthew had no business taking this room."

"Mandy, it's his house. Whatever has gotten into you? You've always been so practical. What would be the use of closing off this room and not using it?"

"It could be a guest room, or a sewing room. Anything but his—but *our* bedroom."

Bonnie took her sister's clenched fist and drew her to sit on the bed. "But it's the largest bedroom and now it even has a private bath. It's meant to be the master bedroom. You can't deny that." She waited for her sister to agree, and when Amanda said nothing, Bonnie looked around the room again, and spotted a painting over the fireplace.

"Why just look at this beautiful painting," she said, leading Amanda toward it, and then, as she stood and gazed up at it, Bonnie said, "It reminds me of you, somehow."

Amanda slowly raised her gaze to the painting of a young lady seated under an apple tree. It was the one she had seen at Matthew's hotel suite the first time she had gone there. She remembered thinking then that it reminded her of something—or someone. But she scoffed at Bonnie's idea.

"It doesn't look like me at all. See there, the girl has darker hair than mine."

"Not by much. And look at the wistful expression about her mouth. See how she gazes out over the orchard, as if she's waiting for someone to come? I've seen that very look on your face many times, when you're dreaming of something. Perhaps Matthew bought it with you in mind."

"That's silly. He's had this for years. He had it at the hotel; I saw it there myself."

"Turn around and look at the room, Mandy," Bonnie told her, taking her by the shoulders to turn her. "Look at it from Matthew's point of view. It had no sentimental value to him. He saw an empty room and made it into the bedroom you would share with him. You shouldn't be angry with him for that."

"A room in which to share lust, Bonnie, not love, as it should be. Our parents loved each other; we were conceived from that love in this room. Can't you see that sleeping here with Matthew would be a sacrilege? I thought you, at least, would understand my feelings."

Bonnie smiled sympathetically. "I do understand; I just don't agree. Matthew loves you, Mandy; I truly believe that he does. He just has a hard time saying it. Go to your husband now. Tell him you like the room. We'll leave so you can be alone with him."

"No!" Amanda cried, grabbing her sister's hand. "Please, Bonnie, don't go. I don't want to be alone with him just yet."

"But you will talk to him tonight?"

"Yes, I'll talk to him," she agreed reluctantly. "Now come down to the dining room with me. I want you to help me plan a party—an evening social just like Mama and Papa used to give."

Matthew and Harper entered the dining room to find their wives bent over the table, chatting excitedly, as Amanda scribbled notes on paper. Matthew took hope that Bonnie had made his wife see reason.

"You look like two schoolgirls doing homework," Harper remarked with a chuckle as he stopped behind Bonnie to kiss the top of her head.

"Amanda and Matthew are going to have an evening social," Bonnie explained.

"And when is this event to take place?" Harper asked.

Amanda stopped writing, her brow wrinkling in thought. "The fifth of May," she announced. She glanced at Matthew to see his reaction, but his features revealed nothing.

He called for brandy. "Shall we drink a toast to our first day at Blake House?" he asked, his dark gaze silently daring Amanda to contradict him. He held out his glass so the others would join him. Harper rose, took his glass in hand, and Bonnie did likewise. They waited until Amanda reluctantly stood and picked up her glass. Only Matthew noticed that she did not drink with them.

Amanda had no choice but to sleep in the bedroom with Matthew that night because there was nowhere else to sleep. As she undressed for bed, Matthew sat in one of the rose silk wingback chairs near the fireplace and read his newspaper. But she felt his hungry gaze following her and knew he watched as she slipped underneath the satin comforter, for he immediately put his paper aside, turned down the lamp, and walked to the bed.

Amanda had turned on her side, facing away from him, and when she felt the bed shift from his weight, she began to tremble. Matthew moved close behind her and wrapped one arm around her, pressing kisses against her hair. She gritted her teeth against the desire that swept through her at the warmth of his flesh next to hers, but when he pulled her tightly against him and she felt his arousal, she froze.

"Matthew, please don't!" she begged, turning to face him. "I can't. Not in this room. It isn't right!"

"Amanda, this is nonsense."

"I didn't expect you'd understand."

He clenched his jaw and glared at her. "This is our bedroom, dammit! Would you rather I take you on the stairs like a whore?"

"Isn't that what you wanted, after all?" She sat up and swung her legs off the bed, but Matthew flung an arm around her waist and pulled her back, rolling her underneath him.

"By God, I won't let you deny me the only thing . . ." He bit off his angry words when he realized how jealous and childish it would sound to say, *"the only thing your family and the college and this damn house can't have!"*

"The only thing you want from me, do you mean?" she cried.

In his fury, Matthew didn't bother to correct her. "Yes, I want you, and by God, Amanda, I shall have you!"

He gripped her white nightgown at the shoulders and tore it down the front, exposing her breasts, but when she turned her face away and began to sob, he muttered an oath and flung himself off the bed, striding across the room to the bathroom, and slammed the door behind him.

Amanda turned on her side and cried herself to sleep.

The following night, Amanda again refused him, but her fumbled explanation only worsened the situation.

"I might be able to understand your feelings if this were still your parents' house," he snarled, pacing in front of the bed, "but it's not, nor does this room even remotely resemble their room, as you've already pointed out!"

Amanda gazed at him forlornly. "But it still feels like their room, especially in the dark."

"Then we'll bring every lamp in the house up here. Will that help?"

"Why must it be in this room?" she cried plaintively. "There are four other bedrooms in the house."

"Because this is the master suite, dammit! This is *our* room."

"It doesn't have to be."

"Forget it, Amanda," he said, striding to the door. "I'm not in the mood anymore."

He came back to bed much later, walking unsteadily and reeking of whiskey. Amanda lay wide awake, hardly daring to breathe for fear he would sense her wakefulness and drunkenly demand his husbandly rights. When he began to snore, she tried to relax, but found herself thinking of Jeffrey Gable's words instead. *"You'll need to prove to the judge the two of you are compatible."*

Amanda turned on her side and chewed her lip. She couldn't deny Matthew his rights. Somehow she had to play the role of mistress without backing down from her position.

Sometime later, Matthew began to toss and struggle until he had freed his legs from the blankets, as if freeing himself from a heavy weight, jolting Amanda out of her light sleep. She recognized the clammy, perspiring forehead and frantic motions from before, and shook his shoulder to wake him.

"Matthew, wake up. You're dreaming again."

He lay on his back, groaning in agony, as tears squeezed out from the corners of his closed eyelids. Amanda slipped her arm under his neck and pressed close against him, murmuring soothing words, cradling his head against her breast. He wrapped his arms around her waist and held her tightly against him as if afraid she would slip away, until, lulled by her comforting words, he fell into a peaceful slumber.

What was it that haunted his dreams? Amanda wondered. All she knew of his past was of a fire that had taken his brother's life. Was that the root of his dreams? She slipped out of his embrace, then lay gazing at him by the dim light of a half-moon. It seemed they were both haunted by the past. The difference was that he knew all about hers. And still he couldn't understand her feelings.

When Amanda awoke in the morning, Matthew was gone. With a despondent sigh, she rolled onto his pillow and hugged it around her face. The scent of him stirred memories of their nights at the hotel. She closed her eyes, missing their closeness, remembering the pleasure of him inside her. Surely there was some way to make peace between them.

"I have to find a way!" she said aloud. With sudden determination, she threw back the covers and began to dress. After a hasty breakfast, she ordered the carriage for a trip to town, but, as the landau pulled away from the house, she changed her mind and ordered the driver to stop first at the lumberyard.

It was Matthew's habit to work at the iron mill until noon and then go to the lumberyard afterward. Amanda knew she would have only a brief half hour to see Michael O'Day and make a hasty escape before Matthew arrived, so with that in mind, she hurried across the hard-packed ground toward the low, wooden building that housed his office.

"Good mornin', Mrs. Blake!" Michael called in cheerful surprise, rising from behind the table.

She returned his smile. "Good morning, Michael."

"Come, sit down here," he said, offering her a wooden chair. "And to what do I owe this unexpected visit?"

"I want to ask you something."

Michael pulled up a chair to face hers. "Ask away," he said with a wide smile.

"Matthew sometimes has terrible nightmares, Michael, and I wondered if you knew of something in his past that might cause them."

Michael was instantly on his guard, but it was not evident in his friendly, concerned expression. "Terrible nightmares, is it?" He lifted his cap and scratched his head. "Well, I suppose just about anything could do that to a man such as Matthew. A slump in business, an angry customer, a new wife." He winked. "I don't think it's anything to worry about. We all have our demons."

"Yes, I'm sure you're right," Amanda said with a sigh. "It's just that these dreams are so violent. It's as if he can't escape from them, or doesn't want to, and I don't know how to help him." She rose and smoothed out her skirt. "I thought perhaps it had something to do with the fire."

"The fire?" Michael asked in surprise.

Amanda gave him a quizzical look. "Yes, the fire that killed his brother. But surely you know about that."

"Yes! Yes! That I do! I'm surprised you know, is all."

"Why does that surprise you?"

Michael knew he had made a mistake. He stood up and began to arrange papers on the table, keeping his eyes averted. "Well, it's just not a subject Matthew will often discuss."

"Why not?"

Michael scratched his head again. "Well," he said, falling into his thick brogue, "I suppose it's simply too upsettin' to him. He and his brother were very close, don't you know."

"What happened, Michael?" Amanda said, putting her hand on his shoulder. "You know the story. Tell me."

"I cannot do that, Mrs. Blake. It's not my story to tell."

"But it is the cause of his nightmares, isn't it?"

When Michael hesitated, Amanda knew she was right. "Thank you, Michael. I think I understand now."

Michael turned to face her, an imploring look on his face. "You won't be tellin' him of our talk, will you?"

She smiled reassuringly. "I won't say a word."

Indeed, Amanda thought as she returned to the carriage, *I won't mention the nightmares again until Matthew tells me about them.* But would he? He had long ago promised to tell her about the fire; he had yet to do it. Perhaps he never would. Perhaps it wasn't something a mistress was supposed to know.

Chapter Thirty

Matthew ARRIVED HOME from work early that day to find a delivery wagon in front of the house and two men walking up the flagstone path carrying in a bureau. He walked inside as the men disappeared around the corner at the top of the stairs. After handing his coat and hat to Prentiss, Matthew followed the sound of hammering to the second floor, where he found two other men busily setting up a brass headboard and bed frame in the room across from his. His attention was drawn beyond them to Amanda, who stood on a chair hanging white eyelet curtains at one of the long windows, humming a tune as she worked.

"What's this?" he asked. "Are we expecting guests?"

Amanda looked around in surprise. "Matthew! You're home early."

"So it seems."

"We're not having guests," she said. "It's"—she paused and took a breath—"for us."

"We have a bedroom," he said, his eyes narrowing.

Amanda's smile faltered and a deep shade of red colored her fair complexion. A muscle in his jaw twitched. He knew exactly what she meant. She meant it to be *her* room. He spun around and stalked downstairs to pour himself a drink.

"Matthew," Amanda said imploringly, walking up behind where he stood in the dining room, staring out the side window, "please let me explain."

"Explain what?" He turned slowly to fix her with a steady gaze. "I think it's pretty clear what you're doing."

"Many wives have their own rooms," she countered.

"My parents didn't. Did yours?"

Amanda bowed her head. "My parents loved each other, Matthew."

He flinched at that.

She kept her gaze lowered. "You may come to my room any time you wish."

In other words, Matthew thought wryly, he could make love to his wife anywhere but *his* bed. He let out his breath. Did it really matter where they made love? "Is dinner ready?" he asked in a tired voice.

At her solemn nod, he held out his arm, and when she accepted it, he led her silently into the dining room.

That evening, Matthew left the house and went to Porter's Saloon for a game of poker. He had announced his intentions to play cards while still at the dinner table and found perverse satisfaction in the panic that had flickered in Amanda's eyes. She was afraid it would get back to the judge that he was spending his evenings in a saloon. Hardly the actions of a happy newlywed.

Yet, now, as he sat in a hard-backed chair facing four stubble-faced, tired men, he was ashamed of himself for punishing her for refusing to share his bed. Dammit, what room they used meant nothing. Why was he so resentful?

He pictured himself lying beside Amanda's warm, sweet-smelling body, burying his head between her breasts, burying himself deep inside her, and he shuddered. Sweet Jesse, how he wanted her.

But all *she* wanted was her family and her damned house.

"Another beer," he snapped.

Amanda lay alone in her new bed, listening for the sound of Matthew's carriage, hoping he would change his mind and come home. She tossed and turned, worrying and waiting, until she finally pulled a chair to the window and sat watching the street, which was just visible between the thick tangle of tree branches outside the house.

At almost three o'clock in the morning, a buggy drew up and a lithe figure climbed down. Amanda watched as the man came around to help Matthew, who sagged against him, and then, propped up by his companion, staggered up the front walk. She hurried to her door and opened it a crack. She heard Prentiss's bass voice talking in hushed tones to a man with an Irish accent. Michael.

They fumbled coming up the stairs. Amanda quickly shut her door as Michael and Prentiss carried Matthew's inert body to his bedroom. It seemed a long while until they left. Finally she heard the two men whispering as they descended the staircase, and then the front door closed again.

Waiting until she was sure Prentiss had gone back to his room at the back of the house, Amanda tiptoed into the hall and stood listening at the bedroom door. Hearing no sounds from within save for a heavy snore, Amanda opened the door and crept up to the bed, where Matthew sprawled naked in the moonlight, the blanket already kicked away.

She caught her breath at the sight of his virile body, and though she tried, she could not draw her eyes away. Her gaze swept down the hard length of him and she imagined waking him with kisses, stroking his firm, silky manhood, bringing him to a frenzy of desire with her touch, her lips, and finally her own body. But then she remembered where she was and was horrified by her traitorous thoughts. Silently, she crept back to her own bed, where she lay tormented by guilt and desire.

"I *must* do something to keep him from going to the saloon every night," she whispered in the dark. "I can't let it get back to the judge that my husband prefers drink to me."

The next morning, Bonnie sought Amanda out in her office at the college, bringing with her disturbing news. "Mrs. Ripley's health seems to be failing," she told Amanda. "She's very weak and has little appetite."

"What do the doctors say?" Amanda asked, setting her pen in its holder.

"They can't understand it. They're of the opinion that it's her nerves."

"Her nerves?" Amanda scoffed. "That old she-cat has nerves of iron. I don't believe she's sick at all. She's just using it as a ploy to keep Gabby by her side."

"Well, it's true that she says she's better when Gabby is nearby. In fact, Gabby is the only one who seems able to persuade her to eat."

Amanda's hands knotted into fists. "She's grasping at straws, Bonnie. If she'll pretend ill health to keep Gabby, there's no telling what she'll do if that fails."

"But what if the judge believes her?"

Amanda tapped her fingers on the desk. "Perhaps I can enlist Dr. Cook to help us. If I can persuade him to pay Mrs. Ripley a visit, he'll see right through her ploy. And I'm sure he would be willing to testify as to the state of her health at the hearing."

"But what if he concurs with the others?"

Amanda frowned. "Then I'll have to think of something else."

When Matthew came home from the mill the next day, Prentiss informed him that Amanda was waiting for him in the morning parlor. She was dressed in a pretty, peach-colored gown and was seated on a new flowered chintz sofa when he walked in. She rose as he approached, twisting her fingers together nervously.

"How do you like the room?" she asked a little too cheerily.

He glanced around at the sofa and the two wicker chairs with their colorful pink and white striped cushions. "Very attractive," he said, turning back to watch her.

"I've ordered curtains and a few tables, but they won't be here for another week yet. Dinner is ready. Shall we eat?" She smiled up at him as she took his arm.

Amanda chattered gaily about her decorating plans over the meal, and of her plans for their first social evening. The only time Matthew saw her mask of pleasantry slip was when she told him of Mrs. Ripley's latest game.

"But I've already talked to Dr. Cook," she added, forcing her confident smile back in place, "and he's agreed to help me."

He could tell she was still concerned. "Do you have a date for the hearing yet?"

"No, but I have an appointment with Mr. Gable tomorrow."

"I'm sure everything will come out all right."

The rest of the meal passed in awkward silence. Amanda watched Matthew surreptitiously, praying her plan would work. When he at last placed his napkin beside his plate, Amanda covered her mouth and yawned. "I think I'll go up and dress for bed."

He studied her speculatively as she toyed with the top button of her shirtwaist. "It's rather early, isn't it?" he asked.

She gave him a sidelong glance. "I thought perhaps you could come upstairs and help me."

Matthew's gaze moved slowly from the opened button at her throat to her blushing face, but he said nothing.

Amanda's fingers shook as she unfastened the second and third buttons. "I thought I'd wear my lavender nightgown tonight. You haven't seen it on yet. It's—nearly sheer."

Matthew's eyes followed her movements; still, he said nothing. Amanda's throat was so dry she couldn't swallow. What if he refused her? "Will you come up with me?" she whispered.

"I think here will do."

Her fingers froze on the fourth button. "Here?"

"Anyplace but my bedroom, as I recall. Close the doors and come here."

Amanda rose stiffly, shut the doors, and walked toward him, her legs trembling, her heart beating a rapid staccato. Surely he didn't mean to make love to her with servants in the next room. He had to be testing her, hoping she'd relent and accompany him upstairs. She stopped before him and waited uncertainly.

"Take off your drawers."

"Matthew—" Amanda hesitated, unsure of what she meant to say. *I can't make love to you here. It wouldn't be proper.* But the proper place was in his bed, and she wouldn't make love to him there. Even worse, the unfortunate truth was that even though the idea of making love in the dining room shocked her, it also excited her. He wanted her—now. And she wanted him.

"What is it, Amanda?"

"Nothing." She started to turn her back on him, but he stopped her. "No, Amanda. Face me."

With shaking fingers and a face red with mortification, Amanda raised her skirts high enough to reach under and pull the ribbon ties on her underdrawers. She stepped out of them, then stood rigidly in front of him as Matthew unfastened the buttons on his trousers and released his rigid shaft. She looked away and swallowed. The sight of him excited her more than she wanted him to know.

"Come to me, Amanda," he said huskily.

He held her on his lap and kissed her deeply, his tongue claiming hers, his hands sliding between her naked thighs, stroking her, until Amanda whimpered with need. He turned her to face him, guiding her hips with his strong hands until she felt him slide deep inside her. With a sigh of pleasure, Amanda moved against him as he opened her shirtwaist and slid his hands beneath her lacy camisole to gently knead her breasts.

"Ah, Amanda," he sighed as she took him in again and again. Her muscles contracted around the hard length of him, sending waves of pleasure throughout her body. She almost felt guilty for letting him believe she was still pretending.

Within minutes, Amanda felt him jerk within her. With a sigh, she leaned her head against his shoulder. "Sleep with me tonight," she whispered. "Make love to me again."

Matthew turned his head and captured her mouth in a lusty kiss that left her panting for more. "Do you really want me to make love to you, or are you trying to stop me from going to Joe Porter's?"

Both she wanted to confess, but she hesitated a moment

too long. Matthew set her off his lap and fastened his trousers. "If you really want to continue this, Amanda, come up to *our* room. I'll be waiting." Then he pulled open the double doors and walked out.

The suite was dark and airless. Alice Ripley thrashed about on her bed until she had twisted the covers around her body, and then she lay there, panting. It was the oddest thing, she thought. She actually did feel weaker than she had only a few days ago. Of course, she'd had practically nothing to eat in a week, which could account for it. That was another oddity, for she really had lost her appetite. And she was sure she'd never had these heart palpitations before.

What if she truly were in a decline?

Alice crawled to the edge of her bed and grasped at the bellpull on the wall. The maid appeared shortly, groggy-eyed from being awakened. Alice did not particularly care. The girl was young and healthy and she, it seemed, was not.

"Laudanum," she called listlessly.

The girl gave a half-curtsy and stumbled across the room to the commode, returning in a moment with a spoon and amber-colored bottle. She poured slowly, but a few drops spilled on the bedcovers anyway.

"Don't waste it!" Alice ranted, gripping the girl's wrist with bony fingers. She gulped the contents, then threw herself back against the pillow with a desolate sigh. She glanced at the young servant, who was staring pityingly. "Don't stare at me!" Alice cried. "This is all Amanda's fault!" She began to sob, harsh, racking sobs that jerked her skinny frame around on the pillow as if she were as insubstantial as a rag doll.

The girl backed away. "I'm truly sorry, ma'am."

Alice was too distraught to answer. She hated Amanda for trying to take Gabrielle away, and she hated Marylou for suggesting such a foolish plan in the first place. Because now it was coming true.

The next evening, Matthew came home to the sounds of laughter coming from the dining room. After shedding his coat and hat, he found Amanda, Curt, Daniel, Ethan, Freddie, and David Hall sitting at his table, looking at him expectantly.

"Good evening," he said, not bothering to hide the irritation in his voice. He took his place at the head of the table as everyone greeted him, but his eyes were fixed on Amanda.

She gave him a hesitant smile, as if sensing her family's presence was the cause of his bad mood. "We have a court date for the hearing," she told him with forced gaiety. "May fourth, the day before our spring social, so I've decided to turn our social into a celebration party instead."

"Where's Gabby this evening?"

Amanda's smile dissolved. "She's sitting with Mrs. Ripley. She didn't want to leave her."

"Is she worse?"

"According to Gabby she is. I won't believe it until Dr. Cook sees her. We're ready to eat, Janie," she called over her shoulder to the girl who hovered just out of sight in the kitchen.

The meal was a pleasant one for everyone, Matthew thought ruefully, except himself. He listened politely as David talked about his travels, smiled at the boys' imaginative tales, and ate what was before him, but his mind was on none of it. Instead, he covertly watched his wife's face as she chatted with Daniel, laughed at Freddie's jokes, and listened, enraptured, to Curt's lumberjack stories.

She was radiant. She glowed with a happiness he knew came from being with her family. Perhaps it was for the best that they were coming to live with her. If he couldn't give her the love she deserved, at least her family could.

Still, Matthew found himself resenting them.

He had been impatient to come home all day. He wouldn't have admitted it to anyone, but he hadn't been able to stop thinking about Amanda. By God, how she had aroused him, letting him make love to her in the dining room with servants hovering just beyond the doors in the kitchen. Until he'd fallen asleep, he'd held out the hope that she would join him in his bed, that she had wanted him as much as he wanted her. He should have known better.

But he wasn't going to let it dampen his own desire.

He had it all planned where to make love to her next. He had decided they would start that evening in the morning parlor and work their way through the entire house, if need be, until she saw how silly she was being about her parents' bedroom. He felt his body react to the image of making love to her in a different room in a different way each night and quickly reached for his wine.

His ardor for her surprised him. Matthew had thought his passion for Amanda would cool the instant she said "I do," but instead, just the opposite had happened. The only thorn in his side was that he could never be sure if Amanda enjoyed his love-play or if she were merely pretending.

At the end of the evening, Amanda saw her family to the door and then walked to the drawing room doorway to bid Matthew good night. He was sitting in a chair before the fire, his long legs stretched out before him, a brandy snifter in hand, staring into the dancing flames. She knew he had been displeased to find her family at his table, but it had been too late to do anything about it. Anyway, she thought, he may as well get used to them being there.

She prayed he was not having second thoughts about taking in her brothers and sister. If Matthew opposed her petition now, her cause would be lost. She could not let that happen.

Amanda waited until his brooding gaze shifted toward her, and then she said softly, "I'm sorry for not warning you about having guests for dinner. It was a spur-of-the-moment idea."

Matthew downed the last of his brandy and set the glass aside. "It doesn't matter." He rose and walked toward her, his eyes burning into her with frightening intensity.

"You're not retiring already, are you? I had hoped you would show me the morning parlor."

Amanda gave him a perplexed look. "I showed you the parlor yesterday."

"Not by moonlight."

Chapter Thirty-one

MATTHEW STRIPPED OFF his clothing and undressed Amanda impatiently, his passion for her burning like a torch inside him. He kissed her ravenously, then lay her back on the new chintz sofa and knelt between her legs. He removed the golden pins from her hair and let the heavy auburn tresses fall freely about her bare shoulders. He kissed her throat, her breasts, her stomach, and the silky skin of her inner thighs. He sucked her toes, one by one, watching her expression closely, tormented by the thought that her breathless gasps were false, that she was only trying to please him.

He used his tongue to bring her to the peak of pleasure, and as her body jerked in spasms of release, he drove himself into her. He felt as though he could not get enough of her. She was like a drug in his blood. *Want me, Amanda. Want me as much as I want you.*

When Matthew had finally slaked his desire, he lay panting against her, his mouth on her breast, and whispered hoarsely, "Come to my room. Let me make love to you all night."

Amanda closed her eyes in anguish. How she wanted to do just that—if only it weren't her parents' room. She smoothed back his damp hair and said against his forehead, "Why not stay here? I—I liked it here."

Matthew sighed miserably. "Amanda, you're not a very good liar."

"I'm not lying. I did like it." Her hand slipped down between their bodies, stroking him until, against his will, he hardened again. He raised himself up with a groan and kissed her as he thrust inside her once more. It was his own fault. He had told her she should lie to make him happy. And if it meant winning her suit, Amanda would do anything to keep him happy. Anything at all, except defile the sanctity of her parents' room.

On Friday evening, Matthew was in a terrible mood when he left the lumberyard and headed home. There were rumors that his iron mill would be hit by vandals that weekend, and so he had doubled his guard, yet he still didn't feel at ease. There had been so many false alarms that his guards were becoming complacent about them. Twice, he had checked on them and found the men engaged in a card game in one of the shanties. He'd finally decided he would have to take a watch himself.

Now, as Matthew walked up to the front door, all he wanted was a few hours to spend in his wife's arms before he had to return to the mill. But he walked into a house ablaze with light and the merry chatter of young voices, and he felt alienated from it. Amanda had no need of him. She was surrounded by the people who mattered to her. He left the house immediately after the meal, muttering that he had business to finish.

That evening, in the darkness of his hiding place in the shanty behind the mill, Matthew groaned and stretched out his cramped legs.

"Gettin' too old for this?" Michael quipped.

"It's too damned wet out here," Matthew growled.

Michael elbowed Matthew in the ribs. "Especially when you could be at home, curled up next to a warm, soft, willin' body."

Matthew grunted in reply.

Michael turned his head to look at him. "Had your first spat, did you?"

"What makes you think that?" he growled.

"Somethin' has your temper up. Come on, 'fess up. It's good for the soul."

Matthew sighed. "I feel like a fool for even admitting this, Mike. I'm jealous of Amanda's family."

"Are you now?" Michael's eyes twinkled. "You wouldn't by any chance be fallin' in love with her, would you?"

Matthew snorted. "Of course not. It's just that my clever little idea seems to have backfired on me."

"Go on. I'm all ears."

Matthew sighed heavily. "I asked Amanda to—pretend for me."

"Pretend what?" Michael asked with a skeptical frown.

Matthew shifted on the hard ground. "That she desired me." At Michael's snort of derision, he hastened to explain. "She couldn't—or wouldn't—let herself enjoy it, Mike. So I asked her to pretend in return for giving her the chance to get her family back. It sounds cruel, but I hoped it would help free her."

"Sure, and I'm one o' the little people."

"Go ahead and laugh, but it worked. Too well. I can't tell now if she's pretending or not."

"Does it matter?"

Matthew dug his fingers into his scalp and raked them through his hair. "God, I don't know why, but it matters."

Michael shook his head. "And this from the man who swore no woman would ever get a ring through his nose."

At the crack of a twig, both men tensed, their hands slowly reaching for the guns lying across their laps. A rabbit darted past, and Michael sighed in relief.

"It won't happen tonight, Matthew, I'm sure of it. Too many rumors about. Whoever 'tis, is smart enough to stay away. I say we call it a night."

"Go ahead," Matthew told him. "I'll stay."

Michael sighed and settled into a more comfortable position. "No, I'll not be runnin' out on you. My conscience would bother me for at least a week if they found your head bashed in tomorrow."

Matthew grunted at his attempt at humor. "Mike, you

may be the only person who cares about me," he said grimly.

"Now, you know that's not true, Matthew. Amanda cares."

"About her family and that damned house!"

"And about you."

"When did you become such an authority on my wife?"

Michael sighed in the dark, reluctant to admit the secret he and Amanda had shared. "She came to see me, Matthew."

"About what?"

"About the nightmares. Now don't get on your high horse. I didn't tell her any more than what she'd already guessed, that they've somethin' to do with the fire. Why don't you tell her about them? She wants to know. She's tryin' to understand."

"She doesn't need to know."

"Doesn't need to know what's inside yer heart? You complain because she doesn't care, then you keep her at arm's length. If you want her to care, my friend, you've got to help her understand."

Matthew was silent for so long, Michael finally peered at him in the darkness. "Well?"

"I can't, Mike," he whispered hoarsely.

The tall, new cherry case clock in the foyer chimed four times. Amanda walked past it and into the formal drawing room to gaze out the front window. She had been expecting Dr. Cook's arrival since three o'clock that afternoon and she was getting nervous.

To get her mind off it, Amanda turned to survey the room. It was taking more time to decorate than she had expected because she wanted to furnish it exactly as she remembered it. She sighed wistfully, recalling that last grand social evening her parents had given, which was still so vivid in her mind. She remembered timid Charlie Edgar standing nervously beside a satinwood lowboy, asking her if she'd like a glass of punch and then spilling the liquid all down the front of his new suit. How long ago it seemed.

She made a mental note to have the new lowboy she'd ordered placed in exactly the same spot.

Amanda glanced out the window again. Surely the doctor's examination couldn't take *that* long. She felt as if she'd been waiting all day, but she'd actually only been home three hours.

Her work at the school no longer took the twelve hours it once had. Now, surrounded by Bonnie's efficient staff, she found her work finished by noon. In truth, Amanda was relieved. The college was no longer her all-consuming interest. Her attention was focused on the house now, trying to make it fill the void in her life until she could get her family back.

At the clop of a horse's hooves, Amanda glanced outside and watched as Dr. Cook pulled the buggy to a stop. She stood in the drawing room doorway, nervously twisting her fingers together as Prentiss admitted him and took his hat.

"Afternoon, Mandy," the doctor said, striding toward her.

"Come in and sit down, Dr. Cook. Can I get you a brandy?"

"Just a tot, Mandy. I can't stay long. Mrs. Cook is expecting me home for supper."

Amanda poured a little of the liquor into a snifter and handed it to him. "How did you find Mrs. Ripley?"

He stroked his full, white moustache thoughtfully. "I wish I could tell you that she's feigning illness, but I believe she's truly made herself ill with worry."

"It's not serious, is it?"

"If she continues this rapid decline, it will certainly become serious. In a very short time."

"She's only doing this to keep Gabby. There must be some way to stop it. Did you recommend a treatment?"

"I gave her a tonic and told her to get out of her bed and take long walks to calm her nerves."

"Did you tell her that Gabby belongs with her family no matter how ill Mrs. Ripley becomes?"

The doctor peered at her from under bushy eyebrows.

"I'm not the judge, Mandy. And if you don't calm down, young lady, you'll be the next one needing a tonic."

After the doctor had gone, Amanda went to Matthew's study to sit at the new mahogany desk and think. She had only finished furnishing the study a day ago. It now looked very similar to her father's room.

Matthew had not yet seen it. In fact, Amanda had not seen him in almost a week. He had been too busy guarding his mill to even come home for dinner at night, and when he stopped at the house in the morning to bathe and change before returning to work, Amanda was at the college.

She sighed miserably. She wished she could talk to Matthew about Alice's little ploy to keep Gabby. The hearing was only a week away and she had no idea what to do about the situation. Alice and Judge Douglas's wife were very good friends. Would that influence the judge's decision? She prayed it would not, but there was no telling how much influence his wife had on him.

Amanda rose restlessly and wandered into the morning parlor, but the sight of the flowered sofa brought back the memory of their lovemaking. She turned around and walked out. That night was the last time she'd seen him.

Amanda prowled the other rooms, yet the solace she expected to find in her home eluded her. But that was only until her family was back, she reassured herself. Because then, everything would be right.

Matthew poured coffee from his tin thermos and handed a cup to Michael. They'd talked quietly in the darkness of the yard behind the mill for two hours that evening, and now paused to sit and drink in companionable silence.

After a week of guard duty, Matthew well understood why his men had grown complacent. It was hard to keep up your edge when night after night passed with no threat. He sipped the strong brew and thought of Amanda, which was what he did most evenings. Did she miss him, he wondered, or did she even notice he was gone?

"Say, Matthew, did I mention my sister Erin was coming for a visit?"

"Erin?" Matthew replied with a laugh. "That scrawny, freckle-faced, carrottop?"

Michael chuckled softly. "Not scrawny anymore, Matthew. She's eighteen now and a real beauty, if I do say so myself. She's been thinkin' about movin' to Wheatener. All the bragging I did in my letters convinced her to come see it for herself. I'll bring her by the lumberyard one afternoon to see you." For a moment, he concentrated on his coffee, and then he said, "I was plannin' on takin' her to the horse races on Sunday. Why not come along? It would do you a world of good to get away from here."

Matthew thought about it for a moment and finally shrugged. "Why not?"

Michael eyed him in the dark. "You'll bring Amanda, of course."

Matthew leaned his head back against the shanty wall and sighed wearily. "She'll be busy with her family, Mike. She's always busy with her family."

"You could ask her, Matthew."

"We'll see."

Amanda woke the next morning to the distant sound of water splashing. Curious, she climbed out of bed, tied the sash of her wrapper around her waist, and ventured into the hallway. The sounds were coming from the new bath, so she tiptoed through her parents' bedroom and peered around the corner, startled to see her husband reclining in the large, luxurious, claw-foot tub. His eyes were closed, his dark brown hair needed a trim, and there was a dark stubble of beard on his face.

Amanda swallowed and stepped back, her heart thumping wildly. With his stubbly beard and unruly hair, he looked like the pirate she had once accused him of being. She leaned against the wall and closed her eyes, wishing she didn't love him so much.

"Amanda?" he called suddenly, startling her.

She backed away from the door. "Yes, Matthew?"

"I could use a back wash."

Her stomach tightened as she remembered their long, intimate bath at the hotel. "Did you want me to call a maid?" she asked, feigning innocence.

There was a pause, and then he said, "If you'd prefer a maid to bathe me, Amanda, then, by all means, call one."

Over her dead body! Amanda hurried into the bathroom only to find him grinning like an ape. Pretending to be annoyed, she rolled up her sleeves, picked up the bath sponge, and began to scrub his bare back.

"Leave a little skin, sweetheart," he said with a wince.

Amanda halted guiltily, then took a closer look. "What are these scratches from, Matthew?"

"Wooden shanties don't make the most comfortable of chair backs."

She sat back on her haunches and shook her head. "Why can't you hire guards to watch the mill?"

"They tend to fall asleep."

"I think you're worrying needlessly about vandals," she told him as she gently washed his neck and shoulders. She leaned closer to wash his chest. "And I hate to think of you spending your nights down at the iron mill. It's not good for your health."

"Do you care, Amanda?" he asked, watching her intently.

For a brief second before she answered, Amanda's gaze met his, then her dark lashes swept down, hiding her feelings from him. "Of course I care. You're my husband."

Matthew's jaw twitched angrily. Of course she cared. It was her duty to care. Amanda was nothing if not dutiful. Yet in that split second before she'd put up her guard, he was sure he'd seen something akin to fear in her gaze. But fear of what?

He wrapped a bare arm around her neck and pulled her closer to nibble her jaw. "Show me how much you care, Amanda. Join me in the tub."

For a moment, Amanda hesitated, then, obediently, she untied her sash and let the wrapper slip from her shoulders, pooling on the tiles around her. Matthew's greedy gaze devoured her nakedness as she pulled her nightgown over her head and stepped gracefully into the tub. He pulled her into his arms, anxious for the taste and feel of her. "Ah, Amanda," he sighed against her damp flesh. "I've missed this."

Yet even after he had slaked his desire, Matthew was haunted by the look he'd seen in her eyes.

What was she afraid of?

Amanda stood naked on the floor of the bathroom in dreamy contentedness while Matthew dried her off with a towel.

He bent his head to nuzzle her ear. "Michael has invited us to go with him to the races on Sunday."

Amanda sighed as his rough beard tickled her skin. "Daniel has a recital on Sunday."

"You've been to his recitals before."

"But he's counting on his family to be there."

Matthew abruptly stepped away from her and began toweling off his own body in furious motions. "What if I were counting on you, Amanda?"

She glanced guiltily at him over her shoulder. A wife's place was beside her husband. Her mother had said it many times. But her brother *needed* her. Matthew didn't. She chewed her lip, her loyalties torn. "Why don't you come to the recital with us?"

"Why is it always with *us*, Amanda, and never with *you*? And to answer your question, I'll be at the races on Sunday." He gave her a hard, piercing stare before stalking out.

Amanda was in her office that morning when her uncle stopped by after his class to drop off some papers.

"Mandy, you look drawn. Are you getting enough sleep?"

She gave him a tired smile. "Don't worry about me, Uncle David. I'm fine."

"I wish I believed you. I thought marriage would agree with you, but it seems I was wrong. Tell your old uncle what it is, Mandy. Perhaps I can help."

"Oh, it's just a silly matter. Matthew and I were invited

to go to a horse race on the same day as Daniel's recital, so I declined."

David appraised her woeful face. "And Matthew didn't, I take it?"

She shook her head unhappily.

"Then simply change your mind and go with him. It's a woman's prerogative, my dear."

"Oh, but I can't miss Daniel's recital."

"Stuff and nonsense! Bonnie and Harper are perfectly able to give Daniel all the moral support he needs."

Amanda sighed. "If I tell Matthew I've changed my mind, he'll think I'm doing it to appease him, not because I want to go."

David stared at the floor, his brow wrinkling in thought. "I have it! *I* shall take you to the races. We'll show up at the track and surprise him."

Amanda stared at him. "Are you certain you want to go?"

"I wouldn't have offered if I weren't. We'll have a delightful time. I shall go buy a newspaper right now and find out what time the races start, while you go straightaway and buy a fancy new bonnet for the occasion."

Amanda stood up and gave her a uncle a hug. "Thank you, Uncle David. I don't know how we ever got along without you."

Chapter Thirty-two

O N SUNDAY AFTERNOON, as soon as Matthew left for the races, Amanda quickly dressed in her mint green and white striped dress and put on her new white straw hat with mint green satin lining and peach and white roses adorning the band. She checked her image in the mirror at least three times before she was satisfied, then hurried downstairs to await her uncle's arrival.

Bonnie and Harper came for Daniel just as Amanda and David were leaving. Amanda kissed Daniel on the cheek for luck, and then, with a happy wave, the two set off in David's new buggy.

"Gabby tells me Mrs. Ripley is worse," her uncle remarked on the way there.

Amanda's brow creased with worry. "Poor Gabby. I've never seen her so depressed. I tried to tell her Mrs. Ripley is not as ill as she seems, but Gabby is convinced the woman is on her deathbed. She says if she leaves her to come live with me, Alice will die and she'll never forgive herself. And I don't know what to do about it."

"Short of letting Gabby stay with her, I don't see that there's anything you *can* do. What does Matthew say?"

"He's been so busy I haven't had a chance to speak with him."

"Is he still sleeping at the mill?"

"He says he's finished for this week, but he may have to start again next." She sighed unhappily. "I can't believe his

guards can't catch that gang of scalawags that keep breaking his windows."

"Is that all it's about? Broken windows?"

"That's what Matthew told me."

They rode in silence for a while, then David glanced at
her sheepishly and cleared his throat. "Mandy, Curt has
asked me to speak to you about his living arrangements."

"Don't tell me he doesn't want his old bedroom back?"

David turned his attention to the road. "Truthfully, my
dear, he wants to stay with me."

"Didn't you tell Curt you'll be selling the house?"

"Well, you see, I've decided not to sell. I rather like
where I am."

"But you must come to live with me!" Amanda cried in
dismay. "And Curt, too! We're family, Uncle David. That
was my whole purpose in getting Hall House back."

"We're family, my dear, whether we live with you or
not. Curt is nineteen, nearly a grown man now. He'd be on
his own if your parents were still here. You must face the
fact that your brothers and sisters are growing up."

But they weren't grown up yet. Amanda pressed her lips
together determinedly. Gabby and Ethan and Freddie and
even Daniel still needed her. If Curt chose not to come
home, she would still have most of her family together
again.

"And another thing," her uncle continued, "you and
Matthew need a home of your own, for your own children."

Her own children. Amanda placed a hand over her stomach. She wasn't carrying a child yet, but it would happen
eventually. And then how would Matthew feel about her?
She would be of no use at all in bed. Would he turn his attentions to one of the comely barmaids down at Porter's Saloon?

She pushed those thoughts away. There were too many
other concerns on her mind to worry about a possible preg-
nancy.

The first horse race was under way by the time Amanda
and David reached the track. People stood seven deep along

the rails, a bright, bobbing sea of colorful parasols and hats. It took careful maneuvering to find a decent vantage point, but finally David found space for them near the starting gate.

Amanda leaned forward far enough to enable her to scan the men's faces along the rail, but she saw no sign of Matthew or Michael. Before the second race began, David left her to place a bet and joined her just as the horses shot out from their starting positions.

"Number seven, Mandy!" David called over the noise of the crowd. "Cheer for number seven to win."

Amanda caught the contagious excitement around her and cheered until she was hoarse, groaning with disappointment when number seven finished in fifth place. She leaned over her uncle's arm to see the paper he was studying, and then she pointed to a name. "Why, here's one called Rachel's Girl. Pick her, Uncle. She has to win."

"Rachel's Girl it is," he called, and disappeared into the throng to place his bet.

When he rejoined her, Amanda grabbed his sleeve, her cheeks flushed with excitement. "The race has just started and she's in first place already. She's going to win!" She cheered exuberantly for the horse and jockey, and when they did win, she threw her arms around her uncle's neck and hugged him, laughing. "I knew she'd win! I knew it!"

"Well, Mandy, as long as you're on a winning streak, pick one for the next race."

While her uncle was placing his bet for the fourth race, Amanda's gaze followed the beautiful, sleek Rachel's Girl as the jockey walked her off the track. As she watched, two men standing along the sideline suddenly stepped out of the crowd and stopped the jockey to talk to him. Amanda's eyes widened when she saw that Matthew was one of them.

Standing on tiptoe, Amanda quickly looked around for her uncle, craning her neck to see above the hats and parasols, and as soon as she spotted David, she hurried toward him.

"I've found Matthew. Come with me." Oblivious to the shouts and cheers from the crowd around her as the next race was run, Amanda quickly threaded her way toward Matthew, with David struggling to keep her in sight.

Suddenly, she saw an attractive young lady with long, shimmering, copper-colored hair link her arm through Matthew's and gaze up at him adoringly. Amanda froze, her heart in her throat, and watched in dismay as Matthew dipped his head to talk to the girl, flashing his charming smile at her, causing the girl to respond with a merry laugh. Amanda pressed her hand to her mouth.

David stopped behind her, followed the direction of Amanda's horrified gaze, and then took her arm. "Come, Mandy, let's go home," he said grimly.

They seemed so perfectly matched—Matthew's handsome darkness and the girl's fresh-faced, copper-haired beauty—that Amanda could not bear to look any longer. She turned away, her heart twisting in misery, and walked with her uncle back across the grass and behind the stables, heading toward the field where the carriages were parked.

Suddenly, a man carrying cups of steaming coffee and three hot sausages on buns came around the corner of the building and nearly collided with them. He started to apologize, but the words died in his throat as he gazed upon Amanda's stricken face.

"Hello, Michael," Amanda said tonelessly.

"Well, Mrs. Blake! And Mr. Hall! Fancy meetin' you here."

"Yes, fancy that." Giving him a scornful look, Amanda took her uncle's arm and walked away.

Michael raised his cap to scratch his head, then turned and strode quickly around to the front of the stables. According to Matthew, Amanda was attending a family function that afternoon. Had she lied to Matthew or had Matthew lied to him? And what was causing her current state of distress?

There was one logical answer, but Michael told himself he had to be mistaken. Yet, the nagging thought that Amanda had seen Matthew and Erin together and had come to the wrong conclusion about them continued to worry him.

Inside the long building that housed the racehorses, Michael found Matthew and his sister talking to the owner of Rachel's Girl. While Matthew continued his conversation, Michael led Erin to a neatly tied bale of hay along one end wall and they perched on it to eat.

"I just ran into his missus outside," Michael said in a low voice, nodding in Matthew's direction.

"Matthew's wife?" Erin asked. "I thought she couldn't come."

"So did I." He stopped to take a bite.

"Didn't she want to see Matthew?"

Michael shook his head. "And I wish I knew why. She seemed greatly distressed and that has me worried."

"I can see that. What are we to do?"

Michael glanced over and saw that Matthew had concluded his conversation. "Say nothin' for the present," he whispered. "Let's see how the wind blows."

"Congratulate me, Mike," Matthew said with a smile as he strode over to them. "I'm the new owner of Rachel's Girl."

Michael stared at him. "Are you now! And what do you intend to do with her?"

Matthew picked up his hot sausage and folded the paper down around the bun. "Race her," he said through a mouthful of food.

Erin laughed. "What did you think he'd be doin' with a racehorse, Michael O'Day, makin' a pet out o' her?"

Michael frowned. "What do you know about racin' horses, Matthew?"

"Nothing yet, but I'll learn. I'm going to hire the same handler. I've heard he's the best horse trainer around. Anything I need to know he can teach me." Matthew finished his food and walked back to the door of the horse's stall to watch the grooms rub her down.

"I thought I'd give her to Amanda," he remarked as Michael and Erin joined him. "Her mother's name was Rachel."

So that's what's behind the sudden interest in horses! Michael thought to himself. *It's to make amends with his wife. And just in time, from the look of things.* His blue eyes twinkled. "I think she'll be pleased, Matthew."

"I hope so. I'd like to keep it a secret until the day of this big celebration she's planning. The only hitch is that the horse will be delivered tomorrow. Would you mind, Erin, if I said she was yours, and I'd offered you temporary quarters for her?"

Erin gave him a bright smile. "I'd be happy to oblige."

Michael lifted his cap to scratch his forehead. The last thing he wanted was to stir up more trouble between Amanda and Matthew. To that end, he had decided that if Amanda wanted her husband to know she'd been there, she'd tell him herself. But if she had spotted Matthew in the company of his sister and had misunderstood their relationship, then he owed it to his best friend to point out the flaw in his plan. Yet what could he say without revealing Amanda's presence at the track?

After a few minutes of deliberation, Michael said, "Don't you think, Matthew, that your wife may find your harboring that animal for Erin a wee bit suspicious?"

"My wife," Matthew said dryly, "is too preoccupied with her family to care what I do, and even if she did, why would she be suspicious?"

"Well, now, she doesn't know Erin, does she? What would she make of your helpin' out this unknown female?"

"Just what it is, a favor for a friend." Matthew put his hand on Michael's shoulder. "You worry too much, Mike."

"I was only tryin' to see it from Amanda's point of view."

"You'll go gray before you do that, my friend."

"But perhaps it would be wise if I took Erin to meet her," Michael suggested, glancing at his sister for help.

"My brother is right, Matthew," Erin remarked. "I'd hate to cause a problem between the two of you."

At their united front, Matthew had no choice but to concede, but he did it on his own terms. "All right then, since you're so certain Amanda will make a fuss over the horse's mysterious owner, I'll see that your names are added to the guest list for Amanda's party. She can meet Erin then."

Erin and Michael exchanged worried glances and then she exclaimed, "Oh, please don't do that, Matthew. I'll not be an unwanted guest."

Matthew smiled down at her. "You won't be. Leave everything to me. And if Amanda should notice the horse, Mike, I intend to stay with my original story."

"You won't get another argument out of me, Matthew," Michael replied with a resigned sigh.

"That man should be horsewhipped!" David Hall ranted on the long buggy ride back to Wheatener. "The nerve of him to appear in public with another woman. This has certainly changed my opinion of your husband, Mandy."

Amanda stared bleakly out the window, too numb to think.

"Haven't you made a fine home for him? Haven't you been faithful? Well, there's simply nothing to do but leave him this very day and come back to my house."

Amanda had barely enough strength to speak. "I can't leave Hall House. It's where I belong."

"Stuff and nonsense! You belong where you're loved and wanted."

She turned to look at him with eyes full of misery. "I wanted Hall House; I won't leave it now. And perhaps we've misjudged Matthew. Perhaps the girl was merely an acquaintance . . ." Amanda stopped, her reasoning sounding feeble even to her own ears. But there had to be an explanation. Surely Matthew wouldn't be unfaithful to her, at least not until after the hearing.

When they reached Wheatener, Amanda realized that they still had time to make Daniel's recital before it ended, and she asked David to take her there. "Please don't mention what happened today to anyone."

He searched her drawn and pale face. "If you're sure that's what you want, Mandy, I shall abide by it."

They slipped quietly into the back of the room, and when the recital was over, only those people in the last row knew they had come late. Or so Amanda thought.

When Amanda, Daniel, Freddie, and Gabby arrived

home late that afternoon, a light meal of biscuits and chicken stew awaited them. Daniel was unusually quiet during the meal, but Amanda was too absorbed in her own misery to notice. She retired to her room directly after dinner with instructions to Prentiss that she was not to be disturbed.

But once in the quiet confines of her room, the scene with Matthew and the beautiful copper-haired girl replayed itself over and over in her mind. Where had he met her? How long had he known her? Those questions and more tortured her thoughts so much that she had to pace about the room to quiet the turmoil in her head.

When she opened the door to a timid knock and found Daniel standing outside, looking at her with concerned blue eyes, she quickly brought him in and closed the door.

"Is Matthew home yet?" she asked in a whisper.

"No, he hasn't come home. Mandy, what's wrong? Why did you come to the recital? You were supposed to be at the races this afternoon."

"I've explained that to you, Daniel. And what does it matter if I went to the races or not?"

"It doesn't matter. I only wondered if there was some way I could help." He stood up and started for the door.

"Daniel, I didn't mean to be cross."

"I know that, Mandy."

"You must promise not to mention anything about this to Matthew."

He dropped his gaze to the floor. "I don't like to deceive him. He's been very good to me."

Amanda gritted her teeth. She had vowed not to tell anyone of what she had seen that afternoon, but Daniel's loyalty was a sore test of that resolve. "I'm not asking you to lie for me. Just do not offer any information."

"All right, Mandy. You know what's best."

As Daniel opened her door to leave, she heard Matthew's deep voice in the downstairs hallway. Daniel cast her a worried look and then quietly left, closing the bedroom door behind him.

Ten minutes later, Matthew rapped sharply and walked

in. Seated at her escritoire, Amanda jumped at his sudden intrusion, her pen making a jagged line on the paper. She turned to look at him.

He was grinning as he strode toward her and his eyes were alight with excitement. *Caused by the copper-haired girl, no doubt,* Amanda thought bitterly.

"Hello, Amanda. How was the recital?"

"Daniel did very well, as usual," she replied stiffly, returning to her writing.

Matthew perched on the corner of the desk and folded his arms across his chest as he smiled down at her. "Luck was with me today. I won twenty dollars. You should have come."

Amanda pictured him as he had looked that afternoon standing with the beautiful girl, and it was all she could do not to cry. She blinked back her tears and began to write again. "Yes, I think I should have come."

"Is something wrong?"

She put her pen in its stand, stood up, and walked to the window. "No, nothing is wrong."

Matthew walked up behind her and slipped his arms around her waist, pulling her against him. "Let's make love, Amanda," he said, kissing her ear.

Had he whispered similar words in the girl's ear only that afternoon? Amanda twisted away and went to her dressing table, where she sat before the mirror and began to take the pins from her hair. "I've had a severe headache all day. And I plan to retire early tonight." She cast him a quick glance through the mirror, but immediately turned her gaze away, for the perplexed, hurt look on his face shattered her heart.

"I hope you'll feel better soon," he replied. When she said nothing further, he strode across the room and left.

It's only what he deserves. Amanda gazed at her reflection for a moment, then picked up her hairbrush and flung it at the jealous-eyed harridan in her mirror.

On Monday, Amanda arrived home from the college to find a sleek black horse being exercised in the fenced-in yard alongside the stables. She was fascinated by the horse's graceful movements, and after stepping down from the carriage, she walked over to the enclosure to watch.

"This horse seems very familiar to me, but it's not one of our horses, is it?" she asked the stableboy.

"No, ma'am," he replied as he walked the high-spirited animal. "We're just stabling her for a while."

"For whom?"

The young man shrugged. "A friend of Mr. Blake's is all I was told, ma'am."

"She certainly is a beauty."

"Yes, ma'am. A thoroughbred. She goes by the name of Rachel's Girl."

"Rachel's Girl? The racehorse?"

"Yes, ma'am."

Amanda was puzzled. Why would a friend of Matthew's buy the horse if he had no stable for her? She turned and walked toward the house, chewing her lower lip.

Shortly before supper, a messenger delivered a slim package for Matthew. Amanda overheard the boy's conversation with Prentiss as she came down the staircase, and offered to take the delivery to Matthew's study on her way to the kitchen to check on dinner. She placed the package on his desk and turned to leave, but as she did, the bell sleeve of her dress swept several papers to the floor and when she stooped to pick them up, a familiar name on one of them caught her eye.

Amanda stood slowly as she read the paper. She was uncertain what to make of it, for in her hand was a receipt for Rachel's Girl made out to Matthew. *Why had the groom thought the horse belonged to Matthew's friend?* She heard Matthew's deep voice in the hall outside and quickly replaced the receipt, then hurried toward the door just as he walked into the room.

"Amanda!" he said in surprise.

"A package came for you," she said, blushing guiltily. "I brought it in here."

"Thank you." He gave her a curious look as he walked toward the desk.

She started to leave, then paused and turned to face him. "A horse was delivered this afternoon, also."

"Yes, I was expecting it." Matthew kept his back to her as he opened his package.

"Is it your horse?"

There was a pause, and then he said, "No."

Amanda eyed the receipt on his desk. "Why are we keeping it then?"

"The horse is for Michael's sister, Erin O'Day. She has no place to keep it right now." Matthew examined the documents inside his package. "And while I'm thinking of it, I've invited Erin to your party."

Amanda saw again the smiling face of the copper-haired girl. Now there was a name to go with the face. Erin O'Day. And now she could no longer deny the truth. Matthew wasn't spending his nights guarding his mill, nor were the scratches on his back from leaning against a wooden shanty. He had taken a mistress. Michael's sister. And the horse was Matthew's gift to her. How could Michael allow it?

At her continued silence, Matthew finally turned around.

Amanda had gone.

Chapter Thirty-three

"Hush, Gabby," Amanda crooned gently, holding her sobbing youngest sister on her lap, smoothing back her damp curls. "Mrs. Ripley will get better."

"Oh, Mandy, I can't hurt her. She's so ill, and she's been so kind to me. And Clara is getting married at Christmas. Who will she have then?"

Amanda's throat tightened painfully. *Who will I have then?* Certainly not Matthew, if she ever had him at all. And Bonnie was married, Curt wanted his independence, Daniel was going to college, and Ethan had decided he wanted to live with David to be near his older brother, leaving her only Freddie and Gabby. And now Gabby didn't want to leave Alice Ripley.

Help me, Mother, she prayed silently. *Tell me what to do.* Since learning of Erin O'Day, Amanda had moved, eaten, lived, without thinking. Her mind seemed frozen, her thoughts locked away where they couldn't torment her. But the hearing was only a day off. She had to think what to do.

"Please, Mandy!" Gabby begged tearfully. "Please come see her for yourself."

"Okay, Gabby. That's what we'll do. Go dry your tears while I call for the carriage."

Amanda was silent as they rode toward the Ripleys' house. Gabby sat, ladylike, across from her, her forehead wrinkled with concern, her head turned toward the window, clean white gloves on small hands that were losing their girlish chubbiness. She had changed remarkably in the year since Amanda's arrival, due to her own diligent effort, Amanda decided, and in spite of Mrs. Ripley's influence. Her parents would be proud of their little girl now.

Amanda squared her shoulders. She had to do what was best for Gabby, no matter who it hurt. Mrs. Ripley could not be allowed to manipulate her family any longer. She closed her eyes and whispered another prayer for guidance.

The maid showed them into Alice's bedroom. It took a moment for Amanda's eyes to become accustomed to the dim light, and then she saw the slight form of a woman propped against pillows on her chaise longue. "Gabrielle, is that you?" a weak voice called.

Gabby urged Amanda forward. "It's me, Aunt Alice. I've brought you company."

"Oh, my dear child, you're so thoughtful." Alice's bony hand reached out for her. "Tell me who you brought. My eyes are rather cloudy today."

Gabby stepped up to her side and clasped the hand. "It's my sister, Aunt Alice. I've brought Mandy."

Amanda braced herself as Alice's head slowly tilted up and her eyes squinted, trying to focus. But rather than flying into a rage, Alice merely sighed tiredly. "Amanda."

Amanda was shocked by the woman's appearance. Her eyes were sunken and lifeless. Her skin was gray and her breathing shallow. She seemed to have aged twenty years since Amanda had seen her last. Dr. Cook had not exaggerated the seriousness of her condition.

Alice turned her head toward Gabby. "Dear child, would you go downstairs and ask someone to bring tea for your sister? That's a good girl." She waited until Gabby had left the room, then turned back to Amanda and lifted trembling arms in a helpless gesture.

"I can't fight you anymore, Amanda. I have no strength left." Her long, narrow chin began to quiver. "I was so afraid you would take Gabrielle from me that I've hastened my own death." She put her hands to her face and began to sob, deep, tormented sobs that alarmed Amanda. "Take her today," she wept. "I don't want her to watch me die."

Amanda leaned over the chaise and put her hand on the woman's shaking shoulder, uncertain whether to pity her or to resist yet another of her manipulations. "Mrs. Ripley, please don't cry."

"You've never understood how much I care for your sister," Alice said between sobs. "How could I not love her? I've raised her for over four years. I've watched her grow from a child to a young lady. I took her to school on her first day. I nursed her through fevers and colds. She's as close to me as my Clara." She blew her nose and wiped her eyes. "And the irony, Amanda, the irony is that I didn't need to fight you. I wouldn't have lost Gabrielle. Distance can't sever the bond between us. But I didn't see that. God help me, I didn't see it."

"You still have Clara," Amanda reminded her gently.

"Clara. She finally caught herself a husband and who does she choose but a traveling sharpener. She'll spend her life wandering the country watching her husband sharpen knives." Her sobs began again. "And she was lucky to get him."

"But what of your husband, Mrs. Ripley? The mayor has always been devoted to you."

Alice tried to snort and ended up having a coughing fit. She groped for a glass of water and took a long swallow, then replaced the glass and sagged weakly against the chaise. "My husband is so devoted that he hasn't been to see me in a week. The only way I've ever been able to get his attention is to involve myself in the town's affairs."

Amanda was at a loss for words. She had long been one of Alice's foremost critics, but what she saw now was not the interfering, insufferable old harpy she had always despised, but an aging, lonely woman who was desperate for affection.

Amanda rose and squared her shoulders. She could not let pity stop her from doing what was best for Gabby. "Mrs. Ripley, please understand that I have no wish to hurt you. I've done what I had to do in order to bring my family back together again, to give them the love and support they lacked because of our parents' death." She began to pull on her gloves, her mouth set firmly. "I'm sorry I won't be able to stay for tea."

"Love?" she heard Alice rasp weakly as she marched to the door. "I've given Gabrielle all the love in my heart, Amanda. And she has given me more than I can ever describe. And look at the others. Do they seem to have been deprived of affection? Have they cried to come live with you since you returned?"

Amanda's footsteps slowed. Had her brothers and sisters clamored to come live with her? Had they seemed unhappy with their new families? She clenched her hands at her sides to keep from shouting her denial. Yes, they had been deprived! Deprived of their parents' love and guidance. They needed to come home!

She swung to fix Alice with a determined glare. "Only *I* can give them back what they lost when our parents died, Mrs. Ripley."

Alice's weak reply cut through the air like steel blades, piercing the armor of self-righteousness around Amanda's heart. "What they lost were their parents, Amanda. You can't give them back their parents."

In the darkness of the shuttered room, Amanda stared at the frail figure on the chaise. She tried to draw a breath, but suddenly it seemed there was no air left to breathe. *You can't give them back their parents.* She turned and groped blindly for the doorknob, her eyes filling with tears, her mind desperately attempting to block out the truth. Instead, it became clearer, as if she had been looking through a murky pane of glass and it suddenly shattered, leaving her with an undistorted view. A view of her brothers and sisters: happy, confident, loving people who had managed to let go of the past. It was only she, herself, who had clung to it, believing if she recreated it faithfully, she could somehow bring her parents back.

She suddenly saw herself as others must have seen her, blindly pursuing a foolish fantasy, arranging lives to fit her dream, even prostituting herself to accomplish her goals. Amanda fled into the hallway, falling to her knees when her tears fell so thickly that she could not see. She had to get home, back to Hall House.

Hall House is a part of your past. Blake House is your future. Matthew is your future.

Amanda shook her head. She had lost Matthew, had lost even the chance to turn his lust into love. She had given it up for a fantasy.

Hearing light footsteps on the stairs, Amanda rose and wiped her eyes with the heels of her hands. She could not let Gabby see her beaten.

"Mandy, are you leaving?" Gabby asked, hurrying toward her. "A maid will be up in a moment with tea."

Amanda gripped her shoulders and stared into her sister's startled eyes. "Gabby, if Mrs. Ripley were not ill, would you still rather live here?"

Gabby's eyes slid away. "I don't know, Mandy. I have a splendid bedroom suite here, and Dorthea, my best friend, lives just across the street, and Aunt Alice buys me ever so many beautiful things, but I'd like to live with you, as well." Her eyes came back to Amanda's. "Couldn't I live both places?"

Amanda gazed down at her small, hopeful face and knew what she had to do. She smiled, and said through the lump in her throat, "If that's what you want."

"Oh, yes, Mandy! That's what I want!"

Amanda gave her a fierce hug. "Why don't you go back and tell Mrs. Ripley what we've decided. I'll go see Mr. Gable and have him change the petition." She gave her one last squeeze and turned away.

"I love you, Mandy," Gabby called softly.

Amanda pressed her fingers to her trembling lips and continued on. *I love you, too, Gabrielle.*

In the early morning hours on the fifth day of May, Amanda lay in her bed waiting for the first light of dawn, when she could begin preparations for the evening celebration to come. And what a celebration it would be! Hall House would ring with music and laughter just as it once had, and the Hall children would be back together again, if only for one magical night.

Judge Douglas had granted her petition for guardianship only the day before. The only modification made to it was to allow Alice to share custody of Gabby. Daniel and Freddie would live with her, but that would change once Daniel went away to school. And Amanda knew that once Daniel had gone, Freddie would probably prefer to join his brothers at their uncle's house.

But that no longer worried her. Amanda had finally accepted that her brothers and sisters were growing away from her, and realized now that nothing could ever stop that, nor could she bring back what she had lost when her parents died.

But there was still a chance that she could bring her husband back, although she knew it would be a difficult feat, considering that she had done everything in her power to drive Matthew away. She had chosen her family over him time and again, demonstrating in every way that her house and family were more important than he was. It was no wonder he had turned his attentions elsewhere.

But on this day, Amanda was possessed with new determination. She would host her celebration and meet Matthew's mistress on the battlefield of her home, fighting for her husband with every ounce of her being. She would show Matthew by her every word and action that she loved him; she would prove that their marriage was more important to her than Hall House—or rather, Blake House.

And when their guests had all gone, Amanda intended to share his bed with him.

She set to work with renewed vigor, supervising her staff to ensure that every detail for her social evening was exactly right. By the end of the afternoon, when she was satisfied that all was ready, she went upstairs to dress.

She walked into Matthew's room for the first time in weeks, momentarily shaken that she had truly thought of it as Matthew's room at last. From the corner of her eye, Amanda caught sight of the painting hanging above the fireplace and turned to study it. Had the wistful girl under the apple tree reminded Matthew of her, as Bonnie had suggested? Was that why he had hung it first in his apartment and then here in his bedroom?

She looked around the room, her heart swelling with hope for the evening to come. On the white dressing table, which had stood bare for weeks, now lay her silver-backed brush and comb and hand mirror, along with several bottles of scented water. Inside the top drawer sat her velvet jewelry case, and in another box were her hair combs and pins.

Amanda walked to Matthew's dressing room and threw back the doors, smiling at the sight of her clothing hanging across from his. She opened a cupboard and found her sheer lavender nightgown in a drawer where a maid had thoughtfully tucked in a sachet of rose petals. She laid the delicate gown on the bed and lovingly smoothed out the material. And then she began to dress.

Amanda chose a gown in royal blue silk because she knew it was Matthew's favorite color. When she had finished dressing, she sat before the dressing table mirror to arrange her hair in a way that he particularly liked, with the sides pulled up and fastened with combs and the back long and loose. She fastened her silver locket around her throat, where it dangled temptingly in the cleft of her breasts, and as a final touch, she added the diamond ear studs Matthew had given her.

When Amanda finally went downstairs, she heard talking and laughter coming from the drawing room. Thinking to find Matthew there, she hurried in with a pounding heart, but it was only Gabrielle and her brothers who waited for her.

Within an hour, the room had filled with people: Harper and Bonnie, Uncle David, Carolyn Tanner, Gabby, and her four brothers, Fred Moore and his wife, Mayor Ripley, and the families who had cared for Amanda's siblings. Except for Michael O'Day and his sister Erin, everyone on the list had arrived, and still there was no sign of Matthew. Amanda was beginning to think it was not by mere coincidence that all three of them were late.

She tried her best to be cheerful as she walked around

the room conversing with her guests, but Matthew's absence cast a pall over any joy she might have found in the event. As the evening wore on, her grand plans began to seem foolhardy and she berated herself for thinking she could so easily make things right between them. Matthew's absence was a clear message; he had found love in someone else's arms, and he no longer cared if she knew it.

Yet, minutes later, when the drawing room doors were suddenly opened, Amanda turned quickly, believing Matthew had come at last.

It was Prentiss. "There's a lady here to see you, madam," he said quietly in his bass voice.

Amanda followed him into the front hall, closing the double doors behind her. There, in the hallway, stood the copper-haired girl in a black and green plaid cloak, her bright hair streaming down her back.

"Good evenin', Mrs. Blake," the girl said with a lilting accent and a confident smile. "I'm Erin O'Day, Michael's sister."

Amanda was astonished at the young woman's appearance in her home, and then indignant. "I know who you are, Miss O'Day. If you've come looking for my husband, he isn't here. In fact, I thought he might be with you."

Erin's gaze darted to the straight-faced Prentiss, and then she said boldly, "I'd like to have a word with you in private, if I may."

Amanda stared at her, seeing not the sincere face of Michael's sister, but the impudent young woman who had filled the empty place in Matthew's bed. Inwardly, she began to quake with fear. Had the girl come to deliver a message from Matthew? Was this how he would end their marriage?

Dread rendering her speechless, Amanda gave a brief nod, then turned and walked down the hallway to the morning parlor, hoping the trembling of her limbs would not be evident to the brazen young woman behind her.

Since that meeting at the racetrack, Amanda had taken pains to avoid Michael's sister, as well as Michael himself, whom she had previously regarded as a friend. His duplic-

ity had deeply wounded her, and when Prentiss had brought
word one afternoon that Michael had come to speak with
her on an important matter, Amanda had instructed the butler to say she was out.

It was more than mere hurt that had caused Amanda to
avoid Michael; it was also cowardice, for she was afraid to
learn how deeply Matthew was involved with his sister.
That Michael might have come for some other purpose had
never entered her mind. Now it seemed she was to find out,
anyway.

Amanda turned to face her. "What is it you wanted to
say?"

Standing just inside the parlor door, Erin calmly laced
her fingers together. "First of all, let me say that Michael
was supposed to come with me tonight to explain every-
thin' to you, but he sent a message sayin' he was held up at
the mill and for me to come on without him. You see, Mrs.
Blake, my brother was afraid you might be misunder-
standin' my friendship with Matthew, and by the way
you've been eyein' me since I came into your house, I can
see he was right. I've known your husband since I was a
young lass; I've admired him that long, as well. But it goes
no farther than that."

Could the girl be speaking the truth? Amanda wanted
desperately to believe her, yet there was too much still un-
explained.

"Your husband has not been unfaithful to you, Mrs.
Blake," Erin continued. "He loves you very much. And
now that I've had my say, I'll be on my way."

"Wait, Miss O'Day."

Erin stopped and looked back. "Yes, ma'am?"

"If what you say is true, why did Matthew buy you the
racehorse?"

Erin broke into a wide smile. "Oh, but Rachel's Girl is
yours, Mrs. Blake!" She clapped her hand over her mouth.
"And now Michael will have my hide for lettin' out the secret."

Amanda was flustered. "But my husband told me *you*
owned the horse."

"Oh, my, no. What would I be doin' with a racehorse? 'Twas only a story made up to hide your surprise. I'm truly sorry I let it out; Matthew wanted to give you the horse tonight, you see."

Erin's blue eyes twinkled as she smiled. "You should have seen his face the day he bought her, Mrs. Blake. He was as thrilled as a young lad at Christmas. He said your mother's name was Rachel; that's why he did it, you know. My, but he was excited."

Remembering the flush of Matthew's face when he had returned from the race track, remembering how she had coldly rejected his advances, Amanda's heart thudded sickeningly. Had she been wrong about everything? She sank onto a chair. "What have I done?" she whispered.

"Oh, you poor thing," Erin crooned, coming to kneel in front of her and pat her hand. "You've been worryin' about this all week, haven't you, and all because Matthew wanted to surprise you. But you mustn't worry anymore, for he told me the day he bought her that he planned to be here tonight." Erin looked around. "Do you want a tot of somethin' to clear your head? I can fetch some brandy for you."

Amanda shook her head. She studied the girl's candid face and felt a stab of guilt for the ill treatment she had given her. As Matthew had pointed out several times before, she had jumped to a conclusion without having the facts.

"It was terribly brave of you to come here, Miss O'Day, knowing how I felt. It seems I've made a very rash judgment; you'll never know how deeply sorry I am for that. I only wish there were some way I could make it up to you."

Erin smiled and sat back on her heels. "Well, now, you can start by callin' me Erin, as all my friends do."

Amanda laughed. "You are so very much like your brother, Erin." She took the younger woman's hand in hers. "Please call me Amanda."

" 'Twould be my pleasure."

As she walked Erin to the front door, Amanda asked, "Won't you stay for a while and have some refreshments while we wait for Matthew and Michael to arrive? I'd very much like for you to meet my family."

Erin glanced down at her clothing and grimaced. "No, Amanda. I didn't dress for your social, so I'll not embarrass you in front of your guests. Perhaps I can come some afternoon for tea instead."

"That would be delightful."

Erin started out the door, but paused to look back. "You're very lucky, Amanda; you've a rare and fine man in Matthew. But then I'd have to say only a special lady would be able to capture such a man's heart."

Amanda closed the door and leaned against it. She owed a huge debt of gratitude to Erin O'Day. She was beginning to understand why Matthew placed such high value on Michael's friendship.

"Hurry home, Matthew. I have so much to say to you," she whispered, before returning to her guests in the drawing room to wait for her husband's arrival.

Chapter Thirty-four

THE WAIT SEEMED endless. Minutes passed like hours. Amanda talked and laughed, but all the while, she felt a sense of detachment from the gaiety around her. Where was Matthew? What could be keeping him so long?

By ten o'clock, most of the guests had departed, leaving only Amanda's family to keep her company. She pretended not to be concerned about her husband's lateness, but she could not fool her brothers and sisters.

Finally, the doors opened and everyone turned expectantly. But it was a worried Prentiss, not Matthew, who appeared in the doorway. He beckoned to Amanda, and when she had stepped into the hallway, he quietly closed the doors behind her. "A messenger to see you, madam."

A tall young man stood near the front door, dressed in blue overalls and a dirty coat, holding his work cap in his grimy hands, his solemn eyes staring from an angular face smudged with dirt. Amanda walked toward him, pricklings of fear raising the hair on her neck.

"You have a message for me?"

The stranger bobbed his head and then handed her a sheet of folded paper. Amanda opened it with unsteady hands.

"I have important work to see to at the iron mill tonight," it read. "Don't expect me home until very late. I would apologize for missing your celebration, but I hardly think my absence would make much difference to you, anyway."

307

There was no signature.

Swallowing her hurt and disappointment, Amanda managed to thank the messenger and send him away. With a heavy heart, she walked back to the closed doors of the drawing room, but hearing the buzz of concerned voices within, she could not face them. Choking back a sob, she turned and fled up to Matthew's room, where she sat on his bed and gave way to her tears.

Did he really believe his absence wouldn't make any difference to her? Did he think she cared nothing for him?

"He wanted to give you the horse tonight, you see. My, but he was excited!"

She remembered again the afternoon he had returned from the races, and the look on Matthew's face when she had sent him away. *"I hardly think my absence would make much difference to you, anyway."* She could feel the hurt and rejection in that simple remark. What a fool she had been.

"He loves you very much." Erin had promised. If only Matthew knew how much that love was returned, perhaps they would have a chance after all.

But that was the answer! She would go to the mill and tell him how much she loved him. Whatever business he had there could surely wait another day.

Amanda jumped up and darted from the room, calling for the carriage to be brought around as she swept down the staircase. She instructed Prentiss to tell her family that she had gone on an errand and would be back shortly, and then she left, pulling a cape over her bare shoulders as she ran down the front steps.

Will, Matthew's burly driver, was reluctant to take her to the iron mill, and only did so when she threatened to walk. He sat forward on his high perch and kept an alert eye all around, and when he pulled the carriage to a halt in front of the yard that separated the mill from the road, he shook his head in worry as he climbed down.

"Mrs. Blake, I don't think Mr. Blake wants you here. I'd better take you back home."

"I have to see my husband first," Amanda replied stubbornly. She gave him her hand and stepped down from the carriage to look around.

Suddenly, two armed men stepped out of the shadows of the trees and pointed rifles at them. The horses pranced and snorted nervously as Amanda sidled closer to Will.

"Who goes there?" one of the men asked in a low, rough voice.

"It's Mrs. Blake," Will exclaimed nervously. "She's looking for her husband."

"He's out back," the man growled. "He can't be disturbed."

Amanda peered through the darkness. "Where? I must see him."

"Behind the mill." The guard turned to Matthew's driver. "Take her home. There's supposed to be trouble tonight."

"What kind of trouble?" Amanda asked, more frightened now by his words than by their menacing presence.

Will tried to explain. "Your husband has enemies who want to see the mill destroyed, Mrs. Blake, and him along with it. He's posted these men here as guards, but it would be best if we went back home. He'd never forgive me if something happened to you."

Amanda was stunned. Matthew's life was in danger, and he hadn't even mentioned it, thinking, no doubt, that she didn't care.

"Has there been any trouble before tonight?" she asked one of the guards.

"Minor incidents is all."

"Broken windows?" At the guard's nod, she said to her driver, "Will, take the carriage back to Blake House. The horses may attract attention here. If I haven't returned home in an hour, come back for me."

"Mrs. Blake, I can't leave you here! Mr. Blake will sack me for certain!"

She gave the driver a reassuring smile. "I won't be unprotected. These two men seem quite capable of lending me assistance if I need it. And you may tell my husband that I threatened to sack you first."

Amanda turned to glare at one of the guards, who had stepped forward to bar her way with his rifle. "Go tell my husband that I shall wait for him in his office." She brushed past the astonished man and set off across the yard as Will climbed back to his perch and clicked his tongue at the horses, shaking his head and muttering to himself as the carriage rolled away. With a smothered oath, the guard hurried after Amanda, and once she had slipped safely through the huge, wooden doors into the silent mill, he left to inform his boss.

In darkness lit only by the feeble light of the moon shining through dingy windows, Amanda picked her way across the vast mill floor. Once inside Matthew's office, she lit a lamp and sat down at his desk, chewing her lip with worry.

She didn't have long to wait. Minutes later, the door crashed open and Matthew stood in the doorway, his fists clenched at his sides, his countenance dark with rage. Amanda stood up, shocked by the look on his face.

"What are you doing here?" he snarled, his shadow on the wall behind him looming large and dangerous as he crossed the room toward her and extinguished the lamp.

"I had to see you, Matthew."

He dragged her to her feet, pushing her toward the door. "Get out of here, Amanda. Go home!"

She turned to face him. "Please, Matthew, this is important."

Matthew gripped her arms and brought her close, glaring into her amber eyes. "You have to leave now! You've put yourself in danger by coming here."

"Why haven't you told me about the danger?" she cried.

He gritted his teeth. "Because, my sweet wife, I didn't think you cared one way or the other. You've been so involved with your family and that damn house that you haven't even noticed what I've been doing these past weeks."

Amanda gazed at him forlornly, tears running down her cheeks. "But I have noticed, and I do care, Matthew; and

I'm so sorry for everything. I see now how foolish I've been about it all."

From out in the mill there came a sudden cry of alarm followed by a pistol shot. Matthew pushed Amanda to the floor. "Stay here while I find out what's going on." Then he was gone, silently shutting the door behind him.

She huddled in the dark beside his desk listening to angry shouts from somewhere close by. There was more gunfire and then a sudden, shattering explosion that shook the floor beneath her and made her ears ring. With a cry of pain, she held her hands over her ears until the reverberations stopped, then realized the bell in the front yard was tolling to alert the town to a fire. She sprang to her feet and ran to the door to peer out.

At the far end of the vast building, Amanda saw a blaze of orange firelight and men's dark forms battling it with blankets and water buckets. She watched, spellbound, until, suddenly, a heavy, moist hand was clamped over her mouth and nose, an arm around her waist, and she was dragged backward into the office. As Amanda struggled to pull the hand away so she could breathe, a thick, gravely voice above her said, "I didn't 'spect such good luck t'night."

She was shoved up against Matthew's desk and the hand was removed. And as Amanda gasped for air, a huge, sweating, bald man loomed over her, his wet lips drawn back in a snarl to reveal rotted and missing teeth.

"You must be the boss's new missus," the man said in a sneer, eyeing the low-cut bodice of her blue silk gown. "Ain't it kind of you to drop by for a visit tonight. Now all we need is yer husband and then we can have us a tea party."

He guffawed as he stepped back, and then, with a jeering grin, he pulled a long barreled pistol from his belt and aimed it at her face. Amanda quickly shut her eyes, thinking she was about to die.

But there was no pistol shot, only five words, uttered in a low, sinister voice.

"Scream, or I'll shoot you."

Amanda's eyes flew open in horror, moving from the giant's grinning face to the end of the long gun barrel, but she did not scream. She *would* not scream, for, if she did, Matthew would come running and the man would kill him. Clutching the desk behind her with cold fingers, unable to draw a breath in her fear, she focused once more on his face and shook her head.

With a roar of anger, the giant leaped forward, grabbed her by the hair on the back of her head, and jerked her head back, causing her to whimper in pain. Still Amanda would not cry out. Thrusting his hideous features close to hers, his rancid breath on her face, he bellowed, "Scream!"

Amanda had no need to reply. The door burst open and Matthew was inside the office before he realized his peril. As the giant pivoted toward him, Amanda screamed, "Matthew, get back!" But it was too late.

The force of the bullet knocked him against the door, pushing it closed. He clutched his left side over his heart, a look of surprise on his face. "Amanda," he rasped, then his eyes shut and he slid to the floor, a red stain spreading onto the white material of his shirt.

A harsh sob escaped her lips as Amanda pushed past the giant and ran to Matthew's side. She quickly felt for the pulse in his neck and found it still strong. Her gaze dropped to the blackened hole in his shirt, and she guessed that the bullet had entered somewhere below his left shoulder, but she had no way of knowing how close it had come to his heart. She knew she had to do whatever she could to get him help quickly before he bled to death, or before they burned alive.

All this took a matter of seconds, and Amanda suddenly became aware of the giant moving toward them, no doubt to make sure Matthew was dead.

She sprang to her feet and lunged at him as if crazed with grief. "You've killed him!" she screamed, clawing at his face and kicking his shins as the man at first cowered in surprise and then, with a bellow of rage, knocked her to the floor with one huge arm.

Before Amanda could get up again, he had straddled her and gripped her upper arms, his brutish fingers digging into her flesh. "You sure he's dead?"

Amanda turned her face to one side, tears rolling down her cheeks. "Yes, for God's sake! He's dead."

He gave her a hard shake, hitting her head against the pine boards. "You're lying!"

Crying uncontrollably now, she cried, "My father was a doctor. I know what death is."

He said nothing for a moment, and Amanda hoped that he would leave her and Matthew before he perished with them in the flames. Instead, he stood up and began to unbutton his trousers.

Amanda cried out and fought to escape as he again straddled her legs and shoved her skirt and petticoats up around her thighs. She clawed at his hands, drawing blood, until he took both of her hands in his steel grip and held them above her head.

"Go on, fight me," he said with an ugly grin. He ripped the thin, silky material of her bodice to her waist, exposing the tops of her breasts above her corset. With his free hand, he pinched the soft flesh, laughing when she gritted her teeth and closed her eyes, forcing tears from beneath her eyelids.

From a distance, Amanda heard the clanging of the fire wagons as they raced toward the mill. Voices shouting orders over the roar of the flames seemed very close now and she knew the fire was spreading rapidly. She began to struggle anew as the giant's hands fumbled between her legs, trying to tear open her drawers.

Suddenly, there was a pistol shot from behind. The man's eyes widened in surprise, then, with a furious roar, he staggered to his feet and swung around. Amanda gasped at the sight of blood coming through the back of his shirt, then her gaze shifted to where Matthew sat with his back braced against the door, his pistol in his hand and beads of sweat on his forehead, making a last attempt to save her.

The giant lunged forward and Matthew fired again, striking him in the forehead. The man staggered backward, reeling like a drunk, and collapsed onto the floor beside Amanda. She stared at him for a moment, too paralyzed to move, until she realized he was dead, and then she scrambled to her feet and flew to Matthew's side.

"Get out!" Matthew rasped, grimacing in pain as he sagged weakly to one side. "Don't go through the mill. Door is hot . . . fire's too near. Use the window."

But when Amanda glanced around at the window in the outside wall, the hopelessness of their situation nearly defeated her. She knew she'd never have the strength to drag Matthew across the floor and hoist him through the small opening. There was only one recourse, and that was to get Matthew away from the door before it ignited, and pray to be rescued.

She stood up and looked around for some way to move him.

"For God's sake, Amanda!" he cried through gritted teeth. "Save yourself!"

"No, Matthew. I won't leave you." She managed to shove aside the heavy oak desk and remove the oval braided rug beneath it to place alongside him. But when she lifted his legs, she saw him clench his teeth against the pain that shot through him.

He reached for her arm, but his grasp was too weak to hold her. "You're wasting precious time. Leave me!"

Amanda ignored his plea and knelt beside him, slipping her arms around his body, grasping his blood-soaked shirt to raise him up. The pain from the movement sent Matthew spiraling into unconsciousness, and she felt him go limp against her.

Slowly, Amanda inched him over the rug and lowered him onto it, but her efforts left her panting for breath, and her remaining energy was quickly being sapped by the suffocating heat. Nearing the point of collapse, she gripped the rug and tugged on it, groaning as she slowly backed away from the door.

Once Amanda had moved Matthew across the twenty-foot room to the far wall, she knelt beside him and opened his shirt to examine his wound. The hole below his shoulder was large and ragged, and he was still losing blood. Using her teeth to make a rent in her petticoat, she tore off enough material to make a pad to press against the wound, and another length for a bandage to wrap around his shoulder to hold the pad in place. It was as much as she could do for him, and she hoped it was not in vain. The roar of the fire was so loud that she had no way of knowing if help was near or if someone would even reach them in time.

Amanda removed the tattered remnant of her petticoat and used it to mop her face. The room had become an inferno. She eyed the window longingly, but feared that a rush of fresh air would only bring the fire toward them that much sooner. She tried to swallow and found her throat painfully parched.

As she looked around for a pitcher of water, she saw thick, black smoke curling under the door and snaking across the room. She snatched the remnant of petticoat and quickly stuffed it beneath the door to prevent more smoke from entering, then she returned to sit beside Matthew and pray.

Her soft murmuring brought Matthew back to consciousness. Slowly, he turned his head and saw Amanda sitting on the floor beside him, wiping tears from her face with the backs of her bloodstained hands. Her lips were moving, and when the fog around his head cleared a little more, he realized she was reciting the Twenty-third Psalm.

"Amanda," he whispered weakly.

"Yes, my love, I'm here," she said with a sob, leaning over him to smooth back his damp hair.

He swallowed with difficulty. "Why did you stay?"

Amanda picked up his hand and kissed it, her tears falling freely onto his open palm. "I love you, Matthew. That's what I came here to tell you."

"Your family . . . needs you."

"Oh, my love, *you* are my family, too."

He struggled visibly to remain conscious. "Amanda," he whispered again.

She put her fingertip against his lips. "No, Matthew. Save your strength. We'll be rescued soon."

He shook his head. "The fire . . . I was lucky the first time. A man doesn't get that chance twice."

Amanda stared at him bleakly, fearing his words would prove true. But her stubbornness and fierce determination would not allow her to give up. She would not let Matthew die. She forced herself to rise on weak legs and stumble to the door. Afraid to open it for the flames on the other side, she screamed for help and pummeled the wood with her fists, oblivious to the searing pain as the paint blistered from the heat.

Suddenly, Amanda heard a man's voice cry out, "Stand clear!" She backed away from the door and stared at it as something heavy hit the wood again and again. Finally, it splintered and gave way, and buckets of water were splashed against the frame. Two men climbed through the smoking timber, their eyes white against the blackness of their faces.

"Mother of God!" one of the men exclaimed, running over to kneel at Matthew's side.

Amanda recognized Michael's voice and began to weep with relief. "Thank God you've come," she said, dropping to her knees in exhaustion as the other man wrapped a dampened blanket around her.

"Mrs. Blake, John will carry you out," Michael shouted. "I'll see to Matthew."

"He's been shot and he's lost a lot of blood. You'll both have to carry him."

Michael looked around and spotted the giant lying on the floor. "Marley! I knew he was behind this."

"He's dead," Amanda told them as she struggled to her feet, adding weakly, "Matthew killed him."

The men wrapped the rug around Matthew and gently lifted him. With one backward glance at the fearsome brute who had nearly killed her husband, Amanda followed her rescuers out, a corner of the blanket pressed against her nose and mouth as she struggled to make her way through the choking, blinding smoke to the fresh air outside.

She was at once surrounded by her family, but she paid them no heed as she followed the two men to the horse-drawn ambulance and climbed into the back, huddling beside her husband as the conveyance pulled away.

Chapter Thirty-five

MATTHEW WAS CARRIED into the hospital unconscious and taken to surgery. Michael paced the hallway as Amanda, the damp blanket around her shoulders, her fists raw and oozing, sat numbly on a bench, shivering. Harper and Bonnie arrived minutes later, and it was all Bonnie could do to coax Amanda to release her grip on the blanket in exchange for a warm cloak.

Bonnie was shocked by the condition of Amanda's torn gown, but cried out in dismay when she saw her sister's hands. She called for a nurse and then wrapped her arms around Amanda and held her close to stop the shivering, murmuring soothing words against her ear.

"Where are the children?" Amanda managed to ask through chattering teeth.

"They're with Uncle David. You needn't worry about them, dearest. Here's the nurse now. Let her see your hands."

An hour later, a young doctor came out of surgery and walked down the hallway toward them. Amanda sat forward, gripping Bonnie's hand with her bandaged ones despite the pain it caused her. "Is he all right?" she asked in a choked voice.

"He's weak from blood loss, but the damage seems to be minimal, and the bullet came out clean as a whistle. Lucky for him, someone stopped the bleeding when they did, or I wouldn't have given him much of a chance at all. Of course, we'll be keeping a close watch over him for signs of internal bleeding, but other than that, I'd say he'll be ready to go home in about a week."

Amanda sagged against Bonnie and began to sob.

"Hush, now, Mandy," Bonnie comforted, drawing her sister's head against her shoulder. "Everything will be fine."

"Can we see him, doc?" Michael asked hoarsely, his voice choked with emotion.

"Not now. In the morning, perhaps, when he's conscious."

When the doctor had gone, Michael knelt before Amanda and took one of her bandaged hands tenderly in his. There were unshed tears in his bright blue eyes. "If I had on my cap, it'd be off to you, dear lady, for savin' his life."

Amanda shook her head, tears rolling down her cheeks. "It was you who saved him, Michael. It was my fault he almost died."

"That's malarkey!" Michael argued.

But Amanda could not be persuaded otherwise. She told them of her suspicions concerning Matthew and Erin, and of how she had gone to the mill to make amends with her husband. "If I had gone home as he'd told me, Matthew would have had no reason to go back to his office. I can only hope he'll forgive me for it."

"No one could have predicted what Marley would do," Michael reminded her.

Bonnie stroked Amanda's hair. "When Matthew regains consciousness, you'll go in and tell him you love him. You'll see that everything will work out between you."

"I wish I had your confidence, Bonnie," Amanda said with a sigh.

Neither Amanda nor Michael would leave the hospital that night, choosing instead to sleep on hard chairs in the second-floor waiting room. Shortly after dawn, a nurse tapped Amanda on the shoulder. "Your husband awoke just a few minutes ago."

Amanda followed the nurse through the ward, past sleeping patients, to Matthew's bed at the end of the crowded room, only to find he had gone back to sleep. She sat on the edge of a chair watching him, willing him to open his eyes, until, half an hour later, the nurse informed her it was time to leave.

"But I haven't had a chance to talk to him," Amanda protested in a whisper, near tears. "Please let me stay."

"I'm sorry, Mrs. Blake. Your half hour is up. I have to follow the rules."

"Let her stay."

Both women turned sharply at the hoarse voice, then the nurse moved to the head of Matthew's bed to take his pulse. She held a glass of water to his lips and after he had taken a sip, she said, "I'll allow your wife to stay ten minutes longer, Mr. Blake, but no more."

As soon as the nurse had gone, Amanda went to the side of Matthew's bed and placed his hand against her cheek. "Oh, Matthew, I'm so sorry about everything that's happened. Please forgive me."

But he only turned her face to both sides and quipped, "You look like you've slept in an incinerator, Amanda."

She wiped away the tears that had slipped from her eyes, smudging her dirty face even more. "Matthew, be serious."

His gaze went to the bandages wrapped around both her hands and then he caught one of her wrists and brought it closer for inspection. "What happened to you?"

Her eyebrows drew together. "I burned my hands yesterday. Don't you remember the fire?"

Gently, he took her fingers and brought them to his lips, his dark eyes on her face, but he said nothing further about her injury or the fire that caused it. "You've spent the night here, haven't you?"

"Yes."

"I suppose Michael is waiting outside."

"He's a good friend to you, Matthew."

The nurse walked toward the bed, shaking her head at Amanda. "Mrs. Blake, you must leave now. Your husband needs his rest."

Amanda looked to Matthew to intervene, but this time he made no protest, as if he would be glad to have her gone. With a brave smile, she bent over him and kissed him gently on the cheek. "I'll come back soon," she said as she backed away.

Michael was waiting outside the ward, and when Amanda emerged, he smiled broadly, but seeing the tears streaming down her cheeks, he checked his smile.

"Is he not doin' well then?" he asked, falling into step with her as she continued down the hallway.

"He's doing fine."

Michael walked beside her, offering her his silent support. At the end of the hallway, Amanda stopped. "He wouldn't say a word about what happened, Michael; he wouldn't even reply when I told him how sorry I was."

Michael put his arms around her and held her as she sobbed into his shoulder. "Now we mustn't forget what an ordeal he's been through these past twenty-four hours. Perhaps it's all murky in his mind right now. Give him a bit of time to sort things out and then he'll talk about it."

Michael saw Amanda to the street and hailed a hack for her, then returned to the second floor, where he charmed the stern-faced nurse into giving him ten minutes with Matthew. With his hands in his pockets, he strolled jauntily through the ward, smiling and nodding at the other patients as he headed toward the last bed, and when he found Matthew propped up against the pillows, feeding himself clear beef broth, he scoffed at him.

"What's this now? Sittin' up and stuffin' yer gab? Why, after seein' your wife walk out of here, I thought I'd find a priest standin' beside your bed givin' you last rites."

Matthew stopped eating and gave him a puzzled look. "For heaven's sake, Mike, what did Amanda say?"

"'Twasn't what she said, 'twas how she looked. Fact of the matter is, she said you were doin' fine. Puzzles me, though, why she should be cryin' when you're doin' so fine."

"She's just exhausted. You look like you could use a

good night's sleep, yourself. I hear you two stayed the night."

"That's true enough, though, speakin' for myself, I would have gladly left; but your wife wouldn't be budged, and I couldn't very well leave her here all alone with no one to look after her."

Matthew finished his broth and leaned back against the pillow, wincing in pain. "Michael, you're the biggest liar ever to come out of County Kerry."

"And you're the biggest horse's arse ever to come out of New York. You could have said you forgave her, couldn't you. But not you, Matthew Blake. You had to make her weep." He clicked his tongue in disgust.

Matthew clenched his jaws. "I can't talk to her about what happened yet, Mike."

"Are you tellin' me you can't even tell her she's forgiven, after she saved your life?" At Matthew's continued silence, Michael said, "You've taken leave of your senses, that's what you've done. And I'll not stand by to watch you hurt Amanda. You can expect my resignation tomorrow."

Matthew raked his fingers through his hair. "I need time, Mike. Please."

Michael gave him a dubious glance, then frowned and scratched his forehead. "Well, I've never doubted you before, Matthew. All right. But one week is all I'm giving you."

During the week Matthew stayed in the hospital, Amanda had no further opportunity to talk privately with her husband. In the brief two hours allotted visitors each evening, Matthew conferred with Michael on business matters and was host to a constant stream of well-wishers. Amanda had to content herself with sitting patiently at his bedside, hoping he would send them away to spend a few minutes alone with her; yet by the day of his release, they still had not discussed the events of that dreadful evening.

Amanda sent Will to the hospital to bring him home, while she nervously paced the upstairs hallway of Blake House. At the sound of the carriage, she hurried to

Matthew's bedroom window and watched with her heart in her throat as he strode up the walk, as confident and as handsome as ever.

By the time Amanda reached the bottom of the stairs, Prentiss had already taken Matthew's coat and hat and was hanging them on the cloak rack as Matthew greeted the housekeeper and maids who had turned out to welcome him home. Then Matthew turned toward her, his dark eyes intent on her face. "Hello, Amanda."

Nervously, she clasped her fingers behind her back and said awkwardly, "How are you feeling today?"

"Almost as good as new."

"Are you hungry? Would you like dinner?"

"I have business to see to first." He turned to the house-keeper and said, "Would you bring coffee to the study?"

Amanda watched as he strode down the hallway and disappeared into his study, then she turned forlornly toward the staircase.

"Amanda," Matthew called from the doorway, "I want you to come, too."

She found him seated at his desk, papers spread out before him. "Would you like a cup of coffee?" he asked, as the maid came in with a silver tray.

Amanda couldn't even think of drinking coffee with the nervous knot in her stomach. She shook her head as Matthew poured a cup for himself. She watched his face for clues to his feelings, but his expression revealed nothing.

"You can sit if you'd like," he said, indicating the chair behind her. As Amanda seated herself, Matthew took a sip of coffee, watching her over the rim of the cup. He placed it back in the saucer, then looked up at her. "I'm deeding Blake House to you."

"To me? Why?"

"I understand the judge granted your petition." His eyes flickered over her. "Now you have everything you've always wanted."

Amanda's mind reeled. Was Matthew leaving her? Her throat tightened. "Not everything," she whispered.

He didn't seem to hear her. "When will your family be moving in?"

"Only Freddie and Daniel will be living here," she answered woodenly. "The others have chosen not to."

Matthew was quiet a moment, then said gently, "I'm sorry. I know that must hurt."

Tears filled her eyes, and over the lump in her throat, she said, "Not as much as if you leave me."

Matthew's dark eyes watched warily as she rose and walked around the desk toward him. She knelt beside his chair and gazed up at him plaintively. "I meant what I said the night of the fire, Matthew. I love you. And if you can forgive me for nearly causing your death, if you feel any affection toward me, then maybe our marriage *can* work."

Her throat ached from holding back tears as he studied her. She wasn't sure what she would do if he rejected her, but she bravely lifted her chin and met his intense gaze.

Suddenly he lifted her up and pulled her into his arms, his lips on her forehead, her cheek, her mouth, kissing her feverishly, desperately, his hands tangling in her long hair. "Ah, Amanda," he sighed, holding her tightly against his heart. "My brave, foolish Amanda. You've never done things halfway, have you? You could have been killed at the mill that night. You should have escaped when I told you to."

"Not without you, Matthew. I wouldn't have wanted to live without you."

She felt him begin to tremble, and then he buried his face in her hair as shudders racked his body. He was crying.

Amanda fought back her own tears as she wrapped her arms around his ribs and held him, unsure of how to help. After a while, Matthew quieted, and finally said in a ragged whisper, "It's time I told you about my brother."

They sat together on one of the overstuffed chairs, Amanda in Matthew's lap, her head against his shoulder. He began to recite the story to her as if he had rehearsed the words a thousand times. "My father owned an iron mill in Upstate New York, a large, profitable business that my brother and I were to inherit. He paid his laborers a decent wage, and most were content there until rumors began to spread about how much better the conditions would be if they were unionized.

"Soon after that, a few men demanded to be allowed to start a union, but my father was so upset by what he saw as their traitorous actions that he fired them and refused to talk to anyone about the subject, until nearly half of his workers rose against him and called a general strike.

"I had come home that summer to work at the mill to earn extra money before entering law school in the fall, and I found myself squarely in the middle: a laborer on one hand and owner's son on the other. I understood the workers' side of it, but my brother, Joshua, who had gone to work for my father after his college graduation, was of the opinion that unionists would never be satisfied, and would always be pressing for more money and more benefits. We argued fiercely about it, until neither one of us would speak to the other."

Matthew sighed heavily. "And then the strike began. Some of the workers, myself included, crossed the picket lines to keep the mill running, but that only caused bitter feelings among those who had given up their wages to walk out for what they believed was the common good of all the laborers. I understood that, and I begged my father to close down the mill until they could resolve their differences; I even suggested starting an association that would be agreeable to both sides, but he wouldn't give in.

"It wasn't long before the strikers grew violent, beating anyone who crossed the lines, and even threatening us with guns and knives. It finally came to a head one steamy afternoon when they threw torches at the building. I think it was only meant as a warning, but they hadn't counted on how quickly the mill would ignite."

Beads of sweat appeared on Matthew's brow, as if he heard again the roar of the fire and the agonized screams of the trapped men, and smelled the charred timber and roasting flesh. He swallowed hard. "Sixty men died in that blaze: sixty good men with wives and children who would never see them again. To this day, I can still hear their desperate cries for help."

He shuddered violently and closed his eyes. "I knew my father was somewhere in the building, and I tried to find him, but a wall collapsed on me, trapping me inside his office. My brother had been away that morning, and when he arrived and found the building in flames, he broke through the line of police and braved the fire to search for us. He found me first, and after freeing my legs, he dragged me to safety. I tried to talk him out of returning to find my father—we both knew that to go back inside would be certain death—but Josh wouldn't listen. He said if he didn't try, he'd never be able to live with himself." Matthew drew a deep breath and let it out again. "They both perished."

Amanda's eyes filled with tears and her throat closed. She turned toward him and slipped her arms around his ribs, hugging him close to her.

"Before he left me," Matthew continued in a choked voice, "I grabbed Josh's arm, apologized for our disagreements, and asked him to forgive me. But he only smiled at me and said, 'Don't ask me to forgive you for your beliefs, Matt. I surely won't ask you to forgive me for mine. Just know I love you.' "

"Oh, Matthew," Amanda said, silent tears streaming from her eyes.

"When my mother learned what happened," he continued, "she had a stroke, and she never fully recovered from it. I lost everyone I loved that night, Amanda. I never thought to find that kind of selfless love again. And when I did, I was afraid—" He broke off, unable to finish.

Amanda hugged him tighter, listening to the rapid pounding of his heart. Slowly, his arms came around her, and when he spoke, his voice was husky with emotion. "I never wanted to fall in love with you. I didn't think there was a place for me in your heart, and I was afraid to risk being hurt again. So I convinced myself that what I felt was merely desire, and I—I forced you to play the part of a mistress to keep those other feelings at bay. I didn't see the truth until Marley attacked you and then it was nearly too late. I love you, Amanda."

Amanda could not answer for the tears clogging her throat. He kissed her then, and Amanda clung to him, starved for the taste and feel of him. When they finally paused to take a breath, she smiled up at him through her tears. "There's something I want you to see."

She led him up the staircase and to the doorway of his bedroom, then left him there while she walked to the middle of the room and turned around to face him, smiling expectantly.

There was a puzzled look on Matthew's face as he watched her, and then he began to look around the room. His eyes fell on the sleek, white dressing table, filled now with her toiletries. He strode quickly to the dressing room doors and threw them open. His gaze moved rapidly along the row of dresses that now hung opposite his own clothing, then raised to the hat boxes on the shelf overhead. He swung around, a look of wonder on his face. "You've come back."

Amanda smiled and walked into his arms.

She was home at last.

Recipes from the heartland of America

THE HOMESPUN
❧ COOKBOOK ❧
Tamara Dubin Brown

**Arranged by courses, this collection of
wholesome family recipes includes tasty
appetizers, sauces, and relishes, hearty main
courses, and scrumptious desserts—all created
from the popular *Homespun* series.**

Features delicious easy-to-prepare dishes, such as:

Orange Nut Bread

2 cups flour	1/3 cup orange marmalade
4 teaspoons baking powder	grated rind of 1 small orange
3/4 teaspoon salt	1 egg
4 tablespoons sugar	1 cup milk
1 cup chopped nuts	2 tablespoons melted butter

Sift dry ingredients. Add chopped nuts, marmalade, and grated
rind. Beat egg into milk and stir thoroughly into flour mixture.
Add melted butter. Pour into well-buttered and floured bread pan.
Let stand 20 minutes, then bake 1 hour at 350 degrees. Do not
cut until cold. Make thin sandwiches with butter and cream cheese
for afternoon tea.

A Berkley paperback coming February 1996

Also by Gregory A. Freeman

LAY THIS BODY DOWN:
THE 1921 MURDERS OF ELEVEN PLANTATION SLAVES

SAILORS
TO THE END

**THE DEADLY FIRE ON THE USS *FORRESTAL*
AND THE HEROES WHO FOUGHT IT**

GREGORY A. FREEMAN

AVON BOOKS
An Imprint of HarperCollinsPublishers

Grateful acknowledgment is made for permission to reprint lyrics from "Cast Your Fate to the Wind," by Vince Guaraldi, Carel Werber © 1947 (Renewed) Atzal Music, Inc. (BMI). All rights administered by Unichappell Music Inc. (BMI), all rights reserved, used by permission. Warner Bros Publications U.S. Inc., Miami, FL 33014.

Photo credits: All photos courtesy of the United States Navy, with these exceptions: 3. courtesy of Gary Shaver; 4. courtesy of Ken Killmeyer; 6. courtesy of Paul Friedman; 7. courtesy of Robert Shelton; 11. courtesy of Bill and Ruth Zwerlin; 29. *Life Magazine*; 32. Gregory A. Freeman. Front cover image: Official U.S. Navy Photograph by J. Nikas, courtesy of the National Museum of Naval Aviation. Back cover image: Official U.S. Navy Photograph, courtesy of Pete Clayton.

AVON BOOKS
An Imprint of HarperCollins*Publishers*
10 East 53rd Street
New York, New York 10022-5299

Copyright © 2002 by Gregory A. Freeman
ISBN: 0-06-054941-6
www.avonbooks.com

First Avon Books paperback printing: July 2003
First William Morrow hardcover printing: July 2002

Avon Trademark Reg. U.S. Pat. Off. and in Other Countries, Marca Registrada, Hecho en U.S.A.
HarperCollins® is a registered trademark of HarperCollins Publishers Inc.

Printed in the U.S.A.

10 9 8 7 6 5 4 3 2 1

This book is dedicated to the 134 men who died on the Forrestal *on July 29, 1967, and all the others on board that day who witnessed the tragedy of men dying young*

It is more useful to watch a man in times of peril, and in adversity to discern what kind of man he is; for then at last words of truth are drawn from the depths of his heart.

—LUCRETIUS
99–55 B.C.

CONTENTS

SAILORS
TO THE END

Chapter *1*

CAST YOUR FATE
TO THE WIND

July 1967

Bob Shelton was still troubled by the nightmare when he reached the bridge of the aircraft carrier. He had hoped that getting out of his bunk and making his way topside to watch the sun rise would help him shake it off, but it was still with him—the puzzling images of fire and smoke on the ship, and the vague sense of dread. He kept going over it in his mind as he watched the horizon begin to glow golden, finally breaking into brilliant sunlight while the USS *Forrestal* sailed in the waters off of Vietnam.

For Shelton, sunrise on the carrier was one of the few reliable indicators that time had passed. Life aboard the carrier could be disorienting and stressful as the young men worked long hours completely separated from the rest of the world. The *Forrestal* was an island where nothing seemed just like home, not even the hours that made up a day.

Most of the crew worked belowdecks, the long workdays and irregular sleep schedules melting together, with few clues from the outside world that yesterday had ended and today had begun. But for those who could see it, the sunrise was a reassuring reminder that there was life beyond the ship.

It hadn't taken Shelton long to realize that he didn't care much for life on board a carrier—even though he had always longed for a job in aviation, one that involved the planes that fascinated him so much. He wanted to be part of the fast-paced, glamorous world of navy flying even if he wasn't the one sitting in the cockpit. His deployment to the USS *Forrestal,* the world's biggest and most sophisticated warship, was a plum assignment by most standards and his actual workstation wasn't far from the flight-deck operations. But still, the novelty had worn off quickly and he had grown weary of standing in line for everything, whether it was a meal or a haircut. Like so many of the other thousands of young men on board, he was riding out his military service and looking forward to going home. Shelton had been in the navy for more than a year and still had a year left to serve on the *Forrestal.* The war in Vietnam was heating up, and the workload on the carrier had increased dramatically since the ship arrived in the Gulf of Tonkin a few days earlier and started launching air strikes against the mainland. He knew the next year on the *Forrestal* would be hard.

In the meantime, Shelton tried to take advantage of the little perks afforded him, and the sunrise was one of them. He reminded himself every day that many men belowdecks rarely got the chance to see daylight, much less something as beautiful as the day slowly breaking over the calm waters.

Shelton had access to this small joy because sheer luck and a few innate skills had resulted in his assignment to a group of sailors who worked on the bridge, standing within feet of the captain in the big control center that rose over the flight deck, the panoramic windows providing a bird's-eye view of everything happening on the flight deck and the world beyond. Shelton didn't work there every day, sometimes rotating through a few other assignments, but even if he wasn't working a shift on the bridge, no one minded if he hung around one of the nearby break areas for a cup of coffee and some conversation.

On this morning in late July 1967, Shelton was arriving even earlier than he had to. He wanted to take some time to relax before reporting to duty as quartermaster of the bridge, keeping detailed records of every order given and nearly everything that happened. It could be a demanding job if a lot was going on, so he liked to relax a bit first. And besides, he couldn't sleep after that nightmare.

Shelton was still a little shaken by it. The whole experience just seemed so unusual. Shelton wasn't the type to have nightmares; he couldn't even remember the last time he'd had one, and he rarely remembered any dreams when he woke up. He wasn't worried or upset about anything, so he was surprised by how much it had grabbed him. The experience was so bad that when he awoke, panicked and breathing like a racehorse, it took Shelton a minute to realize it was only a nightmare. The images were too vivid, the sense of horror too real.

Shelton had sprung up and sat on the edge of his bunk, waiting for his heart to slow down, wiping the sweat from his face. He was glad to be awake. He was glad to see that everything was okay, and yet he couldn't get past the feeling that something wasn't.

Shelton had lain back in his bunk, wide awake and still energized from the nightmare. With the rustling and snoring of his crewmates in the background, Shelton's mind kept flashing with images from the nightmare. There were great bursts of light, loud noises, and fire. Nothing was clear, but he did see fire. More than anything else, though, there was a terrible sense of fear and dread.

Shelton realized he would never get back to sleep, and he wasn't sure he wanted to anyway. After lying in his bunk for a while, wide awake, he got up and dressed. He was assigned to work on the bridge that day, so he had to put on the crisp white uniform instead of the denim work clothes he might wear to other assignments. On the way out of his sleeping area, he passed by his buddy James Blaskis, who was sound asleep just a few bunks away from his. Shelton noticed that Blaskis had a new pinup of a girl taped to the bottom of the bunk above him, yet another added to the collection just a few inches from Blaskis's face. Shelton often wondered how many of those girls were from magazines and how many were girlfriends from back home, but Blaskis never seemed interested in talking about them. It was one of the things Shelton just accepted about Blaskis without question.

Shelton and Blaskis had become close friends soon after coming aboard the *Forrestal,* though it was unlikely that they would ever have met in the civilian world and there was even less chance they would have struck up a friendship. But the military has a way of throwing very different men together in close quarters, giving them no other choice than to be friends or be miserable. When Shelton and Blaskis first met on the *Forrestal,* the only things they had in common were their mutual awe of the massive ship, their assignment to the same division, and their shared duties.

Both of them were also a bit older than the typical crew member. Shelton was twenty-two years old and Blaskis was twenty-one. Once they were thrown together, they found their differences immediately. Shelton was from Longview, Texas, and Blaskis was from Akron, Ohio. Shelton didn't understand much about places where it snowed and nobody rode a horse, and Blaskis couldn't relate to people who drank iced tea so sweet it might as well be syrup. But soon they discovered that their personalities fit well together, sharing a sense of humor that nobody seemed to find as funny as they did. Shelton could see that Blaskis was a real character, a fun-loving type who made everyone comfortable around him. The two young men were soon laughing about their differences and finding more and more things that drew them together.

One of the young men's favorite pastimes was listening to music. After the ship sailed for Vietnam and out of civilian radio contact, they had to rely on their own recordings, and someone in Shelton's division had bought a reel-to-reel tape player when the ship stopped in Rio de Janeiro. The player had become a centerpiece for the crew's recreation.

They would play the same music over and over again while they lounged around between work shifts or wrote letters home to their families. One song in particular had become Shelton's and Blaskis's favorite. "Cast Your Fate to the Wind," written by Carel Werber and Vince Guaraldi, was filled with a youthful optimism and willingness to see what the world would offer.

> *A month of nights, a year of days*
> *Octobers drifting into Mays*
> *I set my sail when the tide comes in*
> *I just cast my fate to the wind.*

They played the tape over and over, losing themselves in its dreamlike melody. The tune came to Shelton's mind as he stood there looking over the water, the sunrise and cool morning breeze helping to clear his head. A few cups of strong coffee also helped. The images from the nightmare were becoming fuzzier and he wasn't at all sure what had made it so scary. When it came time to start his shift, he stepped inside to the bridge and relieved the quartermaster who had worked the overnight shift. Shelton took his position behind the little desk where the logbook lay and prepared for a long day of taking careful notes, documenting any orders given and any activities on the bridge. As soon as he looked at the logbook, he saw that his buddy Blaskis had been there some time earlier.

"Bla is alive!" read a note in the margin. It was Blaskis's graffiti signature. Shelton saw it often.

The day was long, as usual, but fairly routine. The ship had just arrived in the Gulf of Tonkin a few days earlier to begin bombing targets in Southeast Asia, part of the escalating but still undeclared war against the communists trying to take over South Vietnam. Four hundred thousand ground troops were already fighting in the jungles, but the bombers from aircraft carriers stationed off the coast were playing a key role. They mostly targeted North Vietnamese supply lines, and in 1967 the bombing had moved closer to major cities like Hanoi and even to targets just shy of the Chinese border. The *Forrestal* launched bombing missions over Vietnam every day from a spot in the ocean called Yankee Station, several miles out but still close enough to see the coastline across the flat water.

That Thursday morning was uneventful, with the planes launching safely and then returning without harm. By late afternoon, Shelton was relieved from the bridge and he went belowdecks to perform a few small chores before dinner. After eating, he had a little free time to play cards and listen to music with his buddies. The day had turned out to be just another typical stretch of work, standing in line for meals, and a few moments with his friends. By the time he went to bed, Shelton had put the nightmare out of his mind. He fell asleep easily.

And then it happened again, but this time it was even worse.

Shelton was sound asleep when he suddenly shot up from his pillow with a stifled scream, sweat pouring off his face. There were explosions all around him, fire everywhere, and he was trapped. He was blinded by incredible flashes of light and the explosions were striking him as if he'd been kicked by a horse. Things were flying through the air, knocking people down and ripping bodies apart. He had little sense of what was happening, other than loud sounds and men screaming in pain and begging for help. He could see that they were still on the ship, that men were dying all around him, and he was going to die with them.

After he woke up, the details began to blur in his mind, but the nightmare was even more intense than the night before and it held him in its grip as he frantically looked around the dark compartment. He wanted to flee, but he didn't know what to do. Time stretched as he tried to separate the hell in his mind from what he saw around him. No fire in the compartment. No alarms. No explosions.

It was quiet on the ship.

Oh my God. That was worse than the last one.

Last night's had been bad, but Shelton was far more shaken by this nightmare. He couldn't get rid of the fear that it brought, even after he came to realize that he was safe in his bunk.

He was sweating and his chest was still heaving when he swung his legs out of the bunk and walked out of the compartment. There was no way in hell he was getting back to sleep. It was early, about 4:00 A.M., but Shelton had gotten all the rest he was going to get. As on the previous morning, he threw on his white uniform and headed up to the bridge. It was hours before he had to report to duty, but he couldn't have stayed in that bunk any longer.

Again, he had passed by his buddy Blaskis and watched him sleeping peacefully.

Chapter 2

THE SAFEST PLACE TO BE

Bob Shelton and James Blaskis fit right in with the *Forrestal* crew, which was a mixture of young men who were inexperienced in nearly everything and old hands who had been riding the seas for many years. In some ways, they were a slice of America in 1967. The young far outnumbered the older men on the ship, and back home America was just getting used to having teenagers and young adults swarming the country in record numbers. Youthfulness has always been welcome in the military, however, because some jobs can be done only by someone who still thinks he will never die. The old hands on board knew better, because many of them had been through the kinds of experiences that will convince a young man of his mortality. On the *Forrestal*, these veteran sailors guided the youngsters through the daily hazards and lessons of life on an aircraft carrier, providing support that many of the boys would not understand or appreciate until they, too, were old enough to offer advice. It was a common scene to see an older sailor explaining the navy's ways to a lot of younger men who were eager to do the right thing, if only they knew how.

The navy has excelled at turning boys into men, and for many, it represented an opportunity for a career and travel that were otherwise out of reach. Times were difficult for young men in the States in 1967, with the looming possibility of a draft letter arriving in the mail. Even if they hadn't been drafted yet, any day they could be, so employers were reluctant to waste time hiring them.

If a young man did get drafted, he would most likely end up in the infantry and be sent to the jungles of Vietnam. Even though most American youths didn't know much about what was going on in Southeast Asia, they did know that a lot of boys already had been killed in the jungle wars. But if they volunteered instead of waiting to be drafted, they could select which branch of service they would serve in, and might even have some input into the sort of duty they were assigned. That is how a great many of the young men ended up on the *Forrestal.*

If you weren't a gung ho volunteer, eager to be in the thick of things, an aircraft carrier was the plum assignment. Vietnam had little navy to speak of, and carriers did all their work sitting out in the water, far away from any land-based threats. Being assigned to the *Forrestal,* one of the world's biggest and most powerful carriers, was a relief to many because they saw it as the safest place they could be. Safety is a relative matter, of course, and an aircraft carrier actually can be extremely dangerous. But for a young man going to Vietnam in 1967, there was little doubt that he would go home after a year or two on the *Forrestal*. They would ride out their tours of duty there and then return home to pick up the lives they left, satisfied that they had fulfilled their obligations.

Shelton and Blaskis joined the *Forrestal* about the same time as Ken Killmeyer, Robert Zwerlein, and Paul Friedman. When they first reported to the ship, they were all dumbstruck by its size. Especially for youngsters who grew up in small towns and had yet to see anything of the world, the ship looked like the biggest thing on earth. And they weren't too far from the truth.

When she was constructed, between 1951 and 1954, the *Forrestal* was the largest warship ever built. At 1,039 feet long, the carrier would reach the eightieth floor of the Empire State Building if stood on end. Even sitting in the water, she was as tall as a twenty-five-story building. The ship's tall masts, which are full of radar and other equipment, were designed to swing down and lie on the deck temporarily so the ship could pass under the Brooklyn Bridge.

The flight deck was 252 feet wide and as long as three and a half football fields, creating four acres of "sovereign U.S. territory," as the navy likes to brag. The ship displaced eighty thousand tons and was way too big to fit through the Panama Canal, making it necessary to go the long way, an eastern route around South Africa, in order to get from her usual territory in the Atlantic to the Pacific.

The *Forrestal* was so powerful that she was considered to be the crown jewel in the navy's fleet, and she had to be named for a prominent leader from American history—the late James V. Forrestal, a former secretary of the navy and the first secretary of defense, acclaimed for building the modern navy. She was nicknamed "FID" for "First in Defense," a reference to both her namesake and her position as the country's big muscle that would be moved into position against an aggressor. Later, the navy added "Fidelity, Integrity, and Dignity" to the FID moniker.

Military ships tend to get a reputation as they age, and the *Forrestal* was known for always being on time, and also as the "ship with a heart" because of the charity work that her crew always did in the local communities they visited around the world. They would lend a hand with building a clinic or would donate books to a third-world library.

As the new men stood in long lines waiting to board the ship, her gray hulk was all they could see. It took up their entire field of vision. Once they boarded, the size of the ship was underscored by one of the first scenes they witnessed. As the newbies walked by with duffel bags slung over a shoulder and their jaws hanging open in awe, some of the crew already on board were playing football in one of the big open hangar decks. Not a scaled-down game on just a small piece of open deck; they were playing a full-sized football game, with plenty of room to spare.

The men arrived at the ship through slightly different paths, but many of them had similar motives. Shelton and nineteen-year-old Ken Killmeyer had both faced trouble getting work because of their draft status. In his hometown of Pittsburgh, Killmeyer had just graduated from high school and was still living with his parents while looking for work. The first question employers always asked was "What's your draft status?" And when Killmeyer told them he was 1A, meaning he was at the top of the list, employers rolled their eyes and sighed. The employers were as disappointed as Killmeyer that they couldn't hire the tall, lanky kid who obviously wanted to work. "You could be the best guy in the world, but you're only going to be around for a short while and then you're gone," they said.

After a lot of rejections, Killmeyer decided not to sit around and wait to be drafted. He talked it over with his dad, and they decided that the navy was a safe bet.

"Well, you're not going to be shot at. You'll survive it all, and you won't even be in the jungles," his dad told him one night. "You'll be coming home, Ken. We don't know that for sure if you get drafted."

Shelton had arrived at his decision in the same way, but he was out on his own and twenty-one years old by the time he started thinking about enlisting. Shelton had grown up in a little town called Kilgore, Texas, a flat piece of land with oil fields that employed nearly everyone there. He had worked in the oil fields himself as a teenager and then ambled around East Texas for a while before taking a job managing a gas station in Longview,

Texas. It was a decent job, but he was smart enough to know there was no future in it. And when he tried to find a better job, he received the same response Killmeyer heard in Pittsburgh: "Thanks, but we're looking for men who have fulfilled their military obligation." Every time he heard that, it reminded him that he could be drafted and end up in the jungles of Vietnam.

So in August 1965, Shelton took a walk downtown to the air force recruiting office.

I might as well get this over with, he thought.

Shelton had been interested in flying since he was a child, so the air force seemed like a good choice. The recruiter was glad to have him and, after a pep talk about why he should join, sent Shelton home to get his birth certificate. Shelton came back an hour later, ready to sign up with the air force. But when he reached the recruiting office, it was closed. Shelton figured maybe the recruiter had just stepped out for a minute, so he waited outside the door. Before long, someone from the navy recruiting office next door stuck his head outside.

"Hey, it's hot out here. You might as well wait in here if you want."

Shelton took him up on the offer. It wasn't long before he had agreed to join the navy and pursue a career in aviation electronics. It wasn't the air force, but he'd be working in the exciting world of naval aviation on an aircraft carrier.

Killmeyer and Shelton first went through boot camp and studied different fields for a short while before being assigned to active duty. Killmeyer was excited about the prospect of serving in the navy and studied hard for various duties. But his first assignment to an active-duty post at a Philadelphia naval station was to keep the milk machines full in the mess hall. From morning to night, he was filling the machines with plain and chocolate milk. In between, he cleaned the floors.

When he was called to the *Forrestal* in March 1967, Killmeyer was eager to go. No matter what his job would be on board, surely it would be more exciting than filling milk machines.

When Shelton drove into the Norfolk, Virginia, naval base to board the ship, he didn't think much of the drab, utilitarian base. The *Forrestal,* on the other hand, was more impressive, a huge gray monster looming in front of him. He'd worked on marinas around the Texas coast, so he thought maybe he'd like being on a ship. He hadn't yet stood in too many lines.

When Paul Friedman graduated from high school in 1965, all of his buddies received a stern reminder that they might be drafted soon. They all had to strip down to their underwear and wait in line for preinduction physicals, the exams that would help classify them as good prospects or not so good prospects for an early draft. It was a clear warning that Friedman might not get to spend the next few years on the beach and working small jobs, as he had hoped. Like Killmeyer and Shelton, Friedman decided to join the navy as a matter of self-preservation, a way to control his destiny. He could have gone to college and deferred his draft for years, as many did, but Friedman just didn't see himself as college material. Joining the military was not a far-fetched idea for most young men anyway, because they had been raised in the John Wayne generation, an era in which military service generally was seen as honorable, though sometimes inconvenient. If they cared one whit about global politics, they probably believed that communism was a spreading scourge that must be stopped, and also probably believed in the domino theory as much as their parents did. In the early and mid-1960s, the antiwar movement had not yet seized the nation, and though being drafted and sent to Vietnam was scary, there was nothing strange about serving your country. Joining the military was a perfectly reasonable thing to consider, and if it gave you more control over your life, it could be the best option.

When a high school buddy returned from navy boot camp for a visit, Friedman grilled him about which assignments might be best. If Friedman volunteered, the navy would allow him to select his general track, but there would be no guarantees. Like a kid leafing through a toy catalog, Friedman looked through the navy manual to see which jobs he might like. Navy corpsman? No, they're the medics who go in with the marines. He might as well join the marines and go to the jungles. Weather forecasting? Hmmm, maybe. The school was in Lakehurst, New Jersey, so Friedman could spend time sending up weather balloons not too far from home. But then he saw navy aviation, which he knew meant carriers, and that was exciting to him. And besides, carriers never got to within one hundred miles of the real action.

Friedman was very reluctant to leave his home in Rockaway Beach, New York, a real beach community outside of New York City that provided this Jewish kid the opportunity to live the life of a surfer. He'd worked at the World's Fair that summer in New York City, but Friedman spent his days riding his surfboard along the waves and romancing beautiful girls on the beach. It was a sweet life for a good-looking eighteen-year-old. Like many young men in the mid-sixties, Friedman wasn't at all happy about being torn away from a good thing. The only consolation was that he was pretty sure he would return.

Down south in Atlanta, however, returning from the war didn't make Ed Roberts feel much better about going. Sure, he was glad to get in the navy and avoid the jungle fighting, but he just couldn't understand why the government wouldn't leave him and his friends alone. They had worked hard in the past years to make their rock-and-roll band a success, and they were finally getting somewhere. Then the draft notices started showing up.

Roberts grew up in Atlanta. He had started playing the drums when he was twelve years old, first in the school band, then in every other band he could join—the dance band, the all-district band, the all-city band. In 1964, the year he graduated from high school, he teamed up with some buddies and formed a band called the Fugitives, after the popular TV show. The Fugitives started out playing old standards they'd learned in school, like "Give My Regards to Broadway," but then the Beatles hit it big. They started learning all the Fab Four's songs and suddenly they were in demand for parties and were even booking commercial venues around Atlanta. The tall kid banging away on the drums was starting to think his band could really amount to something.

Every one of them knew that the draft could throw a wrench in the plans, and like all young men across the country, they were exploring their options. Roberts's father had seen a lot of combat in Europe during World War II, and he didn't want his son to go through the same thing. They talked it over as Roberts worked with his father during the day in his heating and plumbing business. The older Roberts urged his son to look into the National Guard and the reserve programs that would help keep him out of Vietnam, and Roberts agreed that was a good choice. Whatever he ended up doing in the military, he didn't want to be in a jungle where you couldn't see the people shooting at you. And he had read enough about Vietnam to know that the Vietnamese were using dirty tactics like booby traps. He didn't want to go.

Roberts and one of his buddies started checking into the National Guard and the reserves, but they found that all of the Atlanta units had waiting lists. They couldn't sign up right away, but Roberts made friends with a couple of the recruiters at the naval air station outside Atlanta and started thinking about the navy as an option. When he talked it over with his dad, they agreed that the navy might be his best choice.

"At least you have a place to sleep and regular meals," his father said. "That's more than you're going to get in the army."

Even so, Roberts didn't want to join the navy yet, because the Fugitives were getting bookings and having a good time. He also was studying biology at Georgia State University on a part-time basis. He knew it was risky to wait until he was drafted, so he also hedged his bet by hanging around the naval air station and talking to the recruiters. They treated him to free meals in the chow halls and talked about everything from the navy to the Fugitives. They liked the kid and made it clear that they'd like to sign him up for the reserves if only the list weren't so long already. But they told him they would help if things got desperate.

"If you get your draft notice, come right over here right away," one of the navy recruiters told him. "Don't even go home. Have your mother watch out for it and call you if it comes in the mail, then you come right over here."

Roberts's nineteenth birthday was approaching, and he knew the draft notice could be coming soon. He was worried about what might happen, but he also was excited about what was already happening with the Fugitives. In February 1966, the band landed an audition for a touring rock-and-roll show called "Holiday for Teens." If they could get signed for the tour, the Fugitives would tour the country, which would give them all sorts of opportunities to contact record producers. This was a huge development for a bunch of Atlanta boys, just at the time when nothing was more glamorous for a teenager than being in a rock-and-roll band.

The Fugitives practiced hard in the weeks before the audition. And then just days before the audition, Roberts's mother called him while he was working with his father to say that his draft papers had arrived. Roberts's heart sank, but he did what he had planned. He raced over to the naval air station and told his friends there he had been drafted. Just as they had promised, they bent the rules to get him into the navy reserve program. He'd still have to go in the military, but this way, he got a little more time.

The reserve program required him to sign up right away but he could spend the first year training part-time at the local base. Then he would be assigned to active duty for two years, followed by another year in the reserve. Roberts signed the papers.

Just a few days later, the Fugitives were auditioning for the rock-and-roll tour. They made it and soon found themselves driving around the country in five Oldsmobile Coronados and five Vista Cruiser station wagons plastered with "Holiday for Teens." The tour was a blast, with the Fugitives playing for screaming teens from Miami to Las Vegas. They made a television commercial and were in a parade, and they had girls adoring them. Every time a girl screamed, they were a little more confident that their band had a future.

The tour lasted for a few months and then the band was back home in Atlanta, still playing a lot of shows around town. Roberts still hadn't told his bandmates that he'd signed up for the navy, but now it was time to report to the base for his training. There wasn't very much for him to do, certainly nothing rigorous. Mostly he just learned the basics of navy life, like swabbing a deck and polishing the brass. But the navy made one dramatic change right away. They cut Roberts's hair.

To be in a rock-and-roll band in 1966, you had

to have long hair. Roberts and his bandmates had been cultivating their look for a while, and they all had slightly shaggy hairstyles, not really all that long but enough to set them apart from the crisp hairstyles of Middle America. When Roberts showed up for practice one day with his hair trimmed short, the Fugitives were outraged. How could he ruin his hair that way? Roberts couldn't tell them the truth. He was afraid his friends would be angry that he'd joined the navy, so he lied and told them he cut his hair just because he wanted to look good for his college classes. They were mad at him, but he could live with that.

He kept his secret as long as he could—going to his navy training on the weekends and still showing up for the band's gigs—but finally he had to tell them. He was scheduled to go on active duty in February 1967, and after that, the Fugitives would have to find a new drummer.

Roberts didn't know yet that he would end up on the world's most powerful ship. When the *Forrestal* was put in service in 1955, she was the navy's pride and joy, the biggest, best, and most advanced aircraft carrier the world had ever seen. She would soon start collecting a number of historic "firsts" in naval aviation, and before her long career ended. The *Forrestal* ushered in a new class of aircraft carriers that would follow her design and thus be categorized as "*Forrestal* class." She was the first "supercarrier" ever designed, and she represented everything the navy had learned from the pivotal use of carriers in World War II and the years since. The *Forrestal* was built with more than double the fuel and weapons loads of the most modern *Essex*-class carriers that came before her, and promised to be more useful and versatile than any other carrier on the sea. Her flight deck extended one hundred yards farther than the *Midway*-class ships that were developed at the end of World War II. Built in the early days of the Cold War, it helped fulfill the United States' goal of having the biggest and most powerful military in the world. And it would even carry nuclear weapons at times, ready to deliver them to ground targets within distance of her planes.

Despite her size, the *Forrestal* could move in a hurry. Her four main propulsion engines delivered more than 260,000 horsepower, enough to keep 1,430 1968 Ford Mustangs cruising along at ample speed. Those oil-burning engines powered four propellers that could move the ship at a brisk thirty-three knots, about thirty-eight mph. (A top speed of thirty-eight mph may not sound like much unless you remember that this is a war machine the size of a skyscraper coming your way.) The crew was made up of the sailors assigned to the ship itself, plus the airplane pilots and their own specialized crew. When an air wing was aboard, the *Forrestal* carried a total crew of about five thousand men and about ninety planes.

The *Forrestal* was the first carrier specifically designed to handle jet aircraft. The ship was designed and built at an exciting time in naval aviation, part of the service's huge leap forward in using jets rather than propeller-driven planes. She was the first carrier built with four steam catapults instead of two hydraulic ones, and four deck-edge elevators instead of three. Her flight deck was the first to be designed as a key load-bearing member of the ship's structure, rather than just a flat surface stuck on top of the ship. That change reflected the sophistication of carrier design since the days when they were seen as oddball ships with a runway stuck on top. With the flight deck as a load-bearing part of the ship's structure, the entire ship was strengthened. But there was a cost: if the flight deck was severely damaged, the rest of the ship could be compromised.

Designing such an advanced ship required the very best of 1950s technology. The *Forrestal* was breaking new ground in many ways, and engineers were challenged to come up with new ideas that were difficult to test. Anchoring a ship, for instance, is a fairly simple concept until applied to a ship this big. For such a massive vessel, the anchor chains had to be both heavy enough to hold the ship in place and strong enough not to snap when pulled hard. The engineers designed a 2,160-foot monster weighing 246 tons, each individual link twenty-eight inches long and seventeen inches wide, weighing 360 pounds each. The chain's breaking strain was calculated to be 2.5 million pounds.

Engineers were still refining the ship's design as her keel was laid on July 14, 1952, trying to incorporate the best innovations from the U.S. Navy's own experience with carriers and also the lessons of other countries. The ship was originally designed with the same axial landing deck that most carriers had used up to that point, meaning the "runway" on the deck ran the entire length of the ship from one end to the other. But as the ship was being built, the designers switched to an angle deck design that the British had developed. This method used a landing zone on the rear of the ship that was angled off to the left of the ship's centerline, essentially dividing the ship into a rear landing area and a forward catapult launching area. Previous designs had required the entire deck to be cleared for landings, or necessitated net barriers or similar devices to keep landing planes from running into the other planes parked forward on the deck. With the angle design, the carrier could conduct launches and landings simultaneously, and planes could more easily take off again if they missed the arresting cable. They would continue off to the port side of the ship rather than all the way straight down the length of the flight deck.

The *Forrestal* also was the first ship to incorporate a system of mirrored lights to guide pilots in for landing, instead of the World War II–era method of having a man stand on the deck with signal paddles and wave them at the pilot.

The result was a ship of such strength, size, and endurance that the *Forrestal* was an all-purpose carrier; no other carrier was better at anything. The ship was christened and launched on December 11, 1954, and assigned to the naval station at Norfolk, Virginia. Her total building costs came to $188.9 million.

She also was designed with some previously unimaginable creature comforts. Shelton and Blaskis slept on foam-mattress bunks in cubicles that afforded at least a little privacy, barely realizing this was a substantial change from the bare-bones crew quarters of previous carriers and almost all other navy ships. Another major improvement was the ship's air-conditioning.

Most ships had no air-conditioning at all, and the crew of a carrier certainly could not expect such luxury even when cruising through the hottest climates. But seven five-hundred-ton air-conditioning units on the *Forrestal* provided more cooling power than that used at Radio City Music Hall. The crew could enjoy air-conditioned living spaces twenty-four hours a day, though much of the working space was not cooled. Aviators could even take an escalator up to the flight deck, a more necessary addition than it might seem. Once the aviators were suited up for a flight, they would be lugging nearly one hundred pounds of gear. If they hustled up four flights of steps, they would be perspiring heavily by the time they got to the plane and soaking wet by the time they reached the cold air of high altitude flight.

The *Forrestal* was promoted as the first carrier to try to make the crew reasonably comfortable during long voyages, but the ship's builder explained that the improved accommodations "are not just for luxury, because experts have found that air-conditioning and good recreation and sleeping quarters will make the *Forrestal* a 'happy ship' which will lead to greater crew efficiency."

Though by 1967 she still hadn't seen a single day of combat, the *Forrestal* was known as the very best of naval might. She was the testing site for many new ideas in naval aviation, conducting trials in the 1960s for the introduction of the new F4H-1 Phantom II and A3J-1 Vigilante fighter and attack jets. In one of the most amazing feats, the ship hosted the largest aircraft ever to land or take off from an aircraft carrier: a C-130 Hercules, a fat, cumbersome cargo plane designed to move heavy equipment and troops. The "Herc" is about as different from the sleek carrier-based planes as you can get and still call it an airplane. Just to see if it could be done, the Herc made several takeoffs and landings on the *Forrestal* in 1963 and 1964 with cargo test weights ranging from 85,000 to 121,000 pounds. Though the tests were successful, the navy never again found reason to land a Herc on an aircraft carrier, leaving the *Forrestal* to hold that record.

The ship's size and versatility made her useful as one of the big sticks wielded by American presidents. When a world conflict erupted, the first question asked by American presidents usually was "Where are the carriers?" The *Forrestal* could be moved into position, ostensibly for "training exercises," to remind someone that the United States was the strongest kid on the block. No matter how strong or wild-eyed crazy the other country's leader was, the sight of an American aircraft carrier parked just off his coastline often was enough of a reminder not to mess around too much. To a very large extent, that actually is the purpose of the aircraft carrier in the modern military arena. As part of the American arsenal throughout the Cold War, the *Forrestal* could accomplish much of its mission by simply existing, just sitting in the water and looking fierce. When operating in international waters, an aircraft carrier and its accompanying ships do not need the permission of host countries for landing or overflight rights. Aircraft carriers are sovereign U.S. territory that steams anywhere in international waters—and most of the surface of the globe is water.

That is not to say, however, that the *Forrestal* was all bluster and swagger. The presence of an aircraft carrier off a country's coastline is little more than a curiosity until the residents understand exactly how much power it can aim at them. The *Forrestal* could launch nearly one hundred aircraft in an all-out strike, most of them loaded with the latest, most deadly bombs and missiles. The planes and weapons on the carrier alone often represented more than the entire military resources of the country staring at the big ship on the horizon.

Speed was an essential element of the *Forrestal*'s operations. When the president wanted to intimidate another country, he usually needed to do it quickly. That meant a matter of days, not weeks. That is one reason that modern carriers were designed to be as fast as possible. High speeds, however, are not easy to achieve and sustain when pushing something as big as an aircraft carrier through the water, so they were designed with power plants that are as big as the ship's structure will allow. The *Forrestal* ran on fuel oil, but nuclear power is now the preferred method for powering carriers because it can easily move the ship at the thirty-three knots, or thirty-eight miles per hour, that is considered the minimum top speed for a carrier. Unlike most ships, which are designed only for short sprints at high speed, the navy wants its carriers to be able to sustain a speed of twenty knots, or twenty-three miles per hour, for long distances.

Everything on the *Forrestal* was a wonder to the new sailors on board. When Shelton first reported for duty, he was awestruck by the complexity of nearly everything and every task on board. Simply going from his bunk to breakfast made him feel like a mouse scurrying through a maze in search of the cheese.

One of the first priorities for the young men assigned to the *Forrestal* was to learn just how an aircraft carrier works. This was no ordinary type of ship, and understanding the strange world of a carrier was essential to surviving your time there, much less doing your job well. As the newcomers would soon learn, those two goals often went hand in hand.

The ship could be described as an airport operating under the worst conditions possible. It was like a busy metropolitan airport reduced to just one runway, with planes landing and taking off at the same time, often less than a minute apart. The airport was moving back and forth, and up and down. The airplanes were loaded with some of the deadliest armaments in the world, and live bombs and rockets were stacked all over the runway. Seawater and fuel oil covered everything in sight. There might be an enemy in the vicinity who wanted to destroy the airport. And of course, all the planes taking off that day had to be able to land there in a few hours, no matter what.

Operating an airport under those conditions required a number of special techniques. Taking off from the *Forrestal* was not easy, even for specially designed airplanes. The carriers would always turn into the wind during flight operations, and the crew carefully calculated how to combine the ship's own speed through the water with the existing wind to achieve the optimum wind across the flight deck. With the proper wind speed across the flight deck, planes could much more easily land and take off because the wind created more lift.

Even under optimal conditions, however, airplanes needed a lot of assistance in taking off from an aircraft carrier. The *Forrestal*'s flight deck looked huge when you were walking around on it, but it seemed like a postage stamp when trying to land or take off from it. There was no room for the long acceleration run that would be normal at an air base on land, so the planes had to be artificially accelerated. That meant actually shooting the planes off the deck.

The *Forrestal* used a catapult system that attached to the front wheels of planes and, with a tremendous burst of energy, flung them off the deck at high speed. The steam-powered "cats" took a plane from a dead stop to sometimes 150 mph in as little as three seconds and one hundred yards when everything went well. Otherwise, there was a lot of swearing about "bad cats" and "cold cats." The catapult system consisted of long pistons underneath the flight deck, with a shuttle on the deck surface that was a little bigger than a shoebox. The plane was attached to the shuttle with a tow bar, and the crew carefully calculated the amount of power needed to launch the plane. The calculations were extremely important, taking into consideration the type of plane, the total weight, the wind speed, and other factors. With the proper information, the crew could power the catapult with just the right amount of steam and send the plane airborne. Too much power on the catapult would rip the plane apart, the tow shuttle tearing the front wheel assembly right off the plane. The rest of the plane might or might not stay on the deck. But with too little power, a "cold shot," the plane would be slowly dragged to the front edge of the ship and lightly tossed in the water just ahead of the carrier. Aviators had to be ready to "punch out" with the ejection seats during a cat launch; if things went wrong, there wasn't much time to react.

For the aviators, though, the real nail-biting, sweat-drenching operation on a carrier came when it was time to land. The launch did not require a lot of aviators except to sit there and endure the harsh catapult, ready to respond quickly once they were airborne or headed into the water. But when it was time to land, the aviator had to call upon every bit of training, innate skill, and experience. The difficulty of landing on an aircraft carrier is legendary, and for good reason.

The cliché is that landing on an aircraft carrier is a "controlled crash." Cliché or not, that's an apt description. Unlike anything experienced on a commercial flight or a private plane, a landing on the *Forrestal* was an extremely hard, sudden stop. The plane slammed down onto the deck and was stopped by the arresting gear in a matter of just a second or two. That meant that a thirty-ton plane went from its landing speed of more than one hundred miles per hour to zero miles per hour in about two seconds.

There simply wasn't enough room on a carrier deck to bring planes in for a gentle landing and then a leisurely stop. Instead, they had to be snatched out of the air. The planes were equipped with a tail hook, a bar several feet long that could be extended down from the tail of the plane. When the pilot landed on the deck, the tail hook snagged one of the four big cables stretched across the landing portion of the deck. The cables were only the visible part of the arresting gear, attached below deck to massive machines that controlled how much the cable would give when a plane hooked it, and absorbing much of the force exerted by the plane. The arresting cable had some give to it, extending out a few dozen yards when the plane pulled on it, but the tension had to be just right. When a plane was approaching the carrier to land, the pilot radioed how much fuel, armaments, and cargo remained on the plane so that the arresting gear could be calibrated to stop the plane with just enough resistance. Too much and the tail hook could snap right off the plane and cause it to veer out of control. Too little and the cable would stretch out as the fifty-million-dollar plane continued forward off the side of the ship, right into the water. When a plane went in the water, it was gone forever.

When all went well, the effect was an almost immediate, eye-popping stop. If the plane missed the arresting cable with the tail hook, that was called a "bolter." Though problematic, bolters were not at all uncommon. Even great pilots missed a landing once in a while on a carrier. It could happen because the pilot just didn't hit the landing right, or sometimes because he did everything right but the tail hook still bounced right over the wire he was aiming for. (Even with four wires to hit, the angle of approach and where the plane first hit the deck usually meant there was a chance at hooking only one wire. If the plane missed that one, the tail hook wasn't likely to hit any of the others as the plane continued forward.) When a plane missed the wire, the pilot had to take off again *immediately*. There was absolutely no time to waste, because even a slight hesitation would rob the plane of the boost needed to get off the deck again. The plane would then roll right off the edge of the flight deck and into the sea, or perhaps career into something on the deck. Because there was no time at all for the pilot to react to missing the wire, a carrier-deck landing required the pilot to go full throttle when the plane was just about to touch down. If the tail hook caught a wire, the plane would still stop and the pilot could throttle back when he felt the hard lurch. If the tail hook missed, the plane was at full power and the pilot immediately took off again. The idea was that the pilot would go onto the deck as if he were intending all along to just hit the deck with his rear wheels and then go up again (a "touch and go" landing). That minimized the need to react when, in fact, he didn't catch the wire.

When necessary, the *Forrestal* could "trap" planes for landing as often as every thirty seconds. As soon as they landed, the planes began taxiing away and folding their wings, if necessary, to clear the deck. One crewman, the "hook runner," was always standing by with a long crowbar, his only job to watch the landing and rush forward to disentangle the arresting cable from the tail hook when that happened. Others were in charge of stowing the plane out of the way and chaining it to the deck, a safety precaution that kept planes from rolling off the deck edge in the event of a slight list or a strong gust of wind. The crewmen responsible for chaining the planes down would sometimes challenge one another between landings, conducting little races in which they hustled forward with their heavy chains to see who could complete the chaindown first.

Landings on the *Forrestal* were assisted by a system of landing-signal lights to the left of the deck, known as the "meatball." The meatball was an array of special lights, each about the size of a car's headlight, that the pilot used to determine if he was on the proper approach to the carrier. The lights were configured so that a pilot on the proper glide path would see the middle lens illuminated, but a too-high glide path would show the top lens and a low glide path would show the bottom lens. When a plane was approaching the carrier and given permission to land, the flight controller on the ship asked the pilot to "call the ball." The pilot responded by saying he was "on the ball," letting control know that the meatball was in sight and the pilot was proceeding with landing. If the pilot could not see the meatball, he responded with "Clara."

Besides the meatball, there was the landing signal officer (LSO) to help guide planes in. This person was a descendant of the sailor who used to stand on the deck and wave paddles at World War II pilots to indicate how they should adjust their approach. But with the meatball doing much of that work, the LSO acted more as a coach, offering advice on how to correct a landing and then grading each and every landing or attempt. The LSO was always a highly experienced pilot, and his or her critiques could make or break a naval aviator's career. Too many bad landings and you didn't get to play on the carrier anymore. You had to go back to "the beach," an embarrassing rejection by your fellow pilots.

When the plane was approaching the carrier to land, it was the LSO's voice that came over the radio with commands for improving the glide path. The words were terse, providing only the information needed and not a single word more. A good LSO worked with the pilot's own instincts by telling him what to do, not what was wrong. Since all naval aviators, including the LSO, were egoists who didn't like being criticized, a command for "power!" was received better than the criticism that the plane was "low." When split-second reactions are crucial, such distinctions become important. The LSO watched the lights on the front of the plane to discern whether it was in the proper glide path, and if the plane was too far out of the right path to correct it in time, the LSO hit the "pickle switch" that was always in his hands, and the meatball would signal a wave-off. The pilot had to abort the landing attempt and go around for another try. The LSO also was the one who would warn the pilot when a landing attempt was doomed and the plane was about to crash; sometimes the

LSO's experienced eye could see the crash coming a heartbeat before the pilot realized, and that difference could save the pilot's life. The LSO would shout "Eject! Eject! Eject!" to the pilot, who would probably respond without taking a second to doubt the LSO.

There was always one LSO on the radio speaking to the pilots, but there would be several others on the LSO platform just to the left of the landing area, all watching the landing carefully and administering a grade. The biggest part of a pilot's grade was determined by whether he landed successfully and, if so, what wire he hit on landing. Landing without killing anybody or causing damage usually got you an "OK" grade, which was amended by what wire you caught. Catching wire one was considered dangerous because the plane came in too low, and wire four was bad because the plane almost overshot the landing zone. Wire two was acceptable, but the best grade came from hitting wire three. So an "OK three" was the grade pilots were looking for.

The LSOs were the only people on the flight deck not wearing ear protection, because they had to be able to hear the sounds of the incoming jet to know what the pilot was doing with the engines. The LSO platform put them in an extremely vulnerable position if a jet crashed on landing, so there was a safety net nearby where the LSOs would run and jump if they had to avoid flaming wreckage.

In addition to the violence and split-second timing inherent in a carrier landing, pilots had to contend with a runway that was moving up and down, left and right. The pilots had to land on this small, small, small bit of metal in the pitch-black ocean.

One of the pilots taking that challenge nearly every day was a young John McCain, later to become a prominent United States senator and presidential candidate. In 1967, his assignment to the *Forrestal* was a chance to further his family's legacy. Despite a strong family background in the navy, with his grandfather and father both four-star admirals, his attempt to follow in their footsteps did not start well. He nearly washed out of the naval academy, his bad temper and lack of discretion nearly overcoming his highly praised skills as a sailor and even the family connections that greased the rails for him. But by the time he was assigned to the *Forrestal* in 1967, his reputation had changed. Instead of being known as a naval-academy midshipman with a hearty disdain for the rules, he was now known as a *naval aviator* with a hearty disdain for the rules.

There had been some important changes since he left the academy, however. McCain still was a brash young man who knew how to have a good time, and who was willing to give a lesson to anyone else who might be less innately skilled in that area. And when it came to what he considered the less important conventions of navy life, like how well your bed was made, he still didn't care much. But by the time he hit the deck of the *Forrestal,* he also was known as a serious aviator and people were starting to think he might actually live up to his family's reputation. He was a maverick, but he was good. The navy likes that.

McCain already had served aboard the aircraft

carriers *Intrepid* and *Enterprise,* and those deployments had been eventful for him. He had been aboard the *Enterprise* when she sailed to Cuba for Kennedy's showdown over nuclear missiles, ready to fly off at a moment's notice when the president declared war. Throughout it all, McCain adopted the standard-issue demeanor for military pilots—calm, maybe a bit cocky, but at all times composed and fearless.

It was during his term on the *Enterprise* that Mc-Cain started to think seriously about where he wanted his naval career to go. Though he had been less than enthusiastic about the navy in his younger years, by this time McCain was thinking that he might shoot for the top. Even in his most rowdy days, McCain had always held a deep respect for the notions of honor and service to your country, and as he matured a bit, he saw that he could focus on those aspects of a naval career instead of the meaningless parts he still disdained. The young man who saw no problem with having a water balloon fight in his room and talking back to his superiors at the naval academy was starting to think that he would like to command a carrier someday. Perhaps his service on the *Forrestal,* flying bombing runs over North Vietnam, would be a good step in that direction.

McCain and the other pilots would be put to the test during their time on the *Forrestal.* Flying on and off a carrier strained the skills of even the best, most experienced aviators, not to mention that people might be trying to shoot you down in the meantime. The pilots agreed, enthusiastically, that landing on a carrier deck at night in bad weather was the absolute worst, most difficult, and truly challenging thing they ever had to do. The navy even quantified this challenge during the Vietnam War by attaching biomedical sensors to aircraft-carrier pilots and measuring their physical reaction to different parts of their flights. The sensors showed that the pilots' stress levels peaked when they had to land on a carrier at night, even surpassing the levels registered when they were fighting enemy planes and dodging antiaircraft missiles in combat. It was not uncommon for a pilot to climb out of his cockpit after a night landing on the *Forrestal* with sweat pouring off his pale face, looking like someone who had just barely escaped death.

To make things worse, that challenge was not at all rare. About a third of a navy pilot's landings on the *Forrestal* were at night, partly out of necessity and partly because the navy wanted its pilots experienced in the very worst. Night landings washed out many a pilot who otherwise would have made a fine naval aviator.

The stress level was so high on landing because there was so much that could go wrong. Even with multimillion-dollar airplanes, sophisticated landing systems, and some of the best-trained pilots in the world, landing on a carrier still entailed a huge degree of risk. If the plane came in too steep or too far back, it could hit the "ramp," a slight overhang on the rear of the ship intended to soften the blow a bit instead of having just a hard edge. A ramp strike was the worst landing mistake, a terrible thing to see, as the plane usually broke up and exploded, sending flaming wreckage forward onto the flight deck.

Landing too far to the left or right of the centerline also was risky because the plane might veer off to the side, either rolling off the edge of the deck or into structures and equipment on the deck. Simply coming in too steep or too fast could be deadly as well, causing the plane to smash into the deck harder than intended. Another scenario could occur when the pilot came in too low or received a wave-off from deck control. If the pilot pulled up hard, either trying to correct for a low approach or intending to go around without even touching the deck, the nose could go high enough to throw the tail hook down right into one of the arresting cables. When that happened, the plane was still in the air with no wheels touching the deck but the arresting cable was going to stop the plane no matter what. The result usually was that the plane slammed down onto the deck and pancaked. Even planes specially designed for the rough landings on a carrier could not tolerate such forces.

All of that frenetic activity on the flight deck appealed to some sailors, but Shelton was beginning to doubt his goal of working with the planes. That goal had seemed great until he learned more about how "bird farms" really worked, and realized that flight-deck work meant long hours in very dangerous conditions. By the time he reported for duty on the *Forrestal,* however, he didn't have much say in where he would work, so he assumed he would be out on the flight deck or maybe working in the hangar bays. But one morning he was waiting with some other newly assigned sailors when an officer walked in the room holding seven file folders. He called out the names on the folders, including Shelton's, and said that some of their personnel tests indicated they would perform well in the ship's navigation department. If they wanted to switch to that from their other assignments, they could. Shelton made a snap decision: this was his chance to get out of the aviation assignment. He stood up and accepted the transfer. So did another sailor named Blaskis.

Soon, Shelton and Blaskis found themselves training for duties in the division that supplied sailors to work in the secondary conn, on the main bridge, and in the aft steering compartments. The secondary conn was a spare control center in the very front of the ship, just under the flight deck, that could be used if the main bridge high above the flight deck was knocked out of commission. It was always ready for use in an emergency, but it also was used for storing and updating maps and other navigational materials. When Shelton and Blaskis worked there, they usually spent their time updating navigation charts to indicate changes in the locations of buoys or other landmarks. They also learned to work as quartermaster on the main bridge, the central command center high up in the structure that rose above the flight deck. One of several sailors and officers on the bridge, the quartermaster recorded all activity and orders given on the bridge, creating an official record of the ship's activity. The other duty that Shelton and Blaskis rotated through involved the after steering compartments, little rooms way down in the very bottom of the ship at the rear, near the rudders that made the ship turn. They would work long hours in those compartments, always manned in case manual control of some of the steering devices was necessary in an emergency.

Since Shelton and Blaskis were both new to the ship and learning the same duties, they found it easy to become buddies. They spent much of their free time together, Blaskis frequently teasing Shelton for what they agreed was Shelton's stupidity in signing up for four years instead of two like Blaskis. The friends often worked side by side, and once in a while they would trade shifts when one got an assignment he didn't much care for. Blaskis wasn't too crazy about working on the main bridge, because that meant he had to put on his dress white uniform and be on his feet all day. The bridge was a high-profile workspace, with the captain and other officers eyeballing you all the time, and the easygoing Blaskis didn't care for that. Shelton liked the bridge assignment, on the other hand, because it put him right in the center of the action. When he was on duty on the bridge, he knew everything that was happening on the ship. And it was an air-conditioned space, and out of the weather.

But for Blaskis, the secondary conn was better, since there were no high-ranking officers there to make things tense, and he liked working the steering compartments even more. Many of the sailors in his division, including Shelton, didn't like that steering assignment too much because the steering compartment was small and windowless, below the waterline in fact, and the shift could be boring as hell. Most of the sailors working there always took along a book to read, even though they weren't really supposed to. Shelton knew that was one of the reasons Blaskis liked to work in the steering compartment. He'd rather be left alone with a good book than have the captain looking over his shoulder all day.

Chapter 3

Young men and old

Few of the men on board intended to make the navy a long-term commitment, but for others, the *Forrestal* was a glorious assignment, the high point in their naval careers. John Beling was thrilled when he learned he had been named the new captain of the *Forrestal*, and he was even more excited when he heard that the carrier was going to Vietnam. Though she was the most fearsome vessel on the water, she had never seen a day of combat. When Beling first saw her tied up at the dock in Norfolk, he thought she was like a powerful horse, pawing at the stable floor and waiting to be set loose. He was eager to see what she could do.

Beling knew the ship could fulfill her mission, and then some. Now that the White House was escalating the bombing campaign against North Vietnam, the navy needed another carrier to join those from the Pacific Fleet. The *Forrestal* had not been deployed yet because she was with the Atlantic Fleet, but the war in Southeast Asia had grown and in 1967 the call came.

Commanding a carrier is the ultimate goal for a naval aviator. There are higher posts to reach late in a military career, but for a pilot, the command of an aircraft carrier represents the absolute pinnacle. In a field as rarefied as flying jets off aircraft carriers, it is a huge responsibility, and an equally huge honor. The captain of an aircraft carrier holds a place of great respect within the naval community, and everyone recognizes that he didn't get there easily. A navy career can lead to advanced positions with more money, privilege, and security, but that's not what a man sits and thinks about when he is old and tired. He remembers what he enjoyed the most and did the best.

In 1967, John Beling had reached such a pinnacle. He knew that his assignment to the *Forrestal* would be the glory days he would remember for the rest of his life. No matter what else might await him, he could not imagine anything more fulfilling than serving as captain of this ship.

But he was much more than captain to the men who served him. To many, he was a father figure of sorts, especially to those still making that transition from boy to man. Beling was the leader of the ship, and the young men looked to him, and to the other older and more experienced sailors, for guidance and reassurance.

When he assumed command of the *Forrestal* in 1966, Beling was forty-six years old, an accomplished naval aviator, and one of the rising stars in the navy. A native of Harrington Park, New Jersey,

Beling flew bombers and fighter-bombers in the Pacific during World War II. When the war ended, he studied aeronautical engineering and nuclear physics at the Massachusetts Institute of Technology, and served as operations officer on the aircraft carrier *Intrepid*. Then he was commanding officer of two attack squadrons, and commanding officer of the supply ship *Alstede*. By the time he was assigned to the *Forrestal*, it was clear that the navy trusted Beling with powerful command positions and the lives of many men.

Most of the younger crew on board had only a sketchy knowledge of Beling's background—that is, if they knew anything at all. Some had heard that he was a pilot in World War II and had been shot down, but he rarely told the whole story to anyone. It was typical of Beling to downplay his own involvement in anything noteworthy.

The truth was that Beling had been to Southeast Asia before and almost didn't make it back. He came within a moment of dying in the waters of the Pacific Ocean like so many other pilots and crewmen whose planes went down on raids against the Japanese. Beling was a twenty-five-year-old bomber pilot in 1944, stationed on the carrier USS *Yorktown*. One day in July, he and his co-pilot flew their dive bomber to a tiny island in Micronesia called Yap. The lush tropical island, located just nine degrees north of the equator, was a beautiful green spot in the Pacific Ocean, surrounded entirely by a broad shallow lagoon and nearly ninety miles of barrier reef. The island was held by the Japanese, and Beling's mission was to hit their installations.

As they got to the island, Japanese planes came up to meet the dive bombers and their fighter escorts. Beling, in the front seat, took aim at one of the Japanese planes with his guns and, for just a split second, regretted having to shoot it. The target was a "Betty," which the American pilots considered a beautiful plane. Beling zeroed in on the plane's right engine and squeezed the trigger, watching as his cannon shells cut through the plane and started a fire in the engine. But the fire died out quickly and Beling didn't have time to chase the plane for another shot. The island was almost directly beneath him now and he had to continue on his bombing run.

Beling's escort fighters were taking care of the Japanese planes, so he turned his attention to the island, where antiaircraft guns were filling the air with exploding metal. He was lining up his plane with a good target when he felt a jolt and the whole airplane shuddered. The plane showed no ill effects, so Beling disregarded it and continued to concentrate on the bombing run. He didn't realize that a large-caliber antiaircraft shell had blown through his plane without exploding. Beling squeezed the trigger on his cannons and strafed the island as he lined up his bombing target.

He was low and almost on top of the small island before he realized his plane was on fire. The flames were visible outside the cockpit, but then they died down and Beling thought he might be okay. Then they reappeared inside the cockpit. The plane started to fill with smoke. His co-pilot called for them to bail out, but Beling realized they were right over the island and would land in Japanese hands. Besides, they were too low to bail out.

"No, don't bail yet!" Beling yelled. "Wait! Wait!"

He realized that he still had control of the plane, so he made a big climbing turn under full power to get the plane away from the island and up high enough for their parachutes to do some good. But as he pulled the yoke back hard, Beling felt the fire crawling up his legs. Within seconds, his legs were completely on fire and he thrashed about the cockpit, trying furiously to put out the flames. Beling screamed in pain. He struggled to pull away from the heat, but the tiny cockpit offered no hope of that. His hands and arms were catching fire as he tried to beat out the flames below. With the fire growing larger every second, Beling frantically decided to jump out of the plane *now*, even though he couldn't tell exactly where he was in relation to the island or how high.

It turned out that he was about one thousand five hundred feet high, enough altitude for his parachute to break his fall. Beling watched as his plane crashed into the ocean, then he landed in about three feet of water about a hundred yards off the island. He never saw what happened to his co-pilot. He thought maybe the other man had gotten out in time while Beling was too distracted to notice.

Beling stood up in the shallow water and looked around. He was in agony from the burns that covered his legs and much of his arms. His flight suit was mostly burned off. As he stood there, he could see that the fighter escorts were strafing the antiaircraft gun that had shot him down. He was close enough to see the Japanese installations on the island, but so far no one was shooting at him. Once the antiaircraft gun was out of commission, the fighters circled over Beling and one dropped an inflatable life raft to him. He knew they would send help if they could.

The bundled life raft landed near Beling and he struggled over to it, every movement causing excruciating pain in his legs. He inflated the small one-man raft and flopped into it. He saw that the landing on the coral reef had torn open the dye marker intended to help rescuers spot him, and the green dye was filling the raft as seawater splashed in. He didn't care.

Beling wanted to get away from the island as quickly as possible, because he didn't know if the Japanese would start shooting at him or send a boat to take him prisoner. After trying a few different positions, he found that lying on his back made the raft the most stable in the breaking waves. So he lay there staring up at the blue sky and paddling with both hands. But he soon realized that the coral reef surrounding the island was making his journey difficult. The waves broke hard over the reef and Beling had to contend with higher and higher surges as he got closer to the reef. Paddling was exhausting, and the pain was growing worse every minute. He had to take frequent rest breaks. When he had to urinate, he saw that the urine was fluorescent green because the dye marker had soaked into his body through the burns on his legs.

After more than an hour, Beling saw a navy seaplane headed his way. Landing inside the reef was too risky for the rescue plane because of the shallow water, so it skittered down just outside. Beling paddled with all his might as the Japanese opened fire on the seaplane with mortars.

That's why they didn't shoot at me. I was the bait so they could get a bigger target.

But the rescue plane did not come alone. Fighter planes had come along for support and they strafed the island while Beling paddled furiously to make it over the reef. The shelling stopped and the rescue plane maneuvered as close as it could get. Once Beling made it over the reef, the pilot on the seaplane stepped out on the pontoon landing gear and urged Beling on. He yelled words of encouragement, partly because he was eager to get away from the island.

The pilot had left the plane's engine revving high so they could make a quick getaway, but Beling feared hitting the props as he got close to the plane. The pilot's weight at the door was making the prop on that side dip low and rock in the waves, so Beling called out for the pilot to get back in his seat and move the plane in a slow circle. Beling rolled off the raft and swam toward the plane, trying to reach a rope that the pilot had left trailing in the water. The young man struggled to follow the plane, every kick of his legs sending terrible pain throughout his body, but he finally grabbed the rope. The plane continued to roar forward and Beling was pulled through the water for a while, desperately clinging to the line. Finally, the pilot pulled the line in and grabbed Beling, heaving him into the backseat. The bare metal of the seat was torture on his burned legs, but he had to endure a long, slow ride back to the plane's home, the cruiser USS *Biloxi*.

Medics on the *Biloxi* began treating Beling's extensive burns, but it would be a slow, painful process of recovery. His flying days were over for a long while, and it was weeks before he could walk again.

Beling was a contrast of personality traits, at once brash and cocky as hell but still humble about his own achievements. He was proud of his work in the navy, but like a good officer, he was more likely to defer all the credit for an accomplishment to the men working under him. Like many military leaders with the authority to get away with it, Beling wasn't at all shy about bending the rules just a little or saying whatever would get the job done. And if he tweaked the military establishment a bit, so much the better. Like most accomplished military men who worked their way up the ranks and earned their position through real work, he harbored at least a slight disdain for the desk jockeys back home.

Beling was a strong leader, quiet-spoken and accommodating to his men when possible, but he expected everyone to meet his high standards. He was a very intelligent, well-educated man with a highly analytical mind. Unlike some high-ranking officers whose training emphasizes just doing everything the one "right" way, Beling was a creative problem solver. A smallish man, like most military pilots, Beling nevertheless exuded great authority. He was well liked by those serving with him, but he was known as a real bulldog whenever he was dealing with something that mattered to him, and most things mattered to him. Officers working with him learned not to bring up any problems or ideas at the end of a meeting when what they really wanted was to just end it and leave. No matter how late the hour and how tired everyone was, Beling would insist on hammering out a solution right then and there.

And the cardinal rule in dealing with Beling was never to bullshit him. If you did and Beling found out about it later, God help you. The best policy was to assume that Beling knew the answer to whatever question he was asking and admit when you didn't know. Beling had quite a temper when riled, and nobody wanted to be on the receiving end of it.

The other *Forrestal* officers also learned that Beling was even more determined than most captains about looking out for the welfare of his men—and most of them also had good intentions in that area. Very soon after he took command, the ship's hierarchy discovered that he was a hands-on captain, someone who wanted to see it all for himself. He was not a captain content to enjoy his own privileges while giving no thought to the lowly sailors working under him. To the contrary, Beling didn't hesitate to get right down to what mattered. And to sailors on a long sea cruise, what matters is food. Beling had a habit of touring the ship in the evening hours, accompanied by another officer or two, just to see for himself how things were running. One evening on the ship's first cruise after Beling took command, he opened the door to one of the big coolers used by the enlisted men's kitchen and found that the floor was covered with cockroaches. That set off a tirade that those present still remember as one of the worst they've ever seen from a navy officer. Beling had the supply-department chiefs rustled out of bed and brought down to explain the mess, which they couldn't. First thing the next morning, the whole area was fumigated and the captain was still hot about the incident when he called the supply chiefs in that day to tell them, in very clear terms, that no such scene should *ever* be found on his ship again.

Beling sampled the enlisted men's meals without any notice to those working the kitchen. He would usually grab a fellow senior officer to go with him, and they would get in line with the rest of the men. More often than not, the senior officer accompanying the captain on those surprise trips to the mess hall was Merv Rowland, the *Forrestal*'s chief engineering officer. He was responsible for overseeing a great many of the ship's operations, so he was handy to have around when Beling asked questions or gave orders. Usually, he and Rowland sampled the "night rats," or rations, the meal made available in the middle of the night for men working around the clock. The kitchen sometimes skimped on the night rats, serving a meager or lousy meal just because it wasn't considered as important as the daytime meals. But for those working odd hours, that midnight meal was their primary meal, and Beling knew it mattered a lot to them. The captain's orderly would knock on Rowland's door around midnight and tell him that the captain wanted him to accompany him to the enlisted men's mess, or dining hall.

"Awwwwww, shit. I don't want to do this tonight," Rowland would growl, standing at the door in his underwear and still half asleep.

"The captain says you do, sir," the orderly would reply.

The two senior officers would go through the line with the enlisted men, the suspense in the room building as they approached the servers. They would take trays just like everyone else and then stand right there and taste it. By this time, the mess hall was silent, with all the hungry sailors eagerly watching to see the captain's reaction. On more than one occasion, Beling slammed the tray into a garbage can and loudly declared the food unfit for his men, demanding to see whoever was in charge of handing out that crap.

Rowland would hustle back to his stateroom and get the supply officer, a commander whose stateroom was next to his.

"Sid, the old man wants to see you on the mess deck," Rowland would tell him. No other explanation was necessary.

"I'll kill that goddamn commissary officer," Sid would reply, referring to the man who was in charge of the midnight meal.

"Okay, but first you got to see the captain."

The supply officer would get dressed and rush down to where the captain was waiting to give him hell.

"Get rid of this shit and feed these people!" Beling would yell, dressing down the officer right in the mess hall. He would demand that the midnight meal be just as good as the noon meal, every time. "Goddamn you, *you're* going to feed them, and *I'm* going to work them. Give these men something they can eat!"

The mess-hall workers would trash the food that Beling had sampled and break out something more palatable. Instead of cheese sandwiches, the men might get pork chops just as the day workers had. As Beling stormed out, the enlisted men would cheer, but the captain hadn't done this for the applause. He did it because, by God, nobody was going to treat his men like that.

Though it was hard to keep up with Beling sometimes, Rowland trusted him and had great respect for him. They got along well, and each man admired how the other could get a job done. Rowland had learned to work with Beling's feisty nature, and besides, he was no cream puff himself.

At forty-eight years old, Rowland was hardly an old guy in the civilian world, but on a ship full of nineteen-year-olds, he was one of the sages. He was a tough sailor, gruff as they come and able to take charge of any situation. He'd push his cap back on his round head and start barking orders, and he didn't take crap off of anybody. But like many senior officers, Rowland also relied on his paternal instincts, looking out for the boys as best he could while still getting the job done. The men working for him knew that if they had screwed up in a bad way, they should march right down to Rowland's stateroom and tell him about it. More often than not, they'd leave with blisters on their ears from all his shouting, but no formal disciplinary action in their records. Rowland was like an ornery old dad who would never tell you how much he cared, but who showed it in everything he did. He was tough as nails, but everyone knew he cared about them.

Very few of the men working with Rowland knew what a tough life he'd lived. He was born to a privileged family in Asheville, North Carolina, his father a successful railroad businessman who provided a comfortable home, with a maid and all the luxuries that could be found in the 1920s. He saw a movie every Saturday, and the streetcar that ran down the street in front of his home was a symbol of just how sophisticated his neighborhood was. By North Carolina standards, Rowland was a little rich boy living in the big city. But when the stock market crashed in 1929, Rowland's father lost most of his fortune and the family was forced to move to an old farm where the roads got so muddy that the mail had to be delivered on horseback. The change was a shock to twelve-year-old Rowland and his two sisters, going from the comfortable life of city kids to a run-down farm with no electricity, an outhouse, and water that had to be carried one hundred yards to the house in pails. The kids went barefoot all summer, getting a new pair of shoes only when the first frost hit the ground. Rowland's father struggled through different jobs, trying to put his machinery experience in the railroad to use, and somehow he managed to get all three of his children through high school.

After high school, Rowland struck out with a friend, Lester Millhouse, to find work. Things could not have been much worse for two boys trying to become men. The Depression was in full swing, and there was no work to be found anywhere. Rowland carried letters of recommendation from his doctor, his schoolteachers, the clerk of the court back home, and the county sheriff. They all attested that he was a fine young man, but unfortunately, plenty of other fine young men were out there looking for work.

The two friends hitchhiked all over the Southeast, joining the many others trudging the countryside in search of a few pennies. At one point they took dangerous jobs in a coal mine in Harlan, Kentucky, and worked there for three weeks until the miners went on strike. It seemed everyone there was carrying a pistol during the strike, so Rowland thought he should get out before the shooting started. He and Millhouse hitchhiked to Knoxville, Tennessee, mostly just because that's where the truck they were in was headed. They had seventy-five cents between them.

The two boys spent the night at a Red Cross shelter and then went looking for jobs. There weren't any jobs to be had, so they went to the navy recruiting station, where they underwent preliminary physicals and took written examinations. Millhouse was rejected for being color-blind, and though Rowland had done well on the tests, the recruiter couldn't take him either. You're from North Carolina, he said. You have to go back there if you want to join up.

So the two boys spent twenty-five cents on an all-you-can-eat meal in Knoxville, working hard to get their money's worth, and then they started hitchhiking north. They had a friend in Ohio and hoped they might find work there. But before they got very far out of Knoxville, it started raining hard. They were soaked to the bone when Rowland finally got up the courage to go to a roadside motel and beg the owner to put them up for the night. He was on the verge of tears at that point, tired and cold, scared at what the future might not hold, and the woman gave in. The adventure continued the next morning, the boys slowly hitchhiking north and making their way to Alva, Kentucky, where they got jobs in another coal mine. Rowland and Millhouse were happy to have these jobs, not just because they were desperate for work, but because this was a good mine to work in. Unlike most coal mines, it had eight-foot ceilings, so they could stand up as they worked.

Only three weeks later, these miners went on strike and the National Guard was called in. A friend tipped them off that things were going to get violent soon, and urged them to leave right away. They did. After three weeks of backbreaking work, the boys still had no money in their pockets. They had bought food and work clothing on credit at the company store, but they hadn't been paid yet.

Rowland and his friend stuck out their thumbs again, this time heading back toward Asheville. They survived by eating green apples found along the way. Once they reached Asheville, an uncle put Rowland and Millhouse up for the evening, giving them the first real meal they'd had in days. The next morning, the uncle drove Rowland over to the navy recruiting station, and he signed up. The navy accepted Rowland, but he had to join the long list of other desperate young men wanting to work. The recruiter told Rowland he would be called up at some point, but until then, he was still on his own. It took another six months of waiting, hitchhiking, and scrounging for work before the navy summoned Rowland to duty.

By then, the navy looked like a godsend. For at least a few years, Rowland would have twenty-one dollars a month, a bunk, a doctor, and a dentist. No more green apples.

The navy suited Rowland well, partly because he knew there wasn't much else out there for him. Once he made it inside, Rowland took his job seriously and excelled, soon realizing he could make the navy a lifelong career. He studied engineering as he served on a variety of ships, and when World War II struck, Rowland was right in the thick of things. From Casablanca to Tokyo Bay, Rowland experienced some of the worst.

Rowland made it to the rank of commander, a clear leader for his men. Like Beling, Rowland was a hands-on sort of leader, likely to throw on a pair of coveralls and go crawling through a condensator to find the damn problem for himself. It was his job to keep the ship functioning properly in every way, and he knew the *Forrestal* inside and out. He had his finger on the ship's pulse at every moment, attuned to the slightest changes in her movement, vibrations, and sounds, ready to respond to any problems. When he slept, Rowland dozed lightly. If there was a change in the ship's speed, he could sense it and immediately pick up the phone by his bedside to see what the explanation was.

With Rowland and Beling in charge of the ship, the young men on the *Forrestal* knew they were in good hands. Rowland and Beling, in turn, depended on Washington, trusting their superiors to support the ship well.

The younger men's trust was well placed.

For Beling and Rowland, the *Forrestal*'s deployment to Vietnam was another chance to excel at their life's work. When the orders came for Vietnam, Beling was ready to pull that ship out of Norfolk right then and get going. He was a professional warrior, and this was what they did. There was a war to be fought in Southeast Asia, and Beling was eager to get over there and show the world what the *Forrestal* could do. In addition to his personal stake in performing well, Beling knew that the navy's Atlantic Fleet was looking to the *Forrestal* to do them proud. She had to prove herself among Pacific Fleet carriers that had been on the job for a while already.

Despite his eagerness to get going, Beling knew that there was work to be done before the ship and crew would be ready for war. The navy scheduled months of training time before the carrier's planned arrival off Vietnam in July. Beling took to the training as heartily as he did everything else, and his determination was contagious among the officers he commanded. Rowland felt it directly. They both had been to war before, so the deployment to Vietnam was nothing new in that sense. In fact, the assignment didn't even rank as especially dangerous for the two men who had been shot at by the Japanese twenty-five years earlier. But they knew they were going into a war zone and that thousands of young men under their command would be facing their first real brush with danger. Like many military leaders, Beling saw a certain elegance in striding off to battle. He was proud to be commanding these men, men he considered a good and well-trained crew, and he was determined to do a good job. At the same time he worried about them, hoping that if he lost any of his crew, it would be for a good reason.

Rowland had similar emotions, remembering the first time he was deployed to a war zone, but comforted by the fact that the Vietnamese wouldn't be attacking his ship the way the Japanese had. The two seasoned officers discussed the situation extensively, and they agreed that the men of *Forrestal* would be ready by July. They would step up the training and drills for the crew, just to make sure everyone was on his toes when they got there, but Beling and Rowland knew they had a good bunch of guys on the ship.

Before Beling ever left Norfolk, he went out of his way to make sure the ship was well supplied for its first trip into a war zone. Every ship has a budget for supplies, and on this occasion, Beling made sure to tinker with the budget so that he could get more emergency supplies. It was only a precaution, but he decided to bring on more medical supplies and firefighting equipment than the ship had carried on previous cruises.

Beling made other changes in the ship's operations. He wanted to replace the ship's doctor before leaving Norfolk, but the new doctor wasn't available yet. So Beling called in Dr. G. Gary Kirchner for a talk. Kirchner had just finished his residency in Rochester, Minnesota, when he was drafted and assigned to the *Forrestal*. He was brand-new to the navy and reported to Norfolk thinking he would be one of four doctors on board, in addition to scores of sailors trained as corpsmen, better known as medics. But when he showed up in Norfolk, Kirchner was called to the captain's quarters for more than the usual welcome.

"Well, Doctor, I've looked over your service record and . . . well, it's pretty thin, isn't it?" Beling said. "You have just gotten in the navy?"

"Yes, sir," Kirchner replied. "I don't really know one heck of a lot about the navy, but I am learning."

"Well, I have a piece of bad news for you," Beling said, putting the file down and leaning back in his chair. "The *Forrestal*'s medical officer has been transferred."

"Oh, will his replacement be here soon?"

"No," Beling replied. "In fact, he won't make it here by the time we will go to Guantánamo for the training and the operational-readiness inspection. I'm going to make you the medical officer. You will be the head of the department and I will provide to you any assistance that you will happen to need."

Kirchner stammered a "Yes, sir" and pledged to do his best, but in truth he was scared out of his wits.

Chapter 4

THEIR GREATEST FEARS

The crew of the *Forrestal* learned early in 1967 that they would be heading to Vietnam later that year. In the meantime, they trained and became more familiar with what was to many still a bewildering and frightening place to work.

The flight deck was a busy place during launch and recovery operations, with planes and people making the most of every small bit of space. Newcomers had to trust that the more experienced hands on deck—some thirty-year-olds were called "old men"—would train them well and guide them through the daily hazards. At any moment, planes might be taking off on one end of the carrier while planes landed on the other end, with dozens of others scattered across the deck waiting their turns or being broken down for storage below. Bob Shelton had the same reaction as most sailors the first time he looked on the flight deck during a launch: it seemed a frenetic melange of men and machinery, even though the trained eye could see that it was a carefully choreographed ballet.

There were scores of men on deck, each one in a color-coordinated outfit that signified his role. Their brightly colored jerseys and head-gear gave the flight deck an oddly festive appearance in a navy where gray on gray, with subtle highlights of gray, is the predominant color scheme. Purple indicated fuel handlers, the "grapes" who fueled planes and took care of fuel-pumping stations, while yellow outfits indicated aircraft-handling officers, catapult and arresting-gear officers, and plane directors. Red gear was worn by crash and salvage crews, explosive-ordnance-disposal teams, and others responsible for handling the bombs and other explosives. There were other designations for blue, green, white, and brown outfits.

The color coding resulted in a sea of multicolored dots running around the flight deck, all of them gesturing in carefully orchestrated signals because the incredible noise of jets landing and taking off made it impossible for them to hear one another. Everyone wore a "cranial" that had bulky hearing protection built into a canvas head covering. The cranial cut the noise to a bearable level, but it also had the odd effect of isolating the wearer, creating a lonely effect within a sea of people and activity. For some of the deck crew, the cranial had a two-way radio for communicating with the officers in control areas off the flight deck. But most of them relied on a set of careful, deliberate hand signals, usually large and dramatic gestures designed to be seen and understood clearly. The crew needed to communicate with confidence when moving planes about and conducting various operations that could kill people, so the gestures tended to be sweeping and often were done with a flourish, like those of an old-time baseball umpire adding some drama to his strike call.

When a plane was ready for launch, the pilot saluted the catapult officer, signaling that he was ready to be launched; then the catapult officer, known as the "shooter," would decide whether the plane was ready from his vantage point just outside the plane. From a kneeling position, the catapult officer would then lean forward to signal the launch to the catapult-deck-edge operator, the crewman who actually fired the catapult. Once the aircraft was "cocked" on the catapult, he kept his hands above his head until he received the launch command from the catapult officer. With his hands still over his head, the catapult-deck-edge operator would turn forward and look up the deck to be sure everyone and everything was clear. The catapult-deck-edge operator would then rotate back down the deck to make sure everything was safe to launch the aircraft. Only then would he face his console, lower his hands, and push the catapult trigger. All of this happened quickly, with the plane seeming to fire off the catapult as soon as the shooter leaned forward, the plane's wings just clearing his head by a few feet.

One of the blue shirts on the flight deck was Ed Roberts, the rock-and-roll drummer from Atlanta. He had been assigned to the crews in charge of moving the planes on the deck, a difficult and dangerous job. Roberts had first been given an office job on the carrier, but he quickly decided he didn't like that and asked for a transfer. The office job was easier, but he was really just a gofer and he couldn't stand the piddly-ass work like running down to retrieve laundry and then sorting out everyone's underwear. Plus, he had a fear of being trapped belowdecks if there was any trouble, unable to see what was happening. No one seemed to think there was much risk of the *Forrestal* being attacked, but Roberts had seen enough World War II movies to know that if planes got in to attack his ship, the action would be up top, and that's where he wanted to be.

On the flight deck, one of Roberts's main jobs was to chock the planes, placing heavy blocks on either side of the wheels to keep them from rolling once a plane was parked. He also tied down the planes with chains. The aviators depended on Roberts and the rest of the deck crews to do their jobs well, because the airmen were to a large degree just vulnerable cargo until the plane was actually in the air. Danger was everywhere on the flight deck, and after the aviators were strapped into their jets they depended on the deck crew to move their planes about, arm them with deadly bombs and missiles, and set up the dangerous catapult shots. Each crew had a "plane captain," a sailor who was responsible for that particular plane's preparation, movements, and launch. John McCain's plane captain was a baby-faced twenty-year-old named Robert Zwerlein who, despite his gentle demeanor, gave orders on the flight deck with the kind of authority that was necessary when lives were at stake. Watching him gave no doubt that this young man in the brown jersey could be trusted to get Mc-Cain's A-4 Skyhawk in the air. But when he took off his goggles and headgear, he looked more like the quiet soul his mother knew so well.

Like so many of the young men serving on the *Forrestal,* Robert Zwerlein was an example of good, old-fashioned small-town Americana. Known as Bobby to his family and friends, Zwerlein was the middle child in the family. His father had served three years in the navy, and his older brother also had joined the navy. So when it came time for Zwerlein to make a decision about his future, the navy was an obvious choice.

The Zwerleins were a solid, loving family that stayed close. They ran the local Tastee-Freez stand in the small town of Port Washington, New York, and Bobby and his two brothers worked there after school, handing out ice-cream cones and chocolate sundaes to all the locals. It was the kind of place that everyone in town stopped by every once in a while, and over time, the entire community came to know Bobby well. They watched him grow up, from a little boy barely tall enough to see over the counter to a handsome young man who flirted with all the girls coming in for a cone.

The Zwerleins and their Tastee-Freez were a fixture in the town, and the four men of the Zwerlein family were heavily involved in the community through their volunteer firefighting. Zwerlein's father had been a volunteer firefighter for most of the time that they lived in Port Washington, and he and his brothers hung out with Dad at the firehouse every chance they got. As they got old enough, each one eagerly joined the fire service, making their parents proud that they, too, would want to serve their community. The whole family saw the honor in volunteer service, but Bobby thought that the firehouse was the place to be. It was the Zwerlein men's common hangout, the place their firefighter friends all went to just be with one another, tell stories on one another, and maybe have a beer or two.

The Zwerleins were satisfied that they had raised three young men with good hearts who were ready to take their place in the world as husbands, parents, and whatever else they chose to be. They also knew Bobby didn't relish working at the Tastee-Freez so much; he would be standing at the door when Mom or Dad showed up to relieve him, ready to race out and head to the firehouse. But they knew he was a good kid, like his brothers.

Mom had always considered Bobby a little more fragile than the other two. He wasn't the youngest, but he always got hurt, and always seemed to be sick with one thing or another. He was a sweet kid, never one to raise his voice or lash out. Bobby was the one who seemed just a bit more gentle, and that made Mom worry about him when he joined the navy.

But Bobby saw it as the next big step in his life, the same sort of move his father had made, and his older brother too. It would be a major change to leave his family and the community he loved, but that was part of growing up, and he was ready. Mom wasn't so sure *she* was ready, but she had to trust that he would be okay.

After all, she told herself, he's going to a carrier. And he's got all that training as a firefighter. He can handle himself if anything happens. That was something she repeated to herself over and over again.

Zwerlein's job on the flight deck required him to be right in the worst danger zones, and to stay safe he relied on good communication with the others on deck, as well as a keen sense of his surroundings. Any movements on the flight deck were performed with a deliberate attention to exactly where you were and what was around you, sometimes giving crew members the appearance of operating in slow motion, with a leisurely attitude. But nothing could have been further from the truth. The flight deck of an aircraft carrier often is called the most dangerous workplace in the world, and there are accidents on a regular basis that prove the point. This was no place to let your guard down or daydream. Zwerlein and Roberts both learned quickly that when they were on the flight deck, they had to pay attention at all times not only to operations in their immediate area but also to what was going on elsewhere that might soon come to their immediate area. During landing operations, for instance, their eyes were on the plane coming in if they were not otherwise engaged with their own job. Unless they had something else to concentrate on, they wanted to watch the landing plane so that they knew which way to run if it crashed.

If you were not ever-vigilant, you ran a high risk of being injured or killed on the flight deck. That is why the flight deck was a highly restricted space; no one was allowed there during flight operations without a specific reason. You could not just go hang out there and watch. (There was an area up on the island structure called "vulture's row" that was accessible to most crew interested in watching the operation.) Launching and retrieving planes, and handling deadly bombs and missiles, in such a small space created dangers that were only exacerbated when the crew had to go for speed as well. To make the situation even worse, the crew often had to work in the blazing heat. The carrier was a huge heat sink in the sea, the tons of metal absorbing the sun's rays all day long and not cooling until well after nightfall. Even though Roberts grew up in the heat and humidity of Georgia, never having lived in a house with air-conditioning, he marveled at how hot the flight deck got. He learned to turn his belt buckle to the inside so that it wouldn't heat up in the sun and burn him when he bent over. And when he got caught in the hot exhaust of a jet, he knew that, at least for a moment, his teeth got so hot they would burn his tongue if it touched them.

The heat and long hours quickly could lead to fatigue, and fatigue could kill. The flight-deck crews sometimes had to work twelve hours or more, at physically demanding jobs, and a weary sailor was no match for the hazards that just kept coming and coming.

Ed Roberts and his friend Gary Shaver knew there were dozens of ways to get yourself killed. You could fall overboard, you could be blown overboard by a jet blast, you could be hit by a plane, you could walk into a nearly invisible spinning propeller, an arresting cable could snap and slice you in half, or you could be sucked into a jet engine. The intake of a jet engine posed one of the biggest risks because the crew had to work close by and know just where the dead zone was. A few inches outside the zone, and you would only feel the air being sucked into the engine. Just a little closer, and you would be pulled off your feet and right into the engine before you even knew what was happening. That happened with some regularity, simply because the close proximity of people and jet engines was unavoidable. Surprisingly, the crew member sometimes survived the incident because the strong suction ripped off his cranial and other gear, sucking them into the engine an instant before the person's body would be chewed up. Despite their ferocious appearance, jet engines are delicate machines that can be destroyed instantly by even the tiniest bit of material sucked into the turbines.

With the engines so susceptible to "foreign object damage," or FOD, each flight operation on the *Forrestal* began with what is called an "FOD walkdown." For this vital precaution, off-duty volunteers who rarely got to be on the flight deck because they worked below lined up with the flight deck on one end, shoulder to shoulder, and walked the length of the ship with their eyes cast downward looking for any bit of debris. They picked up anything they found, no matter how small, from an errant screw to a bit of paper. Even a loose bit of the rubbery nonskid surface on the flight deck could be a hazard. During flight operations, the crew was careful to avoid dropping any items that could lead to FOD. Loose items were kept to an absolute minimum on the flight deck, with the crew discouraged from carrying personal items such as an ink pen or spare change.

Roberts had met Gary Shaver when he transferred to the flight deck. Shaver had already been working for a while in the same job, helping move and tie down airplanes. He had joined the navy with some eagerness, looking forward to a job in aviation electronics and thinking seriously about making the navy a career. He was eighteen years old and had started community college in his hometown of Carpentersville, Illinois, when he was hit by what should have been, in a better world, the worst trauma that could befall a young man: his girlfriend broke up with him. Shaver wasn't enjoying college life much and he had already considered joining the navy, so as a way of getting away from a broken heart, he decided to go. Within weeks, he was in boot camp.

Shaver hoped for a job in aviation electronics, but he ended up working on the flight deck as a blue shirt, directing planes as they moved around the deck. It was tough work, but he liked knowing that his job was important, that he had a responsibility to do the job right or else people could get hurt. His crewmates came to know Shaver as conscientious at work, never one to shirk his job or drag ass in hopes that someone else would take up the slack. Shaver and Roberts often worked together, Shaver directing the planes to move about the flight deck and Roberts walking alongside with chocks and chains to secure the aircraft. Shaver had been on the flight deck for a few months already, so he knew just how scary the flight deck could be and he reinforced the main rule of the flight deck for the newcomer: "Be alert at all times. Never let your guard down."

Roberts did his best to stay on his toes, so much

so that he started chugging coffee like never before. (The Atlanta boy couldn't get his favorite "Cocola" on board.) At one point, he reported to the sick bay and very reluctantly told the doctor that it burned when he urinated. He was afraid he had contracted one of the dreaded, but common, venereal diseases that the medics lectured about before every liberty call. He was sure he hadn't done anything to contract a disease, but damn if it didn't burn like hell, just like the docs said it would.

The doctor couldn't find any indication of disease other than the burning, but he had an idea what the problem might be.

"Could be a lot of coffee. You drinking much coffee, son?"

Roberts took a minute to think about it and figure out how much he was drinking.

"Fourteen cups so far today, sir."

Roberts hadn't been working on the flight deck long before he found out how scary it could be. Within weeks, Roberts saw a plane blow all its tires on a hard landing, and on two other occasions, he saw Sparrow missiles fall off a plane during landing and go skittering across the deck. And around eleven-thirty one night, as Roberts was nearing the end of his twelve-hour shift and was dog-ass tired, he suddenly found a pilot's life was in his hands. The plane had just landed and been maneuvered into a parking position. Roberts placed two tie-down chains on one side of the plane and then suddenly the ship changed direction, causing the flight deck to lean to one side. Unfortunately, the tie-down chains were on the downhill side of the lean and the plane started shifting. Roberts didn't have time to put the tie-down chains on the other side, and his mind raced as he thought the plane was about to slip off the ship. The pilot was still inside, helpless unless Roberts could do something. He ran for a set of power-assisted brakes, a device used to move planes around on the deck, and quickly attached it to the plane's front nose gear. There was a heart-stopping moment as Roberts wondered if the brakes would hold, but luckily they did.

Shaver, too, had witnessed an accident that reminded everyone just how dangerous a moving flight deck can be. He had just been briefed on the morning's flight operations and was walking out to begin work when he heard an angry voice booming across the flight deck on the public-address system. It was a controller in flight operations yelling for the deck crew to "Get that tractor! Get that damn thing!" Shaver looked across the deck and saw the *Forrestal*'s "crash tractor" rolling across the deck on its own. The tractor was one of many squat, yellow tractors used on the deck for moving aircraft and other needs, but this one was specially outfitted with a bulldozer blade on one end. With that gear, the tractor was useful in emergencies such as, say, a flight-deck fire. An enclosed driver's area allowed it to be driven right into a fire, and the bulldozer blade could be used to push wreckage out of the way or right over the side of the ship.

Moments earlier, the ship had turned into the wind to prepare for the morning launch and the deck had leaned to the right. The deck crew had used the strong tractor to pull away the heavy deck plating around a catapult that was being serviced earlier that morning, and then they had neglected to secure the tractor with wheel chocks or by lowering the blade to the deck. Now the leaning deck had put the tractor in motion. Shaver joined the crowd of crewmen rushing toward the runaway tractor, but it was picking up speed as it rolled toward the starboard side of the ship. No one had time to catch up to the tractor before it rolled over the edge of the deck, bumped over the catwalk, and fell in the ocean. Shaver reached the edge of the deck in time to see the bright yellow tractor float for just a second and then sink into the ocean.

The crew was embarrassed that they had lost such an important piece of equipment, but more important, someone could have been run over or pushed off the ship. Incidents like that scared the hell out of everybody, because they could happen at any moment.

Shaver had been injured himself when a jet-blast deflector, the big shield that rises out of the deck to deflect the jet's exhaust during takeoff, suddenly lowered. Shaver was hit by the full force of the jet exhaust. In an instant, he was knocked off his feet and sent down the length of the flight deck like a tumbleweed. Shaver frantically grabbed at the deck for anything that would stop him, but the jet blast was so strong that he had no hope of hanging on even if he managed to grab something fixed. His mind was rushing through possibilities as he bumped along the deck, wondering what it would be like to suddenly go off the end of the ship and into the water. As he neared the edge of the deck, the jet's engine shut down and he managed to stop before rolling off. He was badly bruised, and his arms and knees were bloody from scrapes.

On days like that, Roberts and Shaver were glad to have their shifts end and get off the flight deck.

But in any sort of emergency on the ship, another hazard was the sheer complexity of the carrier's inner structure. Except for the flight deck and the hangar bays, all the other decks might as well be a maze, even to those familiar with them. An endless series of identical hatches, doorways, ladders, and hallways, the decks all looked the same and there didn't seem to be any rhyme or reason to how it all worked. Even before the ship was ever launched, workmen at the Norfolk, Virginia, shipyard would get lost in her interior mazes. One welder was lost in the hull all day until a search party found him exhausted and frightened. He had beaten his flashlight to pieces, furiously pounding on the hull all day long trying to help someone find him.

The sailors learned some tricks for orienting themselves within the ship, mostly by knowing what "frame" they were near. The frames were structural elements in the ship's design that were numbered sequentially, so if a sailor was at frame 200, he knew which way to go to get to frame 225. The *Forrestal* also had "you are here" diagrams and placards telling a sailor exactly where he was in numerical code. If he knew how to read the sign that read "01-170-3-Q, FR 170-174, X3," he knew his precise location. But in reality, finding your way around a carrier was difficult even for those who lived and worked on the ship for years. It was not unusual for a sailor to get lost and have to ask for directions from a "local," someone who actually lived or worked in that part of the ship.

Even though they were riding on a huge warship that could kill them in hundreds of creative and gruesome ways, the biggest fear for the men of *Forrestal* was of the simplest, most basic hazard—falling overboard into the sea. It was one of the things that Ken Killmeyer feared the most, and he was not alone. Killmeyer felt the fear intensely in his first few days on the *Forrestal,* and the fear stayed with him on the way to Vietnam, even though he managed to push it aside so he could get his job done.

The first time he walked to the edge of the carrier deck and looked over the side, he felt a queasiness in his stomach and felt as if he were falling forward. He stepped back quickly and learned not to do that anymore, but he thought about the danger often. Killmeyer was glad that he wasn't working right out on the flight deck, where it seemed every step threatened to send you into the sea.

Indeed, there was good reason to fear a "man overboard," because it was not an unusual occurrence. Killmeyer's introduction to the *Forrestal* included a lot of sailors yelling at him to watch out, don't step over there. At a great many points on the ship, very little came between the sailors and the open sea—sometimes little more than a guardrail or a catwalk structure. At some spots, there was nothing to keep a man from walking right off the edge. When the seas were rough and the wind was blowing, it didn't take much more than tripping over your feet to send a sailor over a barrier and into the sea. Once a man went overboard, he probably would be seriously injured either by the long fall to the ocean or by hitting some part of the ship on the way down. Once he was in the water, he had to be rescued quickly if he was to avoid death from exposure. When the water temperature was forty-five degrees, for instance, an uninjured sailor could lose consciousness in thirty minutes and die in one hour. If he was hurt by the fall, death could come much sooner.

Killmeyer's work on the *Forrestal* put him right on the edge of the ship during operations to transfer supplies, and he was constantly aware of what could happen so quickly if he let down his guard. Part of the risk, and one of the reasons sailors feared this accident so much, was that you had no chance whatsoever of rescue unless someone noticed you fall. The accident could happen so quickly it was possible for a sailor to go overboard and for no one to see it happen. And with five thousand men on board, it could take hours or even a full day before anyone missed the sailor. By then, the ship could be hundreds of miles away. That is why carriers always have people scanning the water for a man overboard. If they spot someone in the water, sometimes just by seeing an unusual light or form in the dark sea, they quickly sound the man-overboard alarm. Then the bridge will slow the ship and bring it around, while also launching a helicopter to go back and look for the lost sailor. Other ships traveling with the carrier also may aid in the rescue.

Without an immediate rescue attempt, the sailor had no chance. But even with a quick response, the sailor still might never be recovered. Going in the water is such a nightmare that many sailors say the real enemy is always the sea, not the person shooting at them. For instance, it has often been the sailor's custom to rescue enemy sailors after blowing their ship out from underneath them, rather than leaving them to die as soldiers might do on land. Once the enemy is no longer a threat, one sailor will help his fellow sailor in his fight against their mutual enemy, the ocean waters. And though Killmeyer's fear of falling off the *Forrestal* made him feel like a real rookie, it wasn't just young, inexperienced sailors who went overboard. In March 1942, Rear Admiral John Walter Wilcox, Jr., fell off his own flagship, the USS *Washington*. Despite the frantic efforts of thirteen ships searching for six hours, he was never recovered.

Killmeyer's work in supply transfers put him at risk from the heavy cable assemblies that could knock a man off the upper tiers of the ship or pull him out of the big doors on the side. But up on the flight deck, Zwerlein and his fellow workers were in jeopardy because the flight-deck operations made it impossible to put up much of a barrier on the ship's edge. Sometimes a light wire barrier marked the edge, but that was more symbolic than anything, just a reminder that you were close to walking off the ship. If a man was hit unexpectedly by the blast of a jet engine, that wire wouldn't keep you from going overboard, and neither would the safety netting sticking out a few feet just below the deck edge.

The first man to ever fall off the *Forrestal* provided a good example of how such an accident could happen. On November 25, 1958, the ship was steaming off the coast of Spain, scheduled to pull into Barcelona the next day. There were to be two flight operations that Tuesday, with the first launch scheduled before sunrise. Jim Johnson was a plane director on the flight deck, one of several crew members responsible for directing plane movement on the deck, carefully pulling planes out of the pack where they were prepared for launch and then moving them to the catapults. All the normal hazards of the flight deck were exaggerated because it was still dark outside. The first launch would use the catapults at the midsection of the flight deck, the "waist cats," and not the catapults at the front of the ship, so the plane directors who normally worked up front came back to help out Johnson. As Johnson was directing a plane to move forward from the fantail, the very rear of the ship, another plane director was pulling a plane forward from the starboard side. That plane director, being less familiar with the rear portion of the flight deck, got the plane hung up on one of the fittings that house the arresting cable. Rather than maneuvering the plane back and around the obstruction, the plane director instructed the pilot to rev his engine enough to get over it.

As the pilot blasted the engine over the deck obstruction, the plane cocked unexpectedly to one side and the powerful jet blast aimed directly at Johnson, who was farther back on the deck. He started sliding backward in the strong wind.

Because he was so close to the blast, he could not stop sliding even though he got down on one knee. When he realized that he could not stop and was going over the fantail, he decided to run and jump, hoping to clear the fantail and the screws.

Johnson turned his back to the wind and ran right off the edge of the ship and into the darkness, the jet blast helping to propel him beyond the structures jutting out from the ship and the big propeller blades churning the water below.

After surfacing, Johnson was still holding one of the lighted wands he used to direct planes on the carrier deck. He realized that it was a valuable asset in the dark waters, so he held on to it with all his might. As he bobbed in the water, Johnson could hear two jets being launched off the carrier, which was by now becoming a much smaller cluster of lights in the distance. His heart fell because he thought that the continued launches meant no one had seen him go over.

Johnson was wearing only his yellow jersey over a foul-weather jacket. He tried to take off his shoes, as he was trained to do, but he was too scared he would drop the lighted wand so he gave up on that. He tried pulling off the jersey, which was weighing him down, but he feared getting it stuck on his head and just left it on.

Soon, Johnson saw a ship pass about one hundred yards away with its searchlights on. A destroyer was searching for him, so he found the whistle that he used on the flight deck and started blowing furiously. The ship passed him by, and then Johnson saw two helicopters searching for him. Then the destroyer returned and the searchlights landed on Johnson.

That was when he lost his composure and began yelling for help. Men on the deck of the destroyer shouted back that they saw him and would throw a line as soon as they got a little closer. By the time the line was thrown and Johnson swam over to it, a helicopter had reached him and was hovering overhead. When the helicopter dropped a line, Johnson grabbed it and was hoisted up.

The helo carried Johnson back to the *Forrestal,* where he stepped onto the deck still tightly gripping the lighted wand that he had refused to let go of in the water. He had no injuries, so after a trip below to take a shower and rest for a short while, Johnson went back to work. Despite his ordeal, Johnson still showed the dogged enthusiasm typical of the *Forrestal*'s young men. He had been scared to death while he was in the water, but Johnson showed the attitude of a young adventurer once he was safe. He wished he had stuck with the destroyer's lifeline instead of the helicopter's, because then he would have had to make a daring transfer from ship to ship on a line stretched between the two.

"I could have been high-lined back aboard the *Forrestal,*" he said to a friend. "That would have been quite a thrill."

Chapter 5

JOURNEY TO VIETNAM

In the months before they sailed for Vietnam, the men of *Forrestal* went off on the kind of adventures that make great recruiting posters. As part of the navy's Atlantic Fleet, the *Forrestal* usually ventured to destinations in the Mediterranean—Naples, Rome, Barcelona—as well as all the Caribbean ports of call. In February 1967, the *Forrestal* went on a training cruise to Guantánamo Bay, Cuba, where the men enjoyed shore leave, with the requisite heavy drinking and carousing. Already, the youngsters had stories to tell.

Another physician joined the *Forrestal* when it reached Cuba, and Dr. Kirchner was glad to hand over control of the carrier's medical department. For another four months, the *Forrestal* sailed the Atlantic, stopping in the Virgin Islands and visiting Cuba again. On May 18, the carrier left Norfolk for a roundabout trip to Vietnam. First she had to stop nearby at the Virginia Capes for a one-day "Family, Friends, and Dependents Cruise," a popular day trip in which sailors could invite their loved ones on board to see where they worked and to watch carrier operations up close. These cruises were always fun for the crew and their families, and this one was especially important. Everyone knew the *Forrestal* was heading into danger, at least in theory.

The next day, the carrier was all business. She sailed on to Saint Thomas, in the Virgin Islands, to pick up a group of navy officials so they could conduct an "Operational Readiness Inspection," the final test to see if the *Forrestal* was ready for war. The navy inspectors studied the ship and its crew for three days and awarded a grade of "Excellent" before disembarking again in Saint Thomas.

Plans called for the *Forrestal* to take a southerly journey to the other side of the world, all the way down and around the Cape of Good Hope, at the bottom of Africa. Going through the Panama Canal was not an option for such a huge ship; she wouldn't fit. As she worked her way south, the *Forrestal* crew looked forward to crossing the equator on June 19. Rowland took a lot of flak from the crew for insisting that they not grow beards on the voyage, even though it was common for navy commanders to bend the rules on facial hair when crossing the equator. But a beard prevents an oxygen-breathing apparatus (OBA), the full face mask that supplies oxygen during a fire, from making a tight fit. The complaints made their way to the captain, and he called Rowland in.

"Captain, there ain't no damn way in hell that a

man can fight a fire with an OBA and a beard," he insisted. As a compromise, Beling had agreed to let the crew grow beards until the ship crossed the equator but then everyone had to shave.

Crossing the equator is cause for celebration on a ship. The crew was excited about observing the naval tradition of initiating all those who had never crossed the equator before, the pollywogs, with an elaborate and messy ritual that would make them shellbacks. Those who were already shellbacks would mercilessly haze the others with age-old ceremonies on deck. The shellbacks faced a logistical problem, however. There were only about five hundred of them versus nearly five thousand of their intended targets. Normally, most of the sailors on a ship were shellbacks and they took advantage of their numbers to force the others through a gauntlet of abuse that included paddlings, elaborate costumes, and kissing a fat man's belly.

The night before the crossing, the pollywogs organized a revolt. They wanted to become shellbacks, but they knew the numbers were on their side. Instead of submissively following orders for the hazing, they turned the whole initiation into a good-natured free-for-all and forced the shellbacks to go through some of the same rituals with them.

Four days later, the carrier anchored off of Rio de Janeiro, Brazil. The crew knew that this would be the last big liberty call for a while, so they practically stampeded off the ship. Rio welcomed them; the city was full of nightlife and the kind of entertainment that leaves a young sailor broke and happy at the end of the evening. Rio also turned out to be one of the few episodes that cheered Ed

Roberts's view of his stint in the navy. Soon after coming aboard, Roberts joined one of the bands made up of crew members, and they played for various parties and recreational activities while at sea. Playing drums for the Dynasties made him feel a little better about leaving the Fugitives behind, particularly when they played in Rio de Janeiro. The Dynasties occasionally played for local crowds at their ports of call, and the Rio locals loved them. The rock-and-roll hits that the Dynasties played hadn't made it to Rio yet, so the crowd roared when they played songs by the Doors or Paul Revere and the Raiders. The Dynasties played up their rock-star roles, with Roberts getting furious on the drums. He even had a favorite move where he jumped up, kicked his stool away, and went nuts. He didn't let on that it was just for show and he couldn't really play the drums standing up.

The stop in Rio seemed to provide everyone with a chance to create a memory. Shaver, the blue shirt who worked with Roberts on the flight deck, took full advantage of his opportunity. Drinking with some buddies at a little bar in Rio, Shaver found one of the specialties was a mixture of whiskeys in an unusual flask with a spout at the top. He was already pretty far gone when the bartender challenged him. If he could chug an entire flask of the whiskey concoction, the bartender would give him the flask to take home and another free one to share with his buddies. Shaver was game and managed to swallow it all down, but he was completely shit-faced by the time his buddies dragged him through the dark streets of Rio back to the small boat that would return them to the *Forrestal*. Hey, no problem. All he had to do was get back on the ship, find his bunk, and sleep it off. But the seas were a little rough in the port that night, and Shaver faced one last challenge. He had to leap off the boat onto the little platform floating by the ship, and then onto the ladder that would take him aboard. It required a bit of timing even in good conditions, and Shaver most certainly was not in good condition. He miscalculated one of the jumps and went right into the water. The cold water instantly sobered him and he felt a big marine reach in and drag him up by the collar. He still was holding on tightly to the flask he'd won in the bar.

On another night in Rio, Shaver and some of his pals took pity on a friend who had been unable to get liberty that night. They couldn't stand the idea of him sitting bored on the *Forrestal* while they were having a good time in Rio, so they decided that if he couldn't get to the local flavor, they would bring some of the local flavor to him. It took a little scheming, but they managed to get three prostitutes from Rio aboard the *Forrestal* and deliver them to their very appreciative friend.

After three memorable days and nights in Rio, the carrier hoisted its anchor and continued on its journey. The rituals at the equator and the time spent exploring exotic cities, not to mention the long days at sea, helped the group of strangers bond. They began to form friendships, to get to know people from different parts of the country and people who were very different in some ways. They settled into the daily life aboard ship, learning from some of the more experienced hands who knew more than the basics taught by the navy. Spill fuel oil on your work clothes? Don't send them to the laundry. They'll never get all that stuff out. Just tie a rope to the jeans and throw them overboard. Let them trail in the carrier's wake for a little while and the churning seawater will clean them right up.

The *Forrestal* sailed around the Cape of Good Hope at the tip of Africa. The trip past South Africa was not an easy route, exposing most of the crew to their first big storm on an aircraft carrier. The ship ran into a storm with huge waves, big enough to bat it around like a little boat on a three-hour cruise. It takes quite a rough sea to send a carrier lurching from side to side, but on that night, mashed potatoes and gravy went flying and covered everything in the dining halls.

Then the carrier headed north of Australia and passed close by the tiny island of Yap, where Captain Beling had been shot down years earlier. After a stop at Subic Bay in the Philippines, the *Forrestal* would go on to Yankee Station.

Though the *Forrestal* crew partook of liberty calls just as much as any other ship's crew, their cruise to South America and other destinations involved a great deal of training, both in standard, everyday operations and in emergency operations, like firefighting and man-overboard drills. When the crew was not being trained and drilled on specific operations, the daily tasks of running an aircraft carrier still amounted to practice in procedures that could be vital later on. Ken Killmeyer had been aboard for only a few months, but already he had a number of assignments on board. Though some were as boring as cleaning his crew's sleeping area, others put him right in the middle of the action. Killmeyer served as a messenger on the ship's bridge, standing by to answer the phone and relay messages to others on the bridge, or running messages elsewhere on the ship. As with Shelton and Blaskis, that position put him in the brain of the ship, standing within feet of the captain and making him privy to everything on the bridge. And it also gave him a terrific view of the flight deck.

When he wasn't working that job, Killmeyer was involved in resupply operations, in which a supply ship would pull alongside the carrier and transfer goods along cables suspended between the two. It was a complicated and potentially dangerous operation, but it had to be done frequently, because a carrier requires quite a lot of everything to keep going. The supply ship might provide fuel oil for the ship's engines, jet fuel, food, mail, bombs and other armaments, or just about anything else found on board. Killmeyer was a "phone talker" for the operations, standing on a small deck jutting out from the side of the carrier and communicating to the carrier's crew and also the other ship's crew, helping coordinate the delicate operation. The two ships would remain in motion for the entire operation, carefully matching each other's speed and movements to keep a steady distance between them—about two hundred feet separating them at twelve knots, or about fourteen miles per hour. The maneuvering was a challenge to the captains of both ships, but it was better than bringing both ships to a halt and letting the seas push them around. At least when they were in motion, they had control over where the ships went.

The operation began with the carrier crew firing a line over to the supply ship with a device similar to a shotgun, then both crews would rig the lines for transferring the goods. If fuel was being transferred, the carrier crew hauled over the big hoses from the supply tanker and coupled them to the carrier's intake pipes. With other goods, big crates and wooden pallets stacked with supplies were hauled over. It was customary, however, for the captains to first exchange small gifts. The first package sent over the high wires might be a box of cigars or some cookies made specially by the ship's cook. It was typical for the transfer to last several hours.

Resupply operations were routine, but on a carrier, routine never means safe. There was ample opportunity for error in the operation, especially if the ships did not synchronize their movements precisely. Straying a little too far away from the other ship might mean breaking the transfer cables and dumping the supplies in the ocean, not to mention the danger of high-tension cables suddenly snapping and whipping back toward the crew. Mismatched speeds could have the same results. But if one ship veered in toward the other, there could be a disastrous collision, probably to the detriment of the smaller supply ship. Such accidents happened despite the efforts of captains and crews who performed this operation regularly, sometimes several times a day for the supply ships, because the sea didn't always cooperate. When a sudden wind or current shoved the ship in the wrong direction, or if steering control failed on one of the ships, a captain would call "Emergency breakaway!" and the two ships quickly disconnected their lines and veered away from each other. Lines went flying, fuel gushed from severed hoses, and sometimes a ship got way too close for comfort. Killmeyer had seen a few of those, and they were always scary. One supply ship, the USS *Caloosahatchee,* had two breakaways with the *Forrestal* on successive days. The first day, the supply ship lost steering control and went wild in the water, causing Captain Beling to veer sharply away while the crews slammed sledgehammers on hook assemblies to send the hoses leaping off. Fuel oil covered everything, and one crewman was hit in the head by a flying pulley assembly. The ships tried the transfer again the next day, but the *Caloosahatchee* again veered off too far from the carrier, causing the hose teams on the front of the carrier to abandon the transfer and release the hoses. The crew on the back of the carrier, however, was determined to complete the transfer. They hung on as the rear of the tanker swung in close and its front swung away, popping the other team's hoses.

On the same voyage, the *Forrestal* crew also saw firsthand how dangerous magnesium flares could be. Pilot Ken McMillen was sitting in his A-4 Skyhawk one evening, waiting to be launched off the ship. The deck crew was completing the preparations for arming the plane with bombs and magnesium flares, when suddenly the world lit up behind McMillen. A brilliant white light reflected off the pilot's rearview mirrors and into his eyes.

Nearly blinded, McMillen frantically looked around his plane. He couldn't make out what was happening, but he knew the only thing that could produce such blinding light was one of the flares. But McMillen didn't know for sure if it was from his plane or another nearby. If it was from his plane, was it still on his plane and burning a hole into the fuselage? The pilot twisted around in the tight seat, one way and then the other, desperately trying to see what was happening to his plane.

Out on the deck, the unexpected flare had confused the crew, not to mention blinding those who had been working in the dim light on the deck. No one knew exactly what to do, and crew started giving conflicting directions to McMillen. One person signaled him to pull forward, and then another signaled him to push back. McMillen kept calling the control tower to ask what was going on. "Is it my plane? Is it my plane?"

The tower never responded and McMillen knew that if the flare was burning white hot on his own plane, it could ignite his fuel and everything else aboard. Even if it were on the deck nearby, it still could be a danger to him.

McMillen responded the way most carrier pilots would. He stayed with the airplane. Aviators on an aircraft carrier are trained to stay with their airplanes at all times, and for good reason. The deck of an aircraft carrier is a tightly choreographed stage, and no one wants an aviator moving around on foot when he could be safely out of the way in his cockpit. And more important, the aviator needs to be with the plane in case it has to be moved. So the rule was this: Don't go topside until your plane is ready, then go immediately to your plane and stay there. When you leave your plane, get off the flight deck as quickly as possible. The aviators may have been the glory boys of the aircraft-carrier set, but no one wanted their feet on the flight deck.

McMillen knew the rule, but he still spent several frantic minutes debating whether to leave the airplane. Finally, a petty officer grabbed the flare by its parachute and flung it into the sea. The incident was over quickly, but it gave McMillen a good scare. He never found out if the flare came from his aircraft, and sitting helpless in the cockpit had tested his resolve about staying with the plane. He wondered if he would have the nerve to do that again, or even if it was wise.

Robert Zwerlein and Ken Killmeyer had gotten lucky with the lottery of work assignments. With five thousand men on board the *Forrestal*, not everyone could have a glamorous job, but they at least had not gotten the worst. Zwerlein was in an enviable position with a job as John McCain's plane captain. He had a great deal of responsibility, with McCain relying on him to make sure that everything was in order before they shot him off the ship. It was a high-profile job for Zwerlein, and he loved it. He wrote home to his parents often, telling them how exciting it was to work on the flight deck, how demanding the job was. He told his mother that he enjoyed the fast-paced atmosphere, that it was satisfying to be part of such a great crew.

There were things he didn't tell his mother, though. Zwerlein never mentioned that the flight deck was the most dangerous place he could be on the carrier. Mothers don't need to hear that when their boys are so far away from home. They need to hear that the ocean is beautiful and their boys are having a great time. But the danger was on Zwerlein's mind. He saved those thoughts for when he wrote to buddies back home, knowing they also would not trouble his mother with his fears. The letters Bobby sent them contained plenty of excitement just like the ones he sent to Mom, but he also confided in them that the flight deck was a place where men died.

Paul Friedman, on the other hand, had ended up in an assignment not so directly in the path of danger. He was not pleased with his assignment. He had expected to become a munitions technician, loading missiles onto airplanes. That would put him on the flight deck, or at least up in the hangar bays. Instead, he was assigned to be just another hand working in the kitchen, pretty much the lowest job around. His superiors told Friedman it was only a temporary assignment, something that a newbie might have to do for a while, but he wasn't so sure. He just knew that he didn't want to peel potatoes every day when he could be up in the middle of the action.

Shelton also was not so happy with life aboard the *Forrestal*. He was trying hard to make the best of it, but the Texan used to big open spaces just couldn't stand being crowded on the ship with thousands of men. The carrier was huge, but the living spaces were small. And though he realized that the *Forrestal* had amenities many other sailors would envy, that didn't make it any more pleasant to stand in line every time he wanted to buy a postage stamp. Still, Shelton was a bit of a pragmatist. He didn't enjoy the everyday life on the carrier, but he knew he had it a damn sight better than the guys who had to work down in the belly of the ship every day. And the guys who ended up in the jungles . . . no comparison.

Roberts felt the same way as Shelton about navy life. He didn't want to be here, but he wanted to be in the jungles of Vietnam even less. He kept telling himself that every day when he went to work on the flight deck, but it didn't make him much happier to be out there in the sun, sweating furiously and working harder than he had ever worked in his life. He wasn't used to a cushy life, having done a lot of physical labor for his father's business back home, but working on the *Forrestal*'s flight deck was more demanding than anything he had experienced. In just a few weeks of working on the flight deck, the six-foot, two-inch Roberts dropped from 205 pounds to 175. The quick weight loss left him looking a bit gaunt and feeling less than energetic. In addition to the hard work, he knew that he'd lost weight partly just because he didn't have time to eat. With the long work hours every day, his free time had to be divvied up between sleeping and eating. When he came off the flight deck after twelve hours, covered in soot and grease, he often found he wanted sleep more than he wanted food. At least he didn't have to stand in line to get some sleep.

Another newbie, Frank Eurice, had become a machinist's mate in the engine room, just as he expected. He wasn't thrilled about being on the *Forrestal,* but it wasn't like he'd been ripped away from anything great back home in White Marsh, Maryland. He had been laid off from his job at the local Montgomery Ward department store, where he was the store's expert in drilling holes in bowling balls. When he went home after being laid off, his mother was already crying when he walked in the door.

Eurice asked her what was wrong, but she couldn't speak through her sobbing. She just pointed to the mantel over the fireplace, and when Eurice looked that way, he immediately knew what was going on. Perched on the mantel was a telltale envelope from the United States government. Eurice didn't have to open it to know that he had been drafted.

When he was assigned to the *Forrestal,* he was glad to be on a big carrier. It turned out that for him and Roberts, the rock-and-roll drummer from Atlanta, their assignment to the *Forrestal* would spark childhood memories.

Eurice remembered the mighty *Forrestal* from when he was eight years old. The carrier had just been launched and was hailed as the most magnificent warship afloat. The little boy in parochial school saved ten cents per week from his milk money until he had three dollars to buy the plastic model of the *Forrestal*. He lovingly assembled the *Forrestal* and kept it displayed in his bedroom for years.

Roberts remembered the Christmas when two of his neighborhood pals received the *Forrestal* model from Santa and he didn't. He was terribly disappointed.

Now, at eighteen years old, Eurice was actually controlling that ship's propulsion, receiving orders from the bridge to rev the engines up or down. He was the kid with his foot on the gas pedal of an aircraft carrier.

The training cruises had assured Beling that his crew was in good shape, but he knew that there was no way to anticipate what might happen when the *Forrestal* went to Southeast Asia, so he tried to prepare his crew for the very worst. He was amply supported in that effort by Merv Rowland.

On the voyage around the tip of Africa, he and Rowland stepped up the routine drills and exercises. Rowland convinced Beling that the ship should have "general quarters" drills for two hours every evening. General quarters was an emergency condition that sent each sailor racing to his preassigned station when the alarm sounded, ready to handle whatever was happening. It was used as an all-purpose response to combat or just about any other kind of threat to the ship. The idea behind general quarters was to get all points on the ship manned, but especially those positions that might be crucial in an emergency. Some sailors might be assigned to combat tasks such as manning the defensive guns on deck, while others went to firefighting stations, medical-aid stations, or important engineering work. Others simply reported to certain areas of the ship and awaited further instructions. Even when a position was already occupied by a sailor on regular duty, someone else might rush in to take that position for general quarters because the very best person for each task was to be at the station for general quarters. If the ship was threatened in any way, general quarters assured that the ship's best helmsman was steering the ship, for instance, and not just whatever helmsman happened to be on duty at that time.

Some drills and exercises were carried out all the time, but the pace was increased dramatically on the way to Vietnam; two hours of general-quarters drills every night was much more than the usual routine. And to make the drills even more useful, Rowland decided to simulate damage to the ship. Each department head judged a different zone in the ship each night, making notes of any deficiencies during the drill. The next night, the crew tried to correct those deficiencies.

The crew tired of the constant drilling, but Rowland could not be deterred.

"We're going in harm's way, and repetition is a damn good instructor," he replied. "You go over it and over it, and then when it comes time to do something, you can do it by reflex. You don't have to stop and think or ask somebody. You do it."

Beling and Rowland knew that warships are complicated and, by their very nature, replete with deadly hazards. Over the years, the navy had found that its ships were susceptible to serious accidents at any time, including fire, collision, and grounding. Between 1900 and 1967, the U.S. Navy experienced at least seventy major accidents resulting in the loss of life and substantial damage, as well as hundreds of smaller incidents. Sixty men were killed in 1905 when a boiler exploded on the gunboat *Bennington*, while she was moored in San Diego. Fifty years later, a carrier also named the *Bennington* suffered an explosion and fire that cost 103 lives. The accidents often led to important changes in operations for the navy, with the tragedies providing vivid lessons in what men could do better. And in more than a few instances, such as those involving the grounding of ships in shallow waters, the accidents publicly humiliated the commanding officers and threatened their naval careers.

Of all the accidents that could befall a navy ship, though, fire was at the top of the list. Fires were common, and they were serious. The prospect of a major fire was terrifying to sailors for one obvious reason: there was no way to escape, short of abandoning the ship. The crew could not simply exit the building and wait for firefighters to show up. When a major fire broke out on a navy ship, the crew immediately had to engage it with the same determination they would wield against an enemy firing shots at them. If they didn't, the fire would quickly consume their ship and, at best, they would have to abandon it and take their chances in the sea. At worst, there could be massive loss of life on some of the big ships, with thousands of crew crammed into them, not to mention the tons of volatile materials that could blow the ship out of the water. Some sailors had specialized training in firefighting, but in truth, every sailor was a firefighter. They had to be.

The navy's major lessons in ship fires started just months earlier, on October 26, 1966, when flames broke out aboard the aircraft carrier *Oriskany*. She had already taken a role as a major player in the war in Vietnam, mounting over twenty thousand successful sorties against land targets earlier that month. She had been at Dixie Station off of Vietnam for much of her work, but late in the year she moved to Yankee Station in the Gulf of Tonkin, another ocean grid from which she could launch air strikes on a twenty-four-hour basis.

The crew of the *Oriskany* was planning to launch six Skyraiders and seven Skyhawks on an attack just after midnight. But the weather had turned nasty, so the launch was rescheduled for 7:30 A.M. that day. The rescheduling meant that the crew had to remove and stow much of the ordnance that would have been used, because it was unsafe for it to sit on the flight deck or on the airplanes for more than seven hours.

The attack had been planned for the early-morning darkness, so the ordnance included a lot of Mark-24 Model 3 flares. When activated and dropped from a plane, this parachute flare could provide up to two million candlepower of light for three minutes, lighting up ground targets. The flare created its tremendous light through a combination of magnesium and sodium nitrate, chemicals that were kept separate in the flare until a sharp pull on its lanyard mixed them. When ignited, the chemicals combined and burned furiously at a temperature of four thousand five hundred degrees Fahrenheit. Furthermore, the chemical composition of the flare resisted all firefighting efforts; once ignited, a magnesium flare would burn white hot for its allotted three minutes, and there was practically no way to stop it. Though the pyrotechnic flare was not designed to kill directly, it was one of the most dangerous items on board.

The *Oriskany* had thousands of the flares stored belowdecks, including some in a storage locker in the forward hangar bay just below the flight deck. That storage locker had not been officially declared safe for the dangerous magnesium flares, but the crew used it because it was so much closer to the flight deck than the other designated flare lockers farther belowdecks. What they didn't consider, however, was that the more convenient storage locker was directly above a row of officers' staterooms.

When the crew cleared the flares from the thirteen planes, they started putting them in the unofficial storage locker on the hangar-bay level. Large skids stacked with the magnesium flares were moved down to the storage locker and then the flares were placed individually inside. The night crew left a large pallet of the flares sitting outside the storage locker when they quit for the day, and when the day crew came on at 7 A.M., there was still a big stack of flares to be moved inside. This was a lousy way to start the day, because it meant a morning full of backbreaking work. To make matters worse, the *Oriskany* was scheduled to receive a transfer of armaments later that day. More hard work ahead.

To speed the job, the one sailor responsible for the storage-locker area convinced another sailor to help him move the flares inside. They moved the skids as close to the locker door as they could get it, and then one started passing the individual flares to the other, who stacked them inside. This method worked fine on the first skid parked close to the door, but as they finished with a skid, the sailor outside the locker moved back to another skid and the distance between the two men grew a little farther.

Soon, they were tossing the magnesium flares instead of handing them off.

It didn't take long for the accident to happen. As the sailor outside tossed the flares to the man inside the locker, the lanyard on a flare got caught on something. The outside man instinctively tugged on the flare to free it, and both men heard the loud "pop!" as the flare activated. The sailor dropped the flare to the deck, and almost instantly it began to shine with a tremendous light, the heat radiating out to unbearable levels, and toxic fumes spewing forth. The man who activated the flare immediately panicked and ran away, leaving the other sailor in the locker filled with the deadly flares.

That sailor also began to panic, recognizing the deadly heat produced by the magnesium flares and the danger of fire aboard a carrier. He ran out of the flare locker to a place near where the flare lay burning on the steel deck. In the heat of the moment, the sailor's urge to respond to the accident served him poorly, and he did the most illogical and dangerous thing possible.

Though intensely hot and dangerous, the flare could have been left to burn on the steel deck for its three minutes, after which the incident would have been over unless something else had ignited. Or the sailor could have thrown the burning flare overboard into the sea. Instead, the sailor managed to pick up the burning flare by its parachute and fling it into the flare storage locker where 650 magnesium flares were already stacked. He then slammed the door shut and secured it tightly. Then the sailor ran into the hangar bay shouting "Fire!"

Predictably, the white-hot flare ignited others in

the locker, and soon there was a ferocious chemical fire consuming the forward portion of the *Oriskany*. The flares generated massive amounts of toxic fumes that spread through much of the ship via the ventilation system. The fire spread quickly. By the time the hangar-safety petty officer arrived on the scene, the locker was already buckling from the heat and spitting clouds of deadly fumes. He immediately ordered the crew to throw the remaining skids of flares overboard.

The bridge sounded the fire alarm and then shortly thereafter the general-quarters alarm that signified a serious emergency. Explosions rattled the ship as the fire spread from one compartment to another. The captain maneuvered the ship to help clear the smoke, turning first one way and then another. The ammunition magazines were flooded with seawater to keep them from exploding, a possibility that surely would have meant the end of the *Oriskany*. The fire ravaged the ship for nearly two hours before the crew brought it under control, and then it broke out again with a new vigor when fifty-five-gallon drums of paint in an elevator shaft exploded. The crew continued fighting the fires until 11:58 A.M.

Once the *Oriskany* was under control again, the death toll was terrible. The fire killed eight enlisted men and thirty-six officers, including twenty-four veteran pilots who had survived many combat missions over Vietnam.

The navy conducted a major investigation of the *Oriskany* fire and concluded that it could be traced to the unsanctioned use of the storage locker in the hangar bay, poor training in the handling of flares, and poor performance by the two seamen moving the flares. The navy also cited the *Oriskany*'s executive officers for poor leadership related to the other problems. In addition, the investigation determined that the fire spread as quickly as it did partly because there was not enough fog-foam equipment for firefighting. A number of policy improvements and technical changes in aircraft-carrier operation flowed from the *Oriskany* fire, viewed at the time as one of the worst ever on a naval vessel.

Some of the safety improvements derived from the *Oriskany* fire were put into place on the *Forrestal*, such as the emphasis on adequate fog-foam firefighting equipment. But the navy still had a lot to learn about aircraft-carrier fires as the *Forrestal* made her way to Yankee Station.

The aviators weren't spared from the drills. They didn't get much flight time during the six-week voyage, but their leaders decided the time should be put to good use anyway. They reminded the aviators that they had to be in good shape if they expected to outrun "Charlie" if their plane went down, and so they required daily exercise regimens in the tropical heat. On many days, the fliers could be seen running laps around the flight deck, huffing and puffing in their heavy flight gear.

There were general-quarters drills, firefighting drills, and man-overboard drills, far more than the crew was used to on a normal basis. The men spent many hours fighting pretend fires and rescuing pretend victims from the water, with many others standing around waiting to be counted as part of the man-overboard drill. Counting heads was a major part of the drill, or a real event, for a man-overboard. When the alarm sounded, every single person on the ship had to be counted and then representatives from the different divisions reported the numbers to an administrative officer. If everyone was accounted for, the alarm could be canceled. If not, the count should reveal who was missing.

Killmeyer hated the man-overboard alarms because they reminded him of the risk of falling off the ship, and he couldn't help thinking about the poor guy out in the water if it wasn't a drill. And besides, a man-overboard alarm was always a major headache for everyone. Captain Beling was never happy about going to all that trouble for a false alarm. If a man were recovered, he was likely to get a lecture about staying on the damn ship.

On the trip to Southeast Asia, the *Forrestal* had a number of false alarms for men overboard, plus some incidents in which men actually went overboard, at least one of whom was thought to have committed suicide, a mess cook who jumped overboard on the first day out of Norfolk. Word spread on the ship that some of the crew were getting anxious about going to Vietnam, losing some of their confidence in the safety of an aircraft carrier, and apparently one or more decided to jump. Even in peacetime, it was not unusual for an aircraft carrier to have individuals panic at the thought of going to sea for a long stretch. Sometimes only the prospect of leaving home for a few months of hard work at sea was enough to make men take desperate measures.

All the false alarms and men overboard tried Beling's patience. He declared to the crew one day, over the public-address system, that if anyone else fell off the ship, he wasn't stopping. Other ships would look for the sailor, but the *Forrestal* was continuing on. There were no more false alarms after that.

Beling and Rowland were also mindful of the *Oriskany*'s experience at Yankee Station, when the magnesium flares set off a terrible fire. The possibility of fire was on their minds, and Beling wanted his crew to know what happened on the *Oriskany* and what lessons might be learned from the experience, so he requested a summary from the navy. Nothing was available. Seeing no better option, he ordered reprints of a *Reader's Digest* story and distributed them to everyone on board.

As the ship sailed toward Subic Bay in the Philippines, the last stop before Vietnam, many of the crew were beginning to question some accepted procedures, especially now that they were going into combat for the first time. The men knew they were about to be challenged, and they were as prepared as possible. Even beyond the normal demands of working on an aircraft carrier, a combat situation would put extraordinary stress on standard procedures and the crew's ability to complete all their assigned tasks. The *Forrestal* was about to go into a "high tempo" combat operation, which meant that planes would be launched in large numbers and in a very small time frame, straining the already tense flight-deck operations. Unlike training exercises in which time was not necessarily a critical factor, the launch of aircraft for an air strike against land targets required precision timing and speed, speed, speed. The planes had only a limited amount of fuel and they all had to be in the air simultaneously to carry out a coordinated attack. While they were launching one group of planes, another group might be returning from a mission, low on fuel and eager to land once the deck was cleared. That meant getting planes launched as quickly as possible.

With the need for speed a paramount concern, the crew of the *Forrestal* reassessed some standard procedures. Unfortunately, two separate groups were both contemplating a safety shortcut that, though technically not allowed, they thought would be fine because other safety measures were in place. The weapons systems on the *Forrestal* had redundant safety measures in place so that if one failed, the other could still prevent a disaster. What the two groups didn't know was that each one was relying on the other's safety rule to cover the one they were about to circumvent.

One group, the Weapons Coordination Board, was composed of representatives from the air wings on the ship and others directly involved in arming the planes with rockets, bombs, and other weapons. On June 29, 1967, on the way to Vietnam, the Weapons Coordination Board decided that the *Forrestal* crew could ignore a navy rule regarding "pigtail connectors" in the arming system of rockets on the planes. Called a pigtail because it was a curly cable resembling a telephone handset's cord or a pig's tail, this device connected the triple ejector rack (TER) to the launcher used for various rockets on the planes. Simply put, the TER was a component underneath the plane that ejected and fired the rockets when the pilot activated the system in the cockpit. But the TER could not fire the rockets unless the pigtail connector was attached between it and the actual launching device for the rockets.

Navy regulations clearly stated, "The pigtail connector shall not be plugged into the launcher receptacle until just before takeoff." There was no dispute that "just before takeoff" was when the plane was sitting on the catapult, only seconds before being launched off the deck. This was meant to keep the rocket-firing systems disconnected until the very last moment to prevent a rocket from being accidentally fired while the plane was still on the deck.

There was another rule to achieve the same goal. The firing system also used a device called a TER electrical-safety pin, or just a TER pin. (It also was called an intervalometer pin.) This small device, which was plugged into a receptacle in the rocket-firing mechanism, interrupted the electrical system and prevented a firing command from reaching the rocket. Navy regulations clearly stated that the TER pin was to be in place the whole time the plane was armed on the deck, and the crew was supposed to remove it immediately before launch, as the plane was sitting on the catapult.

The pigtails and the TER pins were a double layer of protection against human error or even an electrical malfunction that could fire the rocket. Without the pigtail in place, the electrical signal could not reach the rocket. Even with the pigtail in place, the firing command still could not reach the rocket because it could not get past the TER pin.

The only problem was that waiting to fully arm the rocket on the catapult was not the fastest way to get planes off the deck and in the air. Everything had to move quickly and smoothly when launching planes, and once the plane was on the catapult, any last-minute steps would just slow the system down, especially if there was a problem. A plane having difficulty on the catapult would delay every plane in line behind it. It was better to take care of as much as possible while the plane was back "in the pack" waiting for takeoff.

So the Weapons Coordination Board decided to circumvent the rule about pigtails, giving the crew permission to plug in the rocket pigtails while the plane was back in the pack. The board acknowledged that this was a deviation from standard practice, but said the rockets would still be safe because the TER pin would be in place. But unbeknownst to the board, other members of the crew had gotten in the habit, without any official approval, of removing the TER pins while the planes were still being prepared for launch. They operated on the same theory that it was much more expedient to remove them before the plane got to the catapult. Those crew members thought the shortcut was acceptable because the rocket pigtails would not be plugged in until the plane was on the catapult. There was a breakdown in communication, one that led to the *Forrestal* inadvertently causing rockets to be fully armed while the planes were sitting on the rear of the ship, bunched up and pointed at one another while being loaded with explosives.

The weapons board's decision to circumvent the pigtail rule was never forwarded to the captain. No one with authority to overrule the weapons board ever saw the board's report, and no one realized the conflict with the habit of removing the TER pins early.

The pigtail decision did not go unnoticed, however. Ken McMillen, the pilot who had the frightening experience with the magnesium flare, heard from an ordnance crewman about the decision. The crewman was responsible for loading the planes in McMillen's division with bombs and rockets, so he was familiar with why the pigtail shouldn't be plugged in early. He expressed some concern to McMillen, who also acted as a safety officer within the squadron. McMillen, in turn, went to his friend and fellow pilot Jim Bangert, who was a safety officer one step up in the chain of command.

"Hey, our people are having some problems with this new thing about arming the rockets while we're still in the pack," McMillen told Bangert one day. "You think that's really safe?"

Bangert said he had wondered about the new policy, too, and said he would look into it. A few days later, after checking with the Weapons Coordination Board, Bangert went back to McMillen and said that was indeed the new policy. Bangert apparently had no idea of the conflict between the pigtail and TER pin shortcuts.

"That's what they say we're doing now," Bangert said. "They say it's the only way to get all the planes launched fast enough."

Chapter **6**

ON YANKEE STATION

The *Forrestal* reached Subic Bay in the Philippines on July 18 and then sailed off four days later for her assigned post at Yankee Station, in the Tonkin Gulf south of Vietnam. She was almost there.

Back home, most people had not paid much attention at first to the buildup of hostilities in Vietnam and the United States' growing presence in Southeast Asia. But by 1967, the country's involvement had reached the point that average Americans were concerned, though not always in the same way. The old guard was worried about the spread of communism and saw North Vietnam as dangerous, generally going along with the Kennedy and Johnson administrations' explanations that U.S. involvement was unfortunate but necessary. The younger generation wasn't buying it.

In 1967, the antiwar movement had not reached a fever pitch yet, but the opposition was making its voice heard. The men of *Forrestal* saw some of the protests before leaving for Vietnam, and on the trip over, they heard about more of it from their friends and family back home. Most of them saw the protests as an affront. Even if they weren't crazy about going to Vietnam or had even thought through the politics enough to disagree with the U.S. involvement, they didn't like being criticized by a bunch of college kids. A great many of the sailors fell in the ranks of Middle America, not necessarily supporting the war but uncomfortable with longhaired kids denouncing their country. It was unpatriotic.

The media were bringing home some images of the war by 1967, and that was starting to turn the tide in the opposition's favor. In April, opponents of the war marched in protests across the country, including two hundred thousand who gathered in New York's Central Park. About 150 young men burned their draft cards at the rally, openly defying the law and signaling a new vigor to the movement. The protestors screamed for Lyndon Johnson to bring home the half a million troops in South Vietnam.

The president was feeling the heat, but not just from the protestors. He could dismiss them as a bunch of misguided college students, naive at best and traitorous at worst, but he could not deny the reports from his own advisers. A year earlier, even those who had pushed for the bombing and ground combat had produced one report after another showing poor results and poor prospects. After two years of the world's strongest country throwing its military might against a supposedly backward jungle nation, victory was nowhere in sight. Johnson was willing to bomb the North Vietnamese mercilessly, but apparently the North Vietnamese were willing to take it and wait for the Americans to leave.

Military leaders pushed Johnson to expand the campaign against North Vietnam, a move encouraged by Secretary of Defense Robert McNamara. He is considered the leading architect of the bombing campaign in Southeast Asia, though by late 1966 he and other civilian leaders had also concluded that the effort was futile. Known for his aggressiveness in pursuing the military effort in Vietnam, McNamara was reluctant to tell Johnson and others in the administration that the Vietnam War might not be winnable. Some other resolution might be necessary, but the question was how to get out.

The buildup in Vietnam had been long and progressive, and the Johnson administration could not back down without losing face. Since July 1965, there had been a steady escalation in the bombing of targets in Southeast Asia, accompanied by a buildup of ground troops. By the end of 1966, the United States had more than four hundred thousand ground troops in Vietnam. After a brief bombing pause in 1966, the administration expanded the bombing again, targeting North Vietnamese supply lines. The bombing moved closer to the major cities of Hanoi and Haiphong, and also to the Chinese border. In 1967, the United States flew 122,960 attack missions in Southeast Asia, hitting 5,261 motor vehicles, 2,475 railroad cars, and 11,425 water craft. Some 3,685 land targets were hit by carrier-based planes.

Fewer than one thousand four hundred Americans had died in Vietnam in 1965, but the figure had jumped to five thousand by 1966 and would reach nine thousand total by 1967.

America's huge military presence in Vietnam came at a high cost, with the country spending millions of dollars every day. The daily bombing runs over North Vietnam pushed the military's supply efforts to the breaking point, and by 1966 there simply weren't enough bombs. Pilots reported going out on bombing runs with only half of what they needed to do the job right, and others were sent out with other types of ordnance, like rockets, that were inappropriate for the mission. The U.S. military couldn't keep enough bombs in the supply line, and the pilots' grumbling was working its way back to the White House and the media back home.

On January 25, 1966, the White House received a cable from Bangkok, Thailand, in which a number of leaders in the American military structure in Southeast Asia assessed the war effort and its future prospects. The cable represented the conclusions reached by General William Westmoreland and Admiral Ulysses S. Grant Sharp, the commander in chief of the U.S. forces in the Pacific, whose carriers had been largely responsible for the bombing runs. Also represented by the cable were General Dick Stilwell, regarded as a slick spinmaster in Saigon who worked hard to suppress negative reports in the media, and several ambassadors: Henry Cabot Lodge, the ambassador to South Vietnam; William Sullivan, ambassador to Laos; Graham Martin, ambassador to Thailand. This was not a whiny complaint from an antiwar crowd; these were the administration's point men for the war effort.

The message they sent to the White House was problematic, especially because it came at a time when the public was starting to question the war effort.

"As far as air actions are concerned, we recognize that the sortie [bombing run] rate may have to be curtailed because of existing and foreseeable shortages in the supply of iron bombs," the cable said. "Iron bombs" refers to unguided, high-explosive bombs, what the public thinks of as simply a bomb rather than something like a missile.

The shortage of bombs was troubling to President Johnson, but more so to McNamara. Though he would soon seek alternatives to the bombing campaign, in early 1966 he still was in favor of it. The intricate plans for demoralizing the North Vietnamese and interrupting their supply lines could not be carried out unless the United States had enough bombs in its supply lines. McNamara was rankled by the cable from Bangkok.

He met with President Johnson in late January to discuss whether to resume the bombing campaign, which had been halted as part of peace negotiations. McNamara expressed his concern that "further delay on resumption of bombing can polarize opinion in this country. I feel we should resume, and send the execute order tonight."

McNamara clearly did not want to slow the bombing campaign for any reason, because he felt that doing so might give the antiwar protesters a foothold. And if it were slowed due to a shortage of bombs, the country would look weak in its enemy's eyes.

McNamara declared that there was no bomb shortage. Years later, he sticks by that assessment, writing in his 1995 memoir *In Retrospect* that he and the military leadership "did our utmost to keep U.S. troops in the field as well supplied and well protected as possible. As the war heated up and passions increased, some critics of the Johnson administration alleged that matériel shortages had compromised our soldiers' safety. This was not the case." He goes on to quote a 1966 letter from General Bus Wheeler, who wrote that "there have been no shortages in supplies for the troops in Vietnam which have adversely affected combat operations of the health or welfare of the troops. No required air sorties [a sortie is an attack mission by one aircraft] have been canceled."

Those who were actually in Vietnam knew the truth was different. Admiral Leighton W. "Snuffy" Smith, Jr., flew over 280 missions in Vietnam during three tours as a navy pilot, during which the military structure in Vietnam encouraged him to do whatever was necessary to send positive reports to Washington, including lying about the success of bombing runs. One day, an intelligence officer told him he should report hitting a target bridge when he had in fact missed it. He felt that an air of deceit had worked its way down from Washington.

The more Smith saw of the lies, the angrier he became. He saw Secretary McNamara on a news report saying, "There's not a shortage of weapons," and soon after he was assigned another mission to bomb a bridge. At the pilot's briefing, Smith was informed that he would be armed with 2.75-inch rockets instead of the five-hundred-pound bombs that he expected.

"Why in the world are you assigning me this target with this weapons load?" he asked.

"That's all we got" was the reply.

Smith complained, and he was not the only pilot unhappy with the shortage of bombs, but the complaints fell on deaf ears in Washington. Sitting in the White House, McNamara and the others controlling the war effort could not be troubled by details like whether there actually were enough bombs to carry out the instructions they sent down the military chain of command.

The White House ordered more bombing. The navy would have to do whatever it took to get enough bombs on those planes.

Like the entire military structure during the Vietnam War, the United States Navy constantly found itself pitted between the directives coming out of the White House and the realities of what was happening in Southeast Asia. The directives from Washington often bore little relationship to what military leaders in combat, or even those sitting in the Pentagon, knew was necessary to fight the war.

Naval officers with both the practical insight and enough authority might have resisted instructions that needlessly put their men at risk, but they needed the right information. As the *Forrestal* would soon demonstrate, the necessary information could be lost in the navy's vast bureaucracy.

The *Forrestal* depended on other ships. Despite her size and strength, or actually because of them, the *Forrestal* did not sail off on her own. Instead, she was accompanied by destroyers and other smaller ships that provided various types of support. They helped defend the carrier from any water-based threats because they were far more maneuverable and carried more weaponry for close combat. Together, the carrier and her support ships were known as a battle group.

The battle group, in turn, was supported by supply ships that rendezvoused with the *Forrestal* and the other ships to transfer all manner of goods. Some ships supplied fuel oil or jet fuel, and others provided food or other goods. And some ships like the USS *Diamond Head* provided ammunition. Among navy ships, the *Diamond Head* was an outcast of sorts, the dangerous cousin that still had to be invited to family gatherings once in a while. Far from glamorous, she was a utilitarian cargo ship that hauled tons of ammunition from storage depots all over the world out to the ships that needed replenishment. At any time, her holds might be chock-full of bombs, rockets, grenades, black powder, small-arms ammunition, and pretty much anything else that could explode. (The irony was that, even with all that ammunition on board, she had only two small guns mounted on the deck to defend herself. One of them usually worked.)

The *Diamond Head*'s task was to load up and then steam out to where the other ships were in transit or already stationed for duty. The work was dirty, especially in a navy that often makes a sailor seem like a fastidious housekeeper with nothing better to do. On the *Diamond Head,* the dangerous cargo was usually dirty and greasy, and there wasn't much hope of maintaining the spotless appearance that other navy ships required. Hard physical labor was routine, with the young men manhandling bombs and other explosives as they moved them on or off the ship. The worst part of working on the *Diamond Head,* however, was knowing that you were on a floating powder keg. All of the sailors knew that they were riding a massive bomb in the ocean, liable to explode with little warning if something went wrong. And with all those tons of high explosives on board, there would not be much left to find. It was a fear that shook many of the 160 sailors when they were first assigned to the *Diamond Head,* but after a while, they became resigned to the possibility of their ship exploding underneath them. Still, there were idle moments on the long voyages out to meet another ship when a sailor's mind could start wandering: *If this thing blows up, what will be the last thing I see? Will I see the deck actually coming up at me?*

The fear was very real for these *Diamond Head* sailors because their ship was not exactly a showpiece. She was old and, though she could still do her job, she was plagued by electrical problems that occasionally started small fires on board. Fires on any ship are serious, but the danger was nightmarish for a supply ship stuffed with explosives. When a fire broke out, the *Diamond Head* sailors had to attack it quickly, and ferociously, because they didn't have a second to spare. The risk of fire and explosion aboard ammunition ships was so serious that they were shunned by navy ports. When the

Diamond Head docked at a naval base, either to pick up ammunition or just to let the sailors off for shore leave, she was not allowed to pull up alongside the other ships. She had to dock far away, sometimes a forty-five-minute bus ride back to the base, or anchor out in the deep water and send her men to shore in small boats.

The *Diamond Head* shared a small honor with the *Forrestal*. She was the first ammunition ship from the navy's East Coast fleet to go to Vietnam, and the carrier was from the East Coast. When the *Forrestal* set sail for Vietnam in June 1967, the *Diamond Head* was already in the area servicing the other ships there. She had settled into a routine of visiting naval ports to pick up ammunition and then running out to where the other ships were at work. She supplied everything from the carriers to the little gunboats that worked their way up the rivers in Vietnam. Most of the time, the *Diamond Head* picked up ammunition at the Subic Bay Naval Base in the Philippines, not far from Vietnam, and then sailed for about three days back to where the other ships were stationed. Once there, she traveled around the area, fulfilling orders for ammunition. The *Diamond Head* might supply six or seven ships in one day.

In the months before the *Forrestal* arrived, the *Diamond Head* sailors had grown accustomed to the routine of docking far out in the undeveloped part of Subic Bay and then driving back to the naval base. With help from Filipinos hired by the naval base, they trucked tons of ammunition back to the *Diamond Head* and loaded it on board. When they stopped for their pickup in July 1967, the sailors were surprised at some of the ammunition they were taking on board. It was old and was clearly not in good shape—dirty, rusty, even leaking. The sailors didn't necessarily know much about the ammunition they worked with every day, but they could tell that this batch was different. Some of the bombs looked different in design, and they clearly hadn't been stored well. When the crew asked the local sailors about this, they learned that the bombs had been sitting in open-air Quonset huts in the Philippine jungles for years, exposed to the humid weather and the occasional storm. No one was sure just how long, but from the grime layered on the bombs, it had been more than a few years.

The *Diamond Head* sailors asked why they were taking on such old matériel, bombs that looked like they should have been destroyed long ago. The local sailors working at the base said they had an order for one-thousand-pound bombs, and these were the only ones they had in that size.

These weren't the first old bombs the *Diamond Head* had loaded in Subic Bay, though the condition was especially noteworthy this time. The sailors had gotten used to loading filthy bombs that had sat out in the jungles. On one recent trip, there was a commotion on the pier as the bombs were being loaded onto the *Diamond Head*. The Filipino workers were shouting and scrambling around one of the stacks of bombs and then, much to the amazement of the *Diamond Head* crew, they pulled out a snake that was long enough to require four men to hold it. The snake had been living in the bomb pallets, apparently for quite a while. On other trips, the crew had found large green tree frogs living among the bombs, a few of which inevitably made their way into the officers' quarters as a prank.

But this ammunition was frightening, even to the *Diamond Head* crew, who were accustomed to the prospect of blowing up at any moment. The young men on the ship were not weapons experts, but they knew that such old and poorly maintained bombs could be overly sensitive, liable to explode with the slightest mishandling. To make matters worse, these were thousand-pound bombs, which were big enough to destroy the ship on their own. The crew didn't like having the old ammunition on their ship, but that was what the navy told them to pick up. At least they could get it off in just a few days when they met up with the *Forrestal*.

As the *Diamond Head* was picking up the old bombs in Subic Bay, the *Forrestal* was just arriving at Yankee Station. The carrier steamed into position on July 25, sixty-seven days after leaving Norfolk.

Yankee Station was a spot in the water off of North Vietnam that looked like any other—except the navy had declared it a staging area for launching air strikes against North Vietnam. Located in the Gulf of Tonkin, about seventy-five miles east of Mui Ron Ma in Ha Tinh Province, North Vietnam, Yankee Station was eighteen degrees above the equator. For sailors on a big steel ship sitting out in the water, Yankee Station guaranteed hot, humid days interrupted only by the occasional rainstorm. Captain Beling was glad to be there, having brought the *Forrestal* for her first days of combat

ever, and his first day of combat as the commander
of an aircraft carrier. Plus, there was the matter of
upholding the honor of the navy's Atlantic Fleet.
The carriers from the Pacific Fleet had been on Yankee Station for some time already, and now the new
kid on the block was determined to show the other
carriers what she could do. The *Forrestal* joined a
number of other navy ships assigned to Yankee Station, including the aircraft carriers *Oriskany* and
Bon Homme Richard. The carriers would cruise
around the Yankee Station area almost constantly,
rarely coming to a halt for any reason.

When the ship arrived at Yankee Station, Captain Beling was confident that his crew and his ship
were ready for combat.

For the first four days on Yankee Station, all seemed
well. Hundreds of planes were launched in those
four days, the crew working fast and hard to meet
the demands of high-tempo combat operations.

On their fourth day at Yankee Station, the crew
started gearing up for what they knew would be a
major air strike the next morning. Two launches
were scheduled for the next day, making up the
biggest air strike the *Forrestal* had launched so far.
Though the specifics were not passed on to much of
the crew, they learned enough to know that this one
would really test their skills.

The pilots always knew a lot more about the missions than nearly anyone else on the ship, so
twenty-six-year-old Rocky Pratt knew the target
for the alpha strike was a rail line north of Hanoi.
Pratt flew A-4 Skyhawks like Ken McMillen and
John McCain, but he was not going out on the al-

pha strike the next day. Instead, he had been assigned to stay back on the ship and wait for others to report on "lucrative targets" they had spotted while on their missions. Instead of those pilots deviating from their flight plan, Pratt would take off and attack the targets they had spotted. Because he wasn't a primary pilot for the alpha strike, he had not attended the briefing for that mission. But by the time he meandered through the *Forrestal*'s big hangar bay that evening, he had spoken with his buddies enough to learn that the planes would hit a rail line—*hard*. He had marveled at how big the air strike was going to be, and he noted that his buddies were excited about the target. The rail line was just south of the Chinese border, in an area that previously was off-limits to air strikes. But now the *Forrestal* had been given the honor of plunging deep into the previously forbidden territory, with the aim of disrupting supply lines to the North Vietnamese. The way Pratt heard it, the plan was to lay bombs on the rail line itself, but also to lob bombs at a mountainside in hopes of causing an avalanche to cover the railroad. The planes were to carry thousand-pound bombs, bigger than the ones they usually carried on such raids.

Pratt was thinking about the mission as he entered the hangar bay, noticing right away that the carrier was taking on some sort of cargo from a supply ship alongside. The other ship was the *Diamond Head*, which had rendezvoused with the *Forrestal* to transfer four hundred tons of ammunition, including the thousand-pound bombs and other armaments for the big alpha strike the next morning. The two ships were cruising alongside each other with lines strung between them, their crews hoisting large wooden pallets stacked with bombs and rockets, cargo nets crammed with rocket fins and other nonexplosives, and box after box of other ammunition.

Pratt watched the transfer for a moment, the careful operation of the two ships always a wonder to anyone nearby, and he strolled past the big open hangar doors to get a better look at the ammunition ship and the operation. As he did, he could hear one of the ordnance officers pitching a fit. The officer was an older man, about fifty, whom Pratt knew casually, so he was curious about what had set him off so badly.

Pratt moved a little closer until he could hear what was going on.

"These are comp B bombs!" the older sailor yelled. "These are goddamn comp B bombs and they're old as hell. Why are we getting this shit?"

The ordnance officer was yelling at two other officers, and all three seemed upset at what they were seeing. Pratt didn't want to get involved in any trouble, and he didn't really know enough about weapons to be sure what all the fuss was about anyway, but he stepped in close enough to take a look at what the officers were yelling about. He saw bombs that looked like nothing he had ever seen before.

They were big and fat, thousand-pound bombs sometimes known as "fat boys" because of their appearance. They looked like the kind of bomb you saw falling out of World War II planes in old black-and-white movies, not the sleeker bombs he usually carried. He also noticed that the bombs were in wooden crates that looked very old, and some of the crates were even rotting. Pratt could read a stencil on one of the crates indicating the bombs had been manufactured in 1935.

Nineteen thirty-five? Geez, that's before I was born!

The older, seasoned sailor was growing red-faced with anger as he talked about how dangerous the bombs were.

"These damn things get real sensitive when they get old and start degrading like that," he said. By then, a group of sailors had gathered around to see what all the commotion was about. "Hell, they'll go off in a fire, and they'll go off just from a bad vibration. There's no telling what could set these damn things off."

The crew working on the arms transfer was used to handling bombs and other ammunition, so they knew the officer was saying that the bombs were far more sensitive than the other ones they used. In normal conditions, a bomb is not extremely sensitive to heat and vibration. In fact, the newer H-6 variety was designed to withstand high temperatures without blowing up at full strength. If exposed to a fire, they would melt and burn, or they might detonate at far less strength than intended. They wouldn't blow up at "high order," the way they were intended to blow up on a target, and they could be trusted to survive some length of time in a fire without any detonation at all.

But the old, decaying bombs sitting on the *Forrestal*'s hangar deck were an entirely different matter.

"Goddammit, these things get a lot more sensitive to heat when they get old like this," the officer explained to anyone close enough to hear. "A fire will sure as hell set them off, and I don't know if they can even take the vibration of a launch. The plane's damn catapult launch might set off the bombs right there."

The ordnance crew was beginning to understand why the officer was so upset, and Pratt was close behind. They were looking at a stack of bombs so old and faulty that nearly anything could set them off, and the blast would be enormous. And of course, the bombs weren't sitting safely in a warehouse somewhere. They had just been delivered to a ship where it was nearly impossible to keep them from exposure to the kind of things that could set them off unexpectedly.

The officer was getting livid, and others in the hangar bay were noticing the commotion. The men working under him were getting scared to handle the bombs, and several suggested tossing them over the side of the ship. The officer considered that option for a moment but then said no. He wasn't sure he could authorize jettisoning ordnance like that without being sure there was an immediate danger. He *was* sure the damn things were dangerous, but making his case with the higher-ups was a different matter. Clearly, the navy had sent these old bombs because the *Forrestal* needed them for its mission the next day. The officer knew that the navy had been short of ordnance for the past couple of years, making it hard to carry out its bombing raids in Vietnam. Throwing these bombs over might make them short on thousand-pound bombs the next morning, and *he* would have to explain why.

The weapons officers passed word on to Captain

Beling that the bombs were too dangerous to keep, and he radioed over to the *Diamond Head* to straighten things out.

"Take these damn things back and give us something we can use," Beling told the *Diamond Head* captain. "Sorry, can't do that," the *Diamond Head* skipper replied. "That's all we have for you."

Beling was angry, but he had orders to carry out the next day and he couldn't do the job without thousand-pound bombs. He'd have to keep the damn things, but he wasn't happy about it.

In the hangar bay, the situation didn't look right to Pratt either, but this wasn't his business. He moved on as the men continued arguing. One of the last things he heard as he walked away was one of the ordnance officers saying, "These goddamn things are not going down in my weapons storage!"

Pratt was curious about the incident, but he had no intention of pursuing it. As a pilot, he didn't get involved in much that didn't directly involve his airplane, and he certainly wasn't an expert at weapons handling. But when he bumped into the ordnance officer later that night, he was still curious about what he had seen. They were friendly enough that Pratt could bring it up and ask why everyone had been so upset.

"Rocky, did you look at those bombs?" the man replied, starting to get agitated all over again.

"Yeah, they looked weird," Pratt said. "What were they?"

"Those are old comp B bombs. Composition B."

"Well, what's that?" Pratt asked, still not seeing what was so wrong.

"Rocky, they don't make those bombs anymore.

The H-6 bombs were built and designed to replace comp B. They're a different type of explosive."

"Yeah, I didn't think they looked like what we usually carry."

"Did you notice that they're banded bombs? You have to put a band around it to hang the damn thing on the airplane!"

"What does that mean?" Pratt asked.

"That is World War Two. Those things have come off an ammunition dump somewhere. They should have been disposed of, and somehow or another here they are in the damn system. And we don't know what to do with them."

"So that's what all the excitement was about? You wanted newer bombs?"

"Rocky, composition B was *very dangerous*," he explained, more than a hint of impatience in his voice. "Did you notice that it was dripping?"

"No."

"Well, if you had looked you would have seen a few spots on the deck. The stuff drips as it ages. That's dangerous because it's a fire hazard. Number two, composition B becomes sensitive to heat and sensitive to vibration when it ages, and it becomes more powerful."

The ordnance officer went on to explain that the old bombs could increase their explosive power by 50 percent under the right circumstances, meaning the thousand-pound bomb could explode with the force of a fifteen-hundred-pound bomb. A huge explosion. That's fine if it blows up on target, but not if it blows up on the ship, he said.

"Did you see the markings on those things?" he asked Pratt. "I know you're not going to believe me, but those dates . . . Damn it, one or two of them were dated 1935! And I know the rest of them have to be nearly that old. They've been sitting in some goddamn disposal area in a weapons depot all this time. They shouldn't be on this ship. That's what the argument was about."

Pratt had gotten the message, and he was concerned. Even if he wouldn't go out with those bombs strapped underneath him tomorrow, his buddies might.

"Well, what the hell are they going to do with them?" Pratt asked.

"I'm not sure. One group wanted to wheel them right across the hangar deck and throw them off the other side of the ship. But I don't know, they're going to need all the big stuff for that strike tomorrow, so it looks like we're keeping them. The captain talked to the skipper of the ammunition ship and they said that was all they had to give us. The captain didn't seem real happy about it, but he said we just have to keep the stuff.

"The weapons officers wouldn't let them down in the magazines with everything else, so they're moving it all topside and just storing it out on the deck."

The conversation upset Pratt, but he still wasn't sure if he had any role to play in the problem. He wondered if he should get involved by telling his superiors, but then he saw the ordnance officer again that same night. This time, some of his fears were allayed.

"Well, it looks like they've decided these things won't go off from the vibration of the catapult shot, so they're going to put them on that big launch tomorrow. We'll just get rid of them as fast as we can."

The ordnance officer seemed less upset, resigned to having the bombs on board for as short a time as possible. Pratt took his word that the bombs would be fine stored up on the flight deck. Hey, with those things, his buddies might have a good shot at bringing that mountainside down tomorrow.

Pratt settled down for the evening, and many of the rest of the ship's crew joined him. There were still men working all over the ship, as there always were at night, and some of the crew were still finishing up the ammunition transfer from the *Diamond Head*. Once the four hundred tons of ammunition was all on board, it still had to be put away, so those men would not be able to call it a night for quite a while. But for a lot of the crew, the day's work had come to an end and they were settling down for a late-night snack, maybe even a game of cards before they hit their bunks and fell asleep.

For others working late into the night, they would not be able to hit their bunks until much later, 2 A.M. for some. Once they did, they fell asleep quickly, exhausted from the night's hard work. Most of them would have to get up early the next morning for the big air strike, so the few hours of sleep were precious.

At 3:15 A.M., the quiet throughout most of the ship was shattered by the man-overboard alarm. Every single man had to get up and assemble in his division for a head count, standing in his underwear or whatever he could throw on, half asleep and barely standing erect. They had done this a hundred times before, but it was especially maddening when it happened in the middle of the night. The men were held in assembly for more than an hour as the division heads counted repeatedly to determine if anyone was missing. Others throughout the ship had to scramble to their stations to aid in the rescue attempt.

One man was missing. Word spread quickly that this was no false alarm, which shook some of the men out of their stupor. After a while, they heard that the man had been spotted in the water but not recovered. That immediately spawned questions. Why couldn't they pick him up? It was nearly dawn before the men were allowed to return to their bunks and try to get some sleep. They went back to sleep, but many were bothered by the sudden loss of a shipmate. Most didn't know the man, or even know who he was, but they knew they had lost their first life on Yankee Station.

They cared because he was a fellow sailor, and they cared because it just as easily could have been one of them. It also was a bad omen, a lousy way to start their long deployment on Yankee Station.

Chapter 7

FIRE ON THE FLIGHT DECK!

The morning of Saturday, July 29, 1967, began early for some of the men, but not all. Even though two launches were scheduled for that morning, much of the ship's crew was given the unusual permission to sleep a bit later than usual to make up for all the late hours. The ammunition transfer had been hard work for much of the crew, and the man overboard had kept anyone from getting rest in the late-night period when the bulk of the crew was off duty. Even on an aircraft carrier where men work around the clock and long days are nothing unusual, the officers still tried to compensate if the crew had been put through an extended period without rest.

A nice gesture, but it didn't help Ed Roberts any. Flight quarters, the call rousting the crew to begin preparations for the day's launches, was sounded at 4 A.M. Roberts and Gary Shaver were already awake, never having gotten back to sleep after the man-overboard alarm. As soon as they heard the alarm, they knew they wouldn't get any more sleep. By the time flight quarters sounded, Roberts had already dressed and started making his way to the flight deck. He was groggy as hell, regretting his decision last night to eat dinner before going to bed. He could have had an extra hour's sleep.

Roberts joined Shaver and the rest of the crew on the flight deck, working in the dark for a long time, testing the catapults and arresting gear, waiting for the sun to rise over the horizon and bring them closer to another full day of combat.

Bob Shelton was on the coffee-break area outside the bridge, still trying to settle down from his second night of sleep interrupted by the nightmare. He was badly shaken and waiting for the sun to rise. Shelton was looking over the sea with a coffee cup in his hand when his buddy James Blaskis appeared.

"Hey man, how's it going?" Blaskis asked, cheerful as usual. Then he saw Shelton's face and gave him a quizzical look. "Geez, what's wrong with you? You look like hell."

Shelton nodded his head and said he wasn't surprised, that he hadn't slept much at all in the past two nights.

"Yeah, that man overboard. I hear they didn't find the guy either."

"Even after that," Shelton said. "I . . . I just couldn't sleep. That's all."

Shelton was still thinking about the nightmare and wondering why he suddenly had such a problem. But he didn't want to discuss it with anybody, not even Blaskis. Too weird.

"Well, almost eight o'clock, about time to go. Where are you today?" Blaskis said.

"I'm in port aft," Shelton said, referring to the port-after steering compartment in the belly of the ship. "Guess I better get going . . ." And then he realized that he was wearing his white uniform as if he were going to work on the bridge that day. He'd put on the wrong uniform and never realized it until then.

"Yeah, I thought you might be. I'm supposed to be on the bridge. Wanna trade?"

Shelton hesitated and Blaskis asked again. "C'mon, you've already got the whites on."

Shelton agreed and he could see that Blaskis was happy to have a quiet day ahead of him instead of working on the bridge. He must have been pretty confident he could make the trade, too, because he was wearing his denim work clothes.

Blaskis called out goodbye to Shelton as he hustled down the ladder, the first of many on his long trip to the port-after steering compartment. As he left, Shelton could see that he had a paperback book shoved in his back pocket.

Shelton was still bleary-eyed, but it was time to go to work. The rest of the ship was getting busy too. On the *Forrestal*'s fifth day in the Vietnam War, the first air strike had been launched at 7 A.M., and that meant that the air crews, pilots, and flight deck crews had made an early start. The second launch was scheduled for 11 A.M. This was the mission Rocky Pratt had heard about the night before, the big assault on the rail line that would require launching most of the *Forrestal*'s planes as quickly as possible.

The mission needed heavy firepower, so the ordnance crews loaded the old composition B bombs that came aboard the night before—anything to get rid of the dangerous ordnance. If all went well, the old bombs would be off the ship by 11:30 A.M. and wreaking havoc over Vietnam. The pilots were never told they would be carrying old World War II–era bombs that were so unstable they scared the dickens out of the *Forrestal*'s ordnance crew.

The day promised to be a beautiful one on the sea, reaching eighty-seven degrees Fahrenheit by midmorning, with 74 percent humidity and calm seas. Cloud cover was scattered at two thousand feet, and once the sun rose, the sailors could see for ten miles. The sea was glassy, as flat and calm as a mountain lake.

All indications were that the *Forrestal* would serve another relatively uneventful day launching and retrieving airplanes in this, its fifth day of combat in its entire history. The previous days' operations had gone smoothly and today's operations shouldn't be any different. Still, the crew knew that nothing on an aircraft carrier was routine or certain.

The ship was set at material condition Yoke, a midpoint status required by the fact that air strikes were being prepared. If the ship were to completely stand down, material condition would be set at X, meaning that the ship is essentially "open" with free access throughout the ship for authorized personnel to travel from one area to another. When the ship was set at material condition Yoke, certain hatches and passageways were closed off as a protective measure so that the ship could be compartmentalized quickly in an emergency and any problems could be isolated. In a worst-case scenario, the ship could go to condition Zebra, sealing off most of the ship into tight portions that help compartmentalize fire, water, and dangerous gases.

A number of other navy ships in the area were providing support or conducting their own activities that morning on Yankee Station. The USS *Oriskany* and the USS *Bon Homme Richard,* two aircraft carriers, were nearby, as were the destroyers USS *Mackenzie, Rupertus,* and *Tucker,* and a number of other smaller vessels. The ammunition ship USS *Diamond Head* was still at Yankee Station after supplying the *Forrestal* with arms for the day's air strikes. Yankee Station was a central work area for navy ships supporting air strikes in North Vietnam and other land-based activities, so a number of ships were always in the area. Once in a while Roberts would look out toward the rising sun and see a ship's silhouette.

Shaver was on the flight deck with Roberts, but Shaver wasn't doing his usual job. He had broken his hand earlier in an accident when he and some other crew were lifting a piece of equipment on the flight deck. His hand was caught between the equipment and a railing, and severely crushed. Dr. Kirchner in the sick bay had put a cast on the hand and then Shaver was reassigned to duties he could perform with limited use of the hand. On this Saturday, he was working with the crash crew, ready to respond in an emergency, and he also was driving one of the tractors that helped start the planes. As he worked that morning, Shaver noticed that some of the bombs looked unusual.

Damn things look like antiques, he thought. *Those things look old as hell.* But ordnance wasn't his job. So what the hell. Work to do.

Roberts was in a foul mood already, angry that he'd gotten so little sleep the night before and feeling like he'd been on the flight deck for days without a break. He knew how tired he was and he knew that put him at risk for an accident, so he tried hard to concentrate. Just recently, before Shaver broke his hand, the two of them had witnessed a grisly accident on the flight deck. Shaver was directing an F-4 Phantom onto a catapult when someone frantically signaled him to stop the plane. The man normally didn't have anything to do with plane movement, so Shaver was puzzled at first. When the man continued his frantic signaling, Shaver ordered the pilot to stop and signaled for the wheels to be chocked. That's when he noticed crew running toward the rear of the plane, on the other side, out of Shaver's view. He felt a knot in his stomach as he saw crew members with white shirts and red crosses running toward the plane. When he stepped around to see what was wrong, Shaver saw a red shirt on the deck. While working on the ordnance hanging from the plane's wing, trying to make the last-minute adjustments so the plane could be launched quickly, the man's red shirt had become snagged on a rocket-mounting bracket. The plane continued to move forward, and the man was pulled off his feet. The man was dragging helplessly as the plane continued forward, and in his thrashing to free himself, one of his feet got caught under the plane's wheel. No one could hear the man's screams over the deafening sounds of the flight deck. Before anyone could react, the plane had rolled all the way up his leg and one side of his body.

Shaver was horrified. Blood was everywhere and Shaver could even see that the man had bitten through his tongue. Shaver suddenly realized that he had directed the plane forward and over the man's body. He took a few steps back, then ran behind the island and fell to his knees, vomiting on the deck. Falling forward, he pounded on the deck in a rage, so upset that he couldn't go back to work that day.

Roberts had also seen the accident up close and the image stuck with him. Now, as he worked to prepare the 7 A.M. strike, he knew the same thing could happen to him if he wasn't careful as he put the chocks under the wheels of aircraft. He had to be alert, no matter how crappy he felt.

There was another big reason Roberts was in a bad mood. Just a few weeks after shipping out on the *Forrestal,* Roberts had received a Dear John letter from his girl back home.

After finishing his work on one plane, Roberts was walking back to another when he saw a couple of crew members writing messages on a bomb hanging under a plane's wing. An old tradition, the messages usually were some sort of taunting toward the enemy. One of the crew was finishing up his message: "Suck on this, Ho Chi Minh!"

Roberts walked over and asked if he could borrow the chalk. With his greasy, gloved fingers, he carefully wrote out "Fuck you Janet."

The 7 A.M. launch proceeded with no problem. By 7:50 A.M., thirty-seven aircraft were launched against North Vietnam, and while the crew waited for the planes to return, they began preparations for the second launch, scheduled for 11 A.M. Roberts and the rest of his team of blue shirts had just finished positioning a plane on one of the catapults and were waiting over by the island for their next task. Their crew leader came over, motioning for them to crowd in closer to hear him. He shouted over the plane noise.

"Do you guys want to break for chow now?"

Roberts and the other crew were surprised because their team didn't usually take a break for another hour. Crew 4 usually went to chow first, but Roberts's crew leader explained that the other team wanted to switch for some reason. Didn't matter to Roberts or his fellow crew members. They shrugged their shoulders and headed off. Roberts was glad to get out of the noise and the wind, not to mention the stench of the fuel and exhaust. They filed around the island structure to the hatch that led them below, walking single file. As they went below, they stopped in their "coffee locker" to stow their gear. The locker was a small area with a coffee urn, used as a general break area and a place to hang your helmet and gloves. As they tossed their gear aside, Roberts pulled a cigarette out of his pocket and then pulled out his lighter. He snapped open the Zippo and sparked the lighter in one smooth move, a motion meant to look so utterly casual but one he'd practiced over and over when no one was looking. Unfortunately, the lighter didn't ignite, causing a few of his buddies to chuckle.

"Damn thing's out of fluid," he said. It probably wasn't, he realized, but he had to save face. "Better see if I can get some av-gas."

Roberts headed down the passageway to one of the fueling stations, where big black hoses were used to pump aviation fuel, or av-gas, up to the flight deck. Checking first to see if any of the purple shirt fuel guys were around, Roberts unreeled a couple feet of hose and squeezed it enough to make a few drops flow from the nozzle and into his lighter. Then he headed back to the coffee locker, where a few guys were still waiting before heading to chow. He started to head out with them, but he was so tired he decided a little sleep was better than food.

"Hey, Dan," he called out to one guy. "I'm not going to chow. I'm going to get some sleep back here in the fuel station. Wake me up when you get back, okay?"

Dan said he would, so Roberts turned around and went to the fuel station again. He stretched out on the floor there, resting his head on his arm and his headgear, and quickly fell asleep.

As 11 A.M. approached, some of the crew belowdecks were just getting into their day because of the late start. Ken Killmeyer had gone to breakfast and then went to pick up the day's mail for his division.

He returned to his berthing quarters, passed it out to the men in his division who were still there, and then stashed the rest to distribute later. Killmeyer's assignment for the morning was dull and laborious, like a great many of the jobs on board an aircraft carrier. While the glamorous work was being done up on the flight deck, Killmeyer was far below cleaning his division's berthing compartment. But before he got to that, he had to read his mail. Killmeyer had received a letter from his six-year-old sister Patty back home in Pittsburgh, and he immediately sat down to write her back.

Like so many others who had worked the night shift and were on their rest period, Gary Pritchard and Paul Friedman were sound asleep in their bunks, ignoring the constant cacophony that would wake anyone who wasn't used to sleeping with airplanes landing on a metal deck just feet above his head.

Captain Beling was still in his stateroom preparing to address the crew about the previous night's activities. Other officers usually handled the preparations for a launch and then Beling would step onto the bridge just before the planes were ready to go. The captain had been on the bridge for the launch of the aircraft in the 7 A.M. strike, but he then retired to his nearby sea cabin before resuming the rest of his working day. He was nearby and ready to take command if necessary, but Captain Beling wanted to take advantage of the lull between flight operations to address the crew about the previous night's man overboard. Losing a man overboard was particularly frustrating for Beling because it was always an unnecessary, wasted loss of life. Some purpose might be found in losing a man to combat or an unavoidable accident, but losing a man overboard was inexcusable for Beling.

As work continued on the flight deck and throughout the ship, Beling's voice got the crew's attention through the 1MC, the public-address system that penetrates every part of the ship. Killmeyer paused when he heard the 1MC crackle to life, putting down the letter he was writing home.

Beling began with the three words that he always used when addressing the crew.

"Men of *Forrestal,* this is the captain. As you know, we just launched our midmorning strike. Pretty soon we will be recovering some of our aircraft. But right now, I want to talk to you about something very, very serious. It is what happened and why it happened, that man overboard that we had early this morning at 3:15 A.M. At that time, a man named Warren saw someone fall overboard from elevator number one, which at that time was at the hangar-deck level. A few seconds later, the alert starboard lifeboat watch, two of them, saw a man in the water. Without hesitation, they threw in a life ring and notified the bridge.

"The life ring had a light attached to it and they put it in the water about twenty yards from the man and heard him shout for attention the word 'Hey!' The starboard quarter watch ran next; a seaman in Fourth Division also was alert. He didn't happen to see the man, but he did see the life ring and the light that was alertly thrown from the bridge. Within minutes HC-2 number twelve [a helicopter], piloted by Lieutenant Gregory, was launched. *Forrestal* maneuvered into position for rescue and stopped dead in the water about five hundred yards from the man's spotted position. A very black night."

Killmeyer listened carefully to the captain's story. Even way down in the port-after steering compartment, Blaskis put down his book to listen. They were curious to learn exactly what happened the night before, and why the man was not recovered.

"There were two destroyers in company, the *Rupertus* and the *Tucker*. They came in close to help. It took the helo about thirty minutes, with the destroyers' help and the ship's help, to find the man in the water. The helo then maneuvered into position over him for rescue and then lowered its rescue seat. The man involved grabbed the seat. However, as the seat was raised just a little bit, a foot or two or three, the man immediately lost his grip and disappeared into the water. *Forrestal* remained on the scene with the two destroyers until daybreak and departed without finding him. We have left the *Tucker* to continue searching. However, there is in my judgment no chance whatsoever that this man will be found.

"Now by taking our muster and subsequent close checking, we have established who the unfortunate individual is. It is Seaman Dyke of the First Division.

"Now some of the rest of this. Seaman Dyke fell from number-one elevator. At this time he was not assigned to the working party on that elevator. Accordingly, he had no business there. Second, three other shipmates appear to have been engaged in horseplay. The man, who must remain at this time nameless, who was fooling around with Dyke was observed to have made a punching motion at him, fooling around. Dyke backed up, lost his balance, and fell over the side.

"Now the rest of this is that horseplay cannot be conducted anywhere at all on a ship like this. It is all very well to give your life for your country, but it is not very smart to foolishly fall over the side.

"On a ship like this there are dangers on every side, and unless one keeps his eyes open and thinks ahead a little bit, we are going to have much more of these needless losses. Let's play heads-up ball and our losses then, if any, will come from the enemy, not from ourselves."

The 1MC fell silent again, and throughout the ship men went back to what they had been doing. The captain's address had captured everyone's attention, partly because it was the first time that most of the crew had gotten the whole story on the man overboard. Word had passed quickly that the man was not recovered, but most of the crew did not know until Beling's address who was lost, or how it happened. Some of the crew were not content with the explanation that the man could not be recovered; they wondered why the helicopter crew did not send a swimmer in to pick up the man, who would have been weak and probably hypothermic after thirty minutes in the night sea.

The planes from the first air strike were recovered without incident and then the deck was configured to launch the second air strike. Because an aircraft-carrier deck is both huge and tiny at the same time, depending on what you're trying to do with it, preparing a launch always required a great deal of planning and meticulous positioning of aircraft. To get all the planes launched as quickly as possible, so that all of the air strike's planes were up at once, the deck crew positioned planes around the edges of the flight deck to go through all the start-up sequences and safety checks that were necessary before flight. Then each plane was taxied forward to one of the four catapults for launch.

John McCain, Jim Bangert, and the twenty-five other pilots were ordered to their aircraft at 10:25 A.M., climbing into their cockpits with the aid of their crews and then proceeding with the sequential steps necessary to get a jet engine up to speed. As the pilots worked in the cockpit, dozens of crew were working around the aircraft to load bombs and missiles, conduct safety checks, and perform various other duties. The flight deck was a sea of colored shirts, with sailors maneuvering around aircraft and other equipment in the deliberate motion designed to avoid the many dangers lurking everywhere on deck. The sound was deafening as twenty-seven jet planes were readied for takeoff.

At 10:46 A.M., moving along at a brisk twenty-seven knots—about thirty-one miles per hour—the *Forrestal* turned so that the pilots would have enough wind over the flight deck to provide lift. The total wind speed over the flight deck was thirty-two knots, blowing from forward to aft of the ship, the equivalent of a thirty-seven-mile-per-hour wind.

Before the 11 A.M. launch of the attack planes, the deck crew launched a KA-3B tanker plane. This was standard procedure for any air-strike launch; tanker planes were always put in the air first so the attack planes could refuel as necessary. This enabled the fighters and bombers to take off with less weight and to fly longer missions than would be possible on just their initial fuel stores. An EA-1F Skyraider was also launched to provide electronic countermeasures that would help protect the other planes.

By 10:51 A.M., all of the flight crews had manned their aircraft and some of the planes had been started. Another KA-3B fuel tanker was being readied for launch, as was an E-2A Hawkeye, a prop plane with a large rotating dish on top that would be used for monitoring the attack planes' flights.

The pilots were in the final stages of their preflight tasks. Bangert was in the forward cockpit of his F-4 Phantom jet. He'd just started his starboard engine and was about to switch from external to internal electrical power. Bangert was a seasoned pilot, so much so that he was the senior landing-signal officer (LSO) for the carrier air wing, a position that made him responsible for guiding other pilots on their carrier-deck landings and also for issuing a grade on each landing. His mission for the 11 A.M. launch was to suppress any ground targets providing antiaircraft flak. Lawrence McKay would be riding in the second seat behind Bangert, acting as the radio intercept officer.

Bangert was informed five minutes before climbing into his aircraft that he would be carrying Zuni rockets rather than the 2.75-inch rockets more commonly used by the F-4 Phantom. Bangert had never flown with Zuni rockets, and during the five days the *Forrestal* was in combat, only 3 aircraft out of 379 planes launched with ordnance had carried Zuni rockets. The change was spurred by some technical problems that made it difficult to load the 2.75-inch rockets on the Phantom, which had been flown just that morning on the 7 A.M. strike and had come back with a five-hundred-pound bomb that had not disengaged properly. The commanding officer of the air wing briefed Bangert about a few flight procedures that needed to be altered because of the Zuni rockets—such as changing the target-sight settings—but apparently the Zuni rockets did not alter the original flight plan much. The MK-32 Zuni rocket could be used by naval aviators for a variety of tasks because of its versatility in both air-to-air and air-to-ground applications. For missions over North Vietnam, it was used almost exclusively against ground targets, often in an effort to suppress antiaircraft fire. Various types of warheads and fuses were installed on the Zuni, depending on the desired effect. On Bangert's plane that morning, the Zuni rockets were equipped with VT proximity fuses that caused them to detonate at treetop level. That made them effective against ground troops, whereas other fuse and warhead configurations could detonate the warhead on contact with a target, or as a "bunker buster" with a delayed-action fuse to detonate the explosive below the surface. At about six and a half feet long and five inches in diameter, the Zuni was long and sleek. Fins on the tail of the rocket were folded into the body until it was fired, and then they popped out to provide aerodynamic stability. Unguided once it was ignited, the Zuni was basically a point-and-shoot type of weapon. The rocket used a solid propellant that burned for about 1.5 seconds. Produced in Belgium, millions of Zuni rockets were fired in combat in Vietnam and in other conflicts.

Only two months earlier, a Zuni rocket had misfired from an F-8A Crusader on the aircraft carrier *Hancock*. Several crewmen near the plane were burned by the rocket launch, but the Zuni did not hit anything on the deck and caused no serious damage.

Bangert's plane was outfitted with twenty-four Zuni rockets, two Sidewinder missiles, and two Sparrow III missiles. The other aircraft on the flight deck were loaded with a variety of weapons, including Shrike and Sidewinder missiles, and many of the bombs that had been transferred to the *Forrestal* the night before.

In all, the planes sitting on the deck were loaded with sixteen of the old, World War II–era bombs weighing 1,000 pounds each, four newer bombs weighing 750 pounds each, and sixty newer bombs weighing 500 pounds each, in addition to missiles, rockets, and twenty-millimeter ammunition. There also were 150 tons of bombs and missiles sitting on the deck on pallets, and more below in storage.

Bangert's Phantom was positioned on the starboard side, at the extreme aft portion of the flight deck, with six more Phantoms parked to his right along the edge of the deck. Looking at the flight deck from overhead, this put Bangert's plane at the extreme lower right of the long flight deck, pointing across the deck at about a forty-five-degree angle. Other planes were positioned along the other deck edges, wingtip to wingtip, with a few looking straight up the flight deck toward the front of the ship, and others across the deck from Bangert, pointing back almost in his direction. The effect was to have the ship's deck ringed in planes, with an open space in the middle so that individual planes could be moved out and then forward to the catapults for launch. In addition, a dozen other planes were bunched up just aft of the island structure and on the two elevators in that area. Those planes included a KA-3B Sky Warrior fuel tanker loaded with twenty-eight thousand pounds of JP5 jet fuel.

Most of the jets on board required an external power source to start them up. Shaver was driving one of the tractors that help start the planes, and he had been working at the very rear of the flight deck before being called to help with some planes farther forward. As he drove his tractor forward, he passed his good friend Lonnie Hudson on a tractor going in the opposite direction. Gary Shaver's tractor had the longer hose needed by the RA-5C Vigilantes that were forward, so he knew that Hudson was going back to do the F-4 Phantoms at the rear. They were swapping places.

As they passed each other, Hudson nodded his head and gestured at Shaver as if to say, "Hey, what's up?" Shaver responded with a friendly shrug of the shoulders and moved on. He had no idea that switching positions with his friend Lonnie would turn out to be such a pivotal moment.

Bangert's plane was being readied by still another crewman in a squat, bright yellow tractor. He hooked up his tractor to the plane's electrical system and hit the juice when Bangert gave him the signal. The crewman then sat back on his tractor and watched Bangert go through the rest of the pre-flight preparations, much of which involved coordinating his cockpit checks with the crew outside arming his plane with the missiles.

Two of the crew members working with Bangert's plane were busy checking the missiles and rockets to ensure that they were properly installed and that the systems were safe. One man began conducting stray voltage checks on the weapons systems, to make sure the electrical system was not malfunctioning in a way that could accidentally trigger the weapons. He found no stray voltage in any of the systems on the port side and then went to the starboard side to conduct the same tests. Having found no stray voltage or other potential problems with the weapons systems, he plugged in the "pigtails," cable connectors that linked the rockets and the plane's launching device. This was the shortcut approved by the ship's administration for the sake of speed. Plugging in the pigtails armed the weapons on the port side.

At 10:51:21 A.M., Bangert had just started his starboard engine. With the engine running, Bangert reached out to press the button that would switch from the external cart's power supply to the plane's internal system. As his gloved finger hit the button, Bangert and McKay both felt a mild explosion shake the plane. Bangert looked up in time to see a small rocket flying across the deck with a yellow-orange exhaust flame.

Oh my God, what was that? Was that from my plane? Frantically, Bangert immediately rechecked all his weapons switches and found that they were in the proper position. *I couldn't have fired a rocket! What happened?*

All over the deck, other pilots who had glimpsed the missile's path were frantically checking their own cockpit systems. They all shared that heart-stopping moment of uncertainty, the blood draining from their faces as they looked to see if they were responsible. None of the pilots found their switches out of place. An electrical surge had fired the rocket on Bangert's plane without anyone hitting a firing switch.

The single Zuni rocket had fired from one of the three launchers installed on the port wing of Bangert's F-4 Phantom. Ironically, Bangert was the safety officer Ken McMillen had consulted about the pigtail shortcut, the officer who said there was nothing to be done about the safety risk.

In an instant, the firing of the rocket initiated a long journey of pain. Two crew members were kneeling under the port wing of Bangert's Phantom when the rocket fired. The one who was checking the weapons systems was burned on the left side of his face, left hand, and his wrist, and he felt like his jersey was on fire even though there were no flames. Several other crewmen working around the Phantom were knocked down by the rocket launch, which happened so quickly that no one actually saw the rocket leave the plane. They all looked back at the Phantom to see smoke rising from one of the rocket pods on the port wing, and small bits of debris fluttering in the wind.

The rocket was flying across the deck at chest height, at hundreds of miles per hour, headed toward a fuel chief who was standing just behind the number-four arresting wire, pretty much in the middle of the deck between Bangert's plane and those parked on the other side of the ship. He was knocked off his feet by the rocket as it passed without touching him.

Another sailor on deck was much less fortunate. An ordnanceman, he was walking along the flight deck in front of a group of A-4 Skyhawks when the Zuni rocket hit him in the shoulder, passing through and instantly severing his arm but leaving him standing.

The rocket then continued on, its course altered to the right by the collision with the ordnanceman. Having traveled about one hundred feet, the rocket then struck the A-4 Skyhawk piloted by John McCain. Like most pilots, McCain was a bit superstitious, and his parachute rigger, Tom Ott, a crewman responsible for the pilot's equipment, had begun a little preflight routine. Ott was carefully wiping McCain's helmet visor clean before handing it to him in the cockpit. This was to make sure McCain could get a clear look at the antiaircraft missiles coming at him over North Vietnam, but the act had taken on more significance over time. It had become an important gesture of friendship, a reassuring, last-minute favor for a pilot who was about to risk his life in combat. Ott had just wiped the visor clean and handed the helmet back to McCain, and then Ott shut the plane's canopy.

Ott gave McCain a thumbs-up signal, and McCain probably returned it with a smile that Ott could not see under the pilot's face mask. That was the last time McCain ever saw Ott.

Nearby, Robert Zwerlein was getting McCain's plane outfitted and ready to move forward to the catapults. Standing just a few feet away, he was focused on the plane and never saw the rocket fire on the other side of the deck.

McCain felt a huge impact as the Zuni rocket tore through his plane on the right side and exited the left side, ripping open his fuel tank with four hundred gallons of JP5 jet fuel. Two crewmen nearby were set on fire as the hot rocket exhaust passed by them. They were already rushing forward toward the island before the jet fuel spreading over the deck ignited.

Just below the flight deck at the very rear of the ship, Edmond McGrew was on man-overboard watch, keeping his eyes trained on the water in his sector, looking for anyone who had fallen overboard. As McGrew watched the water on the port side of the ship, another sailor had joined him on the fantail for a cigarette. Now they both saw the Zuni rocket hit the water on the port side, never exploding. They could tell that the object was not a man overboard, but they had no idea what it was.

The fuel poured out of McCain's torn plane, spreading to the rear of the ship rapidly as it was pushed not only by the thirty-seven-mile-per-hour wind but by the exhausts of at least three jets positioned immediately in front of McCain's plane. The jet fuel was ignited soon by fragments of burning rocket propellant, but there was a delay of a second or so as the fuel spilled from the plane, giving some crew members enough time to realize the danger they were in. With a sudden, deafening "whoomp!" sound, the fuel ignited and soon engulfed all of the A-4 Skyhawks parked on the port side. In a heartbeat, scores of men were in a horrible situation. Some men, like Robert Zwerlein, were doomed by their close proximity to the initial fire. As the fire flashed, he had no chance to escape and was caught in the blaze.

The pilots strapped inside their planes needed help to get out. As they looked out of their canopies, they saw nothing but flames and black smoke, which was so thick that some of them could not see well enough to tell what awaited them if they opened their canopies. And others who could see knew that they were surrounded by a burning lake of jet fuel. In that instant, dozens of crewmen around those planes found themselves soaked in burning jet fuel. Several men stumbled out of the fire scene, covered head to toe in flames. One pilot jumped out of his plane and made his way out of the fire, his entire flight suit in flames. Once he got out of the fire and headed toward safety, he inexplicably turned around and walked back into the fire. Probably disoriented, he disappeared into the heart of the fire and never came back out.

The fire had erupted so quickly that no one had a chance to warn those on the rear portion of the deck to run toward the safety of the center deck and the island structure. The men trapped in the fire had little or no opportunity to escape the huge fireball that grew ever larger as the fuel poured out of the planes, each one adding hundreds of gallons of fuel to the fire.

The rocket's flight was almost caught on film by the plat camera, a television camera located on the island structure. The plat camera was used to record all flight-deck operations for future study, and also to provide images of flight-deck activities to monitors throughout the ship. When the rocket and the subsequent fire caught the camera operator's eye, he was focused farther forward on a plane about to be launched off a catapult. He immediately swung the camera back to the rear of the ship and trained it on the fire, where it remained for hours, but he missed the actual launch of the rocket. The camera operator had to abandon his post after a while because of shrapnel penetrating the space, but the camera continued to record the events. Later analysis of the film showed the reflection of the rocket in a window as it traveled across the deck.

Aviation machinist's mate Robert Mitchell was on routine patrol in his temporary duties with the master of arms that day, and he had stopped by the plat-camera location to watch some of the flight-deck operations as the 11 A.M. launch approached. Mitchell was watching one of the monitors in the area when he saw a flash on the screen and immediately felt a concussion of the ship. When the plat-camera operator swung around and showed the aft portion of the flight deck in flames, Mitchell hastily headed toward the master of arms's office.

He knew the fire was immediately above the office, and his friends there probably didn't know the danger they were in. He hurried down the island structure to the hangar bay below and then sprinted to warn them, himself rushing into an area that would soon be in extreme danger. He was constantly shouting "Fire on the flight deck!" as he was running, to alert everyone he saw. Having seen the magnitude of the fire with his own eyes, Mitchell was not waiting for orders to act.

On the level just below the flight deck, Airman Charles Price was in the squadron storeroom and had just finished his duties in preparing the VA-46 squadron for the 11 A.M. launch. At 10:51, just before the accident and before any alarms sounded over the 1MC, Price informed the other squadron members that he'd finished his work in preparing the launch and was going to go to lunch. To get to the mess hall, Price left the squadron storeroom and went to a catwalk that runs along the port side of the ship and up to the flight deck. Price climbed four steps up the ladder leading to the flight-deck level and was facing the front of the ship when he heard a sudden whoosh as the jet fuel erupted. Price turned around toward the sound and found himself facing a wall of flame.

Near the number-two arresting wire on the rear portion of the flight deck, close to McCain's plane, crewman G. L. Reynolds was making a visual check of the aircraft starts in the A-4 Skyhawks lined up on the port side. The warrant officer in charge of the planes, Donald Hugo, was nearby and about to make a check of his headset communications with Reynolds. Both had their backs to the McCain plane, so neither saw the rocket hit, but at that instant, they both heard the fuel erupt and felt a massive shock wave from the explosion. They turned around to see McCain's Skyhawk in flames and men running away from the fire. They also saw others crawling away, their clothes and bodies on fire. Instead of running away from the obvious danger, Reynolds and Hugo both rushed toward the planes on the port side to "break down" the aircraft by releasing the chains and chocks holding them in place. If the pilots were to have any chance at maneuvering the planes out of harm's way, someone had to release them first. After releasing several planes, Reynolds directed one to taxi forward and away from McCain's plane. Hugo then rushed to the rear to help with the initial firefighting efforts.

Overhead, Leonard Eiland was at the controls of Angel 20, the helicopter flying "plane guard" for the 11 A.M. launch. The *Forrestal*'s helicopters were out of commission for the morning because of scheduled maintenance, so the aircraft carrier *Oriskany* had sent Angel 20 as a loan for the morning. For any aircraft launch, navy regulations require a helicopter to be circling in the air near the ship and ready to rescue any fliers who go down. Most days, it meant just flying in circles until the launch was completed, so the pilot, David Clement, let his co-pilot Eiland have the controls.

Angel 20 was commencing yet another turn from nearly a mile out when Eiland caught something out of the corner of his eye and looked toward the *Forrestal*.

What the hell is that?

Eiland saw splashes in the water followed by a large burst of black smoke on the rear portion of the flight deck. He motioned to Clement, who looked toward the carrier and saw the problem.

"Looks like a plane down, maybe some men overboard," Clement said. "Taking control . . ."

The pilot took over from Eiland and turned Angel 20 sharply toward the *Forrestal,* kicking the helicopter into high speed to close the distance. He called back to the *Oriskany* to report what he had seen, and alerted the two rescue swimmers in the back to prepare for a water rescue. In fact, the first splashes they saw were from the Zuni rocket and debris from the initial ignition of the jet fuel. It also is likely that some men jumped overboard at that moment to escape the flames.

On the *Forrestal*'s bridge, Lieutenant Commander James Bloedorn was in charge while the captain was away. When the fire started he was standing by the windows on the left side of the bridge overlooking the flight deck with a young sailor named W. T. Burgess. Bloedorn had looked away from the flight deck, and when he turned back, he saw Burgess pointing toward the rear of the ship. The young man's eyes were huge white saucers and he couldn't get any words out of his mouth. Bloedorn looked and saw the fireball.

"Plane on fire on the flight deck, aft!" Bloedorn called out.

Bob Shelton immediately glanced up at the clock in front of him and wrote in his logbook: "1052: Aircraft fire on the flight deck." It didn't excite him especially; it was just another fire. The ship had plenty of small ones all the time.

Bloedorn ordered Burgess to sound the fire alarm over the 1MC public-address system. Burgess was a native of Macon, Georgia, with a heavy Southern drawl, and one of his jobs on the bridge was to pass on announcements from the bridge officers to various others throughout the ship. He hustled over to the intercom system and first sounded a whistle tone to call for attention. Then he called out, "Fahr on the flight deck! Aeeyft. Fahr on the flight deck! Aeeyft. Man all foam stations on the double!"

Then after a short pause, Burgess came back on the 1MC to call, "All repair crews man your GQ stations!" A bit of a misnomer, "repair crews" referred to the emergency crews specially trained for firefighting and rescue, as well as actual repairs of damage inflicted in combat, for instance.

Shelton looked up when he heard Burgess call the fire alarm, because he thought Burgess seemed a little too excited for a routine fire. Belowdecks, Killmeyer had written nearly two pages of the letter home to his little sister when Burgess's excited alarms came over the 1MC system. Killmeyer and Burgess were in the same division and were close buddies, so he was used to Burgess's thick Georgia accent. The scratchy public-address system, combined with Burgess's accent and his excitement, made it difficult for some on board to understand his initial fire call. When he called, "Fire on the flight deck. Aft," in his heavy accent, the words were a bit muffled and many crewmen did not understand the initial fire warning. Killmeyer did, however, and he also noticed a change in Burgess's usual calm demeanor. He knew that Burgess was a quiet, mild-mannered guy who never even cursed. Killmeyer thought of him as the kind of guy you want to marry your daughter, maybe. But now Killmeyer immediately noted a sense of urgency in the fire call and began to worry.

Immediately after the first fire alarm, Bloedorn could see that the fire was serious and out of control. He called out, "Sound general quarters!" right after the fire started but then several seconds passed and he still hadn't heard the alarm. He looked back toward Burgess, who was standing directly in front of the general-quarters alarm, and realized the young man had not heard him.

"Sound general quarters!" Bloedorn shouted again, more urgently, and he simultaneously lunged toward Burgess's station to hit the alarm himself. Burgess heard him that time and reached up. As soon as he hit the lever, the ship was filled with a sound that chilled most sailors to the bone, while simultaneously triggering a tremendous adrenaline rush. At 10:53 A.M., sixteen alarm bongs rang out—it seemed an eternity as the bongs sounded and the anticipation grew—and then Burgess called, "General quarters! General quarters! All hands man your battle stations!"

If the first announcement did not get everyone's attention on board the ship, and it didn't, the general-quarters alarm certainly indicated that the ship was in trouble. Sailors throughout the ship dropped whatever they were doing and hustled to get to their general-quarters stations, creating near pandemonium as people rushed to get through the crowds clogging passageways. Killmeyer shoved the letter under the pillow in his bunk and started racing toward his general-quarters station, the magazine-handling room for the five-inch port guns aft and below on the fourth deck. He headed up a ladder and to the port side of the ship because GQ procedures called for sailors to run aft and down on the port side and run forward and up on the starboard side, in an effort to expedite movement.

Not everyone was in position to hear the announcements clearly, however. Frank Eurice, coming off of a long watch on the engine's throttles, had decided to take advantage of his midday break to get some sun. While the 11 A.M. air strike was being readied, Eurice and a friend he knew only as French had made their way out onto the starboard-side gun-mount sponson, a structure that juts out from the side of the ship just below the flight deck to hold the big five-inch guns. This was to be a rare opportunity for Eurice to see sunlight, because normally he worked far belowdecks.

There were huge stacks of potatoes in crates out there, so Eurice and his buddy just spread their beach blankets on top of them. They were enjoying a fine morning up there, oiled down and suntanning, just watching the Tonkin Gulf roll by. Local boats were off in the distance, and the water was as flat as a lawn, making for quite a picturesque scene. The guys were really enjoying the time outside, and Eurice rolled over to get some sun on his back. That's when he noticed the black smoke.

Eurice wasn't concerned at first because from his vantage point he couldn't see exactly where the smoke was originating. The *Forrestal* normally produced a nearly invisible exhaust, but as a machinist's mate, Eurice knew the boilers could churn black smoke if the technicians, known as BTs, didn't get the oil-and-air mixture just right.

"Those dumb BTs," Eurice muttered, looking up at the stack. That's when he noticed there was no smoke coming out of the stacks. *What the hell?*

Eurice called to his buddy, "Hey French! What do you think this is?" They both sat up and lifted their sunglasses to take a better look at the smoke, by now rolling off the deck and down toward the sea. They just sat quietly for a moment and watched the smoke, unable to imagine anything that would cause such a scene.

Up on the bridge, the officers in charge immediately notified Captain Beling of an obviously dire situation. The fire message was delivered to the captain in his sea cabin, his working quarters about twenty feet from the bridge. (The captain's regular quarters were farther away and belowdecks, but the sea cabin allowed the captain some privacy and rest without being too far away from the action.) Having overseen the morning's first launch and then addressing the crew about the man overboard, Beling had retired to his sea cabin to finish getting dressed. As the time approached for the second launch of the morning, he was just finishing the routine that on most mornings he would have done earlier. He was showered and had put on his crisp uniform pants and shoes, but he was still standing in his white T-shirt in the bathroom after shaving. He had just wiped the last bits of shaving cream off of his face and was reaching for his khaki uniform shirt when he heard the phone ring.

The ringing of the phone immediately told him something was wrong because the captain's sea cabin is considered a refuge where you don't bother him without a good reason.

Beling hurried over to the phone by the bedside

and grabbed it. He immediately heard someone exclaim, "Captain, we have a big fire on the flight deck!" Without any other response, Beling quickly put the phone back in its cradle and rushed out the door and straight to the bridge. He arrived in a few seconds, still in his T-shirt, and found a terrible scene awaiting him. He took his seat in the high captain's chair on the left side of the bridge, simultaneously giving him a clear view of the flight deck and putting him in the position that most clearly evidenced his authority.

Beling could see that his officers were understandably excited and frightened by the scene below them. There was a noisy din of voices shouting orders, asking questions, and yelling into microphones to be heard in other portions of the ship. The adrenaline was flowing, and Beling knew it had to be contained if he and his officers were to respond well. Beling immediately established order by taking command of the ship.

He calmly stated, "I have the con." Acknowledging that Beling was officially in control of the ship, Bloedorn called out, "The captain has the con!" and the helmsman repeated, "Aye, aye, captain has the con." Shelton noted in his log that the captain was in control.

Instantly, Beling could see that his ship was facing a major threat. One look out the windows aft showed him a huge fireball and billowing black smoke, with men running out of the curtain of flames, their clothes burning. Others were running toward the fire to help.

Officers and crew were bombarding Beling with

information about the fire and the ship's status, but his own voice overcame any others when he gave an order. His first concern was to reduce the wind flowing across the deck so that the flames would not be fanned unnecessarily. "Emergency full back!" Beling called out, ordering the ship's engines slammed into reverse and to full speed. This was a radical move, akin to throwing a car into reverse while cruising down a highway, but Beling wanted to slow the ship very quickly. The ship shuddered as the order was executed, and soon the ship's speed was cut from twenty-seven knots, or thirty-one miles per hour, to about nine knots, or eleven miles per hour. That eliminated the strong wind that was whipping the flames ever higher. But Beling soon ordered the ship forward again at a slower pace. He did not want to come to a dead stop, because a slight wind would help keep the fire from moving forward from its current location.

Other officers on the bridge were busily giving orders to the crew on the flight deck and were communicating with other key individuals throughout the ship, all the while keeping Beling informed of what they were learning and what they were doing. In the first moment of the fire, the bridge was a hectic but highly organized focal point for the men of *Forrestal*. Shelton, the quartermaster in charge of recording everything happening on the bridge, scribbled furiously in his logbook as every order was given and every report called out over the din of voices. Though the first call of "fire on the flight deck" didn't excite him, Shelton began to realize something very serious was happening. He worked hard to concentrate as orders and reports swirled around him.

On the other side of the bridge, Captain Beling was sitting in control, but he was still half dressed. Having taken care of the most pressing duty in slowing the ship, he took a moment to calm his officers and bridge crew. He reminded them that they all had a job to do and that they should all keep a calm head. The men on the bridge paused to hear the captain's reminder and then went back to their duties.

At that point, the captain turned to the marine orderly who was always nearby to assist him. "Go get my shirt," he ordered. The orderly quickly returned with Beling's uniform shirt, which he then put on.

Now I feel like a captain, he thought, and returned to giving orders.

Word was spreading quickly throughout the ship. Commander Merv Rowland, the chief engineering officer, was in his stateroom belowdecks when he first heard the 1MC calls for fire on the flight deck and then the general-quarters alarm. Rowland had been up most of the night like the rest of the crew for the man overboard, but then he was up even longer because there had been a problem with an evaporator. As chief engineering officer, Rowland was responsible for practically every piece of machinery on the ship, so he had stayed awake all night supervising his crew as they made the repairs. Rowland didn't *have* to be there; he had a good crew working under him that he trusted, but he knew it would be helpful for the old man to be there in case they needed a word of advice. Rowland was far from a softy, but he understood that young sailors can be reassured and encouraged by the mere presence of an older, more experienced hand.

The evaporator repair was completed successfully, and then Rowland headed back to his stateroom for some rest. He had just undressed and crawled into his bunk when the fire alarm sounded. Like others familiar with the frequency of small fires on board a carrier, Rowland did not immediately react to the fire call. He lay in his bunk for a moment, waiting to hear further announcements or the ringing of his bedside phone. He knew that if the situation was serious, the bridge would notify him quickly. But Rowland would be long gone by the time his phone rang. Immediately after the alarms, Rowland's Filipino steward rushed into his stateroom, out of breath. He knocked on the door quickly and then opened it without waiting for Rowland's permission. Having seen the fire on a television monitor, the steward rushed to notify his officer.

"Commander, Commander! Fire! *Bad* fire!" he shouted.

As chief engineering officer, Rowland would play an important role in any disaster aboard the *Forrestal*, directing damage control and repair efforts and reporting directly to the captain about the progress of the problem and the remedy. Like Captain Beling, Rowland was not dressed when he got the alarm. He rushed out of his stateroom wearing nothing but his boxers and a T-shirt, headed toward his GQ station at central control, but then he turned back and got his shoes because he thought the deck might get hot.

As he was putting his shoes on, Rowland felt a mixture of anger and determination.

Here I've done twenty-eight years in the goddamn navy, been in wars and on all kinds of ships, and I come out here and a bunch of goddamn gooks are going to finish my career. Goddammit!

But then his innate ferocity surged within him. To no one but himself, he stood up and exclaimed, "Bullshit! Let's put out this fire!" Rowland raced out into a passageway already crowded with sailors rushing to their stations.

Back on the flight deck, less than a minute had passed since the rocket fired from Bangert's plane and hit McCain's plane. The fire had already engulfed most of the planes parked on the port side alongside McCain, with the JP5 jet fuel spilling aft, toward the rear of the ship. Aviation bosun's mates Robert Menery and D. W. Maxwell were standing near elevator number two, forward on the port side, when Menery spotted the fire. The scene on the deck was already reaching hellish proportions, with a huge wall of flame obscuring the rear of the ship and the dense black smoke billowing hundreds of feet into the air. Like dozens of other men who were well out of the immediate danger zone forward on the flight deck, Menery and Maxwell started running toward the fire to help their shipmates. At the same time, those who were trapped in the fire were running and crawling out of the inferno, fellow sailors and aviators helping them along and struggling to carry injured men out of danger.

Airman T. J. Hunt was also running aft from the same area as Menery and Maxwell, and when Hunt got closer to the fire area, he encountered young Bobby Zwerlein trying to move forward with his clothes burning. Hunt aided Zwerlein, putting him on the deck to help extinguish the flames on his body and then dragging him toward the island structure where men were starting to gather for safety and first aid. As he was aiding Zwerlein, other sailors brought forward the man who had been hit by the rocket as it flew across the deck. His face was badly burned and beginning to swell, but he was not bleeding badly even though his left arm was missing. He was reaching across with his other hand to grab the wound, and crying, "Help me." The sailors laid him down on the deck behind the island, where other wounded were gathering, and then they could see that his trousers were on fire and his abdomen was open. He was conscious and worried that he would lose his arm, not realizing it was already gone.

The aviators strapped into their planes were facing tough decisions, without much time to think. For those parked on the starboard side, near Bangert's plane where the rocket originated, the response to the fire was easier because it did not engulf them immediately. Those aviators were able to see how bad the situation was, but they also could tell that the fire was not in their immediate vicinity.

The first reaction of pilots near the fire or engulfed in it was to stay with the plane as they had been instructed, waiting for the deck crew to extinguish the fire or rescue them. They also had no idea some of them were sitting on top of old bombs that would explode in the fire far sooner than anyone expected. Most of the pilots paused before trying to escape, a pause that cost some of them their lives. The most fortunate pilots escaped from their cockpits with the help of their plane crews on the deck and, like everyone else on the flight deck, they alternately ran for the cover of the island and headed back toward the flames to help others escape. All of the twelve aviators parked to the rear on the right side of the deck, including Bangert and McKay, whose plane had accidentally fired the rocket, managed to escape their planes without serious injury. But beginning immediately to the left of Bangert's plane, on the very rear of the flight deck, and all the way beyond McCain's plane on the left side of the ship, the pilots were in serious trouble.

To the left of McCain's Skyhawk, David Dollarhide had been in his cockpit awaiting the launch when he heard a muffled explosion. As he looked out to the deck, he saw burning JP5 fuel rolling out and to the front of his plane. Initially he was concerned but thought the situation might be handled quickly. Within seconds, however, Dollarhide saw five or six men rolling out of the fire, in flames and writhing on the deck.

Dollarhide reacted quickly, knowing he had to get out of the plane before it was totally engulfed by the fire. He unbuckled his harness, opened the canopy, and stood up in the cockpit, feeling the heat from the flames already growing closer. Before trying to extricate himself, he took the time to pull down the "head knock" on the ejection seat. The ejection seat of a jet plane is an extremely dangerous device that can kill when accidentally activated, so the pilots were taught to carefully deactivate the seat when leaving the plane. The "head knock" was a handle that pulled down from the pilot's headrest, deactivating the ejection system. (The pilot would knock his head on it if the seat were left in the safe mode, reminding him to arm the ejection seat.) Though his plane might be blown to shreds in a few minutes, Dollarhide followed proper procedure in disarming his ejection seat so it would not be a danger to others.

Without his plane crew to help him out with the ladder he normally used, Dollarhide could see that he faced a dangerous leap to the flight deck, which was rapidly being covered with burning fuel. The aviators had not been trained to escape a ground fire surrounding their planes, so he had to improvise. Dollarhide decided that the best way to escape was to go directly forward, over the part of the canopy that jutted up from the front part of the cockpit like a short windshield. If he could get out of the cockpit and up on the nose of the plane, he might be able to leap past the flames.

But the cockpit of a Skyhawk leaves very little room for maneuvering; it is known as one of the tightest cockpits ever made. So the best Dollarhide could do was stand on the seat and lunge forward. He fell awkwardly over the front canopy, landing hard on the nose of the plane and immediately slipping right off onto the deck ten feet below. Dollarhide landed hard on his right hip and elbow. Barely making it past the fire line, Dollarhide lay on the deck stunned from his fall, hurting badly and unable to get up. He lay there on his side for a moment, in pain and feeling the intense heat radiating from the fire, waving his arms to call for help. A few yards away, Airman Price, the one who had stepped up the ladder to the flight deck on his way to lunch and encountered a wall of flame, saw Dollarhide on the deck. Price climbed up onto the deck and ran to Dollarhide, helping the aviator to his feet. Dollarhide took a few steps and fell again, this time into the arms of a green-shirted crewman. Price and the green shirt both helped Dollarhide toward the safety of the island, dragging him eventually.

All of the pilots on the port side were engaged in the same struggle for their lives. Back on the fantail on the port side, Lieutenant Commander Herb Hope's Skyhawk was parked on the extreme back corner of the flight deck, behind where the fire started. He heard a sudden "whoomp!" as the fuel ignited, and as he looked forward to the fire, he saw an orange-red fireball before the sky suddenly turned black. The thick, oily smoke was being blown directly back over Hope's plane, engulfing him in a black cloud that shut out any other indicators of how bad the fire was or what Hope should do in response. Before the black cloud completely engulfed Hope's plane, he looked to his left and saw his friend Lieutenant Commander Gary Stark in the cockpit of the Skyhawk just forward of Hope's plane. Stark's canopy was open, like many others on the flight deck, because the pilots got very hot sitting in their flight gear in the blazing sun. They usually did not put the canopy down until the last minute. Hope had closed his cockpit canopy early because he was annoyed by jet exhaust blowing right into his face, but Stark was sitting exposed in the open cockpit with no gloves and his oxygen mask off.

As the flames crawled up Stark's plane and into the open cockpit, he had no protection. Hope could see Stark react by raising his hands and crossing his arms over his face. That was the last time anyone saw Stark alive. Others would report seeing him later, seeming to sit calmly in his plane as it burned, but he was already dead.

As the black smoke caused the bright Tonkin Gulf morning to turn dark for Hope, he quickly considered his options. No one was nearby to help him, and even if there were, Hope would not have seen them because of the smoke. The fuel from McCain's plane was rushing to the rear of the flight deck, directly to Hope's corner of the world, and he could see flames already beginning to leap up toward his plane. He quickly decided to get out of his plane and make a run for it, but as all the other pilots were learning, getting out on your own is no easy feat once you're strapped in for a carrier launch. The easiest way to get out quickly was to jettison the canopy, actually blowing it off the plane instead of raising it manually, which could be awkward without help. The Skyhawk was capable of blowing the canopy off the plane with explosive charges, as part of the sequence required to use the plane's ejection seat. But even in the heat of the moment, Hope was thinking like a good aviator.

I wonder if popping the canopy will put this plane ACOP, he thought, meaning "aircraft out of commission for parts." Normally, he wouldn't want to put the plane down for repairs because he blew the canopy, but that thought only lasted a short second.

Hope put his head down to protect himself from the blast and pushed the button to jettison the canopy. Instantly, the canopy went flying up and away from the plane, allowing the cloud of smoke to wrap around the pilot. Wasting no time, he used the same maneuver that Dollarhide had attempted in getting to the front of the aircraft, but he managed to get over the front canopy and onto the nose without falling off the plane. Then he wiggled his way out across the nose to the refueling probe, a long metal tube that sticks straight out alongside the nose of the plane. Hope grabbed the refueling probe and swung his legs down, hanging from the probe to get himself close enough to the deck to jump down safely. As soon as he was down, Hope ran a short distance to the edge of the flight deck and leapt into the safety net that juts out a few feet. A little lower than the flight deck and as far away from the fire as he could get for the moment, the safety net looked like temporary safety from the fire and the shrapnel that Hope knew would be flying soon. Hope never slowed down when he got to the edge and threw himself at full speed into the safety net, where he landed right on two green shirts who had had the same idea a moment earlier.

Forward at the origin of the fire, McCain was making the same decision as all the other pilots who found themselves trapped in the fire. Like the others who would survive, McCain wasted no time in getting out of his plane. McCain flipped the switches to shut down his engines, and at about the same time, he heard two loud clanks as the thousand-pound bombs fell off his plane's belly and hit the deck. McCain opened his canopy and threw himself out on the nose of his airplane. He walked out onto the narrow refueling probe and jumped down onto the deck and directly into the burning fuel from his plane. He rolled through the fire to the forward edge of the inferno, tumbling out with his flight suit on fire and covered in fuel. He quickly rolled and patted out the flames on his clothes, then jumped to his feet, wasting no time in running away from the scorching fire and toward the safety of the island. McCain ran as fast as he could, glimpsing Dollarhide lying on the deck and being aided by others. He saw another pilot leaving his airplane in the same way he did, jumping into the fire and rolling clear. That pilot's flight suit was in flames.

All over the flight deck, crewmen were rushing to drag hoses from the fire stations toward the fire. Of the seventeen fog-foam stations on the deck, hoses from eight of them were being led toward the fire within the first minute after it started, one station aft was engulfed in flames, and three were inoperable for mechanical reasons. Belowdecks, sailors were manning the foam-generation stations that fed foam up to the deck. They activated the large pump stations that mix a simple detergent solution with pressurized seawater, creating a foam that the firefighters can use to smother the fire. The twenty seawater firefighting stations on the flight deck also were being manned quickly, with hoses from eight stations led aft in the first minute, two engulfed in flames, and one not functional.

Most of the crewmen were trying to help in the firefighting, even if they initially had sought cover from the fire. Sailors ran to the nearest firefighting stations and dragged the hoses toward the fire as others helped to get the fog foam or seawater flowing. Some difficulties occurred right away, as sailors untrained in the operation of the systems did their best to get them working. The fog-foam generators required activation, and some sailors did not know the procedure, fumbling with the switches and buttons to get the system operational. At most stations, however, the fog foam began flowing quickly, within forty-five seconds.

In the crash-crew shack in the island, William Brooks and Richard Sietz were discussing who would take the next launch and who would take the plane recovery. They were part of Repair 8, the team of firefighters and rescuers who stood by ready to spring into action immediately in the event of a crash or other emergency.

The crash shack was located on the rearmost corner of the island, and the only way you could get into it was from the right side. Various firefighting equipment was kept in the crash shack, along with the silver "hot suits" that allow the firefighters to stride right into burning airplane wreckage and rescue a pilot. But they were not yet geared up for the launch, wearing only the standard pants and jersey worn by all the deck crew, as they sorted out assignments for the 11 A.M. launch. Protected as they were by their position inside the crash shack and hearing nothing of the commotion outside, their first sign of trouble was the call of "Fire on the flight deck!" over the 1MC. When they heard the fire alarm, Brooks and Sietz ran out of the crash shack and were stunned by what they saw. They started to break out fire hoses on the starboard side as aviation chief Gerald Farrier ran by them with a fire extinguisher in hand, headed toward the flames. Farrier was the crewman in charge of Repair 8, and he responded immediately to the fire by charging right into it.

Nearby, Shaver had been hooking up his starter tractor to a plane when he heard a muffled explosion behind him. He turned and saw a plane in flames, and then instantly remembered he was working on the crash crew. Shaver dashed to the crash shack and grabbed a large "purple K" fire extinguisher. Along with several others, Shaver and Farrier ran directly into the fire scene. They were met by a surge of people coming forward, some of them badly burned. Shaver and Farrier struggled to move quickly with the unwieldy, heavy extinguishers, Farrier firing a test shot of the CO_2 extinguisher as he approached the flames. The white cloud was immediately blown into the fire in front of McCain's plane, with no effect.

Farrier's first concern was the pilots trapped in their planes, knowing that they would have more difficulty than the others in getting free of the danger. In the confusion of the fire's initial moments, there was no way to know which pilots already had escaped and which ones were still trapped in their burning planes. Farrier charged forward, taking the lead both physically and in his role as chief firefighter. Shaver wasn't surprised to see Farrier putting himself at risk. He knew Farrier was a good man; they were friends and their wives went shopping together back home. If there was a fire to be fought and men to be saved, Farrier's men knew that he was going to be right in the thick of it.

Dozens of crewmen and aviators saw Farrier rush right to the worst of the fire around McCain's plane, with no more protection than anyone else on the deck, and less than some. Shaver was nearby, struggling to activate the fire extinguisher with his broken right hand. He had to put the extinguisher on the deck and crouch down, holding the metal canister between his legs as he squeezed the lever to spray the purple powder. In what seemed an instant, the canister was emptied.

As Farrier got to McCain's plane, he saw that the two thousand-pound bombs had dropped from its belly and one had rolled about six feet toward the center of the deck. These were two of the old composition B, World War II–era bombs that had so upset the ordnance crew the night before—the ones that they said had decayed so much they were extremely sensitive to heat and vibration. They had said these bombs would explode in a fire, rather than just burning like the more modern bombs. And they would explode with the power of a fifteen-hundred-pound bomb because of their age.

Farrier had no idea. Lying in the flaming jet fuel, the huge bomb was quickly heating up. A longitudinal split had already formed in the outer shell of the bomb.

Other crewmen and aviators alternated between running for their lives and fighting their way toward the flames to help their buddies. About a minute and a half into the fire, dozens of crew members were still in the vicinity of McCain's plane and the fire farther aft, and some pilots were still strapped into their planes. The Repair 8 crew was training hoses on the burning Skyhawks, along with other crewmen who grabbed the first hose they could find, and charged into the danger zone.

Just feet from the flames, Farrier did what he could with the wholly inadequate fire extinguisher. He sprayed clouds of PKP into the flames with little effect. He could see that the situation was reaching a point where it was far too dangerous to have so many rescuers this close by, and he started waving off the other crew, telling them to run for safety. Shaver looked up to see Farrier frantically waving at him and other crew members.

"Go! Get out of here!" he yelled over the roar of the fire. "Get out!"

Some men dropped what they were doing and ran, but many continued to play their hoses on the burning planes. Shaver's fire extinguisher was empty, so he started to get up.

Farrier stayed on the job, never leaving the men he knew were trapped beyond the curtain of fire, doggedly training a portable fire extinguisher on a bomb that was rapidly approaching its cook-off point. As the thick black smoke billowed and swirled, Farrier and Shaver could see that the thousand-pound bomb with the ugly split in its casing had begun to glow a bright red.

Chapter 8

ONE MINUTE AND THIRTY-FOUR SECONDS

One minute and thirty-four seconds into the fire, the thousand-pound bomb from McCain's plane exploded with a fury not felt on the deck of a U.S. aircraft carrier since World War II.

The detonation of a thousand-pound bomb on an armor-plated aircraft-carrier deck is a nearly unbelievable force. At that moment, the bomb's high explosive is converted almost instantly to a gas at very high pressure and temperature. The pressure causes the metal casing to fragment, and the surrounding air is compressed into a shock wave that feels like atmospheric pressure of two hundred times or more. The temperature in such a blast can be ten thousand degrees Fahrenheit even before anything nearby is ignited. The blast of this weapon, designed to take out huge numbers of ground troops or fortified installations, was concentrated on the 1 3/4-inch steel-armored deck of a ship crowded with men already fighting to escape the flames and suffocating smoke. Even though the ship was designed to withstand direct hits from some of the most fearsome of military weapons, the point-blank detonation of such a massive bomb was too much for any armor. In an instant, the bomb blast sent a colossal fireball high in the sky while destroying everything in its immediate vicinity.

Shaver was looking at Farrier and had just started to get up from his crouching position behind the fire-extinguisher bottle when the blast hit. In the tiniest fraction of a second, Shaver saw Farrier thrown into the air and then simply disappear. And at the same instant, he felt the force of the bomb lifting him up and pulling at his body in a thousand different directions. Time slowed to a crawl and he felt as if his body itself were exploding, every part of his body pulling away from the rest. He was aware that he was flying through the air, and he could see yellow and red flames boiling up from the deck. He knew he was on fire. He felt the shrapnel tearing into his guts. Shaver would survive the explosion, but it began a terrible ordeal for him.

In the first milliseconds of the blast, Shaver was protected in part by the fire-extinguisher canister he was crouching behind. Most of the crew members closest to the bomb vanished in an instant, killed immediately by the force of the blast and the intense heat, never to be seen again. The shock wave from the bomb was like an invisible freight train rolling across the deck at lightning speed, hitting everyone and everything in its path with a ferocious force that knocked men to their knees if it didn't send them flying.

The ship shook and rattled at its very core from the bomb blast. The bomb eruption was so ferocious that it was felt throughout the entire ship, down the length of the huge vessel and to the very bottom of the hull. Those who were belowdecks and still unaware of what was going on felt it rocking the ship, signaling serious trouble overhead.

Up on deck, the blast deafened everyone for a moment, and dozens of men were dazed, lying where the explosion had thrown them and trying to get their bearings. Others were scrambling to run and crawl from the blast area, desperately trying to move forward from what had become a hellish scene of death and destruction. The detonation of the bomb had turned an already bad situation into one of absolute horror. It was clear now that the fire was wildly out of control and the *Forrestal* was losing many men.

There had been thirty-five crew members near the bomb when it detonated. In a heartbeat, twenty-seven of them died or received fatal injuries. That twenty-seven included Farrier and five of the other eight members of Repair 8, the specially trained flight-deck firefighters. Most were killed instantly, along with eighteen other crew members, as they fought to contain the initial fire and cool the bombs that were heating rapidly in the burning jet fuel. The three Repair 8 firefighters not killed by the blast were seriously wounded. One minute and thirty-four seconds into the fire, the *Forrestal*'s firefighting team was gone.

All the while, shrapnel and burning debris fell all

over the deck, forcing the men to dodge and weave as they ran for cover. The initial bomb blast had been deadly, but that first split second was only the beginning of the death it would rain upon the men of *Forrestal*. All over the flight deck, men were being hit by bits of debris, some raining down from overhead and some moving horizontally like a speeding bullet. Red-hot, jagged bits of airplanes, tractors, and bombs were flying across the deck, some as large as aircraft wheels, taking down men who had been far enough away to survive the primary blast of the bomb.

John McCain had taken only a few steps out of the fire when the blast hit him. He had turned to look back at the fire and the other men, which meant he was blown backward as bits of metal fired into his chest and his thighs. A larger piece of shrapnel slammed into the radio that hung from his neck, right over the center of his chest. McCain was momentarily stunned by the explosion, staggering backward and ducking to avoid more of the shrapnel, airplane parts, and even body parts that were flying toward him. A headless body flew through the air and thumped down next to him.

Roberts had been awakened from his nap in the fuel station just below the flight deck by the fire-alarm call. He and another man from his crew were headed up the ladder to the flight deck to see if they could help with the fire when the first bomb exploded. The other man had just started out onto the flight deck when the blast blew him back onto Roberts, the huge rush of wind pressing the clothes tight against their bodies. After pausing for a moment, they proceeded onto the flight deck. Once they stood up, they could not believe the hell in front of them. The raging fire drew their attention first and then Roberts saw a man stagger forward and slump down on the deck. He had no face. It looked as if his entire face had been surgically cut off. The man also was burned, most of his clothing gone.

Roberts was terrified at the sight but felt compelled to help the man. He bent down and put his arm around the man's shoulders, supporting him as he sat in a tangle of metal equipment and debris. It was only then that he saw the tattoo on the man's arm. "Justin." Roberts remembered when his friend Justin had gotten that tattoo on shore leave.

"You'll be okay, here, Justin!" he shouted over the noise. Roberts quickly waved over a couple of medical corpsmen with a stretcher basket. They bent down to take Justin, and Roberts patted him on the shoulder. "You'll be okay!"

But that was all he could do for Justin. He felt a wave of nausea building in him and leapt up to get away from it. He then saw two men helping his friend Scotty toward the island. A small, baby-faced eighteen-year-old who was new to the crew, Scotty was considered a mascot of sorts; everyone liked him. Roberts could see that Scotty had lost most of one foot. Still amazed at what he was seeing on the flight deck, Roberts kept looking up in the sky for the attacking planes.

Where are they? If we're under attack, where the fuck are the planes?

He was sure the Vietnamese had managed to attack the carrier with fighter planes, strafing the deck and lobbing bombs. That was the only explanation that made sense. That was the only thing that could cause this kind of shit.

While he was looking around, Roberts noticed a figure lying amid all the tow bars and other apparatus behind the island. It was his own crew's plane director, Kenneth Strain. The man's face was blackened, and the rest of his body was severely burned. Roberts had to fight the urge to run away from the sight, but he went closer and called out to his crewmate.

"Strain! Strain! Come on, let's get you up and outta here!"

The man did not respond, so Roberts tried to grab him under the armpits and drag him closer to the island, farther from the fire. Roberts pulled, and the burned body gave way, his hands slipping on waxy, slick flesh. He fell back hard onto the deck.

"Motherfucking shit!" he screamed. Roberts was overcome with a mix of anger and revulsion. He looked at his hands and couldn't believe what had just happened. He went back to Strain and tried again, this time locking his arms behind the man's back, trying to tug him toward the island. Once again, the slick body slipped through Roberts's hands and he fell back.

"Goddammit!" he yelled. Then he got down closer to Strain's face and yelled at him. "Don't die! Don't die! I'll get you some help!"

Feeling light-headed by now, Roberts got back on his feet and looked around for help. Men were running in all directions. And there were still no planes overhead. Even in the midst of so much horror, this frustrated him greatly. If people were killing his friends, goddammit, he wanted to see them. He stood and looked up at the sky.

"Where are the sorry motherfuckers doing this to us?" he screamed.

When the initial wave of fire and smoke from the first blast died down slightly, those on the bridge and forward on the flight deck could see that the bomb had devastated the entire area near McCain's plane. Where there had been planes and dozens of men fighting the fire, nothing was left but a roiling ball of fire and a cloud of thick, oily smoke. Captain Beling looked down from his perch high above the fire and was astounded. *My God, we've got bombs going off. What the hell is going on here?*

James Bloedorn was still on the bridge after handing control over to the captain, and he too was dumbstruck by the first explosion. Just weeks earlier, he had been in an ordnance-training class that included a film about how modern bombs were supposed to be fire resistant. The film had shown a thousand-pound bomb suspended over a fuel fire, and the instructors said the bomb would last at least ten minutes before exploding. *Why the hell did we have a bomb go off? This fire just started.*

Bob Shelton had walked over to the port side of the bridge in the first few moments of the fire to see what was happening. Along with several others on the bridge, he had been peering down through the armored glass at the fire when the explosion hit. They instinctively ducked for cover as the first bomb went off, feeling the thump as the bomb's concussion hit the armor plating on the bridge and the air exchange as the explosion forced air into the compartment and then sucked it out again. They slowly stood up to look again at the sight below. The officers and crew on the bridge looked down to see no one standing where before dozens of crew had been training hoses on the fire. Instead, men were running toward the island, heading forward on the flight deck, and more than a few were doing so as their clothes burned, trailing blood behind them and desperately crawling or staggering away from the searing heat on their backs. One crewman or aviator could be seen pulling himself slowly along the flight deck, doggedly clawing his way out of the fire and toward the safety of the island, his legs blown off at the waist.

In the worst of the fire and explosions, the men were desperate to get to the island, home base on the flight deck, the only area on a flat ship that represented any real shelter from the hell blowing all around them. The island represented safety, and perhaps more important, it represented the command structure of the ship. These sailors desperately needed to get away from the fire, but in this moment of terror, they also were running and dragging themselves home, to the one spot on that deck they knew as a safe haven. Many would not make it home.

Sailors and aviators were down all over the deck, and the blasts wounded some fliers as they sat in their planes. Others had been blown off the ship by the blast, thrown into the sea by the explosion, sometimes with serious injuries that made their water survival unlikely. Sailors on the other ships in the vicinity could see fireballs falling away from the *Forrestal* flight deck, into the water, and most did not immediately realize that those fireballs were men, engulfed in flames and either leaping into the sea or being blown off the deck by an explosion. On the *Forrestal* deck, Lieutenant James Campbell stood transfixed beneath an F-4 Phantom, stunned by the explosions and unsure where to go or what to do. In the havoc, he could see fireballs hopping and tumbling across the deck. He just stared at them. It took a short moment for him to realize they were men.

Campbell and scores of other men rushed to the burning men and flung themselves on them, rolling around on the burning men, desperately trying to put out the flames. Campbell managed to extinguish the top part of one man's body but saw that his legs were still burning as the medics quickly carried him away. The burned men were screaming.

As those on deck struggled to their feet, they could see that the *Forrestal*'s firefighting crew was gone. Chief Farrier and his men had vanished, leaving charged fire hoses flapping wildly on the deck, most of them shredded by the force of the explosion.

Despite the horror of seeing so many men killed and injured, and the horrific fire that awaited them aft, the men of *Forrestal* headed back to fight the fire and help those who were injured and stranded close to the fire. With burning debris still raining down on their heads, they raced back toward the very area where dozens of people had just been destroyed. Various crew members picked up what remained of the hoses left by the Repair 8 crew and began to fight the fire again, while others started to bring more hoses to the scene.

Nine seconds after the first bomb blast, a second bomb exploded behind the wall of fire with even more violence than the first. This explosion hurled bodies and debris as far as the bow, more than three hundred yards away. Looking down from the bridge in shock and disbelief, Captain Beling watched as a man was lifted up in the air and thrown the entire length of the deck, his body sailing helplessly like a rag doll. An officer standing on the front of the ship, as far away from the fire scene as one could possibly be, was killed instantly when a piece of shrapnel hit him in the heart.

Beling felt particularly helpless to have to sit there in the captain's chair and watch those men out on deck while he was relatively safe up on the bridge.

The first bomb blast had spread the fire significantly, and now the second bomb greatly extended its reach. No longer was the blaze contained mostly to the rear port corner of the ship. Now it had spread across the deck to the starboard side, even approaching dangerously close to the island structure. When the second explosion ripped across the ship like another scythe, the crew on deck realized that the ordnance on deck was cooking off and that the first explosion was not a fluke. *There are hundreds of bombs out here!* Some of the men were surprised that the bombs had started going off so soon into the fire, but they had no time to consider why. The two blasts in quick succession had made it clear that the carrier deck was a deadly place to be. Without any orders being given, the crew realized that they had to take cover while the bombs wreaked havoc on the flight deck. For the moment, simply surviving the explosions was of primary importance. Fighting the fire would have to wait.

The crew members sought shelter wherever they could. Some were trapped out on the deck, seriously injured from the fire and the explosions, missing limbs and suffering from the terrible wounds caused by flying debris and ammunition. Other crew members did their best to help the injured to safety, but in the chaos of the moment, and with the dire need to get out of harm's way, not everyone could be helped. Men crowded around the island structure, seeking shelter behind its thick walls, with some huddling in the Repair 8 crash shack. Others looked at the "bomb farm" directly behind the island on the starboard side, the area where bombs were stored to keep them out of harm's way, and decided they did not want to hide behind thousands of pounds of explosives. They kept running forward.

All across the deck, men were seeking shelter however and wherever they could, diving into catwalks, down ladders and hatches, anything to seek refuge from the hell on the aft end of the flight deck.

Most of the men were in the full throes of a terror-induced adrenaline rush. The mind raced and time slowed. If you leapt into the air, it seemed to take days before you came down. The exertion and excitement made their mouths unbearably dry. And the men worried.

Oh my God, I'm never going to see my momma and daddy again, Roberts thought. *I'm never going to smell fresh-cut grass again.*

* * *

The admiral on board the *Forrestal*, Rear Admiral Harvey Lanham, had not been summoned immediately when the fire first broke out. Though the *Forrestal* was his flagship and he controlled the overall operations of the carrier, the air wings, and the accompanying ships, Lanham did not actually command the ship on a daily basis. That was Beling's job. Lanham was in his quarters when the fire broke out, but when the first bomb went off, he realized there was a serious problem and that he should see for himself.

He dashed for the bridge, knowing from practice drills that he could make it in one minute and fifty seconds. He felt explosions rocking the ship as he made his way. When he got to the bridge, the admiral could see that Beling was already in charge. Lanham surveyed the flight deck and was amazed to see the damage that already had occurred.

As he stared out the window in shock at what was happening, his marine orderly rushed over and roughly grabbed his arm.

"Get away from that window!" the marine yelled. "It's not safe!"

The young man yanked the admiral down to the floor just as another explosion shook the ship. A large piece of shrapnel crashed through the thick Plexiglas where the admiral's face had just been. Captain Beling ordered everyone to stay away from the left side of the bridge where he was, closest to the explosions, but he stayed in his chair looking right out the window.

Things were even worse in pri-fly, the primary flight-control center, one deck above the bridge but sixty feet farther back toward the fire. This was where the ship's air-crew officers controlled flight operations on the deck from a windowed room that looked similar to the bridge. The big windows on three sides of the room provided a clear view of the entire flight deck, but now with the bombs going off, those windows made pri-fly a dangerous place to be. The officers and crew there were ducking for cover as the bombs went off on the deck, and the two crewmen standing watch on the catwalk just outside pri-fly rushed in to take cover from the explosions. They found that pri-fly offered little sanctuary, however. One of the watch sailors made it into pri-fly, but by then, some of the thick, battle-ready windows had been blown out by the blasts and those inside were looking for a way out. As officers and crew started to scramble for a way out, the watch sailor was hit hard by a shock wave from one of the bombs on deck and thrown over some chairs, against a distant wall, and onto the deck. As soon as they could get out, pri-fly was abandoned.

Each explosion rocked the ship, rattling the metal framework and breaking windows. All over the flight deck, men hid behind whatever they could find, but they were also trying to administer first aid to the wounded. No one knew how long the bomb blasts would last. Never knowing if the next bomb blast would be the one to kill you, the men waited and waited for what seemed forever. As soon as one bomb blast faded away, another bomb cooked off. Seven major explosions followed—all from the older thousand-pound bombs. At the same time, rockets and missiles were detonating in the heat. After five minutes, the blasts stopped, and the men started to come out onto the open deck again. The fire was out of control and had to be stopped.

The fire had grown into a massive blaze, enveloping the entire rear portion of the flight deck, and the forty thousand gallons of jet fuel on board the burning aircraft was feeding the fire. The JP5 jet fuel, something akin to kerosene, was not all that easy to ignite, but it would burn furiously. The burning fuel created a shallow sea of fire that was flowing over the sides of the ship. The burning jet fuel poured off the deck and down onto the structures below, setting fires on the sponsons jutting out from the side, the fantail at the very rear of the ship, and Hangar Bay 3 one deck below.

After the initial explosions subsided, Merv Rowland's voice boomed across the 1MC public-address system to tell the crew that they should come out from their cover on the flight deck and go back to work fighting the fire.

"Repair parties, this is control. Re-man your stations! All repair-fleet personnel, this is control. You can now re-man your stations. Stay on the job!"

Men rushed back toward the fire, getting as close as they could to the searing heat and grabbing what remained of the fire hoses that lay sputtering on the deck, most of them ripped to shreds, a frightful suggestion of what must have happened to the men who had been holding them.

As the crewmen moved forward again to fight the fire, Beling looked down from the bridge and saw something that gave him a sinking feeling of fear and despair.

Oh my God . . . The deck is open . . .

The burning jet fuel wasn't just flowing over the sides of the ship. It was flowing down through huge holes that had been blasted in the flight deck by the exploding bombs. Beling knew what lay just beneath the surface of the flight deck—berthing quarters where men were sleeping. All over the flight deck, men were thinking the same thing.

There are men down there!

The first bomb had blasted a hole that was ten feet across, with the heavy metal curled down at the edges as if a fist had punched through tinfoil. And the bombs had opened similar holes in other areas on the deck. Beling could only imagine the devastation that the exploding bombs must have caused belowdecks. Now liquid fire was pouring down into the heart of the *Forrestal*.

The men berthing in the area directly underneath the fire scene had been up on their regular shift all night; the morning was their normal rest period, so they were in their bunks when most of the crew were well into their workday. Others sleeping in the same general vicinity had been given permission to sleep late to compensate for the previous night's operations. These men were used to resting in conditions that most people would find impossible; they had become accustomed to sleeping just feet below the deck of an aircraft carrier, with almost no noise insulation. The sound of aircraft taking off and landing was as normal to them as the creaking of an old bed or the snoring of a sibling. You got used to it after a while, or else you never got any sleep. In this particular berthing area, the men had to get used to the sounds of aircraft slamming down hard on the deck directly above them because they were aft, near the arresting gear where the planes landed. These were men who had learned to sleep through anything, and that would cost many of them their lives.

Just to the rear of the fire area at McCain's plane, Gary Pritchard was asleep in his bunk after a twelve-hour shift. He and his division crewmates had been in a compartment farther back earlier in the trip, not so directly under the arresting gear, but they had been displaced by an air squadron that came aboard and pulled rank to get the choicer spot. Pritchard and his buddies had been forced to move to a compartment directly under the arresting gear and closer to the fire site.

Pritchard considered it the worst place in the world to try to sleep. But they managed, drifting off and ignoring most of the noise, but usually waking with a jolt when a plane slammed down and the arresting cable dragged across the deck.

When the first alarms sounded for fire on the flight deck, many of those sleeping in that area did not even hear it. Those who heard the fire call probably did nothing more than roll over and perhaps listen halfheartedly for further announcements. The fire call did not involve any orders for them to act, and there was no indication that they were in danger. They could not have known that the initial fire call would be their only warning. The men never got a chance to save themselves because the general-quarters alarm came at about 10:53 A.M., just seconds before the first bomb blast hit.

When the bomb from McCain's plane blew up, it smashed through the deck and into the compartment where the sailors were sleeping. Many were killed instantly, never knowing, while others were awakened by the blast and seriously injured. Those who survived the initial blast found themselves under a rain of burning fuel pouring down from the flight deck.

Fifty men sleeping in that berthing area were killed by the explosions and burning fuel, and another forty-one died in nearby areas directly beneath the flight deck. Nine berthing compartments in the aft area were destroyed.

Pritchard's area was just far enough aft of the first explosion that he and his bunkmates survived. But they were close enough to know that they had only *barely* survived.

The bombs were sending concussions through the compartment that were just unbelievable, an incredible, invisible force that rippled through the berthing area, tossing men out of bed and slamming them against walls. The shock waves were so violent that Pritchard was completely disoriented when he woke up. The first thing he knew, he was standing by his bunk with his pants and his shoes in his hands.

The shock waves from the exploding bombs started to come in quick succession as Pritchard and the other crew members in the berthing area responded by donning a bit of clothing and rushing out. Even without any information, they could tell that this area was way too close to whatever was going on outside and they wanted out fast.

Pritchard's buddy Frenchie (not the same "French" who was sunbathing with Frank Eurice) had the bunk right alongside of him and when the two men found each other, Frenchie's eyes were as big as moons. They were temporarily deafened after each explosion, watching the commotion in an eerie silence until the hearing returned, the panicked noise of their buddies swelling to a crescendo again. Pritchard and his buddy tried to stay together as they made their way out into the passageway leading from their compartment, but the area was jammed shoulder to shoulder with men. Some men were wounded already.

"Clear a path! We've got wounded here! Make a hole!"

With general quarters already sounded, Pritchard and Frenchie tried to make it to their GQ stations up on the flight deck, where they could man a fuel-pumping station. The scene was so chaotic on their deck level, however, that they had trouble making any forward progress. People were scared and confused, and no one knew exactly what they should be doing. And no one had any idea what was going on. With all the bombs going off, only one thing made sense.

"We're being attacked! They're bombing us! We gotta get outta here!" The men were shocked to find themselves under attack, but they struggled to make sense of what little they knew. "They're going for the steering! The bombs are all aft. They're trying to knock out our steering!"

Pritchard agreed with most of those around him that somehow the Vietnamese must have gotten close enough to bomb the carrier. He instantly pictured in his head a scene straight out of World War II and countless old movies—a Japanese pilot with a leather helmet diving down on the back of the

When the USS *Forrestal* sailed for Vietnam in 1967, she was the world's largest and most powerful aircraft carrier. The 5,000 sailors and airmen aboard joined 400,000 ground troops already fighting in the jungles, plus the sailors aboard other ships. The bombers who flew off the aircraft carriers played a key role in the ongoing war against the North Vietnamese.

Captain John K. Beling (right) was at the pinnacle of his career when he took command of the *Forrestal*. A World War II pilot who narrowly survived being shot down in the Pacific, Beling was proud to command the carrier and eager to show what his crew could do. Beling is shown with Commander Jack Dewenter of Air Wing 17.

Eighteen-year-old Gary Shaver joined the navy partly as a way to cope when his girlfriend broke up with him. He left his hometown of Carpentersville, Illinois, and thought he might make a lifelong career of the navy. Shaver was assigned a job on the flight deck, directing planes as they moved about the crowded work space.

Nineteen-year-old Ken Killmeyer couldn't find a job back home in Pittsburgh because employers feared he would be drafted soon. After talking it over with his dad, they decided that Ken should join the navy. "You'll be coming home, Ken," his dad said. "We don't know that for sure if you get drafted."

Back home in White Marsh, Maryland, eighteen-year-old Frank Eurice spent his days drilling holes in bowling balls at the local Montgomery Ward. The day he was laid off, Eurice took it all in stride until he got home and found out he had been drafted. Like boys all over the country, he had a scale model of the *Forrestal* in his bedroom.

Paul Friedman was not eager to leave his home in Rockaway Beach, an ocean community outside of New York City. He spent his days riding his surfboard and finding girls to romance, but like many young men in the late sixties, Friedman worried about being drafted. By joining the navy when he was eighteen years old, at least he could be sure to avoid the infantry.

Robert Shelton was twenty-one years old by the time he started thinking about enlisting in the military, and his first choice was the air force. But when the navy recruiter found Shelton waiting in the Texas heat because the air force office was closed, he welcomed the young man inside and pretty soon, Shelton was in the navy.

Gary Pritchard (center) joined the navy right after graduating from high school in Fort Lee, New Jersey, just before his eighteenth birthday. He saw the navy as an opportunity for an education and a career, neither of which was likely if he stayed home. On the *Forrestal*, Pritchard's bunk was right under the noisy flight deck.

In 1966, Ed Roberts (center) was living every teenage boy's dream. His rock and roll band, the Fugitives, was hitting it big in Atlanta and was on the verge of even bigger success. When he was drafted, Roberts kept it a secret from his bandmates for as long as he could.

Milt Crutchley (center) joined the Navy in 1964 right out of high school, when he was only seventeen years old. His older brother had joined already, and his cousin was a navy chief stationed in Norfolk. Crutchley saw the navy as a career opportunity and was glad to be assigned to the *Forrestal*.

The Zwerlein family ran the local Tastee-Freez in Port Washington, New York, and Robert was the second of three boys. All of the sons joined the volunteer fire department just like their dad, who also had served in the navy. Robert's parents hoped his firefighting training would keep him safe on the *Forrestal*.

Dr. G. Gary Kirchner had just finished his residency in Rochester, Minnesota, when he was drafted and assigned to the *Forrestal*. He was overwhelmed at first by the size of the job, caring for 5,000 crewmen along with only a few other doctors.

Merv Rowland, an experienced sailor and engineer at forty-eight years old, was one of the old salts on the *Forrestal*. He had survived many scrapes in World War II, and he would prove vital to the carrier's survival in her worst moment. As chief engineer, Rowland was in charge of damage control and the firefighting response, making him the one individual most responsible for saving the ship.

When a rocket accidentally fired across the flight deck while planes were being prepared for launch, it went right through John McCain's plane. Hundreds of gallons of fuel poured onto the deck and ignited immediately. In an instant, the entire rear portion of the flight deck was on fire.

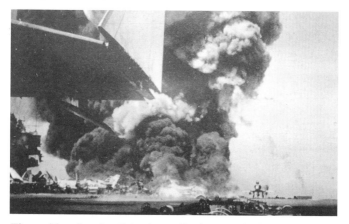

The accidental rocket firing immediately caused a fire, but the situation grew much worse when one of the thousand-pound bombs caught in the fire exploded after only one minute and thirty-four seconds, much sooner than anyone expected.

A huge black cloud rolled off the ship as the fire spread quickly and sailors scrambled to fight it. The flight deck was crowded with planes that had been prepared for launch, loaded with fuel, rockets, and bombs. The fire quickly got out of control.

Sailors did whatever they could to fight the fire, forced to improvise after firefighting equipment was destroyed and the ship's trained firefighters were killed in the first bomb explosion. The deck became so hot from the fires burning below that the sailors had to hoist the fire hoses up on their shoulders to keep them from burning through.

As smoke cleared on the flight deck after the initial explosions, the sailors could see that the bomb blasts had opened huge holes in the armor-plated steel deck. Once the deck was open, burning jet fuel poured through the holes into the decks below, spreading the fire far throughout the ship.

The sailors on the flight deck pitched in to move equipment and planes away from the fire, desperately trying to prevent further explosions on the flight deck. With some planes already damaged and loaded with explosives, the only option was to push them overboard as quickly as possible.

Captain Beling supervised the crew's response from the bridge, where he had a view of everything happening on the flight deck. He witnessed the terrible blasts that blew men overboard and struck down dozens at a time.

One of the main concerns was extinguishing the fires burning inside the ship. Many of the burning sections were cut off by blast damage, so the crew tried to pour water on them through the holes in the flight deck.

As the fires raged for hours, rumors spread that the captain had called for the crew to abandon ship, even though he never did. As the young sailors fought for their lives, some (like this unidentified sailor) donned life vests just in case.

It soon became clear that the bombs were exploding in the fires and word spread that the crew should dump overboard any ordnance that could not be moved safely out of the way. Using brute strength, they moved bombs weighing as much as 1,000 pounds to the deck edge and tossed them over.

In the hangar decks, crew members were concerned that rockets and missiles there could explode in the fire, so they formed impromptu teams to carry the weapons to the open edge and throw them over.

As soon as the scope of the fire on the *Forrestal* became apparent, other navy ships on Yankee Station ceased their own operations and came to the carrier's aid. The carrier crews also loaded helicopters with nearly all of their own firefighting gear for delivery to the stricken ship.

The destroyers nearby could rush in close to the burning ship because, though they were not small, they were highly maneuverable. The destroyers *Rupertus* and *MacKenzie* hugged the carrier close as they glided through the sea, pointing fire hoses at spots the carrier's crew could not reach.

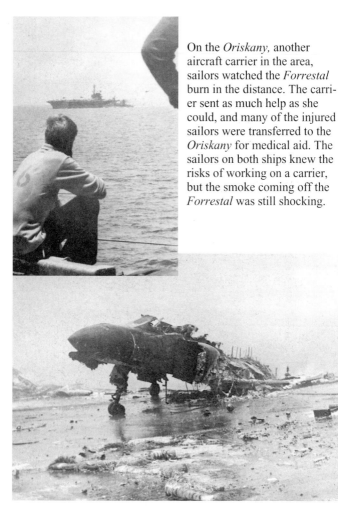

On the *Oriskany,* another aircraft carrier in the area, sailors watched the *Forrestal* burn in the distance. The carrier sent as much help as she could, and many of the injured sailors were transferred to the *Oriskany* for medical aid. The sailors on both ships knew the risks of working on a carrier, but the smoke coming off the *Forrestal* was still shocking.

The *Forrestal* suffered $72.2 million in damage, including the loss of twenty-one aircraft and damage to forty more. Some of the planes pushed overboard that day cost more than $5 million apiece, others $2 million each. The ordnance destroyed or jettisoned during the fire was valued at just less than $2 million.

Once the fires were extinguished, sailors faced the grim task of recovering the bodies of their friends. Some of the compartments could only be reached from above because of blast damage, so sailors were lowered in through the holes on the flight deck to retrieve bodies. For weeks after the fire, crew were still finding bodies.

One hundred thirty-four men died on the *Forrestal* on July 29, 1967. The bodies were first taken to the hangar deck and assembled for identification. Many sailors were stunned by the loss of their friends and tried to find them among the bodies.

Captain John K. Beling returned home from Vietnam much sooner than expected, much to the delight of his children. He was terribly saddened by the loss of his men and the early end to his mission, and he knew the navy would hold someone accountable.

USS FORRESTAL JULY 29 1967

PR2 MARVIN J ADKINS
WEST VIRGINIA
JULY 25 1934

AD13 EDWARD R DORSEY
CONNECTICUT
JUNE 30 1947

AMS3 RUSSELL L FIKE
PENNSYLVANIA
NOVEMBER 27 1947

AE3 LEROY MOSER
SOUTH DAKOTA
AUGUST 27 1944

ATR3 JOHN M PRUNER
MICHIGAN
MAY 14 1948

SN NELSON E SPITLER
OHIO
JULY 2 1946

LT DENNIS M BARTON
IOWA
JANUARY 15 1935

AEI WALTER T EADS
NEW ZEALAND
AUGUST 24 1937

AN JOHNNIE L FRAZIER
TEXAS
JULY 5 1947

AMHC RICHARD L OWENS
CALIFORNIA
MAY 11 1929

AME2 DALE R ROSS
MISSOURI
APRIL 23 1947

LCDR GERRY L STARK
NEBRASKA
DECEMBER 23 1929

GULF OF TONKIN VIETNAM
U S NAVY

AEAN ROBERT J DAVIES
ILLINOIS
NOVEMBER 21 1947

AMEI JOHN J FIEDLER
WISCONSIN
AUGUST 24 1934

ADRAN RALPH E MANNING
ALABAMA
SEPTEMBER 12 1947

AMH2 ERNEST E POLSTON
SOUTH CAROLINA
MARCH 10 1936

AMS2 JOHN F SNOW
NEW YORK
SEPTEMBER 10 1938

AN HAROLD D WATKINS
KENTUCKY
JULY 16 1945

Of the 134 men killed on the *Forrestal*, 18 were never recovered or identified. A monument at Arlington National Cemetery, just behind the Tomb of the Unknowns, marks the resting place of 12 to 14 bodies that could not be identified and memorializes those never recovered.

ship. With adrenaline surging and scared to death, Pritchard clearly pictured a Japanese pilot muttering "Yankee motherfucker!" as he bore down on the *Forrestal*. Pritchard and every other man in that passageway feared they would be trapped belowdecks if the attackers sunk the carrier.

In another berthing compartment a few decks down and farther toward the rear of the ship, Paul Friedman was sound asleep in his upper bunk right up until the first explosion. He had spent a long twelve hours working in the mess hall, and he never even heard the alarms that followed the start of the fire. He had gone to sleep about 6 A.M. and managed to sleep deeply in all the usual noise.

Friedman awoke to the sound of a blast, and when he opened his eyes, the bulkhead to his right was missing. There was some sort of powdery stuff in the air all around him. He was stunned from the explosion and as he lay there, he looked around without moving. He could see fire where another bulkhead was cracked, and he could see other shipmates just lying there motionless, staring back at him. He was stunned, deafened, and was wondering what was real and what was a dream. It was surreal: men awakened from a deep sleep to find themselves in the midst of disaster.

After a few seconds, Friedman looked down toward the foot of his bunk. He could see that his foot was bloody, the red ooze beginning to soak the sheets on his bunk. A piece of shrapnel had gone through the bottom of his foot as he lay sleeping, but he had not yet felt the pain. Then, very quickly, Friedman realized he was not dreaming. His hearing returned and suddenly chaos was all around him. As the explosions continued, he realized the ship was under attack.

Oh shit, we're being attacked by MiGs, Friedman thought, referring to the Soviet-built fighter plane. *God, the five-inch guns are pounding! Why are they firing the five-inch guns? We must really be under attack!*

Friedman sprang out of his bunk, joining the dozens of other sailors rushing to evacuate the compartment. Some already were helping the wounded, carrying injured sailors through the crowd, cradling a head wound, dragging men out of their bunks. Everyone was running to the port passageway to get out, and Friedman was hobbling along on his injured foot, the pain setting in so that it made running difficult. He faltered at one point and fell down in the rushing crowd, but almost immediately, a buddy he knew as Alabama picked him up. A big guy, Alabama picked up Friedman like a twig and eventually helped him get to the sick bay.

Out on the starboard-side gun-mount area where Frank Eurice and his buddy French were sunbathing, the first explosion shook them out of their bewilderment about the black smoke on the far end of the ship. When the explosion occurred, they felt it even where they were, far forward of the fire.

The huge explosion shook them hard and then they could see a sheet of flame, smoke, and pieces of confetti going skyward.

Eurice and French were both momentarily stunned, their jaws dropping open in disbelief. Then

Eurice turned to his buddy and yelled, "I think it's time for general quarters!" and took off.

Eurice hustled through the hatch that led off the sponson and back into the ship, with French close behind him. By that time, burning jet fuel was beginning to come off the edge of the flight deck and French was burned on his shoulder as he made it through the hatch.

With the general-quarters alarm sounding throughout the ship, Eurice bolted down to his station, which was the "2 main stern tube" to the rear of the port steering compartment. He made it there in record speed. *We're in deep shit! This is for real, man. We got some kind of real nasty break and we are really in deep shit!*

His duty during general quarters was to "maintain a good leak" on the propeller shaft at the ship's very rear where it enters the water, keeping just enough seawater on the bearing mechanism so that it was cooled but not so much that the compartment would flood. Failure in either direction would mean that the propeller shaft would become inoperable, crippling the ship's propulsion. Despite its importance, this work was normally extremely boring. That's why there was always a tall stack of *Playboy* magazines in the little compartment, no bigger than your average car interior. On this day, Eurice arrived at his station just as the bombs were cooking off far above him on the flight deck.

Eurice was on a little catwalk trying to get to his workstation when one of the thousand-pound bombs went off far overhead. The noise was deafening and the explosions kicked him over a railing and into the bilges, a pit at the very bottom of the ship filled with seawater and various filth.

Throughout the ship, men were rushing to their GQ stations. Ken Killmeyer was running aft to his GQ station, the magazine-handling room for the five-inch port gun aft and below on the fourth deck. The narrow passageways, cramped even when two sailors were calmly passing each other, became tight thoroughfares as everyone tried to get to their appointed stations and started sealing hatches and making other emergency preparations. As he ran down a passageway, Killmeyer felt the first explosion rock the ship and send the waffle-like fluorescent light covers swinging down toward his face. Dust shook off the hatches, lights, and pipe work overhead, creating an unsettling scene for someone who knew what it took to shake such a big ship so violently.

All along the way, "repair parties" were breaking out emergency equipment from repair lockers and manning their own GQ stations. When Killmeyer got to a hatch he would need to access a ladder taking him down to his GQ station, a repair party was there already and one member was plugging his headset into a communications outlet. Bombs were still going off overhead, and Killmeyer followed another crew member through the hatch and started down the ladder to the magazine-handling area.

As he was halfway through the hatch in the floor, one of the repair-party members stopped him.

"Wait, come here!" he called out. "Don't go down there anymore!"

Killmeyer saw that the man was talking to someone on the phone, and he stopped on the ladder. Scared but pumped full of adrenaline, Killmeyer wanted to keep going. *I don't know what's going on, but I have to get to my GQ station. Now!*

Killmeyer yelled to the repair party that his GQ station was down that hatch and he *had* to go, but the repair party kept telling him to wait.

"They're talking about flooding the magazines!" the guy from the repair party shouted back over the noise of the explosions and the ship rattling. This was not good news. It meant that Killmeyer could not go to his GQ station, even though others already had gone down, but more important, it suggested that things were very bad. The magazines holding ammunition for the ship's guns and aircraft could be flooded with seawater in an emergency to eliminate the risk of a fire setting off the explosives, but that would always be a last-ditch measure. Flooding the magazines put all of that ammunition and ordnance out of commission, and it was generally something you avoided if at all possible. The only reason to flood the magazines was that you needed to save the ship. That decision, if it ever came, would be made in damage control.

Merv Rowland had joined the mass of men running through the ship, shouting questions and orders, everyone wondering what the hell was going on. He made his way to a ladder that would take him down to the deck housing damage control, and that's when he felt the first bomb go off up on the flight deck. The blast almost knocked him off the ladder.

Awwww shit. They've snuck out there with a

goddamn gunboat or something and set off our ammunition.

As Rowland continued making his way, he started thinking about what ammunition was vulnerable to the attack.

Christ, the next strike's ammunition is on the flight deck! That's a big damn strike too. And the next strike's ammunition is on the mess deck, and then another strike is being readied down in the magazines to go up. Son of a bitch, they could blow this whole ship out of the water!

Rowland was scared by what he thought was going on. He counted three more explosions overhead before he got to the damage-control hatch, and then he stopped counting. When he got to central control, Rowland found the room already crowded with sailors assuming their duties for the emergency. A number of men already were manning the phones to get damage reports, and information started flying toward Rowland as soon as his crew saw him dash in.

The first thing he did was to look at the fire-main pressure, the water system that would be used throughout the ship for fighting fires. He told the sailor at that station, "You better make damn sure that fire-main pressure doesn't go below a hundred and fifty pounds." Next, he checked how many generators were on line, knowing all four main plants should be on line because of the scheduled plane launches.

Rowland then took his position in the big chair, assuming control of almost all of the ship's response to the fire. Everything would flow through Rowland's position in damage control. He immediately ordered another generator put on line, in case one of the present generators was put out of commission. Then he turned his attention to the tall Plexiglas plotting boards where sailors were already posting information. Many of the young men were wearing headsets and receiving constant reports from throughout the ship, then posting them on the plotting boards in grease pencil. With that information, Rowland could monitor where the fire was, what systems had been damaged, and the current readiness of vital operations like the ship's propulsion system.

Rowland could visualize the entire ship's operations on the boards, and if he saw something that interested him, he would call the phone talker over and get the information straight from him. Information was key in an emergency, and that put Rowland in a unique position. He was far belowdecks with no direct sight of any fires, damage, or emergency response, but if anyone on the ship knew what was going on, it was Rowland.

He realized he was the only man on the *Forrestal* who knew what was going on throughout the ship. Not even the captain had more information. It was hard to absorb so much, but when he found a hot spot, he would concentrate on that problem and trust his crew to handle the rest.

Rowland was in close contact with the bridge, so it wasn't long before Rowland realized that there was no attack and that the crisis had begun with a flight-deck fire. He couldn't believe a fire on the top deck had gotten so bad.

I know goddamn well we'll get this fire out, but I can't believe we just shot ourselves in the foot. At least some goddamn gook's not going to end my career.

Damage control kept the captain and the bridge fully informed, with Rowland frequently on the phone to Captain Beling, updating him on the fire damage and the emergency response. Years later, Beling would modestly claim that all he did was "steer the ship" while others did the real work in putting out the fires, a vast oversimplification that says more about the captain's respect for his crew than what he actually did during the fire. But still, it is true that Rowland was the man responsible, more than any other individual, for saving the *Forrestal*. He was experienced and capable, and he had no intention of letting his ship and his boys succumb to this fire.

Much of Rowland's attention was directed to the ammunition magazines throughout the ship. No matter how bad things were elsewhere, Rowland knew that the ship could be destroyed in one devastating blast if the fire got to the ammunition. The question of flooding the magazines had arisen very soon in the crisis, once the bombs started going off and burning jet fuel poured down into the lower decks.

Rowland was watching an array of gauges and indicators that gave him a good idea of what was going on anywhere in the ship. His attention was largely focused on the temperature gauges for the ammunition magazines. Each one's temperature was indicated separately, and this was important enough that he wanted *two* sailors standing in front of each gauge, staring at the numbers, ready to scream out if the magazines started heating up even a little.

With the fires spreading, it did not take long for some of the temperature gauges to start rising. Rowland had to be careful with his decision. If he waited too long, the ammunition could ignite in one split second. He called Clark Chisum, the *Forrestal*'s weapons officer, to find out exactly what was in the weapons magazines that were heating up. Chisum told him he thought those magazines held only inert material at the moment, nothing explosive, but he wasn't absolutely sure yet.

"Okay, but the magazines are pretty close to all that hot stuff," Rowland said. "Clark, I think we ought to flood those magazines and make sure we don't have this whole damn ship go up at once."

Chisum didn't argue with him, so Rowland called the bridge to get permission to flood the magazine. Beling couldn't speak to Rowland immediately because he had stepped off the bridge momentarily to get a better view of the fire on the rear of the deck. Though Rowland had authority to do almost anything else he deemed necessary, flooding the magazines was such a serious, irreversible action that protocol required permission from the captain himself.

The navigator on the bridge took the call and told Rowland he could not flood the magazines without the captain personally giving the order.

"The hell I can't!" Rowland screamed back over the phone. "If he doesn't get back and that thing gets any hotter, I'll flood! I'll flood the goddamn thing with or without permission!"

Rowland slammed the phone down and continued to watch the temperature gauges. Beling would most likely have deferred to Rowland's judgment, but fortunately, he soon got word that the magazines in question were devoid of any explosive material, so there was no need to flood. Though damage control constantly produced tense moments like that, full knowledge of the situation made Rowland confident and a damn sight less scared than if he had to wonder about what was going on.

Rowland's confidence stemmed directly from being so well informed, and that put him in a very different position from thousands of other men on the ship. Soon into the fire, Rowland knew that he would save his ship. But others had little or no information to work with, and they were not nearly as sure.

With so many men on the ship, a chaotic situation like a major fire can create vastly different experiences for individuals. Just as Rowland and Beling's experience was far different from those of sailors in the middle of the fire and explosions, so were some sailors' experiences different from other crew members' simply because of where they happened to be stationed for GQ or where they happened to be when the fire broke out. Many men died because they were directly in the vicinity of the fire and the exploding bombs, while many others survived because some quirk of fate or a lucky change in their routine took them out of harm's way. Many survivors would marvel, years later, at how a simple change in their routine had kept them from a place where they almost certainly would have been killed.

Some sailors found themselves isolated from the worst of the danger on board the ship, never truly out of harm's way as the fire and explosions tore through the ship, but far enough away that they didn't immediately fear for their lives. But being that far away also meant that they had little or no information about what was going on, and that could, in its own way, create a different kind of hell. Nineteen-year-old Robert Whelpley, an aviation-supply runner, received exactly that kind of mixed blessing when the fire broke out.

Whelpley's job was to run for aviation parts needed by the aviation squadrons. The mechanics working on the planes would request a part, and Whelpley would be dispatched to the appropriate storeroom to fetch it. It was a fairly simple job that required a lot of running around the ship from one storeroom to another, collecting parts on his list, and then making his way back to the hangar-bay deck to deliver them. On this particular morning, Whelpley had made his way to a supply room that was about midship and three decks down. He had another stop to make at a supply room farther aft, and normally he would have gone to that area first so that he had fewer items to carry on the rest of the trip. But on this morning, Whelpley had decided to stop at the midship storeroom first and have a cigarette with a friend who worked there. He knew the aft storeroom was a busy place that morning, so the midship stop was a better place to take a breather.

Whelpley was shooting the breeze with his friend when the fire alarm sounded, but neither man paid much attention. He was just getting ready to leave and finish his delivery rounds when the general-quarters alarm sounded.

Oh no, not again, Whelpley thought, weary of the many GQ drills and the disruption they always caused. But he immediately put out his cigarette, dropped the parts he had obtained at the store-room, and called out, "See you later!" to his friend. Then he started racing to his GQ station. Because he happened to be at that particular supply room when the GQ alarm sounded, Whelpley didn't have far to go. His GQ station was directly above him on the hangar-deck level, requiring only a short run through a couple of bulkheads and then up a ladder.

Whelpley's GQ station was a small, nondescript passageway on the port side of the ship. At several spots along the wall, there were portals with ladders leading down to the second deck, a quick way to get down into the bowels of the ship from the hangar-deck level. As was the case for a great many men, Whelpley's GQ assignment was nothing exciting or glamorous. He was to report to this passageway area and just wait for further instructions. In an emergency, he might be told to monitor who went down the ladders or to prevent people from going down the ladders into a dangerous area. Or he might be pulled away from the passageway for duties elsewhere.

On the way to his station, Whelpley realized that this was not just another drill. The bombs started rocking the ship and Whelpley could tell that the ship was in big trouble. He knew how many bombs were scattered throughout the ship for the air strikes.

When Whelpley got to his GQ station, no one else was there. He waited, expecting other men to come rushing in right behind him, but they never came. In every GQ drill, there had been dozens of men who reported to that area, all standing around with nothing to do, just waiting for orders or the end of the drill. Now that there was a real emergency, Whelpley was the only one to show up.

It was an odd feeling to be alone at the height of a GQ alarm. Whelpley was out of breath from his sprint, bent over and trying to recover himself, expecting at any moment to see a crowd of men rush into the area. But he waited, and waited, and no one came.

What's going on? Where is everybody? Geez, did I get something wrong here? No, that was GQ, no doubt about that. So where the hell is everybody? This is really weird.

Whelpley remembered all the GQ drills in which the men had put on oxygen-breathing apparatus and sat down next to the bulkhead to wait. There were guys lined up the whole length of the hallway. As Whelpley stood there all alone this time, he began to worry that something was desperately wrong with the ship. *Something's got to be really wrong if all those guys didn't come to GQ.* He could hear the explosions overhead, some of them nearly knocking him off his feet as they rattled through the ship. The longer he stood there, the more uncomfortable he became.

Maybe I oughta go see what's happening out there. I'm sure not doing any good here . . . Hell, there's not even anyone here to give me orders.

But the navy trains sailors to understand one

very important point about general quarters: you go where you have been assigned to go, and then you wait for further orders or act on whatever emergency you find there. You do *not* just go looking for something to do. The whole idea of general quarters is to have people stationed at important points throughout the ship, ready to respond in whatever way might be needed. The idea of standing in an empty passageway while others fight a fire might be difficult to understand for those without military training, but the entire system of military discipline is based on young men and women doing what they are told, even if the reason is not apparent. Whelpley understood that, but his resolve was being tested.

Whelpley stood there for a long while, knowing that there was some sort of serious problem nearby but not knowing exactly what. He kept hoping the phone in the passageway would ring and someone would give him orders. Orders to do something, to go somewhere. Anything. He stared at the phone but it never made a sound.

The only thing he could think to do was to start closing hatches in that area. They had done that on a GQ drill once. Seemed to make sense now.

Finally, he heard another voice. Another sailor stuck his head out of an electronics room down the hall and yelled at him.

"Hey! I'm down here!" Whelpley shouted down the passageway. *Finally, someone else!*

"Well, I guess it's you and me, kid," the other sailor replied. "Just sit tight. This is where you're supposed to be. If somebody needs you, they should come and get you."

And that's exactly what Whelpley did. For hours. He stood his watch in that empty passageway, doing exactly as he had been instructed. He waited for orders that would never come, all the time wondering what was going on on the flight deck and elsewhere. He could tell from the sounds, the rumbling explosions, and the cryptic messages on the public-address system that there was a bad fire and severe damage to the ship. He imagined the worst possible scenario.

God, whatever is going on out there isn't too far away. It sounds like the whole damn ship is blowing up! There's fire everywhere, I can tell that at least. It's not just a normal fire, that's for sure. They never said anything in training about explosions during a fire.

Must have been something really terrible to start all these fires. Could we be under attack? No way! How could the Vietnamese get out here to attack us?

His mind raced with possible outcomes, none of them good. *I hope that fire doesn't come any closer to me. I don't want to be trapped here. I wonder if the smoke will kill me before I burn. I sure hope so.*

The young sailor's mind was filled with images from World War II movies in which the sailors had to abandon ship, scrambling over the side to face their fate in the sea. He wondered if the *Forrestal* would go down. And if it did, would he know in time?

Oh God, what if the ship sinks? Will I hear the abandon-ship call? I don't want to be left behind!

Where do I get a life vest? I haven't seen any around here! Where do I get a life vest???

Whelpley spent hours by himself, getting more and more scared, before he finally couldn't stand it any longer and left his post at midday. He had spent about five hours standing there by himself, just waiting to see how he would die.

Chapter **9**

Stay on the job!

Nine major explosions occurred on the flight deck, all of them from the old composition B bombs. The big fat bombs that had looked so unstable when they were delivered the night before were cooking off in rapid succession. With each blast, the ship vibrated so badly that the men's lower legs became numb.

When all the bombs had exploded, the scene became less hellish, but only slightly. The massive explosions had stopped blowing men and equipment all over the deck, but the fire itself was out of control and spreading. Other materials—fuel tanks, smaller ammunition, various volatile materials on the planes—continued to explode without warning. The fire had spread both forward and starboard, engulfing more planes and equipment, exposing more ordnance to the heat that had caused the other explosions. The fire was getting worse—much worse.

Explosions from the flight deck had spread shrapnel, burning jet fuel, and flaming debris throughout the ship, ripping holes in armor-plated decking and steel bulkheads. With the violent explosions penetrating far beneath the fire scene, the ship was like a crate of fireworks with a bonfire on top, just waiting for one explosion to send one piece of hot shrapnel to the wrong place.

One of the most sensitive spots was the liquid-oxygen-generating plant. In order to supply the pilots' breathing systems in the planes, the ship generated and stored large amounts of oxygen, the quintessential fuel for any fire. The liquid-oxygen plant was located near Hangar Bay 3, on the left side not far below where the fire was raging on the flight deck. On this morning, the tank held 750 gallons of liquid-oxygen stored in the tank there—making it a highly volatile target, far more flammable and explosive than the JP5 jet fuel up on the flight deck. The liquid-oxygen tank was virtually unprotected, with no special armor or protective barriers; an explosion on the flight deck easily could penetrate it and ignite its contents.

The two sailors working there knew how dangerous the liquid oxygen was. John Dickerson and Robert Clark often thought that their workstation was a scary place to be in case of a fire, but like every other *Forrestal* sailor with a dangerous job, they got used to it. The first fire alarm, however, had sparked every latent fear and Dickerson rushed over to the big door leading from the oxygen plant to one of the big hangar bays. He was straining to pull the heavy, watertight door closed when the first bomb exploded. Dickerson kept his grip on the door and went flying with it as the blast flung it wide open. He was left hanging off the door in the hangar bay outside, and when the initial shock wore off, he realized that general quarters had sounded.

I've gotta go, but I have to close this hatch first . . .

Dickerson's general-quarters station was a repair locker some distance away, but he could see that Clark was shaken by the bomb blast and wouldn't be able to secure the hatch right away. He had to get that hatch closed to protect the oxygen plant as much as possible, and to protect his friend Clark, who would stay there for general quarters. Dickerson shoved on the heavy door and threw his body against it, then he started "dogging" the hatch closed by locking all the handles that surrounded the door frame.

Satisfied that the door was secure, he pounded on it a couple times and yelled, "Be careful, man!" before leaving Clark. Dickerson raced off to his general-quarters station.

Back in damage control, Merv Rowland knew what would happen if the liquid oxygen ignited. When a crew member in damage control asked about the vulnerability of the oxygen tank, he made no bones about the result.

"If that thing blows, we're gonna be the biggest damn blowtorch you've ever seen," he said. "It'll blow this ship out of the water, no doubt about it."

In the oxygen-generating plant, Clark recovered from the initial shock of the bomb blast and saw that the fire must be very close. He could feel the heat building to a nearly unbearable level within minutes, and then the bulkheads separating the liquid-oxygen plant from the rest of the ship started to glow red. Clark watched as the paint first bubbled and then burned off. Every time something exploded, red-hot shrapnel would come flying into the compartment. Clark tried to take cover, but he knew that wouldn't help if the shrapnel hit the liquid oxygen. And there was no telling how many more explosions were coming. Clark picked up the phone and called damage control for help.

Rowland had been monitoring the reports from that area closely and personally took Clark's call. The lone sailor sounded scared as he reported that the fire was all around him.

"It's getting hotter than hell out here!" the man yelled over the phone to Rowland. "What do I do, sir? The fire's getting close!"

"Dump it, son!" Rowland yelled back. "Dump it all!"

Rowland wanted the sailor to get rid of the liquid oxygen to eliminate the explosion hazard, but there was just one problem. The *Forrestal* had no emergency dump capability for the liquid oxygen. There was no way to just flip a few switches and send all the liquid oxygen whooshing overboard in a hurry.

Instead, Clark had to hook up a one-inch diameter, sixteen-foot-long hose—no bigger than a typical garden hose—to the liquid-oxygen tank and run out to the platform jutting out from the edge of the ship. There he stood with the hose in his hand, pointing it out to the sea and trying not to spill the super-cold liquid on his flesh. And while he was do-ing this, the fire raged directly overhead, explosions blowing debris onto the sponson and sending burn-ing material directly down on top of him. A bad stroke of luck could ignite the oxygen venting from the hose, leading directly back to the storage tank.

After a moment standing there under the flaming debris, Clark decided to leave the end of the hose dangling off the edge of the platform and retreat back into the oxygen-generating plant. The fires had not let up and the sailor was still scared, with good reason. While he had been venting the liquid oxygen, the fire and the blast damage had spread to the compartments all around him, trapping him there with the big oxygen tank. He had no way out. He called Merv Rowland again in damage control.

"It's still real bad here, sir!" the sailor said, sweat pouring off his face from the heat. "What do I do if it gets worse?"

"Put on your life jacket and go swimming!" Rowland replied. "That's the only goddamn way you can get away from it!"

Clark considered taking Rowland's advice, but he didn't want to. He looked over the side of the ship and thought about how dangerous it would be to jump overboard, trying to weigh that against the fire. Going overboard was a tempting prospect as he watched the oxygen vent and imagined it ignit-ing. It took more than an hour for the liquid oxygen to slowly pour through the hose. He never jumped over, and later, Clark would find out that the bomb shrapnel blew holes in the deck on opposite sides of the oxygen tank, just missing it by twenty feet on one side and fifteen feet on the other. If fate had thrown either piece of shrapnel just a little closer, the liquid oxygen would have been ignited.

A similar situation involved an eight-inch pipe that ran along the side of the ship and pumped jet fuel from the storage tanks belowdecks up to the flight deck, where it could be pumped directly into the planes. The pipe was blown apart early in the disaster, and if the fuel crew belowdecks had not responded quickly, they would have been pumping six hundred gallons of jet fuel directly into the fire scene every minute. When they got word of the fire on the flight deck, the crew immediately initiated a drain-back procedure to stop the flow of fuel to the flight deck and also drain out the fuel already in the pipes.

When Gary Shaver finally landed after being blown through the air by the first blast, he found himself lying far forward on the flight deck. He had witnessed the death of Gerald Farrier, the head of the crash crew who tried to wave off other firefighters when he saw that McCain's first bomb was about to explode. After what seemed a long journey through the air, Shaver tried to get up, but he couldn't. He couldn't hear anything. The cast on his right hand was gone. He felt a burning pain throughout his body, and when he looked down, he could see why. Blood was everywhere, and his clothes were singed and smoking. And his left arm was gone.

Wait a minute, it's not gone. It's over here.

There was a moment of calm and clarity as Shaver realized his left arm was still attached, barely, but it was draped behind his neck and hanging down the front of his right shoulder, the hand resting on his chest. Shaver reached up and grabbed his left hand with the right, hanging on to it to secure the mangled arm. As he looked over to where his left arm should be attached, he could see bones and bright red flesh. He had a tiny second to marvel that no blood was coming from the wound, and then it started spurting out in great jets.

Just then, Shaver was hit by another explosion and went tumbling across the deck. Then the pain hit him. He had been too stunned to feel it at first, but then it came on like a red-hot poker throughout his body. It was unlike anything he had experienced before, so bad that it went beyond anything he could even conceive of as pain. He was in absolute agony.

Screaming, Shaver tried to crawl away from the fire. His mind was totally out of control, certain he was about to die, consumed by the terrible pain and fear that grew worse with every breath.

As he flopped along the deck, someone grabbed him by the neck and pulled him toward the island. The area behind the island was crowded with injured and dying men, some seeking aid on their own, dragging themselves to the only place on the flight deck that seemed safe, while others were carried there by buddies and strangers. Men were tending to others in the crash-crew shack at the island, on the open deck amid the bombs stacked there, and in the battle-dressing station forward in the island structure. The battle-dressing station was the designated first-aid station, but it was quickly overwhelmed by the dozens of injured men.

Men did what they could for the fallen sailors,

but in the early moments of the fire, there was not enough help to go around. The injured were being taken to the sick bay belowdecks as fast as possible, and medical corpsmen were rushing up top to help, but the sheer numbers overwhelmed the first-aid efforts. There were horrible sights all over the flight deck—men with their faces or entire heads blown off by the explosions, limbs missing, bones protruding, severely burned, covered in blood. The victims often were not recognizable even to the men they worked with every day; sometimes only the stenciled name or rank on a man's clothing would give a clue. Some, like Shaver, screamed out in agony, utterly unable to control themselves as they endured the waves of pain and looked at their mangled bodies. Others were too stricken to even speak, and the lucky ones were unconscious.

Shaver was one of the first to be scooped up and carried down to the sick bay. Sailors and aviators did what they could for their fallen friends, using anything handy to try to stanch the bleeding wounds. In lieu of bandages, some were grabbing big fistfuls of coarse brown paper towels and trying to stop some of the worst bleeding. Another ripped off his T-shirt and placed it over a man's exposed intestines, pouring a jug of water over the shirt to keep the wound moist. Their efforts sometimes had little effect on the terrible wounds from the explosions. The deck in that area was covered with a half-inch of blood.

This was the scene that awaited Gary Pritchard and his buddy Frenchie as they made their way out of their berthing area just beneath the flight deck and were fighting the crowds of sailors to get to

their GQ stations topside. They still had no idea
what was going on, other than that it seemed the
ship was under attack. If planes were to be
launched in response to the attack, they thought, it
was important for them to get to that fuel station
on the flight deck and do their jobs. None of the
usual paths to the flight deck were passable, so
Pritchard decided they should make their way to
the island structure on the right side of the ship and
go up to the flight deck there.

When they came up into the daylight, they were
staring at a small piece of hell. Fire everywhere,
smoke, blood, wounded men, screams, alarms.
They thought they were looking at how they
would die.

"Jesus, goddamn," Pritchard muttered, transfixed by the scene in front of him. "Christ, it's all
over. Man, is it all over."

Pritchard's thoughts immediately went to his
young wife of only two years, and how she would
fare without him. In that split second of thought, he
comforted himself with the knowledge that they
had no children yet and he had kept up the pay-
ments on his life insurance.

*Well, at least she'll be all right with the life insur-
ance.*

Quickly, though, Pritchard's attention was diverted to the many injured and dying men who had
gathered behind the island structure. Men with serious injuries were lying all over, and Pritchard
didn't know what to do first. One glance at the
flight deck told him that he was not needed at his
usual GQ station because they sure as hell wouldn't
be pumping any fuel to the flight deck. As he

looked around and tried to decide what to do, Pritchard's eyes fell upon a young sailor sitting on the deck and holding a gravely wounded buddy in his arms. Pritchard still recalls the youthful look of the "kid" holding his bloodied and burned friend in his arms, cradling the man's head in his lap. The kid was crying.

"Help me! Help me!" the kid shouted at Pritchard, his teary eyes looking directly up into Pritchard's. So Pritchard turned to Frenchie and said, "Shit, we gotta help this guy!" The two buddies snapped out of their initial shock and swung into action.

As Pritchard bent down to help lift the wounded man off his sobbing friend, Frenchie ran for a wire stretcher. They lifted the man onto the stretcher, and as they did, Pritchard could see that the man was bleeding profusely. Most likely, the man was dead, but he and Frenchie took him anyway.

"It's all right, we got him," Pritchard told the sobbing sailor. "We'll take care of him."

Pritchard and Frenchie took the dead man down to the sick bay, which was already crowded and filling with the sickening smells of blood, burned flesh, and jet fuel. Then they hustled back up to the flight deck.

There, they could see that the injured men who had made it to the island structure were starting to get more help. But all across the flight deck, more men had not made it that far and many were still fending for themselves amid the fire. That's what happened to Airman Charles Price, the fellow who had climbed up the ladder to the flight deck just as the fire initially broke out. After helping in the first minute of the fire, Price found himself among those seriously injured in the big explosions.

He had been knocked unconscious during the first, and when he came to, he was lying facedown. He tried to get up and run, but he could not lift himself off the deck. When he looked down at his legs, he could see that the remains of his left pant leg were lying flat on the deck from the knee down. The left boot was still there, attached by something, but there was almost nothing left between the knee and the foot. He managed to crawl on his hands and one leg a little farther up the deck away from the fire, where he threw himself into the catwalk on the edge of the ship, just below the edge of the flight deck. Hoping this would be a safe place to take cover until help arrived, Price looked around and realized that it wasn't. He was right next to a fuel-pumping station. The catwalk already had been hit hard by the explosions, the metal railings twisted and torn. Fuel and fog-foam solution were pouring off the flight deck onto the catwalk.

Price tried to pull himself back up the ladder, but he didn't have the strength. The pain was terrible, and he had already lost a great deal of blood, making him weak and light-headed. In addition, he had a number of other shrapnel wounds all over his body that he was only beginning to notice. Realizing that he was very badly injured, Price fell back onto the catwalk and started yelling for help. He soon understood that no one would hear him. Shouting took too much effort anyway, he thought, so he just lay back on the catwalk and breathed heavily. He was worried about the blood loss from his shredded left leg, so he found the strength to pull off what was left of his belt and tried to apply it as a tourniquet. Price was becoming too dizzy to fumble with the pieces of the belt, so he pulled off his T-shirt, which was torn and bloodied already. He managed to wrap it around the remains of his left thigh but was unable to cinch it tightly enough to cut off the blood flow.

Price lay there on the mangled catwalk, rapidly losing strength and unable to do much more for himself. He could see through the perforated surface of the catwalk to the ocean below, and as he began to lose consciousness, he could see a big destroyer maneuvering in close to the ship. He slipped closer to sleep as he lay there looking down through the catwalk, the destroyer slipping in underneath him in a hazy image that might as well have been a dream. The last thing he saw before fading out was his own blood pouring beneath him and dropping into the ocean.

Suddenly, Price heard someone else jump onto the catwalk. He managed to yell for help and look up. As he did, he locked eyes with the other sailor approaching through the smoke. The other man was so startled by what he saw that he immediately turned and ran away, yelling for help. Price's torn body was that much of a shock.

Before long, the man returned with a medical corpsman and a wire basket stretcher. They tried to get the stretcher down to Price, but the catwalk was too mangled, so they decided to lift Price back up to the flight deck first. That was difficult without Price able to help himself, so they improvised by using a two-by-four board underneath Price. The two men lifted Price with the board underneath, hoisting him up to the flight deck and onto the stretcher.

Belowdecks, Ken Killmeyer still was trying to get to his GQ station, but with the warning from the repair crew, he realized he could not make it. He looked back toward the rear of the ship, into a crew berthing compartment, and saw smoke for the first time. It wasn't thick black smoke like what was pouring off the flight deck, but a gray smoke making its way through the berthing area and to the passageway where he stood with the repair crew. Someone closed a hatch to the berthing area, sealing off the smoke, at about the time the explosions stopped overhead.

Soon after the pause in the overhead noise, Killmeyer heard an announcement on the 1MC that anyone not trapped by smoke or assigned to a repair party should move to a forward portion of the ship, away from the danger in the rear of the ship. With about ten other men, Killmeyer made his way forward on the starboard side of the ship and as he approached the sick-bay area, he could see blood on the deck. As he got closer, he saw a buzz of activity with people bringing injured men down from the flight deck and in from other portions of the ship.

He continued to move forward, making slow progress because he and the sailors accompanying him had to stop and open hatches that had been sealed for the GQ alarm.

At one point, Killmeyer stepped aside to let a sailor emerge from the sick-bay area. As the sailor climbed a ladder ahead, Killmeyer noticed that he was carrying a bucket full of blood.

My God, how bad is this thing?

Killmeyer and the other sailors making their way to safety continued forward and up to the second deck, one deck directly above his own berthing compartment where he'd started. At that point, they encountered an officer who ordered them to stay in that area.

At 10:59 A.M., bosun's mate W. T. Burgess came back on the 1MC and called for the ship to set condition Zebra, the most extreme of status conditions for a carrier. Even for those who had no idea what was going on topside, which was most of the thousands of men on board, that was another signal of something very serious.

With condition Zebra, the ship was to be secured as tightly as possible to combat fires and other damage. Hatches were sealed all over the ship and that meant that passing from one area to another was not easy, and in some cases impossible. Crew members would allow others to pass in an emergency, and certainly to allow someone out of harm's way, but otherwise the ship was to be kept tightly compartmentalized. Setting the ship at Zebra made it more difficult for latecomers to access their general-quarters station because, once the ship was locked down, an officer or leading petty officer had to approve opening the hatch to allow a sailor to pass. If an officer wasn't around to approve, the sailor might not make it to his station. That was one reason the crew hauled ass when the general-quarters alarm sounded.

Killmeyer found himself with about forty other

men waiting where the officer had told them to stay. They talked about what they had seen already and what they thought might be going on, all of them excited and trying not to look scared. At one point, they heard tapping on a nearby hatch that led up to the hangar deck.

Killmeyer went over to the hatch and he could hear men yelling. The hatch had been sealed from Killmeyer's side as part of the condition Zebra lockdown. He yelled back to ask if the men were okay up there. They said they were, and asked how Killmeyer and the others were doing in that compartment.

"We're fine. We're not doing anything down here, though. We want to help!" someone yelled. "Let us up!"

"Yeah, hey, let us up!" someone else yelled. "Open the damn hatch!"

Someone waiting with Killmeyer realized he could open the hatch and talk to the men above. Killmeyer could hear the reply.

"I can't let you guys up here," someone from the hangar-deck group yelled. "I'll get my ass in trouble by letting you up. I'm not allowed to. You're going to have to just wait. That's all we're doing up here too."

The hatch was closed again. Soon someone new came into the crowd and told them he had heard the gun mounts were gone and the fantail was seriously damaged. Soon after that, the group of men was allowed into the hangar deck above. What they found was a real mess.

The hangar bays were huge open areas running the width of the entire ship and very nearly the entire length. They were almost directly underneath the flight deck, with only one level between—the level where so many men had been sleeping when the fire started. When the bombs blasted through that level, the inferno poured right down into the hangar bays packed with aircraft, various other equipment, and pallets stacked with bombs. When the fire started, Ronald Williams was at his station in Conflag 3, one of several small control rooms overlooking the hangar bays. His duty was to watch for any fire hazards in the hangar bay and react quickly to prevent or stop the fire, as well as to keep an eye on things in the hangar bay. If you were playing football with some buddies in the big hangar bay, Williams was the booming voice that came over the loudspeakers, warning you to keep your long passes away from that helicopter. Someone was always in the conflag centers, twenty-four hours a day, keeping watch over the hangar bays.

When the fire alarms had first sounded, Williams perked up and prepared for any signs of fire in the hangar bays. He didn't have to wait long for the first explosion to send shrapnel firing down, and that's when he called damage control to report blast damage in the hangar bays. He asked for orders, and damage control told him to activate the sprinkler system and close all hangar-bay doors. The doors were a primary safety feature on the *Forrestal:* mammoth sliding steel slabs more than a foot thick that could be closed to divide the large, open hangar bay into three smaller compartments.

With just a few buttons and switches, Williams initiated emergency measures that would prove vital to saving the *Forrestal*. Within seconds, a heavy rain was falling in the hangar bays, suppressing any fires that had already started and preventing any new fires from taking hold. At the same time, the huge hangar-bay doors started sliding shut, sealing off the different hangar bays from one another so that any fires, smoke, or blast damage could be isolated. The massive doors slid out quickly, accompanied by a loud alarm warning people to clear the way. In less than fifteen seconds the doors had sealed off the hangar bays.

By the time Killmeyer and the other men entered Hangar Bay 1, there was no fire. Others already on the scene, however, told the men that Hangar Bay 2 was full of smoke and Hangar Bay 3, closer to the origin of the fire, was ablaze. The sprinkler system probably had extinguished the fire in Hangar Bay 3 by that time, but nevertheless, Killmeyer could tell that he was now in the middle of the ship's crisis. The hangar bay was filled with the acrid odor of smoke mixed with fog-foam solution, explosives, and burning fuel, plastics, and wiring. An officer soon started yelling for the men to start moving planes out of the hangar bay to get them out of harm's way. Oddly enough, the planes were to be moved onto the elevators and then up to the flight deck. Though the rear of the flight deck was the site of the original fire, the blaze was moving downward at this point, to the hangar bay. The forward end of the flight deck was a safer spot to stow the planes.

Killmeyer joined with a number of other sailors moving planes by hand because there was only one tractor available and operable in the hangar bay. The planes normally would have been very carefully towed by a small tractor attached to the front wheel, but it was necessary to move them quickly and however possible. So Killmeyer and the others grabbed whatever part of the plane they could reach, and started pushing. There was plenty of help, so the planes started moving fairly easily. They found that stopping them was harder, and many planes were damaged when they ran into one another. At that moment, however, minor damage to a plane did not concern anyone.

Indeed, damage to planes and loss of aircraft was becoming an increasingly minor concern. Up on the flight deck, the firefighting effort had resumed with a new vigor, the sailors charging back into the inferno now that the worst of the explosions seemed to have subsided. As crews gathered up the remains of shredded fire hoses and others strung up new ones, the fire finally was being hit with substantial volumes of seawater and fog-foam solution. One of the first priorities was to lay a thick blanket of foam between the island and the fire line, creating a buffer that would protect the all-important command structure and leaving the men a safe zone from which to attack the fire. The deck became a slippery mess as the soaplike fog foam built up in shallow pools. In some areas, the fog foam reached nearly knee-high.

The overall firefighting effort was directed by Merv Rowland in damage control, but on the flight deck, it sometimes seemed like every man for himself. Officers on the deck were trying to organize repair parties and direct a controlled response to the fire, but in the fog of battle, many sailors never saw an officer give orders to anyone. The damage-control and repair-party personnel were not easily identified by appearance, so they had difficulty getting the attention of other crew when giving orders and trying to organize a response. This was particularly true in the hangar bays, where men were working feverishly to control fires and prevent further explosions. In the hangar bays and up on the flight deck, men acted on their own to do the best they could in fighting the fire, manning a hose whenever possible and doing whatever seemed like a good response. Some of those self-directed efforts would turn out to be the best response possible, and others would not.

In the effort to fight the fire, for instance, sailors made the mistake of using both water hoses and fog-foam hoses on the same fire site. In retrospect, many would see this as a major failing of the ship's crew, because the combination greatly impeded the effort to extinguish the blaze. Though the crew thought they were doing their best by pouring as much water and foam on the fire as possible, they were actually making a serious mistake that the *Forrestal*'s trained crash-crew firefighters would not have made if they had survived the first bomb blast. The fog foam is intended to create a blanket over the fire and spilled fuel, smothering it and preventing further combustion. When used by itself, the fog foam can be an extremely effective response to aircraft fires.

But when one firefighting team sprays foam and another sprays water on the same fire, the water simply washes away the foam, leaving only the far less effective water to extinguish the jet fuel. The crew would be criticized harshly for this firefighting

mistake, but Frank Eurice understood the sailors'
dilemma. Unlike him, many of the sailors had no
firefighting training and could not resist when they
found themselves standing in front of a huge fire
with a water hose. He knew they were trying to do
their best.

And besides, the firefighting foam alone does
nothing to cool the weapons that heated up in the
fire. Some of the crew looked at the devastation
wrought by the initial bomb blasts and decided that
water had to be applied to the other bombs and
rockets to cool them off, no matter what effect it
had on the foam.

Eurice had stayed at his station until smoke
started coming into the tiny compartment, forced
in through the ventilation system that normally
pumped fresh air into the otherwise stuffy room.
When the smoke started, Eurice called damage control and asked what he should do. It took fifteen
minutes for them to get back to him and say he
could leave his post. By then, Eurice had breathed a
lot of smoke and was glad to get out, to go anywhere else.

Damage control had also given orders to abandon the ammunition magazines directly above Eurice's station for fear they would explode. He did
not know at the time that that was the reason so
many men were running like hell, just ahead of
him, as he abandoned his own station. As he
brought up the rear, Eurice sealed every hatch behind him.

When Eurice and the others got to the mess
decks, they found the ship was shut down tight for
condition Zebra, and they were not sure where

they should go next. Because Eurice had firefighting training, he decided to organize the men into an impromptu repair party and go looking for some work to do. He found a stash of oxygen-breathing apparatus, known as OBAs, and passed them out. He gave the men a quick lesson in how to use the devices: The mask fits over your face and you pull the straps to create a snug fit. A canister hangs around your neck and sits on your chest. When you insert the activator cartridge, you've got thirty minutes of air. When the bell goes off, *get out,* because you've only got three minutes left.

Eurice led two of the men—he never learned their names—on a path toward the flight deck. When he got to the level just beneath the flight deck, and in the rear portion of the ship, they could see fire damage and feel the heat coming off of the flight deck above. Smoke was everywhere, so Eurice looked for a way out of that compartment and up to the open air. He opened a hatch that he knew led to a walkway that could take them to the flight deck.

But when he opened the door, all he found was a hole where an entire working space was supposed to be. Eurice was looking out at the ocean and a beautiful blue sky instead of the ship interior he expected. Dazzled by the sudden sight of a beautiful Tonkin Gulf morning, Eurice stood for a moment and just stared. Then he slammed the door and moved on.

They were very close to the fire at that point, so Eurice told the other two men to energize their OBAs and he did the same. They found a fire hose on the wall nearby and unrolled it, and the three men started moving forward into the blackness. Breathing heavily in their OBAs, they crept forward with the hose and could feel the heat growing more intense as their sight grew blacker and blacker. Their faces covered by the black masks with the big round eyepieces, rubber hoses dangling from the bottom and attached to the oxygen generators hanging on their chests, they looked like a trio of slow-moving insects merging with the darkness. Finally, they were feeling their way along the passageway, totally blinded by the smoke.

Suddenly they saw a big red glow ahead of them. *Oh boy, looks like we found it,* Eurice thought. *Welcome to Hell: Population 3.*

Eurice opened the nozzle on the fire hose and hit the red glow with a spray of water that immediately turned to steam and rushed back toward the men, searing their skin. Shouting through his OBA mask, he urged the men to keep low, to stay under the heat and steam as much as possible. Before long, Eurice heard the bell go off on one of the other men's OBA, and almost immediately after, Eurice heard his own bell go off and then the other man's. They had to abandon their fight and back out of the fire area, leaving the red glow almost as red as they had found it.

The three of them headed back down to where they had left the rest of the men, showing up drenched with sweat and water, and with black soot all over. After getting a new canister for his OBA, Eurice decided to go off by himself to find a fire to fight. Rather than go back to the fire they had just fought, which seemed too big for a small crew, Eurice decided to head aft, to the rear of the ship, an area he knew well because he worked and lived there. After passing through compartments already blackened by fire, he found himself on the port quarter, the rear corner of the ship on the left side. This was directly beneath some of the worst fires and explosions, and Eurice could see that he'd found the fire. He looked for firefighting gear to use, but all he found was a hose that had been blown apart by the explosions. Ammunition and planes were still exploding just overhead on the flight deck, and a combination of fuel, water, and foam was pouring off the deck right where he stood. With all sorts of debris and God-knows-what raining down on his head, this was not a good place to be. He could see a destroyer coming in close alongside to render aid, but he was not sure what he should do. The hatch he had just come through now had smoke pouring from it, so going back was not really an option. He had backed himself into a corner.

Eurice started thinking about what was around him. He knew that the ship's post office was on one side overhead and on the other side was a magnesium-flare locker. Magnesium flares—the same thing that had caused the devastating fire on the carrier *Oriskany*. Once they're ignited, they burn white hot and can't be extinguished. Desperate to do something, Eurice picked up the shredded fire hose and bent it over itself so that some of the water sprayed out one of the biggest holes. He pointed the spray up at the overhead, toward the magnesium flare locker.

Well, this is a waste of time. I'm not accomplishing a goddamn thing.

Eurice dropped the shredded hose and looked over at the hatch again, trying to calculate his chances if he forced his way back into the smoke. He had used part of another OBA coming to that area, so he figured he had maybe a good seven minutes left on that thing.

I don't know how far I'll get in seven minutes. That's not long.

He had to do *something*. He definitely couldn't stay where he was. Eurice looked up at one of the gun mounts on the side of the ship and saw some sailors working there. *That's not too far a trek from here, so maybe I can make it on this OBA.* He wasn't at all sure, though. Feeling trapped and knowing the danger of running into a smoke-filled passageway without a full OBA, Eurice considered jumping overboard. But he looked over at the destroyer pulling alongside and realized they would not be able to pick him up; the destroyer was keeping pace with the carrier and both would be long gone after Eurice hit the water. He looked aft and could not see any other ships in the carrier's wake. Eurice was trapped between water and fire.

Okay, if I jump over here and nobody sees me, who's going to know? I don't want to just drown out there by myself. He stared at the water for a minute and tried to make a rational decision. *Water or fire?*

Eurice didn't like his choices, but he figured he had a slightly better chance with the fire. He put on his oxygen mask again and knelt down in front of the hatch with black smoke pouring out. After taking one last glance at the bright blue sky, he plunged into the pitch-black hatch and started feeling his way along.

Chapter *10*

KEEP UP YOUR VERY GOOD WORK

The horror continued on the flight deck, but the men were beginning to make progress in fighting the fire. Sailors were manning hoses as best they could, pouring seawater and fog foam onto the burning jet fuel and the wreckage of the planes. It often took a dozen men to man a fog-foam hose, with several holding the hose on the fire and another group manning a water wand, a pipe several feet long with a diffuser on the end to create a fine water spray. The water team held the wand over the heads of the fog-foam team, soaking them as they worked and protecting them from the searing heat of the fire just ahead. (This combination of foam and water was proper firefighting technique because the water did not wash away the foam.)

With the *Forrestal*'s firefighting team wiped out in the first moments of the fire, the sailors had to take over and learn on the job. Some of them had been trained in firefighting techniques but had no real experience, while others had no training whatsoever. As the blazes roared so close it made them flinch from the heat, the men with a little training tried to take the lead. They provided impromptu lessons on how to use the fog foam and the water wands, and they showed the others how to use the oxygen breathing apparatus, the OBAs that allowed the men to get close to the deck fire and some of the burning compartments below. The OBAs were a crucial tool if the men were going to fight the fires anywhere belowdecks, and more was involved than just pulling the mask over your face. Some actually had to sit down and read the instructions that came with the device, while the fires roared nearby and their buddies needed help.

Everywhere they looked on the rear portion of the flight deck, planes were burning furiously and churning heavy black smoke into the air. The entire rear of the flight deck was ablaze, and their first goal was to stop the blaze from moving any farther forward on the deck.

The big explosions during the fire's first moments had spread the fire far beyond its original site at McCain's plane, and smaller blasts of ammunition, fuel tanks, and other items continued for a long time. Ejection seats in the burning planes were firing, sending the remains of a pilot's seat skyward in a weak imitation of their real purpose. Missiles and rockets cooked off periodically, exploding where they lay or their propellant igniting and sending the projectile across the deck at low level, a lightning-fast killer that took out anyone in the way. The warhead on the rocket or missile might then explode with all the explosive power that was intended for ground targets in Vietnam. Every time a bit of red-hot shrapnel made its way to another plane, there was the chance of setting off a whole new fuel spill, fire, and major explosions from the ordnance. Every plane sitting on the deck represented a target for the willy-nilly ways of flying debris. At any moment, the tiniest bit of metal could find a target that could spread the fire much, much farther forward on the flight deck.

There were dozens of vulnerable planes, but none posed more danger than the KA-3B Skywarrior parked on the elevator just behind the island. The Skywarrior was a tanker plane, already loaded with twenty-eight thousand pounds of jet fuel. It was unmanned, having just recently been brought up from the hangar bay below. The plane was to be part of the scheduled air strike, flying off with the attack planes to provide midair refueling. Now it sat on the starboard side of the deck, only yards away from the critical island structure on one side and the roaring fire. If the tanker's fuel exploded, it would probably wipe out everyone on the deck and pour hundreds of gallons of burning fuel down onto the men working in the hangar bays directly below. The fuel tanker was a huge hazard, just sitting there with no protection.

On the bridge, Captain Beling realized the danger posed by all the remaining planes on the deck—and in particular by the Skywarrior and the A-6 Intruders parked just aft of the fuel tanker behind the island.

"Damn it, they're parked right near the uptakes from the boiler rooms," Beling commented, thinking out loud about the dangers to the chimneylike structures that provided ventilation for the ship's vital engine room. "Those planes are armed and loaded, aren't they? If one of those bombs goes, it's going to ruin the draft of the fires"— meaning the boiler fires in the engine room. "We won't have any power."

Losing power would be a major downturn in the ship's effort to survive, preventing it from continuing forward to keep the fire blown back aft and making it impossible to maneuver in cooperation with other ships coming to her aid. Clearly the planes on deck had to be moved, so orders started going out to get them moved in any way possible. Normally the aircraft would be moved either under their own power or by small, low-profile tractors that would attach a tow bar to the front wheel, but that wasn't possible in this critical state.

They had to move the planes by hand, with the sheer muscle power of young men pumped full of adrenaline. All over the deck, they joined together to wrestle planes out of danger and take them much farther forward on the flight-deck, a more frantic and improvised version of the carefully choreographed ballet that was the usual flight-deck scene. The Skywarrior was one of the first concerns, but it could not be moved until a lot of other equipment was first moved out of the way. The tanker plane was parked on the elevator, on the very edge of the deck starboard, and in front of it were two helicopters, a big stack of heavy tow bars, and various other equipment. This area was referred to as "the junkyard" for good reason. Dozens of men set about moving all of this equipment first so they could get to the dangerous fuel tanker. Every minute mattered.

After a while, the path was clear and the men could begin to push the tanker forward. Even with dozens of men pushing hard, they had to find a tractor to take most of the weight. They managed to push the tanker to the center of the flight deck and then turn it right so it could be forced up toward Catapult 1 on the right side of the deck far forward. There they parked the plane as far away from the blaze as they could.

Some planes could not be moved forward, however, no matter how much muscle was applied. Either they were damaged in some way from the blasts, or they already were on fire or were leaking fuel. There was no way to stop a fuel leak in a plane, and they certainly didn't want to move it into the relatively safe area. Some planes ignited from the wheels up, as the magnesium in their brake systems heated from the surrounding flames and the hot deck. Once the magnesium began to burn with its unique ferocity, the plane was a goner no matter what you did. And when the magnesium heated up sufficiently, it could explode like a bomb.

The bombs and missiles loaded on the planes posed their own explosive hazard, of course, and it was not feasible to remove the ordnance in such a crisis. The hazardous planes had to be dealt with, and there was neither the time nor the means to do it delicately. The solution was a fairly universal one on an aircraft carrier: if there's something you don't want on an aircraft carrier anymore, you throw it overboard.

Word of this spread across the deck, from officers trying to organize the men and from orders given by the bridge and by damage control over radio headsets. But mostly the men came to the decision themselves, and it was reinforced when they saw the first plane pushed overboard. Ed Roberts jumped right into the effort to move planes because this was his main job anyway. He joined others who had started forming work parties around individual aircraft, bunching up around the big machines and grabbing whatever they could find to start pushing and pulling. Most of the aircraft were already parked on the rim of the carrier deck, so getting them overboard was just a matter of giving them a good push to get some momentum and then watching the huge aircraft slip over the side of the ship. But others made Roberts curse and scream while he pushed with all his might. The catwalks and various other structures off the ship's edge sometimes made it hard to get the planes overboard in one easy swoop because they got caught, leaving the plane dangling over the edge. Once that happened, it was a tricky proposition to keep pushing it manually because you never knew when the plane or the catwalk would give way and suddenly plummet into the ocean.

Roberts saw that planes and wreckage were being pushed overboard all over the flight deck, but especially at the rear closest to the main fire. That's where the planes were most at risk, and where most of them were already damaged and leaking fuel. While some sailors faced the fire directly with water hoses and fog foam, others worked nearby to manhandle the planes toward the deck edge and over into the sea. Roberts and the other sailors improvised whatever means they could to get the planes overboard quickly, and without taking anyone with them. Much of the deck equipment was burning already or damaged from the explosions, but the men found a few small tractors, a forklift, and, most luckily, the big apparatus known as the "Tillie."

The Tillie, also known as the crash crane, was a big four-wheeled monster that could lift just about any plane, or anything else you stuck in its claws. The Tillie was used to clear out crash wreckage, damaged aircraft, or anything else too big and heavy to be moved easily. Though the Tillie was normally used to lift and carry a load, sometimes without even damaging an airplane, it was also very effective at brutish work. This was a day for getting things done quick and dirty, so the Tillie just ran up to big planes on the deck and forced them right over the side.

But most of the planes were jettisoned with nothing more than muscles and determination. At one point, Clark Chisum, the *Forrestal*'s weapons officer, was on deck helping coordinate some of the plane movement, including throwing some overboard. He was with a group of men pushing a plane toward the edge of the deck, straining to move the heavy machine, when he noticed that one of the men was just walking alongside and making no effort to push.

Chisum was about to ask him why the hell he wasn't pushing when he saw the reason. The man was walking alongside the plane with his index finger jammed into a hole in the fuel tank, stopping a fuel leak that could cause the plane to burst into flames at any moment. Chisum decided the young man was doing a pretty good job.

At one point, Ed Roberts spotted serious trouble with a plane being moved by one of the small tractors on board. The driver of the cart had backed the plane up to the edge of the deck, intending to release it at the right moment and let the plane continue off the edge. But the tow bar did not release, and the plane's weight was pulling the cart and driver back with it. The driver was frantically pushing on the brakes, but the cart was sliding backward in the fog-foam solution. The plane was getting close to the edge, and from the look on the cart driver's face, Roberts wasn't at all certain that the guy would have the presence of mind to jump off in time. He knew from his experience in moving planes that the tractor brakes weren't enough to stop the plane once it got momentum, but he suspected the guy on the tractor didn't. Roberts grabbed a wheel chock and walked alongside the plane as it moved backward, just as he normally would, and tossed the chock into place behind the wheel. The plane was moving too fast and the deck was too slippery; the wheel just spit the chock back out. He kicked it back into place and it came out again.

Roberts kicked it back into place again, and this time he jammed his foot against the chock to hold it in. He had to lean back on his arms and crab-walk backward as the plane continued to move, the chock skipping along as he tried to hold it in. He could see the deck edge getting closer and closer, and then finally the plane stopped six feet from the edge. The tractor driver gunned the engine to get traction as Roberts eased his foot off the chock, and then when it seemed it would hold, Roberts ran up and released the tow bar from the plane. With the tractor freed, he ran back and yanked the chock away from the wheel. With the deck tilted slightly and slippery, the plane began to move on its own and soon crashed over the side, flopping onto its back in the water. Roberts lay panting on the deck from the effort.

One plane aft of the island, a big Vigilante, which was much larger than the Skyhawks and Phantoms, was parked right on the edge of the starboard side when the fire started, just to the rear of where the big tanker plane had been parked and between the two elevators there. The plane clearly was in danger of igniting because of its proximity to the fire; the crew could see that flying debris had already opened the plane's skin in a lot of places. More than a dozen men pushed on the plane and got it rolling backward off the flight deck, but then the wheels got hung up in the catwalk just below the deck. The plane sat there, firmly stuck with its nose pointing up at a forty-five-degree angle, still posing the same explosive hazard but now in a position that made it very difficult for the men to push it. And even if they could, the wheels were caught up in a tangle of metal that would be hard to break.

Quickly, a sailor came rushing up to the big plane in a heavy-duty forklift normally used to move around pallets of bombs and other materials on the flight deck. Wasting no time, he drove the big forklift up to the plane and raised the forks slightly, shoving them hard up under the fuselage. Then he raised the forks higher, forcing the plane into even more of a vertical position, and gunned the engine on the forklift, pushing forward on the plane as hard as he could. The other sailors stood back for the most part and tried to stay out of the way as the determined sailor pushed hard on the plane, the forklift's wheels slipping in the slippery fog-foam solution on the deck. With the forks raised as high as they would go, the sailor kept pushing hard on the plane, the slipping of the truck causing it to rock back and forth into the plane. The sailors nearby were doing all they could to help by pushing wherever they could grab it, but the fight had really come down to one guy in a forklift trying to shove this damn plane off the ship. In doing so, the sailor was risking his own life, because the forks easily could become jammed in the plane's fuselage and be pulled overboard as well.

At one point, another sailor drove up in one of the squat little tow tractors and rammed it up against the rear of the forklift, trying to keep the bigger truck from slipping so much on the soapy deck. After a long struggle, about fifteen minutes of pushing and wiggling, something finally gave way. Whatever parts of the ship and the plane had commingled on the edge of the deck came loose and the Vigilante finally fell into the ocean. The big plane slipped over the side and hit the water hard, floating for just a minute or so as the ship moved on, then sank out of sight in the ship's wake. The crew eventually pushed over three intact RA-5C Vigilantes and one A-4E Skyhawk, not counting other plane wreckage that had been burned and eventually was pushed overboard.

Those planes posed a major risk to the crew, but

not nearly as much as all the ordnance stowed on the ship for that morning's aborted air strike. Tons of bombs were sitting all over, some stacked neatly on pallets in the bomb farm on the flight deck, behind the island where everyone was gathering, and others sitting where they were left on the deck as the fire broke out. Below, more bombs were in the hangar bays, and still more in the magazines belowdecks. In addition, there were hundreds of missiles and rockets on the flight deck and in the hangar bay, each one loaded with fuel and something nasty in the nose that was intended to knock out ground installations, blow planes out of the sky, or wipe out ground troops by the dozens. The rockets and missiles already loaded on the planes were going off as they burned in the big fire, and the crew was worried that the blaze would spread to the others.

And the bombs, of course, had proven to be very sensitive to the heat. Plenty of the old thousand-pound bombs were still left on the ship, not to mention the comparatively smaller ones, and just a handful of explosions from those fat boys had nearly crippled the *Forrestal*. If the crew didn't get rid of the bombs, the fire could set off even more massive explosions, taking more men and threatening the ship's survival.

Beling considered just ordering that the bombs be put on the big elevators and lowered to a safer area of the ship, but the elevators couldn't rapidly handle enormous quantities of ordnance like what was stored on deck. It would be a slow process to get all the bombs belowdecks, and they couldn't risk that delay.

So just as it had with the planes, word spread that the bombs and other ordnance were to be jettisoned as quickly as possible. There was no time to make careful, measured decisions about which bomb was at risk of exploding and which ones could safely be left alone. Officers on the flight deck and in the hangar bays started giving orders to shove it all overboard, *now,* and the crew got the idea fast. Everywhere, men started wrestling the big bombs to the edge of the carrier, sometimes rolling them along the deck, sometimes joining together and straining to lift the heavy weapons. Missiles and rockets were picked up by impromptu teams, sometimes of as many as ten men, drenched from the torrent of seawater falling in the hangar bays, and carried to the big open elevator doors. There they were heaved overboard and lost to the ocean.

This stuff was killing the men, and everybody wanted it *off* the damn ship. They were willing to do whatever it took to get it off.

John McCain had hustled off the flight deck and, after determining that his injuries were not serious, he headed down to the hangar-bay level. There he saw some sailors heaving bombs off of one of the elevators and over the side of the ship. He pitched in.

On the bridge, Captain Beling was concerned that his men would be beaten down by the ongoing fight against the fire and the everyday heat of the Tonkin Gulf. More than an hour had passed and he still didn't have a reliable count of the injured and wounded, but the initial reports indicated the toll would be high. And he could see that men were dropping all over the flight deck from exhaustion.

They had to keep fighting, and Beling thought maybe a pep talk would help. He picked up the mike for the 1MC, the public-address system that reached all parts of the ship.

"Men of *Forrestal,* this is the captain. The forward progress of the fire on the flight deck has been stopped. We've got some good confidence in our ability to get these under control. Keep up your very good work."

Beling's words were welcomed. Ed Roberts just wanted some information—any information—and he liked hearing Beling's calm voice.

Well, okay then. At least he didn't tell us to find life jackets. I guess we're beating this thing.

Beling's encouraging words spurred the men in the hangar bay to get rid of more of the bombs. McCain worked with the group of men on the elevator, two or three of them at a time grabbing a bomb and lugging it over to the deck edge. Some sailors found "bomb carts," resembling a hand truck, to move the heavy bombs, but most of the work was done by energetic, highly motivated young men putting their hands on the bombs. McCain saw that the crew was doing their best to use the equipment at hand, whatever they could find, but sometimes throwing things off a ship isn't as easy as it sounds.

One sailor in the hangar bay, for instance, was using a forklift to pick up a big pallet of bombs and carry them to the open elevator door. With the forklift, he was able to move a lot more bombs at once than the sailors could move by hand, but then he had the problem of actually throwing them off when he got close enough. A forklift isn't designed to actually toss something off it, so the sailor couldn't figure out how to dump the bombs off. He could get close to the edge, but then the big stack of bombs just sat there on his forks. He considered dropping them on the deck and pushing the whole stack off, but there was no clean edge on the deck; the pallet would just get hung up.

But like so many other men on the *Forrestal* that day, the sailor decided to do whatever it took. He drove the forklift, with the bomb pallet still raised high overhead, as close to the edge as he could and stopped. Then he put the forklift in gear, let go of the clutch, and jumped off the truck as fast as he could. As the sailor tumbled to the deck, not far from falling overboard himself, the forklift and its dangerous load flew forward and into the sea.

Extraordinary effort was becoming common-place on the carrier. Men like Otis Kight stepped up and did whatever they had to do. He was one of the older guys on board, and the day of the fire was, in fact, his forty-third birthday. Kight had been on the carrier USS *Yorktown* when it was sunk during the Battle of Midway, and he had been shot down in a bomber over the Philippine Sea. In 1954, he survived an explosion aboard the carrier USS *Bennington,* which killed more than one hundred sailors. So when fire broke out on the *Forrestal,* Kight knew that dogged determination could mean the difference between living and dying. Joining in the effort with men less than half his age, Kight wrestled and heaved the big heavy bombs overboard with a ferocity that amazed those who saw him.

Kight weighed only 140 pounds, but he single-handedly lifted 250-pound bombs, carried them to the elevator doors, and threw them overboard.

Those responsible for the ordnance were doing their best to prevent more explosions, but often that just meant directing the effort to throw bombs overboard and lending their own muscle to the effort. In the hangar bays, however, Chief Ordnanceman Thomas Lawler was trying to put his skills to work on some missiles he knew were dangerous. Lawler had been in his maintenance shop nearby when the fire first started. He had thought the ship was under attack, and when the ceiling of his shop started to glow red in a matter of minutes, he and his assistant fled into the hangar bays. Then he remembered that there were some F4 Phantom jets parked in Hangar Bay 3, already loaded with missiles. Plenty of men were running around already trying to jettison bombs and other ordnance, but missiles loaded on a plane can't just be yanked off by unfamiliar hands. So Lawler ran to Hangar Bay 3 and found the Phantoms parked in the darkness and under a torrent of water. The lights were out and a thick smoke was gathering, so Lawler couldn't see a thing except for the shadows and familiar forms of the planes. With his assistant at his side, he groped from one plane to another, feeling for the missiles and disengaging them from memory alone, unable to see anything they were doing. They felt for the various attachments, and once the missile was free from the plane, they would lower it to the deck and carry it to the edge of the ship.

Like Beling, Merv Rowland was starting to worry that the long fight might get the best of his men. The crew in damage control was performing well, but he knew that the initial adrenaline rush would wear off and then a man's attention could wander. He couldn't have any of that.

"This damn thing's not over yet!" Rowland called out in damage control. "Stay focused on your job and don't get slack on me. We've still got a lot of work to do."

Rowland also used the 1MC system to update the crew and give orders, his gravelly voice tinged with a sense of urgency that contrasted with Captain Beling's ever-calm tone. Rowland sometimes hesitated as he gave instructions to the crew, and in the background, his damage-control crew could be heard feeding him information to pass on, such as where to find needed equipment and electrical controls.

"Repair parties two, three, and four report to your repair party if not needed elsewhere. Do not, I repeat, do not flood out the magazines until directed by the captain!

"All repair parties, this is control. There are two major fires on the fantail, port and starboard one, two, and three levels.

"Order: Make every effort to jettison the fuel drums on the port quarter. On the starboard fantail. I repeat, repair parties fighting the fire on the port quarter, make every effort to jettison the gasoline drums on the starboard fantail! A quick-release will run through the bulkhead, right by the access going to the carpenter shop."

After helping throw bombs overboard in the hangar bay, John McCain made his way to the pilots' "ready room," where they often gathered for briefings and other meetings. Several other pilots were there already, and McCain joined them in watching the flight-deck action on a television monitor. The stationary camera was still transmitting the scene from above, though the operator had long since fled from the danger.

The pilots were impressed with the *Forrestal*'s crew.

"We're professional military men, and I suppose it's our war," McCain said after the fire. "And yet, here were enlisted men who earn a hundred and fifty dollars a month and work eighteen to twenty hours a day—and I mean manual labor—and they certainly would have survived had they not stayed to help the pilots and fight the fire."

The crew was mobilizing to do whatever they could, but they needed help. Fortunately, the ships nearby had sensed the urgency of the situation immediately and sprang into action. Some of the other ships on Yankee Station were within sight of the *Forrestal*, and the moment the fire first started, the sailors standing watch on those ships called in the emergency to their commanding officers. From miles away, the sailors on the other ships could see that something terrible was happening to the *Forrestal*. The ship in the distance suddenly sprouted an ugly black smoke plume that rose high into the morning sun, and they could see debris blown into the air and the splashes made by planes, debris, and people hitting the water.

Even without knowing what was going on, they radioed for help from any U.S. vessels in the area. Soon, messages from the *Forrestal* itself made it clear that the ship was in a desperate fight to survive. The USS *Oriskany* and the USS *Bon Homme Richard,* two aircraft carriers, immediately ceased their own flight-deck preparations and turned their attention to the *Forrestal.* With a fellow flattop in such dire trouble, the crews of the nearby carriers knew that their resources could make the difference in the ship's surviving the fire. At 10:56 A.M., the destroyers *Mackenzie, Rupertus,* and *Tucker* also turned toward the *Forrestal* and awaited orders for coordinating a rescue effort with the other ships. Less than five minutes after the fire started, help was on the way.

Unlike the carriers, the destroyers would be able to maneuver in close and directly aid in fighting the fire. All three ships sounded general quarters and turned toward the *Forrestal.* They poured on the engines to nearly full throttle, rushing to close the distance. By 11:02 A.M., eleven minutes after the fire started, the *Rupertus* was close enough to drop its relatively small "motor whale boat" in the water and start assisting in the rescue of men in the water. The *Rupertus* started maneuvering in close to the *Forrestal*'s left rear, all the time watching closely for men and debris in the water, dodging left and right to avoid them.

The aircraft carriers were launching all of their helicopters to aid in the rescue, and the men already in the water were a primary concern. Some had been blown into the water by the first bomb explosions, and others were still jumping into the sea to escape the fires. A total of forty-seven men went overboard. Up above, Angel 20, the helicopter crew that had been on plane-guard duty and saw the fire start, was the first helicopter on the scene, approaching the *Forrestal* from the right side and crossing in front of the bridge before curving around to the rear of the ship on the left side. As David Clement positioned the helicopter to follow the carrier's wake and look for men overboard, one of the big bomb explosions rocked his craft violently. Clement righted the helicopter and looked in awe at how bad the fire was, then he repeatedly radioed for assistance. His calls for help broke up as his helicopter was buffeted by the shock waves from explosions on the deck, shaking the craft hard and causing it to bounce wildly through the air with Clement struggling to maintain control.

"We have multiple men in the water, repeat, multiple men in the water!" Clement radioed. "Angel twenty requesting assistance!"

The pilot considered pulling away from the stricken carrier because of the danger from the concussions and flying debris, any one bit of shrapnel capable of hitting a soft spot in the fuselage or shearing off a rotor blade. But almost immediately, Leonard Eiland spotted one of several men in the water. He pointed him out and Clement headed in that direction.

Though they had trained extensively for picking up downed pilots and the occasional man overboard, Clement and one of the rescue swimmers, Albert Barrows, had never participated in a real rescue. Eiland and the other swimmer, James O. James, each had one rescue under their belts. Clement dumped seven hundred pounds of fuel in the ocean to make the helicopter lighter and more maneuverable during the rescue. Then he put Angel 20 right over the man in the water and Barrows jumped in with a "fish pole" used to reach the rescue sling lowered from the helicopter and push it toward the victim, who could be panicky. James, the other swimmer, stayed aboard to direct the pilots and operate the winch that would haul the man in once he was in the sling. Barrows used the fish pole to help the first man get in the sling, making the first water rescue only four minutes after the fire started.

James helped the burned man into the helicopter and then the pilots maneuvered over to another man in the water. They picked up two more men in the next ten minutes, both of them badly burned. But after the first rescue, Barrows realized the victims were nearly helpless and stopped using the fish pole, instead swimming directly to the injured men so he could put the rescue sling around them. The swimmer had a hard time hanging on to the victims because their burned skin kept coming off in his hands. The helicopter crews weren't used to seeing so much trauma on the men they pulled out of the water. The men coming off the ship were badly wounded and a great many of them were severely burned over most of their bodies. Many were in shock, unable to help in their rescue, and their clothes had been blown off in the explosions.

As on all the other helicopters working to rescue men from the sea, the crew of Angel 20 was working at a feverish pace, pushing their aircraft to the limit. The helicopters flew at top speed back to the carriers once they had wounded men on board and hovered for long periods while the swimmers tried to save the injured. The prolonged hovering put a strain on the aircraft. As Angel 20 approached a fourth victim in the water, Clement saw that the engine was seriously overheating.

Clement reported back to his flight controllers on the *Oriskany* that he was redlining the engine, and they ordered him back to the carrier. He acknowledged the order, but then he couldn't bring himself to pull away from the men in the water. He kept looking at the instrument gauges and then back at the men in the water. He couldn't do it.

I can't leave them. We've got to get those men.

Clement ordered his swimmer back in the water and he hovered for another long while, watching the temperature gauge creep a little higher every minute. Clement knew he was risking his own life and that of his crew, but he knew they didn't want to leave either.

The fourth man was brought aboard, burned like the others, and then Angel 20 hustled back to the *Oriskany.* They off-loaded the injured men while undergoing a "hot fuel," in which the craft is refueled with the engine running and the rotors turning, ready to jump off the deck as soon as the fuel hose is pulled back. By 11:12 A.M., Angel 20 was in the air again and heading back to the *Forrestal.* Clement was relieved to see the engine temp drop once they stopped hovering so much.

Clement and his crew made one more rescue and then landed on the *Forrestal's* deck to unload the man, using a spot far forward of the fire. With more helicopters on site for water rescues, they headed back to the *Oriskany* to start shuttling supplies between the carriers.

All around the *Forrestal,* surface and air ships were closing in like friends and family eager to help in a crisis. On the other carriers, sailors were hauling their own firefighting gear to the flight deck for transfer, filling big cargo nets with fire hoses, fog-foam solution, and air masks, as well as medical equipment. The air swarmed with helicopters, and a half-dozen ships and smaller boats were coming into sight.

The destroyers were the hard-charging friends rushing in to help the stricken carrier as directly as possible, able to move in remarkably close to the big carrier. The other aircraft carriers nearby could provide much-needed assistance in the way of helicopters and supplies, but they could not maneuver closely enough to actually aid in the firefighting. The destroyers, though not small ships at all, were highly maneuverable and so they were able to rush right to the *Forrestal*'s side.

Captain Beling radioed from the *Forrestal* bridge that the destroyers had permission to move in as close as possible, but he also emphasized that he was *not* ordering the destroyers to do so. Realizing how dangerous such maneuvering would be to the destroyers, he made it clear that the destroyers should move in only at their own discretion.

The skippers of the destroyers did not hesitate to move in close. They steered close in to the big carrier, carefully matching the big ship's speed and diligently keeping a steady course in the uneven water so they could get close enough to direct their own firefighting hoses on the carrier's fires. The destroyers had men stationed on their decks with charged fire hoses, ready to fight the fires visible on the carrier, and when they got within range, the sailors opened the hoses and started pouring water on hot spots that were inaccessible to the carrier's crew. The destroyer crews also stood on the deck tossing life jackets and inflatable life rafts overboard to the men in the water.

In an extreme exaggeration of the supply-ship maneuvering that the carrier experienced all the time, the destroyers maneuvered to within twenty feet of the huge carrier for long stretches, hugging her heaving bulk in a delicate operation that required the very best of the destroyer's crews. At one point, the *Mackenzie*'s upper mast was only five feet away from the *Forrestal*'s elevator deck. Impressive ships in their own right, the destroyers nonetheless were dwarfed by the huge carrier, their tall masts barely reaching the level of the flight deck. With the destroyers at general quarters, the best of the best were manning the bridges, but still, the operation was a tense, extremely demanding exercise in close-quarter steering and propulsion. The young men on the bridges of the destroyers could see nothing but the looming hull of the carrier as they looked out the windows, and at times the clouds of thick black smoke from the *Forrestal* blinded everyone on the destroyers. It took all the concentration they could muster to maintain a steady course without crashing into the side of the bigger ship. Sailors on the bridge and on watch on the bow kept an eye out for men and debris in the water, and periodically they called out for a sudden course change. And as the *Forrestal* crew worked to jettison burning planes and bombs, the destroyers had to zig in and out to avoid them. The crews watched for items being pushed over the carrier's flight deck, and suddenly the destroyer would heave out to avoid the falling debris and move around the plane as it slowly sank in the carrier's wake. Then the destroyer moved back in close again, once again carefully calculating its speed and course to match the carrier's. The destroyers needed to be as close as possible, but all the while, the destroyer crews knew they could be crushed almost instantly by a sudden movement of the carrier. And at the same time, the destroyers had to counter the bigger ship's natural tendency to suck in anything nearby as its huge hulk cut through the water. Steering a straight course with the carrier wasn't enough; the destroyers had to constantly pull away from the carrier just enough to counter the pull toward the carrier. With only twenty feet between the ships, there was absolutely no room for error. Any lurch to the left or right by the carrier could be devastating to the destroyers alongside. Such maneuvering is delicate enough when both ships are in good shape, but it became even more risky when the huge carrier's control was compromised. They had no idea whether the *Forrestal's* steering and propulsion were damaged, praying only that the carrier could maintain a steady course as they cruised alongside. This tense scene would continue for three hours.

The *Forrestal* was surrounded by friendly ships, but there also were a few that weren't necessarily interested in helping the stricken ship. The big black cloud pouring off the *Forrestal's* deck had attracted the attention of everyone on the water for miles around, and that included a number of Vietnamese or Chinese boats in the area. It had not been unusual for the *Forrestal*'s crew to see local boats in the water, often the wooden junks or sampans with big sails that were common to the waters off Vietnam. The officers knew that many of them were enemy boats watching the American ships and sending reports back to the mainland by radio. Normally, the boats stayed a fair distance away, even though the open water allowed them a clear view of the carrier's operations. The crew noticed a couple of boats in the area that morning before the fire, but nobody cared much. They were tiny and far away.

But with the *Forrestal* on fire, some of those junks started moving in closer. By 11:10 A.M., about twenty minutes into the fire, crews on several ships reported seeing the local boats as close as two thousand yards away. With men in the water awaiting rescue, and with the carrier clearly in a vulnerable state, the appearance of the junks was not a welcome sight.

While he was on the flight deck helping with the firefighting, Ed Roberts looked out and noticed that suddenly boats were everywhere. He hadn't noticed any local boats at all before the fire, and now suddenly there were dozens.

"What the hell is that all about?" Roberts asked someone nearby. "They just out here to gawk at us?"

"It's more than that," the other man said. "They get thirty-five dollars if they bring in an American body or an American ID card."

"Motherfuckers . . ." Roberts muttered, shaking his head. The two men forgot about the boats until they heard a thunderous boom from the water nearby. They turned to look and saw that one of the destroyers had fired its big guns on a local boat. The boat disintegrated, bits of wood raining down like confetti. Within minutes, the swarm of boats disappeared as quickly as it had arrived.

As the other ships in the area closed in to help, the *Diamond Head* could only hang back and watch the fire from afar. Still in the area after supplying the *Forrestal* with the faulty ordnance the night before, it could not maneuver close to provide any hands-on help because no one wants an ammunition ship anywhere near a fire. The best it could do was to follow behind at a distance of several miles, the last in a long line of ships following in the carrier's wake. The *Diamond Head* sailors scanned for any men left in the water, but they found only debris. The crew eventually transferred some firefighting gear to the *Forrestal* later in the day.

Not knowing much about what was going on except a fire on a carrier, the *Diamond Head* crew were left to wonder how bad the situation was. The black smoke and the buzz of activity around the ship told them it was serious. Even at a distance, they could see explosions on the flight deck. When word first spread that the *Forrestal* was on fire, the *Diamond Head* crew dropped whatever they were doing and went to the upper deck to see. There they stood, men who had grown accustomed to the daily fear that their own ship might blow up underneath them. They were watching a navy carrier fight for its life, and the explosions on the flight deck were coming from the ordnance they had provided just hours earlier.

As they stood in the bright sun of the Tonkin Gulf, the crew of the *Diamond Head* felt they were watching their own worst nightmare befall someone else, and there was nothing they could do to help. The men were completely silent as they watched the *Forrestal* burn, imagining the horrors that must be happening there, and more than a few cried.

Chapter 11

THEY WERE SAILORS
TO THE END

This was Shelton's nightmare. The fires, the explosions, the flashes of light. The men torn down by explosions and screaming in pain. Shelton was watching his nightmare of the past two nights unfold.

Throughout the *Forrestal*, thousands of men were experiencing their own personal tragedies and crises amid the bigger chaos surrounding them. In different parts of the ship, men found themselves trapped, wounded, and uncertain as to what they should do to help themselves and their ship. Many responded with the kind of fortitude that leads others to call them heroes, none more so than the three men trapped in port aft steering. One of those men was James Blaskis, Robert Shelton's buddy who had traded work shifts so he could work in port aft steering instead of on the bridge.

When general quarters sounded, Shelton had

been relieved from his station on the bridge. He was supposed to go to his station in the secondary conn, but he quickly realized that he couldn't get there with the ship sealed for general quarters—not to mention the fires. With no assignment, he stayed in the bridge area for a while, watching in disbelief as the fires raged and the bombs exploded on the flight deck below. As he looked back toward the rear of the ship and realized how bad the explosions had been, he had a stomach-churning realization.

Oh my God. Blaskis.

Shelton realized that Blaskis could be trapped in the steering compartment. He raced down from the bridge area and headed toward that area. He didn't get far before he reached the infernos of the berthing areas below the flight deck. The smoke and flames were too bad, the fires still at their worst, and there was no hope that Shelton could get to his friend. He reluctantly made his way back to the bridge, thinking maybe he should see if they needed his assistance there.

Maybe Blaskis is okay. The steering compartment is pretty far down. Maybe he'll be fine.

The port aft steering compartment was a small room in the very rear of the ship, on the left side, several decks down from the flight deck and close to the port rudder that steers the ship. The rudder, of course, was a basic but vitally important part of the ship's steering control; turn the rudder and you turn the ship. Each side of the rear of the ship had a steering-control compartment that was about eight feet by eight feet and spanned two deck levels. A massive rudder shaft ran right down the middle of the compartment, disappearing through the floor and eventually going through the hull of the ship and connecting to the rudder itself. There were mechanisms attached to the rudder shaft that turned it in reaction to commands from the bridge.

In normal operations, the rudder was controlled electronically from the bridge without any manual assistance in the steering-control room. But as a precaution, each steering-control room always was manned by two electricians and a machinist who were ready to take over steering control if the bridge was not able to do so. They could receive orders from the bridge and then manually make the adjustments to control the rudder in the steering-control room, bypassing most or all of the electronics that normally made the rudder move.

When the fire broke out, Blaskis and the other two men in port steering control were directly underneath it. The big bomb blasts were powerful enough to penetrate layer after layer of steel down to steering control, blasting holes in the compartment and mangling the only access routes in and out of the compartment. The blasts went all the way through the steering compartment and opened the hull of the ship, the very bottom, and seawater was flooding the compartment below the men. Within minutes, Blaskis, Ronald Ogrinc, and Kenneth Fasth were trapped at their station. By the time general quarters sounded, there was no way for them to leave and no way for anyone else to get in. And within the first few minutes, before the three men even knew what was going on, they were all seriously wounded.

The explosions tore through all the spaces above

the port steering compartment, inflicting grave injuries on all three men. They were missing limbs and suffering a number of other injuries, but they still remained conscious and did their best to protect themselves from the jet fuel that rained down into their compartment from above. With little room in which to hide, they tried to avoid the pyrotechnics—flares and similar devices—that fell down from the storage compartments ripped open above them.

Walls of burning jet fuel were pouring right down over them, by them, above them, and around them. The jet fuel was coming down like a waterfall on fire.

Blaskis managed to call damage control on the phone system and report that they were badly injured and trapped. In the identical steering compartment on the starboard side of the ship, the three men working there listened as their counterparts in port steering explained their situation.

"Central Control! Central Control! This is port steering . . ." Blaskis called. The twenty-one-year-old was in charge of the other two young men.

Soon, a phone talker in Central Control responded and asked for a damage report.

"We got hit bad! The machinist's mate was hit in the hatch, and the electrician's mate's arm is severed. It's bleeding badly! We need medical help bad!"

The phone talker in Central Control assured Blaskis that a repair team was on the way, but reports from that area had already made it clear that the port steering area was a mess. The officers in Central Control studied the situation for any solution, but the repair parties in that area kept saying there was no way they could get to Blaskis's steering compartment. The fire was too intense, and the blast damage was too severe.

"Central Control!" Blaskis called again after a few minutes. "The smoke is getting really thick in here! We can't breathe! Where is the repair party, Control?"

The phone talkers in damage control kept Blaskis on the line, assuring him that help would reach the men soon, urging him to hang on. The dire situation had captured the attention of everyone in the busy room, and several enlisted men took turns on the phone to offer words of encouragement to a sailor they had never met. Just hang in there, they urged, we'll get to you. Every single person who talked to Blaskis that day was left with one impression—the image of a twenty-one-year-old sailor barely hanging on through his own injuries, but concerned only with getting help for his buddies, the men for whom he was responsible. He never mentioned his own injuries to those in damage control, even though they were quite severe.

As the situation in port aft was becoming clear to those in damage control and on the bridge, Shelton was making his way back topside. When Shelton returned to the bridge, everyone noticed when he walked in. He looked like he'd been through hell, his white uniform covered in black soot and grease, his hair matted, and his face filthy from trying to make it to Blaskis.

"Shelton! How did you get out of port steering?" someone called to him. In the confusion, no one seemed to remember that Shelton had been on the bridge when the fire started. When Rowland had notified the captain that the men were trapped and that nothing could be done, the crew on the bridge had looked at the duty roster to see who was trapped in the steering compartment. It said Shelton.

"I wasn't there," Shelton replied, hesitating. "I didn't go there this morning. Why?"

Shelton understood the answer before they explained. Just as he had feared, his buddy was trapped.

He's working my shift. That should have been me.

Shelton volunteered to help out on the bridge, and before long a call came in from damage control with an update on the situation. Someone on the bridge asked Shelton if he wanted to talk to Blaskis. His heart raced as he took the phone.

"How you doing there, buddy?" he asked. There was no immediate answer. "Just hang on, okay? We're going to get you out of there."

Everyone on the bridge watched, knowing that Shelton was talking to a good friend he might never see again. The men maintained a respectful quiet as much as they could, averting their gaze when Shelton looked up.

There was little communication from Blaskis, and Shelton could tell that his friend was in bad shape. He was near tears when he hung up the phone.

Blaskis stayed on the phone with damage control for almost half an hour, occasionally dropping the phone to administer aid to one of the other men. He applied tourniquets to both of Fasth's arms, but the bleeding continued. The enlisted men in damage control continued to encourage Blaskis, but then it became clear that there was no way to rescue the men. The repair parties had tried over and over, but the fire and continuing explosions in that area of the ship were just too great. Someone had to tell the men in port steering the truth, so one of the damage-control crew asked Merv Rowland if he wanted to speak to the men.

He did. The old man got on the line with Blaskis, and his paternal instinct kicked in hard. Rowland always looked at the young crew serving under him as surrogate sons, and they looked up to him as a gruff but reassuring authority figure. Rowland's gravelly voice was uneven as he tried to tell Blaskis that he couldn't help the men.

"Son, I understand you've got a bad situation there."

"Yes sir, it's real bad down here," Blaskis said, coughing through the smoke. "We need some help right away, sir."

"I understand, but the fire and the damage are too bad right now," Rowland said, trying hard to encourage the young man without lying to him. "We keep trying, but it doesn't look like our repair parties are going to make it to you. I'm afraid you're going to be on your own, son. You're going to have to do the best you can."

There was a pause that seemed to last forever for Rowland.

Silence.

And then a quiet, softly spoken response.

. . . "Sir, we're dying."

Rowland stopped for a minute, desperately trying to think of anything he could do. He looked at the plotting board again, even though he knew what was there. Fire was everywhere around the trapped men. Damaged compartments. No way in and no way out. He already knew the truth. These men would die where they lay right now.

"Just hang in there, son. We'll get to you if we can, but it looks real bad right now. I don't think there's anything I can do for you."

Blaskis acknowledged Rowland with a quiet "Yes sir" and then put the phone down. Rowland put down his phone and looked up at the rest of the crew in damage control; they had all been staring at him silently as he talked to the men. Rowland barked an order for the men to get back to work.

Before long, though, Rowland realized that the men's story might not be finished. Though the men were in terrible shape, Rowland started thinking they might have to play an important role in saving the ship. He started to consider giving important orders to the dying men. As the fire progressed and the magnitude of the damage became clear, Rowland began to worry that the ship could lose steering control. All the worst damage was right back on the fantail, and the blasts had penetrated far down to the hull. The damage to port steering control alone was enough reason to worry.

"If anything happens to the steering engines, the ship will be out of control," Rowland explained to one of his crew nearby. The crew member understood already, but Rowland had to say it out loud. He had to remind himself why he was going to give those poor dying men their last orders. "If something happens to the hydraulic steering to move the rudders, the only way to move the ship will be two engines on the port head and two engines starboard back, stuff like that. We can't let it get like that."

And as Captain Beling reminded Rowland, the steering was especially vital at the moment because the two destroyers were so close alongside. If the carrier lost steering control, a destroyer could be crushed. So Rowland made the decision to have the men in port aft steering transfer their steering control to the starboard aft steering compartment. That way, the undamaged steering compartment on the starboard side could control both rudders if the normal control mechanisms were lost.

In most circumstances, this would not be an extraordinary request. But Rowland already knew that the men in port steering were barely hanging on. They were dying and there was nothing he could do about it, and now he had to order them to perform an important task. And Rowland knew, though it pained him to acknowledge it, that he had to give the order soon if they were to live long enough to carry it out. Rowland picked up the phone and instructed the young men to transfer the steering control.

Blaskis was fading fast by that point, but he acknowledged Rowland's orders and set about making the necessary changes to the steering control. Despite their terrible wounds and knowing that they would die where they lay, the three sailors responded well when Rowland ordered them to transfer the steering control. The process was slow, partly because they were so severely wounded, but the men did their jobs. Rowland was on the phone with them the entire time, and then soon after completing the task, he listened as each of the three men died from their wounds. Blaskis told him when the other two died, and then Blaskis fell silent.

Rowland put the phone down and couldn't hold back the tears any longer. They streamed down his face, partly from sheer frustration. There was not a goddamn thing he could do. Not a goddamn thing.

And he cried because he admired the men's determination. The old man had seen some real bravery in his day, but those three young men struck him as the epitome of navy service.

They were sailors to the end. They never begged for mercy. They never whined. They never whimpered.

Chapter 12

I DON'T WANT TO SCREW UP

The ship had become an inescapable scene of drama and desperation, the fire now having spread throughout much of the rear portion of the ship and down many levels. The explosions had ripped open the ship's hull down past the waterline, causing compartments to flood with seawater. That flooding, combined with the seawater being pumped throughout the ship to fight the fires, was beginning to upset the ship's balance and she started leaning to the left. That list was dangerous because it could cause equipment to shift suddenly and slide off the flight deck or across the hangar bay, and, if not controlled, could eventually lead to the ship capsizing.

The list scared the hell out of some of the crew. When they felt the big ship leaning to one side, some worried for the first time that they were going to sink. They were accustomed to the carrier being nearly as stable under their feet as the ground back home, but then they felt the huge ship tipping enough to make them lean hard for balance, and causing water and fog foam, plus any remaining jet fuel, to slosh over the side. They had no way of knowing if this was a temporary problem or the beginning of the end. One thing was certain—they didn't have to be engineers to know that, if it continued, the list would cause the *Forrestal* to fall over on its side, and from there it wouldn't be long before it sank to the bottom. Up on the flight deck, Ed Roberts wondered if the crew would have to abandon ship, and he started planning his own survival. He could see the Vietnamese coastline in the distance, and his mind raced with scenarios that involved him swimming to shore and having to fend for himself. With this in mind, he raced down to his bunk and got the big knife he had just recently bought. He strapped that onto his belt, thinking it would come in handy on shore, and then he grabbed a carton of cigarettes and headed back up to the flight deck. Somehow, in the terror of the moment, it all made sense to him.

But down in engineering, Merv Rowland was on top of the problem. Once the list began, he ordered his men to shift fuel oil from one storage tank to another, compensating for the seawater entering the ship on the other side. Before long, the ship righted itself.

The efforts to fight the fire were taking hold, but all over the ship men found themselves locked in their own individual struggles. Frank Eurice had plunged into the darkness of the smoky passageway to make his way off the fantail, where he had found himself trapped in the worst of the fire, groping his way through the darkness and hoping that the seven minutes of air on his breathing apparatus would be enough to get him out. He wasn't at all sure it would be, and he was relieved to finally see sunlight breaking through the dark smoke. As he threw himself through the hatch and onto the gun mount on the side of the ship, Eurice realized that he had made small progress in saving himself. The gun-mount platform, a small deck jutting out from the side of the ship and holding one of the carrier's big five-inch guns, was only a slightly better place to be than the fantail where he had been trapped. But now he had used most of his oxygen mask in getting here, which meant he was stuck.

Eurice found a few other men already on the gun mount, the ones he had seen from below on the fantail, but they barely acknowledged him as he threw himself out of the smoking passageway and onto the wet, slippery deck. Then one of them came over to help Eurice to his feet and he realized it was a friend from his same division. The other men were manning a hose, so Eurice and his buddy took positions in the rear, helping control the heavy, lurching fire hose. When some of the smoke cleared a bit, Eurice could see that they were cooling down the ammunition-loading assembly for one of the five-inch guns. One of the gun assemblies had exploded already or been torn apart by the explosions above, but the other one was intact. They aimed the hose at the gun to keep it cool, and also because they didn't have much else to do until they could find a way off of the gun mount.

* * *

Over on the other side of the ship, the sailors on the identical gun-mount platform were in far more danger. Located directly under the place where the flight-deck fire originated, the gun-mount deck jutting out from the side of the ship was being drenched in flaming jet fuel and debris, and the situation was no better inside. When the fire first started, twenty-year-old Milt Crutchley was at his usual station in the control room that targeted the five-inch guns. The job usually didn't promise much excitement because the carrier, by its very nature, rarely got close enough to a vessel or plane for its guns to be used in defense. Crutchley's job mostly consisted of maintaining the systems and occasionally honing the crew's tracking skills by using a friendly plane as a target for the radar systems.

Crutchley heard the first alarm for a fire on the flight deck, and as with most of the crew, it only piqued his curiosity. Not expecting much, he started to make his way from the gun-control room to the gun-mount structure nearby so he could take a look at the flight deck. But as he went through the hatch that led to the exposed gun mount, Crutchley heard the general-quarters alarm and turned back inside to man his gun-control station. At nearly the same moment, the first bomb blast rattled the ship and sent flaming debris all over the gun-mount structure.

Two of Crutchley's crew stumbled into the compartment as the explosions continued just overhead, knocking them off their feet. The three of them were shouting and questioning one another about what was happening, but no one really knew.

From the force of the explosions that continued, Crutchley assumed the worst.

Damn it, somebody's snuck in and attacked us! We're going to be the first aircraft carrier to take damage from the North Vietnamese!

The explosions were deafening and kept knocking the three men around the control room, making them work hard just to stay on their feet. Before long, the men could smell smoke nearby. And soon after that, they could see it entering their control room.

The other two crew members were about Crutchley's age, but he was in charge of that control room, so they were his responsibility. He soon got on the phone and called the department that would direct the gun use during combat, but the sound-powered phones designed for combat use had gone dead. The regular phones, expected to go dead in combat, were still operational. Once he got through, the news was discouraging.

"There's a major fire on the flight deck. The bombs are going off," someone told Crutchley. "You might as well abandon your GQ station because we don't have any gun mounts for you to control anyway. They're in the fire."

Crutchley hung up the phone and told the other men they were all going to abandon the space, a relief to the men until they started looking for a way out. In just minutes, they had become trapped by the fire all around them. The smoke was still coming in the room, even though they had closed the door and turned off the ventilation system. They had to get out somehow. They wouldn't live long in this room.

They looked out onto the gun mount and decided that was a lousy place to be, already covered with flaming debris and right under some of the worst fires on the flight deck. The only other option, no matter how bad, was to try to make their way through the ship to a safer area. That meant leaving the smoke-filled room and venturing into the even smokier passageways. Crutchley thought about it for a minute and decided they had to go. But still, he was scared to death. The worst part was that he had to take responsibility for these other two men. At twenty years old, he had to save their lives.

Oh God, I hope this works. I don't want to screw up and get somebody killed.

The men had no oxygen masks, so they had to just rush into the smoky passageway and hope to find clear air before long. They headed out and found that the passage was getting darker and smokier, until finally they reached Hangar Bay 3, the huge open area directly under the flight-deck fire at the rear of the ship. Unbeknownst to Crutchley, the big bay doors had been closed already to seal off the burning hangar space. Once they got to the hangar, the air was even heavier with smoke and there was no light at all. The fire-deluge system was pouring water down from the ceiling, but the water pipes were directly under the flight-deck fires, so the water was scalding hot. Crutchley told the other two men to link arms with him so that they could stay together in the pitch-black darkness, and they struggled along slowly trying to find something by touch, anything they might recognize and that would lead them to safety. They struggled along slowly, choking and hunched over to withstand the hot water pouring on them. Before long, Crutchley decided that this trek was futile.

We're just going to stumble around here in the dark until we suffocate. We have to get out of here!

Still linked arm in arm, the three men snaked back the same way they came and eventually made it back to their starting point. They fell into the control room and slammed the door shut, but the room was filling with smoke nearly as bad as in the hangar bay. The three men were exhausted from their escape attempt, covered in soot and soaked from the water deluge in the hangar bay, choking and coughing up black phlegm. They lay there on the floor trying to breathe and wondering what the hell they were going to do next. Crutchley was starting to think they might die right there on the floor.

He tried calling combat control again, and surprisingly the phone still worked. Breathing heavily, he told them that their escape attempt had not worked and they were trapped. Combat control said they would send help if they could, but made it clear that Crutchley should not wait for rescue.

The three men lay there, feeling the heat seep in with the smoke, trying to stay as low as possible to find the little bit of air still in the room. They could hear the explosions and the fire all around them. Their sense of panic had been left behind in the hangar bay, but the fear stayed with them. Now they were just completely fatigued and concentrating on every breath. They lay there on the floor for an hour, terrified, holding wet rags across their faces and praying that the compartment would have just a little bit more air for them to breathe.

Crutchley's responsibility to save the men in his charge kept him motivated to find a solution. He thought about the hatch that led to the gun-mount structure outside, but he was reluctant to open the armored, watertight door and let in everything that was coming off of the flight deck. Desperate for a way out, he called combat control once more to ask what they knew of the gun mount outside. The gun mount's on fire, they told Crutchley, but we don't know for sure how close it is to that hatch. You can take your chances if you want to.

Crutchley thought about the risk of opening that hatch and stepping right into the fire. He discussed the option with the other two men and they agreed they had to try. Things weren't getting any better in that damn control room.

"We're either going to die in here or we're going out on that sponson," Crutchley said to the other men. "It can't be any worse out there. And even if it is, maybe it'll be quick."

The three men dragged themselves over toward the hatch leading to the gun-mount structure, and with a mixture of dread and hope, Crutchley slowly opened it. He peered out as he opened the hatch just a couple of inches, and the sunlight flooded into the dark compartment. Without opening the hatch too much, he tried to see what awaited them on the other side.

Fresh air!

Crutchley opened the hatch wider and saw that the gun mount was indeed a mess, but the fire was on the other end, away from the hatch. All three men scrambled over the lip of the hatch and fell onto the gun-mount platform, breathing heavily and coughing as they took in the clean sea air. The gun mount was far from a safe place to be, but it was a damned sight better than dying in that smoke-filled control room.

After getting their breath again, the men realized they still could not rest. The gun mount was right under the flight-deck fires, and periodically they had to dodge flaming fuel, debris, and molten metal. There was no other way off the gun-mount platform except the hatch they had just come through, so their only other option was jumping overboard. They started talking about that, but no one liked the idea much. The only good point was that they'd found a bunch of life jackets lying around. The gun-mount platform had a life-jacket-storage bin and one of the explosions had blown it open. Jackets were floating around in the water-and-foam swill that covered the platform, so they started looking for one that hadn't been damaged.

They found three good jackets and put them over their heads, strapping the waist belts around. Then they went to the railing farthest from the fire and debated whether to jump. Nobody wanted to, but it didn't take long for them to decide they had to go overboard, because the gun-mount structure was getting worse every minute. They were scared to death of going in the water, knowing how risky that would be, but Crutchley decided they had to.

The three men climbed over the railing and held on to the ship as they looked down at the sixty feet they would fall before hitting the water. From the railing, there was nothing between them and the water far below. They felt the wind on their faces and turned away as a gust of smoke choked them.

They kept looking down at the sea and back at the fire, holding on tight to the railing. A destroyer was approaching from the rear, giving them some hope that they would be rescued after they hit the water. But they also worried that the destroyer would run over them.

All they had to do was let go. But they hesitated. And in that second, one of the men spoke.

"Milt, I'm not jumping."

"Whaddya mean you're not jumping? We have to!" he replied.

"I can't swim. This vest isn't going to be enough. I can't swim."

Crutchley realized that the man had come to the *Forrestal* through the navy reserve, which didn't require its recruits to prove they could swim as the regular navy did. Crutchley didn't feel like he could force the man to go overboard if he couldn't swim, and they certainly weren't going to leave him behind. Besides, Crutchley and the third man weren't eager to jump overboard either.

So the three men climbed back over the railing and tried to think of another plan. They were arguing about whether there really could be any other plan, and still considering the idea of jumping, when the flaming tail section of an airplane came tumbling down from the flight deck and crashed onto the gun mount right near them.

The men crouched down to avoid the debris as much as possible, and then Crutchley spoke up. They could work their way underneath the railing of the gun-mount platform and then leap down to a little platform that jutted out underneath. It wouldn't be easy, and it was quite a leap to the platform below. There still wouldn't be anywhere to go once they got down there. But at least they'd be farther away from the fire, he told them.

The other men agreed, and they climbed over the railing again, this time close to the ship. They gingerly worked their way down the outside of the gun-mount platform, and when they could climb no lower, they let go and fell about fifteen feet to the other platform. They all made it safely and looked around for the next step. As they looked out, they saw that they were close to the big crane that was used to move airplanes and other large cargo on and off the ship. Its long arm was tucked alongside the ship's body when not in use. Surveying the scene, they could not believe what they saw on the crane.

A man was hanging from the crane's hook. He was in a safety harness but hanging limp as a rag doll. Crutchley supposed the man must have been doing some sort of maintenance work when the fire started, and then he was left hanging there, subject to every one of the explosions going off only thirty yards away. He must have had assistants with him when he was doing the work, but they had left him there, hanging out directly over the water and unable to bring himself back in. He seemed to be barely conscious, probably in shock, and unable to hold his head up.

Crutchley and his crew called to the man to wake him up, to see if he could be helped. After a moment, the man roused and looked over to them but he could not do much more than that. They had to shout encouragement to him for several minutes before he awoke enough to really respond, and then Crutchley took off his own life vest and tossed it to the man. Surprisingly, the man was able to catch it and put it on. Then he seemed to wake up more and, with the encouragement of the guys on the platform, was able to hoist himself up on the crane arm. He got himself on the arm of the crane and then just rested, clutching the steel supports until he could move further.

After helping that man, Crutchley and his crew returned to their own plight. They couldn't stay on the platform because fuel, molten metal, and other material were still raining down on them. The more they thought about it, the more they realized the airplane crane was their best bet. The crane was roughly the shape of a triangle, with a vertical column attached to the side of the ship and a lifting arm that jutted out over the water. From the tip of the crane arm, a third support with cables ran back to the vertical column against the ship. That meant the upper support led right up to the flight-deck level, but it was an awkward path angled up at about forty-five degrees. Luckily, the crane was moved in close to the ship, rather than extended all the way over the water.

If they could get up on that crane support, Crutchley thought they would at least have more options for how to escape. But the crane was not close enough to jump to, and there was no easy way to get to it. Once they did get to it, it would still be a dicey operation. The crane had no walkway that went up the length of the support arm, so they would have to just inch their way along its round pipes.

It all seemed pretty iffy, but they realized that

they had to get out on the crane to help the man who was trapped. He didn't look like he was going to hold on much longer.

But how to get there?

There was one way, but no one was eager to suggest it. In all the mess that had been blown off the flight deck, one of the arresting cables, the big cables that snag the plane's tail hook on landing, had been severed and one end was blown their way. The big heavy cable was hanging down off the flight deck and draped near their platform, out over the crane arm. It was strong enough to hold the men if it didn't shift from their weight. They discussed it and decided once again that they had no better choice. They had to use the cable to get out on the crane.

Reluctantly, Crutchley and the other two men climbed up on the platform railing and grabbed the cable. One by one, they pulled themselves hand over hand along the cable until they could reach the platform. If their strength gave out or the cable dislodged, they would go right into the water, maybe after bouncing off some structure on the ship. Crutchley didn't even have a life vest anymore, having given it to the injured man on the crane.

After a tense while, all four men were hugging the crane arm and looking down at the sea sixty feet below. They stayed there for a while, just trying to hang on and not to move too much for fear of falling off. They were about to start inching their way up when they saw the destroyer *Rupertus* moving in close to the ship, almost right underneath them. As the ship drew closer, they could see that the crewmen were on the deck with fire hoses aimed at the *Forrestal*. When they noticed Crutchley and his crew up above, they shouted at them to offer help.

"Are you going to jump?" they yelled from the destroyer.

The men looked at one another and considered the idea again, not sure if they would safely make it all the way up the crane arm. But then they realized that the prospect of going overboard was worse now than it was before. In addition to the long fall, the possibility of drowning, and being pulled into the carrier's big propellers, now they might also be sucked under by the destroyer or even crushed between the two ships.

"Hell no! We're not jumping!"

After waiting a while longer on the crane, just wondering what to do next, Crutchley decided they had to move. The longer they stayed there, the higher the risk that something would come flying off the deck and knock them off. So he and his crew decided that they had to make their way up the crane arm, inching along the little service walkway and then onto the round arm that led the rest of the way up to the flight-deck level. Crutchley's crew climbed up the arm first, balancing on the piping and holding on to the control cables that ran down the arm. The climb was tricky, up a steep incline on a round pipe covered in slippery foam solution. Near the bottom, the control cables were too high for the men to grab for support, and then as they got closer to the top, the cable converged on the upper end of the piping and was too low to hang on to. After the first two made it most of the way up, Crutchley reached the man who had been hanging there, and helped him up. The guy was remaining conscious, but that was about all. Crutchley wasn't at all sure the guy was going to be able to get up the crane arm and all the way to the flight deck, so he followed along close behind, ready to grab him if he slipped.

As they neared the top, Crutchley could see for the first time just what a mess the flight deck had become. Fires were still out of control, but Crutchley had no doubt that the flight deck still was their only escape. Just then, a fuel tank exploded on one of the planes, showering flaming fuel in Crutchley's direction. The burning fuel and other debris flew past Crutchley, enough of it landing on him and the dazed man to make them wince with pain, the thunder of the explosion already making them duck down as much as they could without losing their grip on the crane.

Crutchley saw that his companions had reached the flight deck already, but the last steps seemed to take forever for him and the injured man. After pausing to shake off the hot debris that landed on them, burning through their uniforms, they inched their way along, slowly getting all the way up to the flight-deck level, where Crutchley's two crew members were waiting, urging them on. They grabbed the injured man and pulled him up on the flight deck as he got close, and then they helped Crutchley up. The injured man collapsed as soon as he was safe, and crew members who had been fighting the fires rushed over to help the obviously exhausted group.

The men had come up on the flight deck near the spot where Jim Bangert's plane had fired the rocket, now in the worst of the fire zone after the fire had spread. Even nearly two hours after the fire started, this still was not a good place to be. But it was a hell of a lot better than where they had been. Crutchley felt a huge sense of relief.

Thank God. I didn't get anybody killed.

On the other side of the ship, Eurice and his friend started heaving overboard anything else on the sponson that could be moved. Crates used to store ammunition, as well as various other debris that had been blown off the flight deck, were burning all around them, so they cleared out the area as much as they could. Periodically, Eurice looked over toward the fantail where he had been trapped, and knew he had made the right decision. That area was now covered in flaming jet fuel and other material.

After about half an hour out on the gun-mount structure, Eurice noticed that the smoke billowing from the hatch was diminishing and turning from black to white, a sure sign that the fire was being extinguished. The smoke eventually diminished to nearly nothing, and the men on the gun-mount structure started thinking it might be safe to venture inside. As they were standing there debating whether to trek through the passageway without a breathing apparatus, a miraculous sight appeared. Out of the sooty, still-steaming hatch came a sailor carrying a tray of orange sodas. He had raided a nearby refrigerator and was passing out drinks to everyone fighting the fire.

It was a small delight that took on massive importance for the men. For the first time in the ordeal, Eurice and the other men on the gun-mount platform got the idea that maybe everything would turn out okay. They still didn't know much about what was going on outside their line of sight, but nobody takes the time to pass out orange sodas when a ship is sinking.

After guzzling several orange sodas, the best he'd ever tasted, Eurice decided to leave the gun-mount platform in search of more fire hose. If they could get their hands on more fire hose to attach to the one they were using already, they might be able to do more firefighting than just cooling down the gun mount. A catwalk had been blown down onto the gun mount in such a way that it provided access to the flight deck, so the men searched for enough hose to go up and help out with the fires still raging topside.

Eurice made his way to Hangar Bay 3, by now a water-soaked mess, and started looking for fire hoses to scavenge. As he searched, he noticed that some of the men were gesturing in one direction, and turned around to see Captain Beling slogging through the hangar with his two marine orderlies close behind. True to his nature, Beling was taking a walk through the ship to see the damage for himself. He had already been to pri-fly and seen the shattered windows, the debris left when the staff there made a hasty retreat. Beling had access to more information than anyone else on the ship, but that wasn't good enough. If his boys were fighting and dying nearby, he had to see it.

Eurice and many other sailors were shocked to see the captain off the bridge in the middle of such a crisis, astonished that he would put himself in harm's way as the fires continued to burn and small explosions continued on the flight deck. His marine escorts were not at all happy to see the captain on the front line of the fire, and they were doing their best to dissuade him from entering some of the more dangerous areas.

Beling strolled through the hangar bay and assessed the damage from that vantage point, stopping to talk to several sailors about what they had seen. From there, he made his way through much of the ship not actively involved in the fires, reaching the conclusion that things weren't nearly as bad as he expected from what he had seen on the flight deck. As he went through one of the big dining halls for the enlisted men, he could see that a meal had been under way when the general-quarters alarm sounded, with trays of food left on tables everywhere. Beling grabbed a couple of carrots as he walked by, and munched on them while he continued his tour.

One thing in particular reassured him that the ship was surviving the damage. Throughout the parts of the ship not actually burning or damaged by explosions, the air-conditioning was working just fine. The *Forrestal* was one of the first warships to have air-conditioning throughout most of the ship, and the cool air was always seen as a luxurious symbol of the ship's bragging rights. Now, Beling found the system's durability comforting in the midst of this disaster.

After Beling's appearance, Eurice went back to searching for fire hose and eventually found enough to lug back to the gun mount. A few other men had brought some back also, so they coupled all the sections together and then headed to the flight deck by way of the catwalk hanging down on the gun mount. When they reached the flight deck, they were stunned. They knew that the situation was bad, but they were not prepared to see the flight deck covered in burning plane wreckage, fires still burning, injured men and bodies still lying where they had fallen. The entire flight deck was a steaming, hazy mess. The smell of burned plastic and explosives hung in the air, along with the stink of the jet fuel and fog foam.

Eurice and the other men surveyed the situation for a moment, brought to a halt by the shock of it all, and then started pulling their fire hose over to the rear portion of the flight deck where they could see that most of the work was being done. When they got closer, they could see that men were aiming fire hoses down into horrendous craters blown in the deck, and nearby, other teams were using an acetylene torch to cut holes in the deck. Compartments below the flight deck were still burning furiously, and the only way to get water in them was to make new holes in the flight deck and fight the fires from above. Black smoke burst out as soon as the torch broke through the armored deck, and a team poured water down the hole. Luckily, Rowland and Beling had authorized the purchase of a special acetylene torch just before departing for Vietnam. The *Forrestal* didn't normally carry one capable of cutting through armored steel, and without it, the crew would have found it nearly impossible to get through the armor-plated flight deck.

As Eurice and his hose team started to pour water down a hole made from a bomb blast, one that didn't have a hose team on it yet, they could see that the other men were yelling and gesturing to them.

"Pick up the hose! You gotta pick up your hose! The deck's too hot!"

That's when they first noticed that the other hose teams were hoisting the heavy hoses onto their shoulders and holding them there as they fought the fires. And that's also when Eurice first noticed that he could feel the hot deck through his shoes, way too much actually. The fires in the compartments below were so hot that the flight deck was becoming unbearably hot to the touch, and several fire hoses had actually burned through as they lay on the deck.

Eurice and his hose team assumed the same position with the hose on their shoulders and fired water down into the hole, standing there for a while before the smoke cleared enough to reveal what they were soaking. As Eurice peered over the edge and into the hole, he could see an unexploded five-hundred-pound bomb about ten feet below.

Chapter 13

I'M READY TO GO

The men battled the fires and their own fears for
the entire morning and much of the afternoon. The
flight deck had become a terrible mess, a remark-
able contrast to its usually pristine order. After the
fire spread across most of the flight deck to the rear
of the island structure, it consumed everything that
could not be tossed overboard. The sailors made
slow but steady progress in extinguishing the blaze.
They were encouraged by the white smoke that signaled a fire under control, and then alarmed when
the smoke turned black again and roiled into the
sky with a new ferocity.

Every few minutes, the 1MC address system
crackled to life, sometimes with a whistle tone to
alert the crew and then orders from Merv Rowland
or someone else directing the firefighting effort.

"You are reminded that the emergency is not
over," Rowland's gravelly voice boomed through-

out the ship. "There are still fires. Re-man your GQ stations and stand fast until you are directed to do something! Do not go wandering about the ship! Re-man your GQ stations and stand fast until directed to secure."

The fire played a cat-and-mouse game with the sailors, roaring up in one spot and then another, then hiding in the many compartments belowdecks. Even when the biggest of the infernos died down, sometimes only because they had consumed nearly everything that would burn, there was still smoldering debris everywhere, pockets of intense heat trapped between the many layers of the ship's steel structure. The fire would not die easily or quickly, and it was taking a toll even on those who had survived the explosions, the searing flames, the deadly gases, and the sea below.

Exhaustion was hitting the men hard. In the initial hours, men had been fueled by adrenaline and the instinct to survive. But by early afternoon, they were losing steam. They had been working feverishly for hours, some with injuries they'd ignored or hadn't even noticed until there was a pause in the action. The combined heat of the fires and the Tonkin Gulf afternoon was wearing them down. All over the ship, men were collapsing in heaps, soaked with sweat, seawater, fog-foam solution, fuel oil, and God knows what else. They were a mess from head to toe, black from the smoke or seared a bright red, their clothes ripped or blown off. Often, they had no idea if the rest of the ship was being saved or not. They knew only that their area, the one problem they were fighting at the moment, wouldn't kill them right away and so they could take a minute to rest. For most of the men, the best they could hope for was a moment to sit down and catch their breath while someone else took a turn on the hose. Maybe they would even find a soft drink to choke down.

A few of the key officers found another way to keep going. As the day wore on and Rowland began to feel fatigued, he could see that more coffee wouldn't be enough to keep him going. He could not leave his post, and he probably wouldn't be able to do so for more than a day. Rowland had to be alert and capable if he were going to help keep the ship alive, so he sent word to the sick bay that he needed some Benzedrine. Known to the rest of the world in 1967 as "uppers" or "speed," Benzedrine was pure energy in a pill. It could keep a man alert and active for days, but eventually at a cost.

When Dr. G. Gary Kirchner got Rowland's request, he didn't even think about it before agreeing. Military doctors often had Benzedrine on hand and it was not extraordinary to administer it in such an emergency situation. Kirchner didn't hand the stuff out like candy, but for someone like Rowland, he knew it was necessary and that Rowland could be trusted with it. Rowland wasn't the only officer who used speed to stay alert for a long period during the fire and its aftermath.

Kirchner dispatched a runner to damage control with enough Benzedrine to keep Rowland alert for a while.

Kirchner's post in the sick bay was the center of the *Forrestal*'s pain. The fire had not reached that portion of the ship, but all of the wounded were being funneled to the small medical department and immediately the magnitude of the disaster had overwhelmed the medical staff. Kirchner was one of four doctors on board, in addition to a couple of "flight surgeons" who worked specifically with the aviators and were attached to their squadrons. There also were sixty-five corpsmen who provided first aid throughout the ship and helped get the wounded to sick bay.

Kirchner had been working on a patient that morning. The young man had been on one of the nearby destroyers when he crushed his hand, so he had been transferred by helicopter to the *Forrestal* for medical care. The injury was serious, more than the usual stomachache and lacerations that the doctor saw on a typical morning. Kirchner had just finished injecting the man's hand with Xylocaine, an anesthetic, in preparation for reducing and casting the hand. That's when they heard the first fire-alarm calls; Kirchner paused, but he was not concerned until he heard the call for general quarters, almost instantly followed by the first explosion. They were two decks below the flight deck and about in the middle lengthwise, but even so, the explosion rattled the tray of instruments at his side and the cabinets full of medicine and gear.

"Damn, that's gotta be a plane striking the deck," Kirchner said to his patient. Both of them were staring up at the sick bay's ceiling as if it would somehow explain the tremendous shaking. Kirchner was already starting to think ahead, realizing that if a plane had crashed he should prepare to receive serious trauma patients.

As he paused and thought about what to do, more explosions caused the lights to flicker and knocked items off the walls all around Kirchner and the patient, both of them reaching out to steady themselves on a nearby counter. The kid with the broken hand looked at Kirchner expectantly, and the doctor realized he couldn't continue treating him.

"Get the hell out of here!" Kirchner yelled at the young man. "Come back when this thing settles down and we're no longer at general quarters! Your hand won't hurt for a while because of the medicine. Just don't do anything with it."

The kid took off running with his injured hand cradled against his chest, and Kirchner headed out of the operating room toward the sick bay's central receiving area. They called it the emergency room, but it was just a small compartment with two beds and some equipment for treating trauma. He had been there for less than a minute, preparing to receive patients, when he felt another huge explosion. Before the noise died down, Kirchner caught sight of his first patient, the first of many.

Several men were dragging a limp body down the corridor, screaming for help. As they carried him through the door, Kirchner's heart sank at the sight but he quickly shifted into the high gear of a trauma surgeon. The young sailor had taken a hit directly in the face and wasn't breathing. His face and neck were a bloody mess, ripped apart by an explosion. Kirchner started an emergency tracheotomy, cutting a hole through the man's neck directly into his windpipe so he could breathe again. Hunched over the patient and working quickly, he inserted a breathing tube through the hole. Only then did he pause to talk to the men who had brought in the patient.

"What the hell is going on out there? What crashed?"

The men started talking over one another, screaming because everyone's ears were ringing from the explosions. All Kirchner could understand was that a fire had broken out on the flight deck and bombs were exploding. That's all he would know for a long time, because within minutes, he was faced with so many patients that he barely had time to think of anything at all.

Patients were pouring into the sick bay, almost all of them gravely wounded, and more help was coming to sick bay too. Explosions still were going off overhead and he was surrounded by bloody, dying men. The sick bay was becoming crowded with the injured, their buddies, and the medical corpsmen who would help Kirchner. Everyone was screaming "Doc!" and "Medic!" and for the moment, that meant Kirchner. The scene in the sick bay was completely chaotic. Dozens of men were dragged in, bleeding profusely, their clothes still smoldering from their flames, charred flesh hanging off their bodies, mangled and fleshy stumps waving where limbs had been blown off. Men arrived with parts of airplanes and bomb fragments still jammed in their flesh, and their buddies sometimes followed behind them, carrying the severed limbs they found on the flight deck. Kirchner regretted that most of the men, even those horribly mutilated in the explosions, were still conscious. With young, healthy men like those on the *Forrestal,* even severe trauma doesn't always knock a man unconscious. What a shame, Kirchner thought. It would have been a blessing for most of them.

The smell was overpowering, and something that the men present would not forget for the rest of their lives: the unique stomach-churning stench of burned flesh mixed with the fumes from jet fuel that soaked many of the men, plus the sickly sweet smells of the fog-foam solution and blood—which was everywhere.

And the sounds that filled the sick bay—these were the sounds of young men in terrible pain, young men terrified and afraid to die in that place, alone in a frenzy. Many lay silently despite horrible burns: third-degree burns can destroy the nerve endings that transmit pain. But others, the ones torn apart by the explosions or the ones who felt their bodies continue to burn, screamed in ways that bore into Kirchner's soul. They moaned and begged for help. And when the pain and the fear became too much, when they overcame the men's minds and there was nothing else in their world, they cried, tears running down their bloodied and burned cheeks. In desperate moments, twenty-year-old men screamed out for their mothers when the pain was too much, when they looked down and saw what had happened to their bodies and knew they would die.

Gary Shaver was still out of his mind with pain when he arrived in the sick bay on a wire stretcher. His left arm still was wrapped around his neck; his rescuers had been too scared to touch it, fearing the whole thing might come off his shoulder. Shaver screamed and cried uncontrollably, even though he had been given morphine before being taken to the sick bay. The morphine had made no difference whatsoever to his pain. The men who brought Shaver down put him in one of the bottom bunks and ran back out.

Kirchner was clearly in a triage situation. In mass casualty incidents, the doctors and others on the scene have to prioritize patients according to their need, as well as the likelihood that medical care will actually save the patient. When the number of patients overwhelms the medical care available, it is necessary to avoid spending time and supplies on patients who are likely to die anyway. Those patients must be triaged as such and left to die while the doctors work on patients who might be saved.

Triage is a familiar concept in military medicine, so Kirchner immediately started this system in the sick bay, aided by the corpsmen and the other ship physicians who were arriving. One of the first tasks was to clear the area as much as possible. The small compartment was clogged with people who had brought patients in and were hanging around to comfort them, but Kirchner started ordering out everyone who wasn't seriously injured. The rest were triaged with tags marking them as needing immediate attention, dying and not to be treated unless there was time, or "walking wounded" without life-threatening injuries. Kirchner tried to ensure that the men tagged as too far gone to treat received adequate pain relief. He could not save their lives or even take the time to try, but he could not entirely turn his back on them either. He instructed the corpsmen to start intravenous lines in those men and provide ample doses of morphine.

The corpsmen and doctors also were administering morphine to those being treated, and even to the occasional sailor who got hysterical with emotional trauma, which meant that many of the men were doped up on the powerful narcotic.

Robert Zwerlein was dragged to the sick-bay area, and Kirchner went to work on him immediately. The boy was burned severely over most of his body after being caught up in the fuel spill outside McCain's plane. Kirchner made sure Zwerlein got an intravenous line and a good dose of morphine, but the young man from the ice-cream shop in Port Washington, New York, was too far gone for him to do much else. Zwerlein lay quietly on a stretcher in the sick bay, covered with a blanket to keep him from getting too cold and going into shock. The morphine relieved his pain, but he was in very bad shape.

Kirchner soon went to Shaver's side, and even in his pain, Shaver recognized the doctor as the same one who had set his broken hand weeks earlier. Kirchner told Shaver that he was bleeding badly inside and that the pressure had to be relieved. The injured man looked down and watched as Kirchner cut a hole in his side and inserted a tube, leaving the end hanging off the side of the bed. Bright red blood poured out of the tube and onto the floor of the sick bay.

Paul Friedman also made his way there and was shocked by what he saw. When he was carried in and deposited on a couch, he couldn't believe the type of injuries he saw all around him. And instantly he felt he shouldn't be there with his relatively minor foot wound. As he looked around, he realized that he knew the man sitting next to him. They had been to a navy school together.

"Howard, hey buddy. You okay? What the hell is going on?"

Friedman poked the man on the arm to get his attention, but Howard never responded, just staring forward with a dazed look in his eyes. Then Friedman looked down and saw that the man had a compound fracture of the leg, with the bone jutting out of his pants leg at a severe angle. Friedman looked down at his own wound and felt lucky.

A corpsman came over to Friedman and offered him some morphine.

"No, I don't need it. I think all I need is a battle dressing and I can get out of here," Friedman said. "But this guy here can probably use it. Give him the morphine."

The corpsman took a look at Howard, still dazed and unresponsive, and never replied to Friedman. He turned to another patient. Friedman sat on the couch dumbstruck by what was going on around him, watching as victim after victim was carried into the sick bay. On the floor in front of him, he saw one man so horribly burned that Friedman could not tell if he was black or white. The man seemed to be conscious, so Friedman was wondering why he did not seem to be in pain. The man was just lying there quietly, his flesh blackened and the features wiped off his face, his eyes open and looking around. Another man was brought in on a stretcher and looked startlingly clean and uninjured, but he was unconscious. The man lay in the wire stretcher in his neat khaki uniform, with no sign of blood or trauma. Soon, Kirchner came over and declared the man dead.

John McCain also visited the sick bay, when he realized he was still bleeding from his chest wounds after helping the crew jettison bombs from the hangar bay. When he walked in, McCain heard a voice calling him over, and though he could not make out the young man's face because of his burns, he suspected the man was part of his air wing's support crew because he called him "Mr. McCain." The charred man asked McCain about a chief petty officer in their squadron and McCain assured him that the man was fine, he had seen him just recently.

"Thank God he's okay," the man said. And then as McCain stood there and watched, the man died.

Overcome with emotion, McCain quickly left the sick bay without being treated.

Kirchner and his staff were so overwhelmed by the severity of the injuries and the number of injured, more than three hundred before the day was out, that he quickly realized they could do little to help the men in the *Forrestal*'s own sick bay. Though the bridge was sending information to him, it was not at all clear how long the emergency would last and how much damage the ship would take. Only minutes after the patients started flooding his sick bay, Kirchner knew there were too many.

I can't handle the patients I have in here right now, and who knows when they'll stop coming? I've got to get them out of here.

Aside from the need to get them out of harm's

way and in the hands of more doctors, space was at a premium. There were forty-eight beds available for patients, but half of those were top bunks. And with the volume of patients coming in, Kirchner and the other doctors only had time to stabilize patients by stopping the flow of blood and helping them breathe. They didn't even have time to suture wounds. Sophisticated first aid was all he could provide. The wounded needed to be taken off the *Forrestal* as fast as possible. Luckily, the other carriers in the area had their own sick bays and physicians, ready to help. Kirchner sent word to the bridge that he wanted to transfer all the severely injured patients to the carriers *Oriskany* and *Bon Homme Richard,* both positioned nearby and already helping out with their helicopters and other equipment. The bridge informed Kirchner that the other carriers were ready to take the wounded, and they passed on another bit of good news. The U.S. hospital ship *Repose* was leaving Da Nang, where it had been stationed to treat soldiers from the jungle war, and would rendezvous with the *Forrestal* the next day.

Soon after the decision to send the *Forrestal*'s wounded to the other carriers, a familiar face appeared to Kirchner in the sick bay. It was a surgeon from the aircraft carrier *Bon Homme Richard* who had trained with Kirchner in the civilian world. He had caught a helicopter ride over to offer his help.

"Gary, what can I do?" the doctor asked as soon as he walked in the sick bay.

Kirchner was glad to have help, but not here.

"Get the hell out of here!" he yelled at his friend. "Go back to your ship! I'll send as many of these people back as I possibly can. You see what this ship is like now. We're on fire and we're at general quarters and this whole situation is just unstable!"

The surgeon followed Kirchner's orders and assisted in transferring some of the most seriously wounded patients back to his ship. By now stressed and unable to waste time with niceties, Kirchner grabbed a corpsman walking by and pulled him close. He put his face close to the corpsman's and talked quietly but firmly.

"What are you doing with a life jacket on?" he asked the scared young man.

"Uh, it looks real bad out there, sir. We're in real bad trouble."

"Take it off. Take it off right now, dammit!" Kirchner ordered. "These men are wounded already and I can't let them see you walking around with a life jacket like the ship's about to sink!"

The fires burned well into the afternoon, but after the crew gained a foothold on the flight deck, Captain Beling decided that the forward portion was safe enough to land helicopters. The rescue helicopters used the free space immediately to return sailors plucked out of the water, and then Beling forwarded Kirchner's request to send all the seriously injured patients to the other two aircraft carriers. They were ready on the other ships. They knew, just from looking at the smoking ship in the distance, that the *Forrestal* could not handle all her injured.

Beling sent word to Kirchner that the transfers could proceed, and from that point, the doctor's main objective was to keep the patients moving.

Stabilize them, and then get them off the ship as fast as possible. Before long, the helicopters were landing on the forward portion of the flight deck every few minutes while the fires still burned on the rear, bringing with them as much cargo as they could carry. The helos were stuffed with canisters of firefighting foam, fire hoses, oxygen-breathing apparatus, and first-aid supplies, sometimes with even more carried below the craft in a big cargo net. When the helicopters landed, crew from the *Forrestal* rushed to unload all the supplies and, with the helicopter still idling at high speed, they loaded stretchers with wounded men and a few who could walk. The helicopters sprang off the deck again and made their way to one of the other carriers.

Gary Shaver, Robert Zwerlein, and Paul Friedman were transferred before too long. Zwerlein was still lying quietly in the wire stretcher basket, calmed by the morphine and mercifully relieved of most pain by the extent of his burns. Two men picked up Zwerlein's stretcher and carried him to the hangar bay, where one of the big airplane elevators was being used to carry the injured to the flight deck forward of the island structure. Once they were moved off the elevator, Zwerlein waited with several other badly injured men until the next helicopter arrived and was unloaded. As it came in, the men carrying Zwerlein leaned over him and used their bodies to protect him from the debris blowing in the downdraft of the rotors. They didn't know Zwerlein, and they probably would not have recognized him if they did, and they weren't even medical corpsmen. They were volunteers who had offered to help with transferring the injured. All they knew was that this badly burned man was a fellow crew member, and they were going to protect him until they put him on that helo.

Shaver regained consciousness while he was lying on the flight deck waiting to be loaded onto a helicopter. He opened his eyes and saw the fires still raging on the other end, and then he looked down at his body. All he saw was a sheet covering him, almost completely red from his blood. The sight terrified him. His vision blurred and he felt his eyes closing. He knew he was dying. As he lost consciousness again, he was sure it was the last time.

They landed on the *Oriskany* in a buzz of activity that mirrored what they had just left behind, except without all the imminent danger.

The carrier had ceased its planned operations for the day and was concentrating solely on helping the *Forrestal*. Indeed, all operations on Yankee Station had come to a halt, and even some "in-country" helicopter units were mobilizing to fly out to the stricken carrier if needed. The *Oriskany*'s crew felt a special urge to help, because it had been only nine months since their own onboard fire that killed forty-four men. They knew from firsthand experience the terror of being trapped on a burning ship.

Lenny Julius, the twenty-five-year-old medical administration officer on the *Oriskany*, had been conducting a fairly mundane task when the *Forrestal* fire started. He was touring the ship with a corpsman trained as the sanitation officer, inspecting all the coffee stations because some of the men had gotten sick from curdled milk. They were in the hangar bay when they saw men running over to one of the open elevator doors, dozens of men gathering to look at something. Curiosity surpassing their need to look for spoiled milk, Julius and the corpsman trotted over to see what was causing all the commotion. As soon as they stepped up to the doorway, they could see the *Forrestal* a few miles away, spewing an ugly plume of rich black smoke. They stood with their jaws dropped open as explosions erupted on the *Forrestal*'s deck, sending bright flaming debris in every direction, and then after a second or two, a loud boom arrived at the *Oriskany*.

"Oh my God! The Chinese!" Julius shouted. "The Chinese are hitting the *Forrestal*! We'd better get back to sick bay!"

Julius and the corpsman took off at full speed for the sick bay, both of them anticipating that the *Forrestal* would very shortly send injured their way. As the medical administration officer, Julius was not a doctor but was charged with keeping the clinic operational while the doctors and corpsmen did their work on patients. In addition, he was trained the same as the medical corpsmen to provide advanced first aid. It was not uncommon for him to provide hands-on care in the sick bay in addition to keeping track of paperwork and supplies.

The *Oriskany*'s four doctors soon showed up, alerted by the 1MC announcement that the *Forrestal* was in dire trouble. Dozens of corpsmen were also arriving to wait for assignments, as were the ship's dentists. Everyone was working fast to get the sick bay ready for the wounded, breaking out supplies to have them within reach and quickly organizing a system of on-site triage so that patients could be channeled in the right direction once they arrived. One surgeon went to the operating room and waited for his first patient, eventually staying there for most of the day without a break.

Julius was concerned that his sick bay run smoothly in this time of utmost need, so he was organizing some of the corpsmen to support the others providing actual treatment to patients. He grabbed one corpsman in the sick bay and gave him an assignment.

"Al, look here. I don't want anybody to suffer because we don't have enough of our supplies," he said. "So your job is not to take care of patients. Your job is to go back and forth and make sure we have everything we need. The minute the doctor sticks his hand out for something, I want it to be right there."

Julius gave the young man a list of items to retrieve from storage and sent him running off.

It didn't seem like much time passed before the wounded arrived. And once they started coming, there was a flood. The *Oriskany*'s medical crew pounced on the first to arrive as soon as they were brought into the sick-bay area, and then the numbers started overwhelming them. With more and more badly injured men arriving every minute, the doctors and corpsmen could not immediately tend to each one as they arrived. Dozens of men were lying in stretchers all over the sick-bay area, quickly turning it into a copy of the frenetic, grisly scene in the *Forrestal*'s own sick bay. All over, men lay with a red "M" scrawled on their foreheads in grease pencil, indicating that they had received a dose of morphine. The red "M," often applied after wiping off enough blood to make a clean spot, served as a warning to others not to overdose the patient. Though the *Oriskany* crew later prided themselves on knowing that every patient left their sick bay with a complete medical chart, there was no time for paperwork while the doctors were trying to save so many lives.

For the *Oriskany* crew who had been through this less than a year earlier, the sight of horribly burned men was distressingly familiar. The *Forrestal*'s injured men, however, included a number who had severe trauma from the bomb explosions, upping the ante in terms of gruesomeness.

Julius was making his way through the sick bay, monitoring everything that made a difference in caring for the wounded. He came upon two *Forrestal* sailors who had just been plucked out of the ocean by a destroyer, then delivered by helicopter to the *Oriskany*. The two young men had no signs of serious injury, though they were covered head to toe in fuel oil. They had swallowed a lot of seawater when they were blown off the *Forrestal*, but they would live. The *Oriskany* crew had told them to sit out of the way and wait until they could be seen, but they grabbed Julius as he was walking by. Their eyes were wide with excitement.

"We've got to get back to our ship!" one of the men said. "Our ship's on fire! We've got to go back to our ship!"

Julius was impressed with their determination to go back and help after barely surviving themselves, but he couldn't let them go.

"You don't need to go back anywhere," he told

the men. "They have enough people to take care of themselves. Just stay here."

The men were frantic and Julius's words did not reassure them. A few minutes later, he looked back in their direction and they were gone. He heard later that they had caught a ride on a helicopter back to the *Forrestal*.

Admiral Lanham jumped on one of the helicopters delivering wounded to the *Oriskany* and visited the sick bay to see the *Forrestal* sailors. He went from bed to bed, speaking with the wounded and unable to hide his own shock and sadness. He could not believe what had happened on his flagship.

Gary Shaver regained consciousness and opened his eyes, but he saw nothing but blackness around him. But then he noted a light above that was getting smaller and smaller and smaller. He felt the pain again as soon as he opened his eyes, and along with whatever medication he had been given, it made his mind fuzzy, almost dreamlike. He remembered the explosion, then lying on the flight deck waiting for the helicopter, and he remembered falling asleep for the last time. That was the last thing he remembered. He remembered dying.

He looked again at the light above him. It kept getting smaller, as if it were moving away. No, *he* was moving away. He became aware of a falling sensation, moving downward steadily, slowly. And he could hear machinery grinding away—gears clacking and chains clink-clink-clinking. He couldn't move. And it was dark. All except for that light, now getting so small above him.

In a flash, Shaver realized what was happening.

He was dead and on his descent to hell. And the pain was still with him. *Oh my God.* His mind suddenly became clear. He was dead, he was on his journey to hell, and perhaps the worst part was that he was taking the pain with him. He began to thrash about, screaming in an all-consuming panic.

No! No! Please, no! Oh God, please, please!

The journey continued and Shaver had time to contemplate his eternity in hell—an eternity of pain—before he passed out again.

It would be a long time before he found out that he had woken up on a dark ammunition elevator on the *Oriskany,* which was being used to move the large numbers of wounded down to the sick bay. At that moment, and for quite a while after, Shaver's trip to hell was absolutely real.

Shaver joined a crowd of seriously injured men in the *Oriskany*'s sick bay. By then, his world was a fuzzy place that came and went, always overwhelmed by pain. He would pass out for a moment and then wake up screaming in agony. Even when he was given morphine or other painkillers, the powerful drugs took the edge off only for a moment. Then the pain would come roaring back. His nightmare worsened a little more when Shaver lost his sight soon after arriving in the sick bay, a temporary effect from trauma and medications.

Shaver lay there wondering how long it would be before he died, wishing it would come soon but still terrified that he would resume the journey to hell—he had not yet realized he'd been on the ammunition elevator. When a dental technician came by to check on him, Shaver pleaded with him for relief.

"Please shoot me," he begged, barely able to make the words come out. He had been crying non-stop and his mouth was desperately dry. The request was sincere. Shaver preferred dying over spending one more minute with the pain. "Please. Please. Go get a gun and shoot me."

The man assured him he would be okay, that they would get him more pain medication. Shaver cried harder when he realized he had to live, that he would have to endure the pain. He looked at the dental tech and made another request.

"Water."

Once again, the man had to say no. Shaver's internal injuries were too severe for him to have any water, no matter how thirsty he was. Shaver begged for just a tiny bit of water, but the answer had to be no. Trying to help, the corpsman went away and quickly returned with a wet washcloth, wiping it over Shaver's face as it contorted in pain. The wet cloth felt good on his face. As it brushed near his lips, Shaver desperately tried to suck the cloth into his mouth to get water.

As Shaver looked around him, he noticed a man lying in a stretcher on the floor nearby. The man's severed legs had been placed across his chest. It looked like the man was staring right at him. And then Shaver saw Lonnie Hudson, his friend whom he had last seen driving his tractor back so he could switch places with Shaver. Shaver had gone forward of where the fire would be, and Hudson had gone back to where the fire would be the worst. It wasn't Shaver's decision, but switching places with his friend would haunt him forever.

Hudson had been trapped behind the fire at the

very rear of the ship, and he was soon manning a fire hose with another sailor. It hadn't taken long for them both to realize the fire was too hot and too close, so they retreated down a ladder on the side of the ship. As they did, Hudson's clothing caught fire from the burning fuel and he had nowhere to go. The other man pushed him off the ship, then jumped in after him.

Shaver stared at his friend's terribly burned and swelling body. Shaver thought that Hudson was dying, and he was right. He turned his face away as the pain surged through him again, and then Shaver finally, mercifully, passed out. Hudson died soon after, along with the man who had jumped overboard with him.

Lenny Julius was aiding patients as much as he could. So many patients were needing attention, and like others in the sick bay, he was working hard to make sure no one suffered without being noticed. As he passed by one of the most seriously injured men awaiting care, Julius wanted to be sure he was not in too much pain. There was no "M" on his forehead or anywhere else because there was nowhere to put it, but Julius assumed that the man had received a dose already. The young man was burned terribly, his flesh charred completely in every visible area. The burns were so extensive, and so deep, that Julius could not tell if the man was white or black. He had no identifying features, the fire's damage having turned him into an everyman for the *Forrestal*'s wounded. The man was lying very quietly, his eyes open and looking around, the whites contrasting with the blackened skin so much that they seemed to gleam. Julius knew right away that the man would die, and that was why the doctors were not treating him yet.

Julius leaned over to speak to him, working hard to suppress the horror he felt at seeing, and smelling, the man up close.

"Do you need any morphine?" Julius asked. "I can get you some if you need it."

The man looked up at Julius and said no, he didn't need it. With a startling grace, as if they were discussing something much more banal, he thanked Julius for offering. The words did not come easily, because the man's throat had been seared from inhaling the flames and smoke, and his lips were mostly gone. Julius nodded and turned to walk away, but then the injured man spoke again.

"Doc?"

Julius turned back to the man. He leaned over so the man wouldn't have to work too hard at speaking loud enough.

"Doc, there is something. I . . . I can't urinate."

Julius understood immediately. Because of his injuries, the man was unable to pass urine and his full bladder was becoming painful. That was a common problem among the injured and ill, and the common response was for a physician to insert a catheter to relieve the pressure. The physicians had no time for that task at the moment, but Julius knew he could do it. He had worked on a urology ward at one point in his medical training, so he found a catheter and proceeded to insert it for the injured man.

Julius started to think that maybe the man was southern, maybe black, because his voice had an accent that came through even though the injuries made his speech difficult. Julius offered him some words of encouragement as he completed the catheter setup, but the patient didn't say anything else for a while.

After a few moments, the man's pain was eased. He was very grateful.

"Thanks, Doc. That feels a lot better."

Before leaving him, Julius asked the man if there was anything else he needed.

The man looked up and then looked away, just staring. Julius stayed, sensing that the man wanted to say something. Finally, he did.

"I'm going to die."

Julius swallowed hard and paused before saying anything. Then he tried to come up with something that might cheer the man up.

"Oh, nobody knows when they're going to die," Julius said, trying his best to sound like he meant it. "None of us knows how long we'll live. Hell, I may die before you."

The man lay there listening to Julius, quiet and not moving. Julius couldn't think of anything else to say. He knew the man would die soon, and it weighed heavily on him that he could not help him pass more easily. He wanted to say the right thing, anything that would make the man suffer just a little bit less. But he couldn't, so he stood there looking down at the dying man and, despite all his efforts, his feelings showed.

When the dying man looked up at Julius's face and saw how sad he was, their roles suddenly reversed.

"That's okay, you don't have to feel bad," he

murmured. "I haven't done anything that I'm ashamed of. I'm ready to go."

Julius was overwhelmed by the man's generosity, his ability to think of someone else even as he waited for his last moment. There was little Julius could say in return, but he wished the man well and turned to leave, holding himself together until he could make it outside into a hallway. That's where he fell apart.

Chapter 14

Injuries, multiple, extreme

Gary Shaver, Robert Zwerlein, and Paul Friedman stayed on the *Oriskany* for the rest of the day as Julius and the other medical crew exhausted themselves providing advanced care for the injured and preparing them for transfer to the hospital ship that was rushing to meet them the next morning. As the day wore on and the most immediate needs were met, Julius left the sick bay to take a break. When he passed by one of the machines that generates fog foam and pumps it to firefighters' hoses throughout the ship, he noticed that all the canisters of foam solution were gone. The *Oriskany* crew had sacrificed most of its own protection to aid the *Forrestal*.

He worried that the *Oriskany* was putting itself at risk if even a small fire broke out, and his heart jumped when he heard the fire alarm sound while he was in the shower. Julius raced to the fire site but found the situation was under control. He wearily went back to finish dressing, and then he returned to the sick bay. Plenty of wounded men still needed help.

Back on the *Forrestal,* the crew was winning its own battle with the flames. By midafternoon, the fires on the flight deck were extinguished and teams of impromptu firefighters were making progress with the ones that had wormed their way through the labyrinth of passageways and compartments deep within the ship. Most of the rear portion of the ship, all the way down the hull, had become a miserable mess of charred and smoking debris, seawater, fog foam, oil, and fuel.

After several hours of intense fear and activity, the men realized that they were not going to sink. But that realization did not come for quite a while. Many of the men expected to hear the captain call "Abandon ship!" over the 1MC at any moment and were prepared to go, some with life jackets at the ready. In the confusion and frenzy of the crisis, rumors even spread that the captain had already called for the crew to abandon the *Forrestal,* often leading those hearing it to a panicky fear that they would be left behind as the ship sank. The rumors always turned out to be false, and on the bridge, Captain Beling had no intention of giving up.

As the fires were controlled, but not completely extinguished, late that Saturday afternoon, Beling addressed the crew on the 1MC. While they continued their efforts to combat the fire and help their injured crewmates, Beling and other officers made frequent announcements on the 1MC either to pass on important information or, in the case of the captain, to bolster his crew's morale.

"Men of *Forrestal,* this is the captain," Beling began. "I want to let you know that *Forrestal* is again making twenty-five knots. We are going to rendezvous just before dusk with the USS *Repose* to get our hurt people off. I want to commend the whole crew today for your heroic actions. You certainly saved the ship with your bravery and you saved many, many lives. We will be back fighting very soon."

Already, Beling's mind was focused on how fast he could get his ship past this terrible incident and back to her job in Vietnam. He had no doubt that she could be repaired and back on duty. The damage was severe in portions of the ship, but the *Forrestal* was far from defeated.

Not everyone would share Beling's determination and dogged optimism, however. The captain was looking at the ship as a whole, with the confidence of someone who has every bit of available information at his disposal. Others were looking only at the charred remains of the structures they had just extinguished, still so hot that molten metal dripped and a fire hose would just create a backlash of scalding steam. And the crisis was far from over. Even as the worst seemed past, fires continued to flare up again all over the ship. As Beling acknowledged in another address to the crew, one of the priorities at that point was to keep crewmen out of the dangerous areas as much as possible. It could be disastrous to have crewmen wander into an area thought safe and then have the fire flare up again.

"Men of *Forrestal,* this is the captain. I want to tell you that it is not all hunky-dory yet. We have got some uncontrolled fires, which at the moment are getting worse and they are all the way aft on the ship, both port and starboard, on the oh-two and oh-three levels. We need to have all personnel stay clear of that area unless they are actually engaged in fighting fires. Take that to heart, please! We are going to slow the ship so as to not fan these fires and we may be just a little late in meeting the hospital ship. Anyway, we have a very good capability ourselves in taking care of our wounded here. In summary, stay clear of the aft part of the ship."

The fires continued to burn well into the night, though the crew had them under control by then. With the immediate crisis behind them, the leadership of the *Forrestal* had to turn some attention back to maintaining the daily needs of the ship and its crew, no small task when a carrier is in perfect condition and a major challenge when it is heavily damaged. As night began to fall on the *Forrestal,* Commander Ralph Smith, the executive officer a step below the captain, addressed the crew.

"Good evening, men. This is the executive officer. The fires are still stubbornly burning in the after section of the ship, therefore *Forrestal* is remaining at GQ. This is to maintain our fighting posture, to keep the ship sealed, and this gives us the best possibility of combating the fires and organizing our work. We are not out of the woods yet. We have much work to do tonight." He went on with instructions to the crew on how to manage the ongoing crisis. In the forward half of the ship, those persons not physically engaged in firefighting or repair work could "stand easy" but had to remain at their GQ stations. All of the crew were instructed to take turns going to the bathroom and to the forward mess deck for chow. And in perhaps the best sign that life was inching its way back to some sense of normalcy, Smith started complaining that the ship was dirty. On any typical day, sailors spend a lot of their time cleaning the ship, so this was another indication that they were recovering, not floundering.

"I have examined, inspected the ship forward to frame one-fifty-four and I noted the decks are getting sloppy and wet from our tracking in from the firefighting area," Smith said. "Tracking fog foam all over the decks has made them slippery and hazardous. We must clean the ship from frame one-fifty-four and forward. People in GQ stations, clean the decks and the area of the ship of your GQ responsibility. The officer or petty officer in charge of the GQ station will supervise this effort. In the island structure from oh-four and above, oh-four level and up, leave your GQ stations, proceed to the mess deck, and report to Lieutenant Kohler. That is Lieutenant Kohler in front of the engineering log room. He will organize your efforts in assisting to clear the mess deck forward and to restore it to the normal mess deck with tables and chairs for the crew's eating. We want a special effort for the next hour and a half, two hours, to clean the ship. Get the berthing area squared away, and the mess deck in condition for chow. Thank you."

Soon after, Smith came back on the 1MC to announce that trash should be dumped overboard at the number-one elevator. "There will be a marine guard posted there to control traffic, and please go single file to prevent another hazard of anyone falling over the side."

Another inevitable task fell on Ken Killmeyer. Even before all the fires were tamed, the crew began gathering bodies. This task would go on for days, and two bodies were found even weeks later, wedged into inaccessible spots where they had been blown by an explosion. Killmeyer was still in the hangar bay after helping jettison bombs and other materials, and then helping move the wounded up to the helicopters on the flight deck. As he walked through the hangar bay, someone called him over to help.

"There's a dead guy out here on the sponson," he said. "Come here and give me a hand."

Killmeyer could see that the sponson, a platform jutting out from the side of the ship like a veranda and directly under the flight-deck overhang, was still a smoky mess. He wasn't eager to go out there, but he couldn't really say no. Someone handed him an air mask, and he put it on, following the other man out there. Killmeyer stepped through the hatch and waited there, not able to see much, and the other man made his way farther out on the sponson. The smoke was still rolling off the flight deck from above, so Killmeyer could hardly see what they were doing. But as he bent close, he could see that the dead man was burned completely black, his arms outstretched in his last moments of life. Nothing was left on his charred body except his boots.

Two other men showed up with a light and a

blanket. Killmeyer was horrified by the body and it took all his willpower to force himself to bend over and help move it. Relieved that the mask kept the others from seeing his terrified expression, Killmeyer helped roll the dead man onto the blanket so they could use it as a stretcher. But as soon as they took a few steps toward the hatch that led back into the hangar bay, he saw a problem. The man's out-stretched arms would not fit through the hatch. Already mortified by the task, Killmeyer turned his head as someone else wrapped a blanket around one of the man's forearms and pushed down. Killmeyer flinched as he heard the bone break and the flesh crackle.

They carried the dead man to a spot in the hangar bay where bodies were being collected. Ten were there already, lying on stretchers or just on the hangar floor, a few in body bags. Blankets covered all the bodies except the ones in bags, but the up-turned limbs and odd postures gave a clue that many of them had been badly burned. Several of the ship's dentists were already there starting to look for identification on the bodies.

Retrieving the body from the sponson had shaken Killmeyer badly, and he started crying. But somehow he managed to keep from falling apart. Plenty of people were in the hangar bay by then, so he took a break and headed down to his division's berthing area. Soon after he got there, he heard someone call for help with the curtain rigging stored nearby. His division often helped set up for ceremonies on board, so there was a supply of heavy blue curtains and stands. The curtain stands were heavy, so they wouldn't tip over easily, and a petty officer in the division was gathering several men to take them to the hangar bay.

"We've got to rig the curtains around the bodies," he explained.

Killmeyer joined the effort and soon found himself back with the bodies in the hangar bay, setting up the curtains to provide some degree of privacy and decorum as the bodies continued to gather in the makeshift morgue. The dentists worked behind the curtains, uncovering the bodies and gingerly looking for dog tags or any other identifying information. Once the curtains were up, Killmeyer was eager to leave again, but then an officer told him and a few others that they had to stay.

"Just guard the bodies," he told them. "We've got too many guys coming up here and trying to see if their buddies are here. Just keep everybody out."

Uneasily, Killmeyer and his companions took up positions around the rectangular curtained area and tried to keep people out. They weren't very successful. The blue curtains just seemed to get everyone's attention in the open hangar bay, so people were drawn over. Once they realized that the bodies were behind the curtains, some men were eager to see if a friend was back there. Killmeyer was a lanky young kid, not much of a match for an overwrought sailor insistent on finding his buddy. He said no and tried to explain his orders, and he even got in a shoving match when the men tried to push through. But he wasn't much of an obstacle, and his heart wasn't in it.

Then Killmeyer saw six marines walking through the hangar bay. They were part of the marine contingent whose tasks included guarding the nuclear bombs on board. Once it became clear that the nuclear bombs were not threatened by the fire, some of the marines went topside to volunteer their efforts. When they saw the bodies, they headed that way. Killmeyer was relieved to see them.

"We're supposed to be guarding these bodies but we can't stop these guys from going in," Killmeyer called out to them. "I'm glad you guys are here!"

The marines took over and quickly established positions around the curtained area. They assumed "parade rest" positions and just stood there with .45s on their hips, as intimidating as marines always are. Killmeyer and his companions were grateful to be done with the task, and as they left, they saw that no one was fighting to see the bodies anymore.

On the evening of the fire, Beling decided it was time to officially address the loss. He waited until the situation was relatively calm, and then he went to the microphone on the bridge. Beling was burdened by the loss of so many men, and he began the address with a heavy heart.

"Men of *Forrestal,* this is the captain. There are no words that say what comes from our hearts tonight. Yet we must try." Beling spoke slowly, evenly. "I ask you to join with me in this humble effort to express our thanks and our deep, deep debt to almighty God. Let us pray: Our heavenly Father, we see this day as one minute and yet a lifetime for all of us. We thank you for the courage of those that gave their lives in saving their shipmates today. We humbly ask you to grant them peace. And to their loved ones, the conciliation and strength to bear their loss. Help us to renew the faith we have in you. We thank you for our own lives. May we remember you as you have remembered us today. From our hearts we turn to you now, knowing that you have been at our sides in every minute of this day. Heavenly Father, help us to rebuild and re-man our ship so that our brothers who died today may not have made a fruitless sacrifice. Amen."

Some of the crew were released from general quarters that night, though others remained at their stations until noon the next day. There was still much work to do, but release from general quarters meant the men had much more freedom to move about the ship and seek whatever aid and comfort they needed. For most of them, that meant rest. Thousands of men, weary and filthy, emotionally exhausted, had to find places to sleep. Those whose living quarters were undamaged welcomed stragglers to share their spaces, handing out spare changes of clothing and whatever else their crewmates needed.

Ed Roberts and some others from his division found that their berthing area had not been burned, but they didn't want to sleep belowdecks; there was still too much uncertainty about what areas were safe. Instead, they found space out on the catwalks and lay there under the Tonkin Gulf night. Some men fell asleep immediately from exhaustion, but others lay quietly. Someone had found a portable radio and tuned in an American music broadcast from Vietnam.

After the song ended, a Vietnamese woman spoke to the crew in English. She was Hanoi Hannah, the propagandist that American soldiers and sailors had to tolerate if they wanted to hear the music from back home.

"Hello, a special hello to all the men on the American carrier *Forrestal*. What happened to you today, huh? Maybe a little accident? Surely you Americans realize now that even the fates are against you now. Why fight us? This is not your war. You are dying so the rich men in America can get richer."

Nobody liked hearing it. "Listening to her is bullshit," Roberts said, and rolled over.

For many of the crew, just lying down in a safe, almost quiet place was a godsend. But exhausted though they were, many could not sleep. They closed their eyes and waited, but their minds were full of images from their day.

And when sleep did come, it often brought nightmares. For a long time after the fire, the sailors would be awakened by fellow crew members screaming out in terror, pleading for their buddies to come out of the fire, or just crying. Those awakened by the screams might throw a pillow or yell a harsh command to shut up, but inside, they had more sympathy than they could express. They knew what it felt like, even if they managed to keep it inside.

The night overtook the *Forrestal* as the ship steamed on to meet the *Repose* hospital ship, the *Oriskany* and the *Bon Homme Richard* following with many of the *Forrestal*'s wounded. The men still at general quarters were exhausted and emotionally drained, but they muddled on through their chores or just tried to stay awake. For many, it was hours or even days before they realized the extent of the crisis they had just survived, and many marveled at how close they had come to dying. There was little opportunity to talk or pass on scuttlebutt while they were at their stations, but when they took their turns heading to the mess hall for chow or when someone came through their compartment on the way to somewhere else, some crew members eagerly asked about news from other divisions, other parts of the ship.

"How bad was it there? Did you see it? I heard the whole aft portion is gone."

And some men asked about specific crewmen, their buddies who were working near the origin of the fire. Sometimes they would find out the guy was just fine, and sometimes they wouldn't learn anything for a long while. A great many of the *Forrestal* sailors would be reluctant to discuss anything about the fire for a long while after. Those who survived seemed to avoid some of the obvious discussions about how bad it all had been, who had been killed, and the horrors they had witnessed themselves. They just avoided talking about it all, as if talking about it made it real.

The last major fire was extinguished at 4 A.M. on July 30. On the way to meet the hospital ship that day, with smoke still seeping from her burned decks, the *Forrestal* rendezvoused with another carrier, the USS *Intrepid*. The *Intrepid* was taking over the duties scheduled for the *Forrestal* on Yankee Station, but the arrival of the carrier was a sad moment for Beling. His ship was being relieved after only four and a half days of combat, sent home like a rookie who couldn't take the heat. Beling knew that wasn't the case, but he cringed every time he imagined how others were looking at his ship. As the two ships steamed toward each other for a predetermined point where some necessary supplies would be transferred to the *Intrepid,* Beling pushed his ship at a brisk twenty-seven knots. He was proud that the damaged *Forrestal* could produce such speed without having to use more than four of the ship's eight boilers. He waited until the two ships were close enough to see each other. When the *Intrepid* was in range, Beling ordered a visual message flashed to the other ship's captain, John Fair, a friend from way back.

"John, how's this look on four boilers?" was the greeting.

After the transfer, the *Forrestal* steamed on with the *Oriskany* and the *Bon Homme Richard.* The three carriers rendezvoused with the hospital ship *Repose* the next morning at a featureless spot in the waters off of Vietnam. The big white ship had rushed at top speed from its station on the coast, where it had been treating soldiers wounded in the jungle fighting. An ungainly big white box on water, with a prominent red cross painted several stories high on the side, the *Repose* clearly was not a fighting vessel. On board, she had dozens of doctors, some of the most sophisticated medical equipment in the world, and plenty of room for the *Forrestal*'s wounded. She was needed.

The crews of the aircraft carriers had prepared for this moment and were ready to transfer patients almost as soon as the hospital ship came within sight. The helicopters swarmed the carriers again, this time in a more orderly and deliberate fashion than the previous day's rescue efforts. Much of the activity was centered on the *Oriskany*, where the most seriously wounded had already been sent. The *Oriskany* crew had stabilized the men and performed some of the most urgently needed surgery, but the patients still needed much more sophisticated care on the *Repose*. The helicopters touched down on the *Oriskany* deck over and over again, ferrying terribly burned and mutilated young men to the doctors and nurses waiting on the *Repose*. Once more, Gary Shaver, Robert Zwerlein, and Paul Friedman were loaded onto helicopters and taken a step farther from the *Forrestal*.

Several times, Shaver woke up on the *Repose* to find the actor Robert Stack, better known as Eliot Ness of the television show *The Untouchables*, sitting by his bedside, talking to him, soothing him. A popular celebrity, Stack was touring Vietnam to greet the troops and had volunteered to see the wounded on the *Repose*. By then, Shaver's pain was controlled enough that he could briefly speak to Stack before passing out again. Paul Friedman got even luckier. He had his picture taken while Connie Francis was singing to him.

The *Repose* offered advanced care, but for many of the wounded, the long journey had just begun. The terrible wounds they suffered would lead to a series of operations, long and slow recuperations, excruciating physical therapy, and prolonged stays in hospitals.

Transferring the wounded to the *Repose* was a relief to Captain Beling because he could rest easy that his injured men were in the best hands, but also because he could get back to his primary job of running the *Forrestal*. Men were finally getting a breather throughout the ship, but not in damage control. The day after the blaze started, Rowland and his crew still had plenty to do, keeping their eyes on each remaining hot spot in the ship and trying hard to keep anyone else from falling prey to the *Forrestal* fire. The mess left by the previous day's fires was creating all sorts of hazards, and one of the worst was chlorine gas. The millions of gallons of seawater sprayed from fire hoses and pumped into the hangar bays had found its way to a battery-storage compartment, where it mixed with the acid from broken batteries to form deadly chlorine gas.

"There is suspected chlorine gas in compartment 03-217-4Quebec," Rowland cautioned over the 1MC address system. His voice sounded weary, almost exasperated. "All hands are cautioned to stay clear of the area. Cautioned to stay forward of frame two-ten. We don't want to have to carry out any more people that went up to help and passed out. Chlorine gas is *deadly* and it *is* up there!"

Despite the warnings from Rowland and others in the area, three men charged into one of the compartments filled with chlorine gas because they mistakenly thought people were trapped there. They quickly succumbed to the gas and were the last three men to die.

By the time he felt confident enough to leave his post on Sunday, Merv Rowland had been on duty in damage control for seventeen hours, and he had been awake nearly forty-five hours because he had been up the night before working on a machinery repair. The Benzedrine from the sick bay had kept him buzzing along and alert enough to do his job, but now that he could stand down, he felt like hell. Rowland was dog-tired but jittery, his eyes wide open but eager to close. His nerves were shot and his hands trembled.

The drug still had him firmly in its grip, propelling him along despite the weariness he felt in every inch of his body, forcing him to hear and see every little thing around him despite his desire to just stop. Thinking he might be able to rest if he got some food, Rowland made his way to one of the mess halls. A lot of others were there in the early morning, milling around and talking about what had just happened to the ship. The mess hall had become a gathering spot for many of the crew, including some of the aviators, who were nicknamed "Airedales." As Rowland made his way through the line and picked up some chow, a few of the men recognized him and knew he could answer all their questions. They waited until he took his tray over to a table and started to sit down, and then someone from another table asked, "Hey, what's the story? What really happened up there?"

The combination of extreme fatigue, stress, and the drug's effects made Rowland nervous and cranky, not a good combination for an officer already known for his hot temper.

"I'll tell you what happened. Those goddamn Airedales blew up the ship!"

The room fell silent. All of Rowland's frustrations from the previous day were coming out at once, and he couldn't stop them. The aviators in the room, not exactly a shy, retiring lot themselves, took exception to Rowland's comment. One of them started to reply, "You're full of . . . ," but whatever else he said was lost in the noise as Rowland leapt off his seat and lunged for the man. Rowland was ready for a fight; once the man opened his mouth to speak, Rowland considered it a personal affront and disrespectful to the ship he had just fought so hard to save. Rowland's mind was a mess, and that aviator had just volunteered to be the whipping boy for everything the old man was mad about.

Rowland swung wildly and had just gotten his hands around the aviator's throat when a dozen others piled on them and tried to pull Rowland off.

"I'll kill you, you son of a bitch!" Rowland roared, his eyes a frightful indicator that he meant what he said.

It took several men to pull him off—with one grabbing him from behind and pulling hard on his neck—but the aviator survived. The men made Rowland sit down as the aviator's buddies hustled him out of the room, but Rowland was still grumbling and yelling at the man. Rowland was breathing like a racehorse and his eyes were wide with adrenaline. The men who pulled him off the aviator realized that Rowland needed help, so they convinced him to walk with them down to the sick bay.

When he got there, one of the doctors could see what bad shape Rowland was in. He told the other men to leave and got Rowland to sit down for a minute. The doctor went to a locked cabinet and then came back.

"Okay, I've got some medicine for you," he said.

"I don't want your medicine!" Rowland snapped. "I've been taking your goddamn medicine and I'm done with it!"

"This is different, Merv. This is what you need."

Then Rowland could see that the doctor had brought out a big bottle of one-hundred proof brandy, kept in the sick bay strictly for "medicinal purposes." Otherwise, alcohol was forbidden on the ship. He filled a water glass with the brandy and handed it over. The old navy officer didn't need any more prompting. He took the glass and drank it all straight down as if it were water.

"Okay, that ought to help," the doctor said. "Now let's get you back to your quarters."

The doctor walked Rowland back to his quarters and told him to just go to bed. The brandy was taking effect by then and overwhelming the Benzedrine. Rowland didn't bother to undress and just collapsed on his bed. He was asleep as soon as his head hit the pillow.

Rowland slept for twenty hours. When he finally awoke, he was disoriented and didn't know how long he had slept. He reached for the phone by his bed to call damage control and get a report, but when he picked up the receiver, nothing. It was dead. *Awww shit. What's that mean?*

He picked himself up off the bed, every muscle protesting after the long rest, and staggered to the door of his room. His mind was foggy. When he opened it, he was surprised to see an armed marine standing there.

Holy shit . . . Captain's put a guard at my door.

Rowland stood there for a moment trying to figure out what was happening. His mind was still foggy, but there was only one reason a marine would be guarding him.

I must have really screwed up. Wait a minute, something happened in the mess hall. Did I beat the shit out of somebody? . . . What did I do in that mess hall?

The marine just looked at Rowland and said, "Good morning, sir." Rowland wasn't sure what he should say in return, but he spoke anyway.

"Yeah . . . Well, what in the hell are you doing here?" Rowland demanded.

"The captain told me to stand here and not let anybody knock on your door until you open the door yourself and come out happy. They disconnected your phones, too, sir."

Rowland thought about it for a minute and realized he wasn't under arrest.

"Okay, well . . . I'm all done."

"Yes sir," the marine replied, and immediately started down the hall. Rowland stood in the doorway and watched him leave, still trying to remember what happened in the mess hall.

Beling knew exactly what Rowland had done in the mess hall, but he understood why. In the day after the fire, the crew began tallying up the number of dead and wounded, plus the physical damage to the ship. Some of the figures would not be complete until later, when there was time to assess the damage more closely and some of the seriously wounded had passed away, but in the end, the numbers were disturbing: 134 men dead or missing, 161 seriously injured. Of 134 dead or missing, 18 were listed as missing and presumed dead. The crew and the other ships recovered the remains of what appeared to be between twelve and fourteen bodies, so four to six bodies were lost completely. Most of the death certificates listed the cause of death as "injuries, multiple, extreme." Many of the others died from burns, some from smoke inhalation, a few from chlorine gas, and some drowned as they were trapped in flooded compartments.

The ship had suffered $72.2 million in damage, including the loss of twenty-one aircraft and damage to forty more. Some of the planes pushed overboard that day cost more than five million dollars apiece, others two million dollars each. The ordnance destroyed or jettisoned during the fire was valued at just under two million dollars.

As soon as word reached the United States, the *Forrestal* fire was front-page news. It was no surprise that everyone wanted to know more about what happened on Yankee Station. Even those who didn't follow the war closely or who didn't have a particular interest in the *Forrestal* wanted to know how an American carrier could shoot itself in the foot and lose 134 men. The *New York Times* featured the fire as its lead front-page story on Saturday, July 29, the day the fire started, reporting only the earliest information that a "raging fire" broke out on the carrier and that deaths were expected. "It would have been impossible to avoid deaths," a military spokesman said.

By Sunday, the *Times* had photos of the carrier ablaze and reported that at least seventy crew were killed and the "craft is out of action." Other papers carried similar coverage, and the August issue of *Life* magazine devoted its cover to a photo of flames and smoke billowing from behind planes parked on the *Forrestal*. Many of the early accounts got the details wrong, understandable because the event was chaotic and the information relayed from around the world. In particular, the early accounts attributed the cause of the fire to an auxiliary fuel tank dropping off of John McCain's plane apparently for no reason, the fuel then igniting from either a plane's exhaust or "the superheated steam" of the catapult launching system. Once it became clear that a rocket had fired, the initial theories were that a plane's hot exhaust or the exhaust of a nearby tractor had overheated the rockets on another plane, causing one to fire. One story in the *Times* described the cause as a plane experiencing "an extreme wet start. This malfunction, comparable to what happens when a cigarette lighter has been overfilled, occurs about once a week on attack carriers, but almost never so severely as it did on Saturday."

That theory was soon discarded, but by then the fire was no longer front-page news. Except in the Norfolk area, where so many families had relatives on the ship, the story was quickly shouldered aside by the other major news of 1967. President Johnson held a news conference on July 31 and did not mention the *Forrestal* tragedy. None of the reporters brought it up either. Three days later Johnson announced that he was sending 45,000 more men to Vietnam, bringing the total to 525,000. By August 1, just three days after the fire, the *Times* front page featured "Shots Fired in Washington as

Negro Youths Rampage" and "Milwaukee Calm After Negro Riot." Another story on the front that same day, "*Forrestal* Blaze Cuts Down Raids in North Vietnam," related the difficulty in continuing air raids on Vietnam without the *Forrestal*. That was one of the last front-page reports on the fire in the *Times*.

For some on the *Forrestal*, a difficult task was still in front of them. Bob Kohler, the ship's administration officer, was in charge of sending messages to the navy offices back home about who was dead and who was missing. He held shipwide head counts every few hours to see if the missing men could be accounted for; if a man who was previously thought missing was found, Kohler insisted that he personally report to him and verify his identity. Kohler wanted to minimize any chance of sending a family bad information.

Many of the crew were eager to let their families know they were okay, but the communications available to them in 1967 were not of much help. The only way to make contact quickly was by telephone, and patching through a call from a ship off the coast of Vietnam to some little town in Minnesota was a frustrating endeavor. And even when such a call was possible it meant standing in line for hours. For those who got through, the call was usually brief, with a young sailor saying, "Mom, I'm okay. I made it okay," and then, "Don't cry, Mom. I'll be home soon." Some gave their wives a list of people they knew were okay, so they could spread the word among those waiting in Norfolk.

Getting word to the families was complicated because some families were on summer vacations and some wives were living with distant relatives while their husbands were away at sea. The news reports were brief at first, indicating only that the *Forrestal* had suffered some sort of bad fire on board. It would be a few days before details emerged and much longer before the media would get access to a reliable list of the dead and wounded. And then the news coverage would fade quickly as the country turned its attention to race riots and other news from Vietnam.

For many of the families, the news gave them only enough information to make them worry that their son, brother, or husband was among the dead or wounded. The worry could go on for days as they waited. Even Captain Beling's wife knew little from the outset.

On the Saturday of the fire, Eve Beling had been moving the family from one home to another, having just sent the moving van off with the final load of furniture from the house. The Belings' oldest son was going off to college that same day, and he kissed his mother goodbye and drove off in his little MG about the same time as the moving van. Eve Beling was left standing in front of the empty house, about to leave herself, when she caught sight of the last thing a navy wife ever wants to see—a navy car driving up to the house with a stern-faced officer and a chaplain. Her heart pounded as she waited for them to pull up and walk the short distance to where she was waiting.

"Mrs. Beling, may we go inside?" the officer asked.

"Well, no. There's no furniture," she said, trying to keep her composure.

"Yes ma'am, I see. Could we sit down right here, then?"

She sat with the officer and the chaplain on the front steps of the house, and listened quietly as the officer told her about a fire.

"What about John? Is John okay?"

"We actually don't know yet, ma'am. We're still getting information from the *Forrestal*, and all we know right now is that there were some deaths and injuries. Mrs. Beling, we wanted you to know about this as soon as possible."

Beling's son heard about the fire on the car radio on the way to school. It would be days before the navy could confirm that Beling was safe, days in which Eve Beling put on a strong face and appeared confident. She had to, because many of the wives of the *Forrestal* crew looked to her for leadership on the home front, for information and support that helped the wives get through their long stints without a husband at home.

Other families all over the country, but mostly the East Coast, were getting visits from naval officers as officials received confirmations of the dead and wounded sailors. Bill and Ruth Zwerlein, Robert Zwerlein's parents, were in Ohio for a friend's wedding on the day of the fire. Some of the wedding attendees had heard about it on the radio, but no one wanted to mention it to the Zwerleins. They were having such a good time, and no one wanted to be the one to break the news.

Two of their sons were working at the family's Tastee-Freez back home when they heard about the *Forrestal* fire on the radio. That evening, they called their parents in Ohio. Bill and Ruth were concerned, but they thought maybe their Bobby would be fine. After all, he had had all that training as a volunteer firefighter. The news reports sounded bad, but they kept hoping that Bobby had been spared.

"He's a fireman," Ruth said more than once. "He'll know what to do."

They flew home from Ohio immediately, but there was no news about Bobby until Monday. Then a navy car pulled up to the Tastee-Freez and an officer came in, causing the shop to fall silent. Everyone in town knew that Bobby was on the troubled ship.

The officer asked to speak with the Zwerleins privately, and when they sat down, he dashed their hopes.

"Reports from the *Forrestal* indicate that your son has been wounded. He was transferred to a hospital ship and his condition is listed as guarded."

Ruth began to cry and Bill worked hard not to, fidgeting and avoiding the officer's eyes. They asked what happened and the officer explained that there had been a major fire on the flight deck and their son had been caught up in it somehow. The Zwerleins sat for a minute, Ruth crying and Bill trying to console her. After a minute, he had to ask.

"Was he burned?" Bill said quietly.

"Yes sir, the report is that he was badly burned. His condition is listed as guarded."

Their hearts fell. Ruth sobbed. The officer promised that the navy would keep in touch and pass on any more information as it came in. But no more information came for the next couple of days. As they waited and worried, Bill and Ruth realized that their son might be dying, alone. The idea tore at them, with Ruth particularly besieged by the idea that her Bobby was hurting and needed his mother. She was tortured by the image of him lying on the hospital ship with terrible burns, in pain and so alone, craving the kind of comfort that can come only from the gentle touch of a mother.

The Zwerleins decided that they could not just sit and wait. They contacted a family friend who had connections with the navy and started inquiring about how they could go to Vietnam. If their son was dying, they needed to be there. They were ready to get on a plane.

But before they could explore that option very much, the naval officer returned to the Tastee-Freez at 11 A.M. one day. Ruth was next door at the beauty parlor, trying to carry on while she worried about her Bobby. When the naval officer appeared again, everyone on the street noticed. There was a hush as Ruth left the beauty parlor and went next door to their shop, everyone anticipating major news, good or bad.

When Bill and Ruth were together, the officer told them the news. Bobby had died on the hospital ship.

For Ken Killmeyer's parents, the news was much better. He had managed to call them soon after the fire, telling them he was okay. It was clearly a relief to his mother, who broke down in tears when she heard his voice. He promised he would write with more details and then he would be home soon.

In the days after the fire, Killmeyer found time to

finish the letter he had been writing when the fire broke out. He retrieved it from where he had stuffed it under his bunk for safekeeping and sat down to complete it.

He had been writing his six-year-old sister, but after the fire the letter turned into something a six-year-old shouldn't read. The page started out with "Dear Patty, Thank you so much for your letter. You don't know how much that letter means out here. Well, we took on bombs last night. Tonight fuel and tomorrow more bombs. I am very tired."

The letter went on to describe the man overboard that interrupted his sleep, and said the man had not been recovered. "They left two destroyers to search for him, but there is no chance. W . . ."

General quarters was called on that last "W." Then Killmeyer resumed writing after the fire. At the very top of the first page, he added "I was writing this letter when it all started. Thank God I am alive."

Halfway down the second page, he picked up the letter again. "Right here is where I stopped writing when fire quarters was called away. I don't have a fire quarters station, so I just sat and was going to keep writing when general quarters stations [sounded]. When I was running aft to my GQ station they said over the 1MC that there was a fire on the flight deck aft. From what I can remember I was about 10 feet away from the hatch I showed you where I go down to the magazine," he wrote, referring to a family day visit when he had shown his parents where he worked on the ship. "When the first bomb went off and then another, everybody froze in their tracks. It was coming from overhead and down the passageway. I was never so scared. I thought we would all be dead soon."

Killmeyer went on for four pages explaining what he did during the fire, including helping to push planes overboard and his grisly assignment to recover the burned body. After the detailed account of his experiences, he told his family how he had escaped injury right up to the end of the day. Finally, an officer had taken a look at the wet, bedraggled kid and told him to take a rest.

"A guy came and gave me a box of K rations and I cut my finger open on the can"— a small irony that would stick with him for years. "I am going to church. Love, Ken."

Ken's father wrote him back to say how grateful he was that Ken had survived and how proud the family was of Ken's work. It was the first time his father had ever written him.

Beling was adamant that his ship was not defeated. He could not stomach the idea that the *Forrestal* had been brought to its knees by an accident on board, the East Coast navy's first carrier in Vietnam sent limping home like a wounded puppy after only four days of combat. This was, at minimum, a matter of pride, and Beling would argue with anyone that it was more than that. From touring the damaged areas and studying the engineers' assessments, he had determined that the ship looked a lot worse off than she actually was, and there was no question in his mind that he could get her back to fighting form. Rowland wasn't so sure, but he agreed that the damage looked worse than it was.

As soon as Washington and Norfolk got word of

how serious the accident had been, officials there started suggesting that the ship should just come home for a major overhaul. Beling was still arguing with them when they ordered him to go to Subic Bay for an assessment, making it clear that they expected the *Forrestal* to leave Vietnam and probably never return.

Beling was determined to avoid that indignity, not only for himself but also for his crew, so he kept pleading his case with the navy. The answer was always the same: head to Subic Bay and then probably on home to Norfolk. Beling still didn't give up hope, though.

It sounds bad to them now, but maybe once we get to Subic and clear away some of this mess, they'll see that the damage isn't so bad. Maybe we can do some repairs and get back to work here.

Admiral Lanham admired Beling's determination, but he could see that the *Forrestal* would be tied to a dock for a long while in repairs, either in Norfolk or in Subic Bay. So he made arrangements to return to the States, where he could be of more use. Lanham flew off of the *Forrestal* and on to the United States, not bothering to make the long journey back with the carrier, even though she had been his flagship. Most of the crew also were eager to get home and see their loved ones, but Captain Beling let them know he had other intentions.

On Sunday morning, Rowland was already sound asleep when the 1MC crackled to life with Beling's calm, carefully measured words.

"Men of *Forrestal,* this is the captain. I want to say a few words to you this morning to sum up the situation that exists at this time and where we are going forward in the future. However, before I do so, the first thing I want to do is to read to you a message which I have just received from the president of the United States. I quote, 'The following is a personal message from the president to Captain John K. Beling, commanding officer of the USS *Forrestal.* I want you and the men of your command to know that the thoughts of the American people are with you at this tragic time. We all feel a great sense of personal loss. Your devotion to duty and the courage of your men have not gone unnoticed. The sacrifices that they have made shall not be in vain.' End of quote. I will answer that on your behalf this morning.

"Now, what for the future. The ship is extensively damaged in the upper after portion. We are going to have to rip off the after section of the flight deck, and most of the structural work down to the main deck will have to be renewed. I think that that is very minor damage for what the ship has been through. It now appears that she sustained explosions of six [later determined to be nine] one-thousand-pound bombs, among other things. A very tough ship. And for your information, the two destroyers which started up to escort us to Subic yesterday are now two hundred and fifty miles behind and we are only using half of the ship's boilers. So there is a lot of spirit left in *Forrestal.* Today at thirteen-hundred we will have a memorial service for those of our comrades who gave their lives for their country. After that we will go into Subic with our band playing and our flag flying. Then we will get started getting fixed. We will be met by a team of experts who will help us assess the damage and where it can best and most quickly be fixed. I do not know at this time whether the damage will be fixed in Japan or on the West Coast. Needless to say, we want to do it in the place where it can be fixed fastest so we can get back on the line."

After his talk, Beling realized that he had a golden opportunity to make his case and keep the *Forrestal* in the fight. He had personally received a message from the president of the United States that morning expressing condolences for the tragedy. Wouldn't it be rude not to reply?

Actually, Beling was rationalizing his own misgivings. He knew that it would be a very cheeky move to make such a suggestion directly to the president when it flatly contradicted the navy's position. But he was willing to take that risk to keep the *Forrestal* in the fight. Beling knew that President Johnson and his advisers would welcome a chance to keep the carrier in Vietnam, and he was willing to live with the fallout from the navy. He was willing to take the chance because he felt he owed it to his men of *Forrestal,* and because he was already thinking that his career might have ended when 134 men died on his watch.

But Beling didn't want to use his trump card too early. He would wait and see if he needed it.

As soon as they had time to catch a breath and start asking questions, the crew tried to figure out what had happened on Saturday morning. On the trip to Subic Bay, the ship's ordnance specialists traced the fire back to its first moments. By interviewing surviving crew members who witnessed the rocket fire, and by reviewing the footage from the flight-deck camera, the *Forrestal*'s investigators pieced together the initial series of events and realized that a Zuni had hit one of the planes on the opposite side of the ship, leading to the fire. How and why the rocket could have fired was more of a mystery, but more investigations would follow once the carrier reached Subic Bay and Norfolk.

The carrier's arrival in Subic Bay, two days after the fire, drew everyone's attention. Those working at Subic Bay or there from other ships were eager to get a look at the big ship and see for themselves how bad the accident had been. They crowded the dock to get a look at the burned ship and as the *Forrestal* drew near, they heard a sound that sent chills down their spines.

"Fire! Fire! Fire!"

Ringing out across the water that separated them, the alarms reached those on the dock, signaling that yet another fire had flared up within the ship, two days after the ordeal began. They had to wait while the fire was brought under control, and only then was the *Forrestal* given permission to dock. Soon after, fifty-two canvas bags containing bodies were wrapped in American flags and borne off the carrier with quiet ceremony. Even then, the tragedy was not yet complete. Crew were still cutting through some mangled portions of the ship looking for more bodies, and smoldering materials still flared up.

While the ship was in Subic Bay for the initial repairs, the crew was allowed liberty for the first time in weeks. Free to roam the Subic Bay bars and nightclubs, the men stood out from the other sailors there because they wore their denim work clothes instead of the spotless dress uniforms usually required for liberty calls. The *Forrestal* sailors couldn't put together enough dress uniforms for everyone after the fire, and that was just fine with them. Going on liberty in their casual work clothes was a treat.

Ed Roberts ended up at a bar with a few of his workmates, and they were more than ready to blow off some steam. When they sat down at a table, someone pointed out a big chart hanging over the bar listing dozens of drinks available, all for about forty cents each. As soon as they saw the chart, they agreed: *That's what we're having. We're going to have one of all those drinks.*

And so they started drinking. They made it through only about seven or eight different drinks, but that was plenty. At one point, one of the guys held up a fried chicken leg and said, "Hey, here's Scotty's foot!" before taking a big bite out of it. It was a reference to their buddy who had lost most of his foot in the fire. The joke was tasteless and not even very funny, but the guys laughed hysterically. They needed to.

Beling was not hitting the bars. He oversaw the inspection of his ship by the engineers at Subic, taking every opportunity to show them how well the ship had withstood the damage. As much as he could, he tried to persuade them that *Forrestal* could get back in the fight. Though they sympathized with Beling, it was clear to everyone that the damage was just too extensive. The navy's instructions were just what Beling expected: Bring the ship home to Norfolk.

Well, okay, then. I've got nothing to lose.

So Beling went ahead with his plan and sent his message to the White House. He reported that inspections in Subic Bay show "our damage isn't anywhere near as bad as we had thought, and if we had six weeks in a Japanese shipyard and replacement of our aircraft, we could operate with at least 80 percent of our normal ability." Beling was stretching the truth a bit, putting an extremely optimistic spin on the engineers' assessments.

Beling waited anxiously for a reply, expecting the Pentagon to send a sharp retort about protocol. He only hoped that the scolding would be accompanied by a change in his orders. But Beling never heard back and the navy's orders were not changed. His gambit had not paid off, but there also was no punishment for his cocky maneuver. At least not right away.

With some of its structural mess cleaned up at Subic Bay, the *Forrestal* headed back to its home port in Norfolk—a journey of thirty-four days. Rear Admiral Forsyth Massey, a highly experienced carrier aviation officer, had met the *Forrestal* at Subic Bay and embarked to begin the navy's official investigation of the fire. Beling knew Massey well and respected him as a capable officer. Massey and his aides would spend the ensuing month inspecting the damage, interviewing witnesses, and conducting tests. They also reconstructed much of the scene on the flight deck and conducted a thorough review of the ship's policies, procedures, and overall readiness.

For much of the voyage, Beling received his orders from the Pacific Fleet command, which instructed him to steam at twenty-two knots. That was a respectable pace for any carrier, and Beling had no trouble keeping up the speed. He pointed out to anyone who would listen that the ship was holding up just fine, not even straining to make the twenty-two knots.

Speed meant power. He was happy to show anyone who was watching that the *Forrestal* was still a fearsome warship. But when they crossed the "chop line" where the Atlantic Fleet command took over, Beling's new orders were to proceed at a more leisurely sixteen knots. He had no choice but to comply, even though it riled him.

First they stopped in Florida to off-load some planes based there and then headed up the coast. When the carrier left the Florida port and headed north, the fleet command was supposed to issue a new order to maintain sixteen knots, but somehow that order never came. With no orders constraining him, Beling immediately kicked the ship's speed to an astonishing thirty knots. By God, he was going to head into the *Forrestal*'s home port with enough speed to dispel any notions that the ship was almost dead in the water.

Soon after leaving for Norfolk, Beling received word that a Soviet spy ship was shadowing them, not an uncommon occurrence even so close to home. Knowing that the sub had been sent to take a look at the damage on the big American warship, the cocky captain couldn't resist sending a message dripping with bravado.

"Let me know if you require assistance," Beling

sent by blinking light. He knew the Soviet ship would get his meaning quite clearly.

As the ship neared Norfolk, Beling had one more trick up his sleeve. The *Forrestal* still had six A-6 attack aircraft in pristine condition. Beling was thinking of one more way to help the ship save face, but this he had to clear with Admiral Lanham, who had flown out to rejoin the *Forrestal* as it neared Norfolk. Beling went to the admiral's quarters one evening and asked to speak with him. Lanham was in his pajamas when Beling entered his cabin.

"So what is it, John?"

"I want to launch all six of those aircraft as we're coming up the channel and approaching the dock," Beling explained. He said it as if he was certain it was a fine idea and just needed Lanham's sign-off.

The admiral looked at Beling for a minute and then said, "John, are you crazy?"

"Oh, the forward catapults are *fine,* no damage at all," Beling said. "We can do it. It'll show that the ship's not as bad off as everyone thinks."

The admiral understood Beling's motivation, but he had to be the voice of reason.

"John, if anything goes wrong, *which it could,* just think what they would do to you. And it would be my butt, too. What if the bridle snaps and the plane goes in the water? Wouldn't that be great, with a thousand or so visitors and crew members' family watching."

Beling tried to think of a response, but then reluctantly decided to just let it go. He agreed with the admiral that the plan was too risky. At least he felt like he had done all he could to preserve the ship's honor.

When the ship arrived in Norfolk, a crowd of three thousand people was waiting. A navy band played as crew members' families strained for a look at the sailors lining the rim of the flight deck, forward of the damage. Most of them were in blue denim work clothes instead of the dress whites they normally would wear for such a homecoming.

Those awaiting the *Forrestal* had heard about the damage and most had seen pictures in the newspaper, but the sight of the once mighty carrier pulling up to the dock was still shocking, even after the crew had cleared away the burned wreckage and cleaned up the ship as much as possible. Joyous grins turned to looks of shock and concern as the *Forrestal* came into view.

Eve Beling and her children were the first to come on board after she docked. The captain couldn't leave the ship right away, but his family wanted to see him. When a reporter tried to bound up the gangplank first, a burly marine stepped into his path and told him, in terms probably still ringing in the reporter's ears, that the captain's family was boarding first.

The crew was allowed to disembark and greet their waiting families. The captain spoke to the press soon after returning and praised his crew as a "concrete demonstration of the worth of American youth," an especially meaningful compliment at a time when the country was starting to see some young people as ill-mannered and unpatriotic. Beling went on to say "there were many examples of heroism" and "not one single example of cowardice."

Continuing his effort to lessen the public impact of the disaster, Beling told the press that the *Forrestal* was "in good shape except for the after section." He put on an optimistic face for the world, but when he turned away, Beling's loss threatened to consume him. The return was not what Beling had envisioned months earlier when the *Forrestal* first sailed away to its destiny. Now she was home, but as a sad imitation of her former glory. And more important, she had returned without nearly three hundred of her crew.

Beling knew someone had to be held responsible.

Chapter *15*

INVESTIGATIONS

The questions started long before the *Forrestal* returned home and they would continue for a long
time afterward. How did the fire start? How did it
get so bad? Why did the bombs blow up so
quickly? Could more lives have been saved? For
days and weeks, the men sorted out who was killed
and who survived, who was missing and who was
injured but alive. Young men like Ken Killmeyer
and Frank Eurice survived relatively unscathed,
while others like Paul Friedman and John McCain
made it through with minor injuries. Rowland survived another tragedy to cap off his long military
career, and Beling survived the fire itself but knew
that he faced more heat from the navy.

The *Forrestal* sailors started reflecting on their
own experiences soon after the fires were out, after
they had a little time to rest and get over the initial
shock. There already was talk of heroics and how

well the crew had responded, but there also was talk of the errors they had made. Fate has a way of showing itself in the aftermath of such a deadly incident, inviting survivors to praise it or curse it, quite often both. After the men had time to compare notes, they marveled at the small coincidences and twists of fate that spared their lives, as well as the ones that killed their buddies. Quietly, a sailor told of going on a coffee break, during which everyone at his workstation was killed. Others told of being on a hose team, fighting to control a raging fire hose with several other men, when one of the big bombs went off. After the blast, there might be one man left, the rest of the hose team on either side of him obliterated by the explosion. That man forever wondered why.

For the aviators on the flight deck, their location when the fire started played a large role in whether or not they survived. The three pilots who died in the fire were all to the rear of McCain's plane, where the fire started, their planes caught up in the conflagration as burning fuel spread to the rear of the ship. Their planes were equipped with ejection seats that could fire while the plane was sitting still, but apparently none of the trapped pilots tried that escape option. Ejecting from a plane is always a last resort, extremely violent and risky, and the *Forrestal*'s situation introduced new hazards that made ejecting even less desirable. The pilot could have floated down right into the fire, and landing out in the water was never a good idea. And why eject if you could just jump out of the plane or wait mere seconds for the firefighters to rescue you? In the end, it became clear that the aviators who made it out of their planes safely were the ones who scrambled out as soon as they saw the fire; even a slight hesitation might have cost some pilots their lives. Those who survived wondered for years if the dead aviators might have been spared by a quick decision to eject, but they also understood why they decided against it.

For most of the sailors, however, there was no accounting for who survived and who didn't. Men tried to reason out the circumstances, certain that there must be a sensible explanation to something so important, but often the answer was nothing more than the capriciousness of a bomb fragment flying this way instead of that way. Over time, odd anecdotes appeared from the tragedy, some merely curious and some more poignant. The crew did not learn for a long time that a father and his own stepson had both died on the *Forrestal* that day. Two brothers were on board as well, one caught up in the blaze on the flight deck and the other fighting his way through the crowd belowdecks to get to him. One brother died. (Though the navy has avoided assigning family members to the same ship since World War II, exceptions were granted if the family requested it and the ship was not thought to be in danger of enemy attack.) They also learned of wives who had been coping with the absence of husbands while they were pregnant, only to receive the horrible news that their children would be fatherless. At least one wife miscarried when she was told her husband had died on the *Forrestal*.

In the days following the accident, while sitting around the table at chow time or in their quarters playing cards at night, the men of *Forrestal* swapped stories about the odd things they felt and saw during the fires. One aviator told his buddies about how he had lost his navy-issued survival knife while escaping the fire on the flight deck. The knife was a specialized piece of equipment for use if the aviator was shot down on a mission, and under most circumstances he could expect a serious reprimand for losing it. Even in the heat of the moment, he feared that reprimand so much that it momentarily outweighed his fear of the fire. He told the story to his buddies and they laughed at the absurdity of it all, but many of them understood because they, too, had seen the strange ways the human mind works in such a crisis.

Not everyone showed the stress. Even for those who managed to cope with what they had seen and experienced, their first weeks back home were rough. Young men tend not to acknowledge that they're hurting inside and they can be remarkably successful at hiding the pain even from their loved ones. But these men and their families found that sometimes the demons would reveal themselves at the most unexpected times.

Gary Pritchard, the sailor who was asleep in his bunk when the explosions started, and ran to the flight deck to help with the wounded, managed to shove aside most of what he had seen, repeatedly assuring his wife and family that he was okay, and offering little explanation of what happened to him. His wife sensed that he didn't want to tell her everything, at least not yet, so she didn't press him. Besides, he seemed to be dealing with it pretty well.

Soon after Pritchard returned to Norfolk, his family threw him a welcome-home party, more of a celebration than he expected, but he knew why. His family wasn't just glad he was home, they were relieved he was alive. Pritchard welcomed the party and had a good time seeing so many relatives and friends, especially because he had expected to be away from them for much longer. For most of the evening everyone enjoyed the food and drink, and no one bothered Pritchard with questions about what happened. But then as the evening wore on and many of the guests had left, the setting became a little more intimate with just Pritchard, his wife, and a handful of close relatives. As they sat and talked, there was a pause in the conversation, and Pritchard's sister-in-law finally asked what had been on everyone's mind all night long.

"Gary, what really happened out there?"

That was pretty much the last thing Pritchard remembered for a while. The next thing he knew, he felt like he was snapping out of a trance. A lot of time had passed and everyone around him was crying. He had no idea what he had been saying, nor could he ever remember.

On the drive home, Pritchard and his wife sat silently for the longest time. Her eyes were still red from crying and he felt bad about making everyone so sad. Finally, Pritchard couldn't resist asking.

"Honey, what did I say?" he asked quietly.

"You did all right, Gary," she replied, with a squeeze of his hand. "You're okay."

Pritchard didn't know exactly what that meant, but his wife wouldn't say anything more. He kept thinking about the tears and the look on everyone's faces, and before he arrived home, Pritchard decided that he should never answer that question again. It would be many, many years before he changed his mind. Like most others who survived the ordeal, he was always reluctant to share the worst memories with anyone, especially anyone he loved, because he preferred to carry that burden alone.

It didn't take long for some of the crew to get a feel for how the navy viewed the fire. The ship was out of commission for a while, so many of the crew were sent to various training programs, including firefighting. Ed Roberts had received no firefighting training before the Vietnam cruise, so he was sent soon after the carrier's return. He was sitting in a classroom one day, just one sailor among a couple dozen from various ships and divisions. The instructor started talking about how to fight fires and said, "Now this is what you're supposed to do, not like those idiots on the *Forrestal*."

Roberts's blood boiled and it was all he could do to sit quietly. *You motherfucker,* he thought.

Rear Admiral Forsyth Massey's investigation continued for months after the *Forrestal* was home. Massey and his team of investigators interviewed nearly every surviving crew member to determine just what happened that Saturday morning. The information they collected was voluminous, the final report eventually reaching seven thousand five hundred pages.

Even with a wealth of data and hard facts at their disposal, the investigators depended on the men on board to help them sort out just what happened. They interviewed anyone who might have even the smallest bit of information that might prove useful, and they meticulously dissected the procedures on the ship to determine how something as devastating as the mistaken firing of a rocket could have slipped through the navy's safety procedures. The big question for the investigators was whether the navy's safety procedures were somehow flawed or whether the crew had simply not followed the proper procedures. The answer was both, but in the big picture, the investigators may have been asking the wrong question.

As it became clear that the Zuni rocket had fired, the investigators focused on the many redundant safety procedures that should have prevented that accident. They interviewed dozens of people involved in the arming procedures for the planes that day, as well as others not working that day, in an effort to determine what was standard procedure on the *Forrestal*. Much of the questioning involved the TER intervalometer pins that should have been left in the rocket firing device as a safety measure until the very last minute before the plane was launched on the catapult. The crew had a habit of removing them early as a way to speed the launching process, but the practice had never been officially approved. When it came time for the crew to explain their actions on the flight deck, more than a few sailors squirmed when asked about removing the pins. They were being questioned under oath by lawyers from the Judge Advocate General's office and by some of the navy's highest-ranking officers. Their answers had to be truthful or they risked criminal penalties and the end of their navy careers. But they also knew that telling the truth might get them in trouble for failing to follow safety procedures to the letter.

Some of the crew who worked on the catapult teams reported that sometimes planes came to the catapults with the TER intervalometer pins already removed, but other planes had them still in place as required by the safety regulations. After many crew members were interviewed, the investigators could see that there had been no official change in the policy involving TER pins, but some of the crew had decided to take a shortcut. One crewman, nineteen-year-old Andrew Sappe, was especially helpful in explaining the circumstances of the TER pins. On the day of the fire, he was working on the forward catapults, responsible for the final arming of the rockets and missiles just before the plane was launched. Among other last-minute adjustments, Sappe was supposed to remove the TER pins to make the rockets fully armed.

Sappe spent an hour being deposed by a naval lawyer on the trip home to Norfolk, resulting in his official written statement to the board. In that statement, Sappe said he did not know what the policy was for removing TER pins.

In August he sat in front of a board of investigation and was advised of his rights not to incriminate himself. Then Sappe changed his story somewhat and said he now understood that the TER pins were supposed to be in place when the plane reached him. He told the investigators that he sometimes found the TER pins had already been removed, but he did not always report the missing pins to superiors because he had heard that some aviation crews preferred removing them early. The investigators insisted that Sappe be specific about who had said it was okay to remove the pins early.

"I don't think anyone said directly that we should take them out," he explained. "This was just a thought, just casual talk, and I didn't say anyone said we should actually take them out. This was just two sides of the story I've heard—why should we leave them in and why should you take them out."

Admiral Massey himself addressed the young sailor with a follow-up. "Why were you so impressed with the pins?" he asked Sappe.

"I think it's safer. It *is* safer. That's what it is for."

"Then it would seem to me that anyone that would advocate pulling it out would be unique. He would be unusual, wouldn't he?" Massey asked.

"Not actually," Sappe replied. "It depends on how your system was set up."

"There are a lot of people that feel that way, is that what you are trying to say?"

"There are some people."

"You can't remember anyone who was for outs?"

"No, sir. Not by name. No one actually said out."

"What did they want to do with them?" Massey asked.

"We were discussing both sides of the story. Nobody said they actually wanted them out."

Massey was losing patience with the sailor's equivocation. "Well, what *did* they want? Halfway in or what?"

Sappe felt the pressure and thought for a moment before answering.

"They wanted them in all the way like they were supposed to be."

Another investigator then asked Sappe who had recommended following the navy procedure and leaving the pins in.

"I guess all the senior petty officers wanted them in," Sappe said. "Anyone that knew anything about ordnance I think would want them in."

Sappe went on to explain that, in actual practice on the *Forrestal,* he saw differences between the way aviation groups armed their planes. The group known as VF-11, Sappe's own squadron, followed the safety procedure and left the pins in until the plane was on the catapult. But Sappe said that he often helped arm planes from the VF-74 squadron, and it was common for those pins to be missing.

"Are you saying, then, that you thought it was VF-74's practice, policy, to take them out?"

"Yes, sir. Well, I couldn't actually say, but that's what it seemed to me from the majority of planes that had no intervalometer pins."

Sappe then told the investigators he remembered one time in which a VF-74 plane had come to the catapult with the pin in place on one side of the aircraft and missing on the other side. When questioned on whether he had always reported the missing pins, Sappe said he hadn't, even though he was fully aware of the rule requiring them and even the purpose they served. He just assumed that VF-74 had their own system and he shouldn't interfere. The investigators noted that a key person in the arming of rockets was confused about what was allowed and what he should do when procedures were not followed.

Others in the system also testified to the same circumstances, and the board flatly accused some crew members of lying to the board when they tried to say there was no habit of removing pins early. In some cases, the safety officers who had been looking the other way when pins were removed early wanted to cover themselves. One safety officer, the last man responsible for ensuring the safety of the arming system, tried to explain away a subordinate's charge that he was ignored when he reported missing TER pins. The subordinate had reported missing pins by holding up the number of pins he had removed from a plane and using hand signals to indicate that some were missing. The safety officer responded by shrugging his shoulders as if to say he didn't care. When the board asked the safety officer for an explanation, he produced an elaborate explanation about how the shoulder shrug actually was a special signal he had developed with another member of the catapult crew and not a response to the missing pins. The board didn't buy it.

Having established that the *Forrestal* crew, or at least certain parts of its crew, were in the habit of removing TER pins back in the pack instead of waiting for the plane to reach the catapult, the board then turned its attention to the pigtail connectors. Even with the TER pins removed, the rocket still should have been safe from accidental firing if the pigtail cables were not plugged in. And navy regulations required that the pigtails be left unplugged until the plane was on the catapult.

This problem was a little easier for the board to

figure out because the deviation from procedure actually had been documented. The board reviewed the records of the Weapons Coordination Board, made up of ordnance experts and other representatives from the aviation groups, which had met on June 29, 1967, just before the *Forrestal* reached Yankee Station. In that meeting, the ordnance experts reviewed some navy regulations that pertained to the safe handling of bombs, missiles, and rockets, with the intention of relating what they considered "ideal" handling to the real-world requirements of a combat situation. The weapons board determined that some requirements for handling weapons in a noncombat situation were impractical in the fast-paced demands of bombing runs on Yankee Station, so they decided to officially circumvent some specific navy requirements. Even so, the *Forrestal* crew was not running wild; as the first East Coast carrier to arrive in Vietnam, they had been advised by the West Coast carriers that some "normal" safety requirements had to be altered for combat. The other carrier crews suggested plugging in the rocket pigtails while the planes were still bunched up back in the pack, instead of waiting until they reached the catapult.

After considering the time demands when launching aircraft and the possible safety risks, the ship's Weapons Coordination Board officially determined that the crew should be allowed to deviate from navy regulations: "Allow ordnance personnel to connect pigtails 'in the pack,' prior to taxi, leaving only safety pin removal on the cat."

The weapons board clearly saw the TER safety pins as their backup, the other safety measure that would still ensure the rocket could not fire until it was on the catapult. To underscore the point, the weapons board stressed in its report that if the pigtails were to be plugged in early, "Safety pin *will not* be removed prior to aircraft being positioned on the catapult."

In hindsight, the conflict was clear. Admiral Massey and the rest of the investigations board could see that there was a terrible convergence. An official change in safety procedures collided with an unofficial change in safety procedures. In addition to that major conflict, the board's investigation determined that the *Forrestal* crew had violated several other safety procedures. Some, such as failing to have the pilot place his hands in view while crew performed certain tasks on the rockets, appeared not to be a cause of the fire but still were safety risks. Others, such as plugging in the pigtails and conducting stray voltage checks before the plane switched to internal power, were considered a direct cause of the rocket launch. The investigation revealed that the rocket had been *able* to fire because the pigtails had been plugged in and the TER pins had been removed. But it *did* fire because a freak surge of electricity jumped through the plane's system at the moment the pilot switched from the outside electrical generator to the plane's internal power system. The voltage surged through five sequential safety devices designed to prevent just such a stray charge from reaching the rockets.

The strange chain of events could not have happened without just one of the sequential causes. All of the causes had to come together at the same time, in the right order, on one plane, to make the Zuni rocket fire.

Now the board knew why the Zuni rocket fired and started the fire. But they still didn't know why that fire killed 134 men.

One of the last steps for the board investigating the *Forrestal* fire was to hear from Captain Beling. He had not been involved in the investigation by the board other than to make available his men and any information he might have at his disposal. He was, after all, one of the chief witnesses to the fire and potentially to blame for whatever failings the board might find. When Beling was finally called to testify, he knew that his career was on the line. He had no way of knowing what the board's findings ultimately would be, but he realized that this was his chance to address whatever problems may have occurred. Accordingly, he prepared a lengthy statement to read to the board before they questioned him.

The room was heavy with anticipation before Beling entered. The board already had some evidence that there had been problems in procedure, and the incident itself was one of the most dramatic that anyone in the navy could remember for many years. When Captain Beling walked briskly to the table in front of the board members, everyone knew that what he said might determine his future.

Beling never showed that he felt the pressure. He maintained his composure from the start and all the way through, addressing the board in a firm voice and never sounding defensive or angry. With the courtly manner that had become his trademark, Beling began his address to the board by reviewing some facts related to how he came to be in command of *Forrestal*, and then how the ship arrived at Yankee Station. The board members and others in attendance listened quietly, their ears perking up when they heard Beling approach the topics that most interested them.

"I have always had a deep respect for the destructive powers of modern ordnance—even in small quantities," Beling said. "Visualizing last summer the potential for disaster inherent in the pattern of operations in Southeast Asia with bomb assembly on the mess decks and bomb farms on the hangar and flight decks, I had extensive discussions with the weapons officer and others searching for safer operating patterns and procedures. The fire on *Oriskany* served as a concrete and shocking example that made it easy to create and maintain a climate of respect for ordnance and of willing adherence to safety regulations."

Beling went on to say that some standard procedures had been altered in anticipation of combat, and he pointed out that the navy had approved those changes in the ship's Operational Readiness Inspection (ORI) before she sailed for Vietnam. But he specifically denied that he had approved any significant changes thereafter.

"It was recognized that in Southeast Asia it would be necessary to vary somewhat from peacetime Atlantic Fleet training procedures. The policy was enunciated to the executive officer, air-wing commander, weapons officer, operations officer, air-wing ordnance officer, and to other key officers that safety was primary. These officers were instructed that variations from peacetime ordnance procedures were to be made only where essential on a case-by-case basis; that current WESTPAC [Western Pacific Fleet] procedures could be used as guides but that they must be upgraded for safety in every respect possible.

"These procedures were discussed with the ORI inspectors by opposite numbers whenever controversy or any question of safety arose. No subsequent relaxation of any aspect of safety ever was authorized by me, either specifically or by implication.

"With reference to the Zuni rocket, which surely has a special role in the matter under investigation, I am certain that the arming procedures validated on the ORI were more conservative, and safer, than those practiced generally on Yankee Station."

In other words, Beling was saying that the *Forrestal* had sailed for Vietnam with a safe policy on arming the Zuni rockets. He did not approve any change in that policy, even if others on board had.

Beling then turned his attention to how the crew had responded to the fire. "Fire prevention, firefighting, and damage control have received heavy emphasis during my tenure in *Forrestal*," he told the board. He pointed out that during the ship's forty weeks of overhaul before she went to Vietnam, there had been sixty-two fires on board, about one fire every five days. (Most of the fires were related to construction work on board.) With pride, he noted that every fire had been extinguished so quickly by the crew that the Norfolk Naval Shipyard's fire department never had a chance to respond. In the navy's major inspection of the ship just before she went to Vietnam, her crew was graded "outstanding" in fighting flight-deck fires. Beling made reference to previous testimony that 1,332 of the crew had undergone firefighting training in the year prior to the Vietnam journey, and then with a note of annoyance in his voice, he explained that he would have trained even more of his crew before going to Vietnam if the navy had let him. The firefighting schools were all booked up.

"Incidentally, my recent request for one hundred quotas on return to Norfolk and one hundred quotas per week thereafter had to be turned down because of present commitments of the firefighting schools," Beling said. He paused to let the board realize what that meant. Even after nearly losing his carrier to a major fire, he still couldn't get his men in the firefighting schools.

Beling was trying to show the board that he did not blindly sail the *Forrestal* into disaster. He knew the risks the ship would face from a high-tempo combat operation, and he had done everything he could to prepare. Beling knew that he had gone out of his way to prepare the *Forrestal* and her men, taking more steps than some captains would have. He hated to sit in front of the board and outline every little thing he did, because it felt too much like a blend of bragging and defensiveness. Neither came naturally to him.

But Beling also was a pragmatic man, a career naval officer who knew exactly why he was sitting there. He had been at the helm of a high-profile warship when disaster struck. If he didn't defend himself vigorously, the board could be expected to put the responsibility at Beling's feet. Without evidence to the contrary, that outcome would be almost obligatory.

Beling went on to describe a host of other precautions he had taken against fire and other accidents on board, noting in particular that he had used the *Oriskany* fire as a teaching opportunity for his crew. He explained that the *Forrestal* had changed some procedures relating to the storage of magnesium flares, for instance, and he showed the board the information on the *Oriskany* fire that he distributed to his crew. Beling also offered proof that he had spent $189,472 in discretionary funds on additional firefighting, medical, and damage-control gear that the ship was not required to have.

The reference to educating the crew about the *Oriskany* fire got Admiral Massey's attention. He soon asked Beling about it.

"You mentioned that you published to all hands a tract of some kind that came from the *Oriskany* fire. I would like to get on the record what that was, where you obtained it, and if it was part of the official board of investigation of the *Oriskany* fire."

Beling welcomed the question. He explained that, no, the article was not a product of the *Oriskany* investigation, and in fact, he had never been provided any official report on the *Oriskany* fire or informed of any lessons learned in that incident. He had sought some sort of report that outlined the seriousness of the fire for his crew and suggested improvements, but the navy had not provided any such materials.

"The document to which I refer, and which was

only an isolated example of the efforts made on this ship to instill an awareness of the dangers of fire into the crew, was taken from *Reader's Digest*," Beling explained. "We wrote to *Reader's Digest* and requested reprints, some three thousand, and offered to pay for them. They said they couldn't provide them because it came from some other publication, and they had used a condensation. Accordingly, we reprinted it on our own and I believe informed them that we had done so. I made sure that every single man had a copy of it."

Admiral Massey was noticeably annoyed by what he was hearing. He took a deep breath and responded, speaking more to the other board members than to Beling.

"Well, it seems to me that for years we have been following this kind of routine where a board of this kind spends a number of weeks intensively looking at accidents of one kind or another, and somehow the system just never provides that the result of the board's work gets to the people that need to know it," he said. "And just for the record, I think this is one of our navy-wide weaknesses that must be corrected. For example, you had to go to the *Reader's Digest* to find out what's happening to carriers, carrier fires today! It just seems to me that is a pretty serious indictment of our system, that after six weeks possibly with a board of officers to determine all these facts, we have to go to a civilian writer to get it."

Beling agreed completely, but he was glad that he had led Massey into stating the absurdity of the situation instead of having to do it himself.

Continuing with his statement, Beling conceded to the board that, based on the evidence presented to it in the previous month, "a decision was made at a low level in VF-11 to shortcut approved procedures." Even though he repeatedly made clear that the Weapons Coordination Board had not sought his approval for the early plug-in of rocket pigtails, Beling told the board he didn't think that was the real cause of the rocket firing. The real cause, he said, was that the crew plugged in the rocket pigtails while the plane was still on external power.

"In my personal opinion, the rocket fired when the pilot of F4B number one-ten moved his generator switches from the external to the internal positions," Beling explained. "If this is in fact correct, it is tragic that squadron personnel were unable to apply enough common sense to conclude that stray voltage checks should be made and pigtails plugged in while on *internal power*. It is at least equally tragic that there does not seem be a recognition in any applicable publication of the wisdom of such an elementary precaution."

But Beling also made an important follow-up point. Though he was critical of how his own crew had made such a serious error, he insisted that the error could not have been overlooked for long. He pointed out that of the 486 aircraft the *Forrestal* launched on Yankee Station, only three were VF-11 planes carrying rockets. That gave the supervisory crew little opportunity to spot the problem.

"It is my carefully considered opinion that had normal Yankee Station operations continued, supervisory authority above the level of squadron commander would have detected these violations soon," Beling said. "I can assure positively that they would have been stopped as soon as detected."

Beling knew the board needed to hear that. It was one thing for the crew to make an error. It was quite another if Beling's command structure was so flawed that supervisors could not detect the problem quickly and take the appropriate action.

Not content to blame his own crew for failing to follow safe procedures in arming the rockets, Beling went on to tell the board that he had serious misgivings about the rocket-arming system itself. Drawing on his MIT education in physics and aeronautical engineering, he provided the board with his own analysis of the circuits and safety devices of the LAU 10 device that fires Zuni rockets, saying he had concluded that the system was fundamentally flawed and overly sensitive to human error. Even if proper procedures had been followed, Beling said, "similar discharge of a Zuni rocket would have been inevitable."

"It is evident that *Forrestal*'s ordnance personnel never had a safe system to work with and never had the technical information needed to design prudent, sailor-proof rocket-loading and -arming procedures. If *Forrestal* were still on Yankee Station, I would not permit any use of the LAU 10 with my present knowledge."

After the lengthy discussion of the rocket firing, Beling moved on to the question of how the sailors fought the fire. He cited information already presented to the board regarding how quickly the crew responded with fire hoses and fog foam, and he emphasized the extremely short interval between the start of the fire and the first bomb blast that killed so many firefighters and others on the flight deck. In his statement to the board, his answers to the follow-up questions, and indeed throughout the entire investigatory process, this was the only point where Beling ever officially addressed the issue of the old, decaying bombs that the navy had sent to his ship. And even then, he referred to them only in an indirect sense by citing the short cook-off time before the first thousand-pound bomb exploded. The explosion of the first bomb after an astonishingly fast one minute and thirty-four seconds in the fire turned a crisis into a catastrophe.

"The diagram shows that a massive effort to control the fire was under way and that hoses from the starboard catwalk and forward were surrounding it," Beling said. "About one additional minute would have been required to bring enough hoses into action to affect the fire and they would have been ideally placed to contain it. I feel, therefore, that had the bomb not exploded, significant headway could have been made against the fire by about three minutes after its inception. However, I consider it utterly beyond the bounds of possibility that the fire could have been suppressed in ninety-four seconds by *any* group of men with the equipment available."

Beling paused before moving on to his closing comments. He had said what he wanted to say, and he did so without directly accusing the navy of killing those 134 men by sending him faulty ordnance. But he wondered if the message had gotten across to the board.

We only needed three minutes. Just three god-

damn minutes and we could have controlled that fire.

Beling took a moment for a sip of water and then proceeded to his closing. It was not just a perfunctory, polite end to his statement. He meant it, and it was the first time in his twenty-minute-long statement that he felt a bit of emotion welling into his voice. His own career was on the line, but at this moment, he was thinking about his men. While everyone was listening, he was going to make damn sure they got the credit they deserved.

"After an intense effort in the fields of material and training, *Forrestal* deployed to Southeast Asia well prepared to do her job. She had made a promising beginning on Yankee Station when a deeply tragic accident occurred. The cause was a combination of faulty rocket-safety devices and inadequate technical documentation of rocket-arming procedures. The quantity of high explosives detonated on board exceeded that in any marine disaster since World War Two."

Beling put down his prepared comments and finished from memory. He wanted to look the board members in the eyes.

"The crew responded with consummate skill and bravery. They saved their ship in a classic demonstration of damage control, so minimizing the injury that *Forrestal* can steam at more than thirty-two knots and retains her ability to launch and land aircraft.

"The men of *Forrestal* return to home port for a full repair looking to the future instead of the past. My pride in their behavior is so immense that I never will have the words to express it adequately."

Chapter *16*

ICELAND

After the board finished its investigation, Beling went back to his temporary assignment at the Pentagon to await the conclusion. Soon after the *Forrestal* returned to the States, the navy had assigned Beling to work in the office of Admiral Thomas Moorer, the chief of naval operations. Moorer was the top man in the navy, and he knew Beling well from the times their long navy careers had intersected. When Beling returned home with a ship in need of long repairs and needing something to do in the meantime, Moorer saw to it that Beling was given a desk job in the Pentagon, working for him. At any other time, Beling would have hated such an assignment. But right after returning unexpectedly from Vietnam and during the investigation, Beling knew that the assignment was a vote of confidence from Moorer. So did everyone else.

Weeks after being interviewed for the investigation, Beling was working in his fifth-floor office at the Pentagon when he got word that the board had found no individual at fault for the fire and the subsequent deaths. An aide to the admiral visited Beling one day to let him know that the report should be on the admiral's desk soon, and Beling could expect to be exonerated. Beling was relieved, but he never showed it to anyone. It just wouldn't be proper for the captain of a ship to rejoice at being let off the hook for such a disaster. Beling never thought he was at fault, but he nevertheless felt a terrible loss for the men under his command.

This is a good conclusion, Beling thought. *Maybe they figured out what the hell happened out there and can put a stop to that ever happening again.*

And Beling also felt a small sense of satisfaction that his testimony to the board had made a difference.

I guess my message did get through. And I didn't have to make a big fuss about it.

Though he would never forget the loss on the *Forrestal,* Beling was eager to put the investigation behind him and get on with his career. Just two days after the *Forrestal* sailed for Vietnam, Beling had received word that in the next year or so he would be promoted to rear admiral. That promotion was still on schedule. He had plenty more to do in the navy, and working at this desk was not in his plans for much longer.

The seventy-five-hundred-page report by the board of investigation found numerous faults that led to the accidental rocket firing and the subsequent fire on the *Forrestal,* but ultimately the board concluded that no individual could be held responsible. The report broke the incident down into tiny parts, meticulously describing what happened and critiquing the action of the crew.

The board concluded that the fire "was caused by the accidental firing of one Zuni rocket," which then struck John McCain's plane, "rupturing its fuel tank, igniting the fuel, and initiating the fire." The report went on to say that "poor and outdated doctrinal and technical documentation of ordnance and aircraft equipment and procedures, evident at all levels of command, was a contributing cause of the accidental rocket firing."

But most important for those whose careers were on the line, including Beling, the board concluded that "no improper acts of commission or omission by personnel embarked on *Forrestal* directly or indirectly contributed to the inadvertent firing of the Zuni rocket." In other words, the bottom line for the board was that no one should be held individually responsible for the disaster.

The board offered many other useful conclusions, addressing the question of rocket pigtails and TER pins at length. After closely studying how the use of rocket pigtails and TER pins affected the accident, the board concluded that the deviation from the rule for plugging in pigtails should have been forwarded to Captain Beling for his approval, but it was not. Even so, the board said such a deviation should have been approved by a navy official higher than Beling. The board went on to say that some of the ordnancemen responsible for arming planes on the flight were "generally competent as individuals but were poorly organized and instructed."

But also, the board gave the crew a break by saying that "at least part of the poor organization and procedures mentioned above, and the failure to uncover them, can be attributed to the short period during which the squadron had been operating on Yankee Station." The board also acknowledged that "the fire could not have been extinguished prior to the explosion of major ordnance (ninety-four seconds after initiation of the fire) regardless of the aggressiveness, readiness, response and expertise of personnel and readiness of equipment." The report went on to say that "the design and operating procedures of fire fighting equipment currently available in attack carriers is totally inadequate to the needs generated by modern combat operations and the concentrations of very large quantities of ordnance and fuel on jet aircraft."

The detailed investigation also led the board to recommend a great number of improvements in carrier operation, from minor procedural and equipment improvements to wholesale revisions. The investigators praised some actions taken by the *Forrestal* crew, such as the decision to cut holes in the flight deck so they could pour water into burning compartments, but they criticized the men for strategic errors in fighting the fire and a general sense of disorganization in some areas. Many of those faults were traced to a basic deficiency in training provided by the navy, plus the horrendous scope of the fire.

"Current fire fighting exercises do not provide

adequate training for the type and scope of fire experienced by *Forrestal* 29 July," the board said.

There was very little mention of the faulty ammunition delivered the night before the fire, with the report detailing the ammunition taken on board but making no mention of it being old, faulty, or unstable. The report noted the quick cook-off time for the bombs, but did not point to that as the primary reason the *Forrestal* lost 134 men. Some navy officials familiar with the facts were realizing that the ship might have faced a much smaller crisis without the old bombs on board, but the official navy report glossed over that fact. The ship still would have suffered the accidental firing of the rocket and a bad fire, but some observers thought that fire could have been contained if not for the bombs blowing up so much sooner than expected. Beling knew that to be the case.

But the official navy report makes no mention of that alternative scenario and devotes scant space to the issue of short cook-off times, concluding only that "cook-off times of ordnance stores in use were not available to *Forrestal* and that considerable injury and loss of life can be attributed to the cook-off of installed ordnance stores at a time earlier than expected." So in that brief statement the board acknowledged that the short cook-off times were the real reason 134 men died, but took that conclusion no further.

There were no recommendations for preventing such a disaster in the future from old and faulty ordnance, and no indication that the navy should investigate the matter further. (The board did recommend that *normal* cook-off times for ordnance be posted at firefighting stations and on the ordnance itself, and it recommended that procedures be developed to rapidly cool ordnance in a fire.)

But even if the board didn't seem eager to hold the navy accountable for the old bombs, at least it did not make Beling a scapegoat for the disaster. The board noted that Beling had demonstrated a personal interest in the training of his crew and the ship's readiness for a fire disaster, concluding that "no blame attaches to Captain Beling in connection with the fire that occurred in *Forrestal* on 29 July 1967."

Instead, the board cited inadequate training for carrier crews and said "the deaths and injuries resulting from the fire aboard *Forrestal* on 29 July 1967 were caused by the negligence and inefficiency of the Headquarters, Naval Air Systems Command."

At the end of the report, the board listed its recommendations. After sixty-one recommendations covering a wide range of topics, recommendation number sixty-two appeared right over the signature of Admiral Massey: "That no disciplinary or administrative action be taken with regard to any persons attached to USS *Forrestal* (CVA-59) or Carrier Air Wing 17 as a result of the fire which occurred on board USS *Forrestal* on 29 July 1967."

Beling was itching to get on to his next assignment, probably the command of another prominent ship, since his experience and skills would be wasted if he remained with the *Forrestal* to oversee her repairs. But first, the Massey investigation had to make its way through the naval command structure and become the official word on the disaster. That would take some time, Beling knew, so he waited, impatient but at least content that he would be moving on to a real job soon.

The normal procedure was for the Massey report to be passed on from one high-ranking officer to the next for approval, until the top man signed off on it. The first officer to review the findings of the Massey investigation was three-star admiral Thomas Booth, commander of the naval air force for the Atlantic Fleet. Booth wrote a two-page response that disagreed with only one point, saying that a board recommendation for changing a test receptacle on the TER-7 rocket-arming device was not a good idea. He noted in his review that he had sent a copy of the board's findings and its "Lessons Learned" to all aircraft carriers in the Atlantic Fleet with instructions to require that it be read by all crew members now on board and all those assigned later.

Booth sent the report on to his superior, Admiral Ephraim Holmes, commander in chief of the Atlantic Fleet. A four-star admiral, Holmes was sort of the number-two man in the navy, one step below Moorer, who was the head of the entire U.S. Navy and Beling's current boss. At this step, Beling started to worry that there might be a problem.

Holmes was new to the job, having replaced Moorer when he moved up to become chief of naval operations. Moorer had been commander in chief of the Atlantic Fleet when the *Forrestal* sailed for Vietnam, but by the time she returned to the States, Moorer had moved up and Holmes was in that position. Beling did not know how Holmes would react to the report, but he did know one thing that gave him pause. Holmes was a black shoe.

In the highly stratified world of the navy, one of the distinctions among high-ranking officers was whether you were a "black shoe" or a "brown shoe." Deriving from the differences in their uniforms, black shoes were navy officers with no direct tie to flying, and brown shoes were aviators or former aviators like Beling. They all worked together on a carrier, of course, but their different backgrounds often led to good-natured rivalries, and sometimes more serious differences of opinion. Massey and Booth were brown shoes, so Beling wasn't surprised that they all saw the *Forrestal* fire from the same perspective. Holmes might be different. And he was brand-new to the job. Beling hoped that didn't mean he was eager to make a name for himself, but he wasn't worried much.

Unfortunately, Beling underestimated Holmes's reaction. Two months after Booth signed off on the report, Holmes issued his opinion on December 1, 1967. In an eight-page response, Holmes flatly refused some of the board's conclusions.

"The Commander in Chief, U.S. Atlantic Fleet, therefore, specifically does not concur in Opinion 115 of the Report of the Investigation wherein it is stated 'That the deaths and injuries resulting from the fire aboard the *Forrestal* on 29 July 1967 were not caused by the intent, fault, negligence, or inefficiency of any person or persons embarked in the *Forrestal*.' Further, the Commander in Chief, U.S. Atlantic Fleet, specifically does not concur in Opinion 4 of the Report which states 'That no improper acts of commission or omission by personnel embarked in *Forrestal* directly contributed to the inadvertent firing of the Zuni rocket from F-4 #110.' "

Specifically addressing Beling's role in the disaster, Holmes wrote that "the conduct of the Commanding Officer and the role played by him in connection with the tragic incident cannot be ignored." The admiral went on to criticize Beling for failing to properly supervise his crew, for failing to be aware of the procedural changes that led to the rocket firing, and for inadequately responding to the fire itself.

As for the Massey investigation's conclusion that the disaster should be blamed "solely on the negligence and inefficiency of the Headquarters, Naval Air Systems Command," Holmes refused to accept that criticism. There were deficiencies in training, he said, but the deaths on the *Forrestal* were caused by more than that. Individuals were responsible, Holmes said.

It didn't take long for word to reach Beling that Holmes had taken a hard-line approach to reviewing the Massey investigation. Beling was disappointed, but he had to let the scenario play out according to navy regulations. It wasn't long before Holmes sent a message to his superior, Moorer, requesting that Beling be transferred from the Pentagon to work under Holmes's command in Norfolk. Moorer's office approved the transfer as a routine matter, the admiral apparently unaware at that point why Holmes wanted Beling. But when he was told to catch a plane for a one-week assignment to

Holmes's office in Norfolk, Beling understood. Holmes could not reprimand Beling unless Beling was serving under his command.

So, like a schoolboy being called to the principal's office, Beling had to go through the motions of transferring to Holmes's office in Norfolk, knowing that he had no duties to perform there. He was to go there and wait for his punishment. It came in the form of a three-page letter delivered to him one day as he sat alone in a temporary office.

Though he had braced himself for the moment, Beling's heart sank as he read the accusations. Holmes cited "loose procedures" and said "these facts clearly establish that your exercise of command was not effective." Regarding the rocket-arming changes and the fact that Beling was not aware of them, the letter said, "Your nonaction in this regard amounted to a dereliction in the performance of your duties, which dereliction materially contributed to the circumstances resulting in the tragic incident aboard the *Forrestal*."

The letter specified that Beling "showed poor judgment" by deviating from established safety procedures, failing to advise superiors of such changes, failing to "devote sufficient time and supervision to administrative and organizational procedures which resulted in a general squadron laxity." And finally, the letter stated, "Your dereliction of duty as pointed out above and your lack of supervision contributed materially to the inadvertent firing of the Zuni rocket and permitted a situation to exist which resulted in the fire of 29 July 1967.

"Pursuant to references (b), (c), and (d), you are hereby reprimanded."

Beling's heart was pounding as he finished the letter, but not loud enough to drown out the words still ringing in his ears: "Your nonaction." "Dereliction of duty." "Poor judgment." "Laxity." "Failure." "Reprimand." Nothing could have hurt him more at that moment.

Beling was right back on the bridge of the *Forrestal,* watching his ship burn. He should have known he would never escape with his career intact. Men died on his watch, and the navy was saying it was his fault.

When Beling returned to his office in the Pentagon after his week in Norfolk, he was still wondering what to do with the reprimand. After the initial shock of the harsh criticism, Beling got angry. The reprimand had hurt so much because it stirred his deep feelings of regret and sorrow at the waste of young lives he had seen on the *Forrestal.* But when he thought about the facts at issue, Beling couldn't sit still and just take the reprimand. To do so would be a sign that he agreed with Holmes's conclusions, a tacit acknowledgment that he was in fact to blame for the deaths of those men. Beling knew he wasn't. He knew the real reason those men died, and all the talk about why the rocket fired missed the point. Sure there were problems that caused that rocket to fire. But that rocket didn't kill 134 men. They died because one-thousand-pound bombs started blowing up only a minute and thirty-four seconds into the fire.

As angry as the reprimand made Beling, he still wasn't sure what to do about it. He didn't want to accept it, but he also was reluctant to make a big fuss about it. Even aside from the personal pain it caused him, and that was no small matter, the reprimand was a major blow to his career. The reprimand would be a red flag every time a superior considered an assignment for him, and it would sully his reputation among the entire navy community. Beling winced at the reception he knew he would receive from his next ship's crew if he showed up dragging that reprimand behind him.

Beling had the right to contest the reprimand, but to do so would require a full-fledged court-martial, the military equivalent of a trial. He would have to take his case before a panel of military judges and, with the help of legal counsel, show why the reprimand was not justified. It was up to Beling—just accept the reprimand or go through a complete court-martial. He struggled with the choice.

I could probably win that court-martial. I know this damn reprimand isn't right, and I could make a good case that I wasn't responsible for what happened out there. But a court-martial would be so public. What would that do to the navy? I'd have to air the navy's dirty linen. I'm not sure I want to do that.

After weeks of soul-searching, Beling decided that he couldn't do it. He couldn't demand a court-martial and accuse the navy, publicly, of killing those men on the *Forrestal*. The idea of just rolling over and accepting the reprimand made him crazy with anger and indignation, but in the end he decided that he'd rather suffer that defeat alone than force the navy to admit to its failings. After all, he thought, the investigations had turned up a great many problems that contributed to the *Forrestal* fire and it appeared the navy was going to correct them. Wasn't that really the more important question? And the country was right in the middle of so much dissension and protests over the Vietnam War. The military was taking a lot of hits already from people who had no respect for the institution or the people serving. John Beling didn't want to add fuel to that fire.

No, it was better that he accept the reprimand, as much as it hurt him. That's what a good officer would do, he told himself. He knew it meant his career might never recover, but he was beginning to think that might be the case even if the reprimand were rescinded. His initial thoughts after the fire were starting to sound more and more on target. A captain just can't recover from an incident like the *Forrestal* fire.

Just as Beling was resigning himself to the reprimand and whatever the future might not hold for him, the final report and reprimand reached Admiral Moorer's desk in the Pentagon. Beling knew that it would be typical for the admiral to sign off on his subordinate's assessment and leave it at that. That would be the final word, since Moorer was the navy's top man. It turned out that Moorer had other things in mind.

Moorer was none too pleased to see that Beling had received a reprimand. Moorer's reading of the investigation's findings, from a fellow brown shoe's perspective, suggested to him that everyone underneath Holmes had read it the right way. But still, Moorer wanted good reasons for concluding what he thought was the case from the investigation—that despite the size of the tragedy, neither Beling nor anyone else on board was personally responsible. To help him make a final decision, Moorer decided to launch yet another investigation.

Moorer called in an old friend and colleague, James Russell, who had recently retired as vice chief of naval operations. Russell was familiar to Beling as well, a former carrier aviator whom Beling considered superbly qualified to assess the situation. Beling still hadn't said a word to Moorer to protest the reprimand, but he was thrilled to hear that Russell had been asked to make a final assessment. Russell came out of retirement, partly as a personal favor to Moorer, just for the investigation.

Months passed as Russell went through the Massey investigation and then went back with his own staff to investigate the incident further. Finally, Beling's phone rang as he was doing paperwork in his office. It was an aide to Moorer.

"Sir, Admiral Russell is going to brief the CNO on his investigation in about ten minutes. Would you like to attend?"

"Yes, I certainly would like to attend," Beling replied. He put the phone down and immediately left for Moorer's office.

When he reached Moorer's outer office, he found Russell and a group of aides already waiting. Beling introduced himself and soon Moorer stepped out. He and Russell greeted each other warmly, just as would be expected of old friends, and everyone went into Moorer's office. Beling sat quietly to the side, knowing that he was there only to observe. After some chitchat to get things settled, Moorer got down to business.

"Okay, Jim, so tell me, what the hell happened out there?"

Russell didn't say anything right away. Instead, he got up and walked closer to Moorer's desk, reaching in his jacket pocket. He pulled a brass slide switch from the TER rocket-arming system, one of several switches that were part of the redundant safety systems designed to keep the rocket from firing. The switch wasn't much bigger than a key.

"That's the culprit," Russell said, handing it to Moorer.

"That switch failed, and so did four other safety devices. That's why that rocket fired."

Moorer looked at the switch in his hand and thought for a minute.

"So you're saying this is the real cause? It was a device failure?"

Russell said yes, and that led him to begin discussing a wealth of technical detail he and his staff had discovered in their investigation. Much of it coincided with and supported the findings of the Massey investigation. The failure of the electrical safety devices didn't negate some of the other problems cited by Massey and Holmes, Russell said, but they were all secondary to the failure of the safety devices. The rocket pigtails, the TER safety pins, and all the other factors still mattered, Russell said, but the rocket fired because the electrical surge made its way through safety switches like that one. They were supposed to stop just such an accidental voltage surge.

"Bottom line, if you want to know what caused the fire, you're holding it."

Beling left with everyone else when the meeting was over, knowing that Moorer would contact him when he was ready. He felt a great sense of relief walking back to his office, confident that he had been exonerated by the highest office in the navy. Within a few days, Beling received a copy of a letter that Moorer had sent to Holmes. It directed Holmes to withdraw the reprimand.

Soon, Beling received notice that he was once again being transferred back to Norfolk for a one-week assignment under Holmes. This time, he was glad to go. As before, he went to Norfolk and sat in a temporary office waiting for a delivery. When the delivery came, it was a much shorter letter. After the usual jargon referencing the investigation and the previous letter of reprimand, the final line was what mattered.

"Your reprimand is hereby rescinded."

Beling finally felt that the investigations were behind him and he could move on. He continued working under Moorer in the Pentagon into 1968 and was assigned to a prestigious task force of military officers and civilian scientists developing sophisticated tools for monitoring activity in Southeast Asia. It was satisfying work, but Beling was still eager to get back to commanding ships. He knew he was in line to be assigned as commander of a carrier battle group in the Pacific. Not only would he be back on a carrier, but as a rear admiral, he would be superior to the captain. The navy takes a while to process appointments like that, so Beling was trying to be patient, knowing that the desk job wouldn't last forever. He was encouraged when the Bureau of Naval Personnel sent word to Beling that the assignment was imminent and he should start preparing for the move to San Diego. Finally, he thought, July 29, 1967, was about to end.

And then, another twist. Before Beling's assignment to the carrier group in San Diego could be finalized, Admiral Moorer's term of office ran out. Beling's good friend, the admiral who had watched out for him in such a difficult time, was to be replaced as chief of naval operations by Admiral Elmo Zumwalt, Jr. This was not good news. Zumwalt was not a former carrier man, like Beling and Moorer and Russellw. Zumwalt had earned his stripes on destroyers, and unfortunately, Beling had had a few run-ins with Zumwalt during his time at the Pentagon. Most of the problems came down to just fundamental differences in perspective because of their different backgrounds, but the end result was that Beling and his new boss didn't get along well.

But maybe it doesn't matter. I'll be out of here any day now for San Diego.

Beling kept plugging away at his desk job, waiting for the final orders to report to San Diego. He was ready to go as soon as the paperwork came through.

Beling waited and waited, and the orders never came. Zumwalt offered no explanation. Beling inquired with more friendly contacts in the navy about why he wasn't being sent to San Diego yet, and one admiral with an aviation background wrote to Zumwalt to ask why Beling was still being held in the Pentagon. Zumwalt did not reply to the letter, but Beling soon received transfer orders.

Beling opened the orders as soon as they arrived. But they did not say San Diego. Instead, Zumwalt was transferring Beling from the Pentagon to a desk job in Iceland.

Iceland. Not only was Beling denied the prestigious command of a carrier battle group as he had been promised, but he was being sent to Iceland, to a desk job that any black-shoe navy officer with none of Beling's experience could handle. The message was clear, and Beling believed it had little to do with his personal disagreements with Zumwalt. No matter how many investigations cleared him, the navy wasn't going to let Beling off the hook for what happened on the *Forrestal*. He was being exiled.

And once again, Beling found himself on the bridge of the *Forrestal*, staring in disbelief as a raging fire killed young men under his command. For John Beling and so many more of the men of *Forrestal*, the fires would never end.

E PILOGUE

Beling did transfer to Iceland and ended his career there, never again commanding a ship. He retired as a rear admiral and is greatly admired by the men who served under him. The other sailors went on with their lives, many of them leaving the navy after just a few years. The ship itself underwent a massive rehaul and then entered service again, but she did not return to Vietnam. She was still one of the country's mightiest warships even after bigger and more advanced aircraft carriers were introduced. The *Forrestal* was on active duty until 1993, when the navy decommissioned her after thirty-eight years. In that time, she saw only four and a half days of war.

The navy maintains the *Forrestal* in a Rhode Island shipyard, the gray hulk sitting quietly in the water with no visitors and no crew, waiting as her veterans continue efforts to turn the ship into a museum. The 134 men who died on the *Forrestal* on July 29, 1967, are memorialized on panel 24E of the Vietnam Veterans Memorial in Washington, D.C. Close by at Arlington National Cemetery, there is a monument to those never recovered or identified after the disaster, just behind the Tomb of the Unknowns. The monument marks the burial site of twelve to fourteen bodies that could not be identified, listing eighteen men whose families were denied the small comfort of taking their loved one home.

A number of sailors aboard the *Forrestal* received medals and other accolades for their actions on July 29, 1967, but none of the injured received a Purple Heart. The navy determined that the injuries were not incurred in combat.

The *Forrestal* tragedy produced a great many improvements in naval firefighting and overall safety. To the navy's credit, the lessons learned caused a major reassessment of firefighting training, techniques, equipment, and fundamental ship design. As a result, many of today's advanced safety precautions in place on aircraft carriers throughout the world can be traced directly to the *Forrestal*. The ship led the way in technological advances when she was launched, and she continued to do so even after suffering the worst disaster in the U.S. Navy since World War II. The *Forrestal* fire led the navy to strengthen firefighting training for sailors, improve the dissemination of pertinent information to both officers and crew, reduce the amount of crew turnover a ship can endure before sailing on a long voyage, and implement a wide range of procedural and policy changes that lessen the risk of accidental rocket firings. Some of the changes were small but significant: all flight-deck crew are now required to wear long sleeves while working, no matter how hot the weather, because long sleeves can make a difference when a sailor is close to a fire. Emergency breathing apparatus was redesigned to make it faster and easier to use. On the whole, safety and fire safety in particular are a higher priority for the navy now than they were in 1967. Some of that improvement is simply the normal evolution of a complex organization, but the navy also remembers the *Forrestal* fire as the singular moment when all its weaknesses in that area were highlighted. The navy's firefighting school in Norfolk, Virginia, is named after Gerald Farrier, the chief who charged into the fire scene and waved off other crew members just before the first bomb exploded.

But some of the most significant changes are purely mechanical. When the navy investigated the fire, its leaders realized that it was completely inadequate to rely on sailors rushing to a major jet-fuel fire with hoses. Instead, they said, carriers needed a way to automatically flood the deck with water or firefighting foam, similar to the way a building's fire-sprinkler system can instantly flood a burning room. At that time, the investigators saw such a system as an ideal solution but acknowledged that it would be difficult to design and implement. Nevertheless, all modern carriers now incorporate a "wash down" system consisting of hundreds of recessed sprinkler heads in the flight deck, and the *Forrestal* was even retrofitted with the system years after the fire. On the bridge and in flight control, a panel of switches can instantly activate the wash-down system on the entire flight deck or just on selected portions. The nozzles send water or firefighting foam arcing in every direction, deluging a fire far more quickly than even the fastest fire-fighting team could put a hose on it. With the wash-down system on board, it is almost unthinkable that a fire could spread as quickly and as far as it did on the *Forrestal*.

Other improvements also were incorporated into new carriers and retrofitted to existing ships. Carriers now have small fire trucks parked on the flight deck, loaded with equipment and manned during all flight operations by silver-suited fire-fighters ready to spring into action. The trucks are designed not only to get the firefighting gear to the scene quickly, but also to bulldoze wreckage out of the way. The oxygen-generating plant, which threatened to blow the *Forrestal* sky-high and had to be drained by a small hose for more than an hour, is now installed on rails so that the crew can push the entire thing overboard if it threatens the ship in any way.

Though the navy deserves credit for acting on many of the lessons learned in the *Forrestal* fire, the role of the faulty ordnance is a glaring omission in every official account of the disaster. The navy investigations and the official navy history of the fire point to a number of shortcomings, both in the navy bureaucracy and on the ship itself, but there is never any mention of the significance played by the decision to deliver old, unsafe bombs to the ship the night before the fire. Even if some criticism of the crew is justified, a full accounting of the incident would show that the overriding cause for the disaster was the navy's decision to deliver faulty ordnance, prompted in turn by the White House's unreasonable demands to escalate the bombing in Vietnam. Instead, the American government has been content to let the men of *Forrestal* shoulder an undue burden, to let them bear the brunt of the blame by pointing out their inadequacies while refusing to acknowledge the much larger danger that it thrust upon them.

The navy's focus on why the rocket fired was useful in preventing a repeat of that accident, but it missed the point in regards to the overall disaster. Though the entire incident began with the inadvertent firing of a Zuni rocket, it is clear that the rocket firing alone would not have led to such a terrible loss of life. Without the faulty ordnance, the rocket firing likely would have been a serious accident, still causing a fuel spill and a fire, but the crew would have been able to extinguish the fire before it spread too far. Men still may have died in that situation, but the facts clearly show that the *Forrestal* lost 134 men because of the bomb explosions, not the original fire. The explosions killed dozens on the flight deck and below, disabled the ship's firefighting response, and opened up decks below to a blaze that should have been contained where it started.

The navy's own analysis of the explosions on the flight deck shows the significance of the faulty ordnance. There were sixteen one-thousand-pound bombs loaded on planes that morning, all of them the older type that so concerned the crew when they arrived the night before, carried two apiece on eight planes. All of the other bombs on planes that morning were the newer type. Nine major explosions occurred on the flight deck during the fire, and all nine came from six of the planes loaded with the old bombs. (One major explosion occurred in between a plane with an old bomb and a plane with a new bomb. It is likely that the second old bomb on the plane is the one that exploded there, rather than the other plane's new bomb.) Of the eight planes loaded with the old bombs, six had their bombs blow up at full strength, and that happened far sooner than anyone would have expected of normal ordnance. The other two were far forward of the fire and never burned.

But perhaps the most telling fact is this: *None* of the newer bombs exploded at anything near full strength, even though some of the planes holding them burned completely.

Thirty-three years after the fire, Captain Beling was willing to speak freely about the role of the faulty ordnance. Referring to the first thousand-pound bomb that exploded only one minute and thirty-four seconds into the fire, Beling said, "It was a World War Two bomb we were required to carry for economic reasons. It was ancient. It was thin-skinned and susceptible to early cook-off."

The tragedy of the *Forrestal* fire continues for many. As the years tore at them, some would not be able to accept that some tragic turn of events was only that, only a coincidence or twist of fate. Some on the *Forrestal* could not escape the guilt that convinced them they were somehow responsible for the death of another crew member—a close friend or a complete stranger. Others took no comfort in the reassurance by their crewmates, superiors, and families back home that someone else's death was not their fault. No matter how tenuous the link seemed to others, they convinced themselves that they bore responsibility. They had survived, but they would suffer for a long time.

Much of Gary Shaver's year after the fire would be a blur of narcotics, surgeries, different hospitals, and nearly unbearable hours alone with his memories and his pain. He would remember terrible smells, the maddening isolation as he lay there for day after day, and the odd moments that his mind chose to save as he drifted in and out of reality. At one point, Shaver was visited by two naval officers with a tape recorder. They explained that his pain medication was being stopped so they could interview him about the fire. He pleaded with them not to stop the medicine, but they insisted. The interview lasted only about fifteen minutes, but Shaver was out of his mind with pain by the end. He wanted so much to jump out of the bed and kick the living shit out of those officers, but the days when that was even a possibility were long gone. He realized later that they had been so insistent because they thought he was going to die soon.

It would take more than a year for Shaver to recover physically, and much to everyone's surprise, he managed to keep his left arm. The extensive injuries to his internal organs were repaired, eventually leaving Shaver with a fully functioning body. He would learn later that, though his body could recover, his mind could not.

Many of the men suffered severe mental stress in the coming years, some bad enough to be diagnosed with "post-traumatic stress disorder," a problem more often associated with the infantry who fought in the jungles of Vietnam. Shaver tried hard to put the horror behind him and for many years, he thought he had succeeded. But as he grew older, he started wondering if some of the demons controlling his life had been spawned on July 29, 1967. He became a police officer after leaving the navy, but he lost two relationships because of his drinking, before seeking help. At that point, he didn't yet understand the underlying cause. He knew he still had terrible memories of the explosions, the pain, the descent to hell, and the loss of his friends, but it took him a long time with PTSD specialists to make the connection between that and his drinking. Even after acknowledging he had an emotional disorder related to the fire, he has found no easy cure. Intensive therapy has helped, but Shaver still is left completely disabled by PTSD. For him, dealing with the aftermath of the *Forrestal* fire may have been more difficult because his terror lasted so long. Instead of just a moment, or even a day, Shaver lived in terror and excruciating pain for a year. More than thirty years later, he can't stop reliving his year of hell, and he can't get rid of the guilt he feels for switching places with Lonnie Hudson. Shaver has come a long way in dealing with his PTSD, but the fire forever altered his life. He readily acknowledges that without the therapy provided by the Veterans Administration, he probably would have killed himself long ago. His daily struggle is a reminder of how a traumatic incident can linger long after the fires are out.

Robert Whelpley, the nineteen-year-old left all alone in the corridor by himself, waiting for orders, never found out why the others had not shown up at his GQ station. He supposed they either were prevented from reaching it by fire damage, or became involved in firefighting efforts or rescues as they tried to get to the GQ station. The hours he spent at his GQ station without doing anything, and without knowing anything, left him shaken. It would take a long time to get over the fear of being left behind as the ship burned and sank.

But that fear is not what burdened Whelpley for decades. He carried another burden, one that gnaws in a way that fear cannot match. Though he was following orders, Whelpley wondered for years if he had done the right thing. He worried for many years that if only he had left his post sooner and looked for something useful to do, someone might not have died. Men died all around him as he followed orders and did nothing. *How could that be right?*

Most would agree that Whelpley did nothing wrong, but he has a hard time believing it.

Robert Shelton, the crew member who was supposed to be working in the port-aft steering compartment instead of his buddy, had trouble living with the terrible guilt he felt for surviving the fire. Nothing was particularly unusual about trading work shifts, but Shelton knew that if he had not done so, he would have been one of the three men trapped in port-aft steering, horribly injured and dying slowly as Merv Rowland talked to them from damage control. Shelton felt that James

Blaskis had died in his place, and not just another man, but *his friend*. The guilt weighed on him so heavily that within days of the fire he requested a transfer from the ship. Not surprisingly, he wasn't the first, and he was told that this was very unlikely unless he went directly to combat in Vietnam.

Shelton accepted the offer. He knew he was going from a relatively safe duty on a carrier, the next year or so tied to a pier in the United States, to being shot at in Vietnam. Within ten days, the navy transferred him to the most dangerous navy duty possible—a small gunboat that patrolled the riverways of Vietnam. This was known as "river rat" duty and it was extremely risky. He survived more than a year, even as his boat sank underneath him. Forever after he would think of it as a way of doing penance, taking some other young man's place the way another man had taken his.

Shelton still vividly remembers the two nightmares that preceded the fire, but thirty-five years later, the terrible images in the dreams are mixed with what he saw during the fire, so much that he can't be sure just how prophetic the nightmares actually were. He is inclined to think that the dreams were some sort of warning.

For years after the fire, Ed Roberts sometimes woke up at night consumed by a sense of doom, convinced that he was about to die. The feeling was so intense that he once got out of bed and wrote his will. Much of his lasting terror could be traced to an assignment he had on the trip back home after the fire. Roberts and his fellow blue shirts were brought to the flight deck one day and handed spoons. Then they were told that they had to clean out the "pad eyes," the little indentations all over the deck that held recessed metal crosses for attaching tie-down chains. The large debris had been cleared away by then, but the pad eyes had to be scooped out individually.

"If you find anything unusual, take it to the medical personnel," the petty officer said.

Roberts went to work with the other men, scooping out the fire debris from one pad eye and then moving on to the next. It was shrapnel, bits of melted plastic, glass, all sorts of things. And then Roberts scooped out something and held it in his hand for a moment. The realization hit him like a baseball bat. He was holding a piece of human flesh. It wasn't the first disturbing thing he'd seen the past few days, and it certainly wasn't the worst. But something about the moment got to him down deep. Ignoring his orders, he stood up and walked over to the deck edge and, with all his might, heaved the mass into the sea.

For the rest of his life, he thought of that moment as the eye of a needle. In his memories, he has to pass through that moment to get to any part of his life before that. July of 1967 seized many families in a similar way, forever changing them. The parents of Robert Zwerlein, who was caught up in the initial blaze and died on the hospital ship, never got over the loss of their Bobby. Years later, when Ruth Zwerlein thought she had learned to get through the day without sobbing, she would still find the sadness hidden in the most unlikely places. On an otherwise enjoyable trip to Disney World with her family, Ruth kept thinking she saw Bobby everywhere in the crowds. Every young man in the distance, every sailor, every face that had just a slight resemblance to her boy sent a jolt of recognition through her, a tiny second of joy followed by a deep sadness as she realized it was not her Bobby.

Merv Rowland, already a crusty old salt by the time of the fire, is still a much-beloved father figure to the *Forrestal* survivors. Eighty-three years old and a grandfather several times over, he regales anyone who will stand still with stories of his days on the sea, his gravelly voice bursting into laughter at regular intervals. But when the subject turns to July 29, 1967—and particularly the three men who died in the steering compartment while he talked to them—Rowland's eyes fill with tears and he sounds like a man who has lost his sons.

Many veterans still have difficulty talking about what they experienced and saw on the *Forrestal*. Some have only recently begun discussing their memories, and many of them report that it is therapeutic. The author noted that many of those interviewed for this book were willing to discuss their experiences more freely with a stranger than with their loved ones. On more than one occasion, veterans lowered their voices and checked to make sure that their wives or other loved ones were not listening.

Few people know the full story of what happened on the *Forrestal,* and why so many men died. Even those who were there that day often know the details only of their own experience. They and the relatives of those who died sometimes have heard only vague reports of "old bombs" but do not know how significant those bombs were. Some of those who know the real cause of the deaths are left uneasy, troubled by the idea that the *Forrestal* disaster was not just a terrible accident caused by an electrical glitch that no one could have foreseen. For Rocky Pratt, the aviator who witnessed the delivery of the bombs and the crew's concern over their safety, the conclusion was so troubling that it led him to leave the navy despite a family tradition of service. The ensuing years without a full accounting from the Pentagon have only compounded his disappointment.

Nevertheless, the men of *Forrestal* are unlikely to ever complain about the navy or the country in any meaningful way. If they know the full story, if they feel mistreated by the navy's compliance in allowing the crew to take more of the blame than they deserved, they aren't likely to say so except when they're having a beer with a trusted buddy. They're too proud to ask for recognition, and they love their country too much to stir up trouble. The 134 men who didn't have the opportunity to grow old probably would have felt the same way.

Killed on board
uss *Forrestal*
July 29, 1967

Marvin J. Adkins
Everett A. Allen
Gary J. Ardeneaux
Tony A. Barnett
Dennis M. Barton
Robert L. Bennett
Mark R. Bishop
James L. Blaskis
William V. Brindle
Bobby J. Brown
Jerry D. Byars
Francis J. Campeau
Jack M. Carlan
Daniel G. Cavazos
Ray A. Chatelain
Richard D. Clendenen
William D. Collins
Robert B. Cotton
James L. Crenshaw
Mario C. Crugnola, Jr.
Robert J. Davies
Thomas J. Dawson, Jr.
Jerold V. Despard
Edward R. Dorsey

Joseph G. Dugas
Paul A. Dupere
John S. Duplaga
Walter T. Eads
James A. Earick
John T. Edwards
Gerald W. Farrier
Kenneth L. Fasth
John J. Fiedler
Russell L. Fike
Harold Fontenot
Johnnie L. Frazier
Gerald G. Fredrickson
Herbert A. Frye
Ramon Garza
Robert E. Geller
Richard H. Gibson
Laurence J. Gilbert
William T. Gilroy
Larry E. Grace
Russell A. Grazier
Charles C. Gregory
William C. Hartgen
Robert L. Hasz

Richard A. Hatcher
William K. Hinckley, Jr.
Stephen L. Hock
Larry D. Holley
Calvin D. Howison
Philip L. Hudson
Julius B. Hughes
Donald N. Hugo
Ralph W. Jacobs
Donald W. Jedlicka
William B. Justin
Thomas M. Kane
Charles D. Kieser
Joseph Kosik III
Edward L. La Barr
Wade A. Lannom, Jr.
William Lee
Robert C. Leonberg
John T. Lilla
Arnold E. H. Lohse
Charles E. Long
William E. Lowe
Kenneth W. Lozier, Jr.
James S. MacVickar, Jr.
Ralph E. Manning, Jr.
Earle E. McAuliffe, Jr.
Brian D. McConahay
George C. McDonald
Frank C. McNelis, Jr.
William V. McQuaide
Allan R. Metz
George D. Miller
Edward A. Mindyas
Hubert H. Morgan, Jr.
Leroy Moser
James E. Neumeyer
Gary E. Newby
James E. Newkirk

Ronald R. Ogrinc
Thomas D. Ott II
Wayne H. Ott
Richard L. Owens
Richard T. Pinta
Raymond N. Plesh
John C. Pody
Ernest E. Polston
Douglas A. Post
Robert M. Priviech
John M. Pruner
Robert A. Rhuda
Charles R. Rich
Jerry P. Rodgers
Dale R. Ross
James M. Runnels
Harvey D. Scofield
Joseph C. Shartzer
William J. Shields
Richard M. Sietz
David W. Smith
Richard T. Smith
John F. Snow
John C. Spiess
Nelson E. Spitler
Johnny W. Spivey
Gerry L. Stark
Walter E. Steele
Wendell W. Stewart
Robert A. Stickler
Kenneth D. Strain
Robert H. Swain
Delton E. Terry
Norman A. Thomas
William F. Thompson
Richard J. Vallone
Robert J. Velasquez
Juan A. Velez

George E. Wall

Harold D. Watkins

Gregory L. Webb

Gerald A. Wehde

Judson A. Wells, Jr.

Richard L. Wescott

Edward J. Wessells

Fred D. White

Kerry D. Wisdom

Robert L. Zwerlein

USS *Forrestal* Flight deck

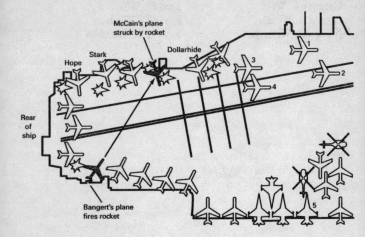

Explosion marks indicate where bombs exploded during the fire.

Planes 1-4 were about to take off. The rest were being armed and preparing to taxi forward to the catapult. Plane 5 was a tanker loaded with 28,000 lbs. of jet fuel.

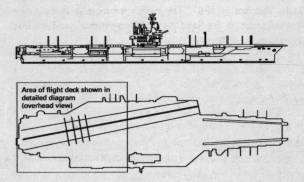

Area of flight deck shown in detailed diagram (overhead view)

NOTES

Chapter 1

Page 7 "Four hundred thousand ground troops." Robert McNamara, *In Retrospect* (New York: Vintage Books, 1995), p. 221.

Page 7 "targeting North Vietnamese supply lines." George C. Herring, ed., *The Pentagon Papers* (New York: McGraw-Hill, 1993), p. 132.

Chapter 2

Page 22 "ground targets within distance of her planes." The navy has a strict policy of neither confirming nor denying that nuclear weapons are on board certain vessels, but retired officers confirm that nuclear bombs were on board when the *Forrestal* went to Vietnam in 1967. The navy's subsequent investigation makes reference to the handling of "conventional (and nuclear) weapons aboard *Forrestal*."

Page 23 "calculated to be 2.5 million pounds." The design of the chain proved sound, and after the *Forrestal* was decommissioned in 1993, the chain was transferred to the *Harry S. Truman*, currently the newest and most sophisticated nuclear-powered aircraft carrier in the world.

Page 24 "$188.9 million." The price of a modern Nimitz-class nuclear aircraft carrier is about four billion dollars.

Page 25 "five-hundred-ton air-conditioning units." R. F.

Dempewolff, "Our Navy's Mightiest Carrier: USS *Forrestal*," *Popular Mechanics*, November 1954, p. 84.

Page 25   "make the *Forrestal* a 'happy ship.'" Ibid., p. 264.

Page 26   "to hold that record." In her thirty-eight-year career, the *Forrestal* continued to undergo design changes to keep her at the head of the pack in terms of usefulness and efficiency. In 1961, she entered the Norfolk Naval Shipyard to have the forward five-inch gun mounts removed when the navy decided that changing trends in warfare made them unnecessary on a carrier. The accompanying ships and the *Forrestal*'s own aircraft would provide much more defense than the five-inch guns, and besides, the heavy concussions from the guns caused too much disruption to flight operations. The five-inch guns to the rear remained on the ship as an extra measure of safety, but no one really expected to use them. The arresting gear, including the huge wires that are used to snag planes as they land, also was modified at that time. Originally designed with six wires, the configuration was changed to just four wires. An updated signal-light system to guide pilots was also installed at that point, replacing the earlier version.

Page 36   "follow in their footsteps." John McCain and Mark Salter, *Faith of My Fathers* (New York: Random House, 1999), pp. 118–152.

Chapter 4

Page 75   "beaten his flashlight." Dempewolff, p. 270.

Page 76   "falling overboard into the sea." On a modern carrier, everyone on the flight deck must wear a "float coat," a color-coded garment that looks like a long vest but actually is an important piece of survival equipment. The float coat is comfortable to wear even while working. It normally is flat and thin like a typical vest, but it can be inflated to act as a life preserver in the water, and it also carries some important gear to help in your retrieval if you go overboard: a dye pack to mark your location in the water, a whistle to signal for help, a flashlight that can be stuck to your helmet with Velcro, and reflective tape on the shoulders and back to make you more visible.

Page 77 "lose consciousness in thirty minutes." *Think Safe* (Washington, DC: United States Coast Guard, 1999), p. 14.

Page 78 "he was never recovered." William Jordan, "USS *Washington* BB56: Man Overboard!" http://home.flash.net/~hfwright/moverbrd.htm.

Chapter 5

Page 97 "hundreds of smaller incidents." Kit Bonner and Carolyn Bonner, *Great Naval Disasters: U.S. Naval Accidents in the 20th Century* (Osceola, WI: MBI Publishing, 1998), p. 5.

Page 98 "fire was at the top of the list." Largely as a result of what happened in 1967, the navy now takes fire safety aboard ships very seriously. Visitors to a carrier, whether civilian or military, are greeted by a safety officer who provides an immediate lesson on fire safety. Before their feet have been on the carrier for sixty seconds, they receive detailed instructions on how to use an emergency breathing apparatus during a fire, where to find one, and how to call for help in an emergency from anywhere on the ship.

Page 99 "Skyhawks on an attack just after midnight." Ibid., pp. 85–91.

Page 109 "They say it's the only way to get all the planes launched fast enough." Ironically, the navy had just produced a training film on board the *Forrestal* earlier in 1967 that specifically addressed flight-deck hazards, including the arming of planes. The film shows *Forrestal* sailors arming planes with rockets and bombs, noting that "most of these weapons have considerable firepower packed into a small space, and need only a tiny electric current to fire them." The film warns that "careful handling alone will not protect you from two prime hazards of arming: the presence of stray voltage and the unintended actuation of the weapons-system firing circuits. Avoid these dangers by professional adherence to ship and squadron safety rules when arming aircraft."

Chapter 6

Pages 112–113 "2,475 railroad cars, and 11,425 water craft." Ibid., p. 212.

Page 113   "assessed the war effort." United States Department of State, *Foreign Relations of the United States 1964–1968* (Washington, DC: United States Government Printing Office, 1998), vol. IV, p. 11.

Page 114   "send the execute order." Ibid.

Page 115   "sorties have been canceled." McNamara, p. 242.

Page 115   "knew the truth was different." http://www.pbs.org/wgbh/pages/frontline/shows/military/guys/smith.html.

Page 117   "provided ammunition." The description of the *Diamond Head* and its mission to deliver bombs to the *Forrestal* is based on an interview with Greg Strain, a sailor aboard the *Diamond Head* in 1967.

Page 125   "been manufactured in 1935." The navy's official report on the incident says those bombs were made in 1953, not 1935 as Rocky Pratt recalls. Pratt allows that he may be mistaken about the exact date he saw on the bomb shipment, but he says it was prior to his birth in 1940. He also suggests that a bomb made in 1953 and stored in the Philippine jungle still would have been dangerous by 1967.

Chapter 7

Page 138   "back to work that day." Official records from the *Forrestal* indicate that the man run over by the plane most likely survived the incident, although he suffered extensive injuries, including the loss of a foot. However, Gary Shaver was certain for the next thirty-four years that the man had died, and his guilt over the incident figured prominently in his post-traumatic stress disorder. Research for this book revealed the discrepancy between Shaver's memory and the records.

Page 172   "put this plane ACOP." *Situation Critical: The USS Forrestal* [videotape] (Arlington, VA: Henninger Media Development, 1997).

Chapter 8

Page 179   "One minute and thirty-four seconds." There is some discrepancy among sources as to the exact length of time before the first bomb exploded, usually one minute and twenty-eight seconds versus one minute and thirty-four seconds. The official navy investigation determined that the bomb exploded after one minute and thirty-four seconds.

Page 179 "high pressure and temperature." http://wseweb.ew.usna.edu/wse/academic/courses/es300/book/chapte 13.htm.

Page 182 "a headless body." Robert Timberg, *The Nightingale's Song* (New York: Touchstone, 1996), p. 98.

Page 187 "fireballs hopping and tumbling." Ibid.

Page 188 "felt particularly helpless." Associated Press, "Forrestal Crewmen Become Fireballs." *New York Times,* August 12, 1967, p. 1.

Page 194 "as the first bomb blast hit." *Manual of the Judge Advocate General: Basic Final Investigative Report Concerning the Fire on Board the USS Forrestal (CVA-59)* (Washington, DC: Department of the Navy, 1967). The navy's report concludes that the Zuni rocket fired at 10:51:21, then the first bomb exploded one minute and thirty-four seconds later, at 10:52:55, then general quarters was sounded five seconds later, at 10:53. It is likely that the time for general quarters was not recorded precisely because of the emergency. Most of the veterans remember that general quarters was sounded immediately before the first explosion, but some recall it sounding just after. All agree that the general-quarters alarm was sounded at almost the same time as the first blast.

Chapter 9

Page 214 "One of the most sensitive spots." *USS Forrestal* (Newport News, VA: Newport News Shipbuilding and Dry Dock Company, 1954). The oxygen-generating plant was another of the *Forrestal's* technical innovations. Previously, it was typical for carriers to keep individual oxygen cylinders for use on board the planes. But enough cylinders to supply the planes for five days would weigh seventy thousand pounds, whereas the oxygen-generating plant itself weighed only twenty thousand pounds. In addition to the weight reduction, the plant made the

Forrestal self-sufficient for liquid oxygen instead of relying on deliveries at sea.

Chapter 10

Page 245   "doing a pretty good job." *Situation Critical: The USS Forrestal.*

Page 251   "explosion aboard the carrier *Bennington.*" Scott Vanier, "A Survivor's Story," *The Flagship,* July 29, 1999, p. A4.

Page 254   "certainly would have survived." "Tragedy's Start: A Blast Is Heard," *New York Times* July 31, 1967, p. 1.

Page 263   "disappeared as quickly as it had arrived." "Chicago Sailor sees 'Great Lady' Burn." *New York Times,* July 31, 1967. There is no official report of a U.S. ship engaging one of the local boats, but Ed Roberts and others on the *Forrestal* witnessed the boat being destroyed. In addition, a newspaper account quotes twenty-five-year old Tony DeBella of Chicago, a tower-control leader aboard the carrier *Oriskany,* describing the same scene.

Chapter 12

Page 275   "That list was dangerous." Associated Press, "Forrestal Fire Took 29 Lives," *Norfolk (VA) Ledger-Star,* July 31, 1967, p. 1. Though Beling and Rowland maintain that they never feared losing the ship, Beling was quoted soon after the fire as saying that it was "absolutely possible" the ship could be lost. He apparently meant the ship could be lost without a proper response from the crew, but he was confident the crew would perform well.

Chapter 13

Page 305   "McCain quickly left the sick bay." McCain and Salter, p. 179; Timberg, pp. 98–99.

Page 305   "more than three hundred." The official count is 161 injured from the *Forrestal* fire, but Kirchner says the sick bay saw far more than that. Not all were serious injuries, especially toward the end of the day, and many may not have been officially recorded if they needed only superficial care.

Page 314   "a dark ammunition elevator." Lenny Julius confirms that the *Oriskany* used the ammunition elevator to transport the wounded. Normally, crew were forbidden to ride on the ammunition elevator because it was designed only for cargo and not considered safe for people. When the volume of patients forced the use of the ammunition elevator, Julius feared the doors at the top of the elevator would not open in time and the patients would be crushed as they were raised to the flight deck.

Chapter 14

Page 340   "photo of flames and smoke." William Mason, a photographer's mate on the *Forrestal*, rushed topside to take photos during the fire, many of which were used in *Life*.

Page 340   "occurs about once a week." R. W. Apple, Jr., "Heroism on Big Carrier," *New York Times*, July 31, 1967, p. 1.

Page 351   "yet another fire." Associated Press, "12 Sailors Still Listed as Missing," *New York Times*, August 12, 1967, p. 1.

Chapter 16

Page 391   "you are hereby reprimanded." The wording of the reprimand is taken from a draft of the letter provided to the author by the navy, which refused to release it until Beling personally intervened. The navy states that the final version of the reprimand letter is not in its files and may have been different from this draft version. Beling did not retain a copy of the letter and does not remember the exact wording, but he confirms that the gist of the letter is correct.

Epilogue

Page 400   "worst disaster in the U.S. Navy." Bonner and Bonner, p. 5. The loss of life on the *Forrestal* was superseded by an incident in 1952 when the carrier *Wasp* ran over the destroyer *Hobson* during nighttime flight operations. The accident killed 176 men, including the captain of the destroyer. Sixty-one men were recovered from the *Hobson*, some without serious injuries. There were no injuries on the carrier. Since 134 men died on the

Forrestal and 161 were seriously injured, the combined death and injury toll was slightly higher for the *Forrestal* incident.

Page 404 "It was thin-skinned." *Situation Critical: The USS Forrestal; Symposium 2000—Valor Under Fire: Forrestal, 29 July 1967* [videotape] (Pensacola, FL: Naval Aviation Museum Foundation, 2000). Vice Admiral Thomas Kilcline stated at a naval symposium in 2000, in reference to the bombs that exploded in the *Forrestal* fire, that the military was compromising by using old bombs. A pilot aboard the *Forrestal* in 1967, Kilcline stated that he overheard the conversation between Captain Beling and the skipper of the *Diamond Head* while the ammunition was transferred to the ship the night before the fire. He said Beling "was not very happy with what he was going to get in the thousand-pounders," but the other skipper replied that the old bombs were all they had to provide. Kilcline said, "We were making a lot of compromises in those days and this was one of them. This was a World War Two bomb. It was not something new. We were buying a lot of new things, but much of our attention was being paid to nuclear weapons and modernization of that type."

BIBLIOGRAPHY

"46 killed, 56 hurt in 'Forrestal' fire." *Norfolk Virginian-Pilot,* July 30, 1967, p.1. *1967 Fire Chronology.* Sterling, VA: Records of the USS *Forrestal* CVA/CV/AVT-59 Association, Inc., 1967

1MC Recording, USS Forrestal, July 29, 1967. Sterling, VA: Records of the USS *Forrestal* CVA/CV/AVT-59 Association, Inc., 1967.

Anderson, Terry. *The Sixties.* New York: Longman, 1999.

Apple, R. W., Jr. "At least 70 dead in *Forrestal* fire; 89 others missing." *New York Times,* July 30, 1967, p. 1.

Apple, R. W., Jr. "Death count on *Forrestal* rises as flooded compartments are searched." *New York Times,* July 31, 1967, p. 1.

Apple, R. W., Jr. "Heroism on big carrier." *New York Times,* July 31, 1967, p. 1.

Arnett, Peter. "Eyewitnesses relate stories of disaster aboard *Forrestal.*" *Lake Charles American Press,* July 31, 1967, p. 8.

Associated Press. "12 sailors still listed as missing." *New York Times,* August 12, 1967, p. 1.

Associated Press. "*Forrestal* crewmen become fireballs." *New York Times,* August 12, 1967, p. 1.

Associated Press. "*Forrestal* fire took 129 lives." *Norfolk (VA) Ledger-Star,* July 31, 1967, p. 1.

At Sea [videotape]. Washington, DC. United States Navy Memorial, 1992.

Beling, Eve. Personal interview with author.

Beling, John K. Personal interviews and correspondence with author.

Bennett, Christopher. *Supercarrier: USS George Washington.* Osceola, WI: Motorbooks International, 1996.

Bonner, Kit, and Carolyn Bonner. *Great Naval Disasters: U.S. Naval Accidents in the 20th Century.* Osceola, WI: MBI Publishing, 1998.

Buckley, Tom. "The *Forrestal* set afire by blast, 29 planes burn; some aboard feared dead." *New York Times,* July 29, 1967, p. 1.

Burner, David. *Making Peace with the 60s.* Princeton, NJ: Princeton University Press, 1996.

Carlin, Michael Joe. *Trial: Ordeal of the USS Enterprise.* West Grove, PA: Tuscarora Press, 1993.

Chesneau, Roger. *Aircraft Carriers of the World, 1914 to the Present: An Illustrated Encyclopedia.* London: Arms and Armour Press, 1984.

"Chicago sailor sees 'great lady' burn." *New York Times,* July 31, 1967.

Clancy, Tom. *Carrier: A Guided Tour of an Aircraft Carrier.* New York: Berkley Books, 1999.

Costello, Joe. *The Pacific War 1941–1945.* New York: Quill, 1982.

Crutchley, Milt. Personal interview and correspondence with author.

Dale, Edwin L. "Johnson asks for 10% surcharge on personal and business taxes; 45,000 more men to go to Vietnam." *New York Times,* August 4, 1967.

Davison, Dog, ed. *USS Forrestal 1967* [cruise book]. Norfolk, VA: Walsorth, 1967. Courtesy of Ed Roberts.

DeBella, Tony. Correspondence with author.

Dempewolff, R. F. "Our navy's mightiest carrier: USS *Forrestal.*" *Popular Mechanics,* November 1954, pp. 81–85, 262, 264, 266, 268, 270.

Department of the Navy. *Manual of the Judge Advocate General: Basic Final Investigative Report Concerning the Fire on Board the USS Forrestal (CVA-59).* Washington, DC: United States Navy, 1967.

Federation of American Scientists. "Military Analysis Network: Zuni 5.0-Inch [130mm] Rocket." http://www.fas.org/man/dod-101/sys/missile/zuni.htm.

Eurice, Frank. Personal interview and correspondence with author.

Fasoldt, Al. "*Forrestal* ablaze." *Stars & Stripes,* July 31, 1967, p. 1.

"Fighting Flare Fires." *All Hands: The Bureau of Naval Personnel Career Publication,* September 1967, pp. 4–6.

Flight Deck Safety: Hazards of the Flight Deck [training film MN-10131]. Washington, DC: United States Navy, 1967.

Friedman, Paul. Personal interview and correspondence with author.

Garrison, Peter. *Carrier Aviation.* Novato, CA: Presidio Press, 1987.

Goshorn, Howard. "New jet fuel, tank may bar fire disasters on carriers." *Pittsburgh Press,* August 10, 1967, p. 17.

"Heroes of *Forrestal.*" *All Hands: The Bureau of Naval Personnel Career Publication,* September 1967, pp. 2–3.

Herring, George C., ed. *The Pentagon Papers: Abridged Edition.* New York: McGraw-Hill, 1993.

Julius, Lenny. Personal interview and correspondence with author.

Killmeyer, Ken. Personal interview and correspondence with author.

Kirchner, G. Gary. Personal interview and correspondence with author.

Kohler, Robert. Personal interview and correspondence with author.

Marwick, Arthur. *The Sixties.* Oxford: Oxford University Press, 1998.

McCain, John, and Mark Salter. *Faith of My Fathers: A Family Memoir.* New York: Random House, 1999.

McMillen, Ken. Personal interview and correspondence with author.

McNamara, Robert S., and Brian VanDeMark. *In Retrospect: The Tragedy and Lessons of Vietnam.* New York: Vintage Books, 1995.

"Navy shipboard disaster." *Fire Engineering,* June 1968, pp. 42–43.

Newport News Shipbuilding and Dry Dock Company. *USS Forrestal.* Newport News, VA: Newport News Shipbuilding and Dry Dock Company, 1954.

No Easy Day: The Incredible Drama of Naval Aviation [videotape]. Louisville, KY: Avion Park, 1998.

Noel, John V., and Edward L. Beach, eds. *Naval Terms Dictionary,* 5th ed. Annapolis, MD: Naval Institute Press, 1996.

Pailthorpe, Robert L., ed. *USS Forrestal (AVT-59)* [1993, final cruise book]. Norfolk, VA: Taylor Publishing, 1993.

Plat coverage, USS Forrestal CVA-59, 29 July 1967 [Film 428 NPC 38757, raw flight-deck film footage]. Washington, DC: United States Navy, 1967.

Pool, Robert. *Beyond Engineering: How Society Shapes Technology.* Oxford: Oxford University Press, 1997.

Pratt, Rocky. Personal interviews and correspondence with author.

Pritchard, Gary. Personal interview and correspondence with author.

Public Broadcasting System. *Frontline: Give War a Chance,* May 11, 1999. http://www.pbs.org/frontline/programs/.about/1715.html.

Roberts, Ed. Personal interviews and correspondence with author.

Rogue Rocket [videotape]. London: ITN, 1997.

Rowland, Merv. Personal interview with author.

Shaver, Gary. Personal interview and correspondence with author.

Shelton, Bob. Personal interview and correspondence with author.

Situation Critical: The USS Forrestal [videotape]. Arlington, VA: Henninger Media Development, 1997.

"Start of tragedy: Pilot hears a blast as he checks plane." *New York Times,* July 31, 1967.

Strain, Greg. Personal interview and correspondence with author.

Symposium 2000—Valor Under Fire: Forrestal, 29 July 1967 [videotape]. Pensacola, FL: Naval Aviation Museum Foundation, 2000.

"The responsibility: White and black." *New York Times,* July 30, 1967.

Think Safe. Washington, DC: United States Coast Guard, 1999.

Timberg, Robert. *The Nightingale's Song.* New York: Touchstone, 1996.

"Transcript of the president's news conference on domestic and foreign affairs." *New York Times,* August 1, 1967, p. 16.

Trial by Fire: A Carrier Fights for Life [training film MN 11204]. Washington, DC: United States Navy, 1973.

USS Forrestal [training film MN 8087]. Washington, DC: United States Navy, 1956.

Vanier, Scott. "A survivor's story." *The Flagship,* July 29, 1999, p. A4.

Whelpley, Robert. Personal interview and correspondence with author.

Wingo, Hal. "Hell aboard CVA-59." *Life,* August 11, 1967, pp. 21–27.

Zwerlein, Bill. Personal interview and correspondence with author.

Zwerlein, Ruth. Personal interview and correspondence with author.

ACKNOWLEDGMENTS

I must thank a number of people who contributed to this book and supported my effort to shed light on the story of the *Forrestal*. First, I thank my dear wife, Caroline, for all the love and support she provided. The productivity kits were greatly appreciated.

I owe a huge debt of gratitude to the veterans of the USS *Forrestal* for sharing their stories with me, many of them intensely personal and painful to remember. Among the *Forrestal* veterans, I extend a special note of thanks to Kenneth Killmeyer, who served on the *Forrestal* during the 1967 fire and has since become historian of the *Forrestal*'s veterans association. Ken was tremendously helpful in explaining the details of the incident, providing original records, and establishing contact with other veterans. Ken's dedication to the *Forrestal* is evident in the way he carefully guards her honor, and I am grateful that he saw fit to aid me as thoroughly as he did. It is no exaggeration to say that this book project would not have progressed without Ken's help.

The USS *Forrestal* CVA/CV/AVT-59 Association

itself, made up of those who served on the ship, deserves recognition. This group of veterans welcomed me to their inner circle and provided all manner of assistance, not to mention encouragement. In addition, I must specifically thank a number of individuals who personally shared their stories with me: John and Eve Beling, James Bloedorn, Milt Crutchley, Frank Eurice, Paul Friedman, G. Gary Kirchner, Bob Kohler, Lenny Julius, Ken McMillen, Rocky Pratt, Gary Pritchard, Ed Roberts, Merv Rowland, Gary Shaver, Bob Shelton, Greg Strain, Robert Whelpley, and Bill and Ruth Zwerlein.

I also wish to thank Christine Burton, Marge Buschman, and Shelly Taylor for their research assistance. A special thanks is due Maureen Hardegree for her invaluable critiques and for commiserating with me as only a fellow writer can.

Mel Berger, my agent, and Henry Ferris, my editor, are trusted colleagues and I am glad to have them on my side. I thank you both for making this book happen. Thank you, Henry, for seeing what I can't.

The staff at the Fire Fighting School in Norfolk was helpful in showing me the state of the art in firefighting education. Bill Natter, a former navy pilot, is due a hearty thank-you for his assistance in getting me aboard an active-duty U.S. aircraft carrier during my research. Some things become clear only when you experience them yourself. Likewise, I thank the U.S. Navy and the men and women of the aircraft carrier USS *Harry S. Truman* for their gracious welcome.

In particular, I'd like to thank one sailor aboard the *Truman*. In my brief time at sea, I encountered hundreds of young men and women on board who gave me a strong sense of confidence about our navy and the generation of young people who serve in it. I was thoroughly impressed when watching them perform some of the most dangerous and demanding jobs in the world. As I prepared to leave the carrier, however, I came upon one young sailor who seemed to embody the essence of the crew.

I never spoke directly with him, and I'm certain he has no memory whatsoever of me, but I had the opportunity to sit and watch him for a long time as I waited for the catapult launch that would send me off the deck and back to Norfolk, Virginia. He was one of the crew in charge of organizing flights off the carrier for visitors like myself, as well as crew who were being flown to the mainland for some reason. It was a big job, as many on a carrier are.

This young man looked to be about eighteen, so youthful and fresh-faced, energetic and eager, exactly like everyone's brother, or son, or boyfriend. A handsome kid with a big smile, he captivated me as I sat there in my float coat and helmet, listening to the noise of the flight deck just outside and waiting for my ride home. As I watched him work, switching effortlessly between a stern demeanor for getting the job done and a wide grin for cracking jokes with his buddies, I realized that so many of the *Forrestal* crew in 1967 would have been just like him. They weren't just names and faces that no one remembers. They weren't just old men with a story to tell. They were young men like this.

I am grateful to that young man and the others who reminded me what this book is really about.

GAF

INDEX

True and Intimate Portraits of America's Warriors
From the Front Lines of Battle

We Were Soldiers Once . . . And Young
Ia Drang—The Battle That Changed the War in Vietnam
by Lt. Gen. Harold G. Moore (Ret.)
and Joseph L. Galloway
0-06-050698-9/$7.99 US/$10.99

One Perfect Op
Navy SEAL Special Warfare Teams
by Command Master Chief Dennis Chalker, USN (Ret.)
with Kevin Dockery
0-380-80920-6/$6.99 US/$9.99 Can

Delta Force
The Army's Elite Conterterrorist Unit
by Col. Charlie A. Beckwith (Ret.)
and Donald Knox
0-380-80939-7/$7.99 US/$10.99 Can

Abandon Ship!
The Saga of the U.S.S. *Indianapolis*,
the Navy's Greatest Sea Disaster
by Richard F. Newcomb
0-380-81904-X/$7.99 US/$10.99 Can

Big Red
The Three-Month Voyage of a Trident Nuclear Submarine
by Douglas C. Waller
0-380-82078-1/$7.99 US/$10.99 Can